Ghost Stories from Hell

Written by Ron Ripley

ISBN: 9781070983851
Copyright © 2019 by ScareStreet.com

Thank You and Bonus Novel!

I'd like to take a moment to thank you for your ongoing support. You make this all possible! To really show you my appreciation for purchasing this book, **I'd love to send you a full-length horror novel in 3 formats (MOBI, EPUB and PDF) absolutely free!**

Download your full-length horror novel, get free short stories, and receive future discounts by visiting www.ScareStreet.com/RonRipley

See you in the shadows,
Ron Ripley

Ta

Boylan House

Chapter 1: Meeting House Road

The Boylan House stood at the end of Meeting House Road in Monson, New Hampshire.

As far as the residents of Monson—all thirty-six-hundred of them—were concerned, the house had always been there.

The house was huge, an ancient beast of a building with a wraparound porch that seemed to beckon the unwary. The colors, perhaps stunning and sensual at one time, had bled into a dull monotony that spoke more of sickness than anything else. A center tower reached up a full story above the first two and, unbeknownst to those who dared a closer look, there were trap doors in the porch's roof, close to the house.

The few windows, on each side of the house, were narrow and set back into the thick walls. Sturdy shutters stood open, but were able to be closed when needed. There were two doors to the house, one in the front, and one the rear. If there had not been the road which ended in front of the house, no one would have known the front from the back. Everything about the house was identical, including the two doors. They were made of thick planks of old oak, bound by iron.

No power ran to the house, and no sewer either. Where the water might come from, if there were water, was also a fair question. The Hassle Brook, which had run near the Boylan House four centuries before, had long since shifted its course. As it was, the Boylan House stood silently upon its hill and looked down upon the world.

Taxes were paid out by way of a trust fund. The checks arrived yearly, on the fifteenth of August, issued by the law firm of Boylan, O'Connor, and Gunther.

The residents of Monson believed that the Boylan House had always been haunted.

Chapter 2: Home Again

Mason pulled into an open parking space on Monson's Main Street and fished around in his ashtray for quarters. He found half a dozen of them amongst the legion of pennies, nickels, and dimes. Holding onto them tightly, he got out of his pickup and closed the door. Ignoring the smell of oil slipping out of the old Dodge's crankcase, Mason stepped up to the parking meter.

The dull gray meter sign read: "No time limit. $.25 = 30 minutes."

Mason looked at his watch. It was ten thirty. He would have to come back and feed meter dimes by one thirty the latest, if he needed more time.

Mason fed the quarters into the meter slowly, making sure that each one bought some time. He didn't want to end up with a parking ticket because he was in too much of a rush.

And he was in a rush.

Mason went back to the truck, opened the passenger side door and grabbed his carry case. He didn't bother locking the doors. If somebody really needed the change in the ashtray, or would even bother to crack the steering column and hot-wire the damned thing, well, more power to them.

His only concern was the Boylan House. It was October twenty-seventh, just a few days away from Halloween and the urban legend that had haunted him for the better part of his life.

4

Chapter 3: Trick or Treat

Halloween. 1980. Meeting House Road.

Mason stood on the road dressed as a Stormtrooper. The vinyl coveralls that served as the black and white uniform were loud as he moved. The elastic of the plastic Stormtrooper mask was biting into his scalp, and the battered Star Wars pillowcase was heavy with candy in his hands.

He looked at the Boylan House, a single light shining through a window on the second floor. His cousins, Matthew and Luke, stood beside him. Both of them were older. Matthew was Han Solo and Luke was, well, Luke was Luke Skywalker.

A few of Mason's cousins' friends were with them, all of them dressed as Star Wars characters. Mason's mom had dropped him off. She was pulling the night shift at the Memorial Hospital ER in Nashua. His dad hadn't been around for years.

Aunt Margaret had been happy to have him. Nobody wanted Mason to miss Halloween. Including Mason.

But he wasn't too happy about being at the Boylan House.

There was something wrong about the place.

It just didn't feel right.

"I'm going up there," Kevin, one of Matthew's friends said. "Anybody else?"

No one answered.

"Bunch of queers," Kevin laughed, sliding his Darth Vader mask up on top of his head.

Kevin was a mean boy. But he hadn't done anything mean to Mason, or to anybody else that night. And just as Mason knew that there was something wrong with the Boylan House, he knew that Kevin was mean.

"Come on, Matt," Kevin said, sneering at Mason's cousin. "Don't be such a girl."

Matthew only shook his head, and Mason saw, in the moonlight, that his cousin's eyes were wet with tears. Matthew was too afraid to even answer.

A soft wind rustled the tops of the trees, the remaining dry desiccated leaves making a low, rattling sound.

"You're a bitch," Kevin said in a low voice and Mason heard the threat of violence in it.

"I'll go," Mason said.

Kevin's head snapped to the right to look at him. Surprise replaced the sneer that the older boy had been wearing. But the sneer quickly came back. "How old are you?"

"Seven," Mason answered.

Again, the look of surprise.

Mason knew he looked younger. His mother always talked about it.

Kevin shook his head, grudging admiration in his voice as he said, "Well, hot damn. Kid, let's make this happen." Kevin handed his bag of candy off to a boy named Chad.

"I'll hold yours," Luke said softly.

"Thanks," Mason said, letting his cousin take the pillowcase.

"Are you okay?" Luke asked him.

Mason nodded, his throat suddenly too dry for him to speak.

Kevin started walking up the slight hill towards the Boylan House. Mason followed a few steps behind. The older boy glanced back to make sure Mason was there, and Mason saw a flicker of relief on the older boy's face.

It seemed to take a terribly long time to get to the Boylan House's front door.

Mason had never seen a door so large. It towered over both of them. Above the door, was a trap door, set into the overhang of the second story and barely visible in the moonlight.

Mason noticed how silent the world suddenly seemed to be, as he stood there, waiting.

The insects and the night animals had seemingly been robbed of their voices. The wind had vanished, and an ancient, sickening smell rose up from the grass beneath their feet. The temperature had dropped sharply, and Mason suddenly felt sick to his stomach; the American chop suey that Aunt Margaret had made threatening to come back up.

In front of Mason, Kevin had noticeably stiffened, a visible tremor in his hands. Instantly, Mason felt sorry for the older boy, even if Kevin was mean.

Kevin was scared.

But both Mason and Kevin knew that the older boy had to do something, even if it was just knocking on that huge and frightening front door.

Mason watched as Kevin took a deep breath, and put his Darth Vader mask back on his face, the older boy's body tensing

6

as he raised his right hand and closed it into a fist.

Movement caught Mason's eye and he looked up.

The trap door above them was opening.

Mason stood frozen, petrified and unable to scream as Kevin knocked, ever so softly, upon the thick and ancient wood of the door.

A pale, white hand shot down from the trap door.

The wrist and forearm, as pale as the hand, vanished into the depths of a black sleeve while the long, yellow-nailed fingers buried themselves in Kevin's loose blonde curls.

With a sudden jerking motion, the hand dragged Kevin up through the trap door and into the house.

Kevin and Mason's screams drowned out the closing of the trap door.

Kevin's shrieks were suddenly silenced and Mason turned and sprinted for the road. Mason's own screaming triggered that of the other boys and sent them racing back along Meeting House Road.

Mason raced after them, breathless, in the October moonlight.

Chapter 4: A Little Morning Research

The Monson librarian looked at him in surprise as she unlocked the door, while he climbed up the last few granite steps.

"Is this a first?" he asked, grinning as she held the door open for him.

She smiled. "It is," she said, "I've never had someone waiting to use the library before."

"I'm Mason," he said, extending his hand.

"Julie," the young woman said, shaking his hand. "Come on in."

"Thank you," Mason said.

As the door closed behind them, she asked, "Is there anything that I can help you with today?"

"Well," Mason said, walking beside her towards the front desk, "I was wondering if you have a local history section."

"You're in luck," Julie said, walking around the desk and taking a key off of a hook hanging on the wall. "We have a large local history section, which I'm sure is a complete surprise to you," she smiled, "and we have both microfiche and microfilm machines."

"Excellent," Mason said.

"May I ask what it is you're doing research on?" she asked.

He nodded. "Yes," he said, "I'm doing some research on the Boylan House on Meeting House Road."

Julie nodded. "Okay. Come on and follow me."

She walked back around the desk and went to a closed door with a brass plate engraved with the name, "Gunther" upon it.

"This," she said, fitting the key into the door's lock, "is the Gunther Room. This is where we keep our local history materials, both published and unpublished work. Monson doesn't have a historical society, so all of that stuff is in here, too. Letters, maps, journals; all of that good stuff. There's even a filing cabinet of photographs."

With that said, she turned the key, and opened the door slowly, taking the key out of the lock as she did so. Julie reached in and turned on the lights.

The room was small, but clean and organized. A large and old reading table with a green shaded brass lamp, dominated the room. Next to it, was an equally ancient reading chair. There was barely any room around the table to get at the shelves that were packed with books of various ages, and neatly-labeled gray manuscript boxes. A pair of sixteen over sixteen windows stood across from the door, letting in the late morning light. They looked out over the Monson cemetery. Row upon row of ancient headstones stood in precise order, with barely an inch or two between the sides of each stone and only a few feet between the rows.

"We're open until four," Julie said, stepping aside so Mason could enter the room. "Don't worry about your truck," she smiled. "I'll give the police a call. My brother's on duty today, he won't write a ticket up on someone who's actually using the library."

"Thanks," Mason said, turning to grin at her. "Is there a place that I could make copies, if I needed to? And also, I have a wand scanner, do you mind if I use that?"

"First," she smiled, "I have a copier, and I can copy whatever you need me to. I'm pretty much caught up on my work, and I just finished a book last night that left me with a book hangover. I can't start a new one until, at least, after lunch."

"Understood completely," Mason laughed.

Her smile widened. "And second, as for the scanner, that won't be a problem at all. The only thing I ask when you're using the Gunther Room is that you leave whatever you take off the shelves or out of the filing cabinet, on the reading table. Things get lost easily."

"They do," Mason said softly, looking into the room. "They do."

Chapter 5: Fear of the Unknown

Halloween. 2000. Meeting House Road.

Matthew smoked nervously, a slight shake in his hand each time he brought the Lucky up to his lips. He looked over at Mason, clearly unhappy.

Mason sat on the lowered tailgate of his Dodge, a cup of Dunkin's coffee in his hands. He looked steadily at his cousin.

"Why the hell are we even here?" Matthew asked, glancing up at the Boylan House.

"We're waiting for darkness," Mason answered.

"No shit we are," Matthew responded. He finished the cigarette, dropped it on the pavement and ground the butt with his foot. Even as he did so, he was fishing his pack of smokes out from his jacket pocket and fumbling with his lighter. It took him a few times, but soon Mason's cousin had the cigarette out of the pack, into his mouth and lit. He exhaled two streams of smoke sharply from his nose. "The last time we were here," Matthew said, stabbing the cigarette in Mason's direction, "Kevin Peacock got snatched and murdered by some goddamn child rapist."

"You know that's not true," Mason said softly. "I don't care how many times you tell yourself, or how many times the psychiatrist and my mom tried to tell me, that is not what happened, Matthew."

"I don't give a shit about what you believe," Matthew said, smoking furiously. "They never found his body. End of story."

"Why," Mason said, taking a sip of his coffee, "did they never find his body, Matthew? They searched for days. Hell, they even brought the National Guard and the Marine Reserve units in to search for Kevin's body."

"They didn't find his body," Matthew snapped, "because there're a hundred acres of wetlands and conservation land behind the damn place."

He refused to look at the Boylan House, keeping his eyes on Mason instead.

And Mason could see the fear in his cousin's eyes. It was deep, old and painful.

"I'm sorry for bringing you out here," Mason said sincerely. "I just wanted someone with me. You're the only one I trust enough."

Matthew merely nodded.

Mason started to take another drink of his coffee when Matthew stopped him with a horrified, "Look."

Mason looked up and saw it.

A single light had come on in the upper left-hand window as night finally settled in completely over Monson.

If they had been in the town, where the electrical wires were strung from pole to pole, and pole to the house, he would have believed that there was a light on a timer. But Mason knew better. Mason knew there was something more.

He set his coffee down on the Dodge's tailgate and jumped off of it. "Watch my coffee," Mason said.

Matthew nodded, as he stared at the Boylan house, the cigarette quickly burning down between his fingers.

Wiping his own nervous sweat off his palms and onto his jeans, Mason started walking up the small hill towards the front of the Boylan House.

His childhood fear came rushing back, settling into his bowels and threatening control over his bladder. He felt like a kid again; following Kevin Peacock, never realizing the simple act of walking up to that house would haunt every night's sleep.

Mason straightened his back and clenched his teeth as he approached the house.

Soon, he stood before it. Mason looked at the door and at the house. Nothing had changed; the air was still; the insects and animals were silent. Something stank beneath the grass.

"Do you remember me?" Mason asked. "Was this real? Was there something here that took the boy? Or did he simply get lost or snatched by some murderer?"

A soft creak answered his question. As if someone was walking in the house, just above the second floor.

Mason looked up and saw the trap door which he had long ago seen open.

A slow, casual opening. No sudden jerking motion. Just a smooth pulling up of the trap.

Something black fell down, landing gently on the granite doorstep. The trap door closed with a whisper.

With a mouth that was suddenly and painfully dry, Mason forced himself to move forward, keeping an eye on both the door and the trap door. When he was close enough to squat down and reach out, he did so.

His hands closed on plastic, but he didn't look at it. Mason kept his eyes on both doors.

He couldn't trust the house.

Mason straightened up, walked backward a dozen feet down the hill, then turned and forced himself to walk calmly down to where Matthew was standing. His cousin had a fresh cigarette shaking in his hands, and he looked at Mason, asking, "What's that?"

He put the item on the truck bed and stared at it. Matthew came and stood beside him.

"Oh damn," Matthew whispered.

On the heavily scraped and worn bed of Mason's Dodge pickup, next to his cup of quickly cooling coffee, was a mask. A thin, plastic, Darth Vader mask.

Chapter 6: Horrors Between the Lines

Mason sat at the reading table, his back to the graveyard and the library visible through the open doorway of the Gunther Room. It had taken him half an hour to find the earliest records from when Monson was first incorporated, back in the seventeenth century.

The records were written on large pages bearing the King's stamp, and the paper was protected in archival Mylar sleeves that allowed him to read but not damage the pages. There were cotton gloves in the gray manuscript box, but Mason didn't want to handle the pages.

He wanted to scan through them, not take in-depth notes. He was only looking for information on the Boylan House.

It didn't take him long to find it.

"A reformed Papist by the name of Liam Boylan has come to us by the Grace of God. He has begun the construction of a Garrison House along the Road to the Meeting House."

This had been written in 1674, although there was no name attached to the document. The rest concerned conflict amongst the local Abenaki tribe. Complaints about the theft of cattle and the pillaging of corn.

Mason moved to the next page and froze as his eyes rested on a sentence.

"Young Master Goodwin, aged 15 years, has disappeared while working on the edge of South Field near Liam Boylan's home. Several Abenaki were seen watering cattle at the Hassle Brooke, earlier in the Day. It is feared that Young Master Goodwin has been taken by them, or murdered by the same."

Taking his new notebook out of his carry case, Mason flipped it open, set it down upon the table and clicked his pen. He wrote down the information on Boylan and the murder.

Putting the pen down, Mason searched through several more documents, but found nothing of interest, until he came upon a page titled, *The Boylan House*. This had been written in the early nineteenth century and was privately printed by a Frederick Gunther, who was also the author.

The reason Mason had stopped was the first sentence of the first paragraph.

"The residents of Monson secured themselves in the Meeting

House and in the Boylan Garrison House when the rebellious Indians attacked. Of the two Houses, only the Meeting House would survive the initial attack unscathed. The Boylan House, however, would not be so fortunate."

Mason quickly flipped through the document until he came to another mention of the house, a section headed, "The Massacre in the Boylan House."

"In late October, when the Indian allies of Philip were making their last raids before the winter snows, the village of Monson was once more attacked. They had barely recovered from an earlier raid on the town, having lost all of their sheep and most of their cattle to the marauding Indians. Their crops, too, had been destroyed. They were relying on the charity of the other towns and villages, in hopes that they might survive the harsh winter.

When the Indians raided Monson the second time, it was only by the sheerest chance that the local militia caught sight of the Indians sneaking in through the fields of the Boylan House.

Liam Boylan held the door for the militia as they came in, and it was through the benevolence of God, that all of the militia made it into that home unscathed. The remaining residents of Monson heard the scattered gunfire and fled to the Meeting House. It would hold those few hardy families which had remained in the village, following the first raid, earlier in the year.

Little, but hearsay, is known of what happened in the Boylan House during the twenty hours that the raid lasted. Those who were in the Meeting House were able to hear, in the pauses of their own battle for survival, the fighting taking place at the Boylan House. The fighting did not last nearly as long as it did for the Meeting House folk. Silence emanated from the Boylan House long before the Indians abandoned their efforts to gain access to the Meeting House.

The next morning, a hardy few left the safety of the Meeting House and made their way to the home of Liam Boylan. What they found outside the home was, what can only be considered as, the aftermath of a battle for survival. Blood stains could be seen upon the grass. There were broken arrows and scorch marks upon the exterior of the home where the Indians had attempted to set the house ablaze.

The men from the Meeting House hailed their neighbors in the Boylan House, but they received no answer. Cautiously, they approached and hammered loudly upon the door.

Still, they received no response. One of the men, Kendall Hall, noticed that the trap above the door was open and convinced his comrades to lift him up so that he might see what had befallen those within. Once inside, Kendall found himself in near darkness; the inner shutters of the second floor having been secured. He opened the shutters and became sick with horror at the sight which he found before him.

Two of the militiamen, who had been stationed at the Boylan House, were dead on the floor. Both of them killed with a small hand ax. The ax, however, was still buried in the back of one of the men. The two corpses, however, weren't what disturbed Kendall, though.

Standing near the chimney, he saw that at some point, Liam Boylan had built some sort of false front around the chimney; false stones made of clay and attached to a wooden door. This door lay open, and within, were the skulls of children. A dozen of them.

After recovering from his horror, young Kendall Hall made his way down the stairs and to the front door. He threw back the locks and the bar to allow his comrades entrance. When they saw his face, they asked him what was wrong but he could only shake his head.

It was at that point, the men stated, that they heard a noise coming from the rear of the house.

The four of them raced to the back and found the rear door open. The last member of the three militiamen, who had been at the Boylan House, sat in the doorway, blood staining his shirt and three bullets in his chest. The shirt he wore, had been burned by the powder of the shots. A brace of pistols lay in the grass near him, as did a musket. His breathing was ragged, and he looked at his neighbors through the veil of death.

He motioned them closer, and Kendall Hall knelt down beside the man.

"They only wanted him," the man hissed, pain marking each word. 'They only wanted him," and gestured towards the rear of the house, before taking his last breath.

Leaving the dead man, for a moment, the militiamen

stepped out into the rear of the house. They looked around before one of them yelled in horror and cried, 'Look!' and the others did.

There, crucified to the rear of the house, was Liam Boylan. He had been stripped naked by the Indians and cut open as one would a pig. The remains of his innards lay in a charred pile by him. He had kept his head, but the Indians had peeled back the skin from his skull, leaving it as two flaps of meat on either side, the lidless eyes staring at them.

The men fled and returned to the Meeting House. There, they gathered more of the men, as well as the Reverend, and returned to the hideous scene. But what they found the second time, was even more disturbing than the first.

Liam Boylan's body was gone. His innards still in a charred pile, and the spikes used to nail him to the house were still bloody and buried in the wood. The militiamen were still dead. But the skulls were gone as well.

The bodies were removed from the house, yet all that was Liam Boylan's, even the precious books he had—and there had been many—were left upon their shelves. The doors were closed, and the people of Monson attempted to burn the Boylan House to the ground. Yet the fire would not catch.

They tried to take the house down piece by piece, yet nothing they did could separate board from board. Any teams, that came close by to try and hitch them to the beams, fled. One team brained a man, killing him.

It was with that death, that the efforts to tear down the Boylan House ceased. Since then, all residents of Monson have given the home a wide berth. Occasionally, people still go missing in Monson, but the disappearances are declared to be the misfortune of wandering around late in October; when the mist is known to rise, and one can easily become lost in the swamps and woods."

Mason sat back and let a deep breath out. His hands were wet with perspiration. Wiping them off on his pants, Mason shook his head.

Standing, he stretched and thought about what he read.

The date had been 1675. That was the time of the King Philip's War. The book was written much later. The writer, Mr. Gunther, could have taken serious liberties with the tale.

I need to look through more, Mason thought, returning to his seat. I need to see what else is there.

Once more, he leaned over the documents that were spread out before him and started to go through them. He scanned through decades of documents; the transfer of deeds and the sale of cattle. Farming disputes, the outbreak of the American Revolution. He didn't find another mention of the Boylan House until October of 1865. A single page in the journal of a young woman.

"My brother Elisha went missing last night."

Mason jotted the information down and then set aside the document by Frederick Gunther to see if Julie could scan it for him. He rubbed his eyes, for a moment, before turning to the next set of documents; a collection of letters written by a Mister Elbridge Copp starting in 1899 and lasting until 1922.

He let his eyes wander over each page before flipping it. He stopped at 1910.

"Dear Harold," the letter began, *"another child has disappeared into the wetlands behind Boylan House. There is, of course, the old superstitious fear that it is the house itself which has devoured the child. I think that they should throw up a fence around it. But, according to Erickson at the town hall, that is strictly forbidden by the contract which has been drawn up between the town and the law firm which pays the home's taxes. Until they do, I fear that people shall continue to think that they can wander at will in a place where even the animals seem fearful to tread."*

Law firm?

Mason jotted the information down. He needed to find out who they were, and if they still existed.

He needed to find out how many children had disappeared.

Chapter 7: A Darkness in the House

Halloween. 2005. Meeting House Road.

It was the third time that Mason had come to Meeting House Road to stand before the Boylan House. This was the only time that he had come alone.

He sat on the tailgate of the truck. The same truck from five years ago, when Matthew had accompanied him. But Matthew was home, handing out candy while his wife and their two little ones were out trick or treating.

Rarely did anyone come down to the end of Meeting House Road anymore, and that was a good thing. No one had believed Mason's story back in 1980. All of the adults had pawned his story off as just that, a story.

Mason knew better. His cousins had been convinced that Kevin Peacock had been snatched by someone, not some supernatural boogeyman that lived in an ancient house.

Mason was the only one who held onto what he had seen that night.

Five years had passed since the last time he stopped by, to visit his cousins. Mason would see them again in the morning. He had rented a room at a nearby motel. Tonight, though, was for the Boylan House.

Whatever was in the house—if there was something in the house, and not the creation of a frightened seven-year-old—seemed to have remembered him. Mason still had the Darth Vader mask; a none-too-subtle hint, that it knew who he was. Perhaps more than anything else, that notion bothered Mason the most. Something knew him there.

Something was playing with him.

Maybe it was the house. Maybe it was something else.

Reaching behind him, Mason took hold of the double barrel shotgun he had brought with him. It was a sawed off. Good for scaring the shit out of someone thinking that sneaking up on your porch was a good idea. Tonight, he had it packed with salt loads. Pure salt from a lick and in shell casings he had put together.

If something came at him tonight, whether human or not, it was going to get a taste of salt that would leave it feeling like hell.

Mason slid off the back of the truck and stood to look at the house.

A single lamp flickered into life in the upper left window. It moved slowly through all four of the second story windows, stopping finally at the far right.

Mason could feel his heart pounding.

But the shotgun was steady in his hands. Holding it easily, he flipped off the safety and started walking up the slight hill toward the front door. When he got about a dozen feet from the door, the light in the window vanished. Mason stopped. The old childhood fear burst up within him and threatened to send him racing back to the safety of his truck.

For the third time in his life, he encountered the abnormal and hideous silence that surrounded the house. The smell rose up around him, and every sense in his body told him that this was no place for him. That this was no place for anyone.

A creak sounded, soft and subtle, just barely audible, but there. The hackles on Mason's neck rose up, and he stiffened.

In front of him, with only the light of the half-moon to show the door of the Boylan House, Mason saw something come down from the trap. As the item landed on the granite step, Mason moved forward with his weapon ready. He reached a shaking hand out and snatched up a burlap bag.

It was full, but light. Mason made his way back to his truck. Back to the safety of the Meeting House Road.

When he reached his truck, Mason put the safety on the shotgun, placed it on the truck bed and held up the burlap sack. He opened it and looked in. But he could hardly see anything. Drawing a deep breath, Mason put his hand in and fished around. He felt something that reminded him of old corn-silk and wrapped his fingers around it.

Taking it out slowly, Mason realized that he wasn't holding corn-silk.

He was holding human hair. And the scalps that went along with it.

He looked closely at one.

The skin was white.

The hair was yellow.

A flicker of light caught Mason's eye and he looked to the Boylan House. All of the windows had light shining from them and somewhere, just faintly, he could hear something laughing.

19

Chapter 8: A Recitation of Events

"How's it going in there?" Julie asked as Mason walked out into the main portion of the library.

"Better than expected," Mason answered, smiling at her.

Julie smiled back. "So, can you talk about what you're researching or is it a big secret?"

Mason laughed, shaking his head. "No," he said, walking up to the desk and leaning against it, "not a big secret at all. Do you get a lot of people, in here, researching big secrets?"

"Oh yes," she answered, rolling her eyes. "You have no idea. It's mostly older people, researching the town's history and whispering about scandals that they've uncovered. Information that will bring down the most influential of the town's families."

"Really?" Mason said, grinning. "I didn't know that Monson was such a hotbed of activity."

"Lascivious in nature, as well," she winked, nodding.

Mason laughed out again. "Oh," he sighed, "that's good. No, my research isn't about lust and passion in eighteenth century Monson."

"Shame," Julie said, "those Revolutionary folks really had some interesting habits."

"I don't even want to know. I'm rather suspicious that it might involve farm animals and cold winter nights."

It was Julie's turn to laugh. "I thought that you said you weren't researching the town's most influential families."

"No," he said. "I'm researching something a little darker, I'm afraid."

Julie looked at him with interest, the smile fading from her face. "What is it, if you don't mind?"

"I don't mind," Mason said. "Do you know the Boylan House?"

"That's the creepy house at the end of Meeting House Road, right?" she asked.

"That's it," he said nodding.

"Yes," she said, frowning, "I know it. I'm not a fan of it. A few of my girlfriends went up there when we were seniors in high school. It was May, almost time to graduate and they decided they'd go up there and see what the fuss was about. Mary Ann, one of my friends, went up there, knocked on the door and ran.

But nothing came out. No, boogeyman."

"Wrong time of year," Mason said softly.

"What do you mean?" she asked.

"Wrong time of year," he said again, straightening up. He crossed his arms over his chest and smiled tiredly at her. "Things only happen at the Boylan House during the end of October. And, from what I can see, by the little research that I've done so far, only boys seem to be the victims."

"So, why are you researching the Boylan House," she said.

"I don't mean to be rude, or crass, but that place is, well, creepy as hell."

"You'll get no argument from me," Mason said. "I was there when something far beyond creepy happened."

"What happened?" she asked.

"Do you know anything about this town?" he asked in turn.

"Yes," she nodded. "I grew up here. Plus, just being around as a librarian, you kind of poke around and see what's old and what's new. Sometimes it gets really slow in here, and I read some extremely unusual things."

"Well," Mason said, "did you know that a boy went missing back in 1980?"

Julie thought about the question for a minute. "I think I read something about it in one of the local histories. It happened around Halloween, right?"

"Right," Mason answered. "It actually happened on Halloween night."

"Yes," she said, nodding, "they think that someone was squatting in the house, grabbed the boy and left his body out in the swamp somewhere."

"That's the theory," Mason agreed. "It's not what happened, though."

Julie raised an eyebrow. "Really?"

He nodded.

"How do you know?"

"I was one of the boys with Kevin Peacock that night," Mason said. "The boy that disappeared."

"What happened?"

"Do you think that you'd believe me?"

She looked at him, confused. "Why wouldn't I?"

"No one did," Mason said, "I was seven years old. Kevin

21

walked up to the door of the Boylan House and knocked on it. I was with him."

"Then why wouldn't they have believed you?" Julie asked. "If you were there, it seems completely logical that they would talk to you and take your statement."

"They did talk to me," Mason said. "And they did take my statement. But they didn't believe me. They tried for over a decade to get me to, well, 'remember correctly' but I never did."

"Well," she said, "will you tell me what you saw?"

Mason thought for a long moment, before nodding. "There is one thing, though," he said.

"What's that?" she asked.

"Even if you think that I'm absolutely insane, will you please let me keep researching? I'm not done, and Halloween is coming up fast."

"Yes," she said, without hesitation. "I promise."

"Thank you," Mason asked and breathed easier, realizing that his chest had been tightening. Julie sat looking up at him, a coffee cup cradled in her hands.

"Kevin was trying to get my cousin, Matthew, to go up to the Boylan House with him. He was riding Matthew pretty hard about it," Mason said, "and Matthew wasn't the type of kid to stand up well to peer pressure. I wasn't exactly a meek kind of kid myself, but I wanted Kevin to leave Matthew alone. Obviously, I couldn't have fought Kevin, he was twelve or thirteen, like Matthew, almost twice my size. I was a tough kid, but I wasn't an idiot. Kevin only wanted someone to go up to the house with him. I told him I would."

"Screw that," Julie said. "I'm an adult, and I wouldn't go up to that house. Sorry. I didn't mean to interrupt."

Mason smiled. "That's okay. Anyway, I went up to the house with him and, like you said, the place is creepy as hell."

Julie nodded her agreement.

"I was standing behind him, just a little bit. I was dressed as a Stormtrooper. Kevin was dressed as Darth Vader. Now these were the 1980 costumes, a plastic pull-down mask and a vinyl jumpsuit that tied in the back. That's important to remember, okay?"

"Okay," she said, taking a sip of her coffee.

"As I stood behind him, and he raised his hand to knock, a

trap door above us opened."

Julie's eyes widened, and she looked like she wanted to ask a question, but she stopped herself.

"I was terrified," Mason said. "I mean I couldn't say anything. I couldn't move. This white hand shot down, grabbed Kevin by the hair and dragged him up into the house."

"What the hell?!" she asked.

Mason nodded.

"Are you serious?" Julie asked.

"Yes."

"Well, why the hell didn't they believe that?" Julie asked.

"Because none of the other boys saw it," Mason said. "Turns out they weren't looking. They looked when they heard Kevin and myself screaming, and all they saw was me. Standing at the door, alone. So, they ran."

"They ran? They left you?" she asked.

"Of course they did," Mason smiled gently. "They were kids. I was a kid. I ran, too."

"But you just saw him pulled into the house," Julie said. "That's understandable. But why didn't the police believe you?"

"Because when they went into the house, there was no one in there. No sign of Kevin ever having been in there. Downstairs had the remains of somebody's camp. Old canned food. Remains of a fire. A blanket roll, some other stuff. The police figured that whoever grabbed Kevin had done it and got out right away. But, they said that he couldn't have possibly dragged Kevin up through the trap door. The dust up there hadn't been disturbed in decades."

Julie shook her head. "Kids know what they see."

"That's what I figure," Mason agreed.

"Okay," Julie said, taking a sip of her coffee, "why are you researching the house? I know the stories, about how kids have disappeared around it for years. But as far as I know, the kid you talked about is the only one who was ever documented. People say the house is haunted, but that's just an urban legend, you know?" she said, "a boogeyman story that kids tell to scare each other."

"See," Mason said, "that's why I'm researching the house. I'm trying to find out whether I'm simply crazy, or whether there really is a boogeyman in the Boylan House. Now, do you remember what costumes Kevin Peacock and I were wearing?"

"You were a Stormtrooper, and he was Darth Vader, right?"

"Right," he said. "Now, those masks were plastic. Cheap plastic that barely survived their one night of use on Halloween, and really got beat to hell once they were played with. So, I've been to the Boylan House twice since Kevin went missing. The second time in 2000, I went with my cousin, Matthew. He didn't want to go. He believed that I remembered everything wrong."

"That sucks," Julie said, frowning.

"Yeah," Mason agreed. "But he did come with me. It was Halloween again, and we went to Meeting House Road. He stayed on the road, I walked up to the house. Just before I got to the front door, something was dropped from the trap door."

"What?"

"Kevin's Darth Vader mask."

"Bullshit" she said. "Oh, sorry!"

"No worries," Mason smiled. "That's pretty much what I felt."

"Have you been back since?" she asked.

"Only once. It'll be ten years ago this coming Halloween."

"Did anything happen?"

Mason nodded.

"What?" she asked, leaning forward.

"Whatever is in the house dropped something else."

Julie looked at him. "What was it?"

"A bag," Mason said, pinching the bridge of his nose and closing his eyes. "A small bag with scalps in it."

Julie inhaled sharply, and Mason opened his eyes.

Surprisingly, she didn't have an expression of concern for his mental well-being on her face. She was shocked and disgusted.

"Scalps," she said in a low voice.

"Yes."

"What type of scalps?" she asked.

"Small scalps," Mason answered. "Caucasians mostly. A few Native Americans."

"Oh Jesus Christ," she murmured. "They were real?"

He nodded. "I brought them to an old professor of archeology down at the University of Connecticut. Nice man. I lied and told him that I had picked up an old chest at a flea market in Hollis and found the bag in a false bottom. I asked him if they were real, and he took a look at them."

"And they were," she said.

"Yes," Mason said. "He told me that he couldn't put a definite age on them, but that he felt fairly certain that they were late seventeenth, maybe early eighteenth centuries. He wanted me to leave them with the University for further study, maybe add them to the University's collection. I told him that I would bring them back when I could, but that I'd purchased the trunk with another buyer and had to speak to him before I made any decision like that."

"Do you still have them?" Julie asked.

"Yes," he said. "I still have the Darth Vader mask, too."

"Wow," she said.

Mason nodded. His throat hurt. He hadn't spoken at such length in a long time.

"Are you okay?" she asked.

"Yes."

"You look like there's something wrong."

Mason smiled. "I'm not used to speaking so much. I don't talk to too many people these days; and definitely not as much as I've spoken to you."

"Well, thank you," Julie smiled, "I'm flattered."

Mason felt his face get hot, and Julie's smile widened.

"So," Julie said, standing up, "would you like a cup of coffee?"

"Yes," Mason smiled. "I would love a cup of coffee. Am I allowed to drink it in here?"

"Of course not," she laughed, "but I'm the only one here, and I'm not going to say anything about it. Come on around the desk," she grinned, motioning him to follow her. "Let's get some coffee."

Chapter 9: A Place to Rest

Halloween. 1977. The Boylan House.

Marcus came out of the woods somewhere in a town called Monson. He was tired. He'd been walking all day. His backpack was heavy, his feet were sore and night was setting. He needed a place to sleep. A glance at the sky showed that the clouds rolling in from the east were thunderheads. An October rainstorm in New England promised to be a miserable experience, and Marcus wanted nothing of it.

He followed a small trail that led through a field, heavy with grass gone to seed. Birds continued their calls and at some point, he scared a small animal, sending it rushing away, the grass waving ever so slightly as it sought refuge.

Marcus didn't need to hunt anything, tonight. He had plenty of canned food, and even a little bit of money tucked away in his boot from the last job down in Nashua.

The trail turned and emptied onto a dirt road. Looking down to the left, Marcus saw a pair of houses and a single streetlamp marking the road. The houses were well lit, and he could make out Halloween decorations from where he stood.

Damn, he thought. It's Halloween. Can't go that way.

Marcus turned to the left and saw a large house, ancient and dark and on a small hill on the left of the road, set back just a little.

No driveway. No cars. No lights.

The place looked abandoned.

In good shape. But definitely empty.

I need to make sure, though, he thought.

Adjusting the pack on his back, Marcus moved forward, keeping to the growing shadows and making his way around to the right. The road ended a hundred yards further down, and Marcus stuck to it. He could smell water and rot. There was a swamp nearby. A good thing to remember.

Fifteen minutes later, Marcus had managed to make his way close to the back of the house. He pulled his binoculars out of a side pouch, brought them up and focused them on the window to the far right.

Nothing.

He moved on to each window and saw nothing. No

appliances. No furniture. Nothing.

Marcus smiled and put the binoculars away. He approached the house carefully. His eyes darted from window to window as he made his way to the back door.

Nothing.

At the door, he found an old iron latch and hinges made of iron as well, and massive boards. The house, he realized, was ancient. Maybe even a landmark. Something on the historical register. But there were no signs. Nothing.

Marcus tried opening the door and found it unlocked. He pushed it open and stepped into the house. The fading light showed him that the home had stood empty for years.

Possibly decades.

The depth of dust on the floor was thick. Not even rodent tracks cut through.

Curious, Marcus thought as he stepped in and closed the door behind him.

It sounded like the house sighed.

Marcus looked around nervously, for a moment. But his stomach grumbled, and he knew he needed to eat. And he knew he needed shelter from the weather.

Just one night, he told himself. *Just one night.*

He walked over to the huge chimney that stood in the center of the house. There was only one room, a giant one that filled the entire first floor. A set of stairs, running along the far wall, went to the second floor. But Marcus had no desire to go up there.

He removed his pack, put it down, and took his flannel shirt off. He used his shirt to sweep away a spot on the floor so that he could sit down without being coated in dust. With that finished, he put the shirt down on one side to be shaken out later and opened his pack. From it, he took his P-38 can opener, a can of peaches, a can of corn and a can of Dinty Moore beef stew. His spoon and canteen followed.

He probably had half an hour before it would be too dark to eat.

Marcus didn't waste any time. He quickly opened each of the cans, neatly stacked the lids on the hearthstone of the chimney, and then began to eat.

It took him only a few minutes to finish off the corn and the beef stew. He was working his way through the can of peaches, when he heard a noise from the upper floor.

Marcus put the can on the floor and pulled his pocketknife out. It wasn't much, but it would be enough to let him either work out a deal with another squatter or get the hell out with his gear.

He looked up at the large beams and the wide floor boards.

The creaks crossed the second floor to the stairs.

Marcus tightened his grip on the knife. Someone started to descend the stairs and pure blackness descended upon the room.

Marcus' heart started racing and his hand was sweating upon the knife.

The creaking continued, the footsteps descending. Suddenly, they stopped, and Marcus tried to control the fear racing through him. He tried to remember where his pack was, where the exit was. He was confused, and his thoughts were racing.

I have to get out, he said to himself.

He leaned forward, reaching out with his left hand, seeking the pack. His hand touched the rough wool of his bedroll, and he sighed, grasping the blanket and pulling the pack to him. *Good, thank God*, he sighed.

"Yes," a deep voice said suddenly in his ear. "Yes, you'll do fine."

And Marcus screamed as something cold closed upon his neck.

Chapter 10: Hunting Liam through History

Mason rubbed his eyes and sat back into the chair. The microfilm reader hummed loudly, waiting for him to put in another spool.

But Mason was done. He was up to date.

Terribly up to date.

A stack of photocopies, printed off from the machine, stood beside his empty cup of coffee. The stack was nearly an inch high. There were dozens upon dozens of articles about missing boys from around the area.

"How are you doing?" Julie asked, coming around the small wall that separated the microfilm and microfiche readers from the stacks of books.

"I'm okay," Mason said. "I finished."

"Really?" she asked. "That was a lot of newspapers you had to go through."

"Not really," he said. "I focused only on October. There might be others, rarities, I would think, but I focused on October." Mason patted the pile of photocopies.

"Damn," she said softly. "That many?"

"Yes and no," Mason said, standing up and stretching.

"How is it 'no'?" Julie asked.

"Well," Mason said, "I figure that Liam Boylan has been killing boys since the late seventeenth century. If he continued to do this after he was crucified and killed, he's only been taking a few boys here and there. This stack," he said, picking it up, "these articles represent missing boys in the surrounding area for the past two hundred years. There can't be more than fifty here. He takes one every so often. Just enough to sate whatever appetite that he has, just enough to leave an urban legend behind him."

"Fifty?" Julie asked in a low voice.

"Fifty," Mason nodded. "And that's just what we have recorded in newspapers from the time. Remember, we don't know exactly what happened before that. But that book by Gunther mentions previous incidents."

"Unbelievable," Julie muttered. Then in a louder voice she asked, "Are you done?"

"For now," he nodded. He pushed the chair back on its wheels. He stood up and stretched and saw her smiling at him.

He smiled back, and she blushed slightly. "Come on up to the front," she said after a moment, "we'll have another cup of coffee." She glanced up to the clock above the microfilm machine. "And we've got to close up, around, I don' know, say fifteen minutes."

"Sounds good," Mason said. He put the copies into his carry case which had become pregnant with the amount of material he had copied and notes he'd made. Turning the microfilm reader off, he smiled at Julie once more and followed her as she led him out towards the front of the library.

Only a few people had come in throughout the day, and none of them had paid much attention to Mason. Now, the library was empty except for Mason and the librarian again.

They walked behind the front desk, and Mason put his carry case on the desk as Julie walked into the small back office. She returned, just a moment later, with two mugs of hot, black coffee.

"Thank you," he said, taking one from her.

"You're welcome," she smiled, sitting down.

Mason sat down after her. He took a sip and smiled at the strength and richness of the coffee.

"Well," Julie said after a moment, "what's your next step?"

"I need to find out if there's a pattern, a schedule, if there's even anything really to it," Mason said. "Halloween's in three days, and I don't know if boys disappear every year, every other year, every five years or what exactly," he sighed. "I don't know if I really saw what I saw. Or if I'm mad, or what. I just know that boys go missing. And they aren't found again when they go too close to the Boylan House."

"So you want to see if it's just terrible coincidences or something sinister?"

"Exactly," Mason nodded.

Julie took a sip of her coffee, her brow furrowing, and then she smiled. "Do you want me to talk to my brother?" she asked.

Mason looked at her, confused. "About what?"

"About the Boylan House," she said.

"Why?" he asked.

"You said that things happen at the end of October," Julie said, "and you want to figure something out by Halloween."

"Yes."

"If you figure it out, or even if you don't figure it out," Julie said, "I could ask my brother to go to the Boylan House on Halloween."

Mason straightened up in his seat. "Do you think that I could go with your brother, or meet him there?"

"I'll give him a call tonight," she said. "Do you want to stop by tomorrow? I can tell you what he said."

"You open at 10:30, right?" Mason asked.

"Yes," Julie answered.

"How about we meet at Anne's Diner across the street for breakfast," Mason said, smiling. "My treat."

"I'd like that," she said, hiding her smile behind her coffee mug. "I'd like that a lot."

Chapter 11: Making his Decision

November 1st. 2014. Hollis, NH.

Mason sat at his desk, drinking his first cup of coffee and wondering if he'd ever be able to sleep past five o'clock in the morning. He doubted it.

He hadn't slept well since 1980.

Turning the computer on, he waited a moment for everything to start up. Finally, he was able to check his emails; notifications of payments from different clients, requests for work, polite rejections of bids and different pieces, and a couple of reminders to pay bills, which he dutifully put in both his computer calendar and his datebook beside the computer.

With his mail read, he opened his web browser and turned his attention to the local news.

There were the usual morning regulars, a shooting in Dorchester, a prostitution drug bust up in Manchester, *The Martian* continuing to rock the bestseller charts, a successful probe launch into space, a heroin operation stopped in Nashua.

Boy missing in Monson.

Mason put his coffee cup down and clicked on the article.

"Jeremy Rand, age 13 years, last seen walking on Meeting House Road after Halloween trick or treating time had ended. Parents had attempted to take his cell phone away as discipline for continued poor grades in school. Police fear that Jeremy has wandered into the conservation land around Meeting House Road. Much of the land is wetland and swamps. Last night, temperatures plunged to fifteen degrees and they are fearful that the boy may have become confused due to hypothermia since he was last seen wearing a pair of basketball shorts and a New England Patriots t-shirt with sandals. The police will be calling a press conference later on to assist in going through the swamp areas in an attempt to find Jeremy Rand."

Mason let out a long breath and picked up his coffee cup. He drank from it several times before putting it down and standing up.

You've known about this for a long time, he told himself. *You need to try and do something.*

There's nothing to be done, he argued with himself. *There's never been any proof that there's something in the house. Never any proof that they had been taken.*

No, he thought. *But there's never been any proof that the boys have disappeared into the swamp either. After all these years, and the people that wander through the conservation land, something should have shown up. A shoe. A bag. A belt. Something.*

Not necessarily, he started, but then he cut his own conservation off.

He walked to the opposite end of his office, the walls of which were lined with hundreds of reference books and histories. At the far end, though, was a shelf with only two items on it.

A bag of centuries old scalps and a Darth Vader mask from a 1980 Halloween costume.

No, Mason told himself. *There's something there, and I need to figure out how to stop it.*

Chapter 12: Gathering Allies

Mason and Julie sat on the steps of the library together. It wasn't time to open the library, and they had just finished breakfast at the diner, which Mason had found, made a hell of a western omelet. In their hands, they held coffees from the local café. The weather was perfect, just warm enough to go around without a jacket, just cool enough to wear a long-sleeve shirt and some jeans.

The granite of the steps, however, were cold under his ass.

"Are you okay?" Julie asked as he shifted himself on the step.

"Yeah," he said, grinning at her. "I'm just old. Pretty sure I'll get arthritis in my hips from the granite."

"You're not old," she laughed.

"Oh no?" Mason smiled. "Don't you know how old I am?"

"No," she said.

"Think about it, just for a minute," he said. "Remember, I was seven in 1980."

Her eyes widened slightly. "Oh. You're forty-two."

He nodded.

"Well," she smiled, "that's still not old. How old do you think I am?"

"Twenty-one," he said without hesitation, taking a sip of his coffee."

She laughed, shaking her head. "Tack on another six."

"Twenty-seven?" Mason said, looking at her. "Honestly, Julie, you really don't look it."

"Why, thank you," she said. "My brother tells me that I look like I'm about fifty and that it'll only get worse, the longer I stay a librarian."

"Brothers are good for that," Mason said. "But trust me, there is a definite shortage of hot librarians around. Don't go and quit on me."

Her laughter echoed off the stones of the library. "I won't," she grinned.

They drank their coffees in silence for a few minutes, simply enjoying the day and one another's company.

"Oh," Julie said suddenly, "I managed to speak with my brother, James, last night."

Mason lowered his coffee cup. "What did he say?"

"He said that he'd meet you in front of the Boylan House a little before six, tomorrow night. Trick or treating is a day early this year, and the kids are out from six to eight. He figured if you two were out there for the whole time, that that would work out pretty well. Plus, he's curious about the House. Nearly everyone in town has been, at one time or another."

"And he won't get in trouble?" Mason asked.

"No," Julie said, shaking her head. "He's just going to bring his personal vehicle. His shift ends at four."

"That's great," Mason said, smiling at her. "Thank you very much."

"You're welcome," she said. "You could pay me back, though."

"How do I do that?"

"Buy me dinner, tonight."

Mason smiled broadly. "I would love to."

"Good," she said, smiling at him. "I was hoping you'd say that."

Chapter 13: A Chat with the Owner

Halloween. 2015. Meeting House Road.

Mason pulled his truck into the dead end of Meeting House Road, turned around and pulled up alongside the grass in front of the Boylan House. He shut the truck down, got out and pulled his flannel jacket off the front seat. Carefully, he buttoned it up, pulled a black watchman's cap from the adjacent seat and put that on, tucking in his ears under the rolled sides. Lastly, he removed his shotgun from the seat, broke it open to double check the loads, then closed and locked it. He patted the pockets of his jacket, making sure the extra rounds, he had, were there.

Mason stepped away from his truck, closed the door and walked around to the back of the pickup. He lowered the tailgate and opened his lockbox. From that, he grabbed a powerful camping lantern and put it on. The light that it cast was cold but comforting, nonetheless. The Boylan House seemed to suck the light from the stars and the sliver of a moon that hung in the night sky.

Next, from the lockbox, he pulled a pair of thin, but warm gloves. He tugged each of them on, flexing each hand in turn. Nodding to himself, he reached in one last time and took out a small leather case. He unzipped it and took out the briarwood pipe that he had packed earlier in the day. Putting the pipe between his teeth, he clamped down on the mouthpiece and took the matches out of the case. He fished a match out of the box, and struck it.

In a moment, he had a strong and steady stream of smoke rising from the briarwood bowl. He put the matches in his back pocket, zipped up the pouch and returned it to the lockbox before closing it.

With his pipe in his mouth, Mason sat down on the tailgate, put the shotgun across his knees and waited.

Only a short time later, a large black pickup with an extended cab pulled up across from Mason's own truck and parked. A younger man climbed out of the truck. He was a little taller than Julie, but he had the same fine features and dark black hair that she had. He wore a hunting jacket and a pair of black cargo pants over boots.

"Mason?" the man asked, walking closer.

"Yes," Mason said around the stem of the pipe.

The man grinned and stopped by the tailgate, extending his hand. "I'm James."

"A pleasure, James," Mason said, shaking the offered hand.

When Mason let go, James nodded to the shotgun. "I have to ask, do you think something bad is going to happen, tonight?"

"I don't know," Mason said honestly. "But it's loaded with salt."

"Salt?" James asked.

"Ghostlore," Mason said. "Salt drives them away. Something to do with the purity of salt and its association with the earth."

"Okay," James said. "Well, I've got my Glock in case something a little less supernatural is creeping around."

Mason smiled. "That sounds fantastic. I'm sorry, does the pipe bother you?"

"No," James laughed. "My grandfather used to smoke one. I love the smell. Reminds me of him. We used to hunt together when I was a little boy."

"Okay," Mason said.

"My sister tells me you've been to the Boylan House before," James said.

"I have," Mason said, looking up at the house. "Back in 1980."

"Really?" James said.

"Yes," Mason answered. "Did she tell you about it?"

"No," James said, shaking his head. "She told me that I'd appreciate it more if I asked you about it directly. 1980 though," he frowned, "that's when the Peacock boy vanished, right?"

"Yes."

"And you were here that night?" James asked.

"Oh," Mason sighed, looking at the house again, "I was certainly here."

"Were you able to see anything from the street?" James asked. The cop in him coming out. "Did you notice anything before he disappeared?"

"I wasn't on the street."

"You weren't?" James asked. "Well if you ..."

Mason nodded.

"You were the boy with Peacock up at the door."

"I was."

37

"Wow," James said, "that would explain you being so interested in the Boylan House."

Mason smiled tiredly at the young man. "Yes."

A few minutes of silence had passed between them before James asked, "What do you think is in the house?"

"Something evil," Mason said in a low voice. "Something that's been preying on boys for centuries. But all I have is an urban legend and the memories of a seven-year-old boy."

"Julie said you'd been back a couple of times," James said looking at him. "That some things happened. Do those count as the memories of a seven-year-old, too?"

"No," Mason said, "but I don't trust myself. I'm not impartial. And, quite honestly, I've always been a little afraid that I didn't look at things the right way. Maybe I saw things that weren't there."

He shrugged. "I'm hoping tonight, though, there'll be something I can hang my hat on. Something definitive I can rule out," he said as he looked at James. "And you'll be able to help me, too."

"I will?"

"Yes, if you see something too, then I know I'm not crazy."

James smiled. "That's a valid point."

"I hope so."

"You know," James said after a moment, "this place scares the hell out of me."

"Why?"

"I've always been afraid of it. Kids used to talk about it at school; how some bum or drifter would snatch you up and kill you if you got too close. Boogeyman stories that I believed."

"I still believe them," Mason said.

"You've got more cause to," the young man said. "I read the report about the disappearance. I read your statement. The cop who took it, wrote on the bottom that he thought you were just too scared to remember what you saw correctly."

Mason nodded. "I know. I had a lot of adults tell me that. They still do. It's one of the reasons why I don't completely trust my memories on the subject."

"Shit," James said.

"What?"

"Look," James said, pointing up to the house.

A single light shined through the window on the far right of the second floor.

"There shouldn't be anyone in there."

"I don't think there is," Mason said softly. He climbed off the tailgate, holding his shotgun in both hands and switching off the safety. James unzipped his jacket, reached inside and drew out his Glock, slipping his safety off as well.

The light moved from one window to the next, then to the next, and then to the next. It stayed there for nearly ten minutes as if someone was watching them.

Then the light moved back, from window to window, until it reached the last window on the right, once more. It faded only to reappear in the lower floor's far right window.

"What the hell is going on?" James asked in a low voice.

"I don't know," Mason said. "I really don't."

The door to the Boylan House opened.

Light shined out.

"Get out!" a voice deep and terrible screamed. "Get out and leave me to my work!"

"You kidding me?" James hissed, bringing his weapon up to bear on the door.

Mason did the same, clenching on the pipe stem so tightly that it hurt his teeth.

The light came out of the house, wobbling as if the hand holding it was nowhere near as strong as the voice to which it belonged.

"Get out! Get out! Get out!" it screamed. "I know you, foul boy! I know your
stench! Boy, no more and man you be, but I'll eat your balls all the same!" it shrieked.

Mason felt a cold, primal fear rip at his stomach. Every childhood nightmare he'd ever had raced into his thoughts, and he frantically fought them back.

"Stop!" James shouted, his voice strong but thick with fear. "This is the Monson police, put the light down and your hands on your head!"

The thing holding the lantern shrieked and started to run down the short hill towards them.

James didn't hesitate.

He put two quick rounds into the center mass of the person

39

holding the lantern, and the result was instantaneous.

The lantern fell, the shape of a man collapsed to the earth. The light went out, and something black leaped up from the man shape and raced towards Mason and James.

And Mason fired both barrels of the shotgun.

An unworldly thing shrieked as the salt struck the shape, turning it around and sending it racing back to the house. The door slammed shut.

Looking at James, Mason nodded, and together they walked up toward the shape on the grass. Mason broke open the shotgun, emptied the casings and put two fresh shells in. He had the weapon ready as they reached the thing lying on the ground.

It was a body.

The body of a man. He wore filthy, foul-smelling rags. James, with a distinct lack of ceremony, put his foot under the body and rolled it over.

"Shit," the young policeman exhaled.

The face staring back up was old, lips pulled back over ancient yellowed teeth. His flesh was white, his nails were long and yellow. Something silver glittered around his neck in the starlight. James squatted down and with a snort of disgust, fished the necklace out.

They were dog tags.

"Henry Marquis," James said. He looked up to Mason. "So this is who I shot. What the hell did you shoot?"

"I don't know," Mason said, "but it's still there."

"What?" James asked.

"Look," Mason said, pointing back at the house.

In the upper right-hand corner of the second floor, the light was shining in the window.

Chapter 14: 12:01 AM, November 1st, 2015, Monson

"What the hell just happened?" James asked, motioning to the waitress.

"Liam Boylan happened," Mason said.

The waitress came over. She was a young woman, and she smiled at both of them. "What can I get for you?"

"Double shot of whiskey," James said, "and a vodka chaser."

She raised an eyebrow but looked over at Mason. "And what about you?"

"Same," Mason said, "except switch the vodka chaser for a bottle of Sam Adams, please."

"You got it."

She flashed them a tired smile and made her way to the bar.

"Who the hell is Liam Boylan?" James asked. He took off his jacket and hung it over the back of his chair. In the pub's dim lighting, he looked pale, with black beneath his eyes.

"Liam Boylan is the owner of the house," Mason answered.

"The owner?" James asked. "I didn't think anyone owned the house anymore."

The waitress came back with the drinks, put them on the table and Mason took a pair of twenties out of his wallet. He handed them to her.

"No change, please," he smiled. She returned the smile and left them to their conversation.

Mason lifted his whiskey and drank it in one swallow. James did the same.

"So," James said, sipping at his vodka, "there's an owner?"

Mason nodded.

"Liam Boylan."

Again, Mason nodded.

"Has he inherited the place?"

"No," Mason said. "There's only ever been one owner."

"What?" James asked, putting his drink back on the battered tabletop. "How is that even possible?"

"I don't know," Mason said. "But according to all of the research I've been able to do, there's only ever been Liam Boylan."

"So what are you saying?" James asked looking at him. "Are you telling me I just killed a, what, a four-hundred-year-old

41

man?"

"No," Mason said, "you didn't kill Liam Boylan."

"Who the hell did I kill?" James asked in a low voice.

"Someone named Henry Marquis," Mason answered.

"Damn," James said. "We're going to have to go back. I still have to call it in."

"The body won't be there," Mason said.

"How do you know?"

"They've never found any bodies there."

James nodded. "I still want to check it out."

"Daylight?"

"Definitely daylight," James said. He drank some of his vodka. "So," he said after a moment, "was the black thing Boylan?"

"Yes," Mason said. He picked up his beer and held the cold bottle in both hands.

"And that's why the light came on," James said.

"Exactly," Mason nodded. He took a drink of the beer and sighed.

"Well," James said, rubbing the back of his head, "how the hell do we kill him?"

"I don't know," Mason said. He looked at the young police officer. "I don't know. But we're going to have to figure it out, and within the next year at the latest."

James frowned. "Why?"

"Because I'm pretty sure," Mason said, "Liam Boylan is going to get his hands on another body before next Halloween. Especially since he didn't get a boy this year, and he was obviously looking for one."

James shook his head and then finished his vodka. "This is pretty screwed up, Mason."

"Yeah," Mason said. "It sure as hell is."

They sat in silence for a minute before James said, "You know what, screw this! You sober enough to drive?"

Mason thought about it seriously for a moment and nodded.

"Good," James said, standing up. He took his jacket off the back of the chair and put it back on. "I need to see whether or not there's a body there."

"Sounds good to me. We'll take my truck, okay?" Mason asked.

James nodded.

Mason led the way out of the pub, waving to the waitress. The young woman smiled, returning the wave. James followed him out into the brisk air and to Mason's pickup. "Door's unlocked," Mason said.

He climbed into the driver's seat, and James got into the passenger's. Mason fished his keys out of his jacket pocket and slid the ignition key into place. A moment later, he had the truck's old engine rumbling, the lights on, and he was pulling out of the pub's parking lot and onto Route 122. He aimed the truck towards Meeting House Road and relaxed in his seat.

James sat silently, looking out of the window.

Mason reached out, turned the heat on and adjusted it.

Within fifteen minutes, he was signaling and turning onto Meeting House Road. He slowed down as they approached the Boylan House, which was disturbingly dark.

Mason stopped the truck a short distance from the house, angling the vehicle, so the headlights shined up the small hill.

"You have got to be kidding me," James hissed. "Where's the damn body?"

The grass was empty.

"I shot someone. I know I did," James said, looking over at Mason.

Mason nodded. "I know, I was there. I saw it. I put two rounds of salt into something, too."

"We need to figure out what the hell's in there," James said. "We need to know."

"Yes."

"I need to know."

Mason nodded.

"Will you be able to find out?" James asked. "I mean, you were able to figure out who Liam Boylan was, is, or whatever the hell it is."

"I'm going to try," Mason answered, looking back at the house. "I'm going to try."

Chapter 15: "What is Liam Boylan?"

Mason was sitting on the top step of the library with the sun beating down and chasing off the November wind. He was holding two coffees, and Julie smiled at him as she walked up the stone steps. She was wearing a pair of dark slacks bloused above black calf-high boots. A gray, mid-thigh fall jacket was belted at the waist, and her hair was pulled back into a loose ponytail.

"Well, good morning," she smiled at him. "Are you here for business or pleasure?"

"Both, I hope," he grinned, standing up.

"Have you been here long?"

"Is that a pick-up line?" he asked with a smile.

She winked at him. "Take it anyway you like, Mr. Philips," she said, unlocking the library's door.

"Then I'd love to have dinner with you this evening," he said, holding the door open for her as she wiggled the key out of the lock.

"That sounds like a date," she laughed.

He followed her into the small vestibule, and she unlocked the second door.

"Speaking of dates," she said, "did you and James meet up at the Boylan House, last night?" she asked.

"We did," Mason said, enjoying the way that she walked to the desk. She caught him looking and gave him a big smile. He smiled back.

"How did it go?" she asked, putting her purse down on the desk and taking off her coat.

"A little rough on both of us, I'm afraid," he answered, handing her one of the coffees.

"Thanks," she said, frowning. "What do you mean by *rough*?"

"We went to the Boylan House last night," Mason said. Julie sat down in her chair and motioned for him to sit down, as well. He did so, and she took a sip of her coffee as she turned on the computer.

"Okay, so you went to the Boylan House," she said. "What happened?"

"We waited a while, and a light came on upstairs in the house," Mason said.

She looked at him. "There's no power to the house."

"I know."

"No one lives there."

"I know."

"Then how the hell was there a light?" she asked.

"It was Liam Boylan," Mason said. "He was possessing someone, as far as your brother and I could guess."

"Possessing someone?" Julie asked, sitting back and drinking her coffee. "Do you know who?"

Mason nodded. "A man named Henry Marquis."

"What happened to him?" she asked.

"Your brother killed him."

Julie's mouth twitched. "He what?"

"Your brother killed him," Mason said gently. "Marquis came out, screaming at us. Your brother identified himself as the police, told Marquis to put his hands up. Marquis screamed and ran at us instead. Your brother never hesitated."

She nodded. "Where is he now? Does he have a mountain of paperwork to do?"

Mason shook his head. "No. Not at all. We left the scene for a little while to get ourselves together."

"Why did you have to get yourselves together?" she asked.

"Because Boylan came out of Marquis when your brother shot the man," Mason answered. "A black shape that I put two barrels of salt into."

"So why isn't my brother writing up reports on an officer involved shooting?" she asked, confused.

"Because when we went back to the Boylan House," Mason said, "the body was gone."

Julie looked at him for a long moment before saying, "You're serious, aren't you? Of course you are. Damn. Damn. That's crazy." She drank her coffee for a moment, then looked at him, giving him a small smile. "So, you're here to do more research?"

"And to see you," he said.

Her smile widened, and her cheeks reddened slightly. "I'm glad. So, you do want to get dinner tonight?"

"Of course, I do," he smiled.

"Good," she sighed. "Okay, you need to get to work, don't you?"

"I do," he said, standing up as she did.

Julie led the way around the desk and back to the Gunther Room. She unlocked it and flipped on the light. "I'll check on you in a little bit, okay?"

"Please do," Mason said, grinning.

She smiled back at him and returned to the desk. Mason entered the room and put his carry case down on the table. He took a sip of coffee, then put the cup down beside the case.

Okay, he thought. *Where do I start today?*

Chapter 16: Reading the Sealed Letter

Mason sat back in the chair and rubbed his eyes. He was still tired from last night's excursion to the Boylan House.

He looked around the room at the shelves of books and files of papers. He'd gone through a lot of them, and he had one more manuscript box that he'd pulled down and wanted to go through before Julie showed up again for coffee.

He smiled at the thought of her. He hadn't had anyone significant in his life in a long time.

He turned his attention back to the manuscript box and read the title on it once more; *Mysteries of Monson, New Hampshire*.

Mason opened the box and found a slim book bound in black cloth. It looked like a small press publication. When he took it out of the box and opened the book, the binding creaked.

The book had rarely, if ever, been opened.

Mason turned to the title page.

"*Mysteries of Monson, New Hampshire*," it read, "*written by Irwin C. Hunt. Published by Morgan Hollis, Hollis, NH, 1957.*"

Mason turned the page and found a dedication printed there.

"*To our town's Sheriff, who has helped me compile some of these incidents and given me unfettered access to any files, which reside solely in the Sheriff's Office.*"

The next page proved to be a table of contents. Mason read the individual titles, which ranged from the mystery of a mountain lion to the local cemetery being haunted by Revolutionary War soldiers. But a title near the bottom of the list, caught Mason's eye.

"*The Abandoned Ford on Meeting House Road.*"

Mason turned to the page indicated, and started to read.

"*Like any small town in these New England states, Monson has had a few abandoned cars. Most of those cars were, of course, dilapidated wrecks, clearly left because the machines would travel no further, regardless of any jerry-rigging which might be done. Mr. Thomas, the owner of the local junk yard, would always come out with his 'wrecker' and take the defunct vehicle away.*

"*In September of 1946, however, there was a vehicle which proved the exception to the rule.*

"Mr. Davis of One Meeting House Road rode his horse into town on a Sunday morning to attend service at the First Congregationalist Church. He also wished to speak with Sheriff Philips about an abandoned vehicle on Meeting House Road.

"According to the report, which the Sheriff filed, Mr. Davis stated the car had been at the end of Meeting House Road for several days. He didn't know if there were men who were hunting, since there was an abundance of deer and small game this season, or what they might be doing. But this is New England, and New Englanders respect the privacy of others.

"It wasn't until several days had passed, without the vehicle moving, that Mr. Davis took a walk to the end of the road, which is something he was not in the habit of doing. He stated that he had a dislike of the old Boylan House, and thus, stayed away from it whenever possible. But he had become concerned that perhaps someone had committed suicide in the vehicle, and he didn't want any wandering child to discover the body.

"Mr. Davis had served with the 9th Infantry in the war, and he was well familiar with death. He had no desire for children to become acquainted with it too early in their lives.

"When Mr. Davis reached the car, he saw it was empty and that it had been for several days. No one had been sleeping in it, and there was no sign of any sort of food or clothing. What was additionally curious, was that the car was new. It was a post-war production Ford, equipped with all of the latest fashions in automobiles.

"This was not the type of car that was found abandoned in Monson.

"It was on Sunday morning when Mr. Davis had made his examination and so he decided that when he went into town for service, he would inform Sheriff Philips.

"When Mr. Davis informed the Sheriff about the car, prior to the start of service, Sheriff Philips immediately left to go to the scene. Mr. Samuel Hackett, the owner of the Hackett Book and Stationery store, accompanied him.

"At the end of Meeting House Road, they found the car exactly as Mr. Davis had said it would be; empty. Sheriff Philips and Mr. Hackett did a quick search of the area and could find no trail leading into the wilderness. Considering that the weather had been fine, whoever the driver had been, would still *have been trackable. The two men even walked up to the Boylan House and wandered around it, looking into the bottom floor and calling out for anyone to answer.*

No one did."

"Sheriff Philips and Mr. Hackett then returned to the abandoned car where they searched for and found the car's registration. It was registered to the law firm of Mr. Frederick Gunther of Boston, Massachusetts. A member of that curious law firm which was the executor of the Boylan House trust.

"Upon returning to his office, Sheriff Philips made several phone calls to the Boston Police Department and received several more from the same place. Sheriff Philips was able to establish that all three of the law firm's senior partners had driven up to Monson to take care of some sort of legal business. It was supposed to be a day trip; one they made every three months together, but none of the men had returned.

"Their wives and junior partners had sought the help of the police to establish that the men were missing and needed to be found. The Boston Police Department were unable to precisely locate where the men had even disappeared from. Neither the men's families nor their junior partners knew where the men were going.

"With that information in hand, Sheriff Philips requested assistance from the New Hampshire State Police and a full investigation was launched into the disappearance of the three men. Search parties combed through the woods and surrounding swamps and wetlands, yet it was to no avail. Nothing could be found regarding the whereabouts of the lawyers. The old Boylan House was even opened up and searched, and that, too, showed nothing.

"To this day, the case of the missing lawyers from Boston remains open. Hunters are constantly encouraged to keep a sharp lookout for any sign of the men. Yet, like all of the residents of Monson know, those who disappear in the conservation land at the end of Meeting House Road, are never seen again. Nor is any sign of them."

Mason closed the book and shook his head. *It was the same,* he thought. *The same, every time. Never a trace of anyone. But why the lawyers? Hadn't they been the trustees of the house? Shouldn't they have been afforded some sort of protection by*

Liam Boylan?

He opened the book once more and moved to the back of it to see if there was an index and when he did, he turned to the back cover first. He went to turn the last page when he noticed the paste down page on the back cover had slightly pulled away from the back cover. There was something in it.

It looked like a thin, folded piece of paper.

Mason reached out, took the edge of the pastedown, and pulled it, ever so gently. It came away easily. Mason saw nothing except old Scotch tape that was much yellowed and folded over to be made two-sided. Still moving carefully though, Mason eased the pastedown away, soon revealing a small envelope. Mason slipped the envelope out of the curious pocket which had held it.

The envelope lacked an address. But it had a date written neatly in script across the center of the envelope. January 1st, 1947.

Mason turned the envelope over and found that it was unsealed.

He opened it carefully, and found a small piece of paper folded within it. He set the envelope down and opened up the letter. The letterhead upon it read "Sheriff Harold Philips, Monson, NH, Sheriff's Office".

Mason started reading.

"To Whom It May Concern," the letter began, *"My name is Harold Philips. I am the sheriff for Monson, New Hampshire. On September 21st, 1946, I executed the three lawyers from Boston that everyone's looking for. They had it coming. They and their fathers have been protecting whatever the hell is in the Boylan House for centuries. It hunts children, that thing. They knew it. That's why they didn't allow the town to put up a fence around the damned thing.*

"Men like that shouldn't be allowed to live. And so I took that away from them. One day, I hope to find out what's in that house, and how I'm going to kill it.

"Because it needs killing.

"Harold Philips, January 1st, 1947."

Mason looked hard at the name. Something pulled at his memory. The man had the same last name as he did, but Philips was a fairly common name. And Harold was common for World

War Two. He'd seen that in his research. *But there was ...* and his thought trailed off.

Dropping the letter to the table, he reached into his bag and pulled out his cellphone. He knew Julie wouldn't care. Scrolling through his contacts, he found his mother's home number and hit it.

A moment later, the phone on the other end was ringing.

By the third ring, his mother picked up the phone.

"Hello Mason," she said brightly, "why are you calling so early in the day?"

"Well," he said, sitting back in the chair, "I had a strange question for you about my father."

"What?" she asked, a noticeable chill in her voice at the mention of the man who had abandoned them.

"Did he have an uncle who served in World War Two?"

"Yes," she said. "Both your grandfather, Mason, and your granduncle, Harold, served in World War Two."

"Where did Harold live after the war?" Mason asked, his heart beating faster.

"In Monson," his mother answered. "That's where they grew up. It was a shame that your grandfather died so young. He did enjoy the little bit of time he spent with you as a baby."

Mason nodded, even though he knew that his mother couldn't see him. "Mom," Mason said, "whatever happened to his brother, Harold?"

"I'm not sure," she said after a moment. "He was the sheriff in Monson for the longest time. I'd get a card from him every Christmas, but that stopped around five years ago, I think. It was a shame, you know."

"What was?" Mason asked.

"He and his wife separated," she said, "unofficially, of course, back in 1946."

"Oh," Mason said. He started to speak again, but she cut him off.

"You see," she said, "their son got lost in the swamp that's out there in Monson, the one that kids always get lost in. They never found him."

A chill raced along Mason's spine. "Do you know if Harold is still alive?" he asked her.

"I'm not sure," she said. "But, like I said, he was the Sheriff there for the longest time. I'm sure that if you get into Monson and ask around, someone will know what's become of him."

"Okay, mom," Mason said. "I'll give you a call tonight."

"Are you coming over on Sunday?" she asked. "Your Aunt will be up from Florida with your Uncle."

"I will," he smiled.

"Well okay, then," she said. "I love you, and I'll talk to you later."

"Love you, too, Mom," Mason said, and he ended the call.

He looked down at the letter on the table and wondered if Harold Philips was still alive.

Chapter 17: Finding Sheriff Harold Philips

"How's it going?" Julie asked from the doorway. She held two cups of coffee and smiled at him as she asked the question.

"Better than I thought it would," he answered, standing up and grimacing as he stretched. "Check this out." He picked up the letter from Sheriff Philips and handed it to her as he took one of the coffees.

He drank slowly as she read the letter, her eyes widening.

"Where did you find this?" she asked. "Was it filed in here?"

"Sort of," Mason said. "It was hidden in the binding of a book on mysteries in Monson."

"Wow," Julie said, shaking her head. "Just wow."

"I know. And I think," Mason said, taking another sip of coffee, "this former sheriff is my great-uncle."

"Really?" she asked.

Mason nodded. "My father bailed out on the family when I was really young, so I didn't get to meet that side of the family. But I just talked to my mom, and she told me my father had an uncle, named Harold, who lived up in Monson and was the sheriff. I just don't know if he's still alive or not."

"James will know," Julie said confidently.

"How do you know?" Mason asked.

Julie smiled. "My brother knows every ex-law enforcement officer in a hundred-mile radius. If your great-uncle's still alive, then James is going to know exactly where he is."

Chapter 18: James Knows Everyone

Mason and Julie were sitting at the front desk when James walked into the library. The young man looked ragged and worn out, dark circles heavy beneath his eyes. He was in street clothes and looked like he would need to sleep for a week before feeling any better.

"Hey Jules," James said, coming to the desk and sitting down on it. "How are you?"

"I think I'm doing better than you," Julie said. "Mason told me about last night."

"Last night was screwed up," James said. "Really screwed up."

"Yeah, it was," Mason agreed.

"Last night aside," Julie said, "Mason has a question for you."

"What's up?"

"Do you know an old Monson sheriff by the name of Harold Philips?" Mason asked.

James smiled. "Damn right I do."

"He's still alive?" Mason said, trying to contain his excitement.

"Yeah," James laughed. "Nothing'll kill that old man. Still lives in his house over on Washington Street. I stop in about once a week and check up on him. He tells me to stop being a Nancy and leave him alone. Of course, he's got coffee on the burner for me when I walk in. Why?" James asked. "How do you know Harold?"

"He's my great-uncle," Mason said.

"No shit?" James asked, and when Mason nodded, James said, "Damn, when's the last time you spoke with him?"

"I don't know if I've ever spoken with him," Mason said. "My father took off a little while after I was born, and my grandfather died a little bit after that. My mom said Harold sent her Christmas cards, but I haven't had any contact with him."

James frowned. "Well, why do you ask then?"

"Come with me," Mason said, "I can show you what he wrote about seventy years ago." He stood up and walked back to the Gunther Room with James following him. The phone rang, and Julie answered it, staying at the desk.

A moment later, Mason was handing the letter that Harold had written over to James. The young man took it, read it and felt his eyes widen. He looked up at Mason.

"Do you think this is true?" James asked.

"Yes," Mason answered. "My mother told me Harold's son went missing in the swamp."

"Dammit," James said. He handed the letter back to Mason. Mason held it for a moment, and then he carefully folded it, returned it to its envelope and put the envelope in his carry case. "Do you want to talk to him?"

"Yes," Mason said. "I'd like to talk to him as soon as possible."

"He should be home," James said. "We can certainly take a ride over there if you like."

"Definitely," Mason nodded.

Julie showed up in the doorway, smiling. "Off to see Harold Philips?" she asked.

"Yes," Mason said. He started to clean up his work.

"Don't worry about that," Julie said. "I'll just lock the door behind you, and if anyone asks, I'll tell them the room is unavailable today."

"Thanks," Mason said, smiling. "You're the best."

"I know," she grinned. "And don't forget about dinner. I'm pretty sure that James and your great-uncle would probably be able to get you side-tracked."

"I won't forget," Mason said. He smiled again at her and followed James out of the room and out of the library.

With the doors closing behind them, James slowed down slightly and looked at Mason. "Dinner?"

Mason nodded.

"You're older than she is," James said.

"Yup. By a bit, too."

"How much?"

"Fifteen years," Mason said, looking at the younger man. "Does this bother you?"

James thought about it for a moment before shaking his head. "Not too much. I'm not happy that my sister is thinking about dating anyone, but I like you, so you get a pass, right now."

"Thank you," Mason said seriously.

"Plus, you seem to know how to handle your shit," James

continued, "and after last night, that means a whole helluva lot."

"Yeah," Mason agreed. "I can see that."

"I'm parked over at Cedar Street," James said. "Do you want to walk there or take your truck?"

"Let's take mine," Mason said, rubbing at his hip. "I'm not too good at walking anymore."

"Arthritis?" James asked as they approached Mason's battered old pickup.

"A little bit," Mason said. "A little hard living, too."

"You?" James asked with a smile as they both got into the cab.

"Yup," Mason said, closing his door and pulling his seatbelt on. "Me."

"What was your hard living?" James asked as Mason started the truck. "You look more like a book kind of guy to me."

"I am," Mason grinned, signaling and pulling out onto Main Street. "Which way?"

"Straight ahead and when you get to the end of Main, turn left onto Sawyer. From there, you'll take a right onto White and follow that until you see the sign for Washington Street on the right."

"Thanks."

"Sure. So," James said, looking over at him, "how does a book guy get some hard living in?"

"Well," Mason said, getting settled into his seat, "this particular book guy thought a stint in the Marine Corps would be the perfect thing to do."

"No shit?" James asked.

"No shit," Mason smiled.

"Wow," the young man said after a minute. "What did you do?"

"I killed people," Mason said.

James laughed and then his laugh trailed off when he realized that Mason wasn't joking.

"Are you serious?"

"Yes," Mason said. "I was a zero three thirty-one. A machine gunner. I saw a little bit of action in the first Iraq war and some time in Bosnia."

"Crazy."

"Yup," Mason agreed. He signaled and turned onto Sawyer.

"Do you know anything about your great-uncle Harold?" James asked after a minute.

"Only that he served in World War Two and his wife left him after his son disappeared," Mason answered. "And the fact that he was the sheriff for a while."

"A long while. I think he retired in the eighties, right when they were phasing out the sheriff's department and making a permanent police force, here. But," James said, "that's not the only thing. He was a Marine. His brother, too. He'll get a kick out of you being his great-nephew as well as you having been a Marine. He loves all that Marine Corps stuff. Has it all over his house."

"Of course he does," Mason laughed. "I've got a whole wall in my den dedicated to my time in the Corps. Meant the world to me. I even hear from some of my friends from the Marines once in a while."

They came quickly up to Washington Street, and Mason signaled again, turning onto it.

"There," James said, pointing, "little white house, four houses down on the left. That's Harold's place."

Mason pulled the truck into the driveway and shut the engine down.

Chapter 19: 3:00 PM, November 1ˢᵗ, 2015, The Boylan House

The light came on in the upper right window of the Boylan House.

Across the field, a trio of teenagers walked steadily, complaining to one another about their parents and the way their teachers failed to recognize their growing maturity.

The light flickered and shined brighter.

None of the boys gave the light any mind.

They were focused on getting up Meeting House Road. Football practice had run longer than usual, but that was because the coach thought they really had a chance against the Bishop Guertin Cardinals from Nashua, this year. The boys, who had played freshman football together the year before, agreed with their coach's assessment.

The light in the window of the Boylan House pulsed, pushing its beam out farther and farther.

But to no avail.

The boys were already on Meeting House Road, and their backs were to the Boylan House. There was nothing the house could do to attract them. Nothing it could do to entice them in.

The Philips wretch had spoiled the hunt.

Something within the house screamed out its rage and hunger. And somewhere deep within, came the sound of glass breaking.

Chapter 20: 3:15 PM, November 1st, 2015, Harold Philips

James stood in front of Mason at the side door to Harold Philips' house as he knocked on it.

A moment later, a voice called out, "Go away and piss off!"

James glanced back at Mason, grinning. "Harold it's me, James!"

There was a moment of silence.

"James?" the voice asked.

"Yup," James answered.

A few moments later, the door opened up a little, and an old man stood in the doorway. He was only a little shorter than Mason, and he wore a buttoned-down shirt tucked into a pair of sharply creased khaki pants.

The man's eyes widened slightly.

"Well," Harold said, "you must be Richard's son."

Mason felt the breath snatched out of his mouth. He could only nod.

Harold smiled at his expression.

"No magic there, son," Harold said. "You're the spitting image of your father. Don't suspect that will please you overly much since he ran like a little bitch when he realized being an adult meant more than sticking your little piss pot in everything that held still long enough." Harold shook his head. "That boy ruined a good thing with your mother and you. Oh well," Harold grinned, "screw him. Right?"

Mason laughed, nodding his head. "Right. I'm Mason, sir," he said, extending his hand.

"No 'sir' necessary," Harold said, shaking his hand. "I earned my stripes. Come on in."

"Same here," Mason said, stepping into the kitchen.

"What branch," Harold asked as James stepped in. "Take a seat at the table."

Mason and James sat down at the old wooden table up against the kitchen's far wall. There were four chairs, and they both sat down on the inside chairs as Harold went about the business of putting the coffee on to boil.

"Marines," Mason answered.

"Really?" Harold asked, looking over at him and smiling. "What did you do for my Corps?"

"Machine gunner," Mason said.

Harold laughed and made his way to the table, sitting down in a free chair. "So was I. .30 caliber."

"Ma Deuce," Mason replied.

Harold's smile got even bigger, showing off the glossy white of his dentures. "Oh yes. You're a good man, Mason. I'm glad to have made your acquaintance." He looked at James and he looked at Mason. "Something by the way you're sitting tells me this isn't simply a family reunion, put together by young James here."

"No," Mason agreed, "it's not. This is about the letter you wrote."

The smile on Harold's face noticeably decreased in size. "Ah. My confession."

James and Mason nodded.

"Well," Harold said, looking at James, "are you here to take me in for questioning?"

"Hell no," James said, shaking his head. "Not after what we saw last night."

"What did you see?" Harold asked, leaning in closer.

"A man came out of the Boylan House," James said, answering him. "I killed him."

"Who was it?" Harold asked eagerly.

"A man named Henry Marquis," James answered. "Disappeared back in seventy-five as far as anyone could figure out. Had a falling out with his wife after he came back from Vietnam, loaded up a camping pack and set off walking. Last time anyone saw him was in Nashua, and that was in seventy-seven."

Harold looked at Mason. "Was it possessing him?"

"Liam Boylan?"

Harold nodded.

"Yes," Mason answered. "Yes, it was. The man, it was inhabiting, was barely alive, and Liam was enraged. Simply by being there, we stopped it from eating. If that's even the right word for it."

"It is," Harold said grimly. "It sure is."

Chapter 21: 7:00 PM, November 2nd, 2015, Route 122, Monson

Nate and Charles walked along Route 122, far into the shoulder to avoid the occasional car racing through Monson to get to Hollis, or the opposite direction to get to Brookline. They'd stayed too late at Mike's house to play Call of Duty, and their mother had sent them a couple of text messages that definitely showed how pissed off she was.

Charles pulled his hat down lower, over his ears. It was cold and getting colder.

"This sucks," Nate complained. "She's really going to freak out when we get home."

"I know," Charles said.

A truck went flying by, high beams on.

"Asshole," Nate grumbled.

Charles could only nod his head.

As they continued along Route 122, nearing the turn for Cedar Street, they saw an SUV backed into the woods on their left, with only the nose sticking out. The finish was dark and looked like one of the new rides the Staties were cruising around in.

Just a little speed trap for the assholes, Charles thought, grinning.

As they came abreast of the SUV, the lights came on, bright, harsh halogens that caused both of the boys to stop.

They heard the door open, and a deep, male voice said, "Boys, it's kind of late to be walking, isn't it?"

Before Nate or Charles could answer, there was the sound of something being launched, a small twang.

And something had struck them both.

Charles looked down and in the bright light of the headlights, he saw two small clips attached to his jacket, wires hanging from them and running back into the light.

"What the hell?" Nate asked.

Less than a second later, Nate's question was answered.

Whoever held the other end of the tasers squeezed their triggers, and electric current raced along the wires and into the two young teenagers.

The boys collapsed and shook on the pavement.

A pair of men came out of the shadows, and into the cone of

light, cast by the headlights. The men were well dressed. Expensive shoes and suits. Gold wedding bands flashed, and the gems of Ivy League schools glittered. Each of the men bent down, one picked up Nate, and the other lifted up Charles. They did it carefully and with respect.

The men carried the boys quickly to the already open hatchback of the SUV. Zipties, duct tape, and blankets waited. The men put the boys down and in a matter of moments, they had the hands of the boys zip-tied behind their backs, their ankles ziptied together. Strips of duct tape went across their mouths, leaving plenty of room for the nose to get oxygen. The prongs of the tasers were removed, and the boys were covered with the blankets.

The men stepped back, and one of them closed the hatchback.

A car went racing by towards Brookline, the vehicle never slowing as the two men got into the SUV, one in the driver's seat and one in the passenger's. The driver shifted the large vehicle into gear, signaled and eased out onto the road. No one was around to see them.

The driver moved the SUV steadily along, taking the appropriate turns until he was signaling to turn onto Meeting House Road.

In the trunk area, they could hear the boys.

Their screams were muffled by the duct tape. Their bound feet thumped against the side of the SUV, but the blankets absorbed most of the impact.

In a moment, the driver was turning the SUV around at the end of the road and parking in front of the Boylan House, turning the lights off. He knew that the few houses at the end of the road were empty. The Walkers were on a weekend trip, courtesy of John Walker's boss, who in turn, had received a significant amount of money to encourage John to have a nice weekend with his wife. Tom Kinney won a trip to Foxwoods down in Connecticut. And Martha Deere had met a wonderful woman up in Concord who encouraged her to explore her sexuality for the weekend.

Liam Boylan's pockets were deeper than anyone could suspect.

The men got out of the car, opened the trunk and looked

down at the two terrified boys.

It was difficult for the men. They had sons of their own, but they knew what they were doing was necessary. It was what had to be done. There was no way around it, and their families had been doing it for centuries, when necessary.

And today was a day when something necessary had to be done.

One of the men picked up Charles, and the other lifted up Nate. Both of the boys struggled violently, but the men were strong. They were in shape. This wasn't the first time they had to perform such an unpleasant task, and they were certain that it wouldn't be the last.

Holding tightly to the boys, the men carried them up to the Boylan House, where the door swung open for them.

The men were thrilled, excited beyond description to be in the presence of Liam Boylan.

They stepped into the house and moved over to the right, towards the stairs. The entire first floor was dimly lit by a single, weak lantern. Holding onto the boys tightly, they climbed the stairs to the second floor. They walked into the darkness, moving by memory toward the top of the stairs. A moment later, the lantern came up and moved past them slowly.

The lantern stopped by the massive fireplace in the center of the room and the holder stepped forward.

It was a middle-aged man, a small cut on his forehead. The clothes were torn, and the face was pallid, the nose and eyes were red. The broken capillaries were the telltale sign of a man who liked to drink.

He was not the man with whom the two men had dealt with before.

But that meant nothing. The voice which issued forth from the man's mouth was the same.

"Two?" Liam Boylan asked, sighing with relief. "Two. You have performed better than before, and I did not believe such a thing was possible."

The men both beamed with pleasure.

"You have honored your predecessors," Liam Boylan said. "I know what I must do will bother you both, so I release you from witnessing it."

"Thank you," the men said simultaneously. They lowered the

squirming boys onto the floor.

Liam Boylan stepped forward, hunger glittering in his eyes.

The two men quickly turned away and went down the stairs. They didn't need the lantern to show them the way out.

Soon, they were walking down the hill in front of the Boylan House, breathing the fresh fall air. They walked down to the SUV, got into their respective seats and the driver started the vehicle.

"What do you have on deck for tomorrow?" the passenger asked the driver.

"I've got to finish up that brief for the Bonano Federal case," the driver replied. "I'll probably be there all day tomorrow. What about you?"

"Taking a deposition for a witness for that car versus bicycle accident in Lexington," the passenger said.

"Who's the defending lawyer?"

"Jones," the passenger said.

"That should be easy, then," the driver said, turning off of Meeting House Road.

"Yes, it should be," the passenger said.

And the two men, feeling greatly pleased with themselves, settled in for the long ride back to Boston.

Chapter 22: 8:30 PM, November 2nd, 2015, The Home of Harold Philips

The three men sat in Harold's library, which took up nearly the entire first floor of the small house. Harold didn't go upstairs anymore. The pain of trying to climb the stairs was simply too much.

"How old are you, Harold?" Mason asked.

Harold finished the whiskey he was drinking and smiled at him. "Ninety-four," he said. He put the empty glass on the table beside his chair and took a pack of cigarettes out of his shirt pocket. Lucky Strikes and an old school Zippo tucked in with the last of the cigarettes.

Harold's hands were steady as he lit the cigarette, returned the Zippo to the pack and the pack to his pocket. He let the smoke stream out of his nostrils, the blue smoke curling up to the old and yellowed ceiling.

"How are you still alive?" James asked laughing.

"Ain't nothing," Harold said. "Every day is an extra one, at this point. Has been since 1945."

Mason nodded, but James looked confused.

"What are you talking about?" James asked.

"Okinawa," Harold said. "But you're not here about that, so let's focus on what we are here for. Finishing Liam Boylan."

Mason and James nodded.

"First of all," Harold said, looking at Mason and James, "you have to understand that he is not the powerful thing he has made others believe he is. Strong, yes, but not nearly as powerful as his little minions make him out to be."

"Are there more?" James asked.

"Of course," Harold said. "I don't know how they continue to breed and produce children dedicated to Boylan, but they do. But that's neither here nor there. We don't have to worry about them for a few months, at least."

"What is he, Harold?" Mason asked, taking a drink from his own whiskey tumbler.

"Just a malevolent spirit," Harold said. "Something that's managed to attach itself to the house, to continue its perversity. Because all Liam Boylan wants, is young boys," Harold said, spitting out the sentence. "From what I've read, he can use the power of the boys to affect various things. Like possessing people, and for long periods.

"But," Harold said, "I don't have anything solid to go on, so this is simply conjecture."

"It's better than nothing," James muttered, and Mason nodded his agreement.

"I think so," Harold said.

"Have you thought of what to do to get him out of the house," Mason said. "Or, even better, kill it?"

"We need a priest," Harold said, looking each man in the eye, one at a time. "A real priest. Preferably orthodox, either Catholic or Eastern European. They're the only ones who are considered to have the ability to drive something like Liam Boylan out. No one else."

"Priests?" James asked. "I'm a protestant, Harold. So are you. How the hell are we going to convince a priest to go into the Boylan House?"

"I don't know," Harold said, tapping the ash off into the standing ashtray on the chair's left.

"I do," Mason said. "My mother raised me Catholic. I'm not a practicing Catholic, but I am on friendly terms with Father Moran in Nashua. He gives the mass in Latin, once a month. That's about the only time I go in."

"So, you'll speak with Father Moran?" Harold asked Mason. Mason nodded.

"Excellent," Harold said. "I'll try to figure out what we're going to need and a pair of arms and legs to get it."

"Ha, you're funny, Harold," James said.

"I know," Harold sighed, smiling a little. "I'm the funniest son of a bitch around."

James opened his mouth to reply, but his cellphone cut him off. It was a short, sharp ring that made him take the phone off his hip quickly. He unlocked the phone and answered the call.

Mason and Harold were quiet, listening.

"What's up?" James asked. There was a slight pause, and he said, "What? When was this?" He paused again.

"Shit," James said, putting his hand to his head. "Did anybody—"

He stopped speaking, his head tilted slightly down, and his hand still on his forehead.

"So, Anderson was out with his dog?" James asked. "Okay, and he said what?" Again silence. "He saw an SUV?"

James straightened up, dropping his hand from his forehead to rub the back of his neck. "Massachusetts plates. Did he get the number?"

"Damn!" James snapped. "No, no. Tell the Captain I'll be down in about twenty. Where's the command center going to be set up?"

Again the pause. "Okay, Hollis Brookline Middle School. I'll swing by the station and get my extra gear. Make sure that somebody calls the Greek out on Hayden Drive and get his dogs out. They can track anything."

Another pause.

"Because what if the asshole who snatched them is hanging around town and not transporting across state lines, Mike?" he snapped. "Call Gus and get those damn dogs down to the high school."

James hung up the phone and looked at Harold and Mason.

"Two boys are missing," he said, trying to keep the anger out of his voice. "Charles and Nathan Verranault. They were almost at their street when two people in an SUV with Massachusetts tags grabbed them."

"Go to the Boylan House," Harold said.

James looked over at him. "We took care of the guy he had."

"That doesn't mean he hasn't gotten another one," Mason said.

"Are you kidding me?" James said.

Harold shook his head. "Think about it for a minute, James. Massachusetts plates. Two boys. And you stopped that monster from feeding before Halloween. It's the only thing that makes sense."

"Shit, shit, shit!" James spat. He looked to Mason. "Are you going to come with me to the Boylan House?"

"Yes," Mason answered. He picked up his tumbler of whiskey and emptied it. "You all set, Harold?" he asked, standing up.

"Of course I'm going to be all set," Harold answered. He pulled out the drawer of the table beside him and took out a Colt model 1911 .45 automatic pistol. The weapon was big, black and deadly. The old Marine smiled at Mason. "I've been killing bastards with this bitch since 1944."

67

"Fair enough," Mason said. "We'll talk to you later, and let you know if anything happened."

Harold nodded.

Mason followed James out of the old man's house, letting the locked door close behind them. The air was cold, the first frost heavy in the night sky. James hit the remote key and start buttons, the truck's doors unlocking and the engine roaring into life. They both got into the truck quickly and in a moment, James was racing towards Meeting House Road. It only took a few minutes.

James left the truck running as they both got out.

"Do you think they're in there?" James asked Mason in a low voice.

Lights burst into life in all of the windows of the house, and Mason felt a chill race up his spine and spread out along his arms.

"No, not now," Mason said with disgust. "But I think they were."

Chapter 23: Father Moran and Father Alexander

Mason didn't bother calling Father Moran. He wasn't sure if he'd even be able to get through to him in the rectory.

Mason sat in his truck in Nashua, in the empty Post Office parking lot, and waited to see the priest. He much rather would have spent the day in Monson with Julie, but that wasn't going to be. They had sent a few texts back and forth, but she was going to be with her mother for most of the day. And both of them knew if they didn't hear from each other, they were still going out for breakfast on Monday morning.

Mason smiled at the thought of it.

He enjoyed Julie's company. She was well-read, intelligent, confident, and beautiful. And she didn't take any shit from anyone. He'd seen her handle a gentleman who wanted to take out reference books which weren't allowed to go out. She'd kept her cool until it was time for the gentleman to leave. Mason helped him leave the building before Julie decided to come around the desk and beat the man senseless with one of the very books he was seeking to use.

And it was still difficult in Monson. The Verranault boys were still missing. There was no evidence other than what the neighbor had seen.

Mason and James and Harold though, they knew what happened. Mason had no doubt that someone from Boston, from the law firm, had come up and brought the boys to Liam Boylan, especially since Halloween had passed.

The lights in the house had helped to solidify that thought in Mason's mind.

Movement at the front of the Church brought Mason's attention back to the now, and he looked, as the tall, ornate wooden doors of St. Patrick's opened. The faithful were exiting the building. Some of them quickly. Others leisurely. Thanksgiving was only a few weeks away, and the attendance at the masses was undoubtedly increasing and would continue to do so until the crescendo of Christmas mass.

A minute or two after the doors opened, Mason saw Father Moran walk out, a head taller than most of his congregation. He was a huge man who looked as though he could easily have led men in the crusades with a mace in one hand and the Bible in the other.

With a grunt, Mason opened the pickup's door and climbed out, his body stiff from having sat in one position for longer than half an hour. He stretched slightly, hooked his keys to a belt loop and closed the door. Checking the street, he crossed and walked against the exodus of Catholics and up the long stairs to find Father Moran shaking hands with the occasional person. Mason waited politely, a step below Father Moran.

As the last of the people left, Father Moran turned to look down on Spring Street and saw Mason. His face broke into a smile, and he adjusted his glasses. "Mason," he said, "how are you?"

"I'm well, Father," Mason said, stepping up and shaking the man's large hand. "How are you?"

"Quite well, quite well," he said. "What brings you to Church, after mass?"

"Something terrible, I'm afraid," Mason said.

Father Moran looked at him then nodded. "Yes, it seems as though it is. Come inside for a moment, please."

Mason followed the priest into the large church. At the dais, a pair of altar boys were putting away the candles. "Jason, Jonathan," Father Moran said.

The two boys looked over.

"Could you finish everything by yourselves today?"

"Yes Father," the boys said in unison.

Father Moran smiled. "Excellent, thank you."

To Mason, he said, "Come along, we'll go through the vestibule to the rectory."

"I didn't know that you could," Mason said.

Father Moran's smile broadened. "It's an old church, Mason. There are a great many little things within it. I'm sure that even I don't know all of them, although I suspect I've found most of them."

Father Moran led Mason back to the vestibule, into the back portion of the room and pressed a bookshelf back, revealing a long, wide and low lit passage. As they entered the passage, the door closed behind them, and the passage angled down slightly, for quite some way, before leveling off.

"We're under the school now," Father Moran said. "Well, the old school. This will come out in the kitchen. Although, I'm not exactly sure why it should start in the kitchen. Or end in the kitchen. Whichever it is," the man chuckled.

The passage started to rise up slightly and soon, they were facing a small door which Father Moran opened, revealing that they were in the large pantry of the rectory's kitchen. He stopped in front of the pantry door, cleared his throat and said, "Martha, it's Father Moran." He turned back to Mason and said in a low voice, "I believe I actually made her wet herself one morning, so I try to give her a warning every time, now."

"Understood," Mason said, suppressing a smile.

Father Moran opened the door, and the kitchen was empty. He sighed, smiling. "Excellent," the priest said. "I really do hate scaring her. Come on, let's go up into my study, and you can tell me what's going on. I've even got a coffee maker in there."

"Sounds good, Father," Mason said. The priest led him out of the kitchen, into the hallway and up a large flight of stairs, the entire rectory resplendent with the ornate beauty of the Victorian era.

Father Moran's study held a pair of large, leather club chairs, a table against the far wall with a coffee maker on it, and several floor to ceiling bookshelves filled with various religious works.

"Take a seat, Mason," Father Moran said, gesturing towards the left chair.

"Thank you," Mason said and sat down.

Father Moran walked over to the coffee maker, plugged it in and started it. As the water heated up, he removed his vestments and hung them on a hanger which he took from a gentleman's butler. In a moment, the water was ready, and Father Moran quickly made two cups of coffee.

He brought the mugs over and handed one to Mason before sitting down across from him. "So," he said, looking at Mason seriously, "in all the times that we've spoken with one another, you've never said that something was terrible. What is it?"

"There is a place in Monson that's evil," Mason said. "It's been evil for centuries."

Father Moran closed his eyes and then opened them. "You're speaking of the Boylan House?" Father Moran asked softly.

Mason blinked. Surprised. "Yes. How did you know?"

Father Moran gave him a tight smile. "The Church knows where certain things are, and where they are not. We know that

71

something is wrong with the house. We know people go missing around it. More than boys, Mason," Father Moran said. "And I know you survived an encounter with the thing in the house."

Mason's hands started to shake, and he put his coffee down on the low table between the two chairs. "How?"

"Because we must," Father Moran said simply. "You are not the only boy to escape, either. There have been others. Not many, but there have been. However, the Church cannot interfere unless we are asked. It is as simple as that." He looked at Mason. "We need to be asked, Mason."

"Will you help me with the Boylan House, Father?" Mason asked.

Father Moran sipped his coffee. "Yes. But I cannot do it alone. I'm the diocesan exorcist, Mason. I need to bring in a colleague, if we are to do this."

"Alright, but, Father, can you exorcise a house?" Mason asked.

Father Moran nodded. He put his coffee down and stood up. "I'm going to make a phone call. I'll be back in a moment."

Mason picked up his coffee and took a sip. He was still shocked that Father Moran was an exorcist.

A few minutes later, Father Moran walked back in, gave Mason a small smile and sat down once again.

"I called my colleague Father Alexander," Father Moran said. "He should be here, shortly."

"What Church is he at?" Mason asked.

"St. Nicholas'," Father Moran said, smiling.

"St. Nicholas'?" Mason asked. "Isn't that the Greek Orthodox Church?"

"Yes," Father Moran said. "The Catholic Church has become much closer to our Orthodox brothers over the past decade or so, Mason. He and I have actually worked together on several exorcisms."

Mason shook his head, confused. "Several?"

Father Moran nodded. "When Pope Benedict the Sixteenth was in the seat at Rome," he said, "he spoke of the emptiness of today's cultures and societies. Of the failings and of the ease and temptations which are available via a disconnected world. We have seen a rise in exorcisms," Father Moran said. "And we cannot work without the support of one another. Father

Alexander is the exorcist for the Orthodox Church in the Metropolis of Boston. Thus, we work together whenever we can."

Mason drank his coffee, thought for a moment and said, "Will you both come to Monson then?"

"Yes," Father Moran said. "He and I have spoken of the house before. We would both like to be rid of it."

"So would I," Mason said.

Father Moran simply nodded and the two men sat in silence, drinking their coffee slowly, for nearly fifteen minutes, before a woman called up the stairs.

"Father, Father Alexander is here," she said.

"Thank you, Martha," Father Moran said. "Please send him up."

A moment later, loud steps sounded on the stairs and shortly after, a priest appeared in the doorway to the study. He was older than Mason and Father Moran, perhaps sixty or seventy, but he was even taller than Father Moran. His head barely cleared the top of the doorframe. He was a solid looking man, as if he should have been working as a longshoreman rather than as a priest. The man's hair was steel gray and long, pulled into a ponytail. His beard, which matched his hair color, was full and stretched to his waist.

Mason put down his coffee and got to his feet, even as Father Moran stood.

"Peter," Father Alexander said, extending his hand.

Father Moran shook it warmly. "Alex. Let me introduce to you my friend, Mason Philips."

When Father Moran released his hand, the Orthodox priest extended it to Mason, who, as he shook the offered hand, realized that Father Alexander's hand was even bigger than Father Moran's.

"A pleasure, Father," Mason said.

"And for me as well," Father Alexander smiled.

"Alex, why don't you take my seat and Mason go back to yours. I'm going to grab another chair," Father Moran said, and he left the room.

Both Mason and Father Alexander sat down. By the time Mason picked up his half-finished coffee, Father Moran was coming back into the room with an antique side chair. He set it down between the other two chairs but a little farther back.

"Coffee, Alex?" Father Moran asked.

"Please, Peter," Father Alexander answered. Silence fell over the three men as Father Moran prepared the coffee for the Orthodox priest. Soon, Father Moran was handing over the hot coffee and sitting down in the side chair.

Father Alexander held the mug and looked at Father Moran. "And I take it that you were serious when you said that we had something of great importance to discuss?"

"This is about the Boylan House, Alex," Father Moran said.

Father Alexander looked from Father Moran to Mason. "You have brought news of the Boylan House?"

"Yes," Mason answered.

"What is it?" the Orthodox priest asked.

"The house has taken two more children," Mason said. "It needs to go."

Father Alexander gave him a large and decidedly disturbing smile. "It does need to go, Mr. Philips. It needs to burn to the ground."

Chapter 24: 6:13 PM, November 8th, 2015, The Home of Harold Philips

Mason pulled the truck into the driveway of the house right after Harold's. The house was empty, the 'For Sale' sign looked abandoned. Mason shook his head at it, turned off the ignition and stepped out of the truck.

He walked to the side door, up the steps and then stopped.

The screen door was open slightly, the screen ripped, and the heavy door pushed back. Mason's hands itched for a weapon.

He slipped into the house and heard the sound of a raised voice. It had a questioning tone, and it was followed by a brutal smack.

Mason moved forward, and he could hear Harold laughing.

"Why the hell are you laughing?" someone asked.

"Because you're a little bitch," Harold spat. "Why don't you send your mother in to take care of this shit. I can't even say you fight like a girl because girls fight better than you can."

There was another harsh smack.

Mason knew Harold could soak it up. But he had to figure out a way to help the old Marine.

"This is crazy," someone said. "I've worked up more of a sweat than I do in the gym. It never looks this hard in the movies or on TV."

"That's because it's the movies or TV," a second voice sighed.

"You want to take a turn?" the first voice asked.

"Not at all. Go get a drink of water or something. Old bastard probably has beer in the fridge."

"No milk, though," Harold laughed.

"Screw you," the first voice said.

Mason heard footsteps, and he stepped back into the darkest part of the kitchen. He caught sight of the butcher's block with the knives, and he quickly slipped a carving knife free. The edge of it, glinted in the little bit of light slipping into the kitchen from Harold's hallway.

And then the stranger was in the room.

He was of medium build, medium height, and with short cropped brown hair. He had on a pair of gold rimmed glasses, and his dress shirt's sleeves were rolled up to the elbow. The man's expensive business shoes clicked on the old linoleum, and he pulled a handkerchief out of his back pocket before reaching for the fridge's handle. His back was to Mason.

With a single step, Mason was up behind the man, covering the man's mouth with his hand and jerking the head up and back as he drove the carving knife up to the hilt into the man's lung. The blade glided smoothly between a pair of ribs and the man struggled for the briefest of moments, his last breath hot against Mason's hand.

Mason eased the body to the floor, opened the fridge, took out a beer and popped the tab before setting it down on the floor beside the dead man.

Stepping silently to the entranceway to the hall, Mason carefully looked around the corner and saw Harold tied to a kitchen chair, his face raw and bloody. One eye was swollen shut, and the man's dentures were on the floor. Blood was splattered on his white tee-shirt.

In front of him, sitting in another chair, was a second man, his back to Mason. The man was dressed as well as the first had been, the sole difference being that he still wore a suit coat.

Harold saw Mason and said to the second man, "Takes a while for the little bitch to drink a beer down, doesn't it?"

"I don't know," the man started, but as he spoke, Mason used the sound of the man's own voice to rush forward. With the hand that held the knife, he punched the second man in the back of the head, right at the base of the skull where it met the neck. He sent the man sprawling onto the floor, grunting. Pre-looped zipties scattered out onto the carpet.

Mason dropped the knife and put his knee on the man's back.

The man groaned as Mason picked up a couple of zipties, looped them around each wrist and then ran a third between them, cinching them all tightly. The man screamed as they cut off the circulation to his hands.

Mason got off the man, stepped over to Harold and cut the old Marine free.

"The other one?" Harold asked.

"Dead."

Harold nodded.

"What were they asking you?" Mason asked.

"Where you were," Harold answered. "The first one might've

hit a little harder if he had known I was the one who had killed their grandfathers."

The man on the floor rolled over, wincing as he looked at them.

Mason kicked the man in the stomach. "I didn't tell you to move."

Bending down, Mason picked up the knife before sitting down in the chair so recently occupied by the gentleman on the floor. "So," Mason smiled, "you're either a Gunther, a Boylan, or an O'Connor."

The man didn't say anything.

"You do know it only takes a short amount of time for loss of circulation to cause permanent damage, which will then lead to amputation?" Mason asked.

The man remained silent.

Mason kicked him in the side of the knee. Hard.

The man screamed.

"He thinks he's a tough one," Harold said, walking out of the room. He came back, a minute later, with a dish towel and the beer that Mason had opened. Harold took a drink and wiped at the blood on his face. "Everybody's tough, once in a while."

"We'll see how tough he is when he's explaining to a jury why he broke into an old man's house and beat him. Of course, it'll be interesting to see how he expresses himself with a pair of hooks for hands," Mason said.

The man looked at Mason, and then he looked at Harold and he smiled. "I won't have to," he said, and he muttered something in a language Mason couldn't recognize.

Mason went to kick the man again, but the bound man burst into flames.

"What the hell?!" Mason yelled, jumping to his feet.

"Fire extinguisher in the kitchen," Harold snapped, and Mason ran for it. He found it by the stove, and he pulled the pin on it, as he raced back into the den.

Harold was using a blanket to try to smother the flames, but the man on the floor was screaming and writhing around.

"Back!" Mason yelled, and Harold moved away, pulling the blanket with him. Mason blasted the man with the fire extinguisher and in a matter of seconds, the flames were out.

But, it was too late. The man was dead, twisted in a fetal

position, the plastic zipties melted into his charred flesh.

"That," Harold said, taking a pack of cigarettes up from a table and fishing one out and lighting it, "is going to be an absolute bitch to get cleaned."

Chapter 25: 7:00 AM, November 15th, 2015, The Boylan House

They had all arrived at the Boylan House in James' truck. The two priests had spoken with their respective superiors and replacements had been found for them. When they got out of James' truck, they were wearing their vestments and armed with the objects of their faith. Mason carried a pump action shotgun that belonged to James, and James carried another. They had spent the better part of the week packing shells with salt from the lick that Mason had used the first time.

James and Mason had received the blessings of both priests, and Mason had received the sacrament of confession from Father Moran. James, being a protestant, needed no such sacrament, but he'd made his peace, nonetheless.

None of them had any illusions about Liam Boylan, or about what might occur within the house.

No one, except the Churches, knew what happened during the day. Harold was at a nephew's house under the pretense of having had a small fire in the den when he had dropped a lit cigarette. Julie was with her mother.

Both Mason and James had written letters explaining the situation and left them in the truck, should things not work out for the best.

It wasn't the first time Mason had to write his will, and he hoped it wouldn't be the last.

He closed the door to the pickup and double checked his pockets to make sure he was carrying enough ammunition.

James, Father Moran and Father Alexander looked at Mason.

"Me first?" Mason asked with a wry grin.

"Honestly," Father Moran said, "you have the most experience with this place, Mason."

"Lucky me," Mason sighed. He chambered a round into the shotgun. "Well, follow me, then."

He crossed Meeting House Road and started up the short hill. Within a heartbeat, he was at the door, refusing to look up at the trapdoor, fearful that it would be open and something would be looking down.

He opened the door and stepped inside, saw the tracks of men in the dust on the floor. Mason stepped off to the right,

James to the left, and the priests came in between them.

The door slammed shut of its own accord, and the house was plunged into darkness as every shutter, on the windows, hammered closed.

Something within the house, sighed audibly with pleasure.

Chapter 26: 7:05 AM, November 15th, 2015, The Boylan House

The darkness stank with the smell of rot and the air was heavy, far too humid for the middle of November.

But they were inside the house.

Inside the Boylan House.

The four of them stood, waiting for their eyes to become adjusted to the darkness and slowly realizing that they never would. The darkness was not natural.

Mason stepped over to a window and peered through a crack in the shutters at the world beyond. A chill shook his body, and his stomach churned violently. The coffee and toast, he had for breakfast, made a valiant effort to leave, but he forced it down.

Beyond the shutter was a different world. An older world.

The woods were farther off, and the land was cleared and occupied by fields of corn. A simple rutted path was where the road had been. James' truck was gone. In the dim light which slipped through the crack in the shutter, Mason looked at himself, half fearful that he would see homespun clothes and a flintlock musket.

"We're somewhere else," Mason said, turning back to the others.

"What do you mean?" Father Moran asked.

"We're in Monson," Mason said, "but out there it's like the seventeenth century, I'm sure of it."

James walked quickly to a window, looked out and swore under his breath. He looked at the priests and nodded.

Above them, something creaked, and a fine film of dust drifted down. For the first time, Mason noticed there was furniture in the shadows. A few chairs and a long table. A hutch of some sort stood on the wall beside the rear door, and shelves had been installed under the stairs.

Someone lived here.

In the wide open fireplace, which was stacked neatly with logs for the evening fire, there were iron hooks and arms. Cast iron pots and pans stood on a wide mantle which ran the perimeter of the entire chimney. A few pewter mugs and a clay pipe could be seen as well. The room was brightening.

Yet even as Mason observed the darkness fading, he realized the creaking change into footsteps. Someone started walking towards the stairs. He and James took up defensive positions around the two priests.

In a heartbeat, the unknown person was at the top of the stairs and started walking down with a rather clumsy gait.

A middle aged man appeared a little thinner than most and grinning through a mask of dried blood on his face. He wore a modern flannel shirt and jeans that looked as though they had been pressed. His feet were clad in tan workboots and a wedding ring glinted on his finger.

"Mike?" James asked. "Mike Sullivan?"

The laugh erupting from Mike Sullivan's mouth told Mason they weren't speaking with Mike, but rather, with Liam Boylan.

"Oh no, young sir," Liam Boylan said, grinning wickedly, "your poor friend Michael Sullivan died screaming as I climbed through his mind. I appreciated his tastes for young boys, mind you, but the body really is designed solely for single occupancy."

Liam looked at Mason, the grin fading away. "You and your family have been a bane for more years than even I care to count, Master Philips," he spat. "I'm pleased that I'll be able to finish you off today even as my colleagues finished off Harold."

Mason nodded. "So it was you who sent those two after the old man?"

"Yes," Liam hissed, the smile returning. "And he must have suffered, I'm sure. A pity he didn't tell them where you were."

"Oh," Mason said, "those two."

The smile on Liam's face drooped slightly. "What do you mean?"

"You sent two men, two lawyers, to deal with Harold Philips?" Mason asked.

"Yes," Liam responded.

"Well," Mason smiled, "I gutted one like a fish and the other set himself on fire."

Liam spat on the floor and took a stutter step towards them.

"No more," Father Alexander said. "Do not exchange any more words with it."

"Ah, priests," Liam said, switching his attention from Mason to Father Moran and Father Alexander. "Always a pleasure. We've met before, myself and your kind. Far away, in Ireland, which is how I ended up here, in this place. So bountiful with young men."

Father Moran started to speak in Latin.

Liam looked at Father Moran, snarling as he responded in kind. Father Moran went pale, yet continued to speak. Father Alexander joined him, speaking Greek, the man's voice powerful, resonating in the room.

Then two voices were erupting from Liam's mouth, one speaking Latin and the other speaking Greek. The thing howled in both languages and started laughing in a third voice.

Mason felt sweat burst upon his own brow, and a glance at James showed that he, too, was sweating, his shotgun trembling ever so slightly.

The two priests never hesitated, never faltered as they spoke. Incense was cast upon Liam and the body he possessed dropped to the rough floor, shaking the broad planks. Holy oil and holy water were dashed at him, and Liam screamed.

Smoke rose from where the water and oil touched the flesh, and a fourth voice tore free of Liam's mouth. This voice spoke in a language which sounded much like the one which the second attacker in Harold's house had used to ignite himself.

Liam Boylan climbed to his knees, and a shriek joined the other four voices.

Neither of the priests raised their voices. They continued on steadfastly.

The entire house started to shake.

The stacked wood in the fireplace fell and the cast iron pots did as well, slamming loudly against the hearthstones. Outside of the house, a fierce wind started blowing, the trees in the distance ripping back and forth while the cornstalks rippled and twisted with the wind's current.

A sixth voice joined the cacophony, screaming the foulest of curses in English. Mason had to ignore the voices and focus on the house. He watched the walls shaking, the stairs undulate, and the chimney seemed to shimmy from left to right.

From somewhere in the house a foul, noxious stench began, drifting down to them and Mason forced his eyes upon Liam Boylan once more.

The man whom he had possessed, Mike Sullivan, was on his hands and knees. Sweat soaked his hair, and mucus and bile hung from his nose and mouth. The voices stopped in mid-sentence.

The priests didn't.

They continued their prayers, and they continued to anoint the man with the holy oils and water.

Mike Sullivan's body shuddered and collapsed to the plank floor. He lay motionless and still the priests said their prayers.

And something black burst up from the back of Mike Sullivan.

Both Mason and James were ready for it, and they squeezed off their first rounds simultaneously. For a moment, the sounds of the shotguns firing drowned out the prayers of the priests and the black thing, that was Liam Boylan, went howling up the stairs.

Mason kept his weapon focused on the stairs as James knelt down beside Mike Sullivan.

"He's dead," James said, frowning as he stood. He looked to the priests.

Father Moran nodded. "I'll give him his last rites."

"I'm not sure he was Catholic, Father," James said.

Father Moran smiled. "I don't think it matters at this point, James."

"We need to go upstairs," Mason said.

Father Alexander nodded. "We do indeed."

"I'll take point," Mason said. He'd walked point before in some scary places, but nothing as frightening as this.

This was something he didn't think he could fight. This was something that made him feel as though he was seven years old again.

In the dim light of the room, with the air still and sick, Mason led the way to the stairs. Father Moran followed behind him, with Father Alexander next and James bringing up the rear of the small group.

The stairs creaked beneath Mason's weight. There was nothing but darkness beyond the last stair.

Above him, Mason could hear breathing.

Deep, heavy breathing, the sound of which threatened to freeze his knees and loosen his bowels.

But he pressed on.

He passed the last stair and entered the darkness waiting for him.

Chapter 27: Mason Philips in the Boylan House

Mason stepped forward, and the blackness faded away suddenly.

He was in the upper floor of the Boylan House by himself. He tightened his grip on the shotgun and found that he wasn't holding it.

He looked down at his hands and saw that they were young and small. Free of scars and age.

And Mason was wearing a Halloween costume.

A Star Wars Stormtrooper costume with the mask pulled down over his face. He could smell the plastic, feel the familiar itch of the old wool sweater which his mother had made him wear that night.

Mason's throat went dry, and he knew if he went to the window, its shutters thrown wide, he could look out into the night sky. He knew if he looked down at the street below the Boylan House, he would see his older cousins waiting. They would be standing there, in their costumes, holding his candy in its pillowcase.

They would be waiting for him to come out.

They would be waiting for Kevin to come out.

Kevin.

Mason heard a soft thump off to his left, and he turned slightly, reaching up and lifting the Star Wars mask up so he could see better.

He couldn't see anything from where he stood, so Mason walked forward a little, his old Zipp sneakers silent on the wooden floor.

Mason stopped as he came around the corner of the chimney, horrified at what lay before him. Kevin was on his back, terror emblazoned on his face. And even though his legs moved and the right heel rose and thumped on the floor, Kevin was dead.

Kevin was dead and never coming back because nobody came back from being dead.

But Mason wasn't really worried about Kevin. No. Not really worried about Kevin at all.

Mason was worried about the thing squatting on Kevin's chest.

It was a dull gray color, and thin. Terribly thin. The thing was naked, and when it heard the sound of Mason's feet it turned and smiled at him.

The face was smeared with blood, its teeth crimson with the same. Blue eyes shined brightly, and it chuckled.

Between its wasted legs, a tremendous, pulsating black cock stood erect, and it seemed to grow even larger as it looked at Mason.

"Sweet boy," the man-thing hissed and stood up.

Mason tried not to scream, but failed.

Chapter 28: Father Peter Moran in the Boylan House

When Mason Philips disappeared into the wall of blackness at the top of the stairs, the scream that followed was perhaps the worst that Father Peter Moran had ever heard.

Without hesitation, Peter went racing up after the man, plunging headlong into a blackness so thick and foul that he felt it wrap itself around his throat. It seemed to be trying to choke the life out of him, and it succeeded in stopping him from calling Mason's name.

Suddenly, light washed over him, hurting his eyes even as the thing grasping his throat let go.

Peter stumbled and gasped for air. He managed to catch himself, and he looked around.

He froze in place.

Peter wasn't on the second floor of the Boylan House.

He was in the backyard of an apartment building in Norwich, Connecticut. It was 1983. He was learning the trade of the exorcist at the hands of a master.

Father Kelly Riordan stood by a rather innocuous looking young black man. The man had a bottle of beer in his hand, and he was talking sagely with Father Kelly. The black man's wife and children stood over with a Hispanic family and an older white couple. All of them looked warily at the black man as he drank his beer happily.

"Do you think you can sit down, Eric?" Father Kelly asked the man.

"Of course I can," Eric said cheerfully. "It doesn't mean I'm going to, though."

"And why not?" Father Kelly asked patiently. Peter stood off to one side. He had positioned himself close enough to Eric so that Peter could step between the man and the others.

They had been coming to this man's house for well over three months. Every Tuesday and Thursday they would come and sit. They would pray with him, and they would recite the prayers of exorcism. Sometimes, the young black man would sweat. Sometimes, he would scream.

These were the regular part of the week.

But today was Saturday.

The family had called. The neighbors had called.

Something was going on.

The man was drinking and drinking and drinking. Every ounce of alcohol that he could find, he was drinking. And Peter had seen the evidence of it. There were beer cans all near the chair that the man had been sitting in.

The wife had told them that he had been drinking for two hours.

There must have been sixty cans and bottles altogether.

"You need to leave now, Kelly," Eric said, grinning as he took another sip. "You couldn't handle me in Wisconsin, what makes you think you could handle me here? This one?" he said, nodding towards Peter. "Do you really think that he'll be able to help you at all?"

Peter looked over at Kelly and saw something that frightened him.

The older priest's face had gone deathly pale. A single blue vein at the top of his temple started throbbing. His mouth worked silently for a moment before allowing the word, "Wisconsin" to come through.

"You do remember," the black man said pleasantly. He finished the beer, and he held it loosely in his hand. "I'm glad, actually," Eric continued. "I had honestly believed you weren't going to remember at all. But you did."

"You were driven out," Father Kelly gasped. "I saw it."

The man shook his head. "Not in the least. Father David and I worked quite hard on that one together."

Father Kelly stiffened, the color completely draining from his flesh.

"Oh yes," the man purred, "Father David belonged to us. Heart and soul. He helped me hide in that poor young girl. And she did taste as sweet as she looked," he grinned. "You can be sure of that, Kelly."

Before Father Kelly could say anything. Before he could even begin the first prayer, the black man lunged forward, dropping the bottle and grasping Father Kelly by the testicles, all in one swift and fluid motion.

In a heartbeat, Father Kelly was screaming, vomiting upon the ground as the young man twisted and pulled. The man's neighbors and family fled screaming, leaving Peter alone with the possessed man and the sickening screams of his mentor.

Chapter 29: Father Stathi Alexander in the Boylan House

Father Stathi Alexander reacted to Mason Philips' scream just as Peter did. He was a few steps behind the man as he disappeared into the darkness, and Stathi was just stepping into it, as well, when Peter's own scream reached his ears.

But then Stathi was in darkness.

Not the pure black which he had entered, but something dim. Something unpleasant. He could smell the sweet incense of Mass, hear the heartbeat of the very Church itself, and he realized where he was.

The Church of the Annunciation.

He hadn't been back to the Church since he was five.

Not since that night.

And suddenly Stathi knew what night it was, and what was going to happen. He understood the meaning of Mason's and Peter's screams.

Father Stathi Alexander knew what was coming, and he tried to steel himself against it. Yet, he was only five. He knew he was seventy-two, but now, in the Church of the Annunciation, he was five, once more. The pews looked right, but wrong at the same time, as if he were too small for them. Dizziness swept over him, and he reached out to steady himself.

The wood of the pew was cool beneath his small hand, and he sighed at the beautiful familiarity of it.

A muffled gasp reached his ears, and Stathi shuddered.

He should have expected it, should have remembered. His mind was fighting the memory, attempting to hold it back as it had done for nearly seven decades.

Stathi dropped his eyes to the floor and looked at his dress shoes, the worn leather was carefully polished. His grandfather had made sure of that. As his grandmother had made sure his clothes were right, neat and clean.

His father had died in Normandy during the war.

And his mother, well, Stathi shook his head at the memory of his mother.

The noises increased.

The candle will fall, Stathi told himself, and he squeezed the pew as the candle on the altar fell.

The grunting and the cursing, Stathi thought. *You know*

what's coming here.

And it all followed. It all came to pass.

And it did pass.

Stathi sighed, looked up as he breathed deeply and began to shriek as Father Satoris, naked, and his genitals red with Stathi's mother's blood, stalked down the center aisle screaming in Greek.

Chapter 30: James Markarian in the Boylan House

Like both of the priests, James heard Mason's scream.

Unlike both of the priests, however, James did not run blindly up the stairs. First of all, the priests were in front of him, and they were both large men. The stairs beneath his feet shook with the hard, heavy steps of Father Moran and Father Alexander.

Second, James was a trained police officer. Yes, he did run toward the sounds of distress and danger, but he had been taught *how* to do it.

And finally, James had something on his shotgun that Mason didn't.

A light.

A small, tactical LED that sent a tight beam out in front of the weapon. As he switched the light on, he heard Father Moran and then Father Alexander scream.

James knew it was a trap, and he walked up the stairs slowly with the light of the weapon cutting through the darkness. Just at the top of the stairs on the second floor, the three men stood. Each of them shook slightly, eyes unblinking as James swept the light across their faces.

His stomach tightened at the looks of terror each of them wore.

James moved up to stand beside Mason.

"Mason," he whispered.

Nothing. Not even a hint that Mason might hear him.

"Mason," he said a little louder.

Still, the terrified expression remained.

James breathed in through his nose and exhaled the same way, calming his racing heart. He brought his shotgun up to his shoulder, put a fresh round in it from his right jacket pocket and slowly started to advance through the darkness. At the edges of his vision, he caught sight of things that surely weren't there.

A little boy in a church being chased by a naked man.

A young priest trying to drag a black man off of an older priest who lay unconscious in a dirt yard.

And a young boy wearing a Stormtrooper costume and staring at something that was advancing towards him, fresh blood upon the face and a dead child behind it.

That, James knew, was Mason's nightmare. He also knew it wasn't a true memory. This memory was being constructed out of fears.

The other two images, though, those had been pulled from the memories of the priests.

James kept his steady pace through the second floor. Like the first floor, there was evidence of someone living in the house. A few books on a shelf beside the bed. The bed itself was a simple thing of rough wood and a strawtick mattress. A tall armoire of dark wood carved and looked as if it had made the trip from Ireland to America with Liam Boylan.

James' stomach tightened as he looked at it.

Swallowing nervously, he approached the armoire, reached out a hand and opened the door.

It swung out on silent hinges.

Hanging amongst the few clothes were two boys.

The Verranault brothers.

The boys were naked and eviscerated.

By some miracle, James managed not to throw up as he closed the door.

"They're pretty like that, aren't they?" a voice asked from the far right.

James spun to face that direction and the beam from the flashlight settled upon a tall, slim man whose face was harsh and unkind. His black hair was shaved close to the head, and he gave James a smile of long, yellow teeth. He wore a black minister's frock and had his hands behind his back.

"You're James Markarian," the man said, a slight lilt to his voice and James realized this was the true voice and image of Liam Boylan.

"And you're Liam Boylan, again," James responded. He kept a tight grip on his sanity.

"I would say we're well met," Liam smiled again, "but we both know that is a lie, and I am many things, Master Markarian, but I am not a liar. I am, however, exceedingly perturbed by your destruction of two of my puppets. They are, as I'm sure you can imagine, difficult to acquire."

"I don't suppose you would do me a kindness and tell me how to kill you, would you?" James asked.

Again the vicious smile.

"No," Liam said, "but I must say, Master Markarian, you and your friends have come uncomfortably close to doing so. And, I must add, I am extremely impressed that you had the presence of mind to use a light and avoid my trap. The good Father Stathi realized that it was a trap, but failed to remember everything he should have. And now," Liam sighed with pleasure, "he's currently preoccupied with avoiding the none-too-gentle hands of his first religious father."

"And Father Moran?" James asked.

"Peter," Liam grinned. "Well now, let's just say that Peter is reliving one of his most exciting moments as an exorcist for the Papacy. Of course, the incident resulted in the maiming and near immediate death of his friend and teacher, so that sort of lowers his enjoyment of the experience. They do say, don't they, the hardest lessons are the ones easiest to remember?"

James nodded, never moving the shotgun off of Liam's face. He didn't know if a couple loads of salt would do anything to what looked like a physical body, but he sure as hell was going to find out if he had to.

"And what about Mason?" James asked. "What's his memory?"

For the first time, Liam Boylan looked angry.

"I've made that special for him," he snarled. "That little wretch has been far more difficult than he should have been. Look at what he's done, brought you and three others into this. His damned relative was the same way. Even his predecessors tried to burn my home to the ground after that raid," and Liam paused, giving a small smile. "But that doesn't really mean anything to you, does it? Let's simply say, I have to work just a little harder to make sure Mason Philips remains where he is."

Liam looked at James and his smile broadened. "Now, however, comes the question of what to do with you, young master Markarian. Do you have any suggestions?"

"Yes," James said. "Tell me how to kill you."

Liam chuckled, nodding in appreciation. "Yes, that would be rather beneficial to you now, wouldn't it? I, regardless of the constant state of flux in which I find myself, enjoy this existence. I don't get to do nearly as much as I would like, but I certainly don't have to worry about my Puritan neighbors setting me alight again either. I don't think that they would have minded terribly about what I was doing with the occasional Abenaki child, but their own precious tots would have proven to be a different story.

"No," Liam sighed, "I'm afraid I cannot help you in that regard. I would, though, like to rid myself of you, and unfortunately for you, I'm afraid, that means killing you." Liam gave him a sad, conciliatory smile. "I promise you. I will receive no pleasure in it. You are far too old and simply no longer attractive to me. You must have been an absolutely delectable youth, though, and I imagine your sweetmeats were ever so sweet."

"I'm just impressed with how you can talk to me, keep the two priests in the past and keep Mason out of the picture," James said, sliding his finger onto the trigger.

"Well, thank you," Liam said, offering a short tilt of his head in a sign of pleasure, "it is difficult. I am thankful that I have enough skill and concentration—"

And 'concentration' was the word that James was waiting for.

He put a single round into Liam's face, spinning the man around, the tails on his coat flaring out.

James followed up with two more quick shots, the noise of the shotgun drowning the outraged screams of the beast across from him.

And then the thing and the darkness were gone.

Chapter 31: The Second Floor of the Boylan House

Mason sat on the wide plank floor of the Boylan House. The shutters were closed. Beside him sat James on the right and Father Moran on the left. Father Alexander sat across from them.

They had listened to James' tale, and they had believed him, of course. Even if they had wanted to doubt him, the fact that he knew exactly what horrors they had all been experiencing, erased all doubt. In the sickening silence of the house, the men tried to gather their thoughts and their courage.

The mere existence of Liam Boylan rattled the men more than they cared to admit.

"What do we do now?" James asked, reloading the shotgun which he had used so effectively.

"We need to find where he is hiding," Father Moran said.

"And drive him out of it," Father Alexander finished.

"And when he's driven out?" James asked. "What then? How do we kill something that is dead?"

"We have to find his place of power," Mason said, rubbing the back of his head. "With that destroyed, he won't be strong enough to resist the prayers of exorcism."

"Will we be able to get home?" James asked.

Father Alexander nodded. "With him gone," he said, sweeping his hand around at the room they were in, "all of this will return to normal."

"And if we don't kill him?" James asked.

"Then we won't have much to worry about anyway," Mason said, standing up. "But the Churches know we're here, James. Even if we don't accomplish this, then others will come to finish the job."

"That's not a lot of comfort," James said as he and the two priests stood.

Mason smiled. "I don't expect that it is." He looked around the room and then his eyes settled on the chimney and fireplace. It was a truly monstrous affair, built out of fieldstones and held together with some ancient mortar. A heavy mantle of thick, dark wood ran along all four sides, much like the one on the first floor.

But Mason remembered something.

He walked to the fireplace and held the shotgun in the crook of one arm, a hand on the butt of the stock. Reaching up, he ran his hands along the edges of the stones that met the mantle, then along those that formed the rounded corners of the chimney.

And he found it, just a slight depression. Enough for him to slip three fingers into and when he did, there was a loud click. With only a slight tug, the entire upper part of the right section of the chimney pulled away, swinging open on unseen hinges.

Stacked neatly, on a dozen rows of polished wood, were small skulls which had been bleached white. A neat hand had labeled each skull, the writing a fluid script that had the curious lettering of the seventeenth century. But the names were easy enough to read, and one of two rows from the top caught Mason's eyes.

Kevin Peacock.

"What the hell?" James asked.

"Hell is right," Father Moran said, and Father Alexander offered up a prayer in Greek.

Looking at the skulls, Mason saw there was a large, iron key hanging at the bottom shelf, barely visible in the small ossuary's shadows. Mason reached in and took the key out.

It was large and bitterly cold to the touch. He put it on the mantle for a moment, pulled a handkerchief out of his back pocket and wrapped it around the key. The cloth helped a little, but not much.

"We need to find a keyhole," Mason said.

"There aren't any doors up here," James said, and he and the two priests looked around.

"There won't be," Mason said. "It will look like a knothole or a stain. But it will be at the height of a doorknob."

Stepping away from the chimney, Mason joined the other men, and they started walking closely around the room. They did one complete circuit around the room, then a second, and then a third. They started their fourth when Father Alexander called out, "Here!"

They hurried to him and found him standing before a shuttered window.

"I didn't think to look at the shutters," he said, pointing to a small keyhole in the left shutter of the window.

"Neither did I," James said.

Stepping forward, Mason slid the key into the keyhole and turned it slowly to the right. A grating sound, like that of old tumblers in terrible need of oil, assaulted their ears.

Something clicked loudly, and Mason let go of the key, his fingers partially numb and complaining loudly.

The shutter swung out towards them, revealing a long dark hallway that stretched into nothingness.

"That really shouldn't be there," James said. "That's just leading out into the open air."

"If we weren't within this house," Father Moran said, "then that would certainly be true, James. But we are beyond reality here. This is Liam Boylan's house, something which he built in both our world and within his own corrupted mind."

"Well," Mason said, flexing his hand to get some of the feeling back into it, "let's get on with this, shall we?"

The other men nodded and Mason stepped up and into the opening beyond the shutter. The floor of the passage was rough wood. The walls were of the same. Light came from somewhere, although he couldn't quite be sure. No windows broke the monotony of the walls and the passage never turned, never dipped, never raised up. It simply continued on.

All too soon, the open shutter behind them was gone, not even a speck in the distance.

Then the passageway began to turn. A gentle curve that rolled out to the right, then rolled back to the left, finally opening to a large, dark field. The sky above had only a smattering of stars and the moon was absent. Corn, nearly ripe, stood in tall rows around the circle which the passage emptied into.

The field's tall grass had been pressed down as if stomped upon by many feet.

In the center of the field was a large fire pit that was dark with blackened wood. The smell of freshly cooked meat hung in the air.

Mason could tell instantly it wasn't from animals, however.

"Smells like a pork roast," James said in a low voice.

"It's not," Mason replied.

"What is it then?" James asked.

"Try not to think about it," Father Alexander said.

"Try not to think about it? Think about what? Do—" James stopped talking. "Oh."

Mason moved towards the fire pit. A rustling sounded from the corn and a trio of shapes appeared.

They were shadows; darkness solidifying and fading.

Three middleaged men. They were Native Americans with thick hair hanging well-past their shoulders, down their backs. They wore breeches, moccasins, and leather jerkins. They all carried muskets.

They looked warily at Mason and the others.

One of them spoke something in his native tongue and looked at Mason.

Father Moran stepped forward and said to Mason, "May I try something?"

"Please, do," Mason said as the newcomers shifted in and out again.

Father Moran said something in what sounded like French and one of the men solidified even further, smiling as he asked a question.

Father Moran answered, and the man translated into his own tongue.

Mason and the others looked at Father Moran.

"What's he saying?" Mason asked.

"He's probably telling them that we're looking for Boylan, too," Father Moran said.

"How did you know he spoke French?" Father Alexander asked.

"Do you see the crucifix upon his chest?" Father Moran asked.

"Yes," Father Alexander answered.

"Only the French were converting Natives at this time. I was lucky he knew the language," Father Moran said.

"So were we," James added.

The French speaking native turned back to Father Moran and told him something.

Father Moran hesitated for a moment before answering. But he did.

The French speaking native swallowed and asked Father Moran something else.

Nodding, Father Moran answered.

The French speaking native turned to his brethren and repeated what Father Moran had said. One of the men solidified and took a stumbling step back.

"What did they ask you?" James asked.

"How long have they been chasing Liam Boylan," Father Moran said. "I asked if he was still alive when they found the way into his secret place."

"And they said yes?" Father Alexander said.

Father Moran nodded. "I had to tell them that they'd been in here for centuries."

The three Native Americans had all solidified completely and sat down around the fire. They looked shocked as if they didn't know they had been chasing the thing named Liam Boylan for so long.

Mason went and sat down with them. A moment later, the others joined them.

The native, who spoke French, looked at Father Moran and asked him a question. Father Moran nodded, answering the man quickly.

"He asked if we would like their help," Father Moran said. "I said yes. They have a fair idea of where he might be if we chased him out of the house itself."

"That's fantastic!" James said excitedly.

The native said something else to Father Moran and the priest nodded. Father Moran turned to the others and said, "The man said that the way is thick with danger. They were six when they began their hunt and even here, in this place, Liam Boylan has destroyed them."

"And they will show us the way?" Father Alexander asked.

Father Moran asked the man, and he nodded. "Yes," Father Moran said. "They will show us the way."

Chapter 32: Within Liam Boylan's Darkness

The world around them, Mason realized, would never see sunlight. It would never see a full moon. It would never see any moon.

It was always night.

Always Fall.

Always the end of October, that time which Liam Boylan loved the most, it seemed.

The Native Americans led the way, more solid than they had probably been in decades, if not centuries.

All of them moved as quietly as they could, wary of the stalks of corn. Any rustling from the corn would be heard for miles, Mason was sure. There were no animals to hide the noise with their night sounds.

The air was chilly, and Mason could smell death; old and new, flesh rotting and bones yellowing.

This was Boylan's world and none of them knew where he was, within its depths.

Father Moran had told them that even the Natives weren't sure how far the boundaries were. But they felt certain as to where the beast was hiding.

The rows of corn suddenly ended and a narrow field separated the corn from the thick forest beyond. And before that forest was a small cemetery.

The grave markers were of intricately carved wood. They bore the names of the boys that Boylan had killed. Rows upon rows of them. The markers were in no sort of order, some clumped close together, others scattered individually. No dates marred the surface, only names.

And amongst them, sitting in a tall chair and looking out at his victims, was Liam Boylan.

One of the natives raised his musket and fired off a shot that splintered the chair and sent Boylan sprawling. And then they were all running towards him, fanning out as he scrambled to his feet.

"Damn you all!" the thing shrieked, its mouth opening impossibly wide and the yellow teeth seeming to grow before Mason's eyes.

"And you, Philips, oh I am not done with thee!"

Boylan reached into a pocket and pulled out something. Screaming in a foul tongue, he threw the thing at them.

Whatever it was, glittered, even in the dim light, and it struck both Father Moran and the French speaking native in the face.

The native disappeared, yet Father Moran was not so lucky.

The priest collapsed to the earth, grasping his face with both hands as a gurgling scream tore its way out of his throat. Mason and James fired again at Boylan as the man fled into the forest. The natives firing their weapons as well.

With Boylan gone, Mason turned to Father Moran and found Father Alexander kneeling beside the fallen priest. The giant Orthodox man was attempting to hold Father Moran still, yet he writhed and screamed. The intensity of his pain nearly shattering Mason's heart and ears.

The shrieking continued as James came to stand beside Mason. Father Alexander leaned over Father Moran, whispering something into the man's ear.

Almost a full minute later, with Father Alexander whispering the entire time, Father Moran suddenly went silent. His body went limp, and the hands fell from his face.

Where the face had been, there was nothing but raw flesh and bone. The teeth looked as if they were being barred at the sky, and the eyes were nothing more than red holes. The nose, too, was gone, a ragged triangle where once had been skin and cartilage. Blood and flesh stuck to the palms of Father Moran's hands.

Father Alexander climbed wearily to his feet, his eyes red.

"What did you say?" James asked softly.

Father Alexander smiled tiredly at the young man. "I told him that he could die, James. I told him that it was alright to die. God would be waiting for him."

Mason felt a cool sensation on his shoulder, and he turned. One of the natives had placed his shaking hand upon Mason. The man gestured with his head, and Mason nodded.

"They'll still come with us," Mason said.

James looked at him. "What are we going to do about Father Moran?"

"We'll come back for the body," Mason said. "Right now, we have to go and kill that prick!"

"Yes," Father Alexander agreed, "our first duty is to kill Liam

Boylan, whatever he is. And I do not think, as we have said, we will be able to leave this place while that beast is alive."

"We can't discuss it," Mason said. "We have to go. If you can't come with us, James, then stay with Father Moran's body."

"I'll do that," James said after a moment. "I don't think I can go into that place," he said, nodding at the forest.

"No shame in that, son," Father Alexander said gently.

"None at all, James," Mason said, "we'll see you soon."

Chapter 33: Harold Philips and Julie Markarian

Harold sat at his small dining table drinking a third cup of coffee. The clock on the mantle in the den, chimed eight. He'd read The Globe, The Union Leader, and The Telegraph.

There was little left of the Sunday morning, unless he wanted to go to Church.

And Harold hadn't been to Church since he'd seen Max Steuben get cut in half by a machine gun on Peleliu. Max had been a good boy.

Harold took a sip of his coffee and looked at the kitchen floor, smiling. No one would ever be able to tell that some prick had bled over there. The carpet in the den had been a little more difficult to take care of, but he did it. And yes, he was supposed to be at his nephew's house, but who wanted an old son of a bitch around?

Besides, Harold liked to be home.

Always had.

The doorbell chimed.

Harold put his coffee down, picked his .45 up and put it on his lap, hidden beneath the table, a round chambered.

"Come in!" he called.

He heard the screen door squeak and then the doorknob to the side door turned and opened. A young, attractive woman stepped in.

She smiled nervously at him. "Mr. Philips?"

"Yes," Harold smiled, keeping his pistol ready.

"I'm Julie Markarian," she said.

His smile fell away. "Come in and close the door, Miss," he said, putting the pistol up on the table as she turned and closed the door.

When she looked back, her eyes widened in surprise at the sight of the weapon.

Evidently her brother hadn't told her about the attack.

"Do you want coffee?" he asked, rising to his feet.

"No, thank you," she said.

"Please, sit," he said, gesturing to the only other chair at the table.

"Thank you," she said, and once she did so, Harold sat down as well.

"What's wrong?" he asked.

"My brother and Mason are gone."

"Do you know where?" Harold asked.

"I'm not sure, but I think they went to Meeting House Road," she said. "I think they went to the Boylan House."

"Did you check?"

She shook her head.

"Good," Harold said. "You and I can go together."

"What?"

Harold nodded. "Yes. We need to know if they're at that house. I can't drive, and you can't go by yourself. It's perfect," he smiled.

After a moment, she smiled, too. "Yes, I believe you're right."

Harold picked up his coffee and finished it before easing himself to his feet. He walked over to the peg rack by the side door and took his gun-belt down and buckled it around his waist. He pulled a flannel jacket on and wandered back to the table. Julie watched him flip the safety on and then slide the automatic into the holster.

"Well," he said, smiling at her. "I'm ready."

Julie laughed and stood up. "That's it?"

"That's it," he smiled, glad to see her relaxing a little. If the two men were up to something that involved the Boylan House, she was going to need to be on top of her game. He couldn't have her distracted and worried.

It never helped.

Julie stood up and reached into her jacket pocket, pulling out her car keys.

Harold opened the door and held it for her.

"Do you need your wallet or house keys?" she asked him.

"No," he smiled. "I've got cash in my pocket and who the hell is going to rob an old man who still has a rotary phone?"

She opened her mouth to say something, closed it and gave a shrug. "You're probably right," she said.

Harold smiled at her again.

"Thank you," she said, opening the screen door as she stepped out into the driveway. Harold stepped down after her, pulling the door closed behind him. Julie's black sedan was parked on his driveway, and she used an electric key to unlock it.

Harold walked steadily to the passenger side door, opening

it and easing himself into the car. He felt the cold in his joints, and it settled into his bones. But it felt good to be doing something. He wasn't angry with the men for not involving him, yet he couldn't help feeling a little useless.

With a grunt, he pulled the door closed as Julie got in.

After she closed her door and started the car, she looked over at him. "Meeting House Road?"

"Yes," Harold said. "Meeting House Road."

Chapter 34: The Whispering in the Woods

Once the graveyard had disappeared, blocked by the ancient trees of Liam Boylan's forest, and James along with the corpse of Father Moran had slipped into shadow, the whispering started.

At first, Mason thought he was the only one who heard the whispers, but one of the natives suddenly glanced around, and Mason saw the fear on the man's face. Looking back to Father Alexander, Mason saw beads of sweat on the priest's forehead. Mason wondered what the priest heard because he knew what he heard himself was different.

Mason heard his mother whispering about how she was molested as a girl by her uncle.

Her uncle telling him how wonderful it was.

A man, who claimed to be his father, saying he left because he couldn't stand the sight of Mason.

His best friend having driven off of the pier in Connecticut, but changing his mind almost at the end, when it was too late.

The last, rattling breath of his Grandmother, telling him that it was all lies and that there was nothing but this world. Nothing next, for there was no next.

And the voices whispered all at once, each one disturbingly clear in Mason's head. They spoke of things he knew were true. Things he remembered hearing, things he remembered seeing.

The whispers that were of combat were the worst, though.

Mason had never been a lover of war. Had never, as they say, fallen in love with the brutality and the camaraderie of it. The bond was tight, of course, between men who fought together, but Mason remembered the horrors of it, as well. Iraqi roads filled with burning cars, the stench of seared rubber and flesh ruining his clothes and his dreams for years.

The discovery of rape squads in Bosnia.

Of killing those men by gutting them and letting them bleed out, zip-tied to the steering wheels of abandoned vehicles.

Mason tried to ignore the whispering, to push it back. Yet all he could do was muffle the voices. Some words slipped through. Occasional sentences, but that was all.

He breathed a little easier even as they stepped out into a small glade, a wide stream running through it, twisting away beneath thick bushes. The stream was silent. The howls of agony from the two natives were not.

Chapter 35: Father Stathi Alexander in the Glade of the Dead

Stathi's mind was in a fog as he stepped into the glade behind Mason. He had spent the short time that they traveled through the woods praying fiercely. He had prayed to the Holy Mother, to God, to the Son, to the Saints and the Martyrs. He had prayed to them all in an attempt to silence the horrific sounds which had assaulted him.

Terrible sounds.

Sounds much like the ones torn from the mouths of the two natives.

Blinking away the daze, Stathi looked about the glade and stumbled.

Crucified between many of the trees were young, teenage boys. They were all natives. All of them eviscerated. Each wore an expression of absolute terror upon their young faces. Each too, had been neatly scalped, the job expertly done. Yet perhaps the most disturbing was the fact that the genitals of each were missing.

Devoured, quite literally, by Liam Boylan.

With a final, combined voice filled with pure rage, the two native men raced across the stream, following the trail and vanished from view.

And then Mason's hand was on Stathi's bicep.

"Come, Father," Mason said gently. "This is no place to stay. We need to follow the trail."

Stathi hesitated for a moment, and then he nodded. "Yes. Of course. Liam Boylan."

"Yes," Mason nodded, turning Stathi away from the dead.

Mason let go of Stathi's arm and led the way to the stream. Stathi followed, trying not to allow the numbness that he was feeling, sweep over him.

He watched Mason cross the stream, the water instantly soaking the man's pants. Mason held the shotgun high, the water just below the hem of his jacket. When he had crossed to the other side, he stood there at the trail, waiting for Stathi.

Stathi nodded and walked to the stream. For a moment, he looked at the running water, remembering such streams in his youth, playing in the woods around Lowell. Smiling, Stathi stepped into the stream.

Something brushed against his calves and Stathi took another step forward through the water, only to feel something wrap around his left leg, then his right. Stathi stopped and looked down at the moving water.

"Are you alright?" Mason asked.

Looking through the rippling filter of the water, in the darkness of the night, Stathi glimpsed a pair of white hands upon his calves. The hands were joined to wrists, wrists to forearms, forearms to elbows, elbows to biceps and the arms disappeared into shadow.

Stathi looked up to Mason.

***

Mason held the shotgun in both hands as Father Alexander stepped into the stream, a tired smile upon the old priest's face.

The man took only two steps in, however, and stopped. He looked down at his legs in the water. Father Alexander seemed lost in thought as he stared down.

"Are you alright?" Mason asked, slipping his finger onto the trigger.

Father Alexander looked up to Mason, opened his mouth and was jerked down and into the stream.

He was gone.

Not even a swirl. No hint of robes. No floating prayer beads.

Nothing.

The priest was gone.

Both priests were gone, and James was still by the graveyard with Father Moran's corpse. And the natives had run ahead for their vengeance. Evidently, Liam Boylan had never shown them that little trick before.

Mason stood alone on the path in the forest. He looked, for a moment longer, at the swiftly moving stream. All traces of Father Alexander having ever existed, now gone.

Mason nodded once, turned and started up the path, following it as the natives had done.

Chapter 36: Harold and Julie at the Boylan House

Harold saw James' truck as soon as Julie turned her car onto Meeting House Road.

The big black vehicle was parked across from the Boylan House, and all of the shutters on the House were closed.

"Why would they close the shutters?" Julie asked, as she pulled in behind her brother's car.

"They didn't," Harold answered softly. "They would never have blocked the light of the sun out of the house. The house closed the shutters."

"Is it that bad?" Julie asked.

Harold looked over at the woman. She was young, but he could see that she was strong and determined. He couldn't lie to her. "It's worse than any of that."

Julie turned the car off.

She opened her door and looked over at him. "Are you coming up to the house with me?"

"I am indeed," Harold chuckled. He unbuckled and unlocked his door, opening it carefully. He walked slowly around the front end of the car to meet her, then together they crossed the road and started up the gentle incline. She had to help him the last few feet to the door, but he made it.

"I'm certain it's unlocked," Harold said.

Julie reached out, tried the latch, and the door was indeed unlocked.

Harold took his .45 out of his holster and followed Julie into the house. "Let's try upstairs," Harold said.

"Are you sure?" she whispered.

He nodded. "There's no sign of anyone here, but someone must have been. We need to check out everything we can."

"Okay," she said.

Harold took the lead and proceeded slowly and cautiously. Something was in the House, and he could feel it. A raw feeling clawed at his stomach. Harold ignored it as he entered the second floor, which was an identical copy of the first floor.

Except for the chimney. This chimney had some sort of false door built into it, and the door was open. He and Julie approached it carefully.

Skulls gleamed and shined upon neat shelves, and Harold

sighed as he looked at them. His breath hitched for a moment and then he cleared his throat.

"Julie, do you think, that you could help me?" he asked her.

She looked at him, concern displayed on her face. "Sure. What is it?"

"Up there, the skull that has 'Michael, 1945' on it, could you take it down for me, please?"

He saw her swallow nervously before reaching up and gently taking the small skull down. Harold holstered the pistol and accepted the skull from her.

He smiled sadly at it and felt tears well up. He tried to blink them away.

"Your son?" Julie asked gently.

Harold could only nod.

She turned and looked back at the skulls. "They were all someone's son."

For a moment longer, she looked at the skulls in their tidy rows. The first ones were labeled simply, 'Indian, 1669' and the last two, Harold saw, were the Verranault boys.

He watched as she took off her jacket, bent over and spread it out on the floor. Without a word, she started to slowly and reverently remove each skull and place it on her jacket.

Harold was silent as she worked, cradling the skull of his only child.

Chapter 37: Mason Philips and Liam Boylan

Mason moved steadily along the path.

He could hear nothing except the sound of his own footsteps and his breathing.

And that was fine.

His hands were cool and calm upon the shotgun. Each step was smooth. His thoughts were focused.

Soon, he found himself stepping into another opening in the woods, yet this one hid the sparse sky. The branches of fir trees were interwoven high above his head. A small fire burned harshly off to the right while Liam Boylan sat on a throne of deadwood. Short pillars of polished wood lined the opening, each with a single skull upon it.

Liam Boylan looked at Mason and sneered.

"If you had been a bit older," the beast said, "then I would have taken you instead of that other boy. That would, I think, have been quite for the best."

Mason came to a stop only a half a dozen yards from the throne.

"Your family has plagued me for centuries," Boylan said, straightening up slightly. "They hunted me in Ireland. Followed me here to the colonies. Found me out shortly before this country's revolution and have generally harassed my business for far too long. I had hoped that with the death of Michael Philips, it would have been done. Yet instead, it has continued."

"And what is your business," Mason asked, looking about him. "The murder of children?"

Boylan chuckled. "That's simply a pleasure. An indulgence, if you will. No, Mason Philips, there are other things at which I work. That is none of your concern, however. You are simply a pest. Like all of your family has been."

"This won't work, will it," Mason said, glancing down at the shotgun.

"Well," Boylan said with a slight hint of admiration, "you are at least smarter than your predecessors. And you are correct. That weapon won't work. Not by itself. Perhaps if you had a priest with you," the thing smiled, "but alas, they're both dead, aren't they?"

Mason nodded, yet he didn't let go of the weapon.

What else would the weapon work with? He thought.

"And now," Liam Boylan said, looking at Mason, "what are we going to do here?"

"I don't know," Mason said honestly. "But I've had just about enough of you, as well."

"Oh?" Boylan asked, grinning.

"You've been in my nightmares for too many years," Mason said. "I want it to stop."

"I truly wish to help it stop," Boylan said. "I think death would be a sweet release for you. I won't deny that I would enjoy your death, tremendously," the thing said, "but I do believe it is the best option for you." he said.

Gesturing at the woods around him, "Trapped here," "well, if there were any Indians left, they could tell you it's a rather unpleasant experience."

Mason opened his mouth to respond when Boylan twitched suddenly on his deadwood throne. The thing looked down at itself as if surprised. Then it doubled over, vomiting black bile onto the dark grass.

"What?" Boylan gasped, looking up at Mason.

Mason really couldn't answer. He stepped back, bringing the shotgun up and focusing it upon the thing on the throne. He scanned the trees, and about halfway around, he stopped. To the left, one of the pillars near Boylan was empty.

The skull was gone.

A soft step sounded beside Mason, and he looked down.

A young boy wearing jeans and a sweater stood beside him. The boy had the classic 1940's haircut.

Boylan started vomiting again.

Another pillar stood empty.

Another youth appeared, and Mason knew exactly who it was.

Kevin Peacock, wearing his Darth Vader costume and stepping up to stand upon Mason's left.

"Hello Kevin," Mason said softly.

Kevin looked up at him and smiled.

Boylan threw up again and again.

Soon, most of the pillars were empty. Liam Boylan lay curled upon the forest floor, vomiting still, in the middle of a giant pool of black bile.

Dozens of teenage boys stood around him, all of them staring at Boylan. All of them waiting to see what would happen next.

Mason looked at the pillars. They were all empty. None of them bore any skulls.

Everyone, whom Boylan had killed, stood once more, staring dispassionately down upon their murderer.

Mason walked up to Boylan, who still vomiting, and looked down upon him and the thing that tormented Monson for centuries looked up at him.

Sighting along the barrel of the shotgun Mason said, "I suppose that this will work now?"

Boylan's eyes widened with fear and rage.

"Well," Mason said, "that's about as close to a *yes* as I'm going to get, isn't it?"

He pulled the trigger.

With the blast of the shotgun ringing in his ears, Mason barely heard the shrieks coming from what was left of Boylan's mouth. Mason fired four more times. He reloaded with five more shells and fired all of those as well.

The thing at his feet finally stopped shrieking.

It stopped moving.

It was nothing more than a smoking pile of clothes. Whatever Boylan had been, it was gone.

Chapter 38: Harold, Julie, and the Zippo

Julie put the skulls in the back of her car while Harold stood at the door to the Boylan House. He took a cigarette out, lit it, and took a long drag. Before taking the skulls out of the house, they had searched the structure from top to bottom. And that hadn't been particularly hard since there were only two rooms and absolutely nothing in them.

The two men were missing, and where they were, he had no idea.

Mason and James were simply another pair of men who had vanished into the wilderness around the Boylan House.

Just another pair of names to add to the long list which already existed.

After a minute, Julie walked up to stand beside him. "Is everything okay?" she asked.

"No," Harold said. "I wish I knew where the two of them were."

"Me too," she agreed. "What are we going to do about the house?"

"What do you mean?" Harold asked, exhaling through his nose.

"Do we tell anyone about the skulls?"

He looked at her and then shook his head. "No, Julie, we're not going to do that."

"Why not?" she asked.

"Because no one would believe us," Harold answered. "Even if we had a forensic artist work with the skulls and everyone of them matched a person they had a picture for, they would only think it was some sick, freak occurrence. They wouldn't believe something like Liam Boylan could actually exist."

"Oh," she said.

"Just because we believe," he added, "doesn't mean anyone else will."

She nodded.

"Now, since those two boys have disappeared," Harold said, "I'm going to burn this son of a bitch to the ground."

"Do you think you can?" she asked.

"Of course," Harold said. "It's ready to burn."

"What?"

"Look at it," Harold said, pointing at the house with his cigarette held between his fingers. "When we walked in, you'd never know the place had been touched in over three hundred years. Now though, you can see how dry and ancient the wood is. There's rust on the hinges. The Boylan House has aged since we arrived, entered, and exited. It's ready to burn."

With Julie watching, Harold stepped over to the left window. He took his pack of Lucky's out and tucked several of them against—the now weathered and flammable—wood. There was no wind for Harold to worry about, and he took his Zippo out of his pocket. Leaning forward slightly, he rolled and snapped the lighter, the flame bursting into life. Harold moved the flame closer until he could light each cigarette in turn. The tobacco started to burn, and he stepped away, Julie taking him gently by the elbow. They turned their backs to the house and walked down to the road. When they reached Julie's car, they turned and looked at the Boylan House. Flames were already eating the first floor, moving quickly towards the second. No smoke rose up from the wood, yet the house burned and burned and burned.

Chapter 39: Trapped in the Forest of Liam Boylan

Mason was fairly certain that the thing, which had been Liam Boylan, was dead.

But, he reloaded the shotgun anyway.

It was then that he realized the boys were gone. He, alone, remained in the small clearing, standing in front of the deadwood throne. That was when he smelled the smoke.

A faint whiff of it at first, and then a little stronger. The smell wasn't one you would associate with a forest fire, or a campfire with a mixture of old and fresh wood.

No, Mason thought. *This smells like a house fire.*

Does it matter? another voice demanded. *There's a fire somewhere, you dumbass!*

And that sane part of himself was absolutely correct.

There was a fire somewhere in the forest that Mason happened to be in. He turned and started to run back down the path he had followed from the stream. By the time he reached the watercourse, there was thick smoke curling up and out of the slim spaces between the trees.

Mason didn't hesitate. He plunged into the stream, the water was bitterly cold. He didn't think of anything. He didn't allow himself the memory of Father Alexander being ripped down into the water. Keeping the shotgun above his chest he made it across the stream and was on the path once more.

Gray smoke started to thicken, piling up on the path and causing Mason to cough. His eyes watered but still he pressed on.

Mason needed to get out of the forest before he burned with it.

He stumbled, almost fell and literally bounced off a tree. Mason's body ached, but he managed to straighten himself and continue forward, running. He was out of shape, and he knew it. Within an exceptionally short time, a stitch had erupted in his side, and his breath was coming in great gasps.

The air around him was beginning to get hotter.

As the heat became nearly unbearable, Mason made it to the graveyard.

James sat listlessly on the ground beside the body of Father Moran.

A twinge of pain raced through Mason's heart as he looked

at the priest. The man had given his all for his God.

"James," Mason called out.

James looked up to him, surprised. Mason reached the young man and gasped for breath.

"We need to leave," Mason said, drawing in deep lungfuls of air.

"Look at him," James said softly.

And Mason did so.

Father Moran's body was nearly one with the earth. The roots of grass had stretched up out of the earth, their small white strands burying themselves into the flesh of Father Moran and the fabric of his vestments.

"James," Mason said, squatting down beside his young friend, "we need to leave now."

"We can't take him," James said.

"No," Mason agreed, "we can't. But he and Father Alexander will help to purify whatever this place is."

James blinked and looked around, realizing for the first time, that Father Alexander wasn't standing beside Mason.

"Oh shit," James said, "Father Alexander is dead?"

"Yes, and we will be, too," Mason said, "if we don't get our asses moving. Now get up."

James nodded, holding his shotgun as he stood.

All around them, the smoke thickened and the heat continued to increase. Mason felt the sweat start to pour out of him.

Together, the two men ran into the cornfield.

But all too soon, the smoke was wrapping around them, choking them, forcing them first to a walk, and then to their knees. Mason held onto his shotgun, crawling forward. He focused on moving just a little bit at a time. Right hand, left knee. Left hand, right knee. Repeat. Repeat. Repeat.

And then Mason heard James scream in outrage and fear. Before Mason could try to see what was happening, he felt hands upon him. On his legs, his back, and then on his arms.

He roared in anger, yet even that expression of anger disappeared into the smothering smoke.

Chapter 40: Harold and Julie and Meeting House Road

Harold stood beside James' truck while Julie stood beside him. Her arms were across her chest as they both watched the smokeless flames devouring the Boylan House.

Even as the fire raged, the sounds of animal life were returning to Meeting House Road.

Yet that was cold comfort to Harold and Julie.

Mason and James had entered the Boylan House, of that, Harold felt certain. Even if, by some unbelievable stroke of luck, the two men had gone into the forest and the swamps to hunt for Liam Boylan, they might never emerge.

So many hadn't.

"What the hell is going on?" Julie asked suddenly.

Harold looked back to the Boylan House and his breath caught in this throat.

He could see shapes in the windows.

Not Mason or James, the shapes he saw were far too small for that.

"Is that them?" Julie gasped. "Oh Christ, did we burn them alive?"

"No," Harold whispered. "No, we didn't."

And then the door to the Boylan House flew off of its hinges, becoming almost horizontal as it was launched away from the house. In the haze of the fire that shimmered in the now door-less doorway, Harold saw both James and Mason. The men hung between the arms of young teenagers and boys.

The boys moved forward. First with James, and then Mason, dumping them unceremoniously upon the grass before sending them rolling down the slight hill where the men came to a tangled mess at the side of the road.

Yet Harold barely noticed this.

In the doorway, standing clear, strong and vibrant was his son, Michael.

The boy smiled at him and waved.

Harold waved back, barely noticing that he wept as he did so.

"Is that your son?" Julie whispered.

"Yes," Harold said. "Yes. That's my boy."

A fist wrapped itself around his heart, squeezing suddenly, and Harold smiled even as he slid down the truck to sit hard on the pavement.

Julie got down on her knees with worry on her face. "Harold?" she asked, and her voice had a hollow, almost distant sound.

He smiled at her.

"Dying," he managed to hiss. "Dying. Finally. I'm dying."

Blackness wrapped around the edges of his vision and gradually moved in towards the center.

Harold closed his eyes and waited to see if he would see his son again.

Chapter 41: 8:00 AM, December 8th, 2015, Mason Philips' Home

Mason poured Julie a fresh cup of coffee before sitting down at the table across from her. She looked up from the morning paper and smiled at him.

"Thank you," she said, picking up the cup and taking a sip.

"You're welcome," he answered. "Anything exciting in the Globe today?"

"Something curious," she said. "It looks like a certain law firm burned to the ground last night."

"Really?" Mason asked innocently. "Well, that certainly is curious."

She looked over the top of the paper at him. "It is, isn't it?"

"Yes," he said, "yes, it sure is."

"There's also another article attached to it," Julie said. "It looks as though two of the three partners in the firm are still missing. No one is sure exactly where they went or what they were supposed to do. Their Lincoln Navigator was just discovered in the long term parking at Logan Airport."

"Well," Mason said, drinking his own coffee, "that is undeniably curious. The firm's offices burn down, and two of the partners are missing?"

Julie lowered the paper and looked at him. "There's also another article here, about the firm's third partner."

"And what's that one about?" Mason asked. "Do they think that the fire is an insurance scam or something?"

"No," Julie said, drinking her coffee and looking at him. "They found the third partner in his black Mercedes at the Gold Club; a place for exotic dancers, in Bedford, New Hampshire."

"Did they catch him with an entertainer?"

"They found him dead," she said. "Apparently from a heroin overdose."

"Ah."

"The strange thing is," Julie continued, "is that he had no history of drug abuse. No history whatsoever."

"Well, that's definitely strange," Mason said. He yawned and rubbed his eyes.

"It is strange," she agreed.

For a minute, Mason ate in silence while Julie drank her

coffee and looked at Mason.

"Mason," she said.

"Yes?" he asked, looking at her.

"What did you and James do last night?" she asked.

"What did we do?" Mason asked. "Well, that's both easy and hard to say. Your brother and I took care of some unfinished business. And it is finished."

"Good," Julie said, picking her paper up again and smiling at him. "I don't like going to bed without you."

Mason smiled at her. Tonight would be a momentous occasion. They were going up to Concord for their first dinner together. Mason's smile broadened. Julie looked up and returned the smile. And the two of them drank their coffee in comfortable silence.

* * *

Bonus Scene Chapter 1: 4:30 PM, Monson, September 21st, 1946, Monson

Harold sat in the cruiser, leaning over the steering wheel with his fingers interlocked.

The war had ended seventeen months earlier.

His son had disappeared eleven months ago.

Martha had gone back to live with her mother. It was easier that way. Whenever he and Martha looked at each other, all they could do was remember Michael.

Harold didn't think of the war too much. He'd done his time in the Pacific with the Marines. Hard times. Hard fighting. Dirty fighting. But he didn't think about it. He didn't need to. He knew that he had done what was necessary to win the war.

But it took a fifth of whiskey every night to fall asleep. A fifth of whiskey to smother the memories of Michael.

And Harold knew that it had something to do with the goddamned Boylan House; that empty abomination at the end of Meeting House Road.

Harold straightened up, stretched a little and settled back against the seat. From his lunchbox, he pulled out his Thermos and opened it. Inside was black coffee. The whiskey would come later. He had a job to do today.

He had the cruiser parked on Main Street, just across from the library. He poured himself a cup of black coffee into the Thermos' cup and took a careful sip. The coffee was still hot and Harold gave a cold smile. The coffee helped to keep him awake.

It was five o'clock in the evening. Well past the time he usually started in on the whiskey, and he was pretty sure that he'd get the shakes if he didn't start soon.

Ah, he thought, taking another sip of coffee, *but there's still work to do.*

While few cars passed by him, Harold sat as if he wore blinders. He was focused solely upon a new Ford. One of the post-war models that was all done up like a whore in church. Everything that couldn't have been put on during the fight was there. So much chrome that it would make your eyes hurt if the sun hit the Ford just right.

Harold didn't care about the car itself, however. Just who had ridden up to Monson in the damned thing.

The car had Massachusetts tags, and it was parked in front of City Hall. The car was registered to a Mr. Frederick Gunther, the Third. Frederick Gunther of Gunther, Boylan, and O'Connor. A stately law firm operating and practicing out of Boston. A firm, according to what Harold had been able to dig up, that had been in operation since the first settlers established themselves in Boston. A firm passed from one generation to the next.

The firm that had control of the Boylan House.

The firm that, according to the trust in the city's records, ensured that no fence would be established around the property known as 'The Boylan House'.

Michael had disappeared near that house.

Michael had disappeared into that house, he corrected himself.

No one believed him. And Harold didn't care.

Harold had hunted the Japanese over Peleliu and Okinawa. He'd been hunting in Monson his entire life. Killed his first deer on the conservation land behind the Boylan House. And when his boy hadn't shown up, Harold shook his head.

Bonus Scene Chapter 2: 5:15 PM, October 31st, 1945, Monson

"Where is he?" Harold asked, looking up from his plate.

Martha turned away from the percolator, frowning. "He said that he was going to play baseball with the Henderson twins. He should have been home by now."

Harold glanced out the window at the darkening sky. "He knows better than this."

Martha nodded, a look of worry on her face. She picked up a dishcloth and a clean dish and started trying to dry it.

Harold bit back the anger he felt at the boy's stupidity. It wouldn't do any good. Martha had had a hell of a time raising Michael while Harold was fighting. Sighing, Harold stuffed the last bit of pot roast into his mouth and washed it down with the dregs of his beer. He took his napkin off of his lap, wiped his mouth and put the white cloth down on the tablecloth beside his empty plate.

"I'll go find him," he said, putting a gentleness into his words that he wasn't feeling.

She nodded. "You don't think that he would have been foolish enough to try and cut through the swamp, do you?"

"No," Harold said, although that was exactly what he was worrying about. The boy was getting more confident in the woods. But confident in the woods didn't translate to being able to find his own ass in the swamp.

"And he wouldn't go near that Boylan House?" she asked, her voice was thick with fear.

Harold shook his head. "No," he said confidently. "Even I, wouldn't go near that place, Martha."

She nodded, put the plate back in the drying rack and twisted the towel in her hands.

"Everything will be fine," Harold said. He stepped in close to his wife and bent down a little to kiss the top of her head. She wrapped her arms around him tightly.

"I'm worried."

"I know."

"Bring him home."

"I will."

She let go of him and stepped away.

Harold walked to the back door, took his gunbelt off the

coatrack and strapped it on. He checked the .45 in its holster before he took down his jacket and pulled it on. His hat followed, and he turned to smile at Martha. "We'll be home soon," he said.

"Okay," she nodded. She forced a smile. "I'll put some hot chocolate on for him."

"And whiskey for me," Harold grinned. "It's cold out, and whiskey'll warm me up faster than hot chocolate."

She gave him a small smile, and he nodded.

Harold took hold of the doorknob and stepped out into the worst night of his life.

Bonus Scene Chapter 3: 5:45 PM, October 31ˢᵗ, 1945, The Henderson House

Damn cold out, Harold bitched to himself as he walked up the long walkway to the Henderson's porch. He had his hands stuffed into his coat pockets and he climbed the stairs two at a time. His blood had gotten thin in the Pacific, and the New England cold was kicking his ass.

And it's not even February yet, he thought bitterly.

Reaching the front door, Harold gave it a knock as if he were delivering a warrant and not checking up on his boy.

A moment later, the door opened, and it was one of the Henderson twins. Harold couldn't tell which one. They were god damn twins after all.

"Hello, Mr. Philips," the twin said.

"Hello," Harold said. He had a fifty-fifty chance of getting it right, but he hated screwing up. He was saved by the boy's mother.

"John," she called out from somewhere, "who is it?"

"It's Mr. Philips, mom," the boy answered.

"Well, let him in and close the door," she said, her voice drawing nearer. "We can't heat all of Monson, you know."

John rolled his eyes and stepped aside. "Please come in, Mr. Philips."

Harold hid a smile by coughing and stepped in, taking his hat off.

Mrs. Henderson came into the room. A short, roundish woman who ruled her household—which consisted of six boys and her rather drunken husband—with an iron fist. She smiled calmly at Harold, asking, "Did something happen to Morgan?"

"No, Mrs. Henderson," Harold smiled, "your husband isn't in any sort of trouble. I came here looking for Michael. He was supposed to have been home by five for dinner."

A frown appeared on Mrs. Henderson's face. "He realized that he was late," she said, "so he took off running."

"Mom," John said.

"Yes?" she asked, looking at him.

"Mike said he was going to run along the swamp trail, cut across Meeting House Road and then through the open field. There's just a little bit of woods between the field and the back of his house," John said.

Harold felt a chill settle into his spine.

"He took the swamp path?" he asked, looking at John.

"Yes, sir," John said. "We saw him right on it."

Mrs. Henderson looked at Harold. "I'll get on the party line, Harold," she said, softly. "Will you wait?"

"No," Harold said. His anger at the boy's tardiness vanished, replaced by a cold fear that started eating at his belly. "But thank you for making the call."

She nodded. "John," she said, turning to her son, "take Mr. Philips to the swamp trail's opening in the yard, but don't you follow. I'll want you and your brother in the kitchen."

"Why, Mom?" he asked.

"We have a mess of hot coffee to make," she sighed. "Now take him, please."

"Lead the way," Harold said, his voice rough and harsh. "I need to find my son."

Bonus Scene Chapter 4: 6:00 PM, October 31st, 1945, The Swamp Trail

The sun was rapidly setting, and Harold wasn't going to have much light to track his boy with.

But he was going to try.

He moved along the path quickly, following the deep indentations left by his son's tennis shoes. The boy had been running, hell bent for leather. Afraid of being late for dinner.

Harold bit back the fear that this was his fault. That if he hadn't been such a hard ass about being on time then the boy wouldn't be lost.

The boy couldn't be lost.

The boy's trail stayed on the swamp's own. It never deviated.

Within ten minutes, he was halfway through the swamp, the trail winding and cutting back, disappearing at times, but each time Harold found it. And Michael had as well. His footprints were always there.

A hundred yards from the end of the swamp, Harold came to a stop. Because Michael had come to a stop. His footprints were solid, shoulder length apart in the soft mud and grass. There hadn't been a hard frost yet, so the boy's marks were easy to spot.

Michael must have waited a few minutes. The footprints were deep. Then the tracks started again. But there was no rush to them this time. Now the tracks were normal, still sticking to the trail.

Harold swallowed drily, loosened his .45 and continued on.

Something wasn't right.

The birds were going quiet. The frogs had lapsed into silence. Nothing rustled the leaves, and no animals made any sort of song which Harold could hear.

And Michael's tracks led on.

Harold followed them until they emptied out into a large stretch of wooded land. In the woods, it was harder to track his son. The earth was soft, but there was a lot of ground cover. Broken branches and fallen leaves.

Still, though, Harold could see the trail his son had left.

A slight impression of a shoe. A bit of khaki string fluttering from a broken branch.

Harold followed them all, through the wooded lot and into

the long grass of the Boylan House's backyard.

Harold stood for a moment, right where the trees made the gradual transition to the grass. He could see Michael's trail through the grass. Bent and broken stalks moved in a disturbingly straight line to the back door of the house.

Harold stared at it for a long time, and then he saw something.

A bit of light in the far, upper left-hand window. A light which grew brighter and stayed bright.

Harold ran for the door.

The light never moved. No voice called out.

Gripping the door latch, Harold ignored the sudden bite of cold that drilled into his hand as he touched the iron. He ripped the door open and raced into the house. Dust flew up from his feet, and he looked around frantically. On the far left wall was a set of stairs leading to the second floor and Harold was racing up them in a minute, his feet thundering in the painful silence of the house.

Yet when Harold reached the second floor, there was no sign of Michael or any sign of the light.

And no one could have gone anywhere.

The stairs were the only way that someone could have left. All of the windows were closed.

The dust on the floor was pristine, an unbroken blanket of light gray.

Harold shook with rage, fear and sickness. He held them all in, though. He kept them all tightly reined in.

A short distance off, he heard the sound of feet and men calling out to their dogs, the animals howling as they followed the trail of both Harold and his son.

Bonus Scene Chapter 5: 4:45 PM, September 21st, 1946, Monson

Harold poured himself another cup of coffee and finished it quickly. He didn't have much left in the Thermos, but that didn't matter.

That didn't matter at all.

He looked at the back end of the Ford at the brake light that was conveniently broken.

No, Harold thought, *it didn't matter at all.*

He finished off the last of the coffee, took a napkin out of his lunchbox and wiped the cup dry. He closed up the empty Thermos and screwed the cap down tightly. Harold put both the container and the napkin away, looked at the sandwich that was still wrapped up and shook his head.

He wasn't hungry.

Was rarely hungry.

He closed the lunchbox and locked it down.

Picking up his .45 from the seat he once more made sure that the safety was off. Seconds would count. He felt that deep in his gut, that place that had kept him alive through months of combat.

And the door to city hall opened outwards. Three men walked out, each in their mid to late forties. Men who hadn't fought in either war.

Men who felt no loyalty to anything but themselves.

They wore obviously expensive suits, carrying themselves well, their very postures speaking of quality upbringing and education. As a group, they advanced to the Ford and climbed in. The car started up, pulled away from the curb and drove down Main Street. Harold watched the Ford turn left onto Route 122 before starting up the cruiser. He shifted into gear and picked the .45 up, steering with this left hand.

Harold drove easily up the street, letting go of the steering wheel once to wave at Doc Mathias as the man walked out of Sean's Bar. Doc, a little wobbly on his feet, waved back happily.

Signaling, Harold turned the cruiser left onto Route 122. Far ahead, he could see the Ford, watched the brake lights flash and was pleased to see that the left brake light was out.

Speeding up a little bit, Harold was soon only thirty yards

behind the Ford. He could see the three men having some sort of animated discussion. They didn't seem to notice him at all.

And why should they? Harold thought with a hard smile. *They weren't doing anything wrong. They weren't even breaking the speed limit.*

He followed them for a short way as they took a few turns. Eventually, they turned onto Meeting House Road and he passed by them, continuing up the road before backing into an abandoned logging road. He left the nose of the cruiser just a little visible. The people driving by would slow down and keep their heads straight, pretending that he wasn't there. Those who did look would be those who knew him. They would think that he was either out of the car taking a piss, or looking again for signs of Michael.

Either way, no one would bother him.

Harold left the keys in the ignition and got out of the car. He shut the door, adjusted his grip on the .45 and started walking into the woods. There was a small game trail that he'd be able to find in the dark. The moon would be nearly full as well, and the leaf canopy wasn't so thick as to blind him.

He kept a steady pace along the path.

The three lawyers came up once a quarter to inspect the house; to make sure that all was well with it, and to ensure that no one had put a fence around it either. They generally spent a good half an hour in the abomination.

More than enough time for Harold to get there.

Bonus Scene Chapter 6: 6:20 PM, October 31st, 1945, The Boylan House

Harold stood on the second floor of the Boylan House, his heart thundering and his stomach a twisted knot.

In the pristine evening air, he heard the men and the dogs. His friends and his neighbors. Men coming to search the swamp for his son. To search the woods for his son. A few would see the trail to the Boylan House. The old stories would leap to mind.

The old stories.

Everyone seemed to know someone who knew someone who had disappeared around the house. Vanished into the swamp, never to be seen again.

The swamp was a killer, they said. *The swamp was dangerous.*

But beneath those stories was another. That of some beast lurking in the shadows of the Boylan House.

Are they real? Harold suddenly thought. *Are all of those nightmares actually real?*

He knew what he had seen. Michael's tracks leading directly to the back door. The door which had been unlocked, even for Harold.

Yet there had been no sign of his son. No sign at all, though a light had been lit on the second floor.

Of that, Harold could be sure. He knew what he had seen.

The men and dogs were getting closer, following the same trail that Harold had followed. The trail would lead them to the house, and then they would search around it, none except Harold would enter it. Harold knew this as surely as he knew that the sun would rise in the east and set in the west.

It wasn't their son who had disappeared into the Boylan House.

Harold turned around and around, looking for some sort of sign of the light. Some sign of his son. He forced his hand to relax its grip upon the pistol.

Something cold whispered across the back of his neck, the faintest of touches, yet still Harold snapped around and he heard a soft, faint chuckle, as though the one he heard was far from him.

"Oh I hear you," Harold growled.

The cold came back, raising the hair on his neck and arms.

"You do, don't you," the voice said. *"I'm impressed. So very, very few men do. It's only the boys, you know, who usually hear me."*

The voice moved to the left and Harold moved his head to follow it. The unknown speaker laughed gently, obviously pleased. Outside, Harold could hear men calling his name, scolding dogs that nipped at one another.

"Where is my son?" Harold demanded, his voice shaking. "Where the hell is my son?"

"Mm, yes, that delicate boy," the voice said, purring from some place behind Harold. *"Well, your son is with me,"* the voice said, a silky tone drifting into its voice as it came to rest in front of Harold, *"and he and I are going to have such a wonderful time."*

Screaming, Harold fired his .45.

Bonus Scene Chapter 7: 7:30 PM, October 31st, 1945, Harold's House

Doc Mathias wasn't too drunk to be able to administer a sedative to Martha, or pour a healthy glass of whiskey for Harold.

Toby Purvis put the glass in Harold's hand and sat down across the table from him. Doc left the room to check on Martha, escorted by Mrs. Henderson, who had taken over the house with her two oldest boys.

"Drink it," Toby said.

Mechanically, Harold obeyed the order, barely noticing the burn of the whiskey racing down his throat.

He drained his glass and set it on the table.

"I'm sorry," Toby said.

Harold looked at him. "Why?" he managed to ask after a moment.

"Because I don't think that they're going to find Michael."

That was the first honest statement that Harold had heard since the men had dragged him screaming, dry firing his emptied pistol, from the Boylan House.

"No?" Harold asked.

Toby took the glass from where it stood in front of Harold, opened the whiskey, poured another large drink for Harold and took a pull from the bottle before capping it. He slid the glass back to Harold.

Harold took a sip and said again, "No?"

Toby shook his head.

"Why not?" Harold asked, his throat tight with fear.

"When you were gone," Toby said, "in '42, a boy from Hollis disappeared in the swamp."

"So?" Harold said between clenched teeth, "what the hell does that have to do with Michael?"

"People don't tell the whole story about that," Toby said, looking uncomfortable. "And there are a few who do."

"What are you talking about?" Harold asked, taking a larger drink.

"I was home, my ship had been shot out from under me," Toby said, pulling at the cuff of his shirt, "and me and my cousins, we were out looking for fisher cats. The Hendersons had lost a few chickens. Same thing with the Halls up the road. Well, we were near the Boylan House, and it was October 28th."

"October?" Harold asked.

Toby nodded. "Late October. We saw that boy, maybe sixteen, or seventeen. We learned, later on, that he was doing a march through the woods because he was getting ready to go down to the recruiter in Nashua. He wanted to make sure that he would do alright marching with the Army. Well," Toby cleared his throat, "we were in the woods when we saw him walk out of the field across from the Boylan House. We figured he would go wide around it, but when he got across the road, he paused and looked to the house."

"Why?"

"I don't know for sure," Toby said. "It looked like he heard something, something from the house."

"You didn't hear anything?" Harold asked.

"No," Toby answered. "We didn't hear a thing. Next, we knew that boy was making a bee-line for the front door of the Boylan House. We just sort of watched. You know, we'd never gone in. Never even heard of anybody going in.

"Well," Toby continued, "when he got to the door, it opened, and we lost sight of him as he stepped in. Next thing we heard was the door slamming and a short, terrible scream." Toby shook his head. "I've heard men like that scream a few times, Harold, and I know you have, too. It's when they know that they're dying. When they know that they're dying badly."

Harold nodded. He knew that sound too well. "Did you go up to the house?" he asked, looking at Toby.

"I couldn't," Toby said softly, lowering his eyes. "God help me, Harold, I couldn't. There's something in there, isn't there?"

Harold waited until the man had raised his eyes once more before answering. "Yes, Toby," he said, "there is. And I don't know how to kill that damn thing."

Bonus Scene Chapter 8: 5:05 PM, September 21st, 1946, The Boylan House

The Ford with the broken light was parked on the dirt road in front of the Boylan House when Harold came out of the trail and into the back yard of the house. Calmly, he walked around to the front, went up to the ancient door and gave it a solid knock that would have woken the dead.

A moment later, the door opened and a man with dark hair that was slicked back gave him a confused look. "Good evening," he man said. "May I help you?"

Harold smiled pleasantly, "Yes, my name's Harold Philips, I'm the Monson sheriff."

The confused look slipped away, and the man smiled, "Ah, Sheriff Philips. We've heard nothing but good things about you. I'm Frederick Gunther. What can I do for you?"

"Well," Harold said, "I've had a few complaints about a Ford driving recklessly and, quite frankly," he said in a confidential tone, "I think that it's a load of shit. But it was Mrs. Kenyon, the mayor's wife who complained."

Frederick nodded in understanding. "How can I help you with this?"

"I'd just like to speak to you about the driving so I can honestly say to her that I did."

"Come in, Sheriff," Frederick said, smiling and stepping back. "I wasn't driving, my friend Charles was. And we wouldn't want you to have to lie to the good mayor's wife."

"Thank you," Harold smiled. "That would be greatly appreciated. The woman can sniff out a falsehood a mile away. I once told her that I'd speak to the Henderson boys about throwing rocks at the old barn on Route 122, and I didn't. She knew it as sure as if she had been standing beside me all day."

"Yes," Frederick said. "My mother was the same way. I thought that she could just tell if I was lying, but it turned out that she was unusually adept at discovering what was true and what was false in a person's voice. I, however," Frederick sighed in mock exaggeration, "did not receive that boon."

Harold smiled and nodded, waiting as the man closed the door and then following him towards the stairs at the far right.

"My two colleagues are on the second floor," Frederick said.

"Evidently, someone fired a weapon in here just before winter, and we're finally getting up to Monson to inspect it. It's part of our job, physically inspecting the Boylan House on a yearly basis, or more, if necessary."

"Yes," Harold said, "I remember the incident. A father was distraught. His son had disappeared into the swamp."

"A terrible place," Frederick said. "Too many people die in places like that."

"Yes, they do," Harold agreed.

They reached the second floor and found Attorneys Gunther and O'Connor standing in front of one of the wooden walls, examining eight bullet holes.

"Gentlemen," Frederick said, "this is Sheriff Philips of Monson. He has the unfortunate responsibility of scolding Charles for his driving."

Charles was blonde, and he turned to look at Harold in surprise. "For my driving?"

"Yes," Harold said apologetically, "the mayor's wife. I have to."

Charles smiled in understanding. "Quite alright, Sheriff."

"Yes, she said that you were driving recklessly where the Henderson family lives, and seeing as how the Hendersons seem to have a new child every other weekend," Harold sighed, "she would like it if you drove a little slower."

"I am quite sorry," Charles said formally, "please inform the Mayor's esteemed wife that I shall drive accordingly."

"Excellent," Harold said. "Excellent." He dropped his hand to the butt of his .45 and pulled the weapon, the false smile he had been wearing, vanished. "Get on the floor and on your goddamned knees!"

The three men looked at him with utter surprise. Shocked, unable to take their eyes away from the barrel of the huge automatic in Harold's hands.

Harold put a single round into the wall between Frederick and Charles. The crash of the shot rang out off the walls, and the men fell to their knees. The third man's trousers went dark with spilled piss.

"I have seven more rounds," Harold said calmly, looking at the men and positioning himself several feet away and facing them. "And I will use them to get some answers from you."

"Answers about what?" Frederick asked. His voice was strained, and the fear was thick in his eyes.

"Why isn't there a fence around this place?" Harold asked.

Charles glanced at O'Connor and Frederick swallowed nervously. "We really can't answer that question."

"I don't accept that answer," Harold said calmly. "I'm going to blow your knee off. Your right knee. Answer the question."

O'Connor straightened up. "The house must be free."

"The house?" Harold asked.

All three of the men nodded.

"Free to do what?" Harold asked.

No one responded.

Harold sighed and gave them a tight smile. "Gentlemen," he said, "my son disappeared in this house. In *this shitty house*. I hope that you understand that."

The men were unmoved. And they were not surprised by his statement.

"Free to do what?" Harold asked again.

The three men straightened up and remained silent.

Harold pulled the trigger and put a round into O'Connor's head. The man's head snapped backward before he collapsed. His blood, brains and skull splattered across the wall.

"Jesus Christ!" Frederick screamed.

Charles opened his mouth to say something but ended up vomiting, instead.

"Free for the hunter to hunt!" Frederick screamed at him. "Free for the hunter to hunt!"

"Who's the hunter?"

"The greatest of us," Frederick said as Charles wiped the remnants of vomit from his mouth with the back of his hand.

"He has his needs," Charles said, glaring at Harold. "He must be allowed to hunt when the time is right."

"When is the time right?" Harold asked.

"October, the end of the month," Frederick hissed at him. "Then is the time right, the youth approaches and hears the call of the hunter."

"And they all answer," Charles said, smiling viciously at Harold. "They all answer, don't they, Sheriff?"

Harold put a round into the man's stomach.

The scream that was ripped out of Charles' mouth brought a

grim smile to Harold's face. He looked at Frederick, whose face was white, sweat breaking out across his forehead.

"Don't worry," Harold said, keeping his voice just above Charles' screams, "he'll be dead in ten minutes. Fifteen at the most. Painfully, too. Gut wounds are terrible," Harold continued. "I've seen men beg to be put out of their misery after being shot in the gut."

Harold looked at Charles. "That won't be the case here, though. That son of a bitch will die slow." Now, Harold smiled, turning his attention back to Frederick, "let's talk about the hunter."

"What about him?" Frederick asked. There were droplets of blood on the side of his face, and he looked too afraid to try and clean himself off.

"How can I kill the son of a bitch?" Harold asked, trying to keep himself calm.

"You can't," Frederick grinned. "He's too strong? That's why he's the hunter. He leads us to glory."

"Hmm, well," Harold said, "that's fine. What is he?"

"He is the spirit made flesh, and the flesh made spirit," Frederick said. "He is the eater of flesh. The devourer of youth."

"A spirit?" Harold asked.

"Yes, but so much more. He is—"

Harold cut him off. "No, no. That's enough of that. I just want to know for certain, is he a spirit?"

"Yes," Frederick snarled. "A spirit that you cannot defeat."

"I can't defeat?" Harold asked.

"You cannot."

"But somebody can," Harold said.

Frederick's eyes widened silently, but he remained silent.

"Well," Harold said, "I guess I need to find somebody who can."

He pulled the trigger for the fourth time and the slug tore out Frederick's throat. Blood sprayed out across the room and the dying Charles.

Harold calmly walked around, picking up his spent shell casings. Waste not, want not, he thought.

Putting the casings in his jacket pocket he stepped over to Charles, who was still weeping from the pain, blood pumping out of the hole in his stomach.

"Not much longer now, Charles," Harold said in a conversational tone. "You'll be dead soon."

"Will you kill me?" Charles gasped. "Please?"

"I already have," Harold said. He squatted down in the blood beside Charles.

"Please?" Charles moaned.

"I've already done that," Harold reiterated, "so I'm going to simply sit here and watch you die."

And with that, Harold held his .45 in his hands, and he watched.

And he waited.

* * *

Blood Contract

Prologue: Ignorance is No Excuse

"Then the motion carries," Alderman Williams said, fairly glowing with his pleasure at the board's decision.

Hollis Blood took his hat off of his knee and stood faster than his old body was used to. He thumped loudly on the chamber's floor with his cane until the cheerful prattle of the alderman stopped. They all looked at him with undisguised displeasure and unease.

Hollis pointed his cane at them. "This, Aldermen, is a poor decision. You've violated the agreement that my family had with the town."

No one responded. *And why should they,* Hollis thought. They've already made their decision.

"Hollis," Alderman Nadeau started, then stopped, swallowing nervously. "Um, Mr. Blood, the agreement was made with the belief that there would never be a need for Thorne to expand."

"I've no issue with expansion," Hollis snapped. "The town needs it. I have issue with you choosing my family lands." Without waiting for another response, Hollis put his hat on his head and left the small aldermanic chamber.

He navigated the long granite steps, ignoring the newly installed handicap ramp. All about him were signs of the town of Thorne moving steadily into the future—or at least playing catch up with the present.

His cane thumped loudly on the old brick sidewalk and the early autumn sun set behind the small, wooden First Congregationalist Church. Hollis moved at a surprisingly fast pace for someone of his age and physical ability, and kept it up until he was well outside of town and came to his own driveway.

The drive was of dirt, the trees heavy around the borders of the property. They were tall and old and angry. Hollis slowed his pace as he walked up the drive, the trees' boughs interlocking a scarce fifteen feet above his head. A long, dark tunnel formed before him, curving slowly up and to the left.

Soon he came to a narrow path, hardly visible even to him.

It had been a long time since Hollis had found it necessary to travel to this part of the family land.

The path ran at a sharp angle from the drive. Beneath the

leaf litter Hollis's cane thumped loudly upon cobblestones which had been set in place by his grandfather's father.

Hollis pushed through thin branches, ignoring the occasional sting of an insect and the cold air that thickened around him.

In a moment, he stood before the wrought iron gate to the family graveyard.

The gate was pure black, untouched by rust or age. The matching hinges were set into a tall granite post, the lock for the gate set into the post's mate standing opposite. A large fieldstone wall, nearly six feet in height, wrapped around the entire graveyard, making a perfect box.

Hollis put his hand on the lock, felt a short, powerful surge, and the lock clicked open. The gate swung in silently.

Hollis walked into the graveyard.

The grass was neat, not rising more than four inches above the ground. The headstones were laid out in even rows, one close to the other. The Blood dead were orderly even in their final repose.

Seventy-one family graves.

Five rows of twelve, one row of eleven.

At the end of the last row, on the far right, was a marker with his name and birth date carved into it. The terminal date had not been set—or if it had, the information had not been shared with him.

Hollis looked at the graves for a moment.

"They've broken the contract," he said simply.

And with that he turned and walked out of the graveyard, leaving the gate open to the coming night.

Chapter 1: Playing Security Guard

Mike and Tom walked among the various pieces of equipment, checking the fuel tanks and the hydraulic reservoirs on everything from the JCB mini-loader to the CAT excavator. It took them nearly twenty minutes to check every piece and to make sure keys weren't in the ignitions.

"Looks good," Tom said, walking with the foreman back to the office trailer that had been set up on the side of Blood Road.

"It does," Mike agreed.

"Do I really have to pull this shift?" Tom asked as they walked into the trailer, the small heater warming up the interior and feeding off of the propane tank outside.

"We've been over this shit," Mike sighed, walking around his desk. He sat down in his chair, pulled a pint of whiskey out of a drawer and uncapped it. Mike took a long pull from it and didn't offer any to Tom.

Tom had been sober for three years, and Mike knew it.

Still, the sight of it made Tom's throat dry.

Mike saw the look, capped the pint and slipped it into the inner pocket of his jacket. "Sorry Tommy," Mike said.

"No problem, Bossman," Tom said, dropping into a beat-up recliner set against the wall.

"I don't know who's screwing with the equipment," Mike said, "but I can't have another morning of dry hydraulic tanks. Somebody managed to pump all of that shit out. I don't see why they'd have to steal hydraulic oil in the first place, but if it's someone who's just screwing around with us, they may decide to move on to bigger and better things."

Tom nodded.

They'd wasted nearly an hour of the workday just filling the tanks and checking out the rest of the rigs before starting them up. Then it was another forty-five minutes before the hydraulic oil was warm enough for the equipment to actually be usable— nearly two hours down the shitter.

"We can't afford another day like today," Mike said.

Tom nodded.

"Winter's coming fast this year," Mike continued.

"I know, Mike," Tom sighed, taking his hat off and rolling the brim for a minute. "I know that another day will screw us on the schedule. I just don't want to have to sit here until, what, eleven?"

"Yeah," Mike said apologetically. "Eleven. That's when the hired security guard is going to come in. I'm paying you time and a half on this, Tom. Eight hours."

"And I appreciate that," Tom said, putting his hat back on his head, "but I want to be home."

Mike nodded.

Tom sighed.

Standing up, Mike put on his own hat and looked at Tom. "Just keep an eye out, kid. And an ear. Let's hope that this was just a one-time deal."

"Yeah," Tom said, "I will."

Mike nodded and left the trailer. A minute later, Tom heard Mike's diesel start, and a moment after that, the big red Dodge went rumbling out of the lot.

Tom was alone.

He dug his phone out of his pocket, checked his emails, his Facebook page, and played a couple of rounds of Candy Crush.

It was four o'clock.

"You've got to be shitting me," he groaned, dropping his phone to his lap. "Seven more goddamn hours."

His stomach rumbled, and Tom suddenly realized that he didn't have anything to eat. He had finished his lunch later than usual, but they had a hell of a time ripping out a stand of pine trees right near the day's end and he was hungry as hell now.

"This sucks," he groaned.

Picking up his phone again, he brought up Google and started searching for any place that would deliver. Thorne, New Hampshire wasn't exactly a hot place to be.

Hell, they had only just had a Dunkin Donuts move into the town and that was because there was going to be construction going on for the next year and a half with all the new developments that were about to be built.

Shaking his head at his miserable situation, Tom scrolled down until he found a pizza place in a nearby town called Monson.

He tapped on the number and hit call.

"Conroy's Pizza," a young girl said, "is this pick-up or delivery?"

"Delivery, I hope," Tom said.

The girl paused for a moment, "Um, what do you mean?"

"Well," he said, straightening up in the chair, "do you guys deliver out to Thorne?"

"Yup," she said.

"There's a new worksite out here, do you know it?"

"Yeah," she answered. "It's on Blood Road."

"Yes," Tom said. "I'm working here. I drive a blue Chevy extended cab, and it's parked right next to the trailer. I can't leave, but if I pay over the phone can you guys send a large pepperoni and a two-liter bottle of Coke out to me?"

"Yeah," the girl said, "that's not a problem. Should the delivery guy go to your truck or the trailer?"

"The trailer, please," Tom answered.

"Okay, that'll be sixteen even then," she said.

"Fantastic," Tom grinned to himself. He read off his debit card information to her, and a moment later he was up and out of the chair, plugging his phone into the extension cord so it could charge.

Beyond the thin walls of the trailer the day was getting darker and the air colder. He pulled his gloves out of his jacket's pockets and put them on.

Need to start the generator for the lights, he thought, opening the door and stepping out into the cold. He walked to the where the generator was chained to the back of the excavator for the night. Tom double checked the fuel, hit the ignition and fired up the generator.

The lights which were suspended from tall, temporary, steel frames flickered into life. Cones of bright, harsh light appeared around the gathered pieces of equipment and Tom nodded to himself. He turned and started to walk back to the trailer and then stopped.

What the hell? he thought, turning back towards the generator.

Standing just inside the tree line, just inside the very edge of the light was a young boy. Maybe six or seven, no older than Tom's youngest brother.

The boy's skin was pale and seemed sickly. He had short, black hair, and he wore a black suit and a white shirt with a black tie. On his feet were battered canvas All-Stars. The suit coat that he wore hung strangely, as if it was too wide in the back, or torn up the center.

Tom took a cautious step towards the boy.

They were out in the middle of nowhere, as far as Tom was concerned, and the only person that he knew of living in the area was the old man who lived up the dirt drive. And that was half a mile farther up the road.

"Are you okay?" Tom asked.

The boy nodded.

A little bit of relief slipped into Tom—but only a little.

"Are you lost?"

The boy shook his head.

"Are you with someone else?" Tom asked.

Again the boy shook his head.

"Are you cold?"

The boy nodded.

"Well," Tom said, "do you have a phone?"

The boy nodded.

"Did you call anyone?"

The boy looked at him, confused for a moment, then shook his head.

Maybe it's not charged, Tom thought, *or bad reception.*

"I've got a phone inside if you want to use it," Tom said, "or I can grab you a blanket out of my truck if you want to wrap up in it. I've got pizza on the way, and I can call someone for you too."

The boy looked at him, hardly blinking.

"Um," Tom said, rubbing the back of his head. "Do you want to come inside and warm up and use the phone?"

The boy smiled and nodded.

"Cool," Tom said, relieved. He didn't want the kid to think that he was some kind of pervert or anything, but he didn't want the kid out in the cold either. Tom would sit at Mike's desk and let the kid sit in the recliner. Then Tom could call the police. That is, if Thorne even had a police department.

He shook his head and then stumbled back.

The boy was right beside him.

"Jesus Christ!" Tom said, his heart thundering in his chest. "I never even heard you!"

The boy smiled happily.

Yeah, Tom thought, shaking his head. *This kid is exactly*

Matthew. Must be the age, he thought, remembering some of the shit that his youngest brother liked to do.

"Okay, kid," Tom said, "come on with me. I'm Tom, by the way," he said, extending his hand.

The boy shook the offered hand, the boy's own small hand was deathly cold to the touch. "I'm Morgan," he said.

"Nice to meet you, Morgan," Tom said, letting go of the boy's hand quickly. He led the boy to the trailer and up the three steps that took them inside.

The boy smiled and walked over to the heater, holding his hands out to it. Tom sat down at Mike's desk and saw that Morgan's suit coat was indeed ripped up to nearly the center of his shoulder blades.

"Does someone know where you are?" Tom asked, reaching for his phone.

"Yes," Morgan answered.

Tom disconnected his phone and saw that the battery was nearly dead. *What the hell?*

Shaking his head, Tom plugged the phone back in. Sitting back in Mike's chair, he looked up and saw Morgan standing in front of the desk.

Tom's heart leaped.

Christ! This kid is way too quiet. He must drive his parents nuts.

"What's up?" Tom asked.

Morgan looked confused, glancing up at the ceiling then back down at Tom.

"Ah, well," Tom said. "I mean, do you have a question?"

"Yes," Morgan said.

"What's your question?" Tom said.

"Why are you tearing down these trees?"

The boy had hazel eyes, Tom realized, and they were fixed steadily on Tom.

"It's my job," Tom answered. "The company I work for was hired to clear the land for houses."

"This is your job?" Morgan asked.

"Yup," Tom answered.

"This is your job," Morgan said again, then he added, "Do you live in Thorne, too?"

"Yes," Tom said again, wondering if something was actually

wrong with the kid's head.

"Then I am sorry."

"Why?" Tom asked, genuinely confused.

Yet Morgan said nothing. He simply stared at Tom.

"Why are you sorry?"

And as the last syllable left Tom's mouth, Morgan leaned over the desk, grabbed Tom by the head with both hands and dragged him out of the chair.

For a moment, Tom was stunned, and then he felt how cold the boy's hands were. There was immense strength in that small frame. At first Tom shouted, then he screamed, flailing at the boy with his fists, trying to get to his feet, yet Morgan jerked him off balance.

Morgan pulled Tom towards the door, which flew open of its own accord as they neared it, and a heartbeat later Morgan was dragging him down the steel stairs and into the yard.

There, just a few feet away was a large hole. One that hadn't been there before.

Morgan moved confidently towards it.

Tom saw the hole, and he knew what was coming.

He shrieked and tried to wrench his head away, but the boy tightened his grip, stars of pain exploding around Tom's vision.

Tom punched at the boy, clawed at Morgan's hands, pulled at the boy's clothes, but nothing stopped the quiet child's steady approach toward the hole. Then Tom was in the hole, Morgan holding him down, looking calm as the dirt started to fall into the opening.

Tom continued to fight, but soon the earth had his legs buried, and then his waist and his chest. One arm became pinned beside him, the other upraised to strike when Morgan settled back, letting go.

"I'm sorry," Morgan said as the earth swept over and around Tom's head, leaving him gasping and in darkness. "It won't be quick."

And it wasn't.

Chapter 2: Checking on the Pizza Man

Jim Petrov was standing in the new Dunkin Donuts in Thorne when dispatch called him.

"Two-Nine do you copy?" Maggie said.

Jim paid for his medium hot regular and stepped off to the side with his coffee, keying the mic on his shoulder strap. "This is Two-Nine, dispatch, go."

"Missing driver from Conroy's," Maggie said.

He looked at his watch. Five o'clock.

"How long, dispatch?"

"Forty-five. And it was just the one."

Jim frowned. "Destination, dispatch?"

"The worksite on Blood Road in Thorne."

"Copy, dispatch. I'm on my way now."

Jim waved to the girls behind the counter and stepped out the backdoor to his Charger. He climbed in, settled into the seat, and pulled the belt on before starting the car. He didn't bother with the siren. Who knew what was going on? The kid could have pulled over for a quickie with his girlfriend, stopped to chat with a couple of buddies, or any number of things that kids did. However, Conroy usually hired kids who stuck to the job and didn't screw around that often, and if Cliff Conroy was worried about this kid, it meant that the kid really wasn't one to drift off.

Jim put a little weight on the gas pedal.

He took a sip of his hot coffee, saw the cars in front of him slow down with the cop-panic setting in. Sighing, he threw the lights on and increased his speed again as the cars happily got out of his way.

Keeping the lights on, he raced along Route 122 and turned onto Blood Road. Up ahead in the darkness he caught sight of work lights glaring down on the worksite. Jim could see a trailer and a small Mazda Miata parked beside a big old Chevy. The Mazda had its lights on, exhaust billowing out of the tailpipe.

The driver's side door was open, and it was empty.

Jim swung into the yard and his headlights splashed across a young man sitting on the ground, a red warming bag on his lap. In front of the young man, sitting on the steps of the trailer, was a boy, perhaps seven or eight. He wore a black suit with a matching tie over a white dress shirt.

Jim put the Charger into park and keyed his mic. "Dispatch this is Two-Nine. I am on scene. I have the delivery driver and a young boy. Something's not right. Send a local from Monson and a bus from Hollis, please."

"Copy Two-Nine," Maggie said.

Jim left the lights on but shut off the car before getting out.

"Hello," he called out cheerfully, stepping around the front of his cruiser.

"Hello," the young man said without looking back. His voice was thick with fear.

The boy on the steps smiled and waved.

Jim returned the wave as he walked closer. He finally stood beside the driver and looked down at the young man.

A look of abject terror was frozen on his face as he stared at something in front of him. Jim thought that it was the little boy on the steps, but as he followed the young man's line of sight he saw something else. Something which caused his spine to ripple with concern.

A hand protruded from the earth nearly halfway between them. It looked almost like a Halloween gag, but Jim knew that it wasn't. The fingers were slightly curled, the wrist slightly exposed, but the forearm vanishing into the dirt.

"It was still moving when I got here," the delivery driver said, staring at the hand. "It was still moving."

"The hand?" Jim asked gently.

The driver nodded, finally tearing his eyes away and looking up at Jim. "The hand was still moving when I got here, sir. I couldn't help. He wouldn't let me."

"Who's he?" Jim asked.

The driver pointed to the young boy.

"Hello," Jim said to the boy.

The boy waved again. He smiled happily at Jim.

"He asked me if I lived in Thorne," the driver said, staring at the boy. "But I don't. He said that was good."

"Do you live in Thorne?" Jim asked the boy on the stairs.

The boy smiled broadly as he nodded.

"Do you?" the boy asked, and his voice was low and happy and raised the hair on the back of Jim's neck.

"No," Jim said evenly, "I don't."

"That's good," the little boy said, standing up.

"Why is it good?" Jim asked.

"Because you won't end up like him," the boy said simply and started walking away.

"Son, you can't walk away from me," Jim said, taking a step forward.

The boy paused to look over his shoulder. He smiled again and said, "Yes I can."

The boy walked towards the tree line hidden just outside the range of the worklights.

Jim started walking after him, stepping around the hand. "Son, don't walk away from me."

The boy didn't answer. He simply slipped away into the darkness. Jim walked quickly after him, slipping his small LED flashlight out of its case and turning it on as he walked into the woods. He stopped and scanned the trees.

He couldn't see anything.

Faintly Jim heard the sound of sirens. It sounded like one of the Monson PD.

Frowning, he turned around, turning his flashlight off as he walked back into the yard. He started following his footprints back towards the trailer when he stopped suddenly and stared at the ground.

Jim could clearly see his own footprints in the dirt.

But his were the only prints there.

No sign of the young boy's footprints at all.

Chapter 3: Hollis and Coffee

Hollis sat on his porch, smoking his pipe and sipping at his coffee. From his chair he could look down through the thinning woods and see the flashes of police lights and the lights of an ambulance. The stark light of the worksite's lights polluted the night sky as well.

Hollis took the pipe stem out of his mouth, exhaled through his nose and took a drink.

In the slim light of the halfmoon Hollis caught sight of a small shape walking up the drive, staying in the center of the dirt. A soft, happy whistling was carried along the autumn breeze and brought a sigh to Hollis' lips.

He put the coffee down and returned the pipe stem to his mouth.

In silence, he watched the small shape move ever closer until he recognized the young boy—not that he hadn't known who it was from the moment he'd seen the walk. and heard his brother's favorite piece from Schubert being whistled.

Morgan walked up the long, winding cobblestone path that their mother had their father install in 1933, a year before pneumonia would claim Morgan's young life. Hollis's brother wore his burial suit, hopping up each granite step cheerfully.

When Morgan's shoes rang out on the broad, wooden steps, Morgan waved at Hollis as he finally stepped onto the porch.

Hollis let out another sigh and waved back.

"Hello Morgan," Hollis said around the pipe stem. "I should have known that you would be the first."

Morgan laughed, a sweet and pure sound that Hollis had forgotten completely, and which brought tears to his eyes.

"I'm so glad to see you, Morgan," Hollis sighed, wiping his eyes before taking the pipe out of his mouth. "I've missed you."

"I've watched you grow," Morgan said, sitting down in the old rocker that their mother had favored. She had never allowed Morgan or Hollis to use it, afraid that they would tip over in it. "I'm very proud of you."

"Thank you," Hollis said, taking a sip of his coffee.

"You're welcome." Morgan looked at him, grinning. "You learned to fly a plane!"

Hollis smiled. "I did. A P-38 Lightning."

"You had a picture of you and me together when you flew," Morgan said, his grin turning into a giant smile.

"I always thought you were flying with me."

Morgan nodded happily. "I was."

Hollis returned the pipe to his mouth, and he smoked cheerfully for a few minutes as they sat in silence. The lights continued to flash down at the worksite and occasionally the sound of a two-way radio could faintly be heard as it echoed off of the trees.

Finally Hollis asked, "What happened down there?"

Morgan glanced over his shoulder, back down the way he had come. "That?"

"Yes," Hollis said, "that."

"I happened."

Morgan's tone was flat. The cheerfulness gone.

"May I ask?"

Morgan looked at him and shook his head. "We've decided that it is best that you don't know what we do. At least not from the family. We don't want you being held accountable for any of it."

Hollis nodded.

His brother stood up and put a cold, but gentle hand on Hollis's shoulder. "Someone will be up here soon, Hollis. A State Policeman. He was nice to me. Tell him to stay away. Some of the others won't care who is from Thorne and who isn't."

Hollis nodded. He looked at Morgan, wishing that they were still little boys, still hunting salamanders under the rocks by Hassell Brook, still picking apples in the family's orchard.

Morgan smiled at him. "I will see you soon enough, Hollis."

Once more Hollis nodded, closing his eyes and listening to the footsteps of his brother fade away.

Chapter 4: Jim Petrov and the Blood Road Worksite

Much to Jim's surprise, his coffee was still relatively warm.

He stood beside Brian Ricard's Monson PT cruiser while the EMTs treated the delivery boy from Conroy's for shock.

Jim and Brian had taped off the area around the hand protruding from the ground, and they had put a call in to the supervisor for the worksite, Mike Pinkham with the Deutsche Development Corporation. The Chevy at the site was registered to a Thomas Pelto, previous arrests for DUI, but that had been three years ago.

Jim had a suspicion that Thomas Pelto's hand was the one sticking up and out of the ground.

According to Cliff Conroy, his daughter had taken an order for a large pepperoni and a two-liter bottle of coke to be delivered out to a Tom at the worksite. Richard MacDonald, the delivery boy, had brought it out to the site.

All they could currently get out of Richard was that the boy whom Jim had tried to follow hadn't allowed Richard to try to save Tom.

The most frightening part of the whole deal—aside from the little boy disappearing into the woods—was that it didn't look like the dirt was even disturbed around the hand.

"It looks like the damned thing just grew out of it," Jim said outloud.

"What's that?" Brian asked.

"The hand," Jim said, taking a drink of his coffee and nodding towards the hand. "It looks like someone planted a seed, and the hand just grew out of the damned ground."

"Yeah," Brian agreed. "Kind of messed up. But what about that other kid?"

"I don't know," Jim said, shaking his head.

One of the EMTs came over, peeling off a pair of nitrate gloves. "We're going to transport him down to Nashua if that's alright," the young woman said.

"Sounds good to me," Jim said.

Brian nodded.

"He says there was another kid?" she asked.

Jim and Brian both nodded.

"Did you guys find him?"

"No," Jim said. "I tried to follow him, but he disappeared into the woods—vanished actually."

"Did you check up at the Blood House?"

"The what house?" Brian asked.

The young woman smiled. "The Blood House. I grew up in Thorne. The Bloods had their main house right up off of the road here. I think the driveway is just a little ways up on the left."

"Didn't even know about that," Jim said.

"Let me know," the young woman said. "My name's Mary."

"Nice to meet you, Mary," Jim said.

She smiled at him, waved goodbye to Brian, and walked back to the ambulance. Just as the ambulance was pulling out, another pair of State cruisers and the crime scene truck arrived.

Jim saw Sergeant Ward step out of the first cruiser and nodded to the man.

The sergeant looked down at the hand, shook his head and walked over to Jim and Brian.

"Hello Pat," Jim said.

"Jim, Brian," Pat said, glancing back at the hand once more. "That's pretty."

"It is," Brian agreed.

"Did you find the other boy?" Pat asked.

"No," Jim said. "One of the EMTs said that there's a house up a little ways on the left. I'd like to go check on that."

"Sounds good," Pat said. "Brian, I hate to ask, but could you run some cones out for me and keep an eye out for the supervisor, please?"

"Sure thing," Brian said. "Things are pretty quiet back in Monson. I'll cover you on this."

Jim gave a wave to both men, walked back to his cruiser and climbed in. He finished his coffee, put the cup down in the holder and started the car. He pulled out of the yard, turned left up Blood Road and in a couple of minutes saw a dirt driveway break the monotony of the tree-lined road.

Signaling, Jim turned the car into the driveway and flipped on his spotlight, guiding it with his left hand and steering the car with his right. The driveway was long and winding, rising up ever so slightly as it continued.

Soon though, the drive turned a little to the left, and a large, grand New England farmhouse stood before him. A few lights shined inside, and a lit lantern hung near the door, illuminating the front steps and the beginnings of a wide, wrap-around porch.

Jim parked the car and keyed the mic. "Two-Nine to dispatch."

"Go ahead, Two-Nine," Maggie responded.

"Dispatch I am at the Blood House, Sergeant Ward is on scene and aware."

"Good copy, Two-Nine."

Once more Jim climbed out of the car, yet he loosened his service weapon in its holster before walking around the car. He moved steadily towards the house, stepping onto a neatly kept stonework path that led unerringly to the wooden steps. He climbed the stairs at a casual pace and almost didn't notice that there was someone sitting in a chair to the left of the main door.

"Hello," Jim said, stepping back down onto the top step.

"Hello," a man replied. Something red glowed in front of the man's face for a moment, and the wind shifted sharply, bringing to Jim the strong scent of pipe tobacco.

"I'm Trooper Petrov, and I was wondering if I could speak with you," Jim said.

"Please," the man said, "come up and have a seat."

Jim did so and as he sat down in the cold rocking chair set at a slight angle from the speaker, Jim saw that the speaker was an old man—an extremely old man. He was probably pushing late eighties or early nineties. The man was smoking an old briar churchwarden's pipe and wrapped in a thick quilt with a knit cap snugly on his head. On a small table beside him there was a cup of half-finished black coffee.

"I don't get many visitors," the old man said politely. "And I do believe, sir, that you are the first State Police officer to ever visit."

Jim smiled, took his hat off and placed it on his knee. "I'm pleased to be the first, sir. However, I'm afraid that I don't know your name."

"Ah," the man said, removing his right hand from the quilt and extending it. "Hollis Blood."

Jim leaned forward and shook the hand. It was old, and it was thin, but the hand was strong. "That's a good New England name," Jim said as he let go of Hollis's hand.

Hollis chuckled. "It is indeed. You should have been here

seventy years ago, Trooper, there were still Coffins amongst the Bloods in Thorne and Monson—Halls and Copps, too. The old names. There are a few Halls about," he continued, "but I'm the last of the Bloods here in Thorne. The Coffins have died out—the Copps too. I believe that I'm the only bench owning member still in the Congregationalist Church in town."

"I suppose, though," Hollis said, "that you're not here for a lesson in the family lines of Thorne. What can I do for you, Trooper Petrov?"

"Well," Jim said, "I noticed that you can see the lights down on Blood Road."

"I can," Hollis said. "Do you mind if I ask what happened?"

"Not at all," Jim replied. "However, I really don't know. The reason that I'm up here is that when I arrived on the scene there was a little boy, perhaps about eight years old. He slipped away into the forest, and I couldn't follow him. I was hoping that maybe he had come up this way, perhaps to your house."

Hollis Blood smoked his pipe for a moment, letting out a slim stream of smoke from his nostrils before responding. "Trooper Petrov," Hollis said carefully, "I don't think that you'd believe me if I told you what I saw."

Jim smiled. "I might, sir. Could you try?"

Hollis nodded. "I believe that you said that you saw a boy about eight years old?"

"I did." Jim leaned forward. Hollis's voice had gotten a little lower.

"I don't suppose that this boy was pale?" Hollis asked.

"Very," Jim said.

"Black hair and wearing a black suit?"

"Yes."

"And the jacket, it was unsewn up the back?"

"I thought it was torn," Jim said. Then he looked at Hollis. "You saw him."

"I did."

"Did you see where he went?" Jim asked. "Do you know who he is?"

"I did not see where he went," Hollis said, "and I do know who he is."

Jim waited a moment for Hollis to speak and when he didn't, Jim asked, "Will you tell me?"

"Yes," Hollis said, looking away. "His name is Morgan Blood."

Sitting back, Jim looked at Hollis. "I thought you said that you were the last."

"I am," Hollis said. He folded back the quilt and stood up. "Please follow me, Trooper Petrov."

Jim stood and walked behind Hollis as the man led him to the front door.

"Who is Morgan, Hollis?" Jim asked as Hollis opened the door and warm light washed over them.

"My brother," Hollis answered, motioning for Jim to follow him in.

Jim stepped into a long hallway that smelled pleasantly of pipe tobacco and a well-used fireplace. Wallpaper that had probably been hanging for at least a century covered the walls and family portraits in thick frames and clear glass hung upon the walls as well.

"Hollis," Jim said calmly, "are you feeling alright?"

"Quite," Hollis answered. He put the pipe stem back into his mouth and stopped in the middle of the hallway and turned to face the left wall.

"Hollis," Jim said.

Hollis let out a bit of smoke, took the pipe out of his mouth, and pointed politely at the wall. "Please," the man said, "simply look at the photographs, Trooper Petrov."

Jim turned and looked at the photographs.

He dropped his hat to the floor as he looked at the black and white photograph of the boy he had seen at the worksite. The boy was smiling at the camera—an old leather baseball glove and ball in his hands.

"Morgan Blood," Hollis said, putting the pipe back into his mouth. "My brother died of pneumonia when he was eight. I don't know what he did down at the edge of the road. He told me that you were nice, Trooper Petrov and that you should be careful."

"Why should I be careful?" Jim asked.

"My relations are angry," Hollis said simply.

"About what?" Jim asked, a sense of the surreal replacing reality.

"Old contracts that have been broken," Hollis said.

"And I should be careful because of that?"

"Yes," Hollis said.

"But why?" Jim asked, looking at Hollis.

"Because," Hollis said, returning his look evenly, "not all of my relatives will be as gentle as my brother."

Chapter 5: Alderman Nadeau and his morning paper

Emil Nadeau watched the paper get delivered by a raggedy looking middle-aged man throwing The Telegraph from the driver's side window. The man was driving on the wrong side of the street and, not surprisingly, he had Massachusetts plates.

Frowning, Emil waited until the man had moved down to the McCalls' house before leaving his own for the paper. The Telegraph, wrapped in a protective sleeve of orange plastic, was light, as usual. Swinging the paper from one hand, Emil looked at his rose bushes and the rose of Sharon growing along the left side of the driveway. Everything had grown in well this year in spite of Daniel moving out.

Well, Emil thought, *I'll certainly be able to find someone to replace Daniel, even if they won't necessarily have his green thumb.*

Their two-year relationship had ended badly, but thankfully the man hadn't gone to the town about their living arrangements. The rest of the country might have been opening up to the idea of homosexual unions, but little towns like Thorne tended to be behind the learning curve.

Emil put the thought out of his mind as he opened the side door and walked back into the kitchen. He closed and locked the door behind him, tossing the paper onto the table before turning to put on a fresh pot of coffee.

He froze and stared at a tall, elderly man, whose back was to Emil. The man played quite happily with a burner on the stove. He turned the front left burner on, then off, seeming to enjoy the ticking sound of the ignition switch before the gas caught flame.

Emil took a deep breath and tried to settle his nerves.

The man looked at Emil, and Emil screamed.

The man's eyes were white as if dipped into a milky cloud. At the sound of Emil's scream the man smiled, revealing old and yellowed teeth.

"Sit, Alderman," the man said, his voice thick and cold. "Sit."

Emil simply screamed again.

Leaving a flame burning, the man took one long stride over to Emil, grabbed him by his throat, and thrust him into a chair.

Emil stopped screaming and stared at the man.

The man smiled again, let go of Emil's throat, and sat down

on the table.

The man looked at Emil and Emil stopped screaming.

"Very good, Alderman," the man said. "Well done. How are you feeling?"

Emil blinked and found that he couldn't answer the man. He simply couldn't.

"Ah well," the man sighed. "I would introduce myself, but I think that you would find little use in that. Although, I must ask you a question. Is that alright?"

Emil stared at him.

"Is it?"

Finally, Emil nodded.

"Excellent," the man said. "Do you understand the phrase contractual obligations?"

Emil nodded.

"I'm surprised," the man said coldly. He looked hard with his milky white eyes at Emil. "When the town of Thorne was signed over in seventeen seventy-seven," the man said, "the town of Thorne agreed to honor the wishes of the Blood family should they render them assistance and protection from raiders drifting down from French Canada. My family held true to their bond."

The man stood, walked over to the stove, and lit another burner. With that done, he turned to face Emil. "As you can so easily testify, Alderman Nadeau," the man sneered, "the town of Thorne did not."

Emil finally found his voice.

"Who are you?" Emil demanded, his voice shaking. "How did you get into my house?"

"You left the door open, you bumbling frog," the old man said, turning another burner on. "And truly, do you wish to know my name?"

"Yes," Emil said, straightening up, "I need to know for when I have a warrant filled out for your arrest."

The man chuckled.

It was a distinctly disturbing and unpleasant sound.

"Well then, Alderman Nadeau, my name is Obadiah Blood," the man said, turning on the last burner. All four of the burners were blazing steadily.

"Obadiah Blood," Emil began angrily, and then he stopped. He looked closely at the tall, old man. "Obadiah Blood," he repeated in a low voice.

"Indeed," Obadiah said.

Emil's heart stutter-stepped and he managed to say, "You can't be."

"But I am."

"Obadiah Blood is dead."

"I am," Obadiah agreed. "In fact I have been for over a hundred years."

"They killed you," Emil managed. "They killed you for murdering the migrant boys. I read that. I read that you were a murderer."

"Oh, yes," Obadiah said, "I've killed in my day. But never boys. Always men. It was a Gauthier, in fact, who killed those boys. But they wrapped those murders around my neck and lynched me in the town center—a blind man."

"They said that you didn't even defend yourself," Emil said.

"No," Obadiah corrected. "I remained silent. They were in a frenzy, led by Gauthier. It was my wish that I could return and gain vengeance upon him through his relatives, but the task of their deaths has been given to another—you," Obadiah grinned, "you, Emil Nadeau, you are my given task." He turned away from Emil for a moment and took one of the decorative towels Emil and Daniel had purchased in York together from its place in front of the sink.

"What are you doing?" Emil asked, standing up.

The old man's head snapped around, and Obadiah snarled, "Sit."

Something pushed Emil back into the chair with enough force to make the chair rock on its back legs. As Emil tried to regain his balance he caught sight of Obadiah holding the towel over one of the burners. It took only a moment for the cloth to catch fire.

"What are you doing?!" Emil shouted.

Holding the burning towel carelessly, Obadiah turned to face Emil. The old man smiled happily.

"Did any of you bother to read the actual contract which the town agreed to?" Obadiah asked.

Emil couldn't answer, staring instead at the slowly burning reminder of a pleasant weekend in Maine.

Obadiah chuckled and stepped forward.

Emil's happy memory was shattered. He suddenly found himself unable to breathe, Obadiah's thick hand gripping his throat. Emil opened his mouth, gasping for air and Obadiah quickly stuffed the end of the towel into it.

Emil gagged, the flames licking at his pajama shirt, slowly setting it alight. Emil tried to breathe, but he could only do so by inhaling as he struggled against Obadiah.

The old man held him firmly, his strength atrocious.

"Now, now, Alderman," Obadiah said softly, "accept your death, as painful as it's going to be."

Emil tried to scream, but he couldn't. He felt his shirt catch fire, and his flesh started to burn. In his nose he could smell it, a stench reminiscent of a pig skin burning. Part of him recognized the fact that he was smelling his own skin burning, part of him wished that Daniel would roll over in bed and wake him from the nightmare.

Emil wouldn't wake up, though, for all of it was true. He was awake.

And finally, Emil found that he could scream.

Chapter 6: Jim Petrov at the Monson PD

"How many months has it been since the divorce, Jim?" Brian asked, handing Jim a cup of coffee.

"Four," Jim answered, nodding his thanks. "Four."

"You know," Brian said, sitting down on the edge of his desk, "you're not going to find your next date in here."

"You never know, Brian," Jim said, taking a sip of his coffee. "You guys just might pull in some extremely attractive DUI one day."

"Have you ever seen an extremely attractive DUI come through Monson?" Brian asked, chuckling. "Hell, have you seen a semi-attractive DUI ever?"

Jim shook his head, laughing. "Now that you mention it, no. No, I have not."

Before Brian could say anything else, the scanner burst into life and Harry, the day dispatcher for Monson, lifted his head up from his Sudoku puzzle.

"Monson Fire and Rescue, all hands, fire at eleven Stark Street," an unknown dispatcher said from the State's emergency call center.

The emergency phone by Harry rang sharply, and the man quickly hit the answer button. "Monson Police Department, Harry speaking," he said, typing rapidly into his computer. A second later he flashed a look at Brian that Jim had seen before. It was Harry's 'You Better Pay Attention' look, and both Jim and Brian waited, listening.

"Eleven Stark Street. Yes, we know there's a fire...you saw someone leave the building as it was burning? What's your address, Ma'am? Ten Stark Street? Phone number? Six Zero Three, Eight Nine One, Zero One Nine Five. Excellent, we'll have a cruiser there in a few minutes."

Brian and Jim put their coffees down, Jim grabbing his jacket off of a wall peg as he hurried out the door behind Brian. He followed Brian to the man's cruiser, got into the passenger seat, and closed the door, buckling his seatbelt.

Jim was off duty. It was officially a day off.

But there was a fire and a man who had walked away from the building.

Brian threw on his lights and siren and took off for Stark

Street.

"Did you hear about last night yet?" Brian asked.

"Thomas Pelto?"

"Yeah."

"No, what?"

"He was buried alive. I saw the initial report this morning when I came in," Brian said. "No one can figure out how it was done. One of the crime techs is an archeology student, and he said that when they were digging Pelto out it looked like the dirt had never been disturbed by digging before."

"But he was alive?" Jim asked, thinking about the strange conversation he'd had with Hollis Blood the night before.

"Yeah," Brian nodded, turning sharply on Ridge Road. "No official cause yet, not until the autopsy is complete, but the medical examiner said that he suffocated."

"That's a suck way to go," Jim said.

"Yup."

The sign for Stark Street appeared on the left and Brian turned hard onto it. Ahead of them, Monson's pump truck and Thorne's fire engine were already on the scene. Brian jerked the cruiser over to block most of the road, leaving room for any additional trucks that might arrive.

Volunteer firefighters from both towns were racing up in their own vehicles as Jim and Brian climbed out of the car. People were coming out of their houses and watching as flames devoured the left side of the house, working their way up the side and into the roof.

A blue Prius with the vanity plate 'NADEAU' sat in the driveway.

"Shit," Brian muttered. "That's Emil Nadeau's house."

Jim wracked his brain for a minute until he found the bit of information that told him that Emil Nadeau was one of Thorne's aldermen. The man was a pain in the ass for both Thorne and Monson. He lived in Thorne but ran an insurance agency out of Monson.

"This'll be more than Thorne and Monson can handle," Jim said.

Brian only nodded. "I've got to speak with number ten."

"Want to pop the trunk?" Jim asked. "I'll grab a vest and make sure no one gets too close."

"Yeah," Brian said, leaning back into the cruiser and hitting the trunk's button.

As the trunk popped open, Brian walked off towards house number ten, and Jim went to the back of the car. He pulled a neon green safety vest with reflective strips out of the back and put the vest on before closing the trunk.

Jim walked away from the cruiser, back towards the intersection with Ridge Road.

An older man, wearing a dark suit and an old fedora, approached Jim slowly, leaning heavily on a well-used cane. The man's eyes, Jim saw, were milky white, and Jim wondered how the man could see at all.

The man stopped a few feet from Jim saying, "Excuse me, but I seem to smell a fire."

"Yes sir," Jim said, glancing around the man to make sure that no vehicles were coming. In the far distance, he heard the sound of more emergency vehicles approaching. Jim looked at the man. "Do you need to get to a particular house, sir?"

"No, no," the man replied. "Could you tell me what house it is?"

"Number eleven, sir," Jim answered.

"Jim!"

Jim turned away from the man to look back, and he saw Brian gesturing to him.

"Thank you, Trooper Petrov," the older man said behind Jim.

"You're welcome," Jim said over his shoulder.

Brian started jogging towards him, yelling, "Stop him!"

The old man? Jim thought.

And then he realized what the old man had said.

Thank you, Trooper Petrov.

Jim whipped around, and the older man was just disappearing around the garage of a nearby house.

Jim ran after him, turning around the corner of the same garage and coming to a stop just in time to avoid running headlong into a tall, chain-link fence. He stood there and looked along the fence's length, through the backyard and past the agitated German shepherd walking the perimeter with its ears back and its tail down. Jim could hear the dog's nervous whines above the noise of more fire trucks arriving.

In a moment, Brian was beside him, breathing heavily. "Where the hell did he go?" Brian asked.

"I don't know," Jim replied, scanning the tree line, which was thin and wide. There were no trees large enough for a man to hide behind, the land itself rolling upwards slightly at a gentle grade for at least a hundred yards.

The man should not have been able to vanish even if he was in the best of health, but he had been old and nearly blind.

"Where the hell did he go?" Brian said again, and the dog let out a long howl.

Chapter 7: At Alderman Nadeau's House

Jim stood with Brian and Travis Hope, the fire inspector out of Nashua. It had taken fire crews from Monson, Thorne, Hollis, Nashua, and the Pepperell, Massachusetts to get the blaze under control.

"The fire started in the kitchen," Travis said, smoking a cigarette and looking at the remnants of the house. A few crews worked around the house, picking apart anything that looked like it might spark and jump to the dry woods around the property. The coroner's van was already gone, taking the body of Alderman Emil Nadeau away.

"How?" Jim asked.

"With the Alderman," Travis said.

"I didn't think he smoked," Brian said.

"He didn't," Travis answered, taking a long drag off of his cigarette. "The medical examiner will have to confirm, but it looked like somebody stuffed a hand-towel down his throat and lit the goddamn man on fire."

"Jesus Christ," Brian muttered, looking away.

"Whoever it was had all the burners on as well. Whoever had the Alderman try and eat the towel also threw the morning paper on the stove. Really set it all going. Place burned quickly, though," Travis added. "Real quickly."

The fire inspector finished his cigarette, put it out, and flicked the butt towards the charred house. "I've got to write this up. See you at the next one, boys."

Jim and Brian watched him go.

"You ready to go?" Brian asked.

"Give me a minute, will you?" Jim asked. Brian nodded, and Jim walked up to the house. He looked at the remnants of the house.

Something was going on, and Jim wasn't quite sure what.

Hollis knows, Jim thought. *Hollis knows.*

Jim turned and walked back to Brian. "I'm ready."

Together they got into Brian's cruiser, and Brian turned off the lights before maneuvering the car around the Thorne fire truck, the only one which remained at the scene.

"Hell of a way to spend your day off," Brian said after a few minutes.

"Well," Jim said, looking out the window, "I don't have much else to do."

"You need a hobby."

"I had a wife," Jim answered.

Brian chuckled. "They may feel like the same some days, Jim, but you know that they're not."

"I know."

"Where are you headed to after we get back to the station?" Brian asked.

Jim shrugged. "I'm not sure. I'll figure it out, though."

A few more minutes passed by before they were back in Monson and Brian was pulling into an angled parking space in front of the station. They both climbed out, and Jim gave his friend a wave goodbye before walking half a block down Main Street to where his Dodge was parked in front of the diner.

Jim opened the door and got into the cab and sat there for a moment before buckling his seatbelt. He rubbed at his chin and looked out the windshield at nothing in particular.

Yesterday afternoon a man was buried alive at a worksite by the supposed ghost of a little boy.

Today a man was burned to death in a house fire. Jim had seen an older man, who was nearly blind, vanish as the boy had from the night before.

And the man had known Jim's name.

Someone had told Hollis Blood about Jim.

There was a connection, somewhere, between the murder at the worksite, the death of Emil Nadeau and Hollis Blood.

Jim started the truck's engines, checked his mirrors and pulled out onto Main Street.

He needed to find out what the connection was.

Chapter 8: The Thorne Historical Society

Jim rang the bell at the small white Victorian that served as the town of Thorne's historical society.

A few moments later, he heard the sound of someone's feet on stairs and then the door was being opened by a middle-aged woman. She had mousy brown hair pulled back into a bun and a pair of reading glasses. She looked over the tops of the glasses at him. "May I help you?"

"Yes please," Jim said. "I was wondering if you could help me with some research on the Blood family."

Her eyes widened a little. "Has something happened to Mr. Blood?"

"To Hollis?" Jim asked. "Oh no. I spoke with him, and I'm just curious about his family's history in Thorne."

"He let you call him Hollis?" she asked in a low voice.

"He did."

She smiled. "Come in, come in. I'm sorry. I didn't mean to grill you on the doorstep like that. There's simply been so much going on with the Blood lands these past few weeks."

Jim stepped in and waited until she closed the door. "Do you mind if I ask what's going on with the Blood lands?"

"You're not from Thorne?" she asked, leading him along a narrow hallway to a large room off to the right.

"No," Jim answered. "I'm a State Trooper, and I spoke with Hollis the other night and he was telling me that his family had been in Thorne for a long time."

The woman laughed pleasantly. "That's an understatement. Thorne is named after Hawthorne Blood, who originally was granted the land for extraordinary service in the French and Indian War. He eventually sold off small lots, or rather they were small when New Hampshire was still young, and eventually he incorporated a town. He made a contract with the other residents when he did, though. Hawthorne Blood told them the town would be theirs so long as the Blood lands were left alone.

"No one knew why, mind you," the woman said, gesturing to a small, Victorian loveseat in the room. The piece of furniture was set just beneath a large window, and Jim settled comfortably in it. "The land which Hawthorne Blood set aside for his own was not the finest by far. In fact, most of the land is unplowable, riddled with small streams as well as Hassell Brook, which tends to jump its bed every decade or so. No," she said, shaking her head, "it's one of those mysteries that New England towns thrive upon.

"Rumors sprang up, of course," she continued as she walked to an old wooden filing cabinet.

"Rumors of what?" Jim asked.

"Treasure stolen from the French. Treasure stolen from the British during the Revolution. Treasure stolen from the Confederates during the Civil War," she pulled a drawer open and glanced over at him, smiling. "Do you get the gist of it all?"

Jim nodded, smiling. "I do."

"I actually have a copy of the contract here as it was drawn up," the woman continued. "The original is at town hall, of course."

"Of course," Jim grinned. "I'm sorry," he said, "but I didn't get your name."

"Groff," the woman said, pulling a file out of the drawer. "Janine Groff." Closing the door, she walked over to Jim and handed him the file. After he had taken it, she went and sat in a high-backed chair standing by the room's door.

"A pleasure, Janine," Jim said, opening the file. "Is this a full-time job for you?"

"It is, but it's unpaid," she said.

"I'm sorry to hear that," he said, looking up at her. "You're extremely knowledgeable about this."

"Well thank you," Janine said, smiling proudly. "I'm a trained archivist, but my husband decided that he didn't want to live in the city, well, in Boston anymore. We moved up here to Thorne, and he works at home, telecommuting. The historical society was looking for help and, well," she laughed, "this also keeps us out of each other's hair."

Jim nodded. "That's completely understandable." He glanced down at the open folder and saw that there were two sets of pages within. One was a photocopy of an old document. The words were cut off on the bottom but continued on the following page. The other set of pages was typed out and looked to be a readable copy of the contract.

Taking the typed pages out, Jim closed the file and set it beside him on the loveseat.

"Be it known that on this Day, the Twenty Third of July, in the Year 1778, the Towne of Thorne in the Free Colony of New Hampshire and Hawthorne Blood enter into this Contract.

"Hawthorne Blood, the Founder of the Town of Thorne, wishes it to be known that all of His Property, extending from the Border of Monson to the Border of Hollis, and down to the Border of Pepperell in the Free Colony of Massachusetts, shall be given to the Towne of Thorne and the Residents therein for the profit and wellbeing of the Community.

"The only Land which the Towne of Thorne shall not dispose of shall be that which currently surrounds the Blood House. This Land shall consist of Four Hundred Acres and the Measurements of the Land shall begin at one hundreds of Rods from the Front Door of the Blood House and two hundreds of Rods on either side of the Blood House. The remainder of the Acres shall continue to the North East until the border of Cannae. These Acres shall forever be the Property of the Blood Family.

"They shall forever be the Property of the Blood Family, and if the Blood Family shall be no more than the Last Will and Testament of the Last Blood shall inform the Town of what is to be done.

"This Contract is never to be Violated, never to be Discarded. The Towne of Thorne with this signing agrees to this and knows that It shall suffer the Wrath of all of the Bloods in Thorne should the Contract be Broken."

Below this text, Jim saw the typed names of those who had signed and agreed to the contract.

Hawthorne Blood, Malachi Coffin, Jebediah Coffin, Alpheus Hall, Richard Arnold, Elbridge Copp, and Harold Lee.

Jim looked up at Janine. She smiled at him, and he returned the smile. "Four hundred acres?"

She nodded. "He was, for that time, keeping an extremely small amount for his family. The other signers were said to have known this, and thus readily agreed to it, and, as you can see, for over two hundred years the town has held to that contract."

"It changed?" Jim asked.

"Just last week," Janine said.

"How so?"

"The board of Aldermen voted to take some of the Blood land

through eminent domain after Hollis refused to sell."

"Why would they do that?" Jim asked.

"They're widening Blood Road, and they're going to erect two private developments—one on either side of the Blood House and well into the Blood land," Janine answered. "Hollis is fighting it, of course, but a state judge has decided that the clearing of the land can continue before the appeal is heard."

"So they broke the contract," Jim said softly.

Janine nodded. "And Hollis Blood was none too happy about it."

"No," Jim said, looking down at the contract, "no I don't suppose that any of them were."

Chapter 9: Alderman Williams Working Late

Dean Williams logged out of his Ashley Madison account, shut down the incognito window, and powered down his laptop. With that done, he unplugged it and put everything away.

Dean had been carrying on a series of affairs for over twenty years, all whilst being married, and he had been able to do that by being careful. He put that concept into practice when it came to his legal practice and his investment methods. He wasn't a rich man, but he was a happy one, with a happy wife who had never suspected that her husband had ever strayed.

Or that he continued to stray.

Dean put that out of his mind—another trick to keeping the various aspects of his life separated—and stood up, stretching slightly. It was after eleven o'clock, and the crickets were singing loudly in the darkness. Smiling, Dean walked out of his office and up the stairs to the bedroom.

The light on his side of the king-size mattress cast a soft glow about the room. He started to unbutton his dress shirt when he realized that Lydia was sitting up at her vanity.

"Lydia?" he asked, turning to face her, and when he did he saw that the woman at the vanity wasn't his wife. His wife lay peacefully asleep on her side of the bed, a Danielle Steel novel open, spine up.

The woman at the vanity was much younger than his wife, perhaps no more than twenty, and she wore a nightgown that Lydia would have referred to as matronly. The woman was pale, her face narrow and had most of her deep brown hair tucked up beneath an old-fashioned nightcap.

Dean slipped his hand into his pants for his phone, and then he remembered that it was still in the kitchen on a charger. His gun safe was under his side of the bed and the only other phone was Lydia's, which more than likely had no charge, or was buried in her purse—or both.

"Who are you?" Dean asked softly.

"My name is Elizabeth Blood," the woman said, and her voice was cold and harsh.

Dean bristled at the name. "Blood? Did Hollis Blood send you in here to harass me about the developments?"

"No," Elizabeth answered. "You did."

"What?"

"You did," she repeated. "You broke the contract."

Dean frowned, trying to figure out what the hell she was saying and then said, "That contract doesn't have any bearing on the eminent domain issue. Hollis was offered fair market value, and he refused."

"Of course he did," Elizabeth said, hate filling her eyes. "He was trying to save you. All of you. That's all any of us have ever done, and this is the repayment."

"You need to leave my house," Dean said, thinking, *She's crazy.*

From the folds of her nightgown, she lifted her hands. She was holding his .22 caliber target pistol. Even from where Dean stood he could see the rounds in the cylinder. The safety was off, and her hands were steady.

"On your knees," Elizabeth said simply.

Dean froze. "Please," he said, swallowing nervously, "the decision is out of my hands now."

"On your knees," Elizabeth repeated.

Shaking, Dean did so, looking at the woman as she stood up. "I didn't—"

She cocked the hammer back, and he went silent, staring at the small, deadly hole in the pistol's barrel. Elizabeth took a step towards him, and he closed his eyes.

The pistol barked, and something thumped softly to the floor, the sound nearly drowned out by Dean's own frightened yell.

When he didn't feel any pain, though, he opened his eyes carefully.

Elizabeth was standing in the same spot. Lydia's book was on the floor, and there was a tiny, neat hole in the side of Lydia's head. A trickle of blood seeped out, tracing the curve of his wife's cheek, gravity pulling the blood down to where it would stain the soft white sheets.

"Lydia?" Dean asked softly.

And then Elizabeth was beside him, the hot barrel of the pistol against his temple, the sound of the weapon being cocked loud in his ears.

Chapter 10: Mike Pinkham and the Mechanic

Damn cold out, Mike bitched to himself. He stamped his feet and clapped his gloved hands together. Way too cold this early in the season, he thought.

He walked through the beams of his truck's headlights to the generator and started it up again. The security guard they'd hired since Tom's death had disappeared in the night. Mike was pretty sure the son of a bitch had gone off and gotten drunk somewhere. The guy's car wasn't even in the yard.

Of course, considering the condition of the guy's Camry he'd have to be drunk to get in it willingly.

Mike stepped back, blinking as the worklights exploded into life. A moment later, the yard and all of the equipment was in sharp definition and—

Mike stopped. He shook his head and tried to figure out what it was that he was seeing.

A moment later, he realized that someone had taken the dozer and driven it over the security guard's Camry. Mike realized, too, that the man's arm was hanging out of the driver's side window, at least what was left of it.

"These new machines are impressive," a voice said behind Mike.

He jerked around and saw a tall, thick man standing with his arms crossed over a broad chest.

"I was surprised," the man continued, "that it could climb up that auto like that."

"You did that?" Mike asked softly. "You, you drove over that guy?"

The man nodded. "Squealed just like a suckling, too. No shame in it, though," the man said after a moment. "No shame in it at all. Terrible way to die."

Mike blinked, confused. "Why?"

"Why did I kill him?" the man asked.

Mike nodded.

"He was here," the man said simply. "He shouldn't have been."

Mike looked back at the arm.

"Why?" he asked.

The man smiled. "This is Blood land that you're on," the man said, "and you don't have the right to be here. None of us have given you approval. Hollis fought it for as long as he could. Now though, now you've left us no choice," the man said, his smile fading away. "Now we have to make sure that you don't come any further onto the land."

"Hell," Mike said, "I'll just get in my truck and go. I've no cause to be here. I don't even live in Thorne, man. I live down in Hudson."

"It matters not," the man said simply. "You're a warning now. A lesson to be learned." The man snapped his fingers, and the excavator roared into life, thick white diesel exhaust belching into the early morning sky.

Mike turned and looked at the excavator, the machine's giant boom unfolding and stretching out, the bucket swinging out and pulling in.

"When I used to work on autos, and the big caterpillars," the man said, smiling at the machine, "I never thought that I would see something as grand as this."

Mike was only half listening. He was watching the bucket at the end of the boom, the hydraulic lines shifting slightly in their harnesses as the machine worked hard in the cold.

"They really are impressive," the man said again. "And they listen so well."

Mike silently watched the boom rise up, the bucket curl in, and then it came crashing down towards him.

Chapter 11: Jim Petrov and Morgan Blood

Jim started his shift hearing about the death of Mike Pinkham, the foreman at the Blood Road job site, and the death of a security guard that had been hired.

The detectives were tight-lipped about it, and the local news agencies were crawling around asking everyone if they had seen or heard anything. The reporters didn't understand that when you lived off the beaten path you usually didn't see or hear anything unless it was at your door. There was also word that there may have been a murder-suicide as well, but that scene was sealed up tightly.

No one was gaining access to that road, though, although there was plenty of speculation that the dead were Alderman Dean Williams and his wife, Lydia.

By the end of his shift Jim had learned that most of the information out there on the State Police grapevine was true. There were two dead at the worksite, and it looked like Dean Williams had shot his wife and then himself although no one knew why.

After Jim got home, changed out of his uniform and put on his .38 revolver in its shoulder holster, Jim climbed into his truck and headed off the long way to Blood Road. He wanted to avoid the reporters and crime scene techs that were sure to be swarming over the worksite.

The drive took fifteen minutes longer than usual, but Jim avoided the mess on the far side of the driveway and turned right into the driveway. His lights cut a bright path up to the house, and within a moment he had the lights off and had turned off the truck. He hooked the keys to a belt loop and hurried up the stairs to knock on the front door.

The door opened a heartbeat later.

It was the small boy, Morgan Blood. Anger filled the boy's face.

"Jim," Morgan said. "My brother's dead."

"How?" Jim asked.

"Age. He was old." Morgan looked past Jim towards the lights. "He could have stopped this, had they listened to him. He wanted to stop this. He was the best of us."

Jim felt the hair on the back of his neck stand up and his balls shrivel into his stomach. Slowly he turned around and looked down at his truck. Dozens of people stood around it.

And they were silent.

Terribly silent.

Most of them were old. A few were middle-aged with several children mixed in amongst them as well. They wore clothes that ranged from those that Jim remembered seeing in paintings of the first colonists to the suits and dresses of the last century.

All of them were Bloods, of that Jim was certain. Thus all of them were dead.

"My kith and my kin," Morgan said grimly.

Jim shook his head, confused as he turned back to face the small boy. "What's going on? Why is everyone being killed?"

"They broke the contract," Morgan said sternly. "Hollis warned them not to."

"How many have to die because of the contract?" Jim asked.

"Whoever doesn't leave is going to die, Jim," Morgan said. "If not by our hands, then by another's."

"Who?"

"There's a darkness in our forest, Jim," Morgan said, "and we've kept the town safe from it for centuries. All of the old families knew of it. Whoever stays in Thorne, well, they're going to know about it too."

The porch trembled beneath Jim's feet. He looked around to see the trees shaking, although there was no wind to speak of. Then the porch trembled again as a large crack ripped through the night air.

"Oh yes," Morgan said softly, looking out into the forest. "They'll know about the darkness soon enough."

Chapter 12: Jim Petrov, Alone with the Dead

Jim sat inside of the Blood house.

Specifically he sat in the kitchen, at an old dining set that served as the kitchen table. It had evidently been where Hollis had taken his meals.

It had most certainly been where Hollis had taken his last meal, for the dead man sat in his chair, an empty plate before him. The fork and the knife were neatly placed at an angle upon the plate and the water glass beside it was half empty. The old man's churchwarden pipe was unlit and on its side. Fresh tobacco spilled across the scarred top of the table.

A book lay closed on the table. The golden title on the green cloth of the cover read: "Gaius Julius Caesar's Gallic Wars." Jim had already opened the book and seen that the writing inside was done in Latin. The book, Jim saw, was well read.

Hollis sat almost perfectly upright in his chair. His expression was slack, his eyes open and seeing nothing. There was no smile on his lips, no hint of pleasure.

Death came in, collected Hollis, and left as quietly as it had come.

Jim reached out, picked up Hollis's water glass and drank the rest of it down.

"Thataboy!" Morgan said gleefully.

Jim put the glass down and looked at the ghost.

"What am I doing?" Jim asked out loud, shaking his head. "I need to call this in."

"There's no time for that now, Jim," Morgan said in a low voice.

Jim looked up at him. "What do you mean there's no time for that now? What the hell am I supposed to do?"

"You have to bury Hollis," Morgan said.

Jim shook his head. "I can't do that, Morgan. I need to call it in and get this ball rolling. There's a lot of shit—"

"Jim," Morgan said gently.

Jim looked uneasily at the ghost. "Yes?"

"Did you feel the tremors earlier?"

"I did," Jim said hesitantly.

"And the cracking trees?"

Jim nodded.

"Well," Morgan said, looking out into the darkness, "I can tell you that if they get closer to us you're definitely going to wish that you were a Blood."

"What made that sound?" Jim asked.

Morgan shook his head. "Simply pray that you never meet them, Jim. Now please, if we're going to carry out our task with any success, we need to get Hollis down to the graveyard."

"You want me to help you bury him?" Jim asked, unable to keep the surprise out of his voice.

"Yes," Morgan nodded. "That is exactly what I want. Once Hollis is buried he will be able to return to us, to help us with the makers of the noise that you heard."

"What are they?" Jim asked.

"It is truly better not to ask," Morgan said. "Speaking their names only perks up their ears and brings them closer to you than you truly want them to be."

Jim rubbed his temples, sitting back in the chair. "I don't know. I don't. Christ, I'm sitting with a dead man talking to a ghost. I have to go back to work tomorrow." He closed his eyes and pinched the bridge of his nose.

"No," Morgan said softly, "you can't go back to work tomorrow. We've too much to do."

"Why?" Jim asked.

Morgan opened his mouth to answer, but the answer came from someone who entered the kitchen.

"Tomorrow will be a terrible day," said the man. He stood tall in the doorway, wearing an elegant three-piece black suit. His hair was trimmed short with just a small forelock hanging over his forehead.

Morgan nodded.

"May I ask who you are?" Jim asked.

"Of course," the man said, coming in and sitting down opposite Morgan. "I am Morgan's grandfather, Ambrose Blood. You will, I trust, forgive my grandson for not knowing exactly what to say."

Jim could only nod.

Ambrose seemed to understand. "I will tell you what I know, and while it is much more than most of my family, it is still less than what is truly out there. Do you understand?"

"Yes," Jim said.

"Excellent," Ambrose said. He looked at Morgan, "Could you start some coffee, please, Morgan?"

"Yes, Grandfather," Morgan said. The boy stood up, walked to the percolator, and went about getting the coffee ready.

"You drink coffee?" Jim asked.

Ambrose smiled at him. "No, Jim, this coffee is for you."

"Oh," Jim said.

Ambrose nodded.

They sat in total silence until the coffee was ready, and Jim could only look at Hollis Blood. All three of the Blood family members were dead, but at least two were actually buried down the driveway in the family graveyard.

Those two wanted Jim to put the third in the ground himself.

I'm a cop, Jim thought. *What the hell am I doing?*

A few minutes later, Morgan put a ceramic cup of fresh black coffee in front of Jim.

"Thank you," Jim said, reaching out and picking up the cup. "I really don't know what I'm doing here."

"You're listening," Ambrose said, polite but firm, "simply listening."

"Okay," Jim said, looking at Ambrose, "okay."

Ambrose nodded. "When the family arrived in the colonies, they did so with indentured servants. These were men and women who had bound themselves to the families that could pay for their transport and passage to the New World. Some of these servants were English. Others were from Wales or Scotch. Several, however, were Irish, and these Irish brought some of the Old World with them.

"When the Blood family came to what would eventually be Thorne village, they had a pair of Irish maids. The Coffins came as well, as did the Copps. It wasn't long before the two families had the Halls, the Lees, and the Arnolds as neighbors. One of the Blood maids fell passionately in love with one of the Lee sons, yet even though Hawthorne Blood released the maid from her contract of indenture, the Lee father would not give his son permission to marry.

"The young man, I am afraid," Ambrose said as Jim drank his coffee, "had a flair for the dramatic. He threatened to kill himself if his father did not grant him permission to marry the girl, and the tale is told that he had a loaded pistol up to the side of his head. The father refused, and as the boy began to lower the pistol, it accidentally fired.

"The boy was killed."

Jim finished his coffee, the caffeine slowly working its way through him. With disturbing silence Morgan took the cup, filled it, and brought it back. Jim nodded his thanks. "What happened to the girl?" Jim asked.

Ambrose gave a small, sad smile. "Unfortunately, she was not nearly as dramatic as the boy. With her freedom, she chose to leave the Blood house and the protection of the small neighbors. She moved deep into the center of the Blood lands, and there she built a small home. Nothing more than a single room house of field stones, but it stands still, close to the Goblins' Keep.

"It was there that she took out what she had brought from Ireland and opened the small lead-lined box she'd carried across the seas from the Old World to the New."

"What happened when she opened the box?" Jim asked. His confusion at what was going on was superseded by his fascination with the story. He didn't even mind the presence of the three dead men.

He just wanted to know the ending of the story.

"Ah," Ambrose said, sighing, "that was truly a calamitous day. When she opened that box, she briefly opened a door between the worlds. A door between our world and that of the fae in Ireland. Soon, there were a number of creatures in New Hampshire that should not have been. There were ogres, trolls, giants, goblins, faery folk of all kinds, banshees and watermen, too many, and by the time the box burst from serving as a doorway, the Old World was with the new."

Jim looked at Ambrose. "What are you saying?" he asked after a moment. "Are you seriously telling me that there are faeries and all of that? You're saying they're real and that they're here? How can that be?"

"Mr. Petrov," Ambrose said gently, "to whom are you speaking?"

Jim opened his mouth and then closed it. He looked at Ambrose, at Morgan standing by the corpse of Hollis Blood, and Jim nodded. "You're right. Either this is all real, or I have slipped the sultry bonds of sanity."

"There is more, though," Ambrose said.

"Of course there is," Jim agreed. "There has to be a reason for the contract. A reason why the Blood lands were protected and cordoned off."

Ambrose nodded. "Exactly. The release of the faery folk did not go unnoticed. In fact, it was the remaining Blood maid who saw the first faery ring and suspected what it was that her countrywoman had done. It is fortunate that Hawthorne was not only a literate man but a rational one as well. When the maid informed him of the ring and pointed out other signs, he could only accept it as fact.

"He released that woman from her bond as well, yet she stayed in the service of the Bloods and helped them to form the barrier that would stretch around the entire perimeter of the Blood lands. So long as those lands remained whole, and so long as at least one direct descendant of the families who signed the contract lived, the village of Thorne would be safe from the dangers of the faery folk."

"But they broke the contract," Jim said softly, looking down into the cold coffee. "Why are you killing them?"

"To scare them," Ambrose said simply. "We're trying to scare the others into leaving."

Jim thought about that for a moment. He wanted to argue that they could simply haunt the residents, but that wouldn't work. Some would leave. Others would simply call in priests or paranormal investigators.

Whatever was deep in the Blood forest would have time to reach them.

"When will the faery folk start slipping out?" Jim asked.

"Soon," Ambrose answered. "They know that there's a breach, down here by the house. They'll be nervous, but they've also been forced to stay in one place for far longer than they would have liked."

"What can be done?" Jim asked.

"An excellent question," Ambrose said. "I doubt there is much that can be done. A certain amount of vengeance is being taken upon those who broke the contract, although I am afraid that there shall be innocents who suffer as well. We can only hope that through terror we can drive the living out of Thorne. A few dead would thus be acceptable.

"If we don't drive them out, Mr. Petrov," Ambrose said, "then they risk slavery, torture, and death at the hands of the faery folk."

Jim looked down at his coffee once more and then he sighed tiredly. Looking back up to Ambrose he said simply, "Well, shit."

Ambrose nodded, and Jim took a drink of the coffee, wondering what the hell could be done.

After a short time, Ambrose stood up and said, "Please, follow me."

Jim did so, and Morgan followed him in return. They left Hollis's corpse alone in the kitchen.

Ambrose led the way down the long hallway to a closed door on the right. He reached out and touched the doorknob. A lock clicked, and the door swung inward silently. The lights came on, and Ambrose stepped into the room. Old books and gathered papers filled most of the shelves of the thin bookcases that lined the walls. On several shelves, however, were weapons.

One was a sword, still in its scabbard, looking ancient. Beside it was a long barreled Colt revolver—one that you'd see in an old spaghetti western. The holster and belt for it were wrapped up and lay under it. A wicked looking knife, with a long blade and brass knuckles with spikes for a hand guard, lay on another shelf.

"This room," Ambrose said, looking around, "holds all of the history of those that protected the town of Thorne from the faery folk. These are the records of those who fought, what or who they fought, and those who died while fighting. Those weapons are the few that the families have found to work on the faeries and their ilk. Others exist, of course, but they were with the families.

"Most of the families, though, they themselves have ceased to exist."

Jim walked into the room and looked around. Most of the shelves were covered with a fine layer of dust, yet one near the door was not. Upon that shelf was a black and white composition book.

"Even until recently," Ambrose said, "Hollis was keeping the faeries at bay. He recorded his experiences there."

"Do I need to read those?" Jim asked, looking at Ambrose.

"No, Trooper Petrov," Ambrose said, "you need to arm yourself with those weapons."

Jim looked at the three weapons and the holster with its belt.

He realized that the belt was designed to allow the scabbard of the sword and the knife to attach. There was no ammunition in the loops of the belt and none in the pistol.

"There's no ammunition," Jim said, glancing at the shelves.

"It isn't necessary," Morgan said from behind him.

Frowning, Jim looked at Ambrose, and Ambrose nodded.

"Morgan is correct," Ambrose said. "It never needs to be loaded when the faery folk are in its sights."

Jim was about to question that statement when he once again remembered he was speaking to the dead.

Wordlessly, he strapped on the belt, tied the holster down to his leg as he'd seen in so many westerns, and attached the sword to the left and the knife to the right. He picked up the pistol, which was heavy and felt beautiful in his hand, and slid it into the holster.

"Where did they come from?" Jim asked.

"The sword came from Hawthorne Blood himself," Ambrose said. "The pistol was used by a Copp throughout the entirety of the Civil War, and the knife," the man said, "my son used it in France during the Great War. As I said, there are other weapons, but they are lost to us, scattered amongst relatives on the wrong side of the family trees."

With everything in place, the belt was heavy, and Jim realized that he liked the weight.

"Good," Ambrose said. "Come now, we have the grave ready for our Hollis, but we need you to carry him down. Then we can hunt down any faery folk who seek to slip through the gap this evening."

"Fair enough," Jim said, loosening the pistol in its holster, "let's get Hollis home."

Chapter 13: Cold and Calm upon the Gauthiers

Ben Gauthier sat alone in the den watching the Raiders getting their asses kicked again. Angrily, Ben finished his Budweiser and put the empty can on the coffee table.

"Susie!" he yelled.

A moment later, his wife came into the room, popping the tab on the fresh can as she handed it to him.

"Thanks, Hon" he said.

"You're already through a six pack, Ben," she said, wiping her hands on a dish towel she had thrown over her shoulder. "We've still got to pick up Mary from the airport at midnight."

"I'll be fine," he said, taking a pull from the can. "It's only Bud."

"Don't be stupid, Ben," she said, "whether it's Bud or Natty, if you're over the limit you're screwed."

"I'll be fine," he said again and swore as the Bengals ran another touchdown straight up the middle.

Susie shook her head and walked out of the room.

The phone rang as a commercial started, so Ben picked up the phone out of the cradle and looked at the caller id.

"Hey Ryan," he said as he answered the call.

"Hi Dad," Ryan replied. "Can I stay over at Bobby's tonight?"

"It's Thursday," Ben said. "You guys have school tomorrow."

"I'll get to school," Ryan said.

"What does he want?" Susie called from the kitchen.

"To sleep over at Bobby's," Ben answered.

"Bullshit."

"Your mom says no, kid," Ben told Ryan.

Ryan groaned. "Come on, we're playing the new Call of Duty."

"You can go over tomorrow after football and play it, but I want you home by ten," Ben said. "Your mom and I have to pick up Mary and I can't worry about you jackassing around after ten. Too much weird shit is going on lately."

"Fine," Ryan grumbled. "I'll be home at ten."

"Bye, kid."

"Bye, Dad."

Ben ended the call and managed to catch sight of the Bengals intercepting a pass. "Oh what the hell," Ben spat.

The doorbell rang.

Ben looked at the clock.

It was nine.

Susie walked into the den as the doorbell rang again.

"Who the hell could that be?" she asked.

"I don't know," Ben answered. He stood up, still holding his beer, and walked to the front door. He flipped on the exterior light switch and said through the door: "Hello?"

"Hello" came a young voice, "do you happen to have a phone I could borrow for a moment? My car's broken down a little ways up the road, and your house was the closest one."

Ben glanced over at Susie, who shook her head.

"No," Ben said, "but why don't you go wait with your car and I'll call the police for you."

"Oh thank you," the voice said, sounding relieved. "I'm just up the street. It's a black Ford."

"You're welcome," Ben replied, smiling. He looked back to Susie and saw that she was smiling too, and then he watched the smile disappear in order to be replaced by an expression of horror as she opened her mouth to scream.

Ben turned around just in time to catch sight of a pale arm reaching through the door, seeming to grow out of it, before the fingers found and grabbed his sweatshirt.

A brutal cold spread out across his chest, and he wondered for the briefest of moments if he was having a heart attack, but that thought was literally driven out of his head as the arm and hand jerked backward through the door, smashing his head against the wood. Again and again the owner of the arm did it. The beer fell from his hands, and Ben felt his legs loosen, his head rolling on his neck. Susie was still screaming. Ben felt Susie's hands on his arms, then around his waist, trying to pull him free.

Then Ben felt himself falling, blood spilling down the door and onto the tiles of the front hall.

Suddenly, Susie was beside him, and all was quiet. He felt the beating of his heart, erratic and shuddering.

He closed his eyes and felt something striking him. The blows were hard, and then they were weaker and weaker.

Ben felt his heart slowing, air more difficult to breathe in. He managed to open his eyes once more, and he saw the back of

Susie's head in front of him. Dully he realized that just beyond the tangled, bloody mess of her blond hair, he could see the gray mass of her brain.

They really are gray, Ben thought, and he closed his eyes once more.

***

Judy pulled up in front of Ryan's house.

"Thanks, Mrs. Showalter," Ryan said, opening the passenger door.

"You're welcome, Ryan. And we'll see you tomorrow?" she asked.

"Yeah," he grinned. "We'll beat the game tomorrow."

"I'm sure that you will," she smiled.

"Thanks again," he waved and closed the door.

Fourteen years old or not, Judy kept the car running at the curb and waited as Ryan walked up the driveway to the side door. She watched him open the screen and try the door.

It was locked.

She saw him knock and ring the bell.

There was no movement inside the house although the shades were up and the lights on.

Ryan knocked on the door again, and she could hear it through the windows. Judy rolled the windows down and turned off the car, leaving the lights on. Ryan took his cell phone out of his pocket and dialed a number. Faintly she could hear the house phone ringing. A moment later the ringing stopped.

Judy watched as Ryan dialed again, hung up after a moment, and then dialed a third time. Shaking his head he put his phone away, walked over to the side of the porch, grabbed a recycling bin, and brought it over to a side window. He climbed up, looked inside, and then stumbled back off of the recycling bin.

Twisting and turning, he finally managed to get to his hands and knees and started crawling towards her car.

Judy had been a parent long enough to know when something was really wrong.

Before she realized what she was doing, Judy was out of the car and running to Ryan as he managed to get to his feet.

"What's wrong, Ryan?" she asked, looking into his horrified

expression.

"They're dead," he whispered, focusing on her. "They're both dead."

Judy looked at the house.

She'd never been exactly friendly with either Ben or Susie—a little too much football and beer for her, but she couldn't leave someone injured if that was the case.

"How do you know, Ryan?" she asked.

"I saw my mom's brains on the floor."

Before she could say anything, Judy heard a rustling sound and something large and brown came out of a forsythia near the front door. She glanced at it then focused on Ryan—

Judy slowly turned her head to look back at the thing.

It couldn't have been taller than three feet, and it wore ragged leather clothing. It had ears that were sharp and tall, standing well past its bald head. A long, thin nose protruded from its face and it had large, black leather boots on its feet. In its left hand it held a wicked looking knife, the blade curved and winking in the light spilling out of the house's windows.

Perhaps the most disturbing thing was the pure black eyes set deep within the gray flesh of the thing's face.

A smile spread and revealed jagged yellow teeth.

More rustling sounded, and more of the things appeared. They varied in shape and size, yet all wore the same clothes and boots and carried either knives or axes.

In a moment, there were a dozen of them spreading out to encircle both Judy and Ryan, the latter of whose shock at losing his parents was quickly being dampened by the horror occurring.

"The boy, woman," one with an ax said, its voice surprisingly deep. "The boy, and you'll meet your maker quickly. Deny us and I'll take a century to kill you."

The air seemed to fill with the sound of her own breathing. She could smell them, a foul, stale smell that curled her nose and set her mind to racing.

"Too slow," one to the right chuckled, "let's take them back to the Keep. It's been far too long since we had one to play with."

The others laughed, and they moved in, laughing and chattering to one another even as Judy wrapped her arms around Ryan and pulled him into her. She closed her eyes, and a large explosion shook her.

Chapter 14: Jim, the Colt, and the Goblins

The loud report of the pistol nearly shook Jim's brains out of his head even as the invisible slug ripped through the jaw of one of the goblins in front of Ben Gauthier's house.

There was a ring of the things—which Jim could only assume were goblins because of the way they looked—around a woman and a teenager. The goblins had been closing in on the pair until Jim had killed one of them.

Now the things were staring at him, nervous glances flickering from one to the other.

"You're not a Blood," one of them said, his nostrils flaring. "Or a Coffin."

"Neither an Arnold nor a Lee," said a second.

'And definitely no Hall," said a third.

"Yet you bear some of their weapons," the first said. "Yes, you do."

Morgan was suddenly beside him. "They're crafty, and false, Jim," the boy said. "Kill them all and don't hesitate. They have every mind to force the boy to be a slave for eternity and to eat the woman."

Before Morgan finished the last word, Jim was firing.

His aim was perfect, the weapon impeccable. Even as the goblins tried to flee, he cut them down. In a matter of moments, there were a dozen corpses littering the front yard of Ben Gauthier's house.

He'd known Ben since high school, and Jim had a suspicion that Ben and Susie were inside and much worse for the wear.

Jim holstered the pistol and walked over to the teenager and the woman, both of whom were looking at him. He didn't know who the woman was, but the boy was Ryan, the Gauthier's' son.

"Ryan," Jim said.

The boy looked at him but didn't recognize him.

Jim didn't push it.

"What were those?" the woman asked, looking around at the bodies.

"Goblins," Jim answered. "Don't ask anything else. Get in your car, get to your house, get your family, and get the hell out of Thorne. Do you understand?"

The woman blinked several times, confused, but she still

nodded.

"Good," Jim said. "Go."

He helped her get Ryan over to the car and into it. She hurried into the driver's side and got the car started. In a heartbeat, she was laying a track of rubber down the street.

"Why did you tell them?" Morgan asked, appearing again.

"They need to know," Jim said, watching the car disappear around a corner. "Even if they don't believe it, they need to know."

Morgan tilted his head slightly and then he said, "There's something coming, Jim. Something bigger."

Chapter 15: Fred O'Dierno and War

Fred had fought in Vietnam. He had more time in that country than he cared to remember, and he'd not only killed men for his own country's sake, but he'd trained men to kill in the name of Freedom.

War had shaped Fred O'Dierno and the way that he looked at the world.

When he heard a gunshot, he knew it for what it was.

When he heard a dozen of them halfway down the street, he knew that something was wrong.

Fred took his reading glasses off and put them down on the coffee table along with the copy of *Harry Potter and the Deathly Hallows* that he was reading. He stood up, walked over to his gun cabinet and took out the M14 that was waiting amongst his other rifles.

From the drawer of the bureau beside it, Fred took a handful of preloaded clips, slipped one into the rifle and the others into the pockets of his shirt.

Walking to his front door, Fred turned off his lights and kept away from the windows. The door was made of heavy oak and thick enough to stop most rounds if need be. Fred found himself breathing smoothly, the rifle a warm comfort in his hands. The weapon had been a yard sale find shortly after he'd gotten back to Thorne from Vietnam. The rifle had been worth its weight in gold in Southeast Asia after the introduction of the M16—that sorry excuse for a rifle which seemed to jam every time Fred was in a firefight.

Fred cleared his mind, though, pushing angry memories back and easing himself to a window where he could look out on the street beyond.

As he did so, the floor shook beneath his feet, the trees swaying haphazardly.

From behind the Gauthier's house, a pair of elm trees came crashing down onto the roof, branches snapping and shingles flying into the night sky. Then it was there.

It stood twenty feet tall, easily, and it was a rough copy of a man. The facial features were blunt, the red hair a tangled, unwashed mass. Thick red hair covered this giant's chest, and a blue, frayed tarp served as a rough skirt around his waist. In the giant's hands, he held a piece of metal that looked like it was ripped off of an excavator or earth mover of some kind.

It was advancing on a man standing on the Gauthier's driveway. The man wore a sword and a pistol and stood still, simply looking at the giant.

Fred pushed the unreality of the situation out of his mind and opened the door, stepping out onto his front step and chambering a round.

***

Jim stood frozen in place on the driveway. Fear and shock rolled over him in waves that sent adrenaline through him, yet he couldn't move.

The giant that had come out of the forest was huge and grinning down at Jim.

"Fresh manmeat," the giant chuckled. "Oh, sweetmeat, I've missed the likes of you these long years."

A rifle cracked out from somewhere nearby, and the giant howled in rage, a sound that both hurt Jim's ears and shocked him into motion.

Jim drew the pistol and backed up, firing as he went, both hands on the pistol as it barked and jumped in his hands. Blood exploded from wounds on the giant's chest as he took a step towards Jim.

"Damnable, man!" the giant howled, and Jim put another four rounds into the giant's chest.

The unknown rifleman continued to fire as well, and Jim watched as the shots from the rifle moved up from the chest to the head, and Jim understood.

Dropping to a knee, Jim steadied himself and fired shot after shot into the giant's head as the rifleman did the same.

The giant's screams of rage ceased as it let go of the metal, collapsed first to his knees, then fell to the left, smashing a blue minivan in the driveway, the windows exploding outwards and showering Jim with glass. Jim struggled to keep his footing as the world seemed to rattle and shake with the falling of the giant.

Carefully, Jim stood up, holstering the pistol once more and brushing the glass off of himself and out of his hair.

"Hello," a voice said calmly.

Jim turned around and looked at a man standing in the center of the street. The man looked to be in his late sixties. He wore a flannel shirt and jeans with a pair of sneakers. His white hair was cut short, and he carried a bolt action rifle with an ease that showed that he had a familiarity with weapons.

"Hello," Jim answered.

"What the hell is going on?" the man asked, perfectly calm.

"Well, that's a long goddamned story," Jim replied.

The man nodded.

"That's Nathan Coffin's rifle," Morgan said, suddenly standing beside Jim.

Both Jim and the stranger jumped.

"Sweet Jesus Christ," the stranger said, "where the hell did you come from?" The man squinted slightly, and then in a lower voice he said, "Oh. You're dead."

Jim looked at Morgan and saw that the ghost-child was smiling.

"Yes," Morgan said. "How did you know?"

"I've seen a lot of death," the man said, "and I know the walking dead when I see them. Now, what did you say about my rifle?"

"It belonged to Nathan Coffin," Morgan said. "He survived the Chosin Reservoir in Korea, where he carried that rifle the entire time. He brought that rifle home," Morgan said, "It's full of his will to survive."

The man frowned.

"Not all weapons work," Jim explained.

"Ah," the man said, nodding.

"You seem to be handling this really well," Jim said, looking at the man.

"I'll freak the hell out about it later on," the man said calmly. "Right now I can't. So I won't."

Jim nodded. He walked to the man and extended his hand. "I'm Jim Petrov, a trooper with the State Police."

"Fred O'Dierno," Fred said. "Retired history teacher, and a United States Marine."

"Well, Fred," Jim said, "care to take a walk with me back to the Blood house?"

"You'll tell me what's going on?" Fred asked.

"I'm going to try," Jim replied.

"Okay," Fred said, "let me grab some more ammunition and I'll be ready to go."

"Sure," Jim said, and he watched the man walk steadily to what was obviously his home.

"He's strong," Morgan said. "We'll need him."

Jim nodded his agreement.

Chapter 16: Scott Ricard and the Dullahan

"Brian," Scott said into the phone, "I don't care what's going on out there. I've got my shotgun and there's no way in hell that I'm going to leave the house or let anyone in."

"Scott," his brother said angrily, "there's something screwed up going on in Thorne tonight. You need to get your ass out."

"I'm fine here," Scott said.

"Then at least send the kids and Marie out. Send them down to Nashua to stay the night with her mom."

"They already left," Scott said, pissed. "She got a call from Judy who said that the Gauthier's' were dead."

"Shit," Brian snapped.

"Exactly," Scott said. "I don't know if it's true or not but Marie took the Jeep and my truck's in the shop. I'm going to have to telecommute tomorrow, and I hate that."

"No, you dumbass," Brian snarled. "Get the hell out of the house. Call a cab. Damn it, if I can get away I'll shoot over and grab you, but we've got multiple fires along the edge of the Monson and Thorne border."

"I'm fine," Scott said. "Talk to you later."

He hung up the phone before Brian could say anything else.

The house was quiet with Marie and the kids gone.

Shaking his head, Scott walked over to the charger and put the phone back on it. He took his shotgun down from the hearth and dug the shells out of their place atop the TV cabinet.

Walking back to his chair, he put on the Raiders game and watched as he loaded the gun. He didn't care about either one of the teams. The Patriots weren't playing until Sunday, but he needed to watch something. With the shotgun across his lap, Scott watched the game, yawned a few times, and felt sleep pulling at his eyes.

Too much chicken pie, he thought, and closed his eyes as the game shifted to commercial with the calling of a timeout by the Raiders.

Scott opened his eyes and saw that the game was over.

Long over.

He hit the 'guide' button on the remote and found out it was two thirty, and he was watching 'Westworld.'

"No, I'm not," he grumbled to himself, turning off the

television.

Holding the shotgun, he stood up, stretched, and yawned.

There was a low rumbling sound that grew louder, coming from the street beyond. Frowning, Scott went to the window and looked outside. He couldn't see anything, but he definitely heard it getting closer. In fact, it almost sounded as if something had turned into his driveway.

"What the hell," Scott grumbled, walking to the front door and flipping the light switch before he opened the door and walked outside with the shotgun. The door clicked shut behind him, and Scott made sure that the safety was off on the gun.

He walked down the stairs and looked up and down his street.

Something was coming towards him. A black carriage drawn by a pair of black horses moved steadily down the street, the wheels loud and harsh upon the asphalt.

The horseman was headless, a wooden pail beside him on the seat.

Scott was fascinated. He couldn't tear his eyes away from the sight, and as the carriage drew abreast of him, it slowed down. The driver let the reins fall to his lap, and then he took up the pail.

A moment later, Scott was stumbling back, screaming and swearing as fresh, hot blood drenched him. His foot caught on a paving stone, and he fell to his knees, the bones cracking and the shotgun skittering away on the walkway.

The rich, sickening scent of iron filled his nose and brought bile up into his mouth. Scott spat it out onto the ground and tried to wipe the blood out of his eyes, his knees sending sharp, piercing pain into his mind. He managed to get into a sitting position, used the bottom of his tee shirt to clean the blood away, and looked out into the street.

The carriage was gone, but the blood remained.

Painfully, Scott got to his feet and turned around, looking for his shotgun.

The driver of the carriage was holding it, the twin barrels pointed at Scott. The driver was still headless.

The shotgun fired, and Scott felt the slugs tear into his chest as the sound of the blast reached his ears. He closed his eyes but never felt the ground when it rushed up to meet him.

Chapter 17: Jim, Fred and Hollis Blood

The air was cold as dawn painted the sky a deep red.

Jim and Fred sat on the porch drinking hot coffee brought to them by a child who had passed in 1933. The two men had weapons that could kill faery folk, and they listened to a gentle rumbling in the distance. Both men, unbeknownst to the other, were wondering if the rumbling came from yet another giant.

From the curve of the road a man appeared, walking upright and easily with a cane. He wore a button down shirt, suspenders and a pair of slacks with well-made shoes.

Hollis Blood.

"This place is full of the dead," Fred said before blowing on his coffee and taking a drink.

"That it is," Jim agreed.

Hollis climbed the steps of the porch and leaned against his cane, smiling at the two men. "Well," Hollis said, "it looks as though things have truly gone to the pot, haven't they, gentlemen?"

"You seem fairly pleased about it," Fred said evenly.

"I'm only pleased that I was right," Hollis said, the smile dropping away. "I have to say that I am upset about the unnecessary deaths. Those, however, I lay at the feet of the men who decided to break the contract which has kept this town safe for centuries."

"Well," Jim said, "what do we do now, Hollis?"

"My suggestion is that you finish your coffee," Hollis said, "then go inside and into the archives, which is where you got the weapons, Jim. In there, I'll show you the document you need to look at. It will tell you of a place where you can ride out the next few hours safely. You'll be able to rest and prepare for the later afternoon and evening."

"We shouldn't do anything now?" Jim asked.

Hollis shook his head. "You not only shouldn't," the dead man said, "but it would be dangerous for you if you did. My family and I are going to do our best to drive out the rest of the town, but the border needs to be mended, and we're not sure how that's going to be done yet."

"So," Fred said, "we hole up somewhere?"

Hollis nodded.

"Will you tell us when to come out?"

"Yes," Hollis answered.

"Sounds good to me," Fred said. "Come on, Jim," he said as he stood, finishing his coffee. "The sooner we're safe, the better I'll feel."

"What about the rest of the town?" Jim asked, standing.

"They'll either get out or they won't," Hollis said. "I can put it no simpler than that. You will serve everyone better by preparing for later on, Trooper Petrov."

After a moment, Jim nodded. "Alright," he said, and he followed Hollis as the ghost led the way back into the house in which he had so recently lived.

Chapter 18: Brian Ricard in Thorne

Brian didn't understand the call that came over the radio.

"What do you mean there's a roadblock set up?" he asked, pulling over on the side of Route 122. "Who the hell put it there?"

"Don't know, Brian," Jane answered. "We just got the call that there's a roadblock at 122 where it crosses over from Monson into Thorne. Can you check it out?"

"Yeah," Brian said, shaking his head. "I'll check it out."

He put the cruiser back into gear and checked the mirrors before flipping on the lights and pulling out onto Route 122. He was exhausted. He'd spent most of the night helping to take care of the fires that had sprung up along the border between the two towns. He'd managed to grab a few hours of sleep in one of the cells, but he was exhausted, and his bladder was full.

The road was absent of other cars and through the vent system of the car, he could smell fresh smoke from somewhere. Brian felt bad for the firefighters. More than likely, there were crews from other towns helping now.

What the hell is going on, he thought tiredly, the road curving slightly ahead of him. Then he stomped on the brakes, leaving rubber on the asphalt.

Ahead of him, dozens of trees had been felled and dragged across the road. It would take a crew with chainsaws and a front-loader at least half the day to clear it, and it wasn't even six o'clock in the morning.

"Damn it," Brian said aloud, throwing the car into park and getting out. He let out a sigh and stared at the mess. "Damn it," he said again. Leaning back into the car to grab the microphone, he stopped.

Something had moved in the corner of his eye.

Slowly, dropping his hand to the butt of his pistol, he backed out of the car and straightened up. He looked at the blockade from left to right, right to left, and up and down.

Nothing.

He waited another moment before he looked at it again.

Still nothing.

Brian closed his eyes and opened them.

Then he saw them.

Small, sharp faces among the gaps in the trees. Their skin

was dark, almost gray.

When they realized that he saw them, they straightened up and climbed onto the trees. The things were small, wiry and wearing an odd assortment of what looked to be children's clothes, though they seemed to have paid no attention at all to what gender's clothing they were wearing, if that even mattered.

What mattered was that they had axes and knives, cudgels, and small bows. They looked at Brian with some interest and chattered back and forth in a language that sounded nothing like anything Brian had ever heard before.

Although, that wasn't true. He had heard something like it before. His daughter loved a movie in which the kids spoke Irish, and that was exactly what the words sounded like.

The strange creatures were speaking Irish, or Gaelic, or whatever it was called.

Brian didn't find himself feeling comforted by that information, or by the way the things started looking at him. They didn't seem to have any desire to leave the safety of the blockade, and that was working out just fine for Brian as well.

"They're goblins," a voice suddenly said from beside him, and Brian screamed.

Several of the goblins screamed as well, and when Brian regained some modicum of self-control he was pleased to see that some of them had left.

"They're not exceptionally bright," the voice said again, "but they are wicked creatures."

Brian looked around, and he saw a young woman standing slightly off to the right, looking at him.

There was something peculiar about the woman, or the old-fashioned black dress that she was wearing. Her deep brown hair hung in curls past her shoulders and her hands disappeared into a dark red, fur muff held properly in front of her stomach.

One of the Goblins called out to her in something that sounded like German, and the young woman responded with kind words. The tone of her voice, though, was vicious, and the goblin, who had spoken, cringed.

She turned her attention back to Brian. "I'm afraid that the only advice which I could offer you, sir, is that of staying away. No matter what you do, you will not be able to stop them. Your weapon is useless, and they will not take kindly to you trying to cross."

"How do you know?" Brian asked.

"Look at what they've done to those on the other side of the barricade," she said, nodding towards the goblins.

Brian looked back and saw the goblins placing aluminum poles in the barricade so that the poles stood up easily. Atop those poles were freshly severed heads, blood still leaking from the necks.

They were heads of men and women of a variety of ages.

The goblins put up perhaps half a dozen, and when they finished, they looked over and saw Brian looking at them. Cheerfully, they waved.

Out of pure reaction, Brian waved back, and then he threw up on the asphalt.

The laughter of the goblins filled his ears, and he tried to block out the image in his mind.

"Go back to Monson," the young woman said kindly. "They won't follow you."

"How do you know?" Brian asked, straightening up and wiping his mouth off with the back of his hand. He looked at her and asked again, "How do you know?"

She smiled at him reassuringly. "They're not the ones who built it."

"But what about the other people?" Brian asked.

"Who?"

"The people on the other side of the blockade," he said.

A cold expression settled on her face. "They don't matter," she said. "They broke the contract."

Brian looked back at the goblins and swore as something wet and soft struck him in the face. The goblins let out peals of high-pitched laughter, and Brian angrily wiped his face, and his hand came away wet with blood. He looked down at the pavement to see what he had been hit with and stumbled, slipping in his own vomit.

Lying on the pavement between the open door and the car's frame was an eyeball, part of the optic nerve still attached—the blue iris still looking surprisingly alive.

Chapter 19: A Place of Safety

Hollis Blood opened the door to the small room that Jim had entered before with Ambrose. With the light turned on, Hollis pointed to a shelf on the far wall.

"On the second shelf," the dead man said, "you'll find a small letter. It's sealed, but you'll need to break it."

Jim walked into the room and walked to the shelf that Hollis had pointed out. Fred stayed in the hallway drinking his coffee and standing between Morgan and Hollis Blood, who watched Jim silently.

On the shelf, Jim found half a dozen leather-bound books, a pair of similarly bound leather journals and dozens of letters. He took the letters down and started going through them. They all seemed to be opened, and it took him a few minutes to find the one that wasn't.

The letter was indeed small, and it was heavy as well. Beneath the thick parchment paper, Jim could feel something small and hard. He returned the other letters back to the shelf and walked out of the room. He turned off the light and closed the door behind him absently, simply staring at the letter.

The paper was old and yellowed. The seal upon the letter was done with green wax and the shape of an oriental dragon.

"That's it," Hollis said.

"It is indeed," said another voice, and Fred snapped the rifle up to his shoulder instantly.

Then the man lowered it, for Ambrose Blood stood beside Hollis.

"That," Fred said, "is an uncomfortable habit that you gentlemen have."

Neither of the dead men responded.

"What's in the letter?" Jim asked.

"Only Hawthorne Blood knows that," Ambrose answered, "and he's quite busy at this time. Open it, please," Ambrose said, "it's time, and time is what we have very little of."

Jim nodded, broke the seal on the letter, and opened it carefully, unfolding each corner of the thick paper. Within, he found a small, old, iron key. Just a simple skeleton key that he'd seen reproductions of at crafts stores when he'd go shopping with his wife, but this wasn't a reproduction key.

He took the key and found it warm to the touch, as if it had been in someone's pocket rather than in the envelope. Still holding the key, Jim read the letter aloud.

"You who have opened this letter fully understand the significance of what has occurred here. For some reason, the barrier is down, the contract broken, and the faery folk rampaging as only the faery folk can. You will need a place of safety while you prepare yourselves for the difficult decisions ahead.

"I have no doubt that few of the residents of Thorne have fled at the first signs of the faery folk. We New Englanders are, by nature, a stubborn breed. In this case, however, stubbornness will cost them their lives.

"Go to Hassell Brook and follow it down as it makes its way to the Nashua River. There is a small pool off of the brook and in and around this pool are great boulders. Here, by the boulders closest to banks, you will find a door. This key will unlock it, and you'll be able to prepare.

"Beware of the pool, though. There is a washer-woman and a korrigan. Beware of them both."

The letter was unsigned.

Jim looked at the others.

Fred shook his head, and the two dead men looked confused.

"We do not know," Ambrose said. "None of us were schooled in faery lore."

"I was," a small voice said, and Jim turned quickly around to see a young woman standing shyly in a doorway. She wore a nightcap and a long, off-white nightgown.

"Mary?" Hollis asked, surprised.

She nodded. "I read everything that I could when I was a little girl, Hollis. That's why, after I heard you and your father talking about the land, I had to go and see if it was true."

"How did you die, Mary?" Fred asked simply.

"The Korrigan, down by the pool with the washer-woman wailing. I heard the washer-woman and went down anyway. When I arrived in the pool, the Korrigan cursed me, and I died at the bottom of the stairs, as you know."

Wordlessly Hollis nodded.

"Both the Korrigan and the washer-woman are still there," Mary said to all of them. "They have no desire to leave the pool.

209

That does not mean, though, that they'll let you pass through without a care."

"Well," Fred said, "I don't see how we have much of a choice."

"No," Hollis said, "there's none."

"We'll be able to guide you to Hassell Brook," Ambrose said, "but you'll need to go the rest of the way yourselves. We have too much work to do while you learn what it is we need to do."

"What work?" Fred asked, looking over to Jim.

Jim shook his head.

Fred looked back to the dead men.

"What work?" he asked of them.

Hollis sighed. "You would know it as scorched earth."

Fred was quiet for a moment. "Stupid assholes," he said, shaking his head. "Alright, gentlemen, show us where this damnable brook is."

Chapter 20: Fires along the Roads

On Friday at six o'clock in the morning, Tom woke not to the alarm he had set for seven, but to the sound of a fire truck and the stench of smoke.

Sitting up in bed, he looked around, expecting to see smoke curling around the ceiling, but there was nothing. Vicki lay asleep on the bed oblivious to the sound and the smell. Tom got out of the bed and walked to the window where he pulled the curtain aside a little to look out on the street.

The fire truck was parked haphazardly on the road, the left front wheel up on the sidewalk. The siren continued to wail, and the lights continued to flash in the early morning light while the Wilsons' house burned brightly. In front of the house, standing on Bill Wilson's prized Kentucky bluegrass was a tall man with a sword. A huge sword, just like the ones that Tom had seen in the movie *Braveheart*.

The man wasn't wearing a kilt, though. He had an outfit on that looked like the man could have stepped straight out of the Revolutionary War. Hell, he even had a cape and a three-cornered hat on.

Tom shook his head. The guy was too tall to be Bill, but he could certainly be one of Bill's buddies still drunk from going out last night. The five volunteer firefighters that had come with the truck were trying to get the man away from the house so they could get at the fire.

Tom grinned, trying to think what the hell they would—

The grin dropped from Tom's face as the man with sword brought the weapon back and with a single, massive swing cut a firefighter's head off.

Tom watched, confused, as the head bounced and rolled, the body falling limply as the other firefighters stumbled back and away from the swordsman. Tom was sure that someone was screaming. Maybe even all of them.

But no one was going to go near that swordsman.

The swordsman, however, was going to go near them.

The man started walking forward, the sword held easily in both hands. Bill's sprinkler system kicked in, the sprinkler heads rising up out of the ground to care for the lawn. As one did, a firefighter tripped and fell, trying to twist away and catch himself.

Then the swordsman was on him, driving the sword through the firefighter's chest and twisting the blade before pulling it out. The firefighter, Tom knew, was dead.

A shape came staggering out of the front door of Bill's flaming house.

"Shit," Tom said.

"What?" Vicki asked sleepily.

"Shit," Tom said again.

A moment later, she was beside him. "Oh my God, Tom," she said.

Even as the words left her mouth, Tom saw the swordsman turn around as if he had sensed Bill's presence. With two long strides, the swordsman was upon Bill, driving the long blade up to the hilt into the soft white flesh of Bill's stomach.

Vicki screamed—a loud, piercing scream that made Tom's ears ring and his head ache.

The swordsman looked up at them in the window.

"Oh no," Tom said. "Oh please no."

Vicki was still screaming as he grabbed her by the wrist and nearly dragged her away from the window and out of the bedroom. She finally stopped when they were in the hallway and by the time that they reached the stairs he didn't have to hold onto her wrist.

When they reached the kitchen, she grabbed her purse from the counter and his wallet from the top of the microwave while he removed the keys from their hook and stepped into his beat-up sneakers. He opened the door, a wave of smoke rolling into the kitchen and a wall of heat waiting for them as Vicki slipped into her flipflops. Even as Tom hit the 'unlock' button on the key, he glanced over at Bill's house.

The swordsman was killing the last of the firefighters, parrying a clumsy ax swing from the man before severing the firefighter's head partially from his neck.

"Oh Jesus," Vicki said. "Oh, Jesus, oh Jesus, oh *Jesus*, Tom. Where are Janet and the boys?"

"Get in the car," Tom said, turning his head away as he saw a small shape run by one of the upper windows of Bill's house. "Just get into the car, Vicki."

They both got in and for a moment, Tom almost laughed

hysterically, wondering if he was going to drop the keys as he tried to get the key into the ignition, but the key went in smoothly, and the engine turned over as he slammed the car into 'reverse', backing up as fast as he could.

Then he lost control.

The car slammed into the back corner of the fire truck so hard that it got stuck part way under it. Cursing and swearing, Tom shifted into drive, but the car wouldn't budge.

Then, Vicki's window was smashed in. A pale hand reached inside, grabbed her by her blonde hair as she screamed, and dragged her out through the broken window. Tom watched in horror as the swordsman wrapped a massive hand around her neck and squeezed.

The breaking of her neck and the sudden, final gasp of breath set Tom to vomiting.

"Coward!" the swordsman snarled.

Out of the corner of his eye, Tom saw the sword driving in towards him.

Chapter 21: Elizabeth O'Grady and the Brownie

Elizabeth O'Grady slept little, if at all, most nights, and this past Thursday had been par for the course. She didn't hear particularly well anymore—one of the sad truths of aging.

She sat at her dressing table and finished the last bits of a ritual that had lasted for decades. She put on her black dress, pinned her hair back into a bun, and made sure that the plain gold wedding band that Murphy had given her was still properly on her finger.

Lastly, she put her crucifix around her neck. The chain was of small, silver links, and the crucifix was of the same, each detail of Christ's suffering exquisitely wrought in the metal. Finishing with her ritual, she offered up a prayer to the blessed Virgin and took her cane off of the dressing table's edge. Using it carefully, she rose to her feet and made her way around her small bed to the hallway.

She traveled along the hall and realized that something wasn't the same.

The hall was spotless.

Not a single particle of dust. The floor was swept, the wooden wainscoting polished. Even the glass shades of the sconces had been washed. When she reached the kitchen, she found that it too had been scrubbed. The metal fixtures positively gleamed, and the few pots and pans which had been from last night's dinner were washed and put away. Fresh vegetables and fruit were in bowls upon the table.

The doors, Elizabeth saw, were still locked, as were the windows.

Elizabeth pulled one of the two chairs out from under the table and sat down. She picked a peach out of one of the bowls and looked at it for a long time.

Finally, she put the fruit back and stood up. She made her way to the refrigerator and took out a small container of cream. From a cabinet over the toaster, she removed a demitasse cup and saucer. She carried all three to the table, set the cup on the saucer, and poured cream into the saucer. With that finished, she returned the cream to the refrigerator, retrieved a paring knife and small plate from their respective places, and took her seat at the table once more.

After taking the peach out again, she carefully cut it in half, removed the pit, and cut the halves in half again. She placed one slice on the saucer beside the demitasse cup.

Elizabeth ate a wedge of peach, wiped her mouth with a napkin, dried her hand and said in a soft voice, "Thank you. Will you join me?"

She sat in silence for several minutes before a creak sounded near the back door. A small creature appeared from a shadow, a small hat held in his hands. He wore a neat pair of knickers and a white peasant shirt with a corduroy. His feet were large and bare, his arms and legs gangly. His hands, like his feet, were large, the fingers gnarled. He stood no more than two feet tall, and when he approached the table he climbed up the other chair deftly, standing politely on the table.

He looked her in the eye and gave her a smile of crooked, yellow teeth. He smelled of smoke and cleanliness.

"Please sit," Elizabeth said.

He nodded and sat down.

"The cream and the peach are for you."

"For me, Ma'am?" he asked, and his small but deep voice was thick with an Irish brogue.

"Yes," Elizabeth said, "in appreciation of the fine work that you did."

He smiled broadly and put the hat down on the table before picking up the demitasse cup daintily. He took a noisy sip and sighed happily. "It is a pleasure, Ma'am," he said, "to find a Mistress who is well bred."

Elizabeth nodded her thanks.

He picked up the peach and tucked the piece fully into his mouth. He chewed and hummed to himself, swallowed, and took another sip.

"You've met no others who know?" Elizabeth asked.

"I tried only one other before you, Ma'am," he said.

"And may I ask who?"

"Your neighbor," he said, "the one across the street in the yellow house."

"The Labries?" Elizabeth asked.

"French, were they?"

"Yes," Elizabeth said.

"Ah," he said, "that would explain it then."

"They were not pleased?"

"Not at all," he answered. "She ignored what I did, assumed it was some other. Not a word of thanks."

"What happened then?" Elizabeth asked.

"I burned their house down," he said simply, finishing his cream, "with them in it."

Elizabeth twisted in her seat slowly and finally could look out the front window. Not much remained of the house. It had burned almost to the foundation.

The place smoldered still, and the Labries' cars remained in the driveway, covered in ash and debris.

No one had tried to put out the fire. That was clear.

"What's your name?" she asked, turning back to him.

"Leabhar," he smiled.

"Leabhar," she repeated.

"Yes, Ma'am," he said. He looked longingly at another wedge of peach.

Smiling she picked one up and handed it to him.

He ate it quickly but politely. When he finished, he smiled at her. "Ma'am, I saw that your woodbox was empty, and winter's coming on. Would you like me to fill the wood box?"

She thought of him with the wood and near the fire.

Elizabeth smiled and nodded. "Please, Leabhar."

As he got off of the table and climbed down the chair, putting his small hat back upon his head, Elizabeth looked out the window.

A pity, she thought. *Here's hoping that it was the smoke that killed them, and not the flames.*

Elizabeth offered up a prayer to the blessed Virgin and smiled as Leabhar made his way outside.

Chapter 22: Down by the Pool

Somewhere, a fire truck, whose siren had been screaming for nearly an hour, suddenly went silent.

Jim looked over his shoulder toward where the sound had been coming from. In the early morning light, columns of smoke were rising up and staining the sky.

"Just keep moving," Fred said, patting Jim on the shoulder. "There's nothing that can be done right now."

Jim nodded and turned his attention back to the narrow path that ran along Hassell Brook. They had cut across the brook nearly half an hour before, and they were keeping a steady pace. The woods were strangely quiet around them. None of the bird or animal sounds were familiar in this part of New Hampshire.

Ahead of them, Jim caught sight of large weeping willow trees filling the spaces between the old trees. Boulders and large rocks started cropping up amongst the trees as well. The sound of water slapping against rocks reached his ears. Jim drew his pistol.

"Take it slow," Fred said softly, "nice and slow."

Jim only nodded.

He moved at a slow pace forward, listening.

Yet he heard only the water, nothing else.

The path they followed curved down slightly, and there before them appeared a trio of large boulders, looking almost like monstrous eggs. A little beyond them grew a massive weeping willow tree. The path led directly to the stones, cutting in amongst them.

Jim walked down, following the path directly to the stones. He passed through a curtain of willow branches, Fred right behind him, nearly bumping into him as Jim came to a complete stop.

In the trunk of the tree was a tall, broad door. There was no window, but there was a doorknob of cut crystal set into a brass plate with a keyhole.

"Well, damn," Fred said.

"You said it," Jim sighed. He put his left hand into his pants pocket and took the key out. Stepping up to the door, he put the key into the keyhole and unlocked the door before grasping the knob and turning it. With a grunt, he pushed the door open.

Within the depths of the living tree, a room spread out before them. It was far larger than the outside of the tree, and thick carpets were laid across a stone floor. A hearth with a small fire occupied the far wall, and torches were set in brackets along walls of smooth stones. Draperies hung from the tall ceiling down to the floor, and a single bed stood off to one side. A writing desk stood opposite of the bed and had a scattering of books and papers upon it.

"What the hell do we do with this?" Jim asked.

In the distance something roared—a terrible sound that weakened Jim's knees.

"We go inside," Fred said.

Jim nodded, took the key out of the lock, and went into the room. Together he and Fred pushed the door closed and found iron mounts on the back for thick boards to be dropped into. Without speaking, both of the men did just that before stepping away from the door.

Whatever they had heard outside roared again, yet it was louder and closer than it had been. Faintly, they heard a splashing sound, and then the sound of two male voices arguing. The voices were incredibly deep, and Jim had a suspicion that giants were the owners of the sounds being made. A third voice suddenly joined the first two and there was a great deal of howling and yelling that arose.

Jim winced, put his pistol back into the holster, and covered his ears. It did little to help the raucous hurting his ears and causing his head to throb with pain. Soon came the sounds of blows. A glance at Fred showed the man to be standing impassively in the center of a rug, his rifle cradled in his arms.

Shortly, the battle being fought rolled away from the pool and silence returned, filled by the small noises of the fire burning in the hearth.

"Let's see if there's any coffee in this place," Fred said. "I've a thirst now."

They found the coffee in a clay jar by the fire, and behind one of the draperies they discovered a hand-pump and some cooking-ware as well. It took a minute to get the water but when it came, the water was cold and sweet. They filled a cast iron kettle and Fred set it on an iron hook before swinging it out over the flame. Jim carried a pair of clay mugs out of the small room and placed them near the hearth.

The two of them sat down on the floor a few feet from the fire and waited for the water to boil.

"So," Fred said, "this has been a hell of a day."

"Yeah," Jim agreed.

That sat silently for a short time.

"I keep wondering," Jim said, breaking the silence, "if any of this is real."

"That's to be expected," Fred said. "It's never easy to face these things."

"All of the killing?" Jim asked.

"That too," Fred said, "but I was talking about the dead and the faery folk."

Jim looked at Fred, surprised.

"What are you saying?" Jim asked. "Have you seen the faery folk before?"

"Not exactly," Fred said. "Not that we're seeing now. I did three tours in Vietnam, you see, and the supernatural is active there. Sometimes we were fighting the Vietcong, some days the NVA, and some days we were fighting things that could be seen but couldn't be defined." Fred looked over at Jim with a wry smile on his face. "Hell, Jim, I even saw a dragon over there. It was really a hell of a thing."

"Jesus," Jim muttered.

"Yeah," Fred said, "we called on Him a hell of a lot."

The two of them lapsed back into silence, waiting for the coffee to boil. When it started to boil, Fred got up, found a poker to pull the iron swing arm out from the flames, and took a rag off of the floor. Using the rag, he took hold of the kettle and carefully poured the steaming coffee into the mugs.

The smell was soothing as Fred handed him a mug, and Jim realized just how tired and worn out he was. All around them, the town of Thorn was being torn down and even though he was a State Trooper, Jim wasn't able to do a thing. He stopped a few creatures.

Hell, he even killed a giant with Fred, but they were losing the town.

The town would be lost.

Jim looked over to the writing desk and drank a little of his coffee.

"I suppose," Jim said after a minute, "that the information we want is over there somewhere?"

"Yes," Fred answered, glancing at the desk. "It probably is."

They both drank their coffee.

Jim watched the fire eat away at the neatly stacked logs before finishing the mug and standing up. Fred did the same a moment later. They walked over to the desk together, and Fred leaned his weapon against the wall.

From what they could tell, the papers on the desk were letters from a professor in England to one Thomas Blood. Jim and Fred scanned through them.

"Here," Fred said, holding up a letter.

"*18th April 1866,*

"*My dear Captain Blood,*

"*I have received your letter and have, as promised, scoured the literature on the question that you asked regarding the binding of a tract of land. Usually, these bindings are made to protect a home and not, as you are seeking, to bind the faery folk in. I have read of only one instance of such a use, and that is in your own state of New Hampshire, though the records do not tell me who or why or when such an event occurred.*

"*With that being said, sir, I have located the name of a book with purports to offer up the applicable information. The title of this book is* Iussitut Ligatis Pedibus Mediocris. *The book was published anonymously in the last years of the last century, and there are many who believe it is simply a satirical endeavor. There are few, if any, copies to be found for sale.*

"*If you wish to purchase the book, please let me know and I will put out a request for further information. Until that time, sir, I have been pleased to assist you, and I do hope to hear from you again.*

"*Sincerely Yours,*

"*Professor Archibald E. H. Wellington.*"

Fred put the letter down and pointed at the pile of books.

There, on the top, was a small leather bound book with gold lettering stamped into it: *Iussitut Ligatis Pedibus Mediocris.*

"Can you read Latin?" Jim asked, looking at Fred.

Grimly, Fred nodded. "As a matter of fact, Jim, I can."

With the fire crackling behind them, Fred reached out and picked up the book.

Chapter 23: Fred O'Dierno and the Book

It had been a long time since Fred O'Dierno had read any Latin other than those found on school mottos and for military units, but he hadn't forgotten what the Brothers of the Sacred Heart had taught him nearly fifty years earlier. It just took a few minutes to get back into the groove of it.

He sat on the bed, the M14 on his lap and the book in his hands. Jim lay stretched out on the rugs in front of the hearth, passed out from the stresses of the past few days. Fred understood that completely.

Fred turned his attention to the book in his hands and looked at the chapter on clearing the area to be bound.

"It is best if only the faery folk are in the area which you are to bind together. Any men, women, and especially children who are caught there will be at the utter mercy of the faery folk. These people, like the faeries, shall be unable to slip free of the bound area."

"Anything?" Jim asked.

Fred looked up at the younger man who had sat up and was rubbing his eyes. "Yes," Fred said, "yes."

"Anything good?"

"That really does depend on our definition of good," Fred sighed, closing the book. He rubbed the back of his head and sighed.

"Well," Jim said, "what's our definition of good then?"

"Our definition of good is that for us to establish the ring around the lands is going to definitely be a possibility."

"What are the negatives on that one?"

"A few," Fred said grimly. "We'll need to have at least seven signers, and it's very specific about that, but we'll need seven people to agree to take up the signing of the contract to bind the lands and keep them protected. That means that you and I have to find five other living individuals to sign the contract. I don't know if there are going to be five people left in the town of Thorne by the time that we get out of here."

Jim nodded his agreement.

"Okay," Jim said, "what about our definition of bad?"

"One of those seven signers is going to need to be inside the ring that'll be set up around the lands," Fred said. "They need to be inside in order to finish the last of the ritual to close the ring up."

"How is that going to be bad?" Jim asked.

"Because once the ring is set up," Fred said, "then anyone in the ring at the time of the final casting will be bound within. That's why it's so effective against the faery folk. The original ring was far from the town's original few roads. And as the town expanded, the ring's distance grew shorter and shorter until it was literally just the Blood lands that the faery folk were bound in. From what I read, it helped that the older families patrolled the original ring. The faery folk couldn't get out, but they sure as hell could be seen.

"The elder families, you see," Fred continued, "didn't want anyone entering the ring and putting themselves at risk, or seeing a giant or a goblin and putting the word out that something strange was living on the Blood lands. That's why the elder families patrolled. They kept the faery folk away from the edges so that no one would see them, and made sure the townspeople knew that no trespassing was permitted.

"But," Fred sighed, "If we can get those seven signers and a new barrier put up, we should be okay. We'll need to patrol the damn thing just like the elder families did. But once the barrier is up, it should work. It'll piss the little bastards off, since they live just about forever. It means that they can't get out."

"But whoever finishes the casting will be trapped as well?" Jim asked.

Fred nodded.

"With a bunch of pissed off faery folk."

Again Fred nodded.

"Wow," Jim said, "that really does suck."

"Yes," Fred agreed. "Here's another part that's a little disagreeable for most folks. The binding is only good so long as there are direct blood descendants in the town of Thorne *and* the ring remains unbroken."

"This was why Hollis was so concerned about the breaking of the contract."

"Yes."

"So," Jim said, "we need to find seven willing participants to sign a contract stating that they and their descendants are never going to move away from Thorn."

"Correct."

"One of them is going to have to be on the inside of the ring and risk almost certain death. And more than likely an unpleasant death."

"Correct."

"And if the ring is broken, like with a development, then the whole deal is going to essentially be null and void anyway."

"Correct."

"Yeah," Jim said, shaking his head, "this is pretty much a miserable situation."

"That too," Fred sighed, "would be correct."

Chapter 24: Brian Ricard and Gilson Road

Brian sat on the hood of his cruiser and looked down the length of Gilson Road, one of the few roads that traveled from Monson into Thorne. At seven o'clock in the morning, someone attempting to get home to Thorne by way of Gilson had discovered that the road was blocked.

For all intents and purposes, it looked as though someone had scraped up an acre of old growth trees and thrown them across the road. In fact, as far as Brian could see through the trees, there was deadfall and the like forming a barrier that curved off to either side.

Downed electrical wires skidded and surged across the pavement. Miraculously, they had ignited nothing in their whip-like passage from one side of the road to the next. The lines were part of the grid that connected Monson, Hollis, Brookline, Pepperell, and Tyngsborough with Thorne. Understandably, the electric company was nervous to cut power to those sections. Granted, there weren't a lot of residents, but schools, businesses, and farms would all be shut down for an unpredictable amount of time.

New Englanders could understand a power outage after a thunderstorm. They would deal with a power outage after a heavy wind, and, well, a snowstorm was a guaranteed loss of electricity.

However, they would not abide a loss of power for no apparent reason whatsoever. Those people unfortunate enough to be trapped within the curious circle which had been made around Thorne, well, they would simply have to remain where they were until the electric company got everything up and running properly.

A few calls had come in on the state's 911 line, but they hadn't made any sense to the State troopers in the area. More than a few of them had joked over the radio about a gas leak somewhere being responsible for the callers' odd comments and descriptions.

Brian knew that the calls weren't jokes, though.

People were calling in giants, goblins, hell, somebody had even called in a troll, and all Brian could think of was Matthew running around the house after having watched the first Harry

Potter movie yelling, "There's a troll in the dungeon!"

This wasn't the movies, though.

Brian took his hat off, checked the brim for the twentieth time, and put the hat back on his head. He looked at the barrier. He didn't have to trick his eyes anymore. He could easily see the goblins guarding the barrier.

"They're afraid to come out," a voice said suddenly from Brian's right.

"Jesus!" Brian yelled, nearly sliding off the hood with the way he reacted. With his heart thundering in his chest, he looked over and saw a young, pale boy standing by the car. The boy wore a black suit, the back of it torn up the middle. The boy smiled at Brian.

Brian gave a nervous smile back. "What are you doing out here?"

The boy looked at him, confused.

Brian put on his policeman voice. "Shouldn't you be at school?"

"I'm dead," the boy said simply, still smiling as he turned his attention to the barrier once more, "and even if I weren't, I would be old enough to be your grandfather."

The policeman's tone died in Brian's throat.

"What's going on here?" Brian managed to ask after a minute.

"Too much," the boy said sadly.

"What do you mean?" Brian asked.

"We've had to erect a barrier around the town of Thorne," the boy explained, "that doesn't keep them in, but it makes them cautious."

"Who?" Brian asked, shaking his head. "I mean, I saw some things earlier, but I don't know what they were."

"Goblins," the boy said simply. "The faery folk have had a long time to think about how they've been ill-used. From what we can tell, many of them are actually working together. The goblins, as you can see, are at the barrier. Further in, the giants are preparing to storm a section of the barrier that they think is the weakest, and somewhere, we're not sure where exactly, we can hear the hounds of the hunt."

"Oh," Brian said. He really couldn't think of anything else to say.

The little boy was next to him for a minute before asking, "Since you're a sheriff, do you know Trooper Jim Petrov?"

"I do," Brian said, suddenly worried. "Is something wrong?"

"No," the boy said. "Nothing's wrong. He's inside of the barrier. I think that he'll be fine. He's with a man named Fred."

"Fred?" Brian asked.

"Yes, Fred," the boy nodded.

Brian thought about that for a moment, and then he smiled. "Mr. O'Dierno, I had him for history in high school. He's a good man."

"Yes," the boy agreed. "They both are. I hope they can save you."

Chapter 25: John Kenyon and the Little Red School House

John had the longest driveway on Indian Rock Road. It stretched for almost a quarter of a mile up into his land. Yes, it was a pain in the ass to plow in the winter, but the seclusion was well worth it. Few political supporters found their way to his door. This was an exceptionally good thing since New Hampshire served as the first in the nation for the presidential primary.

Too much political grandstanding and stumping as far as he was concerned.

John climbed into his beat-up pickup, started the engine and started driving down the long driveway. Faintly, he could smell smoke. It wasn't the good, sweet smoke of autumn and winter.

This was the smell of a house fire.

John stepped on the gas and sped up to the end of the driveway.

Looking left, he saw one of the new houses that had been built a few years earlier. It was burning brightly in the morning sun. Looking over to his right, he saw a car racing towards him.

It had once been a Lexus, although the grille was smashed, and the headlights as well.

And a giant was chasing it—a great, blonde-haired thing perhaps ten feet in height and grinning from ear to ear. The Giant was having a hell of a good time, the ground shaking as it kept after the car, although it was evidently not trying to catch it.

As the Lexus drove by, something screeching in the bearings, John saw a frantic woman behind the wheel. Packed into the car were children of all ages crying.

When the giant started to pass by, John put his foot down hard on the accelerator and blasted out of his driveway, smashing fully into the giant.

The seatbelt stopped John from bouncing his head off of the steering wheel as the truck came to a sudden stop. The giant collapsed as its left knee buckled in the wrong way, howling with pain. John tried to back up the truck, but he heard only the grinding of gears and smelled the sickly sweet scent of anti-freeze.

The truck was dead.

John left his keys in the ignition and unbuckled his seatbelt. He forced open the door and took off running down Indian Rock

Road towards Hollis, New Hampshire. He needed to get out. That thing looked like a secret government project gone wrong.

As John ran up the road, the Giant rose slightly. By the time John reached the top, he could see down the road where the town line was. There was a barrier there—a great mess of trees that blocked the road and spread out into the forest on either side.

The Lexus was there, parked at a haphazard angle in front of the little red schoolhouse. The children were running to the schoolhouse door where one boy, of perhaps ten or eleven, was desperately trying to unlock the door. The woman, who had driven them, was standing behind the last child looking out. She had an extremely large handgun.

Finally, the boy got the door open, and the children flooded into the schoolhouse. The woman followed slowly, looking left and right and then stumbling.

An arrow was lodged deep in her left thigh.

There was another in her right arm.

They were small arrows, John saw as he got closer, but they were arrows nonetheless.

A third arrow zipped in the air and drove into the unknown woman's head.

She collapsed just as John reached the school door. He whipped the door closed behind him as he heard what could only be an arrow striking the building where he had been just a moment before.

John turned around and saw seven children in the room. All of them were young. Not one could have been older than the boy who had opened the door. John glanced around the room at the tall windows. Locking the door behind him, John hurried to the windows, making sure to stay on one side or the other as he drew the blinds. Then he looked to the children, who in turn were looking at him in complete silence.

"Can anyone tell me what's going on?" John asked.

The key boy raised his hand.

"Yes," John said.

"Fairy tales are killing people."

One of the little boys started to cry quietly.

If John hadn't rammed a giant with his pickup, he would have laughed at the boy, but he didn't.

"Were you trying to leave?" John asked.

The boy nodded. "Weren't you?"

"No," John said, shaking his head, "I was just trying to get to work, although that doesn't exactly seem like it's going to happen today."

He looked at the children and forced a smile. "Why don't all of you go ahead and sit down on the floor. You can even lie down if you want to. Someone will come to help us soon, I know that."

A few of the children smiled at him, and all of them sat down.

John walked back to the door and sat on its right side. He crossed his legs Indian-style and adjusted his glasses. God only knew if someone was actually going to be able to come and help them, but he wasn't going to say that and freak them all out.

A gentle knock came at the door.

"Hello in there," a soft, feminine voice said, her voice carrying a gentle Irish accent.

John waited just a moment before saying, "Hello out there."

"We've come to negotiate with you, man," she said pleasantly.

"Negotiate?" Paul asked. "I don't have anything to negotiate with."

"Yes, we want to negotiate," she said. "For the children, you see."

John laughed and shook his head. "Oh. Well, you see, that's not an option. Not an option at all."

"We've simple enough terms," she continued.

"I don't need to hear your terms," John said. "I'm not negotiating with you about the children."

"Oh but you already are, man," she said sweetly. "As I said. We have simple enough terms. Your life for the children."

John sat and smiled at the children who were staring at him in horror and shock.

"No," John said to her. "No. My life is nothing."

"True," she said, her voice carrying a sad note. "But I'll say this for you, there's not many of your kind who would offer up their life to save the lives of children they don't know. I'm sorry that we'll have to kill you."

A moment later, the windows and the door blew inwards, and small, armored creatures came rushing in. All five were slim, with narrow faces and long brown and dark green hair. Their armor shined, and each of them carried an ax.

The children screamed, huddling together as John launched himself to his feet. Two of the creatures came at him, and he managed to avoid the swing of the first ax, but the second caught him in the stomach. He folded over the weapon, gasping as he reached out and caught the thing by the neck. He started to throttle the creature, the thing's bright green eyes growing larger as John squeezed.

Then there was another one screaming at him in some language, breaking his fingers to get them off of the thing's neck.

Next, one blow and then another slammed into his back, driving him to the floor. John watched his blood collect in dark pools around him. He raised his head and saw the children being carried out by the things when John realized that he couldn't hear anything.

He pushed himself to his knees and grabbed one of the creatures passing him. It yelled in surprise, turning on him with the ax. John managed to catch the weapon as it swung down towards him, but another creature had appeared. Even as John wrenched the ax free, the second creature brought its ax crashing down.

John lay on the floor, his face in his own blood. One of his feet twitched spasmodically, and he watched his blood slip away.

Chapter 26: Gerald and the Draugr

Gerald Greene had a scanner—one that he had purchased off of the Dark Net so he could monitor the police. He didn't want to be caught completely unaware when the police eventually came for him.

He knew someone somewhere would talk.

They always did.

He had listened to the scanner all night. He knew that there were fires burning uncontrollably in Thorne. He knew that there were lines down and the state was arguing with the electric company about getting everything back up and running.

He had heard that there was some sort of barrier around the town. A sheriff from Monson had called in two roads that were blocked, and one of the Hollis PD had done the same.

Essentially, Gerald was trapped in his home, which he didn't mind. He had everything he could want. He was, if necessary, completely ready to live off of the grid. He had solar panels, backup batteries, freeze-dried food—the whole deal. Everything.

Bring on the end of the world. Gerald Greene was ready for it.

Except, he had left his laptop in his car. Gerald had moved it earlier that morning to let his roommate drive out for work.

That meant Gerald was going to have to go out to the car and get it. Going out to the car would require him to get off of the couch, use the bathroom, get dressed in somewhat acceptable clothing, and walk the twenty yards to his car. He didn't want to do it, but he knew that he had to do it. If it really was the end of the world, or just a major cluster for some reason, then he wanted to make sure that no one stole his laptop.

It held too much incriminating evidence. There were several police departments that wouldn't be too happy to know how much he knew, and not only about daily operations and such, but interpersonal issues as well.

Oh no, he needed to get that laptop.

Grumbling to himself, Gerald got up off of the couch and wandered into the bathroom where he relieved himself. He washed his hands, went into his small bedroom, and got dressed in his usual fare—sweats and sneakers. Grabbing his keys, he headed towards the side door.

When he stepped outside, he felt the cool air and smiled. Gerald, being as big as he was, had a distinct dislike for heat. Autumn in New Hampshire was a blessing, and being able to sleep with the windows open until February was fantastic.

Gerald paused.

The street was abnormally silent.

He looked around and saw that there were a few people out, walking in a sort of daze as if they weren't quite there. They looked like extras in a mass casualty exercise for some tyrannical police force like the LAPD or the NYPD.

Funny, Gerald thought. *I don't remember hearing anything about a mass casualty exercise.* Shrugging he went to the car. He unlocked the passenger door and bent over to pick up his laptop, which he had hidden under a large, stained white towel. Straightening up, he winced at the pain in his back, tucked the laptop between his large arm and larger breast, and closed the door.

Turning around, he found himself confronted by one of the mass casualty actors.

The man looked spectacular. The torn flesh hanging from the man's face looked so realistic that Gerald had to turn away. The man stared at Gerald with dull eyes that set Gerald's teeth on edge. Something was wrong.

Gerald eased his way around the man, and the man turned to watch Gerald hurriedly walk to the side door, but there were more mass casualty actors between him and the door.

In his path stood trio of teenagers, one of whom had a terrible injury, the lower portion of his right arm having been cut off at the elbow.

All of it looked too real.

"Excuse me," Gerald said, "but I need to get inside of my home."

The three looked at him.

Movement caught his eye, and he turned his head slightly, just enough to see more of the mass casualties appearing on the road, coming out of open doors in his small suburban neighborhood. Gerald looked back to the teenagers and licked his lips nervously. He took a step back and screamed as he bumped into something. Turning around he realized that it was the first man that he'd seen.

The man was staring at him.

What is going on here? Gerald thought, twisting around. He took a few steps away, and all four of the mass casualty actors took a step towards him.

Am I in a movie and no one told me? Seriously, he thought backing towards his car. *What is going here?*

He turned once more to go to his car and found more of the actors around the car. They were all silent. None of them speaking. All of them staring. Each movement they made was rough as if they were marionettes controlled by a poorly trained puppeteer.

"They're interesting to watch, aren't they?" a voice asked from off to the side.

Gerald looked over and saw a small creature sitting on a tree branch. It looked like a miniature woman, her face pulled backward to form an elongated skull. Her eyes were wide and dark blue, the entirety of the orb colored and pulling his gaze back to them. Her hair was short and spiked, a dark brown that was nearly black. She was incredibly thin, almost sickly so, and she smiled a wicked smile at Gerald, her blazing white teeth flashing at him.

"What?" Gerald asked.

"The draugr," she said. "The walking dead. For that's what they are. Dead and walking. Walking and dead." She smiled.

"Zombies?" Gerald asked, twisting around. *Seriously,* he thought, *am I high? Is there a gas leak somewhere?*

She looked at him, confused. "I don't know the word, but they're more troublesome than anything else. Although they have been known to frighten people to death."

Gerald stood against his car as the draugr pressed closer to him.

"Yes," she chuckled, "they can be so frightening."

Gerald fumbled for the door handle on the car but couldn't find it, at least not before the walking dead were on him, arms reaching out and cold, freezing dead hands grasping him. The cold bit through his clothes and his heart started pounding erratically in his chest.

His breath came in great, terrible racks, his whole frame shaking as he squeezed his eyes closed.

Gerald's heart stopped as a hand reached out and cupped his

chin.

Chapter 27: Jim and Fred and Walking Back

Jim checked the laces on his boots one more time and straightened up.

Fred was at the door, waiting quietly.

Both of the men had enjoyed another cup of coffee. They left the fire burning.

"Ready?" Fred asked.

"Ready," Jim answered, holding the key in his left hand and the Colt in his right.

Fred nodded and opened the door.

They stepped out into afternoon light, and Jim quickly closed and locked the door. He put the key in his pocket and moved up to stand beside Fred.

"I'll lead," Fred said. The older man started walking along the thin trail that led back the way from which they had come. The forest was silent, disturbingly so, and there was the distinct feeling that they were being watched, which, Jim realized, they probably were.

Fred set a steady pace that moved them along as the autumn sun rose and reached its zenith before they found the place from where they had started the day before. Neither Ambrose nor Hollis Blood were there. Fred continued on though, not stopping, and that was fine with Jim.

The air stank of smoke and fire. Faintly, Jim could hear the sound of trees crashing down. Soon, the Blood house appeared in the confines of the forest in front of them. There was no sign of anyone either living or dead around the home. Jim could only imagine what was going on in what remained of Thorne.

When they reached the house, Fred said, "Let's stop for a bit, Jim."

Jim nodded and went to the porch, climbing the stairs tiredly. His stomach grumbled loudly, and Fred chuckled.

"Mine, too," Fred said, trying the doorknob. It turned easily, and Jim followed the man into the quiet house. There was no ambient electrical noise. The power had been lost, and more than likely, that had been recent.

They walked to the kitchen and prowled around for a few minutes, digging out dry goods and getting water from the tap. Evidently, the well ran on its own source of power—something

Jim was exceptionally happy about.

With several boxes of crackers, a pair of knives, some peanut butter and a few glasses of water, the two men sat down at the table. Fred leaned his rifle against the table, and Jim put the Colt on it, the barrel pointed at the sink instead of himself or Fred. Silently they started eating, doing so quickly.

Thorne was waiting for them and whatever survivors were still around.

"Where do you think we should look?" Jim asked after taking a long drink of water.

"Town Hall," Fred said simply. "That'll be the most likely place. They may not be able to fight back, but the place is stocked and ready for a hard winter. People would figure that it would be the best place to hole up—wait for the cavalry to arrive."

Jim chuckled.

"What?" Fred asked.

"Cavalry," Jim said, shaking his head. "Maybe we should find a couple of donkeys to ride in on."

Fred chuckled as well. "Yes, that would be appropriate for Thorne, wouldn't it?"

The front door to the house opened, and both men grabbed their weapons.

Ghosts didn't need to open doors.

Fred dropped to one knee and brought his rifle up to his shoulder.

Jim stood behind the man, the Colt up and pointed, held firmly in both hands.

A shape came stumbling towards them.

A young woman came into view, a baby swaddled and held to her breast with one arm. She was bloodied and pale. Her red hair was torn in some places, having been ripped from her head. In her free hand, she held a large meat cleaver, the kitchen tool stained dark with blood.

When her tired eyes focused on Jim and Fred, she came to a stop and brought the cleaver up, angling her body so that the child was protected.

"We're not faeries," Jim said gently, holstering his Colt. Fred stood up, pointing his rifle at the ceiling.

"Neither am I," she said in a raspy voice. Her eyes flicked around the kitchen and stopped on the food at the table.

"Come on," Jim said.

"Yes, there's plenty here," Fred added.

The woman came forward, then staggered to the table. Jim and Fred each caught one of her arms and helped her to sit down. The baby against her breast was sleeping peacefully, although the child's red hair was splattered with dark drops of blood. The woman let the meat cleaver fall to the floor and Fred sat down across from her, putting peanut butter on crackers for her as Jim filled a glass of water and put it down in front of her.

"Thank you," she whispered, taking a drink of water. "Thank you."

The baby grumbled but didn't wake up.

The woman continued to eat. She finished dozens of crackers and possibly half of the jar of peanut butter before she stopped.

Jim handed her a cloth napkin from on the counter, and she smiled at him, wiping her mouth. "Thank you both so much," she said after a minute. She looked down at her baby and kissed the top of the child's head.

"You're welcome," Jim said.

"I didn't think that anyone else was still around," she said. "Everywhere I went, there were dead people, houses burning, and damned faeries everywhere I looked."

Jim looked over at Fred.

"You know that they're faeries?" Fred asked.

She nodded angrily. "My mother was fresh off the boat from Ireland. I cut my teeth on the old faery tales. None of this garbage passed off on kids today. No, I knew what was going on as soon as I saw the faeries. I just didn't think that we would have any here, especially not in Thorne. The town's not exactly a Mecca for Irish Americans."

"True," Fred chuckled, "very true."

"Did that work for you?" Jim asked, nodding towards the cleaver on the table.

"Yes," she said grimly. "I was surprised. It's not an old iron weapon."

"Where did you get it?" Fred asked.

"It was in the house when we bought it," she answered. "My husband and I bought this old farmhouse up on Washington Road. When we were cleaning out the kitchen, I found this in the back of the pantry. I thought it would be an interesting thing to hang over the counter. It was the first thing that came to hand when a goblin came in."

"Is your husband alive?" Jim asked gently.

The woman nodded. "He's on a business trip to New York City this week. It's just Gwen and myself."

"I'm Jim," Jim said, extending his hand. As she shook it, he added, "State Trooper, New Hampshire State Police."

"Rose Mary," she said, letting go of Jim's hand and reaching over to shake Fred's.

"Fred O'Dierno," Fred said, "plain old retiree."

"How did you find this place?" Jim asked.

"A little boy," Rose Mary said. "He was down on the construction site, and he told me that there was a house up the road a bit. He told me that I'd be able to find food here and that I'd be safe.

"What about you?" she asked. "How do you two know about it?"

"That," Fred said, "is a fairly long story."

Chapter 28: Thorne Town Hall, 11:00 AM

Philip Delyani stood at a second story window in the town administrator's small office. From his vantage point, he could look down on the scene below and nothing he saw made him feel any better about life—or rekindle his personal faith in God, for that matter.

Sighing, he pulled his deer rifle in closer to his shoulder, lined up his shot, and carefully squeezed off a round.

The sound of the weapon in the confines of the room was loud and painful, even through the shooter's ear protection that he snuggly wore.

"Shit," he said simply. He lowered his weapon, ejected the spent brass and put a fresh cartridge in before slipping on the safety and taking off his ear protection.

"Anything?" Chris asked.

"Nope," Philip said. "Same as usual. Beautiful head shot and the thing falls to the ground, gets up, shakes its ass at me and keeps on dancing." He put his rifle down on the desk and picked up the board that had been over that part of the window before and replaced it. Philip held it in place as Chris stepped up with a cordless drill and secured the board once more to the window's casing.

With Chris carrying the drill and Philip carrying his rifle, the two men started back towards the basement, where the few survivors were staying as safe as they could from the bizarre storm raging just beyond the walls of the town hall.

Philip waved to the two men standing guard at the front door. Each had a wooden baseball bat, which was proving only slightly more effective than Philip's rifle. The two men waved back, and Philip led Chris into the basement. Nearly fifty people huddled in the basement. Someone had gone into the storage closets and broken out the blankets and the Red Cross emergency cots as well as some of the tastier freeze-dried foods.

Although, Philip couldn't tell if that was an oxymoronic statement or not.

Reverend Schwerdt of the local Lutheran Church had brought a hand cranked radio. The Reverend, along with several others, was listening to the broadcast intensely.

"And now our update regarding the problem in Thorne,

New Hampshire. Authorities are stating that a microburst seemed to have touched down at some point in the night and damaged power lines, causing delays in getting to the sites of multiple fires. There is no word as to when this situation might be resolved."

"Microburst my ass," Chris grumbled.

"I know," Philip said. "Keep it low, though."

Chris simply nodded and walked with Philip into the large kitchen. The heat and hot water of the kitchen were simple. They were attached to the main circuit panel and that, in turn, was connected to the generator outside of the town hall, kept safe in its own covering.

How long that might continue to last though, well, John really had no idea.

Some blessed saint had started a large, twelve-cup coffee maker.

"Do you want a cup?" Philip asked.

"No thanks," Chris said, shaking his head. "I'm all set right now."

Philip nodded, took down a paper cup, and poured himself some coffee.

Always appreciate the little things, he reminded himself.

He leaned against the countertop, enjoyed the coffee, and closed his eyes, listening to nothing whatsoever.

"Philip!" someone yelled.

Never lasts, Philip thought.

"What is it?" Chris called back.

"We've got someone trying to make it to us."

"Wave'em off," Philip yelled, straightening up and walking towards the doorway. "They'll never make it."

"We've tried," Jeff Parker said, coming down the stairs. "We've tried. I even threw a couple of bottles at him."

"Where's he coming from?" Philip asked, heading back up the stairs towards the front door.

"South end," Jeff said.

By peering through a slit between two boards, Philip could see down the road. A stumbling man was weaving between the faery folk. Many of the faery folk laughed at the man, and he could see why.

The stumbling man was naked and nearly dead. It wouldn't

matter if the man reached them or not. He was a dead man walking, but he didn't know that.

Even as Philip watched, a faery tripped the man and he went sprawling, getting back to his feet a moment later. Fresh cuts and scrapes on both knees and hands bled freely, but the man paid them no heed.

"Free the door, please, Chris," Philip said softly. Chris moved forward, undid the screws connecting the board binding the door to the frame. "Jeff, door, please. About an inch should be fine."

Jeff stepped forward, pushing the door open just the slightest bit.

Getting down into a kneeling position Philip brought his rifle up and switched the safety off. He watched the man for a moment, watched the way he stumbled and could almost hear the man's labored breathing from where he knelt in the town hall. Philip took long, slow breaths, and started to take up second pressure on the trigger.

A moment later, the rifle shot cracked out into the air, and the naked man collapsed, his brains blown out in the morning sky.

Philip ejected the casing, put in a fresh round, and straightened up.

"Chris," he said.

"Yes?" Chris asked.

"Please secure the door."

With the sound of the drill in the background Philip returned to the kitchen to drink his coffee.

Chapter 29: Hearing the Hounds, 11:00 AM, the Blood Lands

Evan brought up the rear of his group of friends as they walked their way out of the Blood lands and back towards town. Ever since the town had grabbed a good deal of the property, people had been going in to hunt, and Evan had been one of them. It'd been a while since he'd shot at anything other than people.

Getting fresh venison would be fantastic.

"Would" was the key word, though.

They'd seen nothing and they had been out there since four in the morning, set up on a well-trod game trail. They had seen absolutely nothing. The line stopped, and Paul looked back, a confused expression on his face. He tilted his head slightly, trying to listen better.

Then, Evan heard it too.

The sound of dogs barking. Yipping at one another.

The sound continued to grow louder, and the men started looking at each other, frightened. Evan simply made sure that the safety was off his rifle and that a round was still chambered.

I don't care if it's a poodle or a Great Dane, Evan thought, *it's going to die.*

A heartbeat later, the dogs were howling, bursting into their line of sight.

The dogs were huge—monstrous creatures that Evan had never seen before. They were like pit-bulls the size of Great Danes.

Evan brought the rifle up to his shoulder, squeezed off a shot and smiled as the beast he had hit stumbled, but his smile was erased as the beast got back to its feet and started to run with his siblings once more. Evan turned to tell his friends to run, but they had already done so.

Miserable bastards, Evan thought. With that thought in his mind, he started running northwest, and he kept running, for the hounds seemed to be searching for them all. A short time later, he found a good place to hide and did so, pulling ferns down onto him and settling in just under a thick, rotted dead tree. It definitely wasn't the best there, but it would certainly work for his needs. A few hours of silence and he'd be ready to go.

For two hours, Evan kept silent, watching and listening.

His breathing was slow and regular, his finger loose on the trigger. He had the area in front of him covered from his position, and he knew that he'd have to wait until later before he could move out and head towards town.

So he waited.

And he waited.

Then he heard the noise of the dogs—a combination of barking and baying that set his teeth on edge and urged him to flee as quickly as he could. However, Evan steeled himself and kept his cool, concentrating on his breathing, watching and waiting.

In three minutes, the dogs were there, fifty yards out. They were chasing Mitch.

Mitch staggered and bounced off of a tree. His face was bloody, eyes wide and white in a mask of blood. Mitch bore an expression of pure fear.

The dogs howled joyfully.

They were going to eat Mitch alive.

Evan started to squeeze the trigger—

Mitch fell, and the dogs were upon him.

Evan sighed, relaxed his finger. He watched the dogs devour Mitch, whose agonized screams lasted only a few minutes.

And Evan waited.

Chapter 30: Erin and Klaus at the Bus Stop

Erin Harper had a delayed schedule at the Hollis Co-Operational High School, which meant that she could do her online studying for her advanced college classes in the morning. Unfortunately, her little Volkswagen bug had died over the summer, and they hadn't been able to fix it, so now she had to take a bus to school.

She waited at the end of her driveway, which was shared with her family and the Totenbuch family. The Totenbuch family had a son named Klaus, who also had a delayed schedule. He was a quiet, unassuming boy with round glasses and shaggy black hair. He looked like a tall, German version of Harry Potter, although without the magical ability—or any social skills.

Klaus would say hello to her, and goodbye, but only if Erin initiated it. He always wore a white button down shirt, some sort of vest since the cold weather had started, and jeans with Dr. Martens. His backpack was large and seemed to pull at him. He also stank of pipe tobacco.

Erin knew that he didn't smoke—Klaus's father never seemed to stop smoking, however—but evidently no one in the house noticed the smell.

Other kids at school did, and Klaus had been christened with the unfortunate nickname of 'The Stinky German,' a name which did nothing for him, especially since he was a live action role-player too. No, the boy was a total reject on all levels of the social spectrum at the high school.

The bus, though, was supposed to pick them up at 10:30 AM.

The bus was late.

Erin couldn't call her mother because she worked in Nashua and left the house at five-thirty each morning. Since her parents were divorced, her father lived in Manchester and saw her on the weekends. That is, he did when he could be bothered to. Klaus' parents had left for Germany for a week. Erin had learned that from her mother, who had been asked by Christiana, Klaus's mother, to check up on him while they were away.

Thankfully, Erin didn't have to accompany her mother on the excursions over to Deutschland.

"The bus isn't coming," Klaus said suddenly, breaking the silence.

Erin took one of her ear buds out of her ear. "It doesn't seem like it."

"Something's wrong," Klaus said.

"How do you know?" she asked, trying to keep the dismissal out of her voice.

Klaus pointed, and Erin looked.

Towards the center of town, the air was filled with gray and black smoke.

"We should go inside," Klaus said. "This will not end for us well if we do not."

"Okay," Erin said, nodding, "yeah. Let me call my mom." She took her phone out of her back pocket and went to dial. There were no bars on the phone.

That was ridiculous, Thorne had one of the best reception areas out there. Erin tried to dial, but she didn't even get a dial tone on the phone. Frowning, she put the phone away.

"It is as I thought," Klaus nodded. "You are welcome to come to my home, Fraulein Harper."

She smiled, thinking, *oh hell no*. "No thanks," Erin said aloud, "but thank you."

He gave her a short bow. "If you need me, please call. I believe that your mother has our telephone number."

Erin smiled again and turned away, putting the ear bud back in. Taylor Swift came in full volume, and Erin walked up the driveway, not focused on anything other than getting back inside. She could do more homework on her college classes, which was great, but she was going to miss out on her Latin and history classes, both of which were taught by Dr. Kendall, and which she actually enjoyed.

Plus, she was going to have to try and call her mother from the landline and hope that it was working. She had little faith in the landline and couldn't figure out why her mother always wanted one in the house. The cell phone was usually far more reliable than the landline, especially in the winter when the snow would knock the telephone and power lines down every couple of weeks.

Erin turned up the walkway and then around the side of the house. She took her key out, unlocked the door, and went inside. She dumped her bag on the kitchen table and walked over to the old yellow rotary phone attached to the wall by the fridge. Why her mother kept the thing around, Erin would never understand. It was annoying to use and sounded terrible when it rang.

She picked up the heavy receiver and held it to her ear.

Nothing. No dial tone.

Sighing, she hung up the phone and noticed suddenly that the fridge was quiet. She pulled the fridge door open and saw that it was dark inside.

Fantastic, she sighed, quickly closing the door.

No service, no landline, no power, she thought. *This is going to be a great day at home,* she thought sarcastically.

Groaning, she walked back to her bag, dug out, *The Moon is Down* by John Steinbeck, which Dr. Kendall was having them read for history, and made her way into the den. The room was gently lit by the sun, and Erin settled in on the couch. The cat came in, meowed at her once, and then he wandered away.

Erin shook her head and opened the book to the first page.

Something banged heavily on the front door, scaring Erin into a sitting position.

Maybe it's Klaus, she thought.

Something banged on the door again, and she could see the door shake in its frame.

That's not Klaus.

Slowly, she got off of the couch and started walking out of the room, when the glass in the back door shattered. Erin screamed, and pleased laughter came out of the kitchen. The front door came crashing in, knocked free of its hinges. The steel door bounced off of the wall and slammed onto the floor.

They came in, one from the front door's gaping doorway, the other from the kitchen.

They were tall and thin, faces vaguely human in shape, but their eyes looked like cats' eyes. They wore loose robes with mottled colors of the forest, greens and browns that would have hidden them easily. Their hair was long and brown, twigs and leaves woven into them. The skin of these things looked like the bark of trees, and as they laughed, Erin saw that their mouths were barren of both teeth and tongues.

Erin held back a scream and stepped back towards the wall. She kept her head—which she suddenly realized was one of Kipling's key points in the poem 'If'—and wondered if she had time to unlock the window that she was approaching. Before she could formulate an idea as to whether or not she could, a shape came hurtling into the house through the front doorway.

It was Klaus.

Klaus with a sword.

A *sword.*

It was an old sword, and Klaus used it like it was a part of him, as cheesy as it sounded. He was phenomenal with the weapon, and within seconds, Klaus had literally hacked the thing to pieces, a black ichor spraying out of the thing's body, arms cut off and falling to floor before the thing itself did.

Then he and the second thing fell upon each other, Klaus roaring, literally roaring at the thing in German.

The thing stumbled back, howling in German and raising its arms up in defense, an action which only served to allow Klaus to cut off the left arm before driving the point of the sword home into the thing's breast.

Silently it died, and Klaus used his free hand to push it off.

"KommenSie, Fraulein Harper," Klaus said, looking at her and extending his hand. "We need to leave. Quickly. There are more coming. We must leave."

"What are they?" Erin asked, hurrying over to him and taking his hand.

"Holzmenschen," Klaus said, leading her to the front door. "Wood people. They have no love for us. We must find a place of safety."

"Town hall," Erin said, "if we can make it there. There's food. Water. Lots of supplies."

"Sehr gut, sehr gut," Klaus said nodding. Still holding hands they raced down the walkway to the driveway.

"Not the road," Erin said, pulling him towards a slim path that stretched off to the right before the driveway intersected with the road. "We'll keep to the woods. They're probably setting the houses on fire."

Klaus nodded his agreement, letting go of her hand so she could lead the way.

"Where did you find the sword?" she asked over her shoulder.

"My father's collection," Klaus answered.

"What does your father do?" Erin asked. She had known at one point but could no longer remember.

"He is a professor of classics," Klaus answered. "He collects them as well."

"What type of sword is it?"

"A gladius," Klaus replied.

"Gladius? Isn't that a Latin word?"

"It is," Klaus said. "And this is a Roman sword. One of those which helped to conquer the world."

"I can believe that," Erin said. "I can certainly believe that."

She led them deeper into the woods.

Chapter 31: At the Blood House

"It's getting close to the time," Morgan said, and nearly scared Jim to death. "Sorry," Morgan said.

"That's alright," Jim said, trying to catch his breath. Fred came in from the kitchen with a trio of coffee mugs.

"Hello Morgan," Fred said.

"Hello Fred," Morgan said cheerfully, sitting down on the stairs that led up to the second floor.

Fred handed Jim a cup of coffee, which he gratefully accepted. The older man then walked over to where Rose Mary sat, asleep in a wing-back chair with Gwen sleeping in her arms. The cleaver was on the coffee table in front of her. Fred set the mug down on a coaster in front of the woman before going to a second wing-back chair and sitting down in it. His rifle lay on the floor beside him.

The smell of the coffee alone awakened Rose Mary, and she looked around, confused for a moment. She blinked, stifled a yawn, and smiled at the coffee. With a skill only mothers seemed to have, she reached out with one hand, cradled Gwen and brought the coffee to her own lips.

The young mother sighed audibly and nodded her thanks to Fred.

"It's you!" she said cheerfully to Morgan.

He smiled, "It is."

Neither Jim nor Fred had had a chance to tell her the story of Morgan.

"Did the faeries tear your jacket?" she asked before blowing on her coffee.

"No," Morgan laughed. "This is my funeral jacket."

She took a sip of coffee, and it seemed to take a moment for that statement to sink in. When it did, her eyes widened, and she returned the coffee mug to the table. "Your funeral jacket?"

Morgan nodded happily.

"You're dead, aren't you?"

There was no question implied. Merely a stated fact.

Again Morgan nodded happily.

"And are there more ghosts out there?" she asked him.

"Seventy-one others," he nodded.

"Of course there are," she sighed.

"But," Morgan said, looking over to Jim, "we're getting close to the time."

"What time?" Jim asked him.

"When the faery folk will be able to leave. We're hoping that they won't be able to," Morgan continued, "that you'll have found something in that room."

"We did," Fred said. "We need five more people willing to sign a new contract in order to bind the faery folk within a ring."

"And of the seven of us," Jim said, "one of them will have to cast the rest of the spell from within the ring."

"But that will bind them in as well," Morgan said, looking upset. "They'd be stuck here with the faery folk."

"Yes," Jim said. "That's exactly what would happen."

"What are you talking about?" Rose Mary asked.

Fred briefly explained to her what it was that he had read in the book by the pool.

"Oh," she said afterward. "Wow."

Jim nodded.

"I'll sign," she said after a moment.

"You will?" Morgan asked her.

Rose Mary nodded. "Of course I will. I don't want this to spread."

"That's three of us," Fred said. He reached into his shirt pocket and took out a small folded piece of paper. "I wrote this down earlier," he said, handing it to Jim.

Opening the paper, Jim saw that it was a nearly identical copy of the Blood Contract. Where the names of the town's founders should have been, however, there was only Fred's. Glancing around, Jim saw a pen on the coffee table. He reached out, took up the pen, and put the paper on the table, signing it. He looked at Rose Mary, and she nodded, taking the pen from him and leaning over slightly to sign it.

"Now we only need four more," Jim said, holding the paper out to Fred.

Fred shook his head. "I lose everything. You hold onto it."

"You should go to the town hall," Morgan said as Jim folded the paper in his own pocket. "There are people there. But a great many of the faery folk are gathering around there as well."

Jim stood up and adjusted the knife and the sword on the gun belt. Fear and worry gnawed at him. The trip to the center of town wouldn't be more than two miles. But it would be two miles of faery-infested land that they would have to survive. He bent over and picked up his coffee from a side-table. Quietly, he finished it off and looked at Fred and Rose Mary. "Ready?"

Fred nodded, picking up his rifle and standing up.

"I just need a blanket to wrap Gwen in," Rose Mary said, standing as well, "then I'll be ready to go."

Chapter 32: 4:00 PM, Evan in the Forest

Evan carefully brought himself to a sitting position, and then he sat still for five minutes, listening intensely to the forest.

He heard nothing, which was both relaxing and frightening, the feelings twisting him into a knot. He hadn't heard the dogs for hours, and he liked it that way. However, Evan also feared that it meant the dogs had gotten to his friends.

With a slow, deliberate pace, he picked off the ferns before easing himself up to his feet. His body ached from the forced stillness, but it was better to be sore than to be dead, of that Evan was certain. He flipped the safety on for the rifle and slung it over his shoulder. There's no use carrying a weapon that wouldn't do anything against the dogs that had been, pardon the pun, hounding him and his friends.

The air had gotten remarkably colder, and he had to think about something other than the cold. He knew that he was only ten minutes out from Blood Road, but that wouldn't make the trip into town any easier, or any less stressful for that matter.

No, Evan just wanted to get it done and get into town—preferably before anything tried to eat him.

Evan stepped off smoothly and quietly, moving quickly through the darkening forest. He soon found himself along the edge of the woods and scenes of destruction. Seemingly no house was left untouched, some of them still burning. There were bodies on the ground, on manicured lawns and on asphalt roads. Cars and trucks were stopped, some still idling long after their occupants had fled or been butchered. Some of the vehicles were on their sides, half crushed, as if some giant thing had battered them around.

The sights were terrible, but Evan kept to the tree line, skirting through backyards and thin stretches of open ground that would send his heart racing.

And as he neared Main Street, he could hear them.

The dogs were howling, as were other things. He crept up slowly, having reached the last house before the pharmacy, and he managed to find a position where he could look upon Thorne's downtown and Town Hall.

Evan grit his teeth at the horror laid out before him.

Chapter 33: Town Hall, 4:30 PM

Philip sat by himself on the first floor, looking out the town clerk's window.

The scene on Main Street was horrifying.

A large fire had been built in front of the firehouse, and a spit had been set up over the fire itself. A giant, perhaps ten or twelve feet high, was slowly turning the spit while a trio of gutted men was bound to it. A female giant, her great breasts swinging with each step, stood close to the fire, mashing up something in a dumpster.

Off to the left, in front of Franceur's Bakery, goblins had gathered, dozens of them. They were keeping themselves entertained by eating baked goods as well as banging on a variety of musical instruments taken from Alex's Music Shop, and let's not forget, by forcing a couple of people to dance endlessly.

Crying started on the far right and Philip shifted his gaze to there.

Faeries were crossing the road. Small things, no bigger than three feet. They were wearing bright clothing that they had found somewhere—probably in the same houses from where they had stolen the children.

The faeries were carrying children, some under a year, some as old as four or five. Some of the children cried, but others simply walked along, stunned.

The wind shifted slightly, carrying to him the smell of the flesh roasting on the spit. He turned his head away and closed his eyes for a moment. The flesh smelled exactly like a pot roast slowly basting in its own juices.

With a sigh, Philip stood up and left the room, his stomach rumbling. He needed to find something to eat.

Walking down into the basement he looked around at the few survivors. Chris stood with the reverend, several women of various ages whom he didn't know, and the two men who had been guarding the door earlier. But guarding the door didn't seem to matter anymore. They all knew that the faeries out there would certainly come in whenever they wanted to.

Philip stopped by the boxes of bottled water and took one out, cracking open the top and taking a long drink. He'd have a meal shortly, but for now, just the water.

Although, he'd be happy with a few shots of vodka as well.

He went to an ancient-looking wooden folding chair and sat down, grunting as he settled in, taking another drink. The sun would be setting in another hour, hour and a half at max.

Night would come.

What would the faery folk do?

What would he do? Could they slip away, all of them at once? Would they have to leave singly or in pairs? Would someone panic and give the whole thing away? Would someone refuse to leave, try to stay behind and wait it out?

Philip shook his head.

It was one of those days when he really wished he'd made it to work at the garage so he could wrench on cars all day.

But that wouldn't have stopped what had happened—probably wouldn't even have slowed it down.

Chris came over, took out a chair, and sat down across from him. "How are you doing?"

Philip looked at the man. Chris was a psychiatrist or therapist or life coach or something in Nashua and Philip really didn't want any therapy or New Age bullshit, but hell, he could at least talk to the man.

"Tired," Philip said honestly. "Worried too. I'm worried about what's going to happen tonight."

"Tonight?" Chris asked.

"Tonight," Philip said again, nodding. "We need to try and figure out what we're going to be doing. Are we staying? Are we going?"

"Why tonight?" Chris asked, genuinely confused.

"Too easy for them not to. Perfect opportunity for them to take care of us."

"Oh," Chris said, rubbing the back of his neck nervously. "Oh."

Philip finished the bottle of water, crushed it loudly and put the cap back on. "I'll be right back," he said, standing up.

"What's that smell out there?" Chris asked. "It's driving me crazy. Smells, like they're, have a great big pot roast. I'm so damned hungry for a roast now."

"Well," Philip said, turning away from Chris, "don't eat that one."

"Why not?"

"Because that's the smell of people being cooked for someone's dinner."

Chapter 34: Erin and Klaus in the Pharmacy, 4:30 PM

Erin led Klaus around the back of the pharmacy, when suddenly, he stopped her.

She stopped immediately, looking back at him. Silently, he pointed forward, and Erin saw, in the growing shadows, the shape of a man lying down on the ground. Beyond him were Main Street and a nightmare that numbed her mind.

Then Klaus's lips were close to her ear.

"My friend," he said in a low whisper, "we mustn't be afraid. That man waits and so shall we, with him. We must crawl, though, yes?"

Erin nodded, and together the two of them got on the ground and started crawling towards the stranger. She nearly jumped as Klaus put his hand on her behind and pressed down. It took her a moment to realize that she was moving with her rear nearly straight up in the air, and that he wasn't being inappropriate.

She forced her hips to hug the earth. By the time they reached the shadow where the man was, the stranger had rolled silently to his side.

"Does that work?" the man whispered, nodding to the sword that Klaus carried.

"Ja," Klaus whispered back.

"He's great with it," Erin said softly.

The stranger smiled. "Good. Name's Evan."

"Erin," Erin said, "and this is Klaus."

"Sind SieDeutschlander?" Evan asked.

Klaus grinned, a great big grin and he nodded happily at Evan.

"Are we waiting for night?" Erin asked.

"That's what I wanted to do," Evan stated, "but I'm not sure now."

"No?"

Evan shook his head. "The situation is looking worse. I'm wondering if someone might try to make a run for it. I think that tonight is going to be bad for whoever is in there."

"Yes," Klaus said. "They will move in tonight. They'll try to flush the people within out. They will send in the giants, around three sides, you see, and force the people out through the front and into the arms of the goblins. The people will feel that they have a better chance against the goblins. It will be a rationale of fear."

Evan nodded. "That sounds dead on."

"So," Erin said, looking out once more, "we'll need to open a path through the goblins for them."

"Das istsehr gut, Fraulein Harper," Klaus said. "Very good indeed."

"Well," Evan said, focusing on the street again, "let's try to think of what we can do."

Then the three of them grew silent, listening to the horror of the street beyond and thinking of what it was they might be able to do.

Chapter 35: Jim, Fred, Rose Mary, and Gwen at the Cottage

"Look," Fred said softly, pointing across the street at the pharmacy.

Jim caught the faintest hint of two people moving, and then they disappeared, dropping down and out of sight.

"Definitely not faeries," Rose Mary said. Gwen was against Rose Mary's chest, swaddled and held in place by a blanket. Gwen had a pacifier in her mouth and was looking up happily at her mother.

"No," Jim agreed. "Definitely not."

The four of them were in the front yard of a modest little New England cottage, sitting behind a row of short hedges with an angled view of downtown. They could see the town hall, Main Street, and the pharmacy. The goblins had stopped tormenting the people they had captured, and Jim wasn't sure if the people were dead or simply exhausted.

The giants, in turn, were fighting over their rather disturbing rotisserie, and the sound of bones tearing out of joints actually reached the front yard. Regardless of the sound, the smell was disturbingly good.

Jim tried not to think about it.

"What do you think we should do?" Rose Mary asked.

"We should wait," Fred said, his eyes never leaving Main Street. "Those three by the pharmacy have the right idea."

"Three?" Jim asked, looking over to Fred.

Fred nodded. "I saw the glint of light off of gun metal. There's no mistaking it. Someone else is there, and the three of them have decided to wait."

"For what?" Rose Mary asked.

"The people in the town hall to make a decision," Fred answered.

"I didn't see any people," she said.

Neither did I, Jim thought, looking back at the building. Boards had been nailed up over the inside of the windows, and he suspected that the front door was barred from the inside, but that hadn't meant that anyone was still alive in there.

"Every once in a while a shape will pass by a window, specifically the one to the left of the door on the first floor," Fred said. "Add to that the smoke that occasionally comes out of the vent pipe on the roof. That means someone's in there to monitor the heat. And, finally, the door's closed. The few houses that we saw where the faeries had been through, well, they hadn't bothered to close the doors."

"True," Jim said, shaking his head. "Hell, I'm supposed to be a cop, and I didn't notice any of that."

"So," Rose Mary said, "what do you think they're waiting for?"

"I think the people in town hall are waiting for night. They'll think it's the best time to make a run for it. Pretty sure, though," Fred continued, "that the faeries will think that it's a grand time to force them out. Either way, something'll happen—more than likely right after night falls."

"Well," Jim sighed, looking at the darkening sky, "we shouldn't have to wait too long then."

Chapter 36: Brian and the Dead

Brian zipped up and walked back to his cruiser. Around him, the Blood dead were gathering, dozens of them of all ages. They stood in silence, adding a deep chill to the air as the sun continued its descent.

"It won't be long now," Hollis Blood said. He stood by the cruiser, hands folded neatly over the top of his cane.

"No?" Brian asked.

"No," Hollis answered. "When they come, we will take care of the exit."

Brian looked over at him, wanting to ask what the hell the ghost meant, but then he didn't. The man was dead. Brian was literally speaking with a dead man. He could cut himself some slack in regards to questioning current events.

"We need you to be prepared to help those that come through," Hollis continued. "Morgan told us that the key is to have another contract drawn up. We will have to protect them while it is written and signed. Will you be able to help, Sheriff Ricard?"

"Yes," Brian said simply. He looked out at the barricade of trees. "Yes."

Chapter 37: Night Falls

With the coming of night, all hell broke loose in Thorne, New Hampshire.

***

"You have to leave," Philip said to those gathered around him in the basement of the town hall. He tried to keep the anger out of his voice, but as he buttoned his flannel jacket, his shaking hands betrayed him.

"We can't," the Reverend said. "We just can't. It's safe here. The National Guard will be here soon."

"Soon isn't going to come soon enough for us," Philip snapped, his patience gone. "Anyone who stays here is going to die."

Philip looked at Chris, but the man looked away.

"Jesus Christ," Philip spat, "listen—"

And the walls of town hall started shaking, deep, terrible voices howled, and Philip knew that the giants were attacking the building, seeking a way in.

"We have to go!" he screamed.

The rest of them, though, fled further back into the basement.

Philip dropped his rifle and ran up the stairs towards the front door.

There was nothing banging at the front door, and he knew instantly that it was a trap, all of it. He didn't have a choice, though.

He had no choice at all.

Bending down, he picked up the drill and started taking the screws out of the barrier.

***

"It's happening," Erin said softly.

Klaus and Evan rolled over and looked out at Main Street.

The giants ran, the ground shaking as they surrounded the sides and the back of the house. The great beasts started hammering away at the walls, yelling so loudly that Erin's ears hurt. Goblins gathered around the front of town hall, forming a semicircle around the stairs.

"It is time," Klaus said, standing up, rolling his shoulders back and forth, and swinging the sword with ease. "It is time."

The German teenager looked down at them both. "Be ready to help whoever comes out, yes?"

Erin nodded.

"Sehr gut," Klaus said, and he started walking towards the goblins, the noise of his approach drowned out by the howling of the giants.

***

"Someone's moving," Fred said.

Jim and Rose Mary looked out. In the light of the bonfire, they saw someone approaching the gathered goblins from behind as the door to Town Hall opened. A howl of joy rose up from the goblins, and they started jumping up and down happily.

"Move down to the pharmacy," Fred said, and it was an order, polite but firm. The man stretched out on the ground, his clips on a clean patch of grass, his rifle aimed downtown.

Jim and Rose Mary got to their feet, Rose Mary double checking that Gwen was still sleeping, and then they hurried towards the pharmacy as a goblin shrieked.

***

Klaus killed the first two goblins with ease, the beasts never seeing him as he managed to strike from behind, yet as the door to the town hall opened and a man came leaping down the stairs, Klaus's third target turned at the wrong moment. Klaus killed the thing, but it was a messy kill, and the thing managed to shriek before dying, which alerted its foul brethren to Klaus's presence.

The goblins were shocked, their weapons sheathed or set aside in anticipation of grabbing hold of those who would escape. Klaus killed the next pair neatly and efficiently.

Then the goblins near him turned on him completely, even as the others surged towards the sole runner.

A rifle cracked in the distance, and Klaus was surprised but pleased when a goblin's chest burst open directly in front of him.

The goblins faced towards the sound of the gunshot as more broke through the violence of the night, and Klaus raised his blade and began killing once more.

***

Philip didn't know who was shooting, or how the shooter's rifle was effective against the damn things, but he didn't care.

He was running straight towards the teenager with the sword.

The kid was sprayed with dark blood, and he looked absolutely thrilled to be butchering the little goblin bastards, and Philip thought that was a great thing.

But it was time to leave.

"Run!" Philip screamed. "I'm the only one!"

The teenager gave him a curt nod, finished off another goblin, then turned and started sprinting towards the pharmacy. The tempo of the rifle fire increased, but Philip didn't look back.

He simply raced after the teen.

***

"Hey," Jim said as he and Rose Mary approached the pharmacy from the back.

A teenage girl and a man in his twenties whipped around to face them.

"Who the hell is shooting?" the young man asked. "And how is the weapon working? My rifle didn't do anything."

"Too long to tell," Jim said, drawing the knife and stepping close to hand it to him. "You can use this?"

"Definitely," the young man said, shucking his rifle and dropping it.

Jim turned to the teenager. "Don't suppose you can use a sword can you?"

She grinned, "Three years of fencing."

A moment later, she had the sword in her hand and was checking the swing. "Beautiful," she sighed happily.

"Run!" someone yelled from the street, "I'm the only one!"

Jim and the others turned to look. The man with the sword killed another goblin, then turned and started running, another man close behind him. Fred's rifle fire increased, his accuracy remaining the same.

There was only the slightest of pauses, and then the firing resumed.

Jim drew his pistol as the teenager with the sword and the other man went running by, and started firing at the goblins racing after them.

Each shot found its mark and as goblins closed in, the others started fighting as well. Someone started yelling in German, and beyond the pharmacy, the windows of the town hall started shattering as boards fell to the pavement.

Within moments it was done.

Jim, panting, looked around. No one was hurt, but the ground was littered with goblin corpses.

"The giants," the boy with the sword said with a German accent, "they will be after us soon."

"Not what I'm worried about, kid," the man with the knife said, "the dogs."

Jim was about to ask what dogs when he heard them, great barking things whose cries echoed off of the buildings.

Then Morgan was there, his pale face serious.

"Run," he said, "run for Gilson Road."

***

Fred heard the dogs and held his fire. He had twenty rounds left overall. Not nearly as much as he'd like, but enough to do some more damage.

He could still remember the drill instructors on Parris Island hammering home the importance of shooting properly, and Fred did remember. Every shot he fired was a killing shot, but now he had to wait for the dogs.

The others wouldn't be able to outrun the dogs, especially not dogs of a supernatural nature.

So he waited.

The wait wasn't long.

Half a dozen of the creatures came streaming out from between the music shop and an insurance office. They were followed by what looked like an English gentleman riding on the back of a disturbingly large goat.

Fred ignored the frightening absurdity of it all, sighted on the galloping Englishman and shot him out of the saddle. The goat peeled off, and as Fred had hoped, the dogs were ignorant of their master's death. Working from the rear of the pack, Fred killed four more, and as he was reloading, the last two dogs stopped, suddenly realizing that the rest of their pack was missing.

As the dogs trotted back to examine the dead, Fred killed them both.

Screams rose up from Town Hall as the giants broke through.

Fred stood, gathered the remainder of his ammunition and headed back the way he had come.

**

Brian watched in silent amazement as the ghosts disassembled the section of the barricade which covered Gilson Road.

"They'll be here soon," Hollis said from beside him.

"Who?"

"The survivors."

How many? Brian asked himself silently. And would Jim Petrov be among them? Would Scott?

Brian held no hope for either of them. He didn't know how anyone could survive if even a tenth of the phone calls had been true, but of course, they had to be true. He was standing here with the dead.

Soon, the ghosts had cleared the road, leaving open both lanes for the fleeing survivors.

Brian walked towards the opening and folded his arms across his chest and waited.

**

How any of them made that final run, Jim didn't think that he would ever know. How Rose Mary made the run, with Gwen crying against her chest and a meat cleaver in her hand, he would never know.

Soon, though, they were nearing the town line, and the

barricade of trees had been moved. The blue flashing lights of a cruiser lit up the night, and Jim could make out the shape of a man.

Brian. Brian Ricard.

Brian was running towards them, helping Rose Mary to the cruiser while the rest of them stumbled into the shifting, twisting arc of illumination cast by the lights.

"We need four people to sign this," Jim gasped at Brian, pulling the folded contract out of his pocket.

Brian took a pen out of his pocket as he opened the page. A boy with a sword stood up, having heard Jim.

"Here," the teenager said, "I will sign."

Brian brought the paper and the pen to the boy as a teenage girl stepped up beside him. The boy moved slightly so the girl could read the paper as well, and then the boy and the girl each signed it in turn.

An unarmed man wearing a battered flannel jacket walked up, looked at the paper, and held his hand out wordlessly to the girl. She handed him the pen and as he signed, the last man, carrying a wicked-looking knife came up, accepted the pen from the other man and signed as well.

"Where's Fred?" Jim asked.

Brian looked over at him. "Who?"

"Fred?"

***

Fred stood near the pool, in front of the door, which was open. The key which he had stolen from Jim was in the lock, and Fred held the book that he had read only hours earlier.

A whisper came rippling through the forest and the dead boy Morgan was there.

"The last of them has signed," Morgan said.

Fred nodded, opened the book, and with the light of the stars he read: "*Et ego erudivieostevinctossic ego.*"

The world shifted and far beyond, in the center of Thorne, Fred heard the faeries scream out their outrage.

Morgan smiled at Fred, and Fred smiled at Morgan.

Closing the book, Fred turned and walked into the curious cave, removing the key from the lock and closing the door behind him.

Epilogue: One Year Later

Scientists were still trying to figure out what had happened to the town of Thorne. No one could understand what had caused trees to be uprooted and to form a strange barrier around the town. Some people had attempted to push the State and Federal governments to investigate, but both governments had refused. At least two independent investigative news teams had attempted to discover what had happened to the three hundred and forty-seven missing residents of Thorne.

Neither of the teams, which had slipped over the jersey barriers placed across the sole remaining road into Thorne, had been heard from again.

There were, of course, rumors of a government experiment gone wrong, which caused the death of the residents and poisoned the town, making it unfit for human inhabitation. Others believed that this was the case, and that the news teams were killed for trying to find out what had happened.

A State sanctioned search party went in after each team, yet nothing was found of the reporters and their crews. There was no secret memory card or tape found containing the reasons why—no last video journals.

The news teams—eight men and three women—had simply vanished. Eventually, their cars were towed away.

Theirs were not the only cars, however.

Others came seeking the mystery behind the destruction and abandonment of Thorne. Some never returned, although others did make it into the town and came back. Those that did return said that their various electronic devices were rendered useless during their time in the mysterious circle of trees.

What they had seen in the town had changed them.

Few of the buildings were still standing, and on Main Street they found the remains of large bonfires and the gnawed and broken bones of people. They also reported that the trees lining Gilson Road had human skulls nailed to them.

Jim Petrov and the other five signers of the contract knew all of this. Jim and Evan and Philip had actually been the ones to nail the skulls to the trees. Rose Mary had built dozens of disrupters, which Erin and Klaus had placed in the barrier around the entire perimeter, each connected to a solar-powered battery. These simple devices ensured that no recording equipment or cell phones would work properly within the faery confinement area. None of the signers of the contract were responsible for the deaths, however.

The faeries took care of that.

On the one-year anniversary of their escape from Thorne, the six of them sat in Jim Petrov's new house on the edge of the perimeter on Gilson Road. Brian Ricard was there as well, having full knowledge as to what had occurred. All of them were gathered in Jim's den with after-dinner coffees, yet this wasn't a mere social gathering.

"Have you spoken with Fred?" Jim asked Klaus.

"Yes," the young man said. His voice still had a hint of a German accent. Klaus adjusted his arm slightly, Erin slipping in closer to him. "Erin and I spoke with him on Saturday. We made it all the way to the pool and found him. He was pleased that the note he had thrown over the barrier on the road had been found. Thus, we brought to him those things which he had requested, the books and ammunition."

"Good," Jim said. "What's the word with rumor control, Phil?"

Philip grinned. "Good. The garage is a great place to spread information. Lots of tourists have the bright idea of trying to go through Thorne. I dissuade most of them, but a few get through," he said, the grin fading. "Those I feel pretty bad about. I wish that I could get all of them to stop."

"I know," Jim said, nodding. "Try not to worry too much about it, Phil, we can't stop them all. Rose Mary, what about any new electronics? I know that you were looking for a way to shut down onboard computers for the newer cars."

"I'm still looking," she said, sighing. "The tech's out there, but the Feds have most of it watched. I've got feelers out, but I have to wait until someone contacts me."

"Evan?" Jim said, looking at the man.

"Still patrolling the perimeter at night," Evan said, stifling a yawn. "Every once in a while I'll get a goblin troop that comes a little too close, but a few rounds from the Colt usually settle that business. Most of them are too afraid to come to the barrier now. With Phil spreading the bad news about the barrier and the faery folk kept away from it, well," Evan grinned, "I think that we'll keep accidental sightings to a minimum."

"Good," Jim said. He looked over at Brian. "And politics?"

"Politics is politics," Brian said simply. "We were fortunate that the few descendants of the original signers have as much political pull as they do. Without them, we'd never have been able to shut the world out. As of last week, Senator Copp from Massachusetts managed to get Thorne designated a National site, and Governor Hall of New Hampshire is going to have Thorne listed as a permanent monument. Judge Coffin has also managed to deny the release of any information on Thorne by way of Homeland Security."

"So we're covered," Jim said, "all the way around for now."

"What about the giants?" Evan asked. "What's going on with them? I know that they're kept back by the barrier, but we don't need someone sneaking around the perimeter and spotting one."

"Don't worry too much about them," Jim said. He put his coffee down on the coffee table and stood up. He walked across the den to the bookcases lining the far wall. He moved a small clock and pressed a switch. As he pulled his arm back, the wall started sliding to the right.

"Fred's been busy," Jim said, smiling grimly, "very, very busy."

Revealed by the moving wall was a large trophy case made of dark mahogany and museum-quality glass. Warm lights spilled down from recesses in the ceiling upon six massive, roughly human-looking skulls which had been boiled white. The skulls of the giants stared emptily out from the case with their death's head grins, a bullet hole in the center of the head.

"Damn," Evan said softly as the others murmured, "I guess Fred really has been busy."

* * *

Bonus Scene Prologue: Darkness in New England

There is an old and seemingly eternal darkness that resides and infects New England. You can find it anywhere, tucked into the culverts of brooks, amongst the apple trees, and even in the clear and quiet glens of the forest.

Ancient in their ways, we are less than nothing to these things, and indeed at times we are nothing more than a convenient meal which has walked into their kitchen.

All we can do is take heed of those who know better, and caution our children to do the same.

Bonus Scene Chapter 1: Old Man Copp in the Orchard, 1976

"What the hell is wrong with these trees?" Peter asked.

Dan shrugged, backing the car onto the dirt drive that branched off of Farley Road. The sun was just beginning to set, the Ford's engine running rough at idle as Dan put it into park.

"Hey," Peter said, looking at Dan. "Those trees don't even have any apples on them."

"I know, I know," Dan said, pulling the latch for the trunk so that it popped open. "I'm telling you, though, the best apples in Cross are from the Blood family's orchard."

"I don't know," Peter said, looking at the barren, twisted trees lining the drive, "these trees look like shit, man. And that's not really getting my hopes up for any good apples."

"Shut up and get out of the damn car," Dan sighed. He left the car idling and the door open as he walked around to the back. Peter met him there, and they each pulled a surplus Army duffel bag out of the cluttered trunk.

"You ought to clean this," Peter said.

"You should shut up," Dan replied.

Peter shook his head. "So, just windfall?"

"Yup," Dan nodded. "I'll pick the fresh stuff. Just make sure you fill that bag. I want to get as much for hard cider as we can."

"Me too," Peter said.

Dan led the way into the orchard with Peter following. They passed by rows of truly ancient apple trees. The boughs were heavy with age and absent of fruit, each aged branch hanging low, caressing the grass with each breeze. Gnarled branches and twisted trunks took on sinister appearances as the sun set. Peter felt a growing sense of unease, as though the trees were watching him. He kept close to Dan as they moved further in.

The old trees were quickly replaced though with younger ones, and soon the sweet smell of McIntosh apples was filling the cool, autumn air. Most of these trees, Peter saw, had been picked bare, and the windfall had long since been gathered up early on in the season.

Dan, Peter noticed with relief, kept on a straight track as they walked deeper into what was easily the largest orchard that he'd ever been in.

"Hey, what about the Old Man?" Peter asked suddenly,

glancing behind him.

"What? Old Man Copp?" Dan asked, looking back at Peter.

Peter nodded. "I heard he's a son of a bitch. That the Bloods pay him to run off anyone that even comes near to the orchard."

"Nothing to worry about," Dan grinned, turning his attention back to the trees. "Guy's like sixty or seventy, or something. Pretty sure he's not patrolling the orchard with a shotgun or anything. Besides, I don't think he's going to be too upset about a couple of bags of apples, so don't be such a bitch."

"I don't know, man," Peter said. "Some of the farmers in Massachusetts get pretty upset if you're caught stealing apples."

"New Hampshire isn't that uptight," Dan chuckled. "And besides, things are pretty low key in Thorne. I've been doing field work for the Gauthiers out on Ridge Road since sixty-five. Things are pretty mellow."

Peter looked back again over his shoulder. Something didn't feel right, no matter what Dan said.

Soon they passed a gap in the trees. There were large, dark holes in the earth where trees had once stood.

"Careful," Dan said, giving the holes a wide berth.

"Thanks."

They walked for a good five minutes, the sky getting darker when Peter stopped and said, "Dan."

"What?" Dan asked, turning around and stopping.

"Did you bring a flashlight?"

"Why would I need a—" Dan's voice trailed off as he looked up at the sky, swearing.

It was a moonless night, and it would be pitch black in the orchard.

"Yeah," Peter said.

"Don't sweat it," Dan said after a moment. "We'll have enough starlight to get back."

Dan set off again and with a shrug Peter followed. They walked for a few more minutes before coming to trees with fruit on the lower branches. Reaching up Dan plucked an apple and tossed it to Peter.

"Take a bite of that," Dan said, opening his duffel bag and putting it on the ground.

Peter caught the apple easily, giving it a quick wipe on his sweatshirt. He took a big bite and tasted the sweetest McIntosh he'd ever had. "Wow," he said as he chewed.

"Right?" Dan laughed, picking apples as quickly as he could.

"Damn right," Peter said. He finished the apple in a few bites, tossing the core into the distance and smacking his lips. Grinning at the taste which lingered on his tongue Peter opened his own bag and began gathering up windfall.

"Hey," Peter said after a minute.

"Yeah."

"Have you ever made Apple Jack before?"

"No. Don't think I've even had it," Dan answered.

"It's good," Peter said. "Takes a while to make it, though. It's got to sit for a long time."

"Yeah?"

"Yeah. I've had it, just never made it," Peter said. "Don't like waiting."

"Right." Dan moved to another nearby tree, dragging the nearly full bag with him. "How are you doing?"

"About there," Peter said.

"Me too."

"Maybe we can hit the Indian Leap on the way back into town?"

Dan laughed.

"What?" Peter asked, stuffing in the last apple and zipping up the bag.

"You."

"What about me?

Dan zipped up his bag. "You're sweet on the bartender."

"So?"

"Nothing," Dan grinned, "it's just funny to watch."

"Let's go," Peter snapped, picking up his bag.

"Don't get—"

A loud click cut Dan off.

Peter turned around slowly and saw an old man standing in the fading twilight. He held an obscenely large double-barrel shotgun, both of the hammer's cocked. In his lips, the old man held the stem of a straight briar pipe, smoking casually as he watched them.

"Boys," the old man said softly, "this ain't loaded with rock salt."

Peter looked nervously to Dan.

"Look," Dan said.

The old man shook his head, his long white beard twitching. "Don't really want to look at a couple of thieves."

"They're just apples," Dan said.

"They're just Hollis Blood's apples," the old man corrected.

"How about we just put the bags down, and we'll call it even?" Dan asked.

"Not quite," the old man said. "But you will put the bags down."

Peter and Dan dropped the bags simultaneously, the thuds ringing out loudly.

"Walk," the old man said.

"Which way?" Dan asked, his voice cracking.

"The way you came."

Peter's heart hammered in his chest as they walked, his skin crawling at the realization that there was a loaded shotgun pointed at his back. He had no doubt that the old man would use it. The old man might be in his sixties, but he didn't move or act like it. He'd crept right up on them, right through the orchard—

"Stop," the old man said.

Peter and Dan stopped instantly.

Looking around nervously Peter saw the trees bending in the wind—Peter shook his head.

There is no wind, he thought. *How the hell are they moving?* He looked around and saw that he was standing by the holes they had passed earlier and that young apple trees were moving towards them.

The ground rippled like water, roots appearing and disappearing in the earth which frothed and rolled around the trees as they came steadily on. Peter felt his eyes widen, unable to look away from the sight of the moving trees. They were small, no fruit on their branches, just thin leaves.

"Get into a hole," the old man said.

"No way," Dan said, turning around.

One of the barrels of the shotgun seemed to explode, the muzzle flash lighting up the gathering trees.

Dan let out a scream, his right leg a bloody mess from the knee down as he fell to the grass. Keeping the shotgun trained on Peter the old man walked over to Dan and kicked him into the nearest hole, where he landed with a wheezing sob and a crash.

The old man turned his attention fully to Peter.

"In," he said.

Peter jumped into the nearest hole, which was almost six feet deep. The old man came to the edge and looked down. Dan's sobs were suddenly muffled, then silenced altogether. As Peter stood in the hole, he smelled the old man's pipe tobacco and apples. Peter wanted to ask what the hell was going on, but the old man's grim look and the dull sheen of the shotgun's barrels in the starlight kept him quiet.

Something rustled behind him, and Peter turned to see tree roots snaking out of the hole's earthen walls. Dirt started cascading down from the sides, quickly burying Peter up to his thighs as thicker, and longer roots appeared. Within a matter of moments, Peter could see one of the young apple trees as it pulled itself into the hole, earth and roots crashing onto him.

The weight was unbearable, blackness plummeting down around him. Peter struggled against it but found that he was trapped. While the dirt continued falling between the roots, Peter heard the old man.

"This is the best way to feed them, you know," the old man said. "The reason why Hollis' macs taste the best."

Peter heard the old man chuckle once before the dirt filled his ears, packing his mouth as he tried to scream.

Bonus Scene Chapter 2: Kayaking in Hassell Brook, 2010

"How far into New Hampshire do you think we are?" Ken asked, slowing his kayak down to glide beside Tim.

"A few miles at least. Maybe even five," Tim answered. The two of them kept a steady, leisurely pace, moving along with the current of the Nashua River. The banks were higher than usual, the water level low after such a dry summer. Fall wasn't looking to be any wetter. Birds and squirrels called out from the banks as Ken and Tim kept to the river's center, wary of trees and snags.

"Do you want to pull up soon?" Tim asked. "Figure out how far we are from Hassell Brook?"

"That sounds good," Ken said, scanning the banks for a good spot. "What time are we supposed to meet your cousin again?"

"Eleven o'clock," Tim answered. "She said to just give her a call, and she'd pick us up."

"Cool." Ken smiled at the scenery slipping past. The current was fast but not unmanageable. He and Tim had navigated worse. He kept his eyes open for a grassy spot to pull up. Everything was choked with swamp grasses and deadfall, though, and he didn't want a rough landing if he could help it.

"River's pretty quiet for a Saturday," Tim said.

"Well,   it   is   a   little   cold   today."

"Not that bad," Tim laughed. "You're out here."

"True," Ken grinned. "But soccer season's started, too."

"I keep forgetting," Tim said. "Both girls playing this year?"

"Yup," Ken nodded. "Brenda moved up to U-14, but Sam's still in U-12."

"Do they have games today?"

"Yeah," Ken said. "The ex is there this weekend. We split the games."

"Still tough?"

Ken nodded. "How are you and Melissa?"

Tim shrugged. "I think it's almost done. She's getting a little psychotic."

"How so?"

"Little things," Tim said. "I'll tell you more later. I think I found our spot," he said, pointing.

Ken looked and saw a narrow path through the swamp grass. The path of still water ran along to the bank where it widened into Hassell Brook, curled around a turn and vanished into the tree line.

"Does it look good?" Tim asked.

"That it does," Ken grinned. Dipping his oar into the water Ken guided the kayak into the path. Tim dropped into place behind him, the two of them moving cautiously forward. As they neared the mouth of the brook, Ken felt a slight current, and he smiled, pushing the oar a little deeper into the water.

The brook wound its way lazily into a forest, young trees growing on the banks, branches stiffening with the steady push of fall in the air. The leaves had already begun to change their colors, and as the wind blew a few of them drifted down to rest upon the surface of the water. The leaves drifted past Ken and Tim as they continued on, some of the leaves caught along the banks or made their way steadily towards the river.

Ken steered the kayak around a large branch and hooked to the left, where the young trees sharply and suddenly gave way to ancient oaks and elms. Giant weeping willows clung to the banks, the long branches moving gently with the breeze and rasping against the chain-link fence which crossed from bank to bank and disappeared into either side of the forest. A large 'No Trespassing' sign hung directly above the stream on the fence, and there was barely enough clearance for Ken to get under the fence without rolling the kayak.

He came to a stop, and Tim came up beside him.

"What do you think?" Ken asked.

"Hold on," Tim answered. He set his oar across his kayak, unzipped a pocket on his jacket and took a plastic bag with his phone in it out. Within a moment, he had the phone free of the bag, and he was pulling up his GPS. "Well," he said, "if we go about two hundred meters in it's only a quarter mile to Blackfoot Road in Thorne. I'm pretty sure that Anne can pick us up there."

"Sounds good to me," Ken said.

"Okay," Tim said. He secured his phone and put it away before taking up his oar again. "Lead the way, my friend."

Ken nodded and headed towards the fence. He kept to the left bank, where the fence was a little higher, and he bent low over the kayak, pulling himself ahead with careful strokes. Once he was clear, he paddled ahead to give Tim room to come through.

Around them, the forest sounded and felt different, as though it was older than they could know.

"This place is great," Tim said softly after a minute.

Ken could only nod his agreement. Taking a deep breath he sighed and said, "So, two hundred meters?"

"Yes, yes."

"Okay," Ken said. "Let's go."

The brook remained wide enough for them to paddle side by side. Just before they hit the two hundred meter mark, the brook took a sharp turn to the right, opening into a large pool dominated by a weeping willow. Shadows covered most of the pool, the sounds of fish hunting water bugs on the surface were loud in the stillness. Somewhere a turtle dropped noisily into the water as Ken and Tim steered the kayaks to a sandy patch of banking just beyond the weeping willow.

"Wow," Tim said as they climbed out of the kayaks, hauling them up onto the sand.

"I know," Ken said, looking around. "We need to remember this place," he said, looking over at Tim. "This would be a great place to camp."

Tim nodded.

"Want to—" a whimper cut Ken off.

Ken looked at Tim, who shook his head.

The whimper came again, followed by a splash.

Ken turned, trying to pinpoint the sound.

More splashing and a deep, sorrowful moan.

"I think it came from the tree," Tim said.

Ken nodded, cautiously walking along the banking towards the willow. The splashing took on an odd rhythm while the voice settled into a steady, plaintive cry. When he reached the willow, Ken pushed through the curtain of leaves and whip-like branches. The pool opened up even more around a cluster of water-worn boulders, and Ken's breath caught in his throat as Tim came through the willow's veil behind him.

Standing waist deep in the water was a pale woman. Her back was too thin, and she wore a faded gray dress, shapeless, torn and ragged. Thin, wispy hair hung in wet clumps to her back while stick-thin arms slammed something wet and limp against one of the boulders. The steady cry came from her, the sound pushing itself deep within Ken's chest.

Tim let out a low curse, and the woman heard him.

She turned slowly to face them. Her face was sunken, her eyes a pale white and her teeth a milky green. Her mouth hung slightly open, the cry steadily slipping out. She held her arms out in front of her, a soaking wet jacket clutched in each narrow hand.

"Jesus Christ," Tim said softly, "are those ours?"

Ken looked hard at the blue jacket in the woman's left hand and saw a tear. A small, inch-long tear he'd put in the jacket when they'd taken the kayaks off of the BMW earlier in the morning. Ken glanced down and saw that he was still wearing the jacket, the tear plain to see on the left arm.

"You have got to be kidding me," Ken whispered. His stomach twisted itself into a nasty little knot and bile rose to the back of his throat. "Tim," he said, not taking his eyes off of the woman, "we should probably get out of here."

Tim nodded, and the two of them started backing away. The woman turned back to the rocks, her cries becoming louder as she began slapping the jackets against the boulders once more. Passing through the branches Ken and Tim quickly turned back, walking hurriedly to the kayaks. The horrific noises of the woman convinced Ken that he hadn't imagined it. That and the pale, frightened expression on Tim's face.

"We need to get out of here," Ken said.

Tim only nodded his agreement.

Wordlessly the two of them climbed into their kayaks, quickly pushing off and moving with the current back towards the river. As they rounded the sharp turn which had opened to the pool, there was a loud crack, and Ken snapped his head up in time to see a great oak crashing towards them.

The tree smashed into both kayaks simultaneously, driving them under water and into the soft, sandy bed of the brook. Ken found himself trapped in the kayak, holding his breath as he tried to work his legs free. His face was just inches below the surface, and he could reach his wet hands into the crisp fall air to claw at the bark of the tree.

Growing frantic he looked around for Tim.

Tim sat limply in his kayak, head and hair moving gracefully with the current. Blackness edged Ken's vision, and his lungs screamed for air. He looked to the left for—

Ken screamed the last of his air into the cold water as the woman from the pool settled down on the brook's bed beside him. With an expression of great sympathy, she watched him take in great gulps of water, her long hands gently brushing the hair out of his eyes as she waited for him to drown.

Bonus Scene Chapter 3: Meeting the Baker, 2014

Joel put his truck into park and killed the lights before turning off the ignition. He stifled a yawn and stretched in the confines of the cab, looking at the horizon as dawn started to break. Unbuckling the seat-belt he opened the door and stepped out into the chill morning air, breathing in the deep scent of fall. The noises of the Chevy's engine cooling sounded loud in the morning's stillness.

Smiling, Joel took the keys to the back of the truck, tucking them into a small niche he'd made just for that purpose. From the bed of the truck, he picked up his hiking pack and pulled it on. He adjusted the straps, clipping them into place before he put on his knit cap and leather gloves. Flexing his fingers to loosen the leather he walked over to his toolbox and took out a pair of heavy-duty wirecutters.

With the tool in hand, he left the side of his truck and walked to the chain-link fence which ran the length of woods that he'd heard about from friends down in Massachusetts. The fence, which was surprisingly well kept, surrounded the hundreds of acres of old-growth forest in New Hampshire. Joel had heard that the land belonged to a family, although he didn't know them and didn't care to either.

As far as he was concerned, Joel thought as he stepped up to the fence, no state, and definitely no single family, should be allowed to keep that much of the environment locked away for themselves. It was disgusting, and a prime example as to how the rich had come so far from understanding anyone other than themselves.

Locking the old growth forest away was a crime against the people. And not only should it be illegal, but the people who did such things should be prosecuted for locking away the beauty of Mother Nature the way that they did.

Shaking his head and sighing Joel ignored the 'Warning' and 'No Trespassing' signs bolted to the fence. Whistling he started cutting the fencing along one of the posts, starting at the bottom. In a few minutes, he had the fence cut three-quarters of the way up, and he rolled it back before putting the cutters back in the truck. With a spring in his step Joel walked back to the fence, slipped through without the pack catching, and soon was standing up, rolling the fencing back into place.

Just to be on the safe side Joel took a couple of black zipties out of his back pocket and secured the fencing back to the post in a couple of places. He'd be able to cut through them easily when he was done with his weekend.

Taking a deep breath Joel double checked the straps on his pack, making sure that they were just right. Satisfied he glanced at the trees and saw a small game trail between a pair of elms. Nodding to himself Joel headed out along the trail.

His long legs moved him quickly along the path, which became wider the deeper he moved into the forest. The undergrowth fell away, the forest dark and barely touched by the rising sun. Boulders appeared, and birdsong filled the air. Acorns occasionally settled down, thrown by squirrels from massive oaks. The feeling of serenity and the soft sounds of nature settled over Joel, and he felt great as he moved, the burdens and worries of life falling away as he walked.

Soon Joel passed through a small clearing, the tree's branches forming a thick canopy above. Joel didn't stop, though. He wanted to be further in before setting up camp for the night.

Joel hiked for several more hours before finding the perfect site.

The forest fell away from a small brook, the water whispering around a trio of boulders nearly as tall as the trees. The earth around the near side of the brook was beaten down, and the remains of a tremendous bonfire occupied the center. Amongst the ashes were the charred and broken bits of deer bones.

The site was old and looked as though it hadn't been used in months. Safe enough for a single night.

Joel shucked his pack and gloves, rubbing his shoulders. The sun shined brightly above him, moving steadily towards noon. Leaving his gear near the ashes, Joel started wandering around the brook and boulders. He picked up deadfall and branches, carrying several loads to his gear and stacking them neatly. Within a short time, he had a good supply stocked. Turning his attention to his pack, Joel took out his one-man tent.

He put the tent up and sat down beside it. Pulling his pack close, Joel took out his food, some water and his copy of *The Woman in Black*. Joel tore open an energy bar and ate it slowly, washing every few bites down with some water. When he finished the bar he tucked the wrapper into his pack before stretching out on the ground. He read slowly, eventually taking off his cap and sweatshirt, balling them together to serve as a pillow while the day continued to warm up.

By the time, four o'clock rolled around a definite chill had settled into the air. Putting the book down, and the sweatshirt and cap back on, Joel started preparing the wood for the fire. Disgusted he pushed the deer bones to the edges of the pit, shaking his head at the deep gouge marks in the bone.

Savages, he thought. *Whoever the hell did this, that's all they are. Just savages.* And evidently he wasn't the only one who had ignored the fence. Joel just wished that it hadn't been hunters. The deer had enough problems with the coyotes coming down from Canada and the mountain lions creeping back up through the Berkshires.

Joel pushed those thoughts out of his mind and kindled the fire. He smiled as the flames grew, creeping up around the pyramid of wood. Heat slipped around him as evening came on steadily. Joel took out his dinner, a prepackaged vegetarian meal, and added wood to the fire, building it up. It wasn't nearly as large as the remains of the old fire, but it was bigger than most he'd built. He was deep in the forest, far from the road he'd parked his truck off of.

By the time the sun set, Joel had finished both his meal and the book. He rolled a joint, lit it off of a branch from the fire, and lay back, watching as the stars started populating the sky. His eyes grew tired from the heat of the fire and the grass. With one last pull, he flicked the roach into the flames and let the smoke out slowly.

Too bad Karen couldn't make this one, he thought with a sigh, closing his eyes.

The earth trembled slightly beneath him, and Joel's eyes opened.

The earth trembled again.

An earthquake? he thought, sitting up. He glanced nervously at the giant trees and stones bathed in flickering light.

Again the tremble, and something in the forest fell.

Joel tried to shake away his self-induced haze, forcing himself to think as another tremble rippled through.

That's no earthquake, he thought. *That's got a rhythm.*

He climbed to his feet. *What the hell is that?*

And his answer stepped out of the forest by the brook and came to a stop.

A giant stood opposite him, a man probably a dozen feet tall standing naked in the firelight. He carried a massive wooden cudgel, and coarse, dark hair covered his body. Black hair hung in dreadlocks to his chest and a braided beard reached nearly to his waist. His face was broad, the features thick and he broke into a smile when he saw Joel, his nostrils flaring.

The giant took a step forward, a tremor rippling through the ground.

Joel took a nervous step back, glancing left to right.

The giant chuckled.

"There is nowhere to run, little one," the giant said, his voice deep. "This is Jack's parcel of Blood's Forest, and none knows it better than Jack."

Jack advanced another step, and Joel retreated one as well. Jack swung his cudgel casually. "Which way shall you run, hmm, little one?" he asked. "Back the way you came? Or shall you run right, to the Goblins' Keep?"

Joel licked his lips nervously, his heart beating faster.

"Is it left then, little one, behind the Stones of Coffin's Stand to Blood's dark orchard?" Jack raised an eyebrow. "Or perhaps you shall run by me, into the forest's dark heart where things worse than old Jack await the sweet taste of man?"

"What are you?" Joel blurted out.

"What am I?" Jack chuckled. "I'm Jack, a humble baker."

"A baker?" Joel asked, his blood pounding in his ears.

"Yes, yes. A baker," Jack grinned. "You've not heard the rhyme then, little one?"

Joel shook his head, confused.

Jack laughed, broad yellow teeth catching the firelight. "I'm sure that you have, and you've just forgotten." In a singsong voice Jack called out softly, "Be he live or be he dead, I'll grind his bones to make my bread."

Joel stiffened the full horror of the situation rushing through him.

"See there, little one," Jack winked. "Now you remember. Old Jack's a baker."

Joel bolted.

He ran towards the giant, leaping the brook and cutting hard to the right to stay—

The cudgel caught him in the stomach. Joel folded over it, the breath rushing out of him as ribs cracked. He felt himself flying backward and in a moment he splashed into the brook. He struggled to stand, but Jack was there, plucking him out of the water. Pain ripped through Joel as Jack carried him to the fire. The giant dropped his cudgel to the ground. He started to casually peel Joel's clothes off of him.

Pain wracked Joel's body, but he couldn't move. He was terrified.

Jack made a neat pile of Joel's sopping wet clothes, and then he stood and held Joel at arm's length, examining him. Joel was limp in Jack's grasp, unable to bring himself to do anything.

Jack nodded and set Joel down, turning his attention to the fire. Pain spiked in Joel's ribs, and he shuddered, the pain jarring his mind out of shock.

Jack turned away to throw more wood on the fire, and Joel scrambled to his feet and ran.

He sprinted past the giant, aiming himself towards the game trail which he'd followed in the morning. In spite of the pain in his ribs, he rushed towards the
tree line.

And something struck him in the back of the knee, sending him rolling onto the hard forest floor. He struggled to get up, but Jack was there. The giant picked him up easily off of the ground, shaking his head as he brushed Joel off with a huge, calloused hand.

"Don't run, little one," Jack said, carrying Joel gently to the roaring fire. "You will only die tired."

* * *

Hungry Ghosts

Chapter 1: A Night to Remember, September 5th, 1979

Connor Mann sat on his bed and looked out the window at the cemetery.

Pale moonlight drifted down through a heavy bank of clouds to illuminate the gravestones scattered throughout Pine Grove Cemetery. The headstones, new and old, had a devilish gleam to them, as if the dead lurked in the markers rather than beneath them.

Connor hated the cemetery, and he had for as long as he could remember.

As he looked out through the open window and past the screen, a shape caught his eye. A small creature moved from headstone to headstone, head down, nose to the ground. Connor squinted as the animal moved into a shaft of moonlight and gasped at the sight of a silver fox.

It took him only a moment to realize that the fox wasn't silver, but a ghost. The light of the moon as it reflected off a tall headstone caused the curious color of the fox's fur.

The animal's nose lifted, the head turned, and dark orange eyes stared at Connor.

Horrified, Connor watched as the fox's lips curled up to reveal long, jagged teeth. A tongue, black and worm-like, snaked out of its mouth and glided across the stretched lips.

Connor screamed, tried to wrench the blanket over his head, and tumbled out of bed.

In less than a minute, the light in his room snapped on, and Connor heard the gentle tread of his mother as she came to him. He wiped tears out of his eyes as she removed the blanket and helped him back into bed.

"Connor," she whispered, brushing his hair out of his eyes. "What's wrong, sweetheart?"

Connor's breath hitched in his throat as he tried to speak and his mother's hand went to his back, rubbing it slowly.

"Shh," she said, "catch your breath and tell me."

Connor did as he was told, and then he reported to his mother what he had seen.

She nodded as he spoke, pausing the back rub to tuck her long black hair behind her ears. Her thin face wore a broad smile, love and care filled her eyes.

When Connor had finished with his story, his mother looked out the window, a frown wrinkling the smooth, pale skin of her brow.

"I've asked your father to fix the shades in your room for about three years now," she muttered. "The only thing he can be bothered to do though is get himself a pitcher of beer at the social club."

Connor had heard this complaint before, and he kept silent. There were many repairs and projects that needed his father's attention. Few, if any of them, would ever get done. His father was more concerned with beer than anything else.

"Well," Connor's mother said, looking out the window, "I'm sorry you saw something frightening out there, honey. I don't think it was a fox. You probably just saw a dog. We're too far in the city for foxes to be popping up. Even in a cemetery as big as Pine Grove."

She turned to face him again.

"Now," she said, "here's the deal. You go back to bed without looking out the window again, and tomorrow, as part of your birthday present, we can pick out some new curtains. Something to cover this window a little better. Deal?"

"Deal," Connor said, grinning as he shook his mother's hand.

She stood up, helped him lie back down, and covered him with the sheet and blanket. His mother leaned forward, kissed him on the forehead and said, "Now go back to sleep, my birthday boy. Just a couple more hours and it will be time to get up, and the birthday celebrations can begin!"

Connor smiled, turned his back to the window, and watched his mother leave the room.

She paused in the doorway, blew him a kiss, and turned out the light.

In the darkness, Connor's eyes grew heavy, and as he was closing them, he heard a sound, like the clicking of small claws on the asphalt. He yawned, sank deeper towards sleep, and wondered what dog was out so late at night.

Chapter 2: Happy Birthday, September 6th, 1979

Debra Mann left the house at a little before six in the morning, as she usually did. She liked to walk through the cemetery, enjoying the peace and quiet she could find there. The early morning strolls helped clear her mind and focus on the day ahead.

Debra found herself relying on the walks with a greater frequency. The new manager of the Indian Head Bank was a stickler for all sorts of rules, which was a far cry from the lack of office policies of Mr. Frost, who had recently retired. Added to the stress of a new boss who was nothing like the old, was the concern over Connor's happiness.

A concern her husband did nothing to alleviate.

She shoved thoughts of Cody out of her mind, focusing instead on what she had done, and what needed to be fixed.

A twinge of guilt rose up within her, but Debra smothered it as she walked into the cemetery. Less than a month earlier, she had begun to fret over Conner's birthday. What little money she was able to bring in on a regular basis went to keeping the utilities on and the foreclosure notices at bay. More often than not, Cody managed to get to the social club and drink his earnings away.

When it came to a choice between a beer and anything else in the world, the beer always won out where Cody was concerned.

Then Mr. Frost had announced his retirement, and the following morning, when Debra was in the cemetery, she had an idea. She could borrow some money from the bank, buy Connor that new BMX bicycle he had been so excited about, and then slip the money back in once she got paid.

Because Debra was going to have to steal the money to get Conner his birthday present.

And the strangest part about it was that the idea didn't seem to be her own. It was almost as though a voice had whispered it into her ear when she walked through the cemetery. She had been a conscientious and dedicated employee of Indian Head bank for almost ten years, and she had never once thought of taking even a penny from them.

But she knew she had to.

Connor needed his present.

All boys need a bike.

Debra smiled, thinking about the new bicycle, hidden away in its box in the basement.

She put her hands in her pockets and followed the asphalt road in the cemetery towards the newer headstones. Her favorite place to walk, and where the idea to borrow the money had first sprung up.

***

The loud, abrasive sound of his father snoring woke Connor up, as it did on most days. Connor rubbed the sleep out of his eyes, yawned a few times and cast off his blanket. As he became fully awake, he smiled.

He bounced as he walked around his room, pulling on his clothes before going into the hall. His footsteps became lighter, his mood more sedate, as he approached his father's bedroom.

Connor didn't try to wake the man up. By the heavy, onerous tone of his father's snores, Connor knew that he had gotten far drunker than usual the night before.

Waking his father up for something as small as Connor's birthday would earn him a beating. One his mother wouldn't be able to protect him from.

Connor stopped outside of the bedroom, reached out and took hold of the brass doorknob. Without a word, he eased the door closed and made sure that even the latch was silent as it settled into place.

With his father secured behind the thin, plywood door, Connor picked his way carefully down the hall and descended in the same manner to the first floor. He smelled coffee and toast, his mother's usual breakfast. When he entered the kitchen, his mother wasn't there. Instead, Connor found a card at his chair.

To my one and only, sweet Connor, his mother had written across the envelope. He slipped his small finger in between the envelope's flap and the rest of the paper and tore it free. From within, he took out a note.

Happy Birthday, to my boy, Connor! I've gone for my morning walk, and I will be back soon. I can't wait to show you what I have in store for your birthday, my big, seven-year-old boy!

Holding onto the letter, Connor went to the side door and opened it. He stepped out onto the porch and looked down the driveway into the cemetery. In the early morning light, he strained his eyes to catch a glimpse of his mother. After a moment, he did so, her tall, graceful body moving in long, easy strides along the cemetery's asphalt road.

She made her way to the Oval, the newest portion of Pine Grove. Around the Oval were new stones. Those with polished fronts and names carved in bold letters.

Connor walked to the edge of the porch, stood on his toes, and rested his arms on the railing. He saw his mother as she followed the curve from the left, moving towards the most recent graves.

She glanced back at the house then, and she saw Connor. His mother raised a hand and waved, and Connor returned it.

A moment later, the fox attacked.

Connor didn't see where it had come from, or what it was doing, but he could hear his mother's screams as she fell.

In the stillness of the morning air, Connor heard the crack of her skull against a headstone and her sudden silence. Horrified, he watched as the fox's body pulsated, expanded, shrank, and then violently transformed into a man.

From where he stood, Connor could see the man bend down, reach out, and thrust his hands into his mother's head. The screams started up again, and only when the man faded from view did Connor understand that the screams he heard were his own.

Chapter 3: Therapy, August 1st, 2016

The curtains were raised, the light of the stars visible through the clear glass of Doctor Waltner's windows.

"Connor?" she said, causing him to twitch.

He flashed a nervous smile at her and turned away from the windows.

"How are you feeling?" the doctor asked him.

"The same," he answered.

Her frown triggered anxiety, and he looked down at his hands. She cleared her throat and said, "You've been here a long time."

Her tone was ominous, and he looked at her, suddenly wary. He didn't respond, waiting instead for her to continue.

She adjusted her glasses and said, "It's almost time for you to leave this facility."

Fear caused him to straighten up, his hands to shake, and his mouth to go dry.

"I can't," he whispered. "There's no place for me to go."

"You can go home," Dr. Waltner stated.

"My father's there," Connor replied.

"And that's why you should go. You both have some issues that need to be worked out."

"Why now?" Connor asked.

She hesitated and then said, "This facility doesn't have the ability to care for you anymore."

"What?" Connor said, confused.

"Your uncle passed away," Dr. Waltner said in a harsh voice. "There are no more funds. You are fully capable of taking charge of your own life, Connor. No one else is going to do it for you anymore."

Connor shook his head. "I can't go out there."

"There's nothing to be afraid of," Dr. Waltner began.

"Shut up!" Connor screamed. "You don't know that!"

The door to her office was thrown open, and a pair of large, well-muscled orderlies rushed in.

Connor didn't shrink away from them as he normally would when he had an episode.

He jabbed an accusatory finger at her. "You. Don't. Know. You didn't see it. You didn't see her die."

"Connor," Dr. Waltner said with all the warmth and affection of a piece of steel, "you need to quiet yourself down. These gentlemen will not sedate you. They will not bring you back to your room. They will, in fact, restrain you and hold you until the police can come. I would hate for your first day out of this facility to be spent in jail."

Connor shuddered at the thought.

His shoulders slumped, and he dropped into the chair.

Dr. Waltner nodded to the two men, and they left, leaving the door open behind them. She turned her attention to the file, his file, on her desk.

"You have sufficient medication to last you the next month," she said, closing the manila folder and looking at him. "I believe your uncle prepared for you in other ways, but you will have to speak with his lawyer about that. I am not privy to the particulars of it."

"When do I have to leave?" Connor asked, staring at his hands.

"That's why I called you in here tonight," she replied, "I am well aware of your concern about daylight. I wanted to offer you the opportunity to leave at night. This would allow you to return to your family home or some other establishment before the arrival of the sun."

Connor nodded. "Thank you."

"You'll leave tonight then?" Dr. Waltner asked.

"As soon as I'm packed," Conner stated, "which should be in a few minutes. I don't have much."

She tapped her fingers on the file, and when Connor fixed his gaze upon her, she said, "You have an opportunity here, Connor. Don't squander it. Some people have a golden future laid at their feet, and it goes to waste. Your uncle provided a safe place for you for decades. I suggest you make the most of the time he has given you."

Connor stood up, and as he did so, he noticed how haggard and careworn his psychologist appeared.

"Are you alright, Doctor?" he asked.

A grimace appeared on her face, but it vanished almost as quickly as it had arrived.

"I am now," she answered.

"What happened?" Connor asked.

295

"Let's just say that you're not the only one who was thrust into the cold," she said with a tight smile. Dr. Waltner adjusted her glasses and said, "I honestly wish you the best, Connor."

Connor nodded and left the room.

He never trusted anyone who used the word 'honestly,' and he hadn't trusted Dr. Waltner to begin with.

Stuffing his hands deep into the pockets of his sweatpants, Connor shuffled along the hallway towards his room. Behind him, the two attendants followed, prepared to thrust him into the night as soon as he was packed.

Connor shuddered and wondered what his father looked like after all these years.

Connor doubted it was good.

Chapter 4: Home on Hill Street, August 2nd, 2016

Connor had seen his father a handful of times after his uncle had him committed. The last had resulted in an angry exchange of words, and over three decades of silence from him.

Life had been difficult with his father, and standing outside the family home on Hill Street in the evening reminded him of that.

A single light shone in the den, as it had on the last night Connor had looked at the house. The yellow paint on the wooden walls, which had once been vibrant and inviting, had dulled and faded. Even in the light of the streetlamps, Connor could see how the paint bubbled and peeled. The windows glowed in a dull, feeble fashion. They were filthy, the curtains behind them stained with age and time and his father's cigarettes.

In the driveway was his father's car, a Ford Mustang of dubious vintage, and of doubtful ability. From the leaves and debris gathered around the vehicle's flat tires, Connor suspected it hadn't been in drivable condition for some time.

"You sure this is the place, bud?"

Connor turned, switched his bag from one hand to the other and forced a smile as he answered the cabbie. "Yeah. Been a while. My dad's not in good health."

The older Spanish man nodded. "You're not kidding. Listen, if there's a problem, you just call us right back up. Ain't got a place for you to stay, but we sure as hell can take you away from here."

"Thanks," Connor said.

"Anytime," the cabbie replied, flashing him a smile full of gold teeth. "You call us up, you ask for José Roche. I'll take care of you."

Connor chuckled, smiled without effort, and said, "Thank you."

José grinned, shifted the cab into drive, and pulled away. As the vehicle turned onto Adams Street, music poured out of the car's open windows, and José began to sing along.

Connor kept his eyes on the cab and away from the cemetery. He took a deep breath and stared at the house again.

He had tried to call from the facility, and then from the transfer station when he got off the bus. José had even let him use his cellphone when they were on their way from the cab company's dispatch office.

Each time, the phone had been busy.

Which meant his father had either taken it off the hook or was on the longest call in history.

Connor swallowed, heard and felt a dry click in his throat, and forced his feet to carry him up the slight slant of the driveway. His eyes darted from left to right, settling first on the empty cans of Natural Ice beer in boxes by the front of the Mustang, then on old, broken bottles of wine.

When he reached the stairs that led up to the porch, Connor hesitated. Licking his lips, he took hold of the railing and stepped up. The ancient wood screamed beneath his foot and a dog barked from within the house. As he continued up to the porch, the dog's voice grew louder, the barking intensifying until a gruff, bitter voice yelled for the animal to shut up.

The voice brought Connor to a stop.

It was his father's, and it brought back memories Connor had long forgotten.

Chapter 5: Something Feels Wrong, August 25th, 1980

Connor's mother had been dead for almost a year.

It had been a terrible time.

"Connor!"

His father's voice bellowed up the stairs, and in the tone, Connor could hear the wine and the beer. The man went to bed drunk and started the day the same way.

And his hands swung freer as the day went by.

In less than six months, Connor had suffered two broken fingers and more black eyes than he had excuses for. But he had learned to be quicker, and how to judge his father's moods. He had also discovered how to feed and wash himself and to clean his clothes. When life became unbearable, and his father too drunk or too violent, Connor slipped away to Mrs. Lavoie's house.

She would feed him and clean him, and give him the mothering he still desperately needed.

All of this drifted through Connor's mind as he hustled down the stairs. He kept a wary eye out for his father, passing through the dining room and into the kitchen.

His father sat in his chair at the head of the table. A cigarette burned between his first and second fingers. His eyes were bloodshot, and his dark brown hair was spiked with streaks of white.

Connor didn't pause as he walked into the room, knowing that if he did so, his father would take it as a sign of weakness and lash out at him. Instead, Connor went to the table, grabbed a chair, and dragged it across the floor to the counter. He scrambled up onto the seat, and opened the cupboard to take down the oatmeal and a bowl. His father watched him as Connor made breakfast for both of them.

"There's no work for me today," his father said.

Connor glanced at him, the man's pale face puffy with lack of sleep. The stubble of several days' growth of beard added to his haggard appearance. He wore the same clothes as he had for the previous two days and Connor could feel the violence emanating from the man.

Connor would need to get out of the house soon.

His hands trembled as he poured the oatmeal.

"What are you afraid of?" his father hissed.

"Nothing," Connor answered. His voice was calm and gentle, contrary to the fear ripping through him.

"There's something wrong here," his father said, getting to his feet with some difficulty.

Out of the corner of his eye, Connor saw the man glance about the room.

"It's not right," his father continued, "do you feel it?"

Connor was going to remain silent when he realized his father was right.

There was something wrong; it filled the air. A strange, oppressive layer was added to the late August heat, and Connor knew it was bad.

It reminded him of the morning his mother had died.

The sensation must have brought a similar memory to his father, for the man stumbled back, reaching out and grasping the edge of the table.

"Something's here," his father whimpered. Then he turned and fled from the room.

Connor's hands shook so badly he couldn't hold onto the oatmeal container any longer. He put it on the counter and climbed down off the chair. When he did so, he looked over to the side door and let out a moan.

The ghost fox that had killed his mother stood in the kitchen, sitting on its haunches. Its mouth was open, making it seem as if it were smiling at him. The tail twitched, passing through the door and coming back into the kitchen.

Connor couldn't move as he watched it stand up and step towards him. A single, delicate paw was in the air when there was a knock on the door's glass pane.

Connor managed to tear his eyes away from the fox to see who was there and saw Mrs. Lavoie. She smiled at him, but then the smile faltered when she noticed the fox.

Connor had confessed to her what he had seen in the cemetery the morning of his mother's death. Mrs. Lavoie had shushed him, told him it was nothing more than a terrible creation to deal with his mother's sudden passing.

But in Mrs. Lavoie's wide, expressive eyes, Connor saw that she understood he had told her the truth. The fox had been real. It was not a creation to help him accept his mother's death.

Mrs. Lavoie took a step back. The fox let out a high, pleased yip, and turned away from Connor.

"No," Connor whispered.

The fox's tail swung lazily to the left and then to the right before it passed in silence through the door.

Mrs. Lavoie's scream of terror was hardly muffled by the thick wood of the door.

Chapter 6: Knocking on the Side Door, August 2nd, 2016

The fact that Cody Michael Mann was still alive was proof to Connor that there was no justice in the world. Connor felt, rather passionately, that his father should have died in the cemetery instead of his mother. And if not instead of his mother, then he should have taken the place of Mrs. Lavoie.

His father was alive though, and Connor would have to make the best of a wretched situation.

Connor waited until the unseen dog quieted down, then knocked on the door. The dog let out a series of howls and barks that caused a torrent of profanity to spill from his father's mouth.

"Who the hell is it?" Cody demanded on the other side of the door.

"Connor."

Silence greeted him.

"You're a liar," his father said without conviction.

"Open the door," Connor said. He felt the old anger building up. The rage he had never been able to quench when he was in his father's presence.

"Connor's in a home," his father said, "some place where his mother's family stuffed him."

Connor punched the door, the skin on his knuckles splitting and blood splashing out over the faded paint.

"Open the damned door," Connor snarled through clenched teeth.

A heartbeat later, the sound of locks being turned filled the air. The door opened a crack to reveal darkness. A deep growl emanated from the house, and the dog pushed forward, its nose wet and glistening in the gap between the door and frame.

"Get back, Rex," Connor's father said, and the dog's snout vanished.

"Hell," his father whispered, "it *is* you."

The door didn't open any further.

"Let me in." Connor knew his voice was cold, just as he knew his father was remembering the last time they had met outside of the facility.

"Probably not a good idea," his father said after a moment, a tremor in his voice. "Place is a mess. You know."

"Never bothered you when I was a kid," Connor snapped.

"Open up. Now."

Part of him wanted to smash the door in. He knew he could. The anger would let him. But there was the dog to consider. He was more concerned with any damage it might cause him than the other way around. The police were another matter as well. His father might call them if he had a working phone, and then Connor would end up in jail.

And that wasn't any guarantee of protection from the daylight.

He shuddered as he thought of it, and in a heartbeat, he was plunged into the memory of that morning, of his mother's murder at the hands of the shape-shifting ghost. Connor recalled the terror and the helplessness he had felt when Mrs. Lavoie had been slain by the same creature.

He knew jail wouldn't be a safe refuge either.

Far from it.

Connor didn't think any place was.

Before he could demand entry again, his father opened the door fully, revealing himself and the dog.

The dog was a German Shepherd. Pure black and magnificent. Connor had read a great deal about all manner of subjects in his years in the facility, and at one time, he had been obsessed with dogs. The Shepherd before him had none of the inter-breeding frailties found in the American Kennel Club requirements. There would be no hip problems with the dog before him.

It watched him, brown eyes focused and alert.

Connor smiled at the dog and was pleased to see its tail thump.

His father caused Connor's smile to falter, not only from his hatred of the man but his physical condition as well.

Decades of alcoholism had caused his father's stomach to push out the threadbare fabric of his shirt, the liver swollen. His skin was pale, his hair white tinged with yellow. Red splotches, proverbial 'gin blossoms,' covered his nose and spread across his cheeks. His clothes consisted of a stained and filthy V-neck undershirt with a pair of shredded boxer-shorts. His feet were gnarled, the toenails the color of yellow parchment and curling inward.

While Connor's hatred for the man didn't vanish, it did

lessen as he saw what was left of his boyhood terror.

"You look terrible," Connor said, and he stepped inside the house. The smell of dog urine, filth, and decay washed over him. Connor held back a gag. His nose, long accustomed to the sterile, clean smell of the facility, was in shock at the feral odor of the house.

"Damn," Connor said with difficulty, "you need to open a few windows and air this place out."

His father shook his head, a frantic motion that made him look like a man with a neurological disorder, and he muttered, "He'll get in. I can't let him in. I can't let any of them in."

Connor turned, wanting to ask what the man was babbling about, but his attention was drawn to the lintel as his father slammed the door shut and secured the locks. Dozens of old horseshoes were nailed onto the lintel, and then down either side. Across the threshold were at least a hundred, if not more, ancient, coffin-head nails. They were hammered in a haphazard fashion, each one crossed over another, then twisted, so they met up with the horseshoes on either side of the frame.

Connor looked at his father and wondered if the man had gone insane.

He was surprised that he found no pleasure in the idea. The creature before him was not a beast. Merely a miserable, wretched image of a man.

He was, Connor realized, nothing to fear. If anything, the man should be taken as a warning, an example of what alcohol and cowardice can do to a person.

Connor turned and looked at Rex. The dog returned the look, his ears upright, his eyes alert. Connor closed his free hand into a fist and extended it to Rex, allowing the dog to smell him. When the Shepherd's tail thumped, and the dog got up and left the room, Connor lowered his hand.

"Is my room clean?" he asked. "Or does it look like the rest of the place?"

His father cleared his throat, looked down at the floor and muttered, "Don't know."

"Pretty simple question there, *dad*," Connor said, unwilling to remove the disdain for the title out of his voice.

His father flinched, but he still didn't elaborate on why he didn't know about the status of the bedroom.

"It's a yes or no question," Connor continued. "It either is, or it isn't, a pig sty."

"I don't know," the man mumbled. "I don't go up there."

It took Connor a moment to process the statement.

"What? How can you not go up there? The shower's up there. Your bedroom's up there." Connor shook his head in disbelief.

"I use the first-floor bathroom to get cleaned up," his father said, "and I sleep in my chair. Rex has the couch."

Too shocked to speak, Connor pushed past the man, through the filth of the kitchen and into the den. That room stank worse than the kitchen. It smelled of sweat and sickness, stale air and desperation. Connor grimaced, turned the corner into the small hallway and stopped.

A framework had been set up in front of what had been an open staircase. In the framing was a door made of beaten iron sheets riveted together. His father had followed him and hung back, wringing his hands.

"Why?" Connor asked. "What's the point of this?"

"Keeps them out," his father whispered.

"You said that about the side door," Connor said, frowning. "Who exactly are you trying to keep out?"

"The fox and his friends," the man answered.

Connor dropped his bag to the floor, his breath catching in his throat. Hatred boiled up inside of him. For decades, his father, on the rare occasion when they had seen one another, had denied the existence of the fox. Or of anything Connor had experienced.

"The fox," Connor repeated. He let the word roll off his tongue, enjoyed the bitter taste of it in his mouth. Found pleasure in the blaze which erupted in his mind.

"The fox," he said again, then asked, "and his friends?"

His father answered with an almost imperceptible nod.

"They've been back?" Connor asked, the question difficult to ask as his chest tightened.

"Every year. I see them around the house, and in the cemetery. There are always more," his father whimpered.

Connor bent down, picked up his bag, and said, "Let's hope they're not coming in the morning. I need to sleep."

"You have to leave," his father said, his voice rising. "You can't stay here."

"There's no other place for me," Connor answered. He reached out and took hold of the slim, improvised latch that secured the door to the frame.

"Then sleep down here," his father said. "You'll be safe. I have all the windows and doors secure."

Connor looked at his father, felt the hate and disappointment rise to the surface, and said, "Better to die up there, *father*, than to be in this room with you."

His father made no reply as Connor let himself into the stairwell. As he climbed up the stairs, he heard the door close behind him, and the latch click into place.

Connor's steps carried him into his past, and the nightmare of his future.

Chapter 7: Pine Grove and the Dawn, August 3rd, 2016

The room was dusty and nothing more.

Connor had found a towel in the linen closet and wiped the dust of decades from his belongings. *Star Wars* figures and *Hardy Boys* books, Matchbox and Hotwheel cars. A closet full of old clothes that his mother had folded.

Connor opened his windows and then flipped the mattress on his twin bed. His years in the facility had instilled in him a desire for cleanliness and order. Before he would sleep, Connor needed to make certain the room was as clean as possible.

Once the dust had settled from the mattress, he wiped everything down again, tossed the towel into the rattan hamper, and found a set of old *Star Wars* sheets. They were stiff and had a mingled odor of age and mild decay about them, but they were clean.

He made the bed and stared at it, realizing that his mother was the last one to touch the sheets. To fold them and put them away, never suspecting that the next time Connor used them she would have been murdered in Pine Grove Cemetery.

Connor wiped the tears from his eyes and went to look out the window that faced the cemetery. He looked out at the few headstones illuminated by the red lights the Catholics favored for religious decorations. In the darkness beyond those isolated, glowing graves, was his mother.

They had buried her in the same cemetery she had been killed in, although no one but Connor knew it.

Mrs. Lavoie learned it was true, Connor thought bitterly. *Seems like my father has as well.*

He looked out the dirty window for a moment longer, then turned away, and picked up his bag. For a moment, he rummaged around in it, found his medication, and took out two instead of one of the sleeping pills. Connor didn't think he would be able to sleep with only half a dose.

He took a plastic bottle of tepid water, popped the pills into his mouth, and swallowed them. They left behind an aftertaste of chalk, but they could have tasted like sewer water for all he cared. Sleep was an elusive element in his life.

Putting the water bottle back into the bag, he went over to the bed. Connor stripped down and folded his clothes, placing them on his chair before he climbed into bed. The smell of the sheets washed over him, the fabric rough and cool against his skin. His bed felt too small; his last memory of it when he had been less than half his current size.

Connor yawned, stretched, and rolled over. He closed his eyes and tried not to think of his mother.

The sound of a squeak caused his eyes to snap open, and he sat up, blinking at the bright sunlight streaming into the room.

I fell asleep, he realized. Groggy, Connor rubbed at his eyes, and when he put his hands down, he looked around, wondering what had made the sound. Finally, his gaze fell on the window that overlooked the cemetery, and his throat tightened with fear.

He threw off the sheet, climbed out of bed and stumbled to the window.

In the morning dew that had gathered on the outside of the glass, a message had been written.

Welcome home, Connor, the message read. *Where have you been?*

Chapter 8: Mrs. Lavoie's House, August 3rd, 2016

Exhaustion and the residual effects of the pills had won out over fear, and Connor fell asleep a few hours after the discovery of the message. He woke again at dusk, as was his habit. The shower, he was pleased to find, still worked, and his own toiletries from the facility were put to good use.

Unfortunately, his own fresh scent did little to mask the atrocious smell of the first floor. It took him several minutes to force the makeshift door at the bottom of the stairs, and when he did, he found only Rex.

The dog lifted his head, looked at Connor for a moment, and then dropped his chin back onto his paws. He watched Connor from the dubious comfort of the filthy couch, but his tail wagged.

"Where is he, Rex?" Connor asked.

Not surprisingly, the dog didn't answer.

Connor walked over to him, scratched Rex between the ears, and then went into the kitchen. Trash littered the counters and the floor. Bags of it were piled against the wall where the table had once been. Most of the trash consisted of wrappers for fast food chains and paper plates. A few were empty cans of vegetable soup, a generic store brand, but it gave Connor hope that there might be edible food in the house.

A thorough search of the kitchen resulted in disappointment. All he found was an old tea sampler, recently expired, but Connor was hungry. The tea, he rationalized, might hold him over until he could find a place to eat.

He found the teapot where his mother had left it, rinsed it and filled it, then set the vessel on the stove. For a moment, he feared there wouldn't be any gas, but there was, and soon he had the water warming up. He looked around the kitchen, frowned, and pulled out a black trash bag.

Connor tried not to think about the garbage as he started to clean up the room.

If I'm going to live here for a while, he told himself, *then it's going to be clean.*

By the time the tea water reached a boil, he had filled two trash bags and cleaned off three feet of counter space. Connor put the tea bag in to steep and carried the trash out to the driveway.

In for a penny, in for a pound, he thought with a sigh and carried the rest of the bags out of the kitchen. Rex joined him, watching, snapping up several field mice that tried to scurry away. Connor reined in his disgust, and when he finished with the trash, he found a bar of soap in the bathroom. He scrubbed his hands and forearms in hot water, shook as much of the water off them as he could, and went for his tea.

With Rex following him, Connor walked out onto the porch. He brushed leaves and cobwebs off a faded plastic chair and sat down. The dog stretched out at his feet, and Connor enjoyed the warmth of the tea. From where he was, he could see Mrs. Lavoie's house. Someone had put a fresh coat of paint on the old, Georgian style building, and a well-kept garden could be glimpsed as well.

Everything, in fact, seemed to be in order with her house and yard. The windows shined in the last light of the day, and the driveway had recently been paved. Each bush along the front strip was trimmed, the green leaves in perfect order. The garage, attached by a small breezeway, had a new roof, and through a window, Connor caught sight of a vehicle.

He wondered who might have moved into her home when he saw an Asian man step out of Mrs. Lavoie's side door. The stranger looked to be in his seventies, but he moved with a straight back and sure steps. His hair was silver and clipped short all the way around. The man's skin was almost golden in the twilight, and his long, thin beard fell to his chest. There were no unkempt hairs in the beard, and it was silver like those atop his head. He wore a white shirt buttoned to the neck, and the sleeves were buttoned around his thin wrists. The man's pants were black, as were his shoes.

Connor watched as the man came to a stop in the center of the driveway, withdrew what looked like a rosary from his pocket, and looped it about his wrist. Then the stranger looked up, caught sight of Connor, and took a half step back in surprise.

Feeling badly about being caught staring, Connor raised a hand and waved a cautious hello.

His neighbor did the same, smiled, and turned away.

Connor watched him as he went into the street and moved to walk along the wrought iron fence of Pine Grove Cemetery.

When he finished his tea and stood up, Connor saw that the

man had reached the first entrance to the graveyard and gone in. With a shudder, Connor hurried into the house, Rex close at his heels.

Nights were better than days, but only by a little.

Connor slammed the door and wondered, for a moment, where his father had slipped away to.

Chapter 9: In the Basement, August 3rd, 2016

After he had cleaned the kitchen, and his father still hadn't come home, Connor decided to look in the basement to see if his old man stored anything worthwhile there. It only took a few minutes for him to realize his father avoided not only the second floor but the basement as well. Like the side door, the basement door was hemmed in by iron. When he had managed to open it, a wave of dust had rushed up at him, and Connor spent fifteen minutes in the bathroom, spitting and blowing his nose.

Finally, with the loyal Rex beside him, Connor descended into the basement. Each riser squealed as he went down, and when he reached the cement floor, he looked at the mess before him. Broken chairs and old furniture was piled on one side, his and his mother's belongings on the other. A space was cleared around the water heater and furnace, and another around the corner where the water, gas, and electrical lines came in.

Webs filled the windows and giant, thin-legged spiders hung in them. The air smelled of dust and mildew.

A scurrying sound came from the corners, and a low growl rose from Rex's throat. Connor glanced down at him and saw that the dog's hackles were raised, the ears flat against his head.

"Upstairs," Connor said in a low voice. "Let's go upstairs."

"Send the dog away," a woman said in a whisper, and Connor bit back a scream.

"Send it away," a male said from a corner on the left. "They're ever so wretched to us. Send it away."

"You need to do as we say," the woman said, and it was then that Connor recognized her.

"Mrs. Lavoie?" He choked on her name.

The scurrying came closer.

"Of course it's me," she said, and he could hear the familiar tones of warmth and affection.

But beneath them was a darker current, that of hunger and longing.

"Just send the dog away, Connor," Mrs. Lavoie repeated. "We've wondered where you've been."

Connor didn't reply. Instead, he took a cautious step back and felt something brush his calf.

He screamed before he could stop himself.

Rex snarled and spun around, jaws snapping.

A man cursed, and a chair fell over as a dark shape raced back into the shadows.

"Send it away!" Mrs. Lavoie screamed.

Connor spun around and sprinted up the stairs. Before he reached the top, the door started to close, and he threw himself against it, pain exploding in his shoulder. Behind him, Rex scrambled up the stairs, claws clicking on the old wood. Connor tumbled into the kitchen and Rex came up, spinning to the left and attacking something resembling a rabbit.

The strange animal let out a high-pitched, human-like squeal and fled into the basement.

Connor scrambled to his feet, lurched to the basement door, and slammed it shut. His hands shook and fumbled with the lock, Rex scratching at the bottom of the door and growling.

With a shudder, Connor secured the lock and fell back against the wall, slowly sliding down, coming to a rest. Rex scratched the door for another minute and then backed away. The dog finally settled down beside Connor, staring at the basement.

A thick silence filled the air; Rex's panting was the only sound.

Then, a thin, wavering whisper came through the crack between the threshold and the door.

"We've missed you, Connor," Mrs. Lavoie said. "We all have. Especially your mother."

Chapter 10: News from Beyond the Grave, August 4ᵗʰ, 2016

"That's my dog."

The sound of his father's voice ripped Connor out of sleep faster than any alarm clock could have.

Sitting up, Connor saw the man standing just outside the doorway. Rex lay across the foot of the bed, asleep. Connor's heartbeat resumed its normal pace as he stared at his father.

"Seems like he's his own dog," Connor answered after a moment. "What's going on?"

"You've got mail. Downstairs." His father looked around the room. "Why'd you tack towels over the windows?"

Connor almost told him about the message on the glass and the voices he had heard in the basement. Instead of the whole truth, he gave his father a taste of it.

"I sleep during the day," Connor answered. "That's about it. Towels block out the sun."

"Hmph." His father turned to walk away.

"Where were you yesterday?" Connor asked, the question coming out sharp enough to cause his father to wince.

"Business." The man didn't look back at Connor. "Had things to do."

In the years he had spent in the facility, Connor had learned how to tell when someone lied.

His father was lying.

He didn't press him on the issue. Instead, Connor asked, "Where's my mail?"

"In the kitchen you cleaned," his father answered. The disdain in the man's voice was thick. Without another word, he left, his feet heavy on the stairs.

Connor reached out, gave Rex a pat and got out of bed. He dressed quickly and hurried down the stairs, the dog following him. When they reached the first floor, Connor closed and secured the door. His father dropped into a battered easy chair, took a bottle of wine off the floor, and unscrewed the cap. He drank and ignored Connor and Rex as they entered the kitchen.

On the counter, between the sink and the stove, was a large, padded yellow envelope. It was clearly marked to Connor, and within it was a letter from an attorney, a checkbook, cash in the amount of one thousand dollars, and a debit card.

The letter was short and to the point.

Dear Mr. Mann,

It is with sincere and heartfelt sadness that I greet you, for it means that your uncle has passed away. He was, as I am certain you have surmised, a man of some wealth. After your mother's horrific death, and the sudden passing of your genteel neighbor, your uncle felt it would be best for you to be institutionalized.

However, with his recent passing, the funding for your care at the facility has evaporated, for lack of a better word. He was able to establish a trust fund for you, but in all honesty, it is sufficient only for you to live upon, but not enough to keep you in the facility in which you grew up.

You will, I trust, reach out to me should you encounter any difficulties in this sudden and radical return to society. I have been assured that you have the wherewithal to survive this.

Please feel free to contact me at any time.

Sincerely,
Robert L. Barkis, Esq.

Connor set the letter down and picked up the money. He had handled cash before, but only a little at a time, and that was more to familiarize him with money as a real item than as an abstract idea. The facility had prepared him for an eventual, gradual return to the world he had shunned as a child. Connor knew the basics of cellphones, computers, and even public transportation. He had been taught how to cook, clean, and earned a high school diploma.

And he had been given every assurance that ghosts did not exist.

Some days, he even believed them.

Connor sighed, folded the money, and stuffed it into his front pocket. He put the debit card in a back pocket and walked into the den. Earlier, he had seen a collar and leash. They were draped over the coffee table.

"Come on, Rex," Connor said, patting his leg as he had seen people in movies do. Either his father had done the same, or the dog had watched the same movies, for Rex trotted to him.

"What are you doing?" His father's tone was sharp.

"Taking the dog for a walk," Connor said, his stomach rumbling.

"The hell you are," the man snapped, pushing himself up and out of his chair.

Connor straightened up and glared at his father.

The man's face paled, and he dropped back down, looking at the floor.

"My dog," his father mumbled.

"He's his own dog," Connor corrected, "nobody else's."

He looped the end of the leash around his wrist and followed Rex out of the house. The dog took the lead, going down the steps, onto the broken asphalt of the driveway crossing the street to the cemetery fence. Fear rumbled in Connor's stomach, but he forced himself to deal with it.

Connor had the dog, and Rex would protect him.

The Shepherd put his nose to the ground, tail wagging lazily from left to right. They moved up to the far side of the cemetery, the sun setting to their left. For a short time, the headstones were backlit, and Connor tried not to look at the graves.

The sounds of civilization faded away as they moved further along the street, towards a dead end and old trees. A faint sound reached Connor's ears, and at first, he thought he had imagined it. Then he saw Rex twitch. The dog's snout lifted, and the nostrils flared.

Connor wanted to turn around, but he felt compelled to follow the dog's lead, and the German Shepherd continued.

The sound became more distinct, identifiable.

Those are footsteps, Connor realized.

And they were coming from inside the cemetery. In the growing darkness, someone kept pace with him on the other side of the iron fence, and they were drawing near.

Rex came to a stop and sat down.

Connor caught himself, narrowly missing the dog's tail.

"He remembers."

Connor gasped at the sound of the voice. Rich, pure, and feminine. He turned his head and stared into the darkness.

"Hello, Connor," a feminine voice said, her words thick with sorrow. "You've grown up, my little boy."

"Mom?" Connor whispered, fear spreading through him. *I'm going crazy.*

"Yes," she said. "It's me. You know, dogs don't like us, and the feeling's mutual."

"What?" Connor asked, confused.

"The dog," she continued. "We don't like them. None of us do."

"I don't understand," Connor whispered. "Is this even real? I take a lot of medicine. Maybe it's not real."

"No," his mother said, her voice growing hard, "this is real. I want to be able to tell you what's going on, but I'm not even sure. Memory is tricky."

"What do you mean?" he asked. "I don't understand."

"They're coming for you," she said. "You have to be careful. They want you with us."

"Who?" Connor asked in a hushed tone.

"The hungry ones," his mother answered. "It's because you're special."

"How am I special?" Connor asked her. "What do you even mean by that?"

"If they eat you, if any of us do," she whispered. "We'll be full. And we're all so *hungry*, Connor."

Rex leaped up, straining at the leash and barking furiously.

Connor twisted around, his eyes jerking from left to right. He saw small, animal shapes darting through the shadows.

"A bite," his mother whispered behind him, "that's all I want, Connor. A bite. Doesn't your mother deserve a taste?"

A cold hand raked across his neck, and Connor pulled away. He hurried into the street, stepping into the harsh light of a streetlamp. Around the edges of the light, where it faded into darkness, twenty or thirty dull, green eyes glowed. Some were small, and others were large. All stared at him. Dark, rough paws reached in, but Rex snarled and snapped at them, driving the half-seen creatures back.

Then came the sound of clicking. A faint, delicate noise that silenced Connor's mother. One by one, the sets of eyes blinked out of existence.

Rex's growls faded, and he sat down again. His tail thumped

on the pavement, and a moment later, a man appeared.

It was the old man who lived in Mrs. Lavoie's house. He held a small length of iron in his hand, and he smiled at Connor.

"Hello," the man said, giving a short bow to Rex and then a shorter one to Connor. "I don't believe we've been introduced. My name is Hu Bayi, and you would be Connor Mann."

"Yes," Connor said, nodding and asking. "How did you know?"

Mr. Bayi smiled. "Your mother's told me quite a bit about you."

Chapter 11: Hu and Connor, August 4th, 2016

It had been over thirty years since Connor entered what had once been Mrs. Lavoie's house.

Not surprisingly, a great deal had changed.

New appliances stood in the places where the old refrigerator and range top had been. Tiled floor covered the old wood, and a chandelier had replaced the light fixture. Where small houseplants had once lined the sill of the kitchen window, there was only a small statue of a dog. It looked as though it was made of metal, the hair and the face bearing the intricate carvings Connor had always associated with China and the Far East. The house no longer smelled of the pork pies Mrs. Lavoie had been fond of making, but was instead filled with the lingering scent of fragrant spices.

Connor, and Hu, as the older man preferred to be called, sat at a small dining table. Rex was asleep at Connor's feet. The refrigerator hummed and a clock on the wall ticked away the time at a steady, comforting pace.

Connor had accepted a glass of water from Hu but declined the first offer of beer. He had never had alcohol before, and he wasn't sure a stranger's house was the best place to try it.

And Connor was afraid he might end up liking it too much, as his father did.

"Do you mind if I smoke?" Hu asked.

"I don't think so," Connor replied, adding, "I've never actually been around anyone as they smoked."

"If it bothers you," the older man said, getting up from his seat, and going to a cabinet, "please let me know."

"I will," Connor answered, watching as Hu brought down a small, dark wooden box. From it, the man removed a long, dull white pipe that looked similar to the one Gandalf smoked in the *Lord of the Rings* movies. Hu withdrew a small leather pouch and a lighter. He returned to the table with all three items.

"This," Hu said, holding up the pipe after he had taken his seat again, "was a gift from a British officer I studied with. It is called a churchwarden pipe. Up until a few years ago, he was kind enough to send me some excellent tobacco for it. Unfortunately, he passed away. No one in America seems to sell it, and I can't find anyone willing to ship it to me. I have to make do with what

I can find here, in New England."

Connor didn't know what to say in response, but it seemed as though one wasn't necessary. Hu opened the leather pouch, removed some tobacco and packed the bowl of the pipe down with his thumb. The smell of the dark, shredded leaves was familiar, and it took Connor only a moment to realize that the scent of the tobacco was what he had smelled upon entering the home.

After Hu had gotten the pipe going and put the lighter down, he exhaled a long stream of smoke toward the ceiling. He smiled at Connor around the stem and said, "Now, I suppose you have some questions for me?"

Connor nodded, cleared his throat and asked, "What did you mean when you said that my mother spoke to you about me?"

"I meant exactly what I said," Hu responded, his voice gentle but firm. "You heard her, didn't you?"

"Yes," Connor whispered. His mind was still numb from the experience.

"I have heard her as well," Hu continued. "I moved into this house twenty years ago. During that time, I have walked through the cemetery, and around it, quite often. Your mother and others have reached out to me. They speak about what has occurred, and why they are still there."

Connor's hands trembled, and he slipped them under his thighs, pressing them down against the hard wood of the chair.

"They spoke to you," Hu said in a low voice. "Will you tell me what they said?"

"My mother said she was hungry," Connor answered, his voice nothing more than a hushed whisper. "I don't know what she meant. How can she be hungry? She's dead."

His breath shuddered as the last word passed his lips.

"The dead are often hungry," the older man said, giving Connor a moment of silence to compose himself. "I do not know what your mother hungers for. While their appetite may often stay along a broad theme, there are particulars to each individual ghost."

"Why did she become a ghost?" Connor whispered.

"You will learn soon enough," Hu said, "but for now, I will tell you *how* she became a ghost. I must ask you a painful question."

"Okay," Connor whispered.

"When your mother died," Hu said, "did you see anything strange? Out of place before or after?"

"Before," Connor answered, "and during."

"What did you see?" Hu asked, leaning forward, the pipe held in his hands and forgotten.

Connor closed his eyes and said, "A fox. But it wasn't right. There was something wrong with it. Like it wasn't really there."

"Ah," Hu said with a sigh.

When Connor opened his eyes, he saw Hu lighting his pipe. A grim look was on the man's face, and when he put the lighter down, he let out a stream of smoke from his lips.

"It is as I long suspected," Hu said. "Your mother was slain by a *mèiguǐ*, also known as a trickster ghost. One who can transform into animals."

"A what?" Connor asked, confused.

"A hungry ghost," Hu replied, "and like her killer, she is starving."

Chapter 12: A Conversation, August 4th, 2016

Connor felt physically miserable, and mentally drained. He had his hands wrapped around a tea cup as he stared listlessly at Hu.

The smell of the tobacco was pleasant as smoke curled up from the dark rim of Hu's pipe. After a moment, he removed the pipe stem from his mouth and said, "I suppose you are confused about all of this?"

Connor thought that was the understatement of the century.

"Yes," Connor said, sighing, "you could say that."

Hu nodded, puffed on his pipe shortly, and then, with smoke coming from his mouth and nose, said, "China has a long tradition of ghosts, as it does for a great many different items. But our ghosts are not as simple as Western ghosts. Your ghosts frighten you, and at times attack, but they are, in the end, only ghosts."

"A ghost is just a ghost, isn't it?" Connor asked, confused.

Hu shook his head. "Not in China. In China there are a great many types of ghosts, and the one that seems to have been imported here, to Pine Grove Cemetery, is the *èguǐ*, the hungry ghost."

Connor put the teacup down on the table and said, "What does that even mean? What are they hungry for? Seriously, Hu, I have no idea what you're talking about!"

"I know that you do not." Hu said, a note of anger creeping into his voice. "Please listen, Connor. I am attempting to tell you."

Connor pushed himself deeper into his chair and remained silent as Hu continued.

"When a Chinese individual is murdered, or their family has treated them shamefully, or if they are wicked," Hu said, "there is a good chance they will become a hungry ghost. This applies to those who were consumed by some passion in life as well. Someone who was gluttonous, or filled with greed, a person whose thoughts were enthralled with lust. All of these could lead to an afterlife of hunger. Death did not sate their desires. Instead, it magnified them."

Hu looked at Connor to see if he understood what was being said.

"But, my mom wasn't Chinese," Connor said, "and neither was Mrs. Lavoie. German and French-Canadian, respectively."

Hu inclined his head once and said, "I know, but there is a curious phenomenon that has been noticed, at least amongst the Chinese ghost-hunters. Those slain by our dead are affected as if they were native born. Do you follow me so far?"

Connor nodded and Hu took up the lesson once more.

"There are many different types of hungry ghosts," Hu said. "Some can take the form of animals, such as *mèiguǐ*, or there are the *wǎngliǎng-guǐ*, who can join themselves to rocks and trees."

"How can that even happen?" Connor asked, unable to shake his confusion. "I mean, ghosts here, in the States and Europe, they don't do that."

"It is a question of belief," Hu responded. "Look at your religion. When you die, you go to one of three places."

He ticked them off on his fingers as he said, "Heaven, Hell or Purgatory. For us, we await rebirth, or we are sent to various hells of our own devising. Not so for a western man or woman. There seems to be a general consensus as well in regards to what a ghost can or cannot do. The Germans have their poltergeists, and those of Celtic stock have an impressive variety as well. But the modern westerner is as mundane with his afterlife as he was with his life. So, when we boil it down, it is belief and culture."

Connor shook his head with disbelief. "Are you telling me someone can will themselves to be a certain type of ghost?"

"Of course," Hu said, "if the spirit is strong enough. I have read of such cases here in America. The internet is a source of wonder at times. There was, for a short while, a husband and wife team from New Hampshire, the Roys, I believe, who spoke of people who were able to remain after death."

Connor didn't believe everything Hu told him, but he kept the opinion to himself, feeling the older man wouldn't receive it well.

"Why is my mother still around?" Connor asked, his voice small.

"She must have had a hunger," Hu said gently. "From what little I have gathered from your mother, she made a poor choice, trying to acquire a birthday gift for you. It was a small act of theft, the most miniscule portion of greed that caused her to remain hungry after her death. I suspect Feng had some large part in her fall. He is a persuasive speaker."

Connor shuddered at the memory of his mother's death, and at the idea that her imprisonment was a result of her desire to make him happy on his birthday.

"So," Connor asked, fighting back a wave of depression, "not everyone who is killed by a hungry ghost becomes one?"

"No," Hu replied, "it is rare, in fact. But it seems as though these particular ghosts have a sense for kindred spirits, if you will pardon the pun."

As Hu paused to relight his pipe Connor asked, "Why do they want me?"

Hu shrugged his shoulders. "That is a question for which I have no answer. Not yet. My concern right now, Connor, is that we take great care from here on out. The dead have taken an interest in you. I do not know how many ghosts are in Pine Grove, or how many of them can be classified as *hungry*. But I do know you are their primary concern, which, in turn, makes you mine."

"Why?" Connor asked.

"Because," Hu said, the line of his jaw hard with determination, "I don't want you to die."

Connor didn't disagree.

Chapter 13: The Priest, June 7th, 1979

The sun was warm on his face and hands, the black fabric of his suit absorbing the light and warming him pleasantly. Robins sang in the trees, and a pair of squirrels chased one another across the street, up one side of an elm tree and down the other before they vanished from view.

The Priest smiled and hummed an old marching tune his father had been fond of.

When he reached the end of Adams Street, he turned left, past the Mann house and on towards Cushing Avenue. This he followed to the first entrance of Pine Grove Cemetery and made his way in. The air smelled of lilacs and freshly cut grass.

The Priest's smile broadened as he caught the scent of turned earth and paused to look for a new grave.

Near the far fence, across from the Mann's house, he saw a pile of dirt, an empty hole beside it. Evidently, the grave-diggers had paused in their work.

Perhaps for coffee, the Priest thought as he changed direction.

The grave occupied all of his attention, as they often did.

He had no great love for baptisms, and he found he despised performing the sacrament of marriage. But that of Extreme Unction, one of the Last Rites, thrilled him. The knowledge that he might well be the last person seen before the dying penitent went to their judgment thrilled him.

The Priest squatted down beside the unoccupied grave and stared down at it. Soon a coffin would be lowered into the ground. Mourners would stand and weep and gnash their teeth, rend their clothes and beat upon their breasts.

He wished he could offer them some peace of mind, let them know that their loved one would not be in the ground alone.

No, the Priest thought, reaching into the inner pocket of his suitcoat, *not alone at all.*

He removed a cigarette case. It was made from aluminum, the metal cut from the fuselage of a German fighter plane, an Me 109 his father had seen shot down in France.

The case, while it held a certain sentimental value to the Priest, carried something far more precious within it.

With a pleased sigh, he opened the cigarette case and looked at the beads within. There were one hundred of them. Dark brown and smooth, with a hole bored all the way through each. They had once been strung along a thin red cord, but the Priest had severed it. Each was far more effective alone.

At least, for his purposes.

The Priest selected one, rolled it between his fingers, and enjoyed the graceful texture of the bead. He smiled, leaned forward, and dropped the bead into the grave. It fell with a thud, much louder than an object its size should have made, and the Priest gave a chuckle.

Yes, he thought, *it will serve admirably.*

The Priest stood up, closed the cigarette case, and returned it to the safety of his inner pocket. He wondered who might interact with it first. The seventh month was drawing nearer, and someone was bound to see it.

The Priest looked out at Hill Street and saw Mrs. Mann step out onto her porch. She noticed him and waved, he did the same. His smile transformed itself into a grin. There were three members of the Mann family. Husband, wife, and child.

Perhaps, if the Priest was lucky, it would be one of them.

God willing, the Priest thought, *God willing.*

Chapter 14: With Hu, August 5th, 2016

"Can we free my mother?" Connor asked. He had regained some small measure of composure, but the idea of his mother trapped as a ghost had rattled him.

Hu hesitated before he responded. "Yes. But it will not be easy."

Connor waited for the man to clarify the statement.

At last, Hu turned away from the window and returned to the table.

"There are a great many ways to free a ghost," Hu began, "and some work for all, while others only work for a few. In your mother's case, we must deal with the hungry ghost who has trapped her."

"Okay," Connor said, "how do we do that?"

"I am hopeful," Hu said, "that we will only need to find that ghost."

"Hopeful?" Connor asked. "What do you mean by that? Is there something else? Something more that we might need to do?"

Hu nodded. "There is a chance."

"What?" Connor said, trying to keep the question from sounding too demanding.

"Connor," Hu said, "there is a strong chance that there is someone who is controlling the hungry ghost."

Connor opened his mouth to respond, closed it, and then shook his head. "I don't understand. How in God's name can someone *control* a ghost?"

Hu tapped the ashes out of the pipe's bowl into a small ashtray. When he had finished, he gave Connor a tight smile and said in an apologetic tone, "I don't know."

Connor didn't know why the answer took him by surprise, but it did.

"I wish I had an answer for you in that regard," Hu continued, "but I confess myself as little more than a novice in the area of ghosts. I grew up with folklore and myths. I know what is supposed to help keep a ghost out of my house, and what my ancestors did to protect themselves. Beyond that, I am a student, and I have discovered that there are few hard and fast rules when it comes to ghosts in general. Your father, I trust, still has the doors and windows protected with iron?"

"Um, yeah," Connor said, "on the first floor."

"Iron is crucial to keeping the dead at bay," Hu said. "And salt as well. Dogs are excellent deterrents. The hungry dead will not cross them. They fear them."

"What else?" Connor whispered. "What else works?"

"I don't know," Hu confessed, "but if we're going to help your mother, we need to learn, don't you agree?"

Connor nodded. "What do I need to do?"

"Change your sleeping pattern," Hu stated, "and we can work from there. As for myself, I must attempt to sleep. While I no longer sleep as much as I did in my youth, it is still a requirement."

"Alright," Connor said. He stood up. "Thank you, for speaking with me."

"It has been my pleasure," Hu said. "Will you come tomorrow evening, or shall I stop by?"

"My father's house is filthy," Connor answered, "and I'd rather you not have to deal with the mess. Once I get it clean, we can meet there."

"Excellent," Hu said, smiling. "It has been a pleasure speaking with you."

"Same here," Connor said, shaking the man's hand.

He and Rex left Hu's house and walked down to the steps in to the driveway. Connor stared at his own house and wondered, with growing fear, if anything would try to stop him.

With Rex close on his heels, Connor fled home.

Chapter 15: Fear in His Heart, August 6th, 2016

Connor sat on the kitchen floor with Rex beside him, the dog's chin on his leg. They had walked down to a 7-11 together, and Connor had picked up food for himself and some canned food for the dog. When they had arrived back at the house, Connor's father was gone again.

Where does he go? Connor wondered. It was three in the morning, and he had no idea where the man might have gone. A small part of him was concerned, but more out of self-preservation than for his father's well-being. Connor wasn't sure if he would have a place to live if his father died.

A scraping sound caught his attention and Rex's as well.

They both looked to the basement door.

The scraping became a knocking.

Then the person on the other side pounded on the door, causing it to shake in its frame.

And it stopped as suddenly as it had started.

A voice chuckled from the other side.

"Connor," Mrs. Lavoie said. "Are you there?"

He didn't answer, but Rex did. The dog got to his feet, snarling at the woman's voice.

Mrs. Lavoie let out a laugh. "Oh, you are there. That dog likes you, Connor. And who wouldn't? You were such a sweet little boy. I bet you're sweet now, too. Come back into the basement, Connor. Won't you give your old friend a hug?"

Other, deeper voices laughed. And a chorus called out, "Come down, Connor!"

"Or," Mrs. Lavoie said, "we can come upstairs and see you."

"Stay where you are," Connor snapped, "stay in the basement!"

"Connor," Mrs. Lavoie said in a soothing tone, "do you know how hard it was for us to get into the basement? How long it took us to find our way in from the graveyard? Too much time passed, even for the dead. Now let us in."

"I can't," Connor said, his voice sinking to a whisper. "You all need to leave. Go back to the cemetery."

"No," the voices said together.

"Please," Connor begged.

Heavy objects slammed into the door. The hinges groaned,

then squealed, and finally snapped. Connor watched in horror as the door flew across the short hall and crashed into the bathroom.

Darkness filled the hallway, and a high-pitched shriek cut through the air.

"Take the iron down!" Mrs. Lavoie screamed.

Rex's barks took on a frenzied pitch, and he moved forward, snapping at the shadows.

The ghosts in the basement howled, and it sounded as though bowling balls were thrown down the stairs.

And then there was silence.

Connor's blood raced through his veins while Rex's barks transformed into a low growl.

A creak sounded, a vague, muffled noise that sent a chill down Connor's spine. Rex's head snapped toward the sink.

Then the floor thumped from behind the battered cabinet doors.

A heartbeat later, they exploded outward, and the dead raced into the room.

They were small and difficult to see. There were three of them, and they were no bigger than rats. Rex lunged forward and the dead scattered, screaming in a high-pitched mixture of rage and terror. They avoided the dog's snapping jaws and sped towards Connor.

He leapt to his feet, narrowly avoiding one of the dead who screamed at him in a man's voice. Connor tried to twist away from a second but tripped over his own feet and crashed into the cabinet beside the stove. In addition to his own groan, Connor heard the rattle of pots and pans behind the thin cabinet door.

An idea burst into his consciousness, and he ripped open the cabinet as Rex defended him, chasing away the dead as they converged upon him. Connor plunged his hands into the depths of the dark cabinet and found what he sought.

He ripped the old cast iron skillet out and slammed the nearest rat-like dead with it. Before it vanished, the creature let out a horrific scream. A terrible, painful sound that caused stars to explode around the edges of Connor's vision, and sent a spike of pain through his head.

Despite the agony that the sound had plunged him into, Connor got to his feet. With the help of Rex, he chased off the last two of the dead, driving them back under the sink. Gasping and trying not to retch from the pain, Connor staggered away, clutching the pan.

Rex stayed near him as Connor tried to find where his father had hidden the hammer and iron coffin nails.

He found them near his father's chair, and they were the only items in the room, other than the sprung Lazy-boy, that weren't covered in a fine layer of dust.

Connor gathered up the hammer and the half dozen nails he found and made his way back to the kitchen. He slammed the door back into its frame and drove the nails in as best he could. Connor also tried to hammer in the original nails, but the force of the earlier blow had made them too weak to do much more than help keep the door upright.

I'll have to get more nails later, Connor thought numbly, retreating to the kitchen and dropping the hammer to the counter. For several minutes, he stared at the battered cellar door. Then, with Rex at his side, Connor hurried to his bedroom.

Chapter 16: Contemplation, August 7th, 2016

In the quiet and solitude of his garden, Hu considered his conversation with Connor. He had been saddened by the need to keep information about the dead from him. The man was an unknown variable in Hu's quest. Hu hoped to be able to finally find a starting point for his investigation. After twenty years of searching, he had begun to believe that he would never progress beyond Pine Grove Cemetery.

He knew that the first clue was there. The death of Connor's mother and the subsequent deaths over the years convinced Hu of the truth of his belief. Yet conviction and proof were two entirely separate animals, and Hu preferred hard evidence to faith and belief.

The sound of a commotion in Connor's house reached his ears. Hu didn't move. Instead, he continued to listen.

After the screams had faded away, a short silence followed. A growing dismay filled his heart, and Hu wondered if he had been wrong about the younger man.

Perhaps I should have asked him to remain with me a while, he thought.

Then the sound of hammering interrupted his self-reflection, and Hu smiled.

Connor Mann was not much to look at. He was tall, almost six feet, and what could only be described as rail-thin. Connor couldn't have weighed more than 150 pounds, and his light brown hair was cut short. His face was neither handsome nor ugly, bland features easily seen and easily forgotten. But Connor had an inner strength that Hu felt would be difficult to beat. He had seen it before, in men much younger than Connor. In his years as an officer, he had come across many of them, and some he had been terribly wrong about.

Hu remembered a youth who had been overweight, even in the heat of Vietnam. The boy had come from a small village at the top of the Gansu province. Hu had expected nothing but trouble from the young soldier, but he was proven wrong.

"Li Chuan," Hu murmured around the stem of his pipe.

The soldier had died defending the platoon during an attack.

Hu sighed and cleared his thoughts. He would have enough time to reflect upon the past later in his life. The dead needed all of his attention.

He drew on the pipe casually, letting the smoke eke out of the corners of his mouth. Hu came to a stop at the edge of his garden. Stones marked the boundary, and flowering plants grew between them. And every few feet stood ceramic statues of dogs.

They kept the dead at bay.

It had taken a great effort to get the statues into the United States. They had been smuggled in through Canada, into Boston, Massachusetts, and then back to him in New Hampshire. A long and twisted path of active agents and sleepers.

If it had not occurred before the attacks in New York City, Hu thought, *then it would not have been accomplished.*

It was an idea that he considered on a regular basis. When he had been sent to the United States from China, there had been many holes in the American security system. These had been exploited, allowing him to establish an outpost in the house across from the cemetery.

The last known area of the Priest.

Hu let out a long sigh, realized that he had allowed his pipe to go out and removed the lighter from his breast pocket. With the tobacco burning once again, he dropped his free hand onto the head of the nearest dog statue. The ceramic was cold to the touch, the paint faded and weathered. Each statue—and he had thirty of them—was several hundred years old.

Hu remembered the effort it had taken, the scouring of entire provinces looking for those statues not destroyed during the Cultural Revolution. But they had been found.

From the depths of the ceramic, there came a scrambling, scratching sound. Hu let out a pleased chuckle and in his native Chinese asked, "Are you awake now?"

The centuries old dog spirit confined within the statue let out a sharp yip, a noise taken up by the twenty-nine other canines guarding his home.

Hu gave the ceramic statue a reassuring pat and turned away. He felt his age in his knees and in his back, the old complaints and aches of a soldier.

Perhaps we will find you now, Priest, Hu thought. *Perhaps I will bring our dead home.*

Stifling a yawn, Hu left behind the baying dead dogs.

He was tired, and there was a great deal to do.

Chapter 17: Somewhere in Connecticut, August 7th, 2016

The Priest sat in his office. Sunlight streamed in through the open windows and fell upon his desk. Delicate tendrils of steam rose from his coffee, thick with cream and sugar, and a plate of dry, scrambled eggs with several slices of well-done bacon beside them, and a slice of toast. His notepad was blank, a ballpoint pen resting on it, waiting for him as he was waiting for inspiration.

The Priest smiled, picked up his toast, and ate it, careful to do so over the plate. Mrs. Soares disapproved of crumbs on the floor. He dunked a section of the crust into the coffee and enjoyed the sharp, bitter tang of the drink.

Within a few minutes, he had finished his simple morning ritual, and a moment later, there was a gentle knock on the door. Mrs. Soares didn't wait for him to answer, but opened the door and came in. After three years in the parish, she knew his habits well. She cleaned up the dishes, nodded with approval at the lack of crumbs, and exited as silently as she had entered.

When the door latch clicked, the Priest picked up the pen and focused on the notepad. Sunday was fast approaching, and he needed to have a sermon prepared. He considered the members of his parish and frowned.

The Priest missed his days as a missionary, stealing his way into mainland China and ministering to the faithful trapped there behind the godless, communist wall.

Little does my current flock know of suffering, the Priest thought.

He hesitated, then put the pen down and opened the center drawer of his desk. From it, he withdrew his father's cigarette case. The Priest set it down beside the pen and opened the case. Smooth beads were still within the metal walls, but there were far fewer than there had been over the past thirty years.

Is it time? he asked, a smile dancing on his lips. *Shall we help them know what suffering is? Will we show them the fear and glory to be found in an all-loving and forgiving God?*

On the table beside the desk stood an old black rotary telephone that seemed to be almost as old as the Priest. The device let out a shrill ring that caught him off guard and almost caused him to spill the beads. He glared at the phone, snapped the cigarette case closed and put it away.

Mrs. Soares answered the phone before it could ring a second time, and the Priest had shut the desk drawer only a moment before she came in.

"You have a call, Father," she said, speaking with a heavy Portuguese accent.

"Who is it?" he asked.

"He would not give his name," Mrs. Soares replied, "but would say only that it is important that he speaks with you."

"It always is, is it not, Mrs. Soares?" the Priest said, sighing.

Mrs. Soares nodded.

"Thank you," he said, picking up the handset from the cradle.

She smiled, backed out of the room, and eased the door shut behind her.

"Hello?" the Priest asked.

The man on the other end cleared his throat nervously.

"Hello," the Priest said again, "may I help you?"

"Is it you?" The caller's voice was cracked with fear, and it sounded familiar.

"Yes," the Priest answered. Before he could ask whom he was speaking with, the man continued on.

The words rushed out of the stranger's mouth.

"He's back," the caller said. "And they're here. They're after him. They broke in! They haven't gotten in before!"

The man's voice rose higher as he spoke, a frantic, frenzied pitch to each word as they chased after one another.

"I've seen them," the caller continued, "do you understand? They're going to get in. They want him. *She* wants him."

When the man said 'she,' and stressed it, the Priest knew who was on the other end of the call. He straightened up in surprise.

"Is he really?" the Priest asked in a soft voice. "I didn't think anyone would come back from such an event. Then again, I suppose it should have been expected. Children are remarkably resilient. Well, I do thank you for the call."

"What are you going to do about it?" the caller demanded, his voice shaking with fear.

The Priest almost laughed, but he managed to restrain himself. "I suppose I shall come for a visit. The festival will be occurring soon."

"What?" the man asked, confused. "What festival?"

"Never mind," the Priest said, chuckling. "I will be there soon

Hungry Ghosts

enough. Thank you for calling, Cody. It is greatly appreciated."

Before the man could say anything else, the Priest hung up the phone.

For several minutes, he sat and considered the return of Connor Mann, and then the Priest let out a joyous laugh.

He picked up the pen, leaned over the pad and jotted down the title of his sermon.

The Tale of Lazarus.

Chapter 18: Defending Oneself, August 8th, 2016

"What did you do?"

The angry and drunken tone of his father's words snapped Connor awake, and Rex too. Connor watched the dog spring from the bed and land in front of the doorway to the bedroom, snarling at his father.

The man took a hurried, surprised step back and looked from Rex to Connor.

"What are you talking about?" Connor asked, groggy from lack of sleep and the residual effects of his medications.

"Look at this, the wood's all split," his father replied, gesturing furiously at the casing of the door. "And where the hell is the door?"

"In the spare bedroom," Connor answered. "The dead got in here last night. Do you understand that? I don't care about the wood. All I care about is making sure that they didn't come into the bedroom while I was trying to sleep. Hell, if I'd bothered to think about it, I would have thought you'd be happy to have another room protected by iron."

"Maybe you should have left them alone," his father snapped. "You know, just stayed the hell out of the damned basement. Did you ever think about that? And hey, since we're thinking about stuff that maybe should have happened, maybe you should just pack your crap and get the hell out of here!"

"You're still drunk," Connor said, smelling the cheap wine and beer on his father's breath.

"Doesn't mean I'm wrong," the man spat.

"No," Connor said, "but it still makes you look and sound like an idiot."

His father swore and clenched his fists.

"And what did you do in the kitchen, *Connor*?" the man asked, his voice filled with spite. "Why in the hell are the cabinet doors nailed shut? Huh? How the hell am I going to get anything out of them now?!"

"Like what, cleaning supplies?" Connor sneered. "You're a pig. Don't worry about the cabinets."

His father grumbled, stepped forward, and then threw his arms up as he stumbled back. Rex's voice had risen to a fierce growl, and there was no doubt as to what would happen to

Connor's father if the man stepped across the threshold.

"You better watch your mouth," his father snapped, eyes darting from the dog to Connor, "I can still beat you."

Connor got out of bed, his face hot with anger.

"Go downstairs and sober up," Connor hissed, "or go down there and shut up. Either one is fine with me."

His father's jaw worked feverishly for a second, as if he were about to speak, then the man grumbled and retreated down the stairs.

When Connor heard the door slam shut, he sat down on his bed, body trembling from the surge of adrenaline. Rex came over, tail wagging. Dim light outlined the towels on the windows and Connor wondered what time it was.

I don't even own a watch, Connor realized.

Then a frightening thought occurred to him.

I have to go out. Into the world.

The thought terrified him. His breath came faster, racing out of his lungs and leaving him gasping. Rex whined, pushed his nose into Connor's hands and remained there.

The reassuring touch of the dog helped Connor control himself. He forced his heart to slow down, breathed in through his nose, and closed his eyes.

I faced the dead last night, he told himself. *I can go to a store.*

Connor nodded, opened his eyes, and stood up. He went to the window facing the cemetery and took down the towel.

Connor froze, squeezing the towel in his hands.

Another message had been left, but it hadn't been written, although Connor wished it was.

Instead, four dead birds had been driven into the window screen, their small heads pushed through the wire mesh. The dull black eyes of the birds stared at him, their wings and feet limp.

Connor dropped to his knees, barely registering the sharp pain of the floor against his joints. He shook, unable to control himself, and let his chin fall to his chest.

From somewhere in the house he heard a deep, pleased laugh, and knew it was not his father.

This, Connor realized with horror, *is only the beginning.*

Chapter 19: Alone in the House, August 8th, 2016

Cody Mann sat in his chair, as he had for the majority of his time in the house. Connor had left, exhausted and haggard, with the dog.

Cody grimaced at the memory. The dog had belonged to him, not his weak, simpering excuse for a son.

With a scowl, Cody reached out, snatched up his can of beer, and popped it open. It frothed, foam spilling out over his hand. He sucked the beer off his hand, then lifted the can up and drained it in one long, well-practiced motion.

Cody felt better with the cold drink in his belly and dropped the empty can to the floor. He settled into his chair, took a second beer off the battered end table beside him, and opened it. This one he drank slower, but he still finished it within a few minutes. He went through the rest of the six-pack in less than half an hour, and he felt good when he was done.

The beer was followed by a bottle of cheap red wine, and the world had taken on the soft glow he appreciated. He stared at the blank television. While he couldn't afford cable—not with the stipend he had been given following his wife's death—he had been able to get his hands on a used DVD player when the world stopped making VHS tapes.

He looked at the television, tapped his fingers on his thighs, and wondered what he should watch. At Goodwill, he'd gotten a copy of *Red Dawn*.

Should watch that tonight, he thought. *Need to get a few more beers in me first.*

His thoughts were cut off by a dull thud from the basement, followed by a heavy crash, then a soft scratching sound in the room with him.

Cody had learned not to worry about the random noises in the house. Especially those coming from beyond the iron and salt. The scratching sound was irritating, so he focused on that.

It came from beneath the old dresser upon which the television was set.

Cody stared at the piece of furniture, trying to decide what was making the noise. The boy had cleaned the kitchen, and Cody knew there had been mice in it, living under the trash.

He had decided it was the displaced mice when a rattle

joined the scratching.

The bottom drawer of the dresser shook. A gentle, almost probing motion. The old television shivered and moved a fraction of an inch towards the edge.

Cody watched, fascinated.

The drawer eased out a little, then a hair's breadth more.

Cody leaned forward, grinning and wondering what was hidden in the drawer. He knew it couldn't be a mouse, and it couldn't be the dead. The iron around his doors and windows had kept them at bay for over twenty years. They had never been able to pass through the basement door, or descend the stairs from the second floor.

He chuckled and dropped back into the sprung comfort of his chair.

The thought crossed his mind that he wasn't even awake.

I'm dreaming, his words slurred even in his own thoughts. *Passed right out, didn't I?*

Before he could answer his own question, the bottom drawer slid out.

Cody held his breath, waiting to see what would emerge.

A small, silver nose appeared. It was followed by a snout, equally silver, which in turn was attached to a head of the same color. Soon a fox was before him, sitting upright in the drawer and looking at Cody.

Cody let out a giggle.

Then the sound died in his throat.

The fox was familiar.

Somehow, he had seen it before.

Then the memory came to him unbidden.

The night Ida Lavoie had died, on the porch. Connor had been in the kitchen, and the silver fox had been there, sitting in front of the side door with the same patience it was showing from its seat in the drawer.

Then the fox shimmered, shifted, and grew. By the time Cody had drawn in a shuddering breath, a man stood in front of him.

The stranger was as silver as the fox, his skin rippling, and fluid. He was middle-aged, a sly smile on his face. A chill filled the room, accompanied by the stench of decay.

And Cody understood that he wasn't dreaming. Along with that understanding came the knowledge that Connor probably hadn't secured the basement door properly. That the crash he had heard wasn't a noise made by the ghosts to irritate Cody, but the sound of the dead getting into the house effortlessly because of his mind-numbingly stupid son.

Whimpering, he tried to get to his feet, but the man stepped forward, a single, graceful motion that brought him to Cody's side. The man reached out, brushed Cody's hair out of his eyes, and then thrust his hand into Cody's mouth.

The pain was immediate and complete.

Gagging, Cody tried to escape, but he couldn't move, couldn't breathe.

And in a moment, it didn't matter anymore.

Chapter 20: Magpies in the Window, August 9th, 2016

They stood on the street with their backs to the cemetery, the wrought iron fence separating them from the graves as the two men looked at Connor's house.

Despite the warmth of the sun upon him, Connor felt cold. He crossed his arms over his chest and clasped his biceps, trying to keep himself from shaking.

Hu stood beside him, hands behind his back and moving a string of beads through his fingers one at a time. The older man examined Connor's window with a critical eye, remaining silent for a long time.

Rex paced back and forth on the street, his claws clicking on the pavement.

Connor glanced at Hu. The man's face was tight, his lips pressed close together. Finally, the beads ceased their movements through Hu's fingers. He looped them around his left wrist and let out a small sigh.

"What is it?" Connor asked. "That isn't good, right?"

"Correct," Hu said after a moment, "that is not good, Connor. In at least two ways."

Connor waited for the man to clarify his statement.

"Those birds," Hu said, gesturing towards the dead animals, "are magpies. They are often viewed as a symbol of great joy. To kill them in such a way, to use them so callously, well, let us say that we can assume that you are not being wished happiness."

Connor swallowed, and a dry click sounded. He cleared his throat and said, "Okay. That's the first."

Hu nodded. "The second inauspicious aspect of this message is the number of birds used. Four is an unlucky number in China, the unluckiest, in fact."

Connor looked at Hu. "And that's bad?"

"Yes," Hu said in a soft voice. "It is bad. Worse, in fact, than I originally thought."

"Worse?" Connor asked, laughing in disbelief. "What the hell do you mean?"

Hu raised an eyebrow at the note of panic in Connor's voice, but Connor didn't care. He pressed on.

"Seriously," Connor said, "how bad is this going to get?"

"That, I do not know," Hu said, "but the symbolism tells me

that we are dealing with a hungry ghost who is well aware of what they are, and what they want."

"And what's that?" Connor demanded.

"Evidently, you, Connor," Hu said.

Connor's stomach twisted. He tried to speak, but couldn't. His mind didn't accept what Hu said. Connor had heard the dead say it, but he hadn't believed.

They were dead. He had a difficult time believing *in* them.

But Hu's pronouncement had such an air of finality, of truth that Connor had to accept it.

He had no choice.

As the cold mantle of realization settled over him, the house seemed to shimmer. He cast the idea away from him, dismissing it as a reaction of his mind to the strange reality Hu's statement had thrust him into.

And then Hu spoke.

"What was that?" the older man asked.

"You saw it?" Connor asked in reply.

Hu nodded, a grim look on his face. "Is your father home?"

"I don't—" Connor started, then caught himself. "Yes, yes, he's home."

"Come," Hu said, crossing the road and hurrying towards the porch, "we must make certain he is safe."

Connor didn't care if his father was well or not, but he didn't want to be outside without Hu. He found himself jogging to keep up with Hu, the older man far sprightlier than Connor would have thought.

Hu reached the porch a few steps before him, sped up the stairs, and tore open the screen door. It slammed against the side of the house as he forced his way in.

"Cody?" Hu called as they entered the kitchen.

Connor came to a stop, and his father shambled out of the den. His gait was stilted, his movements awkward.

"He's drunk," Connor said, his voice filled with bitterness.

"No," Hu said. "He's not."

Rex growled, snapping at the air as Connor's father took another trio of steps towards them.

Hu yelled at Cody Mann in Chinese.

Connor's father laughed and answered in the same.

343

Chapter 21: A Warning Unheeded, August 20ᵗʰ, 1986

Avery Christiansen pulled into the small, dirt parking lot behind the caretaker's office in Pine Grove Cemetery.

There were no other cars.

And the curtain was still down in the caretaker's office, which meant Mr. Strafford wasn't in.

Avery was the newest hire, having been with the cemetery for only a month. When Mr. Strafford had informed him that there would be no work on Wednesday, Avery had assumed it was a joke. The other guys in the crew had pulled some good ones on him.

And when Mr. Strafford had said they had a paid day off in the middle of the week, at the end of August, Avery had figured his two coworkers had gotten the boss to go in on a gag.

Frowning, Avery put his Volkswagen into park, turned the engine off, and got out. The August air was sticky and uncomfortable, and it was only a quarter to seven in the morning.

He got out of his car, stuffed the keys into his pocket, and went to the back door. Avery jiggled the handle and twisted it to the right, which was what Danny had told him to do if Avery ever needed to get into the building after hours.

The lock popped, and the door swung in.

Avery hesitated, listened, and when he didn't hear anything, crossed the threshold. Mr. Strafford's office door was open, and Avery went in, flicking on the light as he did so.

His boss's desk was neat and organized, nothing out of place on the leather blotter, not a speck of dust to be found on it. A large calendar, devoid of any pictures or decorations, hung on the wall closest to the desk. The calendar was separated into weeks and each week into days. But the blank squares were huge, information regarding burials and schedules filling them.

Avery walked to the calendar and leaned in, squinting a little to read the words written on August 26.

C. Lawson's funeral, East Orleans, Massachusetts.

Shaking his head, Avery straightened up and turned away.

He still couldn't believe there was no work, just because of a funeral for someone Mr. Strafford knew. Frowning, Avery called out in a loud voice, "Hello?"

The walls of the building deadened the impact of his voice,

and Avery grumbled before he yelled, "Anybody here?"

No one answered him.

He left the office, wandered down the hallway and went into the kitchenette. The coffee pot was off and cold. A sure sign that no one had come in and then hidden from Avery.

They all needed their coffee in the morning, except for Mr. Strafford, who drank tea. At least a gallon a day from what Avery had seen.

He walked over to the two-burner stove, where Mr. Strafford's teakettle sat, and gave the metal a cautious touch.

It too was cold.

Avery shook his head, confused.

The rear door rattled, and Avery backed out of the kitchenette, looking down the hallway to the open door.

"Hello?" a female voice inquired. "Is someone in here?"

"Yeah," Avery said, walking down the hall. "Come on in."

A shape appeared in the doorway, silhouetted by the daylight. The stranger stepped in, closing the door behind her. Avery blinked, his eyes adjusting to the change in light. His breath caught in his throat and he licked his lips self-consciously.

The stranger was indeed a woman, young and beautiful. She wore a simple summer dress of light green, and her blonde hair was piled in a loose bun on the top of her head. Her limbs were slim, and when she took a step closer to him, she moved without sound, almost as if her feet didn't touch the floor.

Goosebumps rippled along his flesh, and Avery smiled at her.

She came to a stop a few feet away from him, her fingers interlocked in front of her. From beneath long lashes, she looked at him, her lips parted slightly.

Avery had a difficult time hearing his own voice when he asked, "Do you need some help, miss?"

"My name's Ethel," the young woman said, and her voice caused him to tremble with excitement.

Avery stuttered as he introduced himself.

She gave a crooked smile that weakened his knees.

"Are you the only one here today, Avery?" she asked.

He nodded, noticing the pale gray color of her eyes.

"When are your employees going to be here?" Ethel asked. "Later in the morning?"

"Oh, they're not mine," Avery whispered, unable to keep his eyes off her lips. "In fact, my boss, Mr. Strafford, he gave us the day off. I thought he was joking."

"You're the only one?" she asked, taking a small step forward.

Avery's heart hammered against his chest as he nodded.

"Well," she said in a husky voice, "I'm a lucky girl then."

Before Avery could respond, Ethel transformed in front of him. Her youth and beauty were torn away by some unseen hand, leaving behind a face and body ravaged by time and disease. The gray eyes vanished, sinking into her skull as her teeth yellowed, blackened, and dropped from her mouth.

Avery turned to run, but Ethel sprang at him, far too fast and strong for him to get away. She slammed into him, sending him sprawling into the wall. The plywood panels cracked beneath his weight and he twisted as he fell, landing on his right elbow. Pain tore through his arm, and he felt the same shoulder dislocate.

Before he could get to his feet, Ethel scrambled onto him, ripping his shirt off him.

"Give it to me!" she shrieked, long, cracked nails digging into the flesh of his chest.

Avery screamed as she struck bone and broke his sternum. She dug through it with the tenacity of a dog, his blood splashing up and through her. He took another breath for a scream and then choked on it as she tore into his lungs, shredding them as she ripped them out of his body.

"No!" she howled. "There is nothing sweet about this one!"

Then her cry of anger shifted into a shout of pure, animalistic joy as she held his heart aloft.

My heart is so small. Strange, Avery thought and closed his eyes as Ethel squealed with pleasure.

Chapter 22: An Unexpected Conversation, August 9th, 2016

Hu managed to keep his face blank, hiding the surprise he felt at hearing his mother tongue spoken out of the dirty mouth of Cody Mann.

But he knew, even if Connor did not, that Cody was dead and his corpse a host for a hungry ghost.

"And what is your name, Little One?" the ghost asked in Chinese. "Do you speak your own tongue?"

"Why would I not?" Hu asked in return.

The ghost chuckled and switched to English, saying, "Excellent. And do you know who I am, Little One?"

"I know," Hu said, "that you are a Backdoor God, and nothing more than that."

The ghost let out a pleased laugh, nodding. "Let me give you a name, Little One. Backdoor God, while appropriate, is cumbersome. Feng, I think, shall suffice."

"And would you like to know mine, Feng?" Hu asked.

Feng shook his head. "There is no need. You are a little one, a child to me, though you might be a hundred. I have marked the passage of decades when still alive, and after by the festivals I have seen."

"Why don't you tell me why you are here, Feng?" Hu asked.

Feng shook his head, then he smiled and nodded in the direction of Connor.

"He is interesting though," Feng said, his voice dropping to a barely audible whisper. "Strong. The younger ones, they are afraid of him. He can sense us. He saw me a full day before I butchered his mother, and still, he saw me for what I was when I killed the woman who lived where you do now, Little One."

Feng's smile widened, and, still whispering, he asked, "How do you think he will act when he learns I have made him an orphan?"

"I'll show you!" Connor screamed from behind Hu.

Hu pushed the younger man back and kept his attention on Feng.

The dead man leaned forward and continued softly, "I think he'll go mad with rage eventually. It is a pity I was not able to kill his father in front of him. The boy's reaction would have been thrilling to see."

"Will you not step out, Feng?" Hu inquired. "Come into the air and speak with me."

The dead man sneered. "Too much iron, Little One, though I suspect it is why you made the suggestion."

Hu allowed himself a small smile.

Feng chuckled.

"No," the dead man continued, raising his voice, "I will not be stepping outside. Even if there were no barrier, I would refrain from such an act. The *dog* does not agree with me."

As if he knew that he was the subject of the statement, Rex let out a dark, low bark that caused even Hu's hair to stand on end.

"Yes," Feng concluded, "I will stay here. Where I do not have to contend with the beast."

Then the dead man narrowed his eyes and grinned, asking, "Will you come in with me, Little One? You and your friend?"

Hu shook his head. "No. I have no desire to die today, Feng."

Feng shrugged. "We all die sometime. Some of us even remain past our death. I could help you with both of those if you are so inclined."

"I am not," Hu replied.

"Ah well," Feng said. Then he looked past Hu to Connor and smiled. "I wish I could linger in this meat, but it will stiffen soon enough, and then it will be far too unwieldy."

Feng stretched, let out a brief laugh, and focused his dead eyes upon Hu.

"Look for me soon, Little One," Feng advised, "for the Festival is coming upon us, and I will be stronger then."

As the last word passed the dead man's lips, Feng turned and shambled towards the window over the sink. With a laugh ringing out, Feng launched Cody's body into the glass, shattering it as he broke through. The ghost slipped out of the body, and the corpse of Cody Mann collapsed, hanging half in and half out of the window.

Chapter 23: The Safety of Hu's Garden, August 9th, 2016

They sat on chairs in Hu's garden. Each piece of furniture was crafted from dark wood, scenes of ancient battles carved into the surface. A gentle breeze made its way through the manicured landscape and carried with it the smell of flowers Connor had no name for.

Only he and Hu were in the garden.

Rex, his tail between his legs and a steady whine in his throat, had refused to enter it. The dog remained in the house, lying down at the back door and staring out at them.

After several minutes of silence, Connor interwove the fingers on both hands together and said, "He's made an orphan of me."

Hu looked over at him. "He was thrilled about that."

Connor nodded and stared at one of the many dog statues that encircled the garden's edge. "Can he be destroyed?"

"Not destroyed," Hu said, "but sent on his way. I suspect he will have a Hell of his own waiting for him."

"I'd like to help him find it," Connor muttered. "Tell me something, Hu. If this ghost was able to turn my mother into a ghost, and Mrs. Lavoie into one, would they be able to do the same to someone else?"

Hu sighed and nodded.

"How many could there be?" Connor asked, looking at him.

"First," Hu said, "you must understand the nature of this ghost. He is strong. Far stronger than others you will encounter here. He will be able to kill when he chooses, but he will be strongest during the seventh month."

"What, July?" Connor asked.

Hu shook his head. "Not your seventh month, China's. We move through the year on a lunar calendar, and so the seventh lunar month is different each year than your calendar."

"Alright," Connor said, taking a deep breath, "when is it going to be this year?"

"This month," Hu replied, "and there is a particular day in the seventh month, one on which the dead will be especially powerful."

"And that is?" Connor asked, anger mingling with anxiety.

"The seventeenth," Hu said. "That will be the most

dangerous day."

"The seventeenth," Connor whispered. "That's only eight days away."

Hu nodded.

"And now you're saying that there might be others," Connor said, anxious, returning to the original concern. "Will they be more powerful that day, too?"

"Yes," the older man replied, "without a doubt."

"How many are we talking about," Connor said, shifting in his chair to look at Hu, "when it's all said and done?"

"The ghostly community could have grown exponentially," Hu said. "First, in 1979, the ghost murdered your mother. The next year he slaughtered Mrs. Lavoie. We know both of these because you witnessed them. But, from what I have learned, their deaths are listed as natural."

"How did you get that information?" Connor asked in surprise.

Hu waved the question away.

"Now," the older man continued, "what if your mother killed someone the same night that the first ghost murdered Mrs. Lavoie? And, for the sake of argument, what if the ghosts of your mother, the person your mother killed, and Mrs. Lavoie all killed someone the next year. What if this continued?"

"Until last year?" Connor whispered.

Hu nodded.

"I don't know," Connor said, shaking his head. "I can't even do the math."

"The math wouldn't be correct," Hu said, a comforting tone in his voice. "Not all would have been able to kill. Not all who were killed would have become ghosts. There is a large set of variables, special circumstances, if you will, concerning Chinese ghosts."

"I still don't understand," Connor said, angrily, "how my American mother can be a Chinese ghost."

"To your Western sensibilities," Hu said a trifle coldly, "ghosts have a set pattern then?"

"No," Connor said, "there shouldn't be ghosts at all. None of this makes any sort of god-damned sense. My whole life, I was told that ghosts didn't exist. I merely had a *curious reaction* to the trauma of seeing my mother die on my birthday."

"They do exist," Hu said, looking away and staring at a dog statue. "They are to be found everywhere. In each culture, no matter how civilized or how primitive. It cannot be denied, Connor Mann, that some of the dead do come back."

Connor wanted to argue the point, but he found he couldn't. The old man was right.

Connor had heard it, and he had seen it. He had heard both his mother's voice and Mrs. Lavoie's.

"Why?" Connor whispered.

Hu returned his attention to Connor, frowning. "Why what?"

"Why is my mom a ghost?" Connor asked, blinking back tears. "Why hasn't she moved on, or whatever? What's keeping her here? Is it me?"

"That, I cannot answer," Hu replied, his words tinged with bitterness. "Not at first. Perhaps not at all. When I am able to speak to her at greater length," Hu explained, "I will be able to tell you why she is a ghost, and what we might do to help her."

Connor nodded and said nothing more.

After several minutes of silence, Hu cleared his throat.

Connor glanced over at him.

"There is still a task left unfinished," Hu said.

Momentarily, Connor didn't know what the man meant, then he shuddered. His father's body remained in the house and Connor suddenly understood the man was dead. After Mrs. Lavoie's death, and his subsequent institutionalization, Connor had not been forced to deal with death or fatalities. In the facility, someone was either there, or they weren't.

With a sigh, Connor nodded, stood up and asked, "May I use your phone?"

"It is in the kitchen," Hu answered.

Connor walked into the house and Rex scrambled to follow him. In the kitchen, he found a black, rotary phone on the wall. He picked it up, held the receiver to his ear, and heard a dial tone. Connor dialed 9-1-1 and told the woman who answered that his father was dead.

Chapter 24: Pine Grove Cemetery, June 4th, 1987

Mr. Lloyd Strafford was alone in his office. It was 3:47 in the afternoon and the last of the laborers had left seventeen minutes earlier. He glanced around his office, still surprised after two years on the job that it was his. The building had been a wreck when he had taken over. Windows had been sealed shut with thin iron bars, salt had been stuffed into openings in the floor and packed into windowsills and the thresholds. His first task had been to get the building serviceable as an office, which meant he had stripped it of all the items he had found.

Lloyd shook his head and fingered the small cross he had fashioned from a pair of old, iron coffin nails. He doubted the religious aspect of his homemade talisman would have any effect on the dead, but he had learned that the metal itself worked wonders.

His hand shook as he squeezed the iron in his palm.

It was too early in the season for all of them to be out, but it was never too soon for the fox to prowl among the headstones.

His mouth went dry as he thought of the fox, the strange creature that had appeared almost a decade earlier. Shortly after the silver animal's arrival, the woman had died in the cemetery.

Since that first death, there had been more, all of them within the confines of the cemetery's fence.

Lloyd stood up and walked out of his office.

He suspected the fox lived within the cemetery. That somewhere it hid among the graves. Possibly within one.

Lloyd went to the kitchenette and took a bottle of Coke out of the refrigerator. He tried not to turn and look at the stain on the wall, where Avery had been murdered.

The young man's death weighed on Lloyd, for he felt as though he had failed him. It wasn't true, of course, but it didn't stop him from believing it. Nor did it stop Lloyd from waking up screaming most nights, seeing Avery's mutilated corpse.

Meredith, Lloyd's wife, had even taken to sleeping in another room.

Back at her mother's house.

Lloyd frowned, opened the bottle of Coke, and dropped the cap on the small counter. He drank half of the bottle in one long, greedy gulp.

A poor substitute for bourbon, Lloyd thought, finishing the drink, *but infinitely better in its own way.*

He put the empty bottle on the counter and stared at the small sink.

Lloyd shuddered, took the iron cross out of his pocket, and looked at it again.

After Avery's death, and the lack of even a hint of a suspect for the crime, Lloyd had sought out alternative answers. He had spent all of his free time in libraries, and one late night, he had had a conversation with a researcher at the library at St. Anselm's College. In the course of their chat, Lloyd learned the man was a professor of Chinese mythology and folklore. St. Anselm's had recently acquired a small collection of older Chinese works, and the professor was on sabbatical in order to study them. Lloyd, feeling undereducated, explained how he was researching ghosts.

Whether it was because he didn't have anyone to talk to, or that he was overtired, or a combination of the two, Lloyd told the academic everything that had occurred at Pine Grove Cemetery.

To his surprise, the man didn't laugh or snicker, or do anything of the sort. Instead, he had asked about the timing of the deaths. Lloyd told him, and the man's face had paled, and he brought him to the small, secure room where the Chinese manuscripts were being held. On the desk where the professor had been working, was a small book. It was written in English. Lloyd saw the book was about ghosts and the supernatural.

It had been an older work, published in the late nineteenth century. Not only did it cover the gamut of Western ghosts, but that of the Orient and the Far East as well. And it was in that book, in a chapter on Chinese folk tales revolving around the ghosts, that Lloyd had found the fox.

Nothing more than a paragraph, but it had contained a description of how certain ghosts had the ability to take on the shape of animals.

And the fox had been one of them.

Reading that information had been an epiphany for Lloyd, and it had changed the direction of his research. He had delved deeper into ghost lore, regardless of cultural or geographic boundaries. Lloyd had learned about the power of iron and salt, and how Chinese ghosts were powerful, especially during the

Ghost Festival.

And he had discovered how Avery had been murdered on the day of the festival. Further research and telephone calls to professors at both Boston College and Boston University had confirmed Lloyd's suspicion about the other deaths as well.

The woman who had died in the cemetery in 1979, and the one who had died across the street in 1980, both during the Ghost Festival.

No, Lloyd corrected himself, *they were murdered.*

He reached into his pocket and squeezed the iron cross, the metal hard against his flesh. A comforting sensation.

Lloyd took another Coke out of the refrigerator and left the kitchenette. It was time to go to his house. The thought held no attraction for him. Without Meredith, it was no longer a home, merely a place of shelter.

Nothing more.

Lloyd walked through the small building, turned off lights as he went and double-checked the lock on the filing cabinet. There wasn't much in the petty cash fund, but he saw no reason to tempt fate by leaving it unlocked. When he left his office, he heard a soft bark, as if someone had let a dog loose in the cemetery.

Lloyd shook his head, faced the back door, and froze.

The silver fox blocked Lloyd's exit.

He watched as the animal tilted its head first to the left, and then to the right, the gesture so uncannily human that sweat broke out across his brow.

The fox's body fluctuated, shrinking and then growing larger in fits and spurts. Soon an Asian man stood before him, the same silver as the fox. He wore loose fitting robes and had a long, thin string of beads around his neck. They hung down to his waist, and his hands were held in front of him. His face was old and cruel, a sneer on his thin lips. The man's nose was equally thin but short, like the point of a knife protruding from the center of his face. His head was shaved and his eyes pulsed in their sockets.

The ghost gave a short, mocking bow, the necklace of beads swinging freely. When he straightened up, he leered at Lloyd and asked a question that was unintelligible.

Lloyd didn't speak Chinese, and it didn't seem as though the ghost spoke English.

The ghost voiced a question again, and when Lloyd didn't answer, the dead man chuckled, nodding to himself. He held up a thin hand and beckoned Lloyd with long fingers.

Lloyd remained rooted in his spot.

The ghost frowned and snapped a statement at Lloyd.

"No," Lloyd whispered. He plunged his hand into his pocket and removed the iron cross.

Lloyd wasn't sure what he had expected when he had envisioned the use of the cross. Perhaps a rearing back, maybe even a hiss and shying away as a vampire was supposed to do.

The silver ghost did neither of those.

Rage filled the dead man's face, and he pointed at the cross, yelling at Lloyd.

The man's intention was clear.

Put it away or suffer the consequences.

Lloyd remembered Avery's corpse and decided he wouldn't roll over and offer himself as a victim to the ghost.

"No," Lloyd said, his voice shaking but firm. "You get the hell out of my office."

The ghost snarled, spoke in a vicious tone, and gestured again for Lloyd to come forward.

"I'll come to you," Lloyd said, holding the cross out in front of him. "Do you want this?"

The dead man let out a laugh that shrank Lloyd's courage and caused him to stumble closer to the ghost. A wicked grin spread across the dead man's face, and it seemed to grow wider the further Lloyd moved toward the back door.

Then the smile vanished, a concerned look replaced the grin, and the dead man disappeared.

Lloyd hurried to the back door, throwing it open. He looked around wildly, trying to see where the dead man had gone.

The ghost had disappeared.

With his heart pounding in his chest, Lloyd forced himself to examine everything he saw. Within the cemetery, there was nothing different. No mourners, no people taking a stroll, no kids on bikes.

The only item out of the ordinary was a moving van, parked on Hill Street. Someone had purchased the old Lavoie house, which had been empty since Ida Lavoie had died at the Mann house seven years earlier.

It was then that Lloyd saw the silver fox, seated beside a headstone and staring at the moving van.

The animal was still there when Lloyd hurried to his car and fled the cemetery, stunned by what he had witnessed.

Chapter 25: The Priest Returns, August 10th, 2016

The Priest wore street clothes, his faith, and his role in society hidden as he walked through Pine Grove Cemetery, a cane in his hand. In the forty years since the planting of the bead, a great many graves and headstones had been added. It made finding the resting place of the bead difficult.

But not impossible.

The Priest came to a stop in front of the grave of Andrew Smythe, aged 82. A smile crept onto the Priest's face, and he held his hands behind his back as he looked down at the vibrant, green grass.

"I have returned," he said in Chinese, the words coming out rough and ungraceful. It had been years since he had spoken the language aloud. He would sound ignorant, and stupid, but that couldn't be helped.

A cold breeze moved around his legs, and a moment later a silver fox stood in front of Smythe's polished granite headstone.

"You're larger than I would have expected," the Priest admitted, the words flowing easier. "I am impressed."

The animal blinked out of existence, replaced by an ancient Buddhist priest. A smile came onto the ghost's face.

"Priest," Feng said with a chuckle, "you are old."

"Of course, I am," the Priest said. "I'm still alive."

The dead man's lip twitched as he snapped in English, "Your Chinese is worse."

The Priest shrugged. "There are worse things. Trapped here with you, for one, would be a rather unbearable situation."

Feng swore, a long, impressive stream of vulgarity and profanity. When the dead man stopped, the Priest asked, "Are you through?"

"For now," the ghost replied. "Why are you here?"

"I have heard of Connor's return," the Priest answered. "I've come to see what he does. Have you confronted him about his mother yet?"

"No," Feng said. "Although his mother has sought him out."

The Priest raised an eyebrow as he asked, "How did that go?"

"He has a *dog*," the dead man spat, as if the word left a bitter taste in his mouth.

"Ah," the Priest said, nodding.

"How did you learn of the boy's return?" the ghost inquired.

"Cody, Connor's father," the Priest explained. "I had an agreement with him. An understanding, if you will. He was able to stay and drink while I ensured all of his bills were paid. It kept him quiet, and he informed me whenever there was a death nearby."

Feng nodded.

"Have you spoken with the father?" the Priest asked.

"In a manner of speaking," the dead man said.

"What do you mean?" the Priest asked.

"Through actions," Feng said with a smile. "I showed the father that he was no longer needed. Now that the boy had returned a man."

"But he was needed," the Priest said, an angry chill racing up his spine, "he was to be left alone."

"And so he was," the dead man said, "for the most part. He kept himself sealed away and drunk."

"Where is he?" the Priest demanded.

"Being prepared for his burial, I assume," Feng said, waving his hand dismissively. "It was time to confront my countryman, and I needed a vessel. The boy's father seemed appropriate."

"You're a fool," the Priest grumbled.

The dead man flared up with anger. "Who are you to speak to me in such a way?"

The Priest watched as Feng lunged forward, and when the ghost had nearly reached him, the Priest twisted the end of the cane open. An angry growl emerged, and Feng leaped back through the granite headstone so that it separated him from the Priest.

"What is that?" Feng hissed.

"The spirit of a dog," the Priest answered. "I took the precaution of slaying one before I came today. Its spirit is here, and should I need to, I will let the beast off its leash. Am I understood?"

Feng glared at him and remained silent.

The Priest took the silence as an assent and nodded. He kept the cane's top open and his eyes on Feng.

"Now," the Priest said, "what is done is done. I am displeased that you killed Cody Mann, but we shall move on. I have not finished planting the beads, and I will not be interrupted by

Connor."

"He is not the one you should be concerned with, Priest," Feng grumbled. "My countryman is more than he seems. Much more. Your Cody was far too stupid to realize it. He had drunk far too much for him to see what was in front of him."

The Priest frowned. "What do you mean?"

"Your father was a fool," Feng said, grinning, "and not nearly as clever as he thought. They realized that he stole the beads, but they didn't know what happened to them. Somehow, they found me, and so they placed a man here. A soldier to watch and to wait. He has done both."

"Who is *they*?" the Priest demanded. "And what do you mean by a soldier?"

Feng ignored the questions as he said, "He is not the only one, Priest. No, not at all. There is another. An older man. I am already dead, perhaps I am ready for the next life. Perhaps I do not care if they cast me out of this world. You had best pray, Priest, that the two men do not meet the third."

Before the Priest could repeat his questions, Feng vanished.

The dead dog whined in the cane, and the Priest snapped the top closed and sealed it. He seethed as he stood in front of Smythe's grave. Beyond the iron fence, he saw Mann's house, and Lavoie's.

In that pair of houses were two men who could deprive the Priest of the only pleasure he had left.

And there was a third man as well.

Which meant the Priest couldn't strike out until he knew the identity of the third.

Grinding his teeth together in rage, the Priest turned and stalked out of Pine Grove Cemetery.

Chapter 26: Alone in the House, August 10th, 2016

Connor wasn't sure what to do first.

The coroner's office had removed his father's body, and when the police had decided that there was no overt evidence of a crime, Connor had been told he could go back into the house.

They didn't ask him if he wanted to.

Connor had no desire to enter his home, but he had to.

It was his.

With Rex beside him, Connor had gone up the stairs, crossed the porch, and entered the kitchen. It had been both difficult and frightening. The air was heavy with a foul, fetid odor. A low growl constantly rumbled from Rex's throat, the dog pushing his snout into dark corners while questing for something hidden in the shadows.

A nagging sense of guilt ate at Connor, the idea that his father had died because Rex had been with Connor, and not in the house.

It was a difficult thought, because as much as he disliked the man, he hadn't wanted his father to die.

Connor sighed and turned on the light over the sink, the old bulb flickering for a moment before staying lit. He went to the stove, put the water on for tea, and then got a plastic bag. Cleaning would help take his mind off his father.

The light above the sink flickered again, sputtered, and went out.

Connor shook his head, walked back to the light switch, and flicked it up and down several times. When it still refused to return to life, Connor made a mental note to buy bulbs.

Rex snarled behind Connor as the rattle of bottles came from the den.

Connor's stomach knotted with fear as he turned around. His blood pounded in his ears, and a pain sprang up in his head. He took a short, nervous step toward the den when he heard a soft chuckle.

The sound was familiar.

Connor passed by Rex and came to a stop in the entryway to the den. A dark shape moved along the far wall.

"Who's there?" Connor asked, hating the quivering way the words came out.

The shape vanished into a corner.

"Hello, Connor," his mother said, her voice coming from near the floor.

Connor shuddered at the sound.

There was no love. Merely desire, a longing without a shred of maternal devotion within it.

"You're not my mother," he whispered.

Her laugh was cold and cruel, but it was still his mother's voice.

"We both know you're wrong about that," she said, her laughter fading away. "Send the dog away."

"No."

"Do it!" she snapped.

"No," he repeated.

She changed her approach, saying in a voice false with sweetness, "Do it for me, Connor. I'm your mother. I miss you. Terribly. Don't you miss me?"

"Yes." The word was little louder than an exhalation.

"Then send the dog away," she implored. "We can be together, for a little while. I'm cold, Connor. And you, my sweet, *sweet* boy, you can warm me."

The child he had been, the one deprived of his mother and witness to her death, begged him to send Rex out.

But Connor wasn't that little boy.

"You need to leave," he said, raising his voice. "You need to get out."

"You can't make me," she said, the shadow rising up in the dim room.

He watched as the darkness spread across the entire far wall, the house seeming to ripple in front of him.

"I will learn how," Connor said, anger filling him. "You're dead. Leave."

She swore at him, and the shadow pulled off the wall. It formed into a shape, and when Connor realized what it was, he took a desperate step back.

A spider, absent of definition but as tall and as large as Rex, stood in the center of the room. Connor was horrified; spiders terrified him. For his entire life, he had been afraid of them, regardless of their size.

And his mother knew it.

The spider stepped forward and from it came his mother's voice.

"Come, Connor," she said, laughing. "Embrace me. See if this form of mine has fangs as well. Wouldn't you like to know? Can you imagine their size?"

Fear took control of him, took the strength out of his knees, and dropped him to the floor. He sank down and stared at the dark arachnid as it approached him, his blood racing and drowning out all other noises.

Then Rex leaped over him, smashing into the shadow spider.

His mother's pleased laughter changed into a terrified shriek, and she vanished.

A moment later, Rex stood before Connor, the Shepherd's tail wagging. Connor leaned forward, wrapped his arms around the dog's thick neck, and held onto him. With his face pressed into Rex's fur, Connor wept and tried to drive the memory of his dead mother out of his mind.

He failed.

Chapter 27: Ashland Avenue, August 10th, 2016

Lloyd Strafford sat in his chair, book forgotten on his lap, and stared out the front window of his house. Through the clear glass, past the small yard and the freshly paved road, he looked down into Pine Grove Cemetery. From his seat, Lloyd could see his old place of employment, the caretaker's office still the same ugly shade of brown as when he had worked there.

He knew the young man who ran the cemetery, and most of the staff who did the burials. Lloyd even knew the men and women who served as the honor guard for the various military burials.

He had warned them all about the ghost.

Lloyd had tried to warn others when he was still employed as the caretaker until the town had threatened to have him removed. Then he had taken his own, quieter steps to ensure public safety while remaining employed.

Even then, he had made himself a pariah in the town in general, and within the community of municipal employees in particular.

He brushed aside the bitter feelings as they attempted to rise up and focused his attention on the cemetery. On the small, tilt-top tea table beside his chair was a pair of powerful binoculars. His hands, the fingers crooked with arthritis, picked up the binoculars, adjusted its focus and looked down into what he still thought of as the 'new' section of Pine Grove.

For several minutes, he observed the cemetery. He would allow his gaze to linger on a headstone for a full five seconds, and then he would move on to the next.

Lloyd sought out the hiding place of the silver fox, something he had failed to do while he was employed at the cemetery.

And it was a task which remained unaccomplished, well into his retirement.

He returned the binoculars to their place on the table and settled back into his chair. His fingers tapped out a nameless tune on the book on his lap, and his eyelids began to weigh heavy. He fought against sleep, but the older he became, the less he slept at night, and the more he napped in the day.

Lloyd yawned, closed his eyes, and rubbed at them.

When he opened them again, it was night once more.

His body ached, his neck stiff and crooked.

Lloyd braced himself, straightened up, and stifled a moan of agony. He had fallen asleep in the chair more times than he cared to remember, and each time was worse than the last.

He waited for his heart to slow down, its pace always quickened by the pain.

When it had assumed a more natural rhythm, Lloyd pushed himself up. He tottered for a moment, keeping his hands close to the arms of the chair. If he fell, he might be able to catch himself.

He didn't have to.

After several anxious moments, he had retained his precarious stance and straightened up. He walked to the television and turned it on. It was permanently set on the weather channel, which always gave him the time, and more importantly, the date.

There had been more than one occasion where he had lost an entire day in the chair, having slept almost around the clock.

The date and time revealed that he had only nodded off for a few hours.

With a sigh of relief, Lloyd turned the television back off and limped into the kitchen. He fixed himself a bowl of cereal, sat down and ate it in silence. When he had finished his meal, he cleaned up his dishes, put them in the sink to soak and let out a scream of surprise when he looked up.

Through the kitchen window, he saw the silver fox that he had seen so many decades before. The one that had killed Avery, and the women across from the cemetery.

It was in the yard, looking at something in the distance Lloyd couldn't quite see.

The creature was just beyond the buried PVC pipes in the yard, the ones that were packed with salt and protected Lloyd's home.

Lloyd's heart thundered against his chest as he stared at the back of the fox. He grabbed hold of the edge of the counter to keep his balance as his body shook with fear.

Lloyd nearly jumped out of his shoes when he heard the sharp whoop of a siren from the front of the house. He blinked and saw that the fox was gone.

A sense of panic welled up within him and Lloyd raced to the bathroom window. He caught sight of the fox as it passed around the side of the house towards the front yard. Quick steps brought Lloyd into the den and he watched as the fox broke into a run.

The animal slipped between the open gates of the cemetery's back entrance, raced by a police cruiser parked near the old Hall Mausoleum, and down the winding asphalt road.

In the darkness of the night, the silver fox was still visible.

Lloyd's hands shook as he picked up the binoculars and trained them on the creature. He followed it as it sprinted through the cemetery. It would vanish behind headstones and trees to reappear a moment later. Soon the animal reached the far gate and slipped out onto Cushing Avenue.

The animal turned to the left, picking up speed until it became a blur. It became difficult to keep track of as it raced around the corner of Cushing and Hill.

But Lloyd never lost sight of the fox, and he watched it travel a short distance along Hill Street before it came to a stop. It hesitated for a moment, then snuck up the driveway of the first house on the street. For a heartbeat, the creature lingered near the stairs.

Then the side-door of the house opened, and the fox vanished.

Lloyd's hands had become steady, all hints of tremors gone as he lowered the binoculars. He had recognized the house that the fox had stopped at, for it had once been the home of Mrs. Lavoie.

In 1987, someone new had taken up residence in that particular house, and it had caught the fox's attention then.

Lloyd's heartbeat quickened, and he sat down in his chair, forcing his aged heart to slow its pace.

No! he thought. *I need to know. I need to know what it is. Why it's here!*

He repeated that single train of thought over and over, until his heart had calmed down and he could breathe without pain in his chest.

Then Lloyd closed his eyes and willed himself to live until morning.

He had too many unanswered questions.

He had no time for death.

Chapter 28: Pure Rage, August 10th, 2016

The Priest had found lodging with the Order of the Sacred Heart, the Brothers of the community having a spare bedroom they had been able to let him use. He found them to be Brothers considerate and mindful of his desire for silence. Brother Joseph Guertin, the head of the house, believed the Priest was there on some personal issue in regards to a family member.

The Priest didn't correct him.

The Priest sat at the room's small desk, his father's old aluminum case in front of him. He had it propped open, and he stared at the beads contained therein.

The Priest prodded several with his index finger, wondering how such small, almost insignificant items could be so terrible. For all the years he had possessed them, he had never once had the desire to know *why* the beads were important. Nor had he examined the how of it. His control over the dead who had been bound to individual Mala beads was tenuous at best. He knew, from speaking with Buddhist monks and reading on his own, that a ghost bound to such an object would need to be placed with their bones or incinerated for them to move on.

There had been an added layer of security as well. None of those Feng had bound to the Mala in China would be able to go to the next world until they were all gathered together again. None of them would rest until the Priest allowed it. And since he alone knew where the beads were, none of the dead would threaten him.

Thus, the Priest had been content to use them as he saw fit, which was to sow death and sorrow along the East Coast of the United States.

A smile twitched the corners of his lips and broke the bad mood that had hung about him since his conversation with Feng.

The Priest sighed, closed the case, and put it away. He stood up and went to the window that looked out over the narrow street that curled past the house. His first parish, St. Lloyd's, was only a few miles away. He remembered the ripples the woman's death had caused, the way the community had reeled at the unexpected death of a young mother.

If they had only known, the Priest thought, humming a soft tune. It took him several heartbeats to recognize it as the one his father had sung so often.

The memory of that first death, much like the memory of his father, always made him happy. The Priest imagined the horror that must have gripped the woman as Feng assaulted her, the absolute terror.

It caused his heart to race and his breath to quicken.

The Priest could picture it perfectly.

A knock on his door interrupted him, shattering the idea.

He took a shuddering breath, forced himself to remain calm, and called, "Yes?"

"May I come in, Father?" a voice asked.

The person sounded familiar.

Frowning, the Priest replied, "Perhaps later. I am not feeling particularly well."

Whoever it was on the other side of the door tried to open it, the doorknob rattling.

"I just want to talk, Priest," the voice hissed, and it was deeper, angrier.

The Priest backed away from the window, pressing himself against the far wall. He was vulnerable, without the salt or iron he needed to defend himself.

The doorknob continued to twist back and forth, and after a minute, the lock broke with a loud, nerve-jolting crack. An unseen hand thrust the door forward, and the intruder was revealed.

A man stood in the hallway, wearing only a pair of boxer shorts. He was middle-aged and flabby, and dried blood covered most of his pale skin. The stranger had evidently committed suicide, as evidenced by the long straight cuts that ran from the wrists to the elbows. Each wound was deep, the flesh spread apart to reveal the severed remains of veins.

There was no light in the man's brown eyes.

The dead man took an awkward step into the room, moving with the same jerky, imprecise actions of a broken marionette.

"Hello, Priest," the man said, a foul, horrific stench rolling off the corpse.

"Hello," the Priest said, his voice hoarse.

"Do you know who I am?" the dead man asked.

The Priest shook his head, trying not to breathe through his nose. His head ached from the nauseating smell.

"Why should you?" The laugh that followed the question caused the Priest to flinch.

"Here is a name," the corpse said. "And see if you remember it, yes?"

The Priest nodded.

"Geoffrey Mulvanity."

It took a moment for the name to register, for the Priest's mind to recall the history behind it.

Geoffrey Mulvanity had been a good Catholic on Sundays, if no other day of the week. He had been a brute of a man. One who had been so despotic that he had driven his wife and daughter to suicide. Although many, including the Priest, believed that Mulvanity had actually murdered both of the women.

But Mulvanity had still been relatively young when the Priest had been transferred to another parish. The years had passed, but not so many that Mulvanity should have died.

The Priest felt his eyes widen with surprise as he whispered, "You're dead?"

"Of course I'm dead," the ghost of Mulvanity snarled with scorn. "How else would I possess a corpse? Hm? Yet he was not dead meat when I first slipped in. Oh no. He was a drunk, Priest. Deep within the bottle he was, when I snuck in. It was the old Buddhist who showed me this trick, how to take control. Oh, the things I've done, Priest. But, then this man cast me out when he became sober. You see, Priest, we can slip into drunks, so easily, they cannot refuse us. Not at all."

The dead man shook his head and made a 'tsk-tsk' sound before he continued. "That I could not have. So when he drank again, I barreled in and made sure he made himself available to me."

The ghost of Mulvanity lifted up the arms of the corpse, allowing the Priest a good look at the open gashes down his forearms.

"So, in a word, yes. I am dead. Long ago and far away," the ghost of Mulvanity confirmed, laughing. "Did you know what would happen when you trapped the old Buddhist within Pine Grove?"

"Yes," the Priest answered, "but how did you fall victim to him?"

"To him?" Mulvanity asked, a twisted, insane tone to his

question. "You mean the old Buddhist? Oh no, there are so many more now. So many created by him within the cemetery. In fact, the one who created me was a woman, the first one he had slain. You know her, and her husband, I suspect. She, Debra Mann, helped to spread the old Buddhist's hatred. It is like a sickness. Your little bead spread death. To so many, and they, in turn, spread out. And I am here. Stuck here."

"But why?" the Priest asked.

"Because!" Mulvanity screamed. "Because God hates me as He hates you! I have long dreamt of killing you. And then I heard your voice yesterday. Saw your face. Fatter and paler, but your face still. I sought you out, I remember where the clergy lay their heads. This corpse, so near myself, served me well, did it not?"

The Priest could only nod in agreement. Mulvanity did not seem sane. Not anywhere close to logical. A far cry from the control Feng exerted over himself.

And the Priest had nowhere to run.

Mulvanity did his strange, stiff-legged walk and came closer to the Priest. The dead man's face looked as though it were mottled porcelain, the pale skin shot through with deep blue veins and broken capillaries. As the lips curled into a wider smile, the Priest thought he heard teeth and bones break.

"God hates you," Mulvanity whispered, "and so do I."

He lifted his hands up and shambled the last few steps forward. When the dead man's fingers brushed his chest, the Priest screamed with fear and struck out with both hands. His fists smashed into Mulvanity's cold, dead flesh, and the ghost let out a shriek of pain and terror.

The corpse fell backward, slammed into the desk, bumped into the chair, and fell to the floor.

And there the body remained, dead eyes staring at the old plaster of the ceiling.

The Priest's hands tingled, a curious, pulse that left him with a strange sensation. It felt as though energy coursed through his bones. He flexed and relaxed his fingers, feeling the power within them.

His attention returned to the corpse of Mulvanity.

No, the Priest told himself, *not Geoffrey Mulvanity. Only a corpse the ghost of Mulvanity had possessed. Where is he?*

Then the Priest looked at his hands and had an epiphany.

He had driven the ghost out of the stolen corpse.

The Priest looked down at his hands again, turning them over and chuckling. On his ring finger, the plain, silver ring he wore throbbed and pulsed with a pleasant, curious heat. It had been a gift to him from his late mother, and it had belonged to her uncle, who had been a priest in Ireland.

The silver, normally dull and unnoticeable, glowed.

A smile spread across the Priest's face.

He felt stronger.

The ring, he thought, *there's something about it. It's special, and I need to know more.*

The Priest lowered his hands, stared at the corpse, and wondered, suddenly, how he was going to dispose of such a large body.

Chapter 29: Seeking Help from Hu, August 11th, 2016

By noon of the day after his father's death, Connor made a decision.

He would ask Hu if he could live with the man.

Connor knew that continued use of his old, childhood home was detrimental, not only to his physical health, but his mental health as well.

After he had packed his few belongings and those of Rex, Connor and the dog went to Hu's house and knocked on the door.

There was no answer.

Connor knocked again, a little louder. Hu was old and perhaps needed hearing aids.

By the time Connor knocked a third time, waves of anxiety crashed over him at a pace that threatened to disable him mentally. He imagined Hu on the floor, unconscious, or dead. Connor wondered what was capable of such an act.

Or the thing that had been his mother.

He had a sudden fear that his father would be a ghost as well, both of them out for his blood.

"Hello?"

Connor shouted in surprise as he jumped and turned around. At the end of Hu's driveway was a man in his seventies or eighties. He looked at Connor and Rex, then glanced to Hu's door.

"Hey," Connor said, trying to decide if the man was friendly or not. "Can I help you?"

"I certainly hope so," the man said, "though I'm not quite positive as to how to proceed from here."

Rex didn't growl or move towards the stranger, so Connor waited.

The man cleared his throat, gave a nervous smile, and said, "I'm going to say something odd, and I hope you don't think I'm insane."

"Go for it," Connor said. The calm tone of his voice belied the frantic beats of his heart.

"Did you, ah, well, did you see a silver fox run past?" the man asked, his voice a low whisper.

Connor was too shocked to speak, but he was able to nod.

"You did," the stranger said, his voice only a hint above

audible. "My God, you did."

Connor nodded his head several more times. "Yeah. And a long time ago, too."

The stranger gasped and said, "You're Mann's boy!"

"Yes," Connor agreed.

"I remember you," the man said in a soft voice. "I remember you were the one who found your mother after it had killed her."

The stranger's statement ripped through Connor's mind. Each syllable slammed into him, sent his thoughts into a wild tailspin he couldn't control. For he remembered the stranger. Much younger, sturdier. Helping Connor to his feet, turning him away from his mother's corpse.

"You were there," Connor said, his voice raw, and each word like broken glass in his throat. "I remember you."

The man nodded. "Yes. I was the first to find you and your mother. My name is Lloyd, Lloyd Strafford."

"Thank you," Connor murmured. "Thank you for helping me."

Before Lloyd could reply, the side door opened and Hu stepped out. His beard was a mess, his clothes rumpled. There was a wary, dangerous look in the man's eyes as he fixed them on Lloyd.

"Who are you?" Hu demanded.

"Hu," Connor said, stepping forward, "he's okay."

Hu shot a withering stare at Connor, but he remained firm, saying again, "He's okay. He saw the fox."

Once again, Hu focused his attention on Lloyd.

"Come into the house, both of you," Hu said after a few seconds of silence. "If you truly saw the fox, then it is best for you to speak of it to us. And you, Connor, have you come to rest for a bit?"

Connor nodded. He almost told Hu what had occurred in the house, but he could get to that after he was inside.

Connor moved aside, and he and Rex waited for Lloyd to put his bike against Hu's garage. With Lloyd in front of him, they went into the house. Connor hesitated at the top of the stairs, turned and looked at his house. Around the foundation, hiding in the shadows and clinging to the overgrown bushes, he saw small shapes.

Each dark and not truly defined.

Connor knew what they were, and he had a terrible, gut-wrenching realization.

The ghosts weren't bothered by daylight.

Keeping his blossoming fear to himself, Connor hurried into the house after Lloyd and Hu. He followed both men into the kitchen where the three of them sat down at the table. Hu looked expectantly at Lloyd, and after several seconds of silence, Lloyd cleared his throat and began to speak.

Connor listened as the man told them of his job in the cemetery, of the death of a man named Avery. Admiration for the man's determination grew as Lloyd presented his evidence as to why the ghosts in the cemetery had to be Chinese in origin.

Lloyd ended his short monologue with a description of the fox outside his home, and managing to track it to Hu's.

Fear settled into Connor's heart as he listened to Lloyd speak about the way the fox had run when the side-door had been opened.

Connor had been the one to step out onto the side steps. The one who had frightened off Feng in fox form.

Would he have run off if he had known it was me? Connor wondered. With growing trepidation, he thought. *No. He would have stayed to say hello.*

And the idea terrified him.

Chapter 30: Henan Province, China, January 3rd, 1988

Hu sat in the outer chamber of the Monk's rooms, wrapped in an overcoat and with thick boots on. He had tucked his hands into the sleeves of the coat and sat in silence, waiting to be invited into the room.

A short time later, the Monk's assistant, a young monk with a shaved head and the orange robes of a Buddhist, offered up apologies for the delay and invited Hu in.

Hu stood up and followed the young man into the senior Monk's quarters. The younger monk remained only long enough to pour tea and then left on quiet feet.

"Hu," the Monk said, "it is a pleasure to finally see you. I must confess I did not quite picture you as so militant. There is a gentleness to your words, an elegance to your writing."

"I am afraid that I can barely make myself understood," Hu said, nodding his head humbly.

The Monk smiled, took a sip of his tea, and said, "Have they told you anything about your task?"

Hu allowed himself a small smile.

"No, sir," Hu said. "I know only that I am to watch the cemetery."

The Monk frowned, returned his teacup to the tray, and said, "I am afraid that there is much more than that. You are looking for something dangerous, Hu. An item which was stolen from us after the war against the Japanese had ended."

"Ah," Hu said, and he waited for the Monk to continue.

The Monk straightened his long beard, tugging at the ends of the gray hair.

"In the past," the Monk said, half closing his eyes as he spoke, "there was a Monk. His name was Feng for he was like a hot wind bringing famine and death as it dried out the fields. Feng was a wicked and terrible man, a creature of the past who had loved to sow confusion. The man was brilliant. His ability to persuade a person was not supernatural in nature, but merely through a careful study of the individual he spoke with. He was, when he desired to be, exceptionally charismatic. Feng was a man who could, over the course of several months, convince the weak-willed to do the unthinkable. Feng once led a husband to murder his wife. A mother to slay her children. Numerous cooks to poison their patrons. Even disciples to turn against their masters. And he would linger, to serve and say the prayers over the dead."

The Monk paused, took a sip of his tea, and straightened his beard once more.

"Feng lived to be an old man, and he had taught himself a terrible ability," the Monk said, sighing. "How to trap a spirit in an object. For Feng, this was a set of Mala beads. Each bead was carved from a child's bone. In some cases, the spirit bound within the bone was from the same child."

Sorrow flashed across the Monk's face, but it vanished, replaced by the calm and stoic expression he usually wore.

"When Feng died," the Monk continued, "he bound himself to his 100 bead Mala. This was discovered shortly afterward. A silver fox was seen on the grounds of a monastery in the Yunnan Province. Several of the monks passed away rather suddenly. At the Ghost Festival, Feng and those he had bound were unleashed upon the monastery."

"Did the monks survive?" Hu asked.

"A few," the older man replied, "though only because one of the bound ghosts told them about Feng's Mala. The surviving monks went into the pagoda by the monastery and removed his Mala. They placed it within a dog statue, with the animal's spirit, and sealed it. There Feng's Mala remained until the defeat of the Japanese and the expulsion of the Nationalists. An American soldier, traveling through the Yunnan Province, came upon the monastery, and he stole the statue."

Hu shook his head, repressing the anger he felt.

The Monk waited until Hu regained his composure, and then picked up the tale again.

"Until several months ago we did not know the name of the American, or what had happened to the Mala," the Monk said.

"What happened?" Hu inquired.

"A death," the Monk replied, "seemingly innocuous. A young mother died in a graveyard, suddenly. Her son was a witness. The following year the woman's neighbor died."

Hu frowned. "How were these deaths significant?"

"They both occurred at the beginning of the Ghost Festival," the Monk said, "and the boy reported seeing a silver fox."

Hu leaned back in his chair and nodded.

"We have had monks searching for the Mala for close to fifty years," the Monk said. "It is time for a soldier to go and retrieve it for us."

Hu straightened up in surprise, but before he could question the statement, the older man raised a hand and silenced Hu.

"Your commander was my disciple when he was younger before he joined the army," the Monk stated. "I had always hoped he would return and seek enlightenment, but China, it seems, needed him elsewhere. With the discovery of Feng's Mala, I reached out to him and asked for the finest officer he had. One willing to sacrifice himself for humanity."

While pride flushed through Hu, so too did a sense of dread. He did not know what the Monk was going to ask of him, but he knew it would be difficult.

Hu cleared his throat and asked, "What needs to be done?"

"You need to move to America," the Monk replied, "and seek Feng there. He must be found, and bound, and then brought back."

Hu's mind raced, thoughts swirling through it and difficult to control. He strained and focused his thoughts. After several deep breaths, he said, "Yes. I will."

"Thank you," the Monk said.

"Is there more information about the deaths?" Hu asked. "Is it known why Feng has appeared after all this time?"

"Nothing certain, I am afraid," the Monk said, "but we have found out that there is a man in the vicinity of the deaths who bears the same name as the soldier who stole the statue."

"It cannot be the same person," Hu said, unable to keep his surprise to himself.

"No," the Monk said, "it is certainly not. But we believe his father was the soldier."

Hu nodded. He understood.

"What is this man's name?" Hu asked.

"Michael Goyette," the Monk answered. "Father Michael Goyette. You will be hunting down a priest for more information. He may not know what he did and thus released Feng accidentally. Or, as I fear, he may be helping Feng willingly. If that is the case, you may have to hurt him. Is that an issue with you?"

"No," Hu said, picking up his tea, and taking a sip, "I have no issue with that at all."

Chapter 31: The Wrong House, August 11th, 2016

Tom Brewer crouched behind an elm tree by the Pine Grove Cemetery. In the darkness of the night, he was able to see the house of Cody Mann. The gentleman had passed away the day before, and from what Tom had heard at the morgue, there was only an estranged son to worry about.

Tom had watched the house for over an hour, and he hadn't seen or heard anything from the house. No lights came on as darkness had settled in, and no sounds were emitted from the house. It looked abandoned. The building was in general disrepair, and there was a large pile of trash bags at the top of the driveway.

Around the morgue, there had been the usual chatter, gossip about co-workers and the newly minted dead. Word about Cody Mann had been that he hadn't worked since his wife had died in the seventies. And he had never been in for any sort of medical treatment.

And that, to Tom Brewer, sounded like an old miser who had hidden his money away.

Tom had worked at the morgue for three and a half years, and after the first six months, he had figured out that dead people were the best to rob.

He did his research on each person that ended up on a slab in front of him. They weren't slabs of meat with 'Y' incisions anymore. The corpses represented lucrative paydays.

Over the years, Tom had stolen and sold cars to chop shops in Lowell and Billerica, Massachusetts. He had dumped jewelry off in pawnshops from Bangor, Maine to Brooklyn, New York. And there had always been a little cash. Sometimes in bills, but more often in coins.

Tom had read about the mistakes people made when it came to theft, and the biggest one was spending the money.

Like any sound financial plan, Tom lived below his means when it came to appearances. He didn't have jewelry. No brand name clothes. And he drove a beat-up Ford Taurus that was twenty years old.

At his bank, Tom had four lock boxes, with a total sum of $76,120 in cash. The plan was to get enough tucked away to buy a house and find a job where he didn't have to clean up after autopsies.

Tom brought his thoughts back around to the job at hand.

Breaking into Cody Mann's house.

He straightened up, crossed the street and walked up to the porch. He climbed the stairs and gave a bold knock on the door.

It swung open and caught him off guard.

A foul odor drifted out of the house, and Tom coughed.

Too bad someone didn't leave a window open, he thought, stepping into the house. *Damn, guy didn't smell this bad on the table.*

Tom tried the kitchen light, and nothing happened. He shrugged, took a flashlight out of his back pocket, and flicked it on. He turned to close the door and found it was already shut.

Did I do that? he wondered, trying to remember if he had or hadn't. Finally, he went the rest of the way into the kitchen.

The room had recently been scrubbed, and Tom could smell a faint scent of cleanser beneath the stench of decay. He passed through the kitchen, the cabinet doors hanging open on broken hinges, and then into the first room. It was a den of some sort, and it looked as though it was where the recently deceased had spent most, if not all of his time.

Tom smiled.

This is where it will be, he thought, using his flashlight to probe the dark corners of the room. *This is it.*

Grinning to himself, Tom took a step forward and then stopped as a creature darted to the right, its tail illuminated for a split second in the flashlight's LED beam.

He hesitated, unsure whether he had seen a cat or a big rat.

A scurrying came from the left, and Tom snapped the flashlight towards the sound.

He watched as a dull gray rat raced into darkness.

Tom grimaced. Revulsion swept through him, forced him to take a step back and reassess the house. Tom hated rats. He had seen corpses gnawed on by the rodents and it disgusted him on a primal level.

Snarling, Tom stepped forward and aimed a kick where the rat had vanished. His foot plunged into the darkness and connected with something hard and cold. The force of the impact jarred his leg, caused his hip to flare with pain and a gasp to explode past his lips.

Tom jerked his foot back and found he couldn't.

Something had a grip on him. A harsh chill penetrated the leather of his boot as Tom tried to free himself again. He brought the flashlight's beam to bear on his foot and regretted the act instantly.

There wasn't one rat, but three, and as he watched, they shifted, twisted, and expanded. They pulsed with a sickening, flat yellow light, and as they grew larger, Tom saw that they were people and not rats at all.

Tom dropped the flashlight, the tool shattering and going black. He twisted and tried to run but only succeeded in falling flat on his face. Hands raced along his limbs, locking them down to the floor. Tom opened his mouth to scream, but something wet and foul was stuffed between his teeth, pressing his tongue into the back of his throat. Gagging, he tried to breathe and could only do so through his nose.

He struggled, twisting and jerking, but nothing worked.

The strange, nightmare creatures had him pinned to the floor.

His flesh became numb, the cold too much to bear.

Tom exhausted himself, unable to continue without more oxygen for his efforts. When he lay still, dragging in shuddering breaths through his nose, someone got down onto the floor beside his face.

A woman spoke, her voice thin and wicked, each word like a lash and shredding his sanity.

"You're not my boy," she said, "not at all. And you are *not* sweet. No. We can smell your stench. You are nothing more than one of us, merely drawing breath instead of rotting in the ground. That will change soon enough. We cannot feed on you, thief. Your soul will not satisfy our hunger. But we will take what we can get."

And as they fed on him, and jagged spikes of pain pierced Tom, the gag muffled his screams.

No one living heard him suffer, and no one living watched him die.

Chapter 32: Protected but Not Safe, August 11th, 2016

At a little before midnight, Connor was still awake. He had yet to break himself of the habit of sleeping during the day, and he doubted he would do so anytime soon. The dead were still too active during the day. Night was preferable.

His mother had died during the morning, and daylight would always be far more threatening than the night.

Connor climbed out of the bed, and Rex lifted his head, blinked, and then lowered his chin back to the mattress. A smile crossed Connor's face as he gave Rex a quick pat on the head.

Connor's feet whispered across the wooden floor. He came to a stop at the window and pulled the shade over to the right, allowing him to glimpse his own house. A fog had risen up from the ground and hid the same from his eyes. Shadows passed behind the windows of the house he had so recently fled from and Connor wondered if one of the shapes he saw belonged to his mother.

His throat tightened, and he ground his teeth, letting the shade fall back into place.

He walked to his bag, took his clothes out, and got dressed. The dog remained asleep as Connor left the room. From behind a closed door, Connor heard Hu snore. He crept along the hallway, not wanting to wake his host up.

The stairs creaked as he descended to the first floor. Once in the kitchen, he clicked the light on over the stove and found the long, fireplace candles he had seen earlier. He took several before he exited the house.

Standing on the cracked asphalt of Hu's driveway, Connor stared at the dilapidated building that had once been his home.

His shoulders sagged, and for a moment his heart ached, tears filling his eyes. He swallowed his sorrow back, wiped his eyes with his hand, and walked through Hu's yard to stand beside his father's car. Leaves and debris were piled around the foundation, dead bushes and plants crowded against the cement. The trash that Connor had so industriously bagged and removed from the kitchen was still stacked against the house. Ancient paint hung in great strips from the wooden siding and all around the building was a void of silence.

Nothing moved.

Nothing *lived*.

There were no crickets, no night birds.

Connor walked to the house, and he heard thumps and scrapes against the interior walls. Fingernails clawed against the filthy glass, and people hissed his name at him.

They would be out soon, and they wanted him.

The idea of it drove nails of fear into his temples, bright white spots exploding around the edges of his vision while the pounding of his own heart almost made him deaf.

Without further reflection, Connor hurried to the foundation to the left of the porch. He crouched down, and with shaking hands, struck the matches against the rough cement. The heads flared up. The strong smell of sulfur assaulted Connor's nose, and he dropped the matches to the leaves.

The debris burst into flame, the heat sending him tumbling backward. He scrambled to his feet, ran to Hu's driveway, and turned to see what he had done.

Flames climbed up the walls, the fire devouring the uncared for wood and the memories of Connor's childhood.

"Get in!" Hu commanded from the door.

Connor turned his back on his old pain and hurried into the safety of Hu's home.

Chapter 33: An Investigation, August 12th, 2016

Detective Noah Rattin popped another piece of Nicorette gum into his mouth and ignored the disdainful glance from Lieutenant Meg Ward. They stood together by the iron fence of Pine Grove Cemetery and watched as the fire inspector talked to a couple of firefighters.

Noah yawned and ignored the desire to get a cigarette in spite of the gum.

"You having a tough time this morning?" Meg asked.

Noah paid no attention to the tone of her voice as he replied, "Every morning is a tough morning, Lieutenant."

"You know," she said, scratching the back of her head with a thick finger, "I don't know what's worse, the fact that you gave up cigarettes, or the idea that you're using gum to help you."

"I could always go back to bourbon," Noah retorted.

"And as your sponsor," Meg said, turning to face him, "I'd have to counsel you. As your commander, I'd chew you out. And as your friend, Noah, I'd drag you into the gym and beat you seven ways to Sunday."

"Looks like Pete's done," Noah said, interrupting her tirade and gesturing towards the fire inspector.

Pete Babcock, seven years past retirement and looking more like the Michelin man than a firefighter, crossed the street and took his helmet off. His thin, gray hair was plastered to his forehead with sweat, and his puffy cheeks were red.

"What's the deal, Pete?" Meg asked.

"Definitely got a body in there," Pete said, jerking a thumb back towards the burned out structure, "and the place was lit up. Doesn't look like any accelerant was used, but the fire started to the left of the side porch. Shouldn't have. No wires, nothing at all."

"Intentional?" Noah asked.

"That's what it looks like," Pete said, "unless your body had a partner and that one was smoking outside. But it isn't likely."

"When can we get the body out of there and bring the arson team in?" Meg asked.

"Couple more hours," Pete said, his tone apologetic. "Still got a couple of hot spots in there, and we've got part of the second floor still up. Body's not there, but I don't want to see anyone get hurt. You know?"

Noah and Meg nodded their agreement.

"I got to get out of this gear," Pete said. "Sweating like a pig in this, plus I had about a gallon of coffee before I got the call."

"Nice, Pete," Meg said, frowning, "too much information. Neither one of us needed that."

"Speak for yourself," Noah joked.

Pete snickered, said goodbye and left as Meg gave Noah a punch in the arm.

"Damn," he complained, shaking his arm. Meg had been an Olympic finalist in the hammer throw straight out of high school, and her arms had never lost their superhuman strength.

"Let's take a look," Meg said, leading the way across the street.

The cloying scent of burned wood and trash hung in the air as the morning fog dissipated. Several firefighters manned hoses, keeping steady streams of water on the hot spots Pete had mentioned. A tarp had been set up around the location of the body. Fire trucks and engines were parked on the street. Yellow and dull gray hoses snaked out from the vehicles and from a nearby hydrant.

Noah had been on his share of investigations with a body, and while most turned out to be accidental deaths or occurred due to natural causes, there was the occasional homicide.

The corpse in the burned out house was a first. He had never helped conduct an investigation with a body and arson.

He and Meg came to a stop a short distance away from the house.

"So, we're going to Sherlock this," Meg said, and Noah rolled his eyes.

She hit him in the arm again.

"Jesus," he muttered and walked around to the other side of her.

"Why did you change sides?" she asked.

"I don't want a bruise on only one arm," he answered. "I like symmetry."

Meg sighed and shook her head. "You are in rare form this morning, Noah."

"Whatever. Now, what were you saying, my dear Watson?" Noah asked.

She hit him again, and Noah swore, rubbing his arm.

"I'm Sherlock here," she said, "and now let's look at this. We know the body in the building can't be the owner, right?"

"Why not?" Noah asked.

"He died a day or two ago at home," Meg said. "So, unless he got up and left the morgue on his own and set fire to his house, well, it's not him."

"Anybody else live here with him?" Noah asked.

She nodded. "A son who recently returned and they had a German shepherd, according to the report filed the other day."

"A son. Where's he at?" Noah wondered aloud. "Where's the dog? Did the son have a car? Do we have a number on file for him?"

Meg pulled at her left ear lobe, a habit she had when she was thinking hard on a case.

"No car that I know of," she said after a few seconds of silence. "Means he has to be around, or he took off."

"I suppose we're going to have to start talking to some of the neighbors?" Noah said, the idea distasteful. While he didn't have the legendary Sherlock Holmes's investigating abilities, Noah's dislike of people certainly ran a close second to the great detective's.

"Yes," Meg agreed, "here's hoping someone saw something."

"If life were that easy," Noah said, "I wouldn't have been an alcoholic."

Meg gave him a hard look.

"Fine," he said, sighing, "I know it was because of my choices. I was just running my mouth."

"Well, don't," Meg snapped. "Come on, let's go meet the neighbors."

Noah grunted a response, rolled his eyes, and popped another piece of gum into his mouth.

He absolutely hated people.

Chapter 34: The Priest Decides, August 12th, 2016

Father Michael Goyette had reached physical exhaustion.

All of the television shows he had watched over the years made the dismemberment of a human look easy.

They had lied.

For three days, he had kept the body in the bathtub in his room with the Brothers of the Sacred Heart. He was fortunate in that they left him alone, and that they had left cleaning supplies in the bathroom sink.

Father Goyette shifted in his chair and winced. His shoulders and arms ached, and his lower back was a massive knot of pain. The worst pain resided in his stomach, the core muscles worked the hardest. He flexed his hands and then massaged them, first the left, then the right. The fingers were stiff, the palms cramping at odd times.

He had found a hacksaw in the basement and a package of replacement blades. The task had been difficult and distasteful. He had been fortunate in how close to the woods the brothers lived.

Father Goyette closed his eyes and leaned his head against the chair. The situation had changed, and in a way he hadn't anticipated. Feng had gone from being an interesting experiment to a distinct threat. Goyette understood the fault lay with himself, but it was still a bitter pill to swallow.

Goyette had no idea how he might contain or control Feng. When he had been a young man, Goyette had believed any supernatural problems could be solved through his belief in God's grace and might. His faith and spirituality had lapsed when he had finished seminary and taken his vows. Goyette had lacked the desire to do something different, and being a priest was easy for him. And he was addicted to death.

There was a thrill in the observation of death that filled him with the same ecstatic sensations that prayer once did. He had spent years moving from parish to parish, planting the beads at various cemeteries and ushering dozens of people to the hereafter. Finally, in 2012, he had been given a great gift.

The diocese had assigned him to an aged community in Rhode Island, a place where the median age was seventy, and death was commonplace. So much so that no one seemed to notice the slight increase when Goyette sowed more of the beads.

Death was natural, and nowhere more so than in a community that had come of age in the turbulent sixties.

Someone knocked at his door, and Goyette's eyes snapped open, a brief flash of panic sweeping through him. He regained his composure and said in a clear voice, "Come in."

The door opened, and Brother Dominic walked in, smiling.

"Michael," Dominic said. "We're doing some shopping this afternoon, and we weren't sure how much longer you were staying. We would like to make certain we have some of your preferred foods in if you plan to remain for a time."

Goyette smiled, saying, "I appreciate the concern, Dominic, but I plan on leaving in the morning. I have a flock to attend to after all."

"Of course you do," Dominic said, giving a small nod.

"I would like to thank you," Goyette continued, "for showing me such hospitality, especially considering I was such poor company."

"That is nothing," the brother responded. "We were quite happy to have you here, and you were not poor company. I am glad you are returning to your parish, Father. Some of the old parishioners here remember you and speak well of you."

"That is very kind of them," Goyette said, adding, "perhaps I will come back soon and see if the new priest will let me speak at Mass."

"I'm sure he would," Dominic said, smiling. "I will leave you to your packing, Father, and I hope to see you before you leave."

When the brother left the room and closed the door behind him, Goyette got up and went to the desk. He took out his father's case and tucked it into the inner pocket of his suit coat. The beads rattled and filled him with a mixed sense of anticipation and excitement.

He would plant the others on his return trip to Rhode Island.

Perhaps, he thought, smiling, *I will find a cemetery alongside of the highway. What would occur then? Will the dead intercept the living at seventy miles an hour?*

The idea brought a chuckle to his lips, and he hummed his father's marching song as he began to pack for the trip home.

Chapter 35: Questions without Answers, August 12th, 2016

Connor didn't like police officers.

He had been impressed with them as a boy, seeing them as saviors, people who would be able to find the creature that killed his mother.

They hadn't. And they had ridiculed and mocked him, one officer telling him to stop being a baby and grow up. Connor had always suspected his father had put the man up to it, but the experience had soured him to the police.

Thus, his reaction to the ones who knocked on Hu's door after the fire was colored with anger.

When the introductions had been made, and all of them sat in Hu's garden, there not being enough furniture in his house for so many guests, the female detective led off.

"Mr. Mann," Lieutenant Ward said, "did you have anyone staying in the house with you?"

"No," Connor answered, his voice flat and cold. "It was only the dog and myself."

"Did you see or hear anything last night?" she asked. "Did you go out anywhere?"

"No," Connor answered.

"No to both?" Detective Rattin asked.

"No to both," Connor said.

"Are you feeling alright, Mr. Mann?" Lieutenant Ward asked, her voice hard. "You look a little peaked."

"I'm fine," Connor said.

"Mr. Bayi," Detective Rattin said, shifting his attention to the older man. "Did you see or hear anything out of the ordinary last night?"

"No," Hu said with a smile, "our neighbors are the quietest."

Rattin chuckled and nodded.

"I guess the obvious question here is, Mr. Mann," Lieutenant Ward said, "do you think anyone had any sort of reason to burn your house down?"

Connor looked at her and replied, "It wasn't my house. Belonged to my father. I was cleaning it. I had every intention of selling it and moving on. Now I can't even do that."

"Sorry to hear that," Detective Rattin said without anything resembling sympathy.

"Were you both here last night?" the lieutenant asked.

Connor nodded, and Hu said, "We were. My new friend here is a loud sleeper, I am afraid. His nightmares became my own, and I ended up spending a good deal of time reading. I didn't even know his home was on fire until the first fire engines came racing along the street."

"You didn't call it in?" Detective Rattin asked.

"No," Hu said, "I was reading. Connor was asleep."

Lieutenant Ward took a business card out of a pocket and handed it to Hu. "We may need to speak with you both at a later point, depending on where the body takes us."

Connor looked at her in surprise, and Hu blinked several times as he tucked the card away in his breast pocket.

"Did you say body?" Connor managed to ask.

"Yes," Detective Rattin said as he and the lieutenant stood.

"We're not sure who the person is yet," she stated. "At first, we were afraid it was you, Mr. Mann. We are quite glad you are alive, but it does leave us with the problem of identification. Which makes me ask you again, did you have anyone staying in the house with you?"

"No," Connor said in a soft voice. "No. The only one in there with me was Rex, and we were here last night."

"So you said," Detective Rattin said. He nodded to Hu and added, "A pleasure, sir. Thanks again."

Connor remained in his seat as Hu got up and escorted the detectives out. The older man returned a few minutes later and sat down again.

They were silent for a short time, Hu finally breaking it with a muttered sentence in Chinese.

"What did you say?" Connor asked.

"I said," Hu grumbled, "that you've created wind and fire."

Connor shook his head and replied, "I don't understand."

"Of course you don't," Hu snapped, getting to his feet, "you've created trouble for the both of us."

"What should we do now?" Connor asked, looking down at his hands and avoiding the anger in Hu's eyes.

"I'm going to smoke my pipe," Hu said, "and I am going to attempt to find a way out of this situation. Try not to do anything stupid while I am inside, Connor Mann. We may not survive if you do."

Connor winced as Hu slammed the door closed.

Fear rose up in him, fear that he would be alone, cast away by Hu.

Connor shuddered, dropped his chin to his chest, and waited to learn his fate.

Chapter 36: Quelling the Anger, August 12th, 2016

Hu sat in his office, smoking with long, deep breaths. He let the pipe smoke curl out of his nose, the effect painful and clarifying. It chased his anger away and allowed him to focus. In front of him was the small statue of the dog he had kept on the sill of the kitchen window. It reminded him of what was to come, why it must be done, and how it could all be finished.

Hu understood why Connor had burned the house down, even if the younger man did not. The building had been a pit of sorrow and rage. Setting the fire had helped him mentally, but it served as another hurdle for Hu to overcome in regards to the Priest and Feng. For decades, he had tried to hunt down the Priest, but the Catholic Church was far more diligent with its secrets than the American government tended to be.

Father Michael Goyette had been a discipline problem, from what Hu had gathered, and so he had been sent on to another church.

And Hu had never been able to discover where the church had been.

Hu had scoured newspapers and death certificates for years, but to no avail. With the return of Connor, there had been a glimmer of hope. Perhaps one of the dead would speak, a new lead for Hu to chase down.

There had been hope. Feng had appeared, made contact. Then there was Lloyd Strafford, who had seen the dead man as well.

After a dearth of information, Hu had been graced with a glimpse into the future. One where the Mala of Feng was gathered and returned to China.

The task would be harder than he had anticipated.

Hu shook his head, relit his pipe, and considered his options.

He had Strafford as an avenue of research, which would enable Hu to cut Connor loose if necessary. But aside from the younger man's worth as a connection to Feng and the other dead, Hu found he liked Connor. He enjoyed his company, and that of the dog as well.

You know he didn't kill anyone, Hu told himself, *and the dead seem enthralled with him. Didn't his own mother refer to him as sweet? She had not been affectionate when she said it.*

No. There is something more about him. Some essence the dead want.

The answer suddenly made itself clear.

Connor could satisfy their hunger. His spirit would satisfy their needs, free them of the world, and allow them to move on to the next world.

Hu doubted the act would be painless, or that Connor would survive it.

No, Hu decided, *I will not leave him behind.*

Satisfied with his decision, Hu left his office and returned to the garden. He needed to speak with Connor.

It was time to remove Feng, and imprison him.

Chapter 37: A Bike Ride, August 13th, 2016

Annie liked to pretend she was a pilot when she raced her bike through the narrow paths and between the headstones of Pine Grove Cemetery. Her parents hated how reckless she was, but Annie couldn't care less.

At twelve years old, she knew what she could and couldn't do on her bike, and using the cemetery as her own private obstacle course was definitely manageable.

She cut the bike hard, hopped to the right, and slid the rear wheel over a low headstone. Her laughter rang out, her loose hair damp with sweat and snapping around the sides of her face and along her neck.

Annie took a sharp left onto an asphalt path and leaned over the handlebars. The wind rushed past her as the path dipped and curved. Around her, the warm air smelled of summer and freedom. She didn't have to be home until the streetlights came on, and she didn't need to worry about anything.

Without warning, Annie found herself sailing over her handlebars. The world turned, and she slammed into a tree with enough force to drive her breath out of her body. Gasping for air with her head spinning from the impact, Annie rolled onto her stomach, pushed herself upward, and stood up. She needed to check for broken bones. She knew that.

But she couldn't.

Her bike occupied all of her attention, even her breath returning was a pale second to what she found herself watching.

The roots of a tree had broken through the asphalt, and they were slowly crushing her bike. Dimly she heard the sound of metal crunching, then both tires popped and the light on the front shattered. More roots, dark brown with stones and dirt clinging to them, followed the others. They snaked out along the asphalt, seeking something.

Me, Annie thought, and she knew it was true.

Despite this knowledge, Annie couldn't move. She was terrified.

The roots continued their approach. They seemed to sense her presence, and their speed increased. Within a heartbeat, they had covered half the distance to her, and she still couldn't force herself to move.

Fear had gripped her and controlled her. Part of her screamed for her to run, but she couldn't.

She froze, except for her eyes, which continued to observe the roots as they closed the space between them. They seemed to understand her fear and they slowed their approach, lazily snaking from left to right as if they were playing, teasing, and taunting her with their movements.

The foremost root stopped a short distance from her right foot, and the other roots followed suit.

Annie hyperventilated as she watched them, eyes locked on the lead root.

It rose up like a king cobra, bobbed and weaved, dipped down and rose up. Then with a quick motion, it lashed out, striking at Annie's foot.

As the root touched her, a horrible cold penetrated her sneaker, and Annie screamed.

The scream jarred her into movement.

She ripped her foot back, leaving her sneaker in the root's clutches, and she ran.

Annie kicked her other sneaker off and sprinted onto the grass. Behind her, as she darted between the headstone, she could hear the roots tearing through the asphalt.

And something's enraged shrieks hounded her as she fled.

Chapter 38: The World is Too Much, August 13th, 2016

Connor's hands shook as he sat in Dr. Waltner's waiting room.

The short trip from Hu's house to her office had been petrifying. When he had traveled from the facility to his father's home, Connor had done it at night.

Dr. Waltner could only see him in the late evening when the sun still hung in the sky. Which meant the dead could get at him if they chose.

He chided himself, clasping his hands together to quell their shaking. The dead had made it abundantly clear they could get to him regardless of the time. But knowing that didn't do anything to help him deal with his fear.

The door to her office opened and cut off his trepidation.

She gave him a small, stern smile and a nod as she stepped aside. Connor got to his feet and managed to walk in. He took a seat on a couch set against the wall while she closed the door.

Connor waited for her to sit down at her desk.

"You look tired," Dr. Waltner said, watching him.

"I'm exhausted," he replied.

"Why is that?"

"I'm trying to change my sleeping pattern," Connor answered. "I have to learn how to function in the outside world."

"How are you finding it?" she asked. "The outside world."

"Terrible," Connor whispered. "My father died the other night."

Dr. Waltner raised an eyebrow. "I didn't see an obituary."

"I didn't put one in," Connor said, his tone sharper than he had intended. "But he's dead all the same. The lack of an obituary doesn't bring him back."

"Do you want him back?" she asked.

Connor snorted. "Good God, no. I'm fine with him being dead. It's just kind of strange to be an orphan, but all in all, no, I'm not upset."

Dr. Waltner took out a pad of paper, jotted down a few lines, and said, without looking up, "What else has been going on since your release into life?"

"Someone was murdered in my father's house," Connor stated.

Her head snapped up, and she asked, "What! How?"

Connor shrugged. "We don't know yet. Someone burned the house down afterward."

She reclined in her chair, tapped her pen on the pad, and asked, "Did you burn the house down?"

With his face blushing, Connor lied. "No."

Dr. Waltner gave him a hard look and said, "Connor, I want you to remember two things. First, I am your doctor. Nothing you say to me will be relayed to anyone else. Second, I am your doctor, which also means I know when you're lying. Why did you burn your house down?"

"The ghosts," Connor muttered.

"What?" she asked with a frown.

"The ghosts," he repeated in a louder voice. "My mother was there. And Mrs. Lavoie. There were others, too."

A disapproving expression settled on her face. "Those were products of your imagination."

Anger flared up, and he spat, "I know my own imagination. They weren't it. I heard my mother. My *mother* told me how much she looked forward to feeding on me. That wasn't my imagination. It was real."

She switched subjects as she asked, "Why did you kill the man in your house?"

Connor laughed in disbelief. "No. No, I didn't kill anyone. I couldn't. Damn, I can't even step on a bug without feeling guilt. How could I kill someone?"

"I don't know," Dr. Waltner replied, "you're no longer in a controlled environment, Connor. You could do anything if enough pressure is exerted over you."

"No," Connor said in a soft voice, "I couldn't. I wouldn't even if I had to."

Dr. Waltner watched him for a short time, then capped her pen and put both it and the pad on her desk.

"Tell me," she said, folding her arms over her chest, "what exactly has happened since you returned to your father's house?"

Connor licked his lips, cracked the knuckles of his fingers, and looked down at his lap.

"Connor," Dr. Waltner said, her stern tone a comforting reminder of the safety of the facility, "I'm your psychologist. You need to trust me. Now, without any embellishment, tell me what has been going on."

Connor cleared his throat, looked down at his feet, and mumbled, "I'm worried you'll think I'm crazy."

Dr. Waltner let out one of her rare laughs and said, "Connor Mann, I am your psychologist. I know you're disturbed. What you tell me won't make me think any less of you. Perhaps it will even help us find a better treatment plan for you."

He hesitated a moment longer, and then he told her.

Connor told her everything.

Chapter 39: A Phone Call is Made, August 13th, 2016

Hu had retired to his bedroom and sat on the floor, back straight and eyes closed. His body was sore, pleasantly so. The slight pain was a reminder of the physical exercise he put himself through daily. A habit he had formed when he still served in a regular military unit. His constant state of physical fitness was a testament not only to the strength of his body, but the discipline of his mind.

Meditation was also a part of his mental well-being, a way to focus himself at the end of each day. Hu had one last task before he could go to bed. He had a phone call to make, and he didn't want to. Not at all.

But what he wanted had been supplanted by loyalty and duty in China, long before he had accepted the task in America. Hu took a deep, calming breath and let it out through his nose.

When he had regained his composure, he opened his eyes, reached out and picked up the phone. He dialed the area code and then the number. It rang once on the other end and the call was answered.

"Hello?" a woman asked in Chinese.

"Good evening, Mei Ling," Hu said.

"Colonel," she replied. "I am surprised to hear from you. I do believe it has been eight years since we last spoke."

"You would be correct," he said, unable to keep the tightness out of his voice.

She laughed, a deep, American sound that reminded him of the alien nature of some of his American cousins.

"I know I'm correct," Mei Ling said, a pleased note in her voice. "I was looking through my calendar yesterday. You were due to call soon. You think you've found someone to help you with Feng."

Her sentence wasn't a question, but a statement. How she knew the information was a question he did not ask, knowing she would not answer.

"Yes," Hu said. "He is the son of Feng's first American victim."

Mei Ling hesitated and then said in a thoughtful voice, "She tells him he is sweet."

"Yes," Hu said, nodding and switching the phone from one

hand to the other.

"He's the one," Mei Ling said without hesitation.

"How do you know?" Hu blurted out.

"The sweetness," she answered, her voice soft. "He was a child when the attack happened. I have seen it. His love for his mother never soured. It is sweet. Pure. All want to partake in it, though they do not understand that to do so would destroy them and send them to their own personal hell. He does not grasp that this sweetness is strength, that he will be able to command them, so long as they understand his native tongue."

A silence filled the space between them, then Mei Ling chuckled and added, "Best to do it quickly, Colonel. There are a great many seeds your Priest has sown."

Before Hu could thank her, she ended the call.

He held onto the receiver for a few moments longer, then he put the phone back in its cradle. A nagging sense of worry grew within him. The idea that Connor Mann was the answer to some of the issues concerning Feng and the Priest had been faint at best. Mei Ling's statement about the younger man's importance overall was disconcerting.

Hu saw strength in Connor, but he also acknowledged the weakness.

In the silence of his room, Hu wondered if there was enough courage in the younger man to overcome the deficiencies created by a lifetime spent in a mental hospital.

Do we have another choice?

Hu got to his feet and readied himself for bed. He didn't bother answering the question.

He already knew.

Chapter 40: A Ruckus in Pine Grove, August 14th, 2016

When Lloyd Strafford walked out to gather his newspaper from the front steps, he was surprised to see police officers in the cemetery. He counted at least ten of them, and as he stood with his front door open, trying to fathom what the officers were doing there at 6:30 in the morning, a policeman noticed him. The young man pulled the iron gate open a little further and passed through.

Lloyd waited for him, and when the man arrived, he greeted him.

"Hello, I'm Officer Pappas," the young man said. "I was wondering if I could speak to you."

"Certainly," Lloyd replied. "Do you want to come inside?"

"Let's hold off on that for now," Officer Pappas said with a tired smile, "but I was wondering if you noticed anything odd in the cemetery over the past few days."

Lloyd kept his initial response to himself, saying instead, "Not really. May I ask what's going on?"

"We've got a teenager who's gone missing," the young man said, his face becoming grim. "There was an incident reported two days ago where a girl said she had been chased by a tree in the cemetery. Everybody thought she was nuts, of course. Then this teenager went missing last night, and one of his friends said the same thing. Damned tree chasing after them."

Lloyd felt cold, and sick to his stomach.

"Has anything been found?" he asked in a tight voice.

Officer Pappas shook his head. "We're hoping someone saw something. Now, you haven't seen anyone new hanging around the neighborhood, have you?"

Lloyd shook his head confused. "No. Why?"

"There have been some new, designer drugs put out on the market," the officer said. "A few of them have some lethal side-effects. Others cause massive hallucinations, so there's a possibility the kids could have had a bad reaction to some recreational drug."

"No," Lloyd said, "I am sorry to say I haven't seen anyone new. Or even the children you spoke of. I tend to keep to myself."

"I don't blame you," Officer Pappas said, smiling. "Thank you for your time, sir. We may be back to question you again."

Lloyd nodded, waved goodbye to the officer and watched the young man cross the street and reenter the cemetery. Feeling numb, Lloyd walked back into his house, closing and locking the door behind him. He dropped the newspaper onto the coffee table and sat down on the couch. His heart was heavy as he thought of the unknown teenager. As well as the girl who had been chased by the tree.

Lloyd could hardly wrap his head around the idea of it. The mental image of a tree chasing someone was absurd and made him physically ill. He knew what the ghosts in Pine Grove Cemetery were capable of committing against adults, and the thought of those same pains being visited upon children brought the bile up into his throat.

He choked it back down and sank further into the couch's old, spring cushions. Part of him knew he was too old to be concerned with the ghosts in the cemetery. To be worried about the silver fox.

Lloyd needed to let young men such as Officer Pappas pick up the mantle and save the day. Connor Mann could make an effort as well to keep people safe. Lloyd was too old. It would be far too dangerous for him to risk a confrontation with the fox, or any of the dead who haunted the cemetery.

And what of Hu? Lloyd asked himself. *What about his age and what is he planning to do? Can you do no less?*

He sat for another minute, then pushed himself to his feet and got ready to visit Hu.

Chapter 41: Investigating Pine Grove, August 14ᵗʰ, 2016

Meg Ward chewed on her thumbnail as she stood in the late afternoon sun. Her shift had finished hours earlier, but the disappearance of the teen from the cemetery upset her. In her gut, she felt it had something to do with Connor Mann, although she knew there was no evidence or reason to think so.

She pulled off a small bit of nail, spit it out, and clenched her hand into a fist.

Meg, along with half of the police force, had scoured Pine Grove. Their search had revealed nothing except a New York Yankees baseball hat. The missing boy's mother had identified it as his.

Over the years, Meg had grown a thick skin when it came to investigating crimes. Children and grieving relatives always left her drained and wanting to do more.

Which was why she was alone in the cemetery going over the ground again.

She scanned all around, searching for anything odd. Her head stopped and her eyes locked onto a shape. An animal. A small, silver fox. It stood in front of a headstone and stared at her. The creature was the strangest she had ever seen. It was as if someone had dipped the fox in a vat of silver paint. The idea that it might be a pet dyed in the way some people did to French Poodles caused Meg to take a cautious step forward.

When the fox didn't move, Meg advanced several more feet.

The animal seemed amused, its tail flicking from the left to the right and back again, the rhythm casual and hypnotic. Meg found it fascinating, and she lost all sense of caution.

"Hello," she said, coming to a stop a few feet from it. "Are you okay? Are you lost?"

The words sounded stupid and absurd, but she couldn't stop them. She was worried about the fox.

Its tongue slipped out, licked its chops, and watched her.

A small part of Meg realized the entire situation was unnerving.

Meg latched onto that thought and forced herself to take a step back.

The fox lunged at her, shifting its shape.

By the time Meg reached for her pistol, and the weapon

cleared the holster, a man had replaced the animal.

He was old and Asian, and she could see the hatred in his eyes.

She fired off three rounds, each passing through the man without any effect.

He struck her, the force knocking her backward, her head slamming into a gravestone. Meg was plunged into darkness, but she could still hear and feel. Something warm coursed down from her cracked skull, and she knew, without any doubt, that there were more brains than blood running down her neck.

As she lay immobile, Meg felt a cold hand reach out, caress the side of her face, and several voices rang out with laughter.

"Thank you," a woman said in Meg's ear, "our master was ever so hungry."

Meg found she couldn't scream when teeth as sharp as razors burrowed into her flesh.

Chapter 42: A Harsh Awakening, August 14th, 2016

Connor jumped out of bed, his heart pounding. Rex was up as well, pacing the room and growling. Connor's head throbbed as he made his way to the window and pulled up the curtain. A second later, he heard the door slam and saw Hu hurrying across the street towards the cemetery.

Connor looked to see what had caught the older man's attention.

There was movement in Pine Grove. One woman was bent over another, who was propped against a large headstone. Connor rubbed sleep from his eyes as he tried to focus on what he saw. As the image became clear, a sense of horror welled up within him. The woman who was propped against the headstone was at the mercy of the other, who was tearing at her flesh.

A scream tore out of Connor's throat and the attacker's head snapped around.

It was his mother, and her mouth was twisted in a vicious grin.

Hu, in spite of his age, grabbed onto the crossbar of the wrought iron fence and pulled himself up.

Connor's mother pushed herself away from her victim and vanished.

Clamping a hand over his mouth, Connor was able to silence himself. Yet when he saw the victim, a fresh scream built up in his throat.

It was the police lieutenant from earlier in the week.

Gagging in horror, Connor turned and stumbled to the door of the bedroom, wrenching it open. He staggered to the stairs, clung to the railing and made his way down to the first floor as quickly as he could.

In the kitchen, he found the man, Lloyd Strafford, looking pale and concerned.

"Hu told me to wait here for you," Lloyd said. "I think something bad has happened."

Shaking, Connor settled down across from the man, and they sat in silence until Hu returned several minutes later. The man walked to the phone, picked it up, and called 911. Connor listened as Hu described the condition of Lieutenant Meg Ward, and heard that she was dead.

After he hung up the phone, Hu faced Connor and Lloyd.

"I will be in the cemetery," Hu said, his voice stiff. "I will sit with her until someone comes."

"My mother killed her," Connor whispered.

Hu raised an eyebrow, and shook his head. "She may have quickened the Lieutenant's death, but she did not kill her. When the woman fell she struck a headstone and cracked her skull open. Most of her brains were literally knocked out."

Connor shook his head. "It doesn't matter. I saw my mother's face. She enjoyed it. She needs to be stopped. They all do. Can I stop her? Is it even possible?"

"I don't know," Lloyd confessed.

"Of course it is," Hu said. "The most difficult part is finding someone strong enough to cast her out, and burn her bones."

"Where would we find someone like that?" Lloyd asked.

"He's already here," Hu said, taking his pipe and packing the bowl with tobacco.

It took Connor several seconds to realize both Hu and Lloyd had fixed their attention on him.

"Yes, Connor," Hu said around the stem of the pipe, "it's you."

"No," Connor said, shaking his head. "Why would you say that?"

"It certainly isn't me," Lloyd said, shaking his head. "If it were, I would have been able to do something decades ago."

"And I would have found Feng long before you ever returned to your father's home," Hu added, putting his lighter away. Smoke curled up from his mouth and the pipe's bowl. "No, you are the only one. I have received confirmation of this."

"From whom?" Connor demanded, trying to keep fear out of his voice. "Who told you that?"

"Someone I trust," Hu said, "and we shall leave it at that. You are the only one."

Connor shook his head, panic building.

"Listen," Connor said, glancing frantically from Hu to Lloyd, "I can't do anything. I can't. Come on, I wasn't even supposed to be out of the facility. If my uncle hadn't died, I'd still be in there. I should never have been let out. You know that, right?"

The older men looked at him with impassive expressions.

Connor's shoulders slumped.

"I can't do anything," he whispered. "I can never do anything. Why don't you believe me?"

"There isn't time for a pep talk, son," Lloyd said. "People are dying. Faster now since you're out, and you can't think that's only coincidence."

Connor looked down and saw Rex, the dog's brown eyes staring into his own.

"What do I need to do?" Connor whispered.

"Nothing yet," Hu responded. "There are some steps and precautions I must take first. When those are complete, then we will begin our hunt for Feng's bead."

"I think I know roughly where it is," Lloyd said, and both Connor and Hu looked at him in surprise.

"Where?" Hu asked, an excited note entered his voice. "Where is it?"

"Shortly before Debra Mann was killed," Lloyd said, looking apologetically at Connor, "only a few graves had been dug in the section where she died. I have seen the fox linger near them, but I thought he was at Debra's grave. There is the distinct possibility that he was at his own resting place. It would make sense for the bead to be deposited there. In one of the deep, pre-dug holes."

"Yes," Hu agreed, "it would make sense. Could you draw a map from here to the grave where you believe you saw Feng. I do not wish you ill luck, my friend, but I would hate for you to become injured or slain. Such an event would leave us without the information we need to carry on."

Lloyd gave a wry smile and said, "Bring on the pen and paper then."

Connor watched the interaction between the two men and felt neither confidence nor joy. Instead, a black cloud settled over him, and he wondered what would happen to them if he failed.

Chapter 43: Preparations are Made, August 15th, 2016

For hours on end, Hu worked.

He gathered iron and salt and went into a small room in his basement he rarely frequented. There were basics of ghost lore that spanned cultures and civilizations. Iron and salt formed the keystones of those essentials, and while they could be found in America, it was not as easy as it seemed.

The United States had long ago focused upon steel, as had most nations, and so iron was no longer in abundance. Recent economic downturns in America also factored into that supply as more and more people sold their scrap metal to private businesses. Hu, in turn, spent the better part of three days traveling up into the northern parts of New Hampshire, and the southern parts of Maine. He rummaged through indoor flea markets, stopped at junk yards, and prowled through antique stores.

In the end, he had done well. He had gathered up enough old and pure iron to protect himself, Connor, and Lloyd. With the metal in hand, Hu had found a man with a forge, a retired blacksmith in Brookline, New Hampshire, who had agreed to forge the items Hu needed.

And for a cost that didn't put a dent in Hu's limited operational budget. China wanted Feng's Mala back, but they were being notoriously cheap about it.

Hu snorted and looked down at what the blacksmith had created for him.

Three pairs of leather gloves, courtesy of the Home Depot garden center, were studded with small, iron spikes. The gloves would allow them to defend themselves from any attacks they could see.

Salt gathered from a local lick that Hu had found years earlier would serve as a rough barrier. A circle of it spread out around them while they worked would prohibit the passage of any of the dead.

As long as the circle remained unbroken.

Hu nodded, lit his pipe, and felt satisfied with their preparations. If all went well, they would gather the bead. He hoped it would solve the problem of the other ghosts created by the Priest.

If not, then Hu would be forced to find himself a Buddhist monk to assist him.

And they were in short supply.

Hu lit his pipe, inhaled, and let the smoke out through his nose.

After decades, Hu was looking forward to running the Priest to the ground.

Chapter 44: With Silent Fury, August 16th, 2016

Noah Rattin took out a cigarette, lit it, and stared out of the window of his car at Pine Grove Cemetery. The world had taken on a bleak tint, his vision fuzzy from the half-pint of sloe gin he had picked up.

With Meg's death, he had lost any sort of reason to remain sober or quit smoking.

She had encouraged him and wanted him to be better.

He tapped the ash of the cigarette into an old Pepsi can and tried not to imagine how angry Meg would have been with him.

Noah would have given anything to be able to listen to her yell at him.

He took another drag from the cigarette and then followed it with a swig of gin.

Noah glared at the cemetery, hating every aspect of it. He despised the fact that a teen had disappeared there, and when Noah thought of Meg, his skull ached.

He ground his teeth together and shook with rage.

Her death was inexplicable.

For three days, they had combed through every inch of cemetery within a hundred feet around Meg's body. They found the shell casings from her pistol. Trace evidence from Hu had been discovered, but the older man had been ruled out as a suspect.

For Hu to have been the cause of Meg's fall and subsequent death, there would have been some sort of powder residue on his clothes. Noah and anyone who had ever watched Meg qualify with her pistol knew Hu would have been wounded, if not dead.

Meg never missed her target.

Every round hit the target center mass. She wasn't a sniper, but she never missed what she shot at. The fact that she had fired off three rounds and there hadn't been any blood, disturbed Noah. Something was wrong with the entire situation.

He reached out, ignored the gin and picked up the old manila folder from his passenger seat. It contained all of the information gathered in 1979 when the death of Connor Mann's mother had been reported. Connor, as a boy, had talked about a fox that had transformed into a man.

He had spoken of the same animal when Mrs. Lavoie had

409

been killed almost a year later.

Connor had then spent decades in a private psychiatric facility, and since his release, Connor's father had died, a teen had disappeared, and Meg had fallen and split her skull open.

And don't forget the thief, Noah reminded himself.

They had finally gotten an identification on the body in Connor's house. A morgue attendant, the one who had handled and processed Cody Mann's body. Noah and Meg had dug into the attendant's past and finances and discovered he had been picked up on petty larceny charges as a teen. In addition to the previous record, the paperwork for numerous safety deposit boxes had been found. A subsequent warrant had revealed over $70,000 in cash.

While they knew who the attendant was, and could surmise as to what he was doing in Connor's house, there was still no official cause of death. It wasn't a suicide, and the man didn't die of smoke inhalation. The coroner was still waiting on tissue samples that had been sent off.

Noah dropped the folder back onto the seat and made a decision.

It was time to go into the cemetery and find out what was going on.

He reached for the door handle and stopped. Across the corner of the cemetery, he saw a light come on in front of Hu's garage. Within a minute, Hu, Connor, and a third man came out of the house. Noah watched them walk inside the garage and emerge a short time later. Hu and the third man carried backpacks.

Connor carried a shovel.

Noah continued to watch as they crossed the street and followed the fence to the cemetery's first gate. They were an odd procession as they passed through the entrance, turned right, and walked towards where Meg had died.

Noah snatched up his cigarettes, opened the car door, and eased it shut. With his heartbeat quickening, he hurried after them.

As Noah got closer, the distinct sound of a shovel striking earth rang out, and he wondered whose grave they were disturbing.

Chapter 45: Chinatown, Boston, March 10, 2011

Hu didn't enjoy traveling to Massachusetts.

The Massachusetts State Police had a tendency to pull him over, although he was never given a satisfactory reason why. Hu wasn't foolish enough to argue with the officers or to let on that he understood everything they said to him. He was content to play upon the stereotypes the men brought to him.

Hu had given up driving in the state because of those situations and relied upon public transportation.

When the train rumbled into North Station, he moved along with the steady pace other travelers set. Soon he was on a bus, edging ever closer to Chinatown.

The sun partially hidden by a bank of dark clouds had begun its descent toward the horizon when Hu stepped off the bus. The smell of the Chinese enclave wrapped around him, a reminder of some of the smaller cities he had been stationed in back home.

A pang of regret rose up as he remembered China, and he wondered if he should ever have left.

Hu did his best to ignore the unspoken question. His country needed him, and he had answered. It had always been the case, and it would remain so.

Patriotism was not the sole domain of the Western world.

Hu made his way through the streets, the air cold and sharp against his cheeks. He passed the Winsor Dim Sum Cafe, reached a green-grated door, and opened it. Warm air rushed out to greet him, and Hu hurried in, closing the door behind him. Several bare light bulbs illuminated a narrow passage, and Hu followed it to a trio of stairs that led down to a landing. There he found another green-grated door. This one was locked, and he had to ring a doorbell.

He stood in silence, listening to the dull thrum of some sort of machinery behind the walls, and then took a step back as the door opened.

A young woman looked at him and asked in Chinese, "Who are you?"

"Hu," he replied.

She raised an eyebrow. "I'll need more than your first name."

"No," Hu disagreed, "you won't. Tell her it is Hu."

The young woman shrugged and closed the door on him.

She was back in less than a minute, a fearful and apologetic expression on her face. As she opened her mouth to speak, Hu shook his head and smiled.

"No apologies are necessary," Hu said, stepping into the brightly lit room beyond. "You were doing your job, and did not know who I was."

"Thank you," she whispered.

Hu nodded and waited until she had closed and locked the door before he walked towards Mei Ling's office. She looked up from the table next to where she stood and smiled at him.

"You have caused my apprentice no amount of concern," Mei Ling said, stepping away from her work and looking up at him. "You seem tired, Hu."

"I am," Hu admitted.

"Sit," she said, gesturing towards a wooden chair.

Hu did so, removing a small pile of books from the seat and placing them on the floor before he sat down. He looked at Mei Ling and wondered how she seemed to stay so young. She appeared to have aged only a few years since the last time they had met when he first arrived in the United States.

Mei Ling seemed to feel his eyes on her, and she turned to glance at him, a crooked smile on her face. She brushed a lock of long black hair behind her ear and said, "What are you thinking about, my friend?"

Hu hesitated before he told her the truth.

She shrugged. "Do you wish to know my age, Hu?"

He felt as though the question were a trap, that an answer either for or against would be unwise.

"If you wish to tell me," he said, "then I will be happy to hear it."

"A pity you're not married," Mei Ling said, chuckling and turning back to her work. "You would have made an excellent husband. So few happy marriages exist."

"I was married," Hu said in a low voice, "a long time ago."

She straightened up and turned to face him, a concerned look on her face. "How did she die?"

"She was murdered," Hu answered.

Mei Ling nodded. "I am sorry."

Hu didn't trust his voice not to break if he spoke again.

"I am nearly done here, Hu," Mei Ling said, walking to a set of thick shelves on the far wall. "I will have what you need shortly."

Hu sat and waited, letting his eyes roam over the strange and fascinating artifacts Mei Ling had collected. There were books and scrolls by the dozens, weapons and containers, toys and puzzles, and all of which, Hu knew, were dangerous.

There was not a single item in her office, including Mei Ling herself, which did not have some deadly purpose.

"Ah, finished at last," she said, interrupting his train of thought.

Hu looked and saw she held a small statue. It was of a dog, painted in deep, vibrant shades of red, purple, and blue. Jade stones glittered in its eyes, and teeth the color of ivory grinned from its mouth.

The dog stood perhaps six inches tall, and the way the muscles stood out on Mei Ling's forearms, it seemed to be heavy.

"Take it," she said, and for the first time Hu heard pain in her voice and saw beads of sweat standing out on her forehead.

He got to his feet and took it from her, gritting his teeth against the surprising weight of the statue. His hands grew hot, as if the dog were alive.

Mei Ling looked at the statue and spoke sharply in a dialect Hu neither recognized nor understood.

But the statue did.

Instantly it became cool to the touch.

"What is it?" Hu asked, impressed.

Mei Ling smiled, dragged a chair over, and sat down across from him.

"It is a container, and little more," she said. There was a hint of a smile on her lips, and Hu waited for her to add to the statement. After a minute of silence, the smile appeared fully, and she chuckled again. "Perhaps much more than that, yes, Hu?"

He nodded.

"Good," she said, "very good. Now, what you hold in your hands is more than a container. It is a safe. A box with a lid that locks. The heat you felt, it recognized you."

"How can it recognize me?" Hu asked, looking down at the statue in his hands.

Mei Ling waved away the question. "Never mind the how.

413

Merely understand that it does. Do you?"

"I do," Hu answered, shifting his gaze from the statue to the woman.

"Yes," she whispered, leaning closer, "I see you do. Good. I have always liked you, Hu, and your honesty is one of the reasons why. Now, let us continue. You cannot open the dog's mouth. It will do that on its own."

Hu didn't ask how. He listened.

She winked at him and continued. "When the dog opens its mouth, it means you will have found something important."

"Feng's Mala?" Hu asked.

Mei Ling face hardened, her eyes draining of joy.

"Do you really think," she asked in a low voice, "that his Mala has been left intact?"

Hu thought about the question and then replied, "No. No, I don't believe it has."

"It has not," Mei Ling said, "and the statue you hold will help you contain each ghost when it is found."

"How?" Hu asked, turning the statue over in his hands before looking back to Mei Ling. "How will it do that?"

"Two ways," she answered, holding up two fingers. "First, the inner casing is of lead, which is why the statue is so heavy. Second, I have bound a dog's spirit within it as well. He will not let any of the dead that you place within escape. And once closed, the lead will serve as a double layer of protection."

Hu looked at the statue in his hand. He thought of how the object had cooled down when commanded by Mei and said, "I didn't think a dog's spirit could listen and obey."

"He was not always a dog," Mei said, nodding to the statue. "He was once a hungry ghost, who had chosen the form of a dog. It was both a curious and rare choice for him to make, as dogs are their bane. But, it was as a dog he was caught, and bound."

Mei gave Hu a grim smile and added, "Fitting, is it not, to bind such a ghost to this?"

Hu nodded as his throat tightened, and he gazed upon her with a newfound fear.

Chapter 46: A Lonely Vigil, August 16th, 2016

Antoinette Felicia Francour sat in a rocking chair with a soft light behind her. The lamp cast enough of a glow over her shoulder so she could see her rosary and little more. Her eyes were not fixed on anything except the cemetery beyond her house. She had buried both of her sons and her husband, and since neither of her children had produced heirs, Antoinette was alone in the world.

Alone except for the Church, which always made certain to send someone to pick her up for confession on Saturday and Mass on Sunday. She had been a devout Catholic her entire life, and she often wished that God had called to her to become a Sister, and not a wife.

Antoinette never questioned His choices for her. She had only longed for something different.

Movement in the cemetery caught her attention and pulled her out of her memories. She watched a trio of figures at a grave, and it took her several seconds to realize what it was.

People were excavating a grave.

She stared at them for a long time, judging the distance from the open gate to where they stood. Then she did the same from the right corner post of the wrought iron fence.

Whoever the grave robbers were, they shouldn't have been there.

Antoinette's hands trembled, her heart beat quicker than it had in decades. She reached out and picked up her address book. In less than a minute, she found the phone number she sought and took the receiver out of its cradle.

Her breath was short and shallow as she dialed the number, then listened to it ring.

After the sixth ring, the call was answered.

"Hello?"

"Father," Antoinette said, her voice quivering, "someone's here."

"You can see them?" he asked.

"Their shapes," she answered. "One of them is digging."

"Excellent. Thank you, Antoinette."

"You're welcome, Father," she whispered and hung up the phone.

Antoinette settled back into her chair and picked up her rosary.

Father Michael had been such a good priest. Kind and caring. He had visited her every day for the first few weeks after her husband, Emil's death.

Everyone, including the priest, had agreed that Emil's passing had been strange. He had been such a healthy man. Every day he had walked through Pine Grove Cemetery, so it had been a terrible surprise when he had been found dead of a stroke.

So very strange, Antoinette thought, *but he certainly wasn't the first person who had passed away suddenly in the cemetery. And he wasn't the last either.*

But he had been the only one she had cared about.

Antoinette was mildly curious about Father Michael's interest in the grave in question, but she had never pressed the issue. He had his reasons, and it was not her place to pry.

And besides, he had been so kind after Emil's death.

So kind.

Chapter 47: Preparations for the Conflict, August 16th, 2016

Michael had forgotten about Antoinette. When he had heard her frail voice over the phone, he recalled her status as observer. He had encouraged her to reach out to him if she saw anything in regards to the grave Feng was buried in.

And she had.

Her husband had been another victim of Feng, or possibly one of Connor's mother. Regardless as to who did the final deed, it had been done, and Emil Francour was dead. For several weeks, Michael had remained with Antoinette. Anyone who looked at his constant visits saw his concern and care.

Which were nothing more than tools to observe the house.

Father Michael had no interest in the woman's sorrow or empathy for it. His concern revolved around Emil.

He had been curious as to whether or not Emil would return. He knew little of the man, so he was unsure what unnatural appetites he might have. Some overbearing desire for food, perhaps a need to acquire possessions, some sort of lust that would condemn Emil to be hungry after death.

From what Michael had been able to gather, the man had been without base desires.

A boring result.

Michael had consoled himself with the hope of better luck at the next festival, and wondering if Feng would grow strong enough to strike outside of the limited time period the festival offered.

The ghost had, with each year, grown stronger, the energy of the dead he had created boosted his own.

Michael chuckled at the thought of all of the people he had helped usher into the next life. He laid back down in bed and stared up at the dim light on the ceiling. A sense of nervous anxiety began to build up within him. His mouth became dry and he plucked at the sheet beneath him, his fingers unable to stay still.

Michael wasn't sure if he would be found, but he had a nagging suspicion that he would. Being discovered would be far more than inconvenient. It could be disastrous, not only to his goals, but to his own personal safety.

He would be traveling back to Rhode Island soon, to his new

parish. The Greenbriar Nursing Home fell within his domain, and it was from there he would be able to recruit personal guards.

Michael needed to build a refuge for himself, and he could think of no better guards for such a place than the dead. They did not need to sleep, and since they were always hungry, well, there were always plenty of people to feed to them.

The Priest closed his eyes, doubtful if he would be able to fall asleep. His mind raced with thoughts on preparations, and the growing idea of how he might trap those coming after him.

A smile settled onto his face as he thought of how enjoyable it would be to watch them die.

Perhaps, Michael thought, *I might even kill them myself.*

He pushed that pleasant idea away and focused on what he would need to secure a place for one of his last beads at Greenbriar. The item would have to be buried in a grave, and to create a grave, Michael would need consecrated ground and a body.

The ground he could consecrate himself, the body he would have to procure.

Ideally it will be small, he thought, *and easy to transport.*

Chapter 48: Andrew Smythe's Grave, August 16th, 2016

Connor held onto the handle of the shovel, his hands sweating in the leather gloves Hu had given him. A rough circle of raw salt encompassed the three men and the grave, with a little room to spare. The headstone read *Andrew Smythe*, and he had died a few weeks before Connor's mother. Andrew's grave was one of the three that had been dug in the days preceding his mother's death. Connor prayed this grave, the third and last one, was the right one.

At the edge of the circle of salt, dark shapes sat, and Connor knew the dead were watching.

There was absolute silence in the cemetery. The birds and night animals had been frightened away by the presence of the dead. Small shapes darted around the outskirts of the salt line, but none of them were Feng's silver fox.

Connor could feel his mother's presence, but he couldn't see her, and that worried him. He had no reason to feel concerned, not if what Hu had said about the salt was true. Connor's mother and the others wouldn't be able to get by.

"Connor," Hu said.

He looked at the older man and saw a look of concern on Hu's face in the moonlight.

"Yes?" Connor asked, conscious of the sweat clinging to his back for the first time.

"You need to dig," Hu said, his voice firm. "Lloyd and I are too old. This part of the task is up to you."

Once more, Connor's eyes were drawn to the object Hu had brought with him from the house. It was a small dog statue, jade eyes glittering in the moonlight. The sight of it chilled Connor, but he didn't know why. Lloyd, too, had seemed uncomfortable in the object's presence.

Hu paid it no mind, holding it with almost reverent attitude.

"Dig, son," Lloyd said, patting Connor on the arm. "The sooner you're done, the happier we will all be."

Connor nodded his head in agreement and started to dig again. The soil was heavy on the shovel, and his hands felt as though they would swell with the sweat gathering within the leather.

He pushed that concern, and the worry over his mother, to

the back of his mind and focused on the task at hand. Even while the muscles of his shoulders and arms protested, Connor continued to dig, and the hole got deeper. Somewhere, according to Hu, a bead from Feng's Mala was in the grave.

The bead Feng had bound himself to, if what Hu had been told was true.

All Connor wanted to do was stop his mother.

He wanted her free, and unable to torment anyone else. But what he wanted and what would be reality were separate, and he had no guarantee of success.

The idea of ghosts being a harsh and brutal reality caused him to hesitate before he drove the steel edge of the shovel into the dirt again. He had always defended his statements, his memories, to the legion of doctors and do-gooders who had attempted to wear him down over the years. Men and women who had tried to convince him that what he had seen wasn't real.

A small slice of Connor's personality finally felt justified, yet the remainder horrified him.

He was in a cemetery, digging up a grave to find a small bead that once held the spirit of an evil man. And around this man were ghosts, and all of them bent upon keeping Feng safe.

"Connor?" Hu asked in a gentle voice.

Connor looked up, the man's face a mixture of shadows and highlights from the moon's light.

With a nod, Connor went back to digging. Regardless of how strange and disconnected he felt from the world, he still had a grave to rob.

Chapter 49: In the Name of the Law, August 16th, 2016

Noah picked his way through the cemetery with as much caution as he could muster. Which, considering how much alcohol he had in him, wasn't an impressive amount.

He knew, in fact, that if the trio he had seen weren't digging, they would have heard him.

But they were the ones committing a crime, and he was a cop.

And Noah was certain they were behind Meg's death.

He loosened his pistol in its holster and kept his hand on the grip as he came to a stop behind a large tree. Thirty or forty feet ahead he saw one of the men digging; the other two stood close by. None of them spoke, and Noah was impressed with their disciplined silence.

Noah maintained his own reticence as he crept forward, the whisper of his shoes on grass lost beneath the sound the shovel striking the ground. The thump and slide of dirt on a growing pile obscured whatever noise the shovel didn't.

His steps carried him to a tall headstone, and he crouched behind it to look at the trio.

Noah recognized two of them, Hu and Connor. The third was an old man, roughly the same age as Hu if Noah had to guess. A dull white substance caught his eye and Noah scanned the area around the men and the headstone.

One of them had created a large circle made up of what looked like rock salt. Noah stared at it for a moment and wondered if it was, and if so, then why it would be around a grave?

The question was too much for his inebriated brain to handle, so he didn't.

Movement close to the ground caught his eye, and he turned his head to watch what looked like the tail-end of a rabbit slip into the darkness. Other, similarly sized shapes moved in the shadows, and Noah shook his head. He would need to contact Park and Recreation in the morning, if he remembered, and tell them about the rabbit problem in the cemetery.

Noah shook his head and thought. *Enough distractions.*

He took a deep breath, stood up and advanced toward the grave. He stepped over the salt with his right foot, but stumbled and broke the continuity of the line with his left.

"Stop!" Noah commanded, the word slurring as he spoke.

The three men looked at him, staring, surprise on their faces.

Hu's gaze went to the line of salt, and his surprise became fury.

"What have you done?" Hu demanded.

Before Noah could answer, something struck him in the small of his back and knocked him to him knees. As he struggled to his feet, the creatures he thought were rabbits barreled towards him.

In a heartbeat, he realized they weren't rabbits, and with that realization came shock as the creatures transformed into people and moved past him.

A heavy blow landed against the back of his head, and the world went black around him.

Chapter 50: Defending Themselves, August 16ᵗʰ, 2016

Connor dropped the shovel, waves of fear threatening to push him to his knees. A deeper, more primal part of himself screamed for him to run, to race for the fence and scramble over it. Hu's house would be safe. The statues around and within it would protect him.

But Connor knew he couldn't run.

He had to stand and fight.

Hu depended on him.

Clenching his hands into fists, Connor stepped forward and swung a wide, clumsy punch towards a ghost. It was a man in his early forties, wearing a business suit and a Boston Red Sox baseball hat.

The ghost, with a smile of twisted joy on his face, leaped towards Connor, allowing Connor's blow to pass through him.

The dead man's eyes widened with rage before he vanished.

A fierce joy surged through Connor and the adrenaline that had demanded he flee suddenly changed, urging him to fight. Connor had never had much cause to fight while living in the facility, and so his punches were amateurish, and poorly thrown, but they were thrown. Some of them even connected. His focus was upon the ghost in front of him, and he rarely noticed either Hu or Lloyd.

Connor turned to find another ghost, and he saw the detective, Noah Rattin, get to his feet. Yet the man's eyes were disturbing. In the moonlight, they looked almost silver, as if the pupils were gone.

Connor watched as the detective staggered forward, reached out, and grasped Lloyd's arm. The old man turned, a shocked expression on his face.

Noah brought his fist back and struck the old man in the face, knocking him out. The detective allowed Lloyd to collapse to the ground and faced Hu, raising his fists to strike the man.

"No!" Connor commanded. "Stop!"

All of the ghosts stiffened, and Noah did as well. They looked at Connor, horror etched on their dead faces.

Hu faced Connor and said in an awed tone, "Tell them to leave."

"Get out," Connor spat. "Go away."

The ghosts vanished, and Noah's silver eyes rolled up in his head as he fell backward, landing with a thump on the ground.

Hu shook his head as he asked, "Can you get the detective onto his feet and out of here?"

"I think so," Connor answered.

"Good," Hu stated, "I will carry Lloyd. I do not know how much time we have, I suggest we move as quickly as possible."

Connor could only nod in agreement as he picked up Noah.

He half dragged, half carried the unconscious detective towards the gate. And as he did so, Connor's mind raced, trying to understand why the dead had listened to him.

He tried to understand what was going to come next in the strange new world he had been thrust into. And wondered if he would survive it.

Chapter 51: Explanations, August 16th, 2016

Both the detective and Lloyd were unconscious, and Connor worried that the men should be brought to the hospital and not kept in the kitchen. The two of them were stretched out on the floor, but Hu had assured Connor they would be fine.

While he trusted Hu, Connor was still concerned for their well-being.

He and Hu sat in the garden, their chairs turned to face the kitchen. They had been quiet for a long time, each lost in their own thoughts.

"I didn't see my mother there," Connor said, interrupting the silence and unable to keep the horror out of his voice.

"I did," Hu replied.

Connor glanced at him, wondering how the man could be so unperturbed by what they had experienced in the cemetery. He pushed the thought away, cleared his throat, and asked, "How are we going to find a bead in a grave?"

Hu let a small, wry smile slip and he said, "We will feel it. *You* more than the rest of us, I think."

The tone of the man's voice made Connor ask another question, one that had arisen only recently.

"Hu," Connor said, "why did the ghosts listen to me?"

The older man looked down at his teacup for a moment, then smiled and said, "Do you recall when your mother spoke about your sweetness?"

Connor nodded. The memory was an uncomfortable one.

"There is something special about you, Connor," Hu said, "something that attracts the dead to you. There is a purity to you that draws them like moths to the proverbial flame. Yet at the same time, they seem bound to listen to your commands. This is an aspect to you that we need to explore further, my young friend."

The sliding door that led from the kitchen to the garden opened, and Detective Noah Rattin stepped out. In the glow of the exterior light, the officer looked queasy, his face pale and his forehead slick with sweat. His gait was unsteady, and when he reached them, Noah sank down and sat on the ground.

He blinked several times and asked, "What happened?"

"In the cemetery?" Hu inquired.

Noah nodded, wincing as he did so.

"Ghosts, Detective," Hu replied. "They made an appearance, and when you broke the salt line, you let them in. We were attempting to retrieve an item."

"You were robbing a grave," Noah retorted, closing his eyes. "Someone hit me on the back of the head. And it sure wasn't a ghost."

"Believe what you want," Hu said, turning his attention back to Connor, "we have little time for the likes of you."

Noah frowned. "Ghosts don't exist."

"Ghosts," Hu snapped, "are what killed Lieutenant Ward. There is no other explanation. I do not believe she fell through her own fault."

Noah's face grew whiter, but he didn't argue the point. He swallowed and asked, "How can there be ghosts?"

Hu chuckled. "Better to ask why the sun rises in the east and sets in the west, young man. For some questions, there are no answers. Ghosts are one of them."

"Tell me this," Noah said, looking at Connor, "did you know there was a body in your house when you set it on fire?"

Connor kept his gaze steady as he lied. "I didn't set my house on fire."

Noah snorted, shook his head, and said, "Sure."

"Connor!" a woman yelled.

Connor stiffened while Noah looked around, frowning.

"Don't answer," Hu whispered. "Let her fester beyond the dogs. It will keep her off balance, which is how we want her when we retrieve the bead."

"Connor!"

"Who's yelling?" Noah asked. "Why aren't you answering her?"

"That's my mother," Connor whispered.

"Bull!" Noah snorted. "Your mother's dead."

"Yes," Connor agreed, "but look."

He pointed to a spot beyond the nearest dog statue, where his mother stood and glared at them.

The detective let out a string of curses that brought a laugh from Connor's mother as she took a step closer to them.

"Tell me, Connor," she said, "what did you do to us in the cemetery?"

"Not enough," Connor replied.

"Perhaps not, my sweet, little boy," she agreed, "but let's talk a little more about it, shall we? Come to your mother, let me hold you. If only for a little while."

Connor shuddered and looked away as Detective Rattin got to his feet and walked towards the edge of the garden, an expression of disbelief on his face.

Connor wondered if the man would be foolish enough to step beyond the dogs. Then he realized the detective didn't know about the statues, but before he could react, Hu was on his feet, racing for Noah.

Connor's mother smiled, beckoning the detective to come closer.

Chapter 52: Detective Rattin and Disbelief, August 16th, 2016

Noah saw the woman at the edge of the garden, standing in a shadow and not quite visible. He knew it couldn't be Connor's mother because he had read the report about her death. Why Connor would say the unknown female was his deceased mother wasn't something Noah was concerned with.

He wanted to know who she was, if she had anything to do with Meg's death, and he was tired of listening to the lies coming from the two men about ghosts.

Noah had walked only a few steps towards the woman when someone grabbed his arm and stopped him. The grip was like a vice, each finger digging deep into him, the pain sharp and ripping a gasp from him.

Noah twisted around, tried to free his arm, and got ready to yell at Hu.

The look on the man's face was as hard as his grip. There was no humor in it, or in his voice when he spoke.

"Detective Rattin," Hu said, "let me assure you that the woman you see before you is dead and that she would like nothing more than to kill you."

"Don't listen to him," the woman said, laughing. "He's jealous that my attention is on you. And what woman wouldn't be interested in a man such as yourself? A police officer and handsome. Yes, come closer, Detective, I think we would have a great deal to talk about."

A curious tingle rose up in his stomach, and Noah glanced from her back to Hu.

The old man shook his head, took a small flashlight out of his pocket, turned it on, and aimed it at the woman.

Noah couldn't tell if she was attractive. He didn't notice the color of her hair or the clothes she wore. All of the identifiers he had been taught to notice as an officer were forgotten as he stared at the light.

The beam passed through her, illuminating the shrubs behind her. She didn't cast a shadow, and when she saw his face, the strange woman let out a laugh.

"A shame, is it not?" she asked. "But there are still ways I can entice you, Detective. Come a little closer, and we can discuss it."

Hu leaned close to him and whispered, "Ask her to come to

us."

Noah did so, and the woman sneered at him.

"Don't listen to him," she snapped. "Come to me."

Noah shook his head; the idea that Hu and Connor might be right was gaining credence.

"You come here," Noah said. "Step into the garden. I'll get us each a beer."

The woman sneered as she replied, "You're a coward, and worse than a child. Why are you listening to that old fool?"

Noah's head had cleared from both the blow received at the cemetery and the alcohol he had consumed earlier.

"No," Noah replied, "I don't think so. And from what I can see so far, Hu here has his head on straight. Who are you?"

The woman scoffed, then answered the question. "I'm the boy's mother, although he's a little older than when I died."

"Why are you here?" Noah asked, a chill racing up his spine and settling into the base of his skull.

"I'm hungry," she whispered, "so *hungry*, Detective. Do you understand that? Have you ever been so hungry that you couldn't stop trying to eat, and when you were eating you couldn't put the fork down? That's how hungry I am. How hungry we *all* are."

"How many of you are there?" Noah asked.

She smiled. "Enough. More than enough. Eventually, you'll leave this little garden, Detective, this small oasis. When you do, one of us will be waiting for you. And then we'll feed."

Noah's stomach twisted, sick with a growing fear. He had a horrifying image of the dead devouring his flesh.

"We will eat you," she continued, and a wicked grin spread across her face, "and I will shred your flesh, leave it hanging from the trees in the cemetery. How do you think your colleagues will react to that?"

Noah didn't have an answer.

But Connor did.

The man had appeared at Noah's side, and the woman smiled at him.

"Hello, sweetheart," she said.

"Be quiet," Connor said in a soft voice.

His mother's eyes widened and looked at him with a shocked expression. She tried to speak, but her mouth wouldn't open. Terror filled her eyes.

"You're going to return to the cemetery," Connor said, staring at the ground. "You will not speak to any of the others. You won't do anything except remain in Pine Grove. You will wait there until you are freed."

Noah watched the woman as Connor spoke. She shook her head and tried to pry her mouth open with her hands. Despite all of her efforts, she wasn't able to speak. Her hands fell limp to her sides, and she glared at her son in silence.

Connor didn't look at her.

"Go now," he said, "and remember what I said. You will not speak or communicate in any way with the others in the cemetery."

Noah watched as the woman vanished.

Hu let go of him, went to Connor, and patted the man on the back.

"Well done," Hu said. Then, to both Connor and Noah, he inquired, "Would either of you like some tea?"

Noah could only nod. The world had become much darker than he had ever imagined.

Chapter 53: A Bad Night's Sleep, August 17th, 2016

Later in the night, after Connor's mother had been cast back to Pine Grove Cemetery, Hu had explained the circumstances behind Feng and the beads to Noah. While the detective still appeared skeptical at times, he kept his thoughts to himself. When Hu had shared a great deal of information about the dead man, they had found separate places to sleep in the house. Connor had fallen asleep on the couch, Rex on the floor beside him. Lloyd had been helped upstairs, and Noah had stretched out on some blankets in the kitchen.

Connor had woken up several times, each preceded by a nightmare of his mother and father. In the dream, his parents had chased him through the cemetery. Dozens of silver foxes had darted out from behind headstones and trees, cutting off his escape and forcing him deeper into the cemetery, which had become limitless. The light had been a dull, hazy gray, the morning sun revealing each new horror.

Finally, unable and unwilling to sleep any longer, Connor had gone into the kitchen. Rex had followed him, laid down beside the detective, and returned to sleep.

Connor gave the dog a wistful glance, then went about making breakfast. By the time he had finished, Hu arrived. They moved in silence, not out of respect for Noah, but because they were used to the quietness.

When the two of them had eaten, Hu sat back, lit his pipe, and looked at Connor.

"You do not look rested," Hu said.

"I'm not," Connor replied. "Nightmares."

"Ah," Hu said, nodding, "I am sorry to hear that. It will make the day's work a little more difficult for us, I am afraid."

Connor rearranged his dishes on the table before he asked, "Are we going to try and dig Feng up today?"

"This evening," Hu confirmed, "and we will have a difficult time ahead of us. Once Feng realizes what power you hold over the others."

"Will my mother listen to me?" Connor asked. "Will she do what I told her to?"

"She should," Hu answered, "for while she is strong, I do not believe she is strong enough to disobey your command."

"But why?" Connor asked, unable to keep the anxiety out of his voice. "What is it that makes me special?"

"Part of it is your isolation," Hu said, speaking slowly as if he was choosing each word with care. "There is a reason why so many stories revolve around the pure of heart and the pure of flesh. You spent decades away from the world, Connor. But that, as I said, is only a part of it. The remainder, I am not quite sure. There have been others like you, from what I can gather in my reading. Yes, there have been plenty who can hear the dead. Plenty who can speak to them. But those who can command them? Ah, no, my young friend. Your kind are few and far between."

Hu leaned forward, smiled and said in a low voice, "They are afraid of you, and rightfully so. For the wicked ones, you are their downfall."

Hu's words weren't comforting. Instead, they placed a heavier burden on Connor, and his face must have shown it.

Hu smiled at him, an expression of understanding.

"This will be difficult for you," Hu said, "but I am confident in you, Connor. You showed remarkable strength as a child, and while you may not be sure of yourself, you were last night, when it was important. The detective is alive because of you, and I do believe you have removed your mother as a threat."

"I hope so," Connor said in a low voice.

"So do I," Noah said, sitting up and rubbing the sleep out of his eyes. "Your mom's a pain, and I don't think she's a fan of any of us."

Connor nodded and gave a bitter laugh.

Noah looked at them and said, "How do you plan on getting this bead out of the grave?"

"We will dig," Hu said, "then we'll have to get one of the dead to show us where it is so we can retrieve it."

"Are we bringing Rex along?" Connor asked hopefully.

Hu shook his head. "We cannot. As much as the dead are frightened by him, he would be at risk, and it would be for nothing. He is a good and faithful dog, Connor. It is best to reward him with safety. And, to be quite honest, to keep him here to aid with our own protection should we fail in Pine Grove."

"I have a question," Noah said, glancing at them. "Why not just get one of them to pull it out for you, without all this digging around?"

Connor opened his mouth to reply, closed it, and looked at Hu.

Hu's expression was one of surprise. "I think it could work. Yes, yes, I don't see why it wouldn't."

"Do we need to wait for night then?" Noah asked.

Connor shuddered at the idea of going into the cemetery in daylight. Memories of the silver fox flashed across his mind's eyes, but he choked back his fear and said, "No. We don't need to wait for the night. Let's get it done. As soon as possible."

Hu leaned forward, smiled and said softly, "It is alright to be afraid, Connor. There is no shame in it."

"That's good," Connor said, nodding and swallowing, "because I'm terrified."

Chapter 54: Preparing to Enter the Cemetery, August 17th, 2016

Lloyd felt sick to his stomach, and his head throbbed. His mouth was dry, and he realized the last time he had felt so terrible was when he had gotten out of the army. He had spent three days drunk and ended up miserable for a week afterward.

He sat on the edge of the bed in Hu's house, wearing the same clothes from the day before. A small part of him wanted to return home, shower, and put on a clean outfit.

He knew it was not only vain, but pointless.

They were going into Pine Grove to retrieve Feng's bead.

And Lloyd was filled with doubt. He wondered what it was that he could bring to the confrontation. The brief battle of the night before had reminded him of not only his age but how frail he was. It was a bitter realization.

His pride had forced him out the door, following behind Hu as the man led them towards the cemetery. Through the iron bars of the fence, Lloyd could see a tarp had been spread over the grave they had partially excavated in the search for Feng. The groundskeepers in Pine Grove had evidently returned most of the dirt to its proper place.

Memories of the various deaths that had occurred within the confines of the cemetery and outside of it flooded Lloyd's mind, causing his feet to stumble. Connor reached out a hand and steadied him, asking, "Are you alright?"

Lloyd didn't trust his voice, so he nodded.

Connor gave him a friendly pat on the shoulder and silence fell over the small group again.

Lloyd wondered what the detective thought of it all. The man hadn't seemed overly impressed with what they had told him, and Lloyd had a suspicion the detective would arrest them for disturbing a grave when all was done. He glanced over at Rattin and saw the man slip a flask back into his pocket.

The detective smiled sheepishly at him, stumbled and muttered, "Liquid courage."

Lloyd wondered if there was any alcohol left in the flask, or if Rattin had drunk it all.

Then all concerns other than what lay ahead flew from his mind as they reached the gate for Pine Grove.

Hu stopped and turned to face them all. There was a soldierly bearing to the man, a sense of military pride and confidence.

It didn't help Lloyd.

"We are going in now," Hu said, looking at each one in turn as he spoke. "We must remember to be wary. Why they did not attack as soon as we left my home, I do not know. I do not believe we will reach the grave unharmed. Keep your iron ready and understand that we all go together to Feng. It is safest that way."

"Yes," Detective Rattin said, "that would be the safest way."

There was a strange note in the man's voice, and when Lloyd turned, he saw an odd glint in the detective's eyes. Detective Rattin's arm caught Lloyd's attention, the limb coming up with a jerking motion, a flat black pistol held in his hand.

And then Lloyd knew how he could help.

Chapter 55: The Plan Goes South, August 17th, 2016

Lloyd's brains and bits of skull struck Connor in the face as Detective Noah Rattin pulled the trigger and killed the old man.

Connor fell to his knees and vomited, the action saving his life as the detective fired. The bullet passed through where Connor's head had been. As fear nailed him to the earth, Connor watched in horror as Rattin swung his pistol towards Hu.

Hu had dropped the bag he had brought with him and closed the distance between him and the detective, the older man's hands a blur. In a heartbeat, he had taken the weapon from Rattin and tossed it aside. Rattin threw a punch, but Hu was too close to him, and unlike the detective, Hu wasn't concerned with punches.

Connor watched as Hu used his elbows, shoulders, and head to drive Rattin backward. Hu's strikes were precise and incapacitated Rattin in a matter of seconds. From where he knelt, Connor saw the detective's eyes roll up, the whites revealed as he fell backward. The man's limbs flopped with all of the grace of a dying jellyfish, and he lay unconscious on the ground.

"Are you hurt?" Hu snapped.

Connor shook his head.

"Then on your feet," Hu said, extending a hand.

Connor took it and let the man pull him to his feet.

"What happened?" Connor asked, shaken. "Why did he do that?"

"I suspect, and hope, he was possessed," Hu said, glancing down at Noah.

"You hope?" Connor said.

"Yes," Hu said, "I hope. If he was not possessed, then we have a police officer who wants to kill us for other reasons. Now we must hurry, the gun shots will undoubtedly be reported, and we will face enough challenges attempting to induce Feng to bring us his bead."

Connor nodded, shuddered at the idea of Detective Rattin bent on murder for the sake of murder, and looked down at the man's unconscious form.

"How did you do that?" Connor asked. "How did you disarm him and knock him out?

"I was an Eagle," Hu replied, picking up his bag and turning his back on Rattin.

"What do you mean an 'Eagle'?" Connor asked, confused.

Hu gave him a small smile and said, "When I was younger, I belonged to a military unit known as the Eagle. Part of the Chinese Special Forces, if that helps. I will tell you more when we are done with Feng. Come, I think I hear sirens in the distance."

Connor nodded and followed Hu into Pine Grove Cemetery.

Chapter 56: An Awakening, August 17ᵗʰ, 2016

Noah pushed himself up, his head pounding. He scanned the area and saw Lloyd on the asphalt. Noah stared at the man, understanding Lloyd was dead. A vague memory sprang up, and Noah saw his own hand, with his pistol, aiming the weapon at Hu.

Lloyd had stepped in the way, and Noah had executed him. Then he had tried to kill Connor.

A laugh filled his ears, and Noah knew it came from within his own head.

"Did you enjoy that?" a voice asked. It was old and terrible, filled with hate and spite. "I know I did. It has been so long since I possessed someone, and never have I employed a weapon such as yours. It was exceptional. Tell me, how does it work?"

Noah clenched his teeth together, squeezed his eyes shut and tried to drive the voice out of his head.

The voice laughed, saying, "That is alright, I will find the information I seek, although you may not find it pleasant."

Noah didn't.

A whimper escaped his lips as needles of pain were driven through his skull.

"Ah," the voice said with satisfaction, "you call them bullets. And you have more! Many more. Do you know what we can do with them, my Little One? Do you know how many we could slay with these bullets?"

Noah shook his head, trying to force the voice out.

"Oh no, Little One," the voice said, chuckling. "You will not expel me so easily. I rather like it here. You're quite young. Imagine what I could do with your flesh. No, pick up your weapon."

Noah tried to resist, but it was useless. The voice had all control, and in a moment, he found himself crawling towards his pistol. He found it in the grass, the grip cool in his hand. The voice allowed him to sit back on his heels.

"Show me," the voice commanded, "that we have enough of these bullets in your pistol."

Panting with the effort, Noah ejected the magazine and looked down at the exposed round.

The voice purred and said, "Excellent, Little One, now we

will commence our killing. We shall start with Hu and the other with the pure voice. I think that will be our best course of action. What say you?"

As the stranger laughed, his grip on Noah loosened, and instead of casting the pistol aside, Noah turned it on himself.

He was able to pull the trigger faster than the voice could react, and Detective Noah Rattin died with a sense of satisfaction as the voice screamed with rage.

Chapter 57: A New Threat, August 17th, 2016

Connor jerked around when he heard another gunshot. At the gate, he saw Noah sprawl backward, the pistol in his hand.

Shuddering, Connor turned to speak to Hu and tripped, tumbling forward and catching himself with his hands. He twisted onto his back and sat up, trying to see what had tripped him up, and saw only the root of a tree that had grown up through a crack in the asphalt.

As Connor looked at it, the root curled, the end facing him.

Before he could react, the root snapped out with the speed of a rattlesnake and wrapped around his ankle. Within a heartbeat, it was squeezing Connor hard enough so he could not only feel, but hear the bones in his leg grinding together.

A shriek of pain escaped his lips and Hu was there. Without hesitation, he grabbed Connor's trapped leg, pulled it up, and wrenched the root off. Connor screamed again, and blackness swarmed over him.

When he came to, Hu was dragging him away from the tree. Hu realized Connor was awake and snapped, "Tell them to stop, Connor. Tell them now!"

Dazed, Connor glanced around to see what Hu meant, and he saw them.

Seven trees had wrenched themselves out of the ground, trailing roots, and shedding dirt while shambling towards him and Hu. Ten or eleven ghosts could be seen, moving from tree to tree, hiding from Connor and Hu, not quite certain if it was safe to attack.

"Connor!" Hu shouted.

"Stop it," Connor yelled, the effort causing stars to appear in his vision. "Stop!"

The trees came to a shuddering halt, each of the dead frozen in their tracks, some half-hidden behind trees and headstones. They all stared at Connor and Hu.

"Thank you," Hu said, sinking down to the ground beside Connor. "I do not believe I would have been able to continue much longer. Not dragging you, my young friend."

"No," Connor said, sitting up and grimacing at the pain in his leg, "thank you. Noah's dead."

Hu nodded. "I am not surprised. One of them must have

taken possession of him. We were lucky."

Connor didn't think losing Lloyd and the detective could count as luck, but he kept his opinion to himself. Instead of responding to the statement, he looked at the trees, gestured towards them, and said with unfeigned confusion, "Why were trees chasing us?"

Hu gave him a grim smile and replied, "Some of the dead can possess them, but they lack the ability to take possession of people. The same is true of animals. It seems that some of the dead have discovered such an ability in themselves. Are you ready?"

Connor was far from ready, but he nodded anyway.

"Good," Hu said, standing up. "Let us try and find Feng's grave."

Before he could answer, Connor's eyes were drawn to a ghost standing near one of the three graves Lloyd had marked as possibilities for Feng's bead.

Connor's throat tightened and his heart raced.

His mother stood by the grave, a look of desperation and sadness on her face. When she saw that she had his attention, she pointed at the headstone.

Connor mouthed the name *Feng*, and his mother nodded once before she vanished.

"I know where to find him," Connor whispered.

Hu looked sharply at him. "How?"

"My mother just pointed it out," Connor answered, the words painful to speak. "She showed me."

Connor stood up, yelping in pain, and wavering on his feet. Hu reached out a hand and steadied him.

"Come, Connor," Hu said, "we are nearly done here."

"I hope so," Connor muttered.

As soon as the words left his mouth, something struck him in the head and he found himself falling back.

Chapter 58: Alone with the Dead, August 17th, 2016

Hu grunted as he caught Connor, the unconscious man nothing more than dead weight in his arms. He lowered him to the ground, opening his eyes to peer into them. The man's eyes contracted with exposure to the light, and Hu let the lids fall back in place.

Hu pushed the gloves down tighter on his hands and considered what to do next.

He had little time.

Movement in his peripheral vision caught his attention and Hu snapped around to face it. An old woman crept towards him, her eyes a dull gray and her teeth bared. The woman's hair was thin and a sickly yellow, hanging in weak clumps about her face. She snarled at him, and Hu felt a cold hatred roll over him.

He glanced around him and saw no other ghosts advancing on him.

Hu stood up, eyed her, and wondered how he would deal with her while protecting Connor simultaneously.

"And what is your name?" Hu asked.

She cocked her head to one side, stared at him and said in a loud, slurred voice, "What?"

And Hu knew why she hadn't been affected by Connor's command.

She hadn't heard him.

"Leave," Hu said, making a shooing gesture with his hands.

The corner of her mouth curled up into a sneer as she flexed her hands. On the tips of her long fingers, each one segmented and narrow like a spider's leg, were yellow and cracked nails.

"I'll gut you," she hissed, "if you stand between me and the sweet man behind you. I can smell him from here. Get out of the way and let me eat. I'm *hungry*."

Hu set his bag with the statue down by Connor's feet and straightened up. He smiled at the ghost and said in a pleasant tone, "No, I will see you starve first."

She howled, hands extended as rage and hunger propelled her forward.

Hu planted his feet and waited for her to reach him.

Chapter 59: Forced to Fight, August 17th, 2016

When Connor opened his eyes, he was on his back and struggling to get to his feet. Around him, Hu continued to battle the dead, but Connor could focus only on the ghost in front of him.

Feng.

The ghost wore orange robes, with a beaded necklace hanging down almost to his waist. His face was lined with age and malice, his eyes a bright silver, his head shaved.

When Feng spoke, it was a voice both smooth and vile; a curious mixture that enticed Connor to listen even as a visceral part of himself screamed to flee.

"Connor," Feng said, "it is a pleasure to speak with you. We have known each other for quite some time, and yet we have never once exchanged words."

Connor faced the dead man with anger building up within him.

"This is where you first saw me," Feng said, chuckling, "peering out of your window at night. A brave act from a boy so young. Especially one so frightened of the graveyard across from his home. Tell me, Connor, are you still fearful of the cemetery?"

"Yes," Connor confessed, "I'm terrified of it."

"There are not many who would admit to such a fear," Feng said, stepping forward, "I admire your courage."

Connor didn't respond. He remained silent and waited to see what Feng would say next.

Feng hesitated, then stated, "I have a proposition for you. You are far stronger than I suspected. I thought of you as nothing more than a meal. If not for myself then certainly for your mother. However, I think we can form a union, the pair of us. We can work together, and satisfy urges that I have denied for far too long, and ones you are not yet aware exist. Everything would work out beautifully for us."

"You need to leave," Connor said, his voice low and rough. "You can't be here. I won't allow it."

Feng flinched as if struck.

"You don't have a choice," Feng snapped once he had regained his composure. "Either you will join with me, or I will grind you beneath my heel and take your flesh for my own. There is no other option here."

"Get out," Connor commanded.

Feng growled as his head twitched back.

The ghost sprang forward and Connor found himself within arm's reach of the dead man. Feng's hand lashed out and caught the front of Connor's shirt, jerking him the last few inches toward Feng.

"No!" Connor screamed, pulling back at the same time.

Feng's grip was firm though, and the smile that spread across the dead man's face was simultaneously vicious and victorious. He lifted Connor up with an ease that dropped a cloud of fear over Connor's eyes. With a snorted laugh, Feng threw him.

Connor flew backward, unable to regain control until finally, after far too long, his back smashed into a headstone. His breath rushed out of him as he fell forward.

Connor slammed into the ground, the force of the impact wrenching a cry of agony from his lips.

He forced himself up, first to his knees, then to his feet, and looked around. Connor's head swam, his eyes unable to focus as he tried to look at Feng.

The dead man sneered.

"Look at you," Feng said, his voice smooth and gentle, "so weak and so delicate. You're a rare flower waiting to be picked. And I think I shall do that for you. Will you stay with me, once I have helped you shed your flesh? When your corpse is rotting, will you sit with your mother and hunger, attempting to satiate some secret need?"

Connor shook his head.

Feng chuckled, stepped forward, and grabbed hold of Connor's shirt once more.

"No," Connor hissed, and he struck the dead man's arm.

Feng's eyes widened as he shrieked with a voice filled with pain, his body fluctuating, his hand letting go while Connor went tumbling back. The ghost vanished as Connor caught himself. Feng reappeared a moment later with a shocked expression.

The dead man's face had a large black swath across it as if someone had struck him.

"You need to get the bead for me," Connor said, pouring rage into the words.

Feng gasped, and as Connor watched, a second patch of the

dead man's face turned black.

Connor steadied himself, took a deep breath, and then jumped back as Feng launched himself forward. The dead man's hands sped toward Connor, one landing a blow against his chest. A bright blossom of pain caused stars to explode around the edges of his vision, and a metallic taste filled his mouth. Connor tried to speak again, but Feng smashed a backhand into Connor's cheek, causing his ears to ring.

"Who are you?" Feng howled. "Who do you think you are to command me? Do you think I will be stopped by some infant in a man's body? I lived to twice your age before I died, boy, and I have killed hundreds. You have nothing with which to fight me."

"Shut up!" Connor spat, and the venom he put into the words caused Feng to hesitate, a grin spreading across his face.

"Ah," Feng said, laughing, "there is some strength to you. Well, let us see how deep it goes."

The dead man sprang forward, smashing an open palm into Connor's chest and sending him tumbling backward. His head spun as he slammed into the ground. The pain in his breast was terrible, each breath like fire as he inhaled.

Feng laughed and moved forward with a burst of speed, a foot lashing out, racing towards Connor's head.

Grunting, Connor threw up an arm, absorbing the impact of the blow on his shoulder. His arm went numb and collapsed, useless, to his side.

Feng struck him again and again, stars exploding across Connor's vision.

Then a single image drifted up through the pain and misery.

The memory of his mother, dying at Feng's hands.

Connor found himself screaming, barreling into Feng. He threw punch after punch, the ghost vanishing with each blow, and what he lacked in skill, Connor made up for with furious rage. His entire body howled with pain as he drove fists, knees, elbows, and shoulders into Feng. The dead man tried to back away, a shocked expression on his face.

Connor knew, suddenly that he was in control.

Completely.

Glaring at Feng, Connor stepped forward and smashed the dead man in face again.

A howl of agony erupted from the dead man's mouth as he

vanished and then reappeared, collapsing to the ground.

The dead man lay sprawled out.

"I am Connor Mann," Connor growled, "and you are going to do what I tell you, is that understood?"

Feng glared at him as he got to his hands and knees.

The dead man looked as though he might challenge Connor again, so Connor sprang forward and slammed a gloved fist into Feng's head.

Feng vanished again, and when he reappeared he let out a guttural growl, but he lowered his eyes.

"I asked you a question," Connor snapped. "Do you understand me?"

"Yes," Feng hissed, hatred in his voice as he raised his head to glare at Connor.

"Do you believe me?" Connor asked.

"I do," Feng spat.

"Good. You'll bring the bead up," Connor said, his voice filling with hatred. "You will find it and carry it."

Feng's face was a mask of pain and fury as he managed to climb to one knee.

"Do you understand?" Connor demanded. "Remember this, when you go back, because if you don't do it, I will dig that damned bead out myself, and I will torture you for as long as I live."

Feng nodded his assent.

"Then go," Connor commanded the dead man.

Feng vanished into the earth, and Connor realized he was looking at the charred remains of his home beyond the iron fence of Pine Grove Cemetery. Behind him, Hu's battle continued. Connor turned to assist but he stumbled as the adrenaline drained out of him. He struggled to remain upright, but he felt himself fall, succumbing to the sudden exhaustion he felt.

Connor blacked out before he hit the ground, and his fight was over.

Chapter 60: Hu and Feng, August 17th, 2016

The dead woman's grave must have been close by, for each time Hu dispatched her, she was back within a minute. He decided he didn't like her.

Hu had slapped her again with an iron-studded glove and sent her back to her bones when the top of the dog statue sprang open. Twisting around, Hu saw Feng. The dead man looked horrible, as if someone had taken hot irons to him, which was a ridiculous thought considering Feng's status as a ghost.

"You are not looking well," Hu said in Chinese.

Feng gave him a bitter smile. "It is an understatement. I have something for you, from Connor Mann."

Hu waited and watched as Feng extended a hand, the fingers opening to reveal a small bead. It was yellowed bone, and Hu knew it belonged to the dead man's Mala.

Weary of Feng, Hu stepped forward cautiously.

Then the old woman appeared, reaching once more for him.

"Go," Feng said, and she vanished.

Hu stood there, surprised.

"My power fades," Feng said, his voice filled with suppressed rage. "Somehow the one with the pure voice bested me. Me! And has forced me to do this, to capitulate to the likes of him. Here is the bead, damn you! And remember this; you will not win. You will not complete whatever task you have been assigned, little soldier. Nothing you can do will change your fate, a fate which will leave you rotting here, far from your ancestors. I will tell you this. This bead I am bound to, it is not unique. There are ninety-nine others, and the Priest has planted them. One of us will kill you. There's even a bead in a place called Hollis, in a cemetery behind a church."

"Why would you share such information?" Hu asked warily.

"Because I know you. You can't resist being a hero. And the next will kill you," Feng snarled, "if not him, then the next one, or the one after. I'm ushering you to your death just as I've done for so many others."

"I hope in the next life you will return as an insect," Hu said softly, "trapped in the bowels of a pig."

Feng snickered, his lip curling into a sneer. "Our curses are exchanged. Go then, and die."

Hu held out his hand, and Feng dropped the bead into it.

Without further conversation, Hu retrieved the dog statue, and deposited the bead. Feng vanished.

Hu secured the statue, placed it in his bag, and went about the task of reviving Connor.

Chapter 61: Standing at Her Graveside, August 17th, 2016

The fighting was done. He was exhausted and battered. His throat hurt and he felt as though he had been thrown down a flight of stairs while tied to a chair. Every part of him ached and he wondered what would come next.

Connor limped to his mother's grave and stood there.

A moment later she appeared.

She was dressed in the clothes she had worn on the last day he had seen her alive. Her hair was pulled back into a loose ponytail. She was, as always, the most beautiful woman he had ever seen. Her eyes were filled with love, and the smile on her face was formed from a mixture of sadness, exhaustion, and maternal devotion.

"You can speak now," he whispered. "I'm sorry I had to tell you to be quiet."

"It's okay, Connor," she said, the sound of her voice bringing tears to his eyes. "I know why you did it. I've missed you so much, Connor, so much."

She started to say something else, but her body shimmered.

A pained smile flickered across her face.

"This is difficult for me," she said. "It's hard to make myself stay. There's something pulling me. Telling me it's time to leave."

"Please, Mom," Connor begged, "can't you stay a little longer? It's been so long since I've seen you."

"I'll try," she said, her smile tight. A heartbeat later, her body took on a firmer look, her voice stronger. "I'm sorry you saw me like that."

He shook his head. "I know what happened, and why. Don't talk about it, please. We probably only have a few minutes. I spent a long, long time thinking about you."

"Where have you been?" she asked. "I never saw you with your father. Not after Mrs. Lavoie was killed. What happened to you?"

"Don't worry about that, Mom," he said, forcing a smile. "I just want you to know that I was thinking about you. I missed you. A lot."

"I missed you too," she said, her physical form fading away for a moment. "I always thought about you, deep down. Always. You look like a good man, Connor. And you freed us. All of us.

You've made me proud, just like I always knew you would."

Pride and sadness mixed within him, and Connor found he couldn't speak. He nodded, tears stinging his eyes.

"You'll keep making me proud, too," his mother said, her voice beginning to fade. "If I'm able, I'll be watching you. You're the best son any mother could ever hope for, Connor Mann, and I love you. More than you can possibly know."

"I love you too, Mom," Connor choked out, but before the last syllable left his lips, she was gone and he was without his mother again.

For the first time, Connor could hear birds. They were flying in over the wrought iron fence and landing in the trees. Their songs filled the air and reminded him of his childhood, when his mother had still been alive and all had been right with the world.

Connor sank to the ground, dropped his head to the cool grass, and wept.

Chapter 62: Hu's Garden, August 18th, 2016

Connor had an icepack pressed against his forehead. The cold allowed him to focus on something other than the constant pulse of pain at the back of his skull. Several glasses of water and a generous amount of sugar added had helped him calm down.

The police were in Pine Grove Cemetery, investigating the murder-suicide committed by Noah Rattin. They would be canvasing the neighborhood soon enough, but Connor was certain they had nothing to worry about. If anything, people would have seen Hu and himself trying to get away from Noah.

There would be no need to tell the police about Noah's possession because no one would believe it.

Hu came back out into the garden and sat down.

"Have you made a decision?" Hu asked.

Connor shifted uncomfortably in his chair and then nodded. "I'd like to take you up on your offer to stay here. At least until we can figure out what we'll need to do about the Priest."

"Excellent," Hu said. "It is for the best, I believe. We will be able to better coordinate our attacks and gather intelligence."

Silence filled the garden until Connor broke it with a statement.

"Did you feel it?" Connor asked.

Hu frowned and asked in return, "Feel what?"

"When everything was done," Connor said, "there was a lightness to the air in the cemetery. Before, it always felt as though the atmosphere was a little heavier there. Was it because of Feng?"

"Yes," Hu replied. "His presence and that of the other ghosts created an unpleasant air, one that pressed down upon the world. When he was removed and imprisoned, his hold on the other ghosts was destroyed, and so they all were released. That is why the air is lighter. So not only did you see your mother freed, but all of the other ghosts in the cemetery as well, Connor. All of them are gone."

"Do you think," Connor asked, hesitating, "that she's in a better place now?"

Hu nodded. "So I believe."

Connor picked at a bit of lint on his pants leg. After a minute he asked, "Any idea on where the next one might be?"

"In the town of Hollis, in a graveyard behind a church," Hu answered.

"When will we go and check it out?" Connor inquired.

"Tomorrow," Hu replied, "after you've had a day of rest."

"Alright," Connor said, then asked, "Will we meet this Priest at all?"

"Yes," Hu answered, "I believe we will."

"Good," Connor said, closing his eyes. "I want to hurt him. I want to hurt him a lot."

"So do I," Hu said in a soft voice.

The silence returned, and Connor imagined all the ways he could make the Priest suffer for the death of his mother.

Chapter 63: Greenbriar Nursing Home, August 19th, 2016

Michael sat back, wiped the sweat from his brow, and wondered why the weather had gotten so warm. The morning paper had said nothing of the sort in regards to the day's temperature. But, even if it had, he wouldn't have stayed away. Visiting members of his congregation in Greenbriar, as well as amusing himself with the question 'who will die next,' was something he looked forward to.

"Are you alright, Father?" someone asked.

Michael looked around, spotted Scott Lange, and smiled.

"Yes," Michael said to the young man, "quite alright, Scott. I forget sometimes how old I am."

"You're not that old," Scott said.

"No, older," Michael chuckled.

Scott grinned and asked, "Do you want a drink?"

"I would love a glass of lemonade, Scott, thank you," Michael answered. The young man nodded and left the small garden in the back of the nursing home. Michael was left alone and he glanced at the flowers he had planted. The air smelled pleasantly of turned earth, and his mind drifted to what he had heard from Antoinette Francour.

She had awoken to police activity in Pine Grove Cemetery, and she had later learned all the details. The old woman had relayed them to Michael, and he had been forced to accept that his plans were in jeopardy.

He needed to prepare himself for his eventual discovery by Connor Mann, although he wasn't certain as to what might come of it.

Better safe than sorry, he thought, quoting the old maxim.

He picked up his small satchel and made certain the zipper was secure. Within its brown leather were his travel vestments, the book which contained the necessary prayers to consecrate ground, and a now small, empty bottle that had contained holy water.

Michael reached into his breast pocket, removed the tin, and withdrew a single bead. Of the one hundred beads he had started with almost forty years before, only five remained. He had buried them in graveyards and cemeteries along the eastern sea-board, in every town he had been a priest in. In other cities and towns that had been nearby. His goal had been to send as many to their deaths via the hungry ghosts as he could, but he had used the beads sparingly.

He rolled the bead he had removed between his fingers for a moment, knowing that after he buried it, he would have only four left to him. Michael looked down at the freshly turned earth before him. Beneath it lay a cigar box, and within that were the earthly remains of a child who had never seen the light of day.

Michael smiled, dug a small hole, and placed the Mala bead in it. He put the box away, placed a violet on top of the bead, and then patted dirt down around the plant.

After he had watered the flower, Scott appeared in the doorway. The young man carried a pair of tall, plastic glasses filled with lemonade and handed one to Michael.

"Ah, thank you, Scott," Michael said, standing up.

"What type of plant is that?" Scott asked.

Michael told him and the young man nodded. "I bet it'll grow real nice, Father."

"Yes," Michael said, looking at the nursing home's tall brick wall and the multiple windows facing the garden. "Yes, I'm certain it will do quite well here."

Michael finished his lemonade and wondered who the first victim would be.

* * *

Bonus Scene Chapter 1: Yunnan Province, 1846

Magpies sang from the rafters of the roadside shrine, the song gentle and powerful in the evening light.

Monk Feng Huiliang entered the shrine and sat down to the left of the Buddha statue. Feng was ninety-two years old, and at that moment, he could feel the weight of every hour he had been alive pressing down upon him.

Death was close.

He could sense it.

And how can I not? he thought with a smile. Death was his favorite past-time. The one recreational activity he allowed himself. Unlike some of the other monks he knew and had known, he kept the strictures in regards to meat and alcohol.

He was neither enlightened nor on his way to becoming so.

In fact, his actions had removed him from even a consideration of such a status in his lifetime.

His smile broadened as he thought of all the trouble he had caused. The animosity he had sown. His stomach rumbled and he reached into his travel bag, removing a rice ball and biting into it. Most of his brethren found such simple fare to be too boring, seeking spices, and other such enhancements for their food.

But not Feng. Food was nothing more than fuel, the substance which his body needed to keep him alive.

The sound of feet on the road brought his attention back to the world, and he stared out the door to catch a glimpse of the traveler.

A middle-aged woman came into view and she glanced in, paused, and then turned to face him.

She gave him a shy smile and said, "Good evening."

"It is indeed," Feng agreed, nodding. "Will you come in and sit with me?"

The woman hesitated, then entered the shrine. She sat down across from him and Feng examined her with an appraising eye.

He was certain she was a merchant's wife. Her clothing was rough, her hands the same. There were no gentle lines about her face, merely the stamp of hard work and hard living.

"Have you traveled far?" Feng asked her, passing a rice ball to her.

She nodded, saying, "I have."

There was a slight accent to her voice, vaguely familiar, and Feng tried to place it. After several moments, he gave up. He had traveled to far too many villages in the province to know the subtle lingual hints of all of them.

Feng suppressed a smile. She would be easy to convince to kill herself, and it would be a pleasant way to relax before he had to sleep. He would be surprised if it took more than an hour or two to lay the groundwork, then perhaps another hour to get her ready to end her life in front of him.

The only interesting part of the challenge was to find a way for her to kill herself. He didn't carry any weapons, and he doubted if she had any either.

She took off the small pack she carried and placed it on the dirt floor between them. Her fingers, which were crooked and twisted, worked at the knot on the pack until it was undone. She drew a bottle out, removed the cap, and took a small sip. Bowing her head, she offered the bottle to Feng.

He accepted it with a nod of thanks, and took a sniff to reassure himself that it was not alcohol.

It wasn't, but there was a bitter scent that made his nose wrinkle.

"My apologies," she said, seeing his reaction, "but the water was brackish. I had no choice but to take it from that well. I had found no other source."

Feng bowed his head and drank a small portion. He was too thirsty not to drink, and he knew that a refusal would alienate her.

And he needed her to be comfortable for his words to have any effect.

He took a second drink and passed the bottle back to her. She smiled, had another sip, and then set the bottle between them on the floor, with the cap off.

"Have you far to go?" Feng asked.

The woman nodded. "I must travel to Old Peng village, on the other side of the monastery. I am gathering money for my husband."

"A dangerous occupation," Feng sympathized. "I trust you have not met with any bandits."

She shook her head. "No. They leave me alone."

"They do?" Feng asked with a smile, picking up the bottle

456

and taking a longer drink of the brackish water. The taste of it wasn't too bad, he realized. He took another longer drink before he set it down again.

"They do," she said, smiling and revealing a mouth full of broken and black teeth. "Do they leave you alone?"

"Of course they do," Feng chuckled. He reached out for the bottle again, smacking his lips before taking another gulp. He finished the water and handed the container to her.

"Did you like it?" she asked.

Feng nodded, went to speak and found he couldn't.

He tried to move, but his body refused to listen.

Surprised, he looked at the woman, who had gotten to her feet.

"I'm glad," she said, "because now I can do this."

Feng wanted to ask what, but his lips wouldn't cooperate, and by the time he got control of them, it was too late.

The woman was bringing the bottle crashing down onto his head.

Bonus Scene Chapter 2: Behind the Shrine, Yunnan Province, 1846

When Feng awoke, he was stiff, uncomfortable, and unable to see a single star in the sky.

Then he slowly remembered what happened to him in the shrine, and regardless of the darkness, he should have been able to see the stars.

"You're awake," the woman said, her voice muffled. He realized something was wrapped around his head.

"I am," Feng replied, trying to keep his voice calm. The anger within him threatened to break free, but he knew it would be to his advantage. He needed to convince her to free him, and then he could take his revenge upon her.

And he would drag it out. He wouldn't convince her to kill herself, in fact he would do it for her. With a small, dull rock, Feng would beat her to death.

The thought of it caused him to smile.

He grunted with a mixture of surprise and pain as she tore away the cloth that had covered his face. Feng blinked several times and saw that the moon was near its zenith. He was upright and he found his head was the only part of his body which he had command over. Fighting back his growing rage, Feng locked his eyes onto the woman.

She sat down across from him, her hands tucked into the wide cuffs of her sleeves.

"Why have you done this?" Feng asked, letting his anger subside.

"It is less than what you deserve," she answered.

Feng gave her a small, gentle smile. "You did not answer my question."

"No," the woman said, "I did not."

Frustration welled up, but Feng kept it out of his words. "I am only a monk. I have nothing to be stolen. Come with me to the nearest monastery and I will feed you."

She stared at him. After a long silence, she responded.

"I am not hungry," she said, "nor are you."

Feng realized she was correct. He had neither hunger nor thirst.

"I am an old man," he continued, "what have I done to you?"

Her face was cold and expressionless as she answered.

"You have destroyed my life," she said, "and I shall do the same to you."

Feng suppressed a chuckle. "And how did I destroy your life? I have never seen you before."

"You spoke with my husband," she answered.

"I have spoken with many husbands," Feng said gently. "How did that ruin your life?"

"He was not a smart man," she said, glaring at Feng, "and so when you spoke with him, he listened. He listened, and he listened, and then he did as you suggested. My husband went home and murdered our family. He drowned the children. His father, he gutted. His mother, he strangled. And had I been home, Feng Huiliang, I too would have been killed."

Feng listened impassively, considering her tone of voice, searching for the weaknesses within her heart that he could exploit.

"My husband then killed himself," she continued. "He drank a poison, one that left him immobile. But only after he gutted himself, as he had his father."

Feng smiled and said, "You must have me confused with someone else, dear lady."

"No," she whispered. "I passed by you on the road outside of Yunnan-Fu. Little did I know the damage you had caused."

"Enough," Feng said, putting all of the power of command he could muster into his voice. "Release me!"

She smirked. "From what?"

"These ropes," Feng snapped. "You have held me prisoner long enough."

"But you're not bound," she said, her smirk fading away. Pure hatred filled her eyes. "Did you not notice the curious taste to the water, Monk? Or did you believe me when I lied to you?"

Feng's eyes widened as he realized what had happened.

"You poisoned me," he gasped.

She shook her head. "No. I poisoned both of us. You may have had more, but it only means you will die quicker."

"No!" Feng yelled. "It is not my time. Not yet! I have more to gather. More to speak with! Do you think your husband was the first, woman?"

"No," she said, smiling, "but I know he was the last."

Bonus Scene Chapter 3: At the Roadside Shrine, 1846

Brother Bohai hurried along the road, tired and anxious to be back at the monastery. He had been gone for ten days, and the allure of his bed was strong. Yet as he neared the shrine, his nose wrinkled at a foul odor.

One he recognized instantly.

His shoulders sagged and he stopped at the shrine, peering in. He was surprised when he found it empty. Bohai gagged on the scent of putrid flesh and walked around to the back of the shrine.

There he found a pair of bodies. One wore the orange robes of a monk. The other was a woman. Both of the dead had been picked over by animals, and their features were gone, the meat having been stripped from the skulls.

Bohai bent his head and offered a silent prayer. When he straightened up, he turned away. He needed to gather some of the other monks and return for the corpses.

Which meant sleep was that much further away.

Bohai sighed and hurried back to the road. A small, selfish part of him wished he hadn't discovered the bodies.

They had ruined any sort of rest he had looked forward to.

Bonus Scene Chapter 4: Yunnan Province, 1847

Monk Lau Fei stepped back and looked at the small courtyard in front of the temple. The stones were free of weeds, and the dust had been swept away. His face remained impassive, and hid the joy and pride he felt at the cleanliness before him.

Lau's pride was a constant source of bitterness to him. When he sat in meditation, he found his thoughts often drifted back to some small task he had done well. And it always seemed as though Brother Zhu knew when those thoughts entered Lau's mind.

Invariably, he would look up and find Brother Zhu's eyes upon him, leaving him with a sense of frustration.

The sound of raised voices caught his attention, and Lau hurried towards the disturbance. It was unusual for someone to argue inside the narrow confines of the temple's walls.

When he reached the scene, he found Brother Zhu and Brother Bohai with one of the local farmers, a man whose name escaped Lau.

Both of the older Brothers had concerned expressions on their normally impassive faces.

"Brother Lau," Zhu said, beckoning him closer, "come and hear what Jiang has to say."

Lau quickened his steps and joined the trio of men. The farmer was an older man, not one given to flights of fancy or spastic episodes. His brown eyes danced with terror, and he wrung his hands together as he repeated his story to Lau.

It was simple and unbelievable.

Jiang had seen a silver fox. A graceful animal that had slain four of his chickens and would have killed more had Jiang's dog not chased away the beast.

"Where did it go?" Lau asked.

Jiang glanced at Zhu, and the Brother nodded.

Licking his lips nervously, Jiang answered, "It disappeared."

"So I assumed," Lau said, frowning, "but where did it disappear to? Was its den nearby?"

Jiang shook his head and said, "No, you don't understand, Brother. The fox vanished into thin air. One moment I was looking at it run, the next, it was gone."

"Do you see the dilemma?" Bohai asked.

Lau nodded, rubbed his chin and said, "Did the fox eat the chickens it killed?"

"No," Jiang said, "it seemed only to delight in the slaughter, and nothing more."

Lau glanced at Zhu who asked, "How does an animal delight in slaughter?"

"The way it moved," Jiang answered, "as if it were a cat and not a fox. It toyed with the birds before it killed them."

"I would suggest," Lau said, "you take ample precautions against the fox. You are still alone in your home?"

Jiang nodded.

"Keep your dog with you at all times," Lau advised, "we will look into this matter more. The Ghost Festival is almost upon us, and we may succeed in learning who this ghost is and what they need to be able to move on to the next life."

Jiang thanked them all and left, his steps carrying him quickly away from the monks.

"Brother Lau," Zhu said, "do you think it will be as simple as that?"

"We can only hope," Bohai said, answering for Lau. "We may have to intervene if the fox does not leave of its own accord."

Lau nodded and glanced at the farmer, the man's broad shoulders hunched as if against a cold wind.

A tremor of fear rippled through Lau, and he wondered if the ghost would torment something larger than chickens.

Bonus Scene Chapter 5: A Costly Meal

Chow watched a young monk place food and drink before the small roadside Buddha. When the monk had finished and left the statue, Chow's stomach grumbled loud enough to disturb a small bird that had settled down next to him.

As the animal flew away, complaining with harsh chirps, Chow smiled. Life on the road was difficult, and there were many nights when he went to sleep hungry.

During the Ghost Festival, he was sure to find food wherever he went, the superstitious country folk always put out food for the ghosts.

Chow snorted. The idea of a ghost eating was ludicrous, but he couldn't scoff too much at the practice.

It had kept him fed during the festival, and similar fears and offerings left at roadside temples had done the same. The thought brought his attention back to the stone Buddha. The smell of freshly cooked rice drifted to him and his mouth salivated.

Standing, Chow glanced up and down the road. It curved at either end, and a grin settled onto his face. There was no one on the road, so it was safe for him to approach the food. While the young man would have invited him to dine at the monastery, Chow disliked the sense of obligation he felt when he ate with monks.

And others, fellow travelers or local people pausing at a shrine, invariably disagreed with Chow eating the offerings.

Chow rolled his eyes at the thought of their disapproval and walked to the shrine. He gathered up the rice as well as some vegetables someone else had left there. Tucked beside the Buddha was a small drinking gourd. Chow removed the cork, sniffed it, and laughed.

Someone had hidden rice liquor.

The Buddha does not drink, Chow thought, chiding the unknown individual who had left the wine. *But I do.*

Chuckling, Chow took his feast and retreated to his hiding place. He sat down and started his meal with a drink of the liquor, which caused him to cough and his eyes to water. Next, he ate the vegetables, frowning at how chewy they were. While he wasn't fond of the way they tasted, he was too hungry to leave them.

Soon Chow finished both the vegetables and the rice and was able to concentrate on the liquor. He settled back against a tree and watched the sun set at a lazy pace, the sight of it reassuring.

Chow picked at some food in his teeth and wondered where he might head to in the morning. There had been rumor of work further to the east.

A soft bark drove the thought of employment out of his mind, and he sat up.

He held the gourd tight in one hand and looked around, listening.

The sound was not repeated.

Chow waited a little while longer, shrugged, and drank again.

He had only a small portion more of the liquor when several delicate yips sounded off to his right. The noise was unfamiliar to him. Chow had been born in a large town, and so he was ignorant of most sounds that various animals and birds made. In spite of his lack of knowledge, Chow wasn't intimidated by the yips. They seemed almost playful, as if they were made by some cheerful beast.

He smiled at the thought of such an animal, and he raised the gourd to the unknown creature in a silent salute.

A shimmer of silver caught his attention and Chow jerked his head to the left, almost spilling his drink. He glimpsed the tip of a tail as it vanished behind the tree.

Chow stared after it, attempting to see what it was. In all of his years of travel, he had never seen a silver animal before, and the idea of one piqued his curiosity. While part of him knew he should remain with his drink and wait for the creature to leave, Chow was far more eager to seek out the beast. The liquor had emboldened him, and he wanted to know what it was he had glimpsed.

Still holding onto the gourd, Chow got to his feet, wavering. The drink had been stronger than he thought, and he felt a lopsided grin spread out as he realized how drunk he was.

Fortified with the liquor, and knowing he had survived far worse surprises than a silver creature beside a Buddhist shrine, Chow staggered after the animal.

He had gone only twenty or so paces when the beast's silver tail flicked off to the right. Chow hurried after it. He saw it again a little farther in the woods, but straight ahead rather than off to one side.

Chow kept after the creature and soon he had come to a small pagoda outside of a monastery of equal size. From where he stood, he saw the silver animal, standing beside a large marker.

The beast was a fox, and it looked at him with eyes of the same color. It stared at him, tail flicking left and right.

Chow took a drink, wiped his mouth with the back of his hand, and took a step forward. When the fox didn't run, Chow took another drink and then several steps toward the animal.

The fox continued to sit still, tilting its head to one side and watching Chow approach.

"What are you doing?" Chow asked, grinning at the animal. "Hmm?"

"Me?" the fox asked in return. "I'm trying to decide on how best to kill you."

Chow's surprise died almost as quickly as he did.

Bonus Scene Chapter 6: A Traveler Found

Sleep had eluded Lau, and he had been up and about his chores well before the sun had risen. There had been some muttered complaints from his brethren, but they knew him too well to believe he had begun early on a whim.

With all of his work completed, Lau decided he would take a walk to farmer Jiang's house, and see how the man had done overnight. If the fox was a ghost, then the man's dog should have protected him. Should the fox only be a fox, then again, the dog would have served its purpose.

The road that led from the monastery to Jiang's farm was long and solitary. In most places, it was narrow, only large enough for an ox-cart to make its way through. Other sections would allow for the passage of ten men to walk abreast of one another. Like all of the roads, it curved in, which was an effort by the villagers to confuse ghosts and keep them far away. The local farmers weren't pleased with them, believing that some ghosts became lost and trapped within the loops and curves.

Lau wasn't quite certain how he felt about the roads. There were enough stories to give credence to the idea of trapped spirits. He was also able to understand the points of view for both the farmers and the villagers.

Lau's nose wrinkled as the scent of iron suddenly filled his nostrils. His steps faltered, then he came to a complete stop. He looked around and listened. Silence hung heavy in the air.

Lau glanced at the woods on either side of the road, an uncomfortable sense of being watched settled over him.

The absence of birdsong, the complete void of animal and insect noises, caused his stomach to roil with unease. He cleared his throat to be certain he hadn't gone deaf in the short time since he had left the monastery.

He had not.

Lau took a deep breath, attempted to slow down the quickened beat of his heart and failed.

His feet refused to move, fear rooting him to the road. After several more breaths and a prayer, Lau was able to walk again, his fear no longer controlling him.

The smell of iron grew stronger, a scent reminiscent to that of the small village Lau had grown up in. Near Lau's home had been a butcher, and whenever the man prepared an animal for sale, the entire street had stunk of blood.

Lau rounded the next curve in the road, and an involuntary gasp escaped his lips.

There was a man, or the remains of a man, spread out on the road before him.

Blood and flesh were strewn about the road. The stranger, whose back was to Lau, was suspended several feet above the ground, arms and legs stretched out at angles unnatural to the human body. Curious, braided rope was wrapped around his wrists and his ankles to anchor him securely to the trees.

Lau took a few, hesitant steps forward. Blood had pooled in several low places in the road, and he avoided the puddles as best he could. The edges of his robes brushed against the ground and became stained a dark, sickening red. When Lau had passed around the man, he came to the realization that the victim before him had not only been stripped of his clothes but of his skin as well.

With his throat clenching to keep back the vomit, he came to a stop and forced himself to turn and face the man.

What he saw churned his stomach and weakened his knees.

The stranger had been disemboweled, and it was not rope that had been used to string the man up.

Unable to control himself any longer, Lau rushed to the side of the road and fell to his hands and knees, vomiting into the grass. His stomach went into spasms and what little he had eaten was soon in front of him. Trembling, Lau wiped his mouth with the back of his hand, his eyes watering as he took in great, shaking breaths.

He pushed himself onto his haunches and felt his eyes widen as he found himself face to face with the silver fox. It was only a few feet away, head cocked to one side as if curious about his reaction to the murdered man suspended from the trees.

A heartbeat later, the fox was gone, replaced by an ancient monk. The man's face was a mask of wickedness and guile. There was neither gentleness nor mercy in the set of his jaw, and the lines that sprawled out from the corners of his eyes spoke of a man who delighted in the suffering of others.

The ghost monk seemed to understand what Lau could read in him, and he smiled.

"And what is your name, Brother?" the ghost asked.

Lau told him.

The ghost bowed, saying, "I am Brother Feng. I must say, I enjoy your community. Their fear is a joy to behold. Except for this man."

Feng gestured toward the body. "Do you know what I found him doing?"

Lau shook his head, forced himself to remain calm and answered, "No, Brother, I do not."

Feng grinned at him with appreciation for Lau's humbleness and said, "I caught him eating the offering to Buddha."

"Ah," was all Lau replied.

Feng chuckled. "I imagine you are wondering if I truly care about the offerings to the Buddha."

Lau cleared his throat and answered, "I confess, the thought did cross my mind, Brother Feng."

"Well, I don't," Feng said, sitting down and gesturing for Lau to do the same. "What I do care about is respect. And my own entertainment. Last night, those two concerns were married perfectly in the form of, well, whatever his name was. I didn't bother to ask him."

Lau didn't know how to respond to the ghost's statement, so he remained silent.

Feng watched him in silence for a short time before he said, "You have quite a few monks in your monastery."

"We do," Lau replied.

"It is always a pleasure to see our brethren working together, is it not?" Feng asked, reaching a hand out to the Mala that hung around his neck. The ghost fingered the beads as he waited for Lau to respond.

"I agree," Lau said, trying to ascertain what it was the ghost was implying. He doubted Feng said or did anything without some ulterior motive. And, judging from the corpse hanging from the trees, Lau didn't believe the outcome would be pleasant.

Finally, Feng dropped the Mala and smiled. "You are a perceptive young man. I appreciate intelligence. It is far more entertaining than stupidity. Stupid people can be afraid, but they cannot be truly terrorized."

Feng leaned closer, saying in a soft voice, "No, only the intelligent ones can know terror in its purest forms. I believe you can know what that is. I can sense your strength as well, Brother Lau. I will tell you this, to see if you can overcome your fear. To see if you will survive because I find it an interesting test. The Ghost Festival will be upon you soon. My power grows and will reach its zenith on that night, as you should know. I will come for our brethren, Brother Lau. But not for you. You must convince them of what you have seen and heard. You must learn where I am, and stop me."

Before Lau could respond, Feng shifted into the silver fox, and trotted away.

Lau glanced over his shoulder at the traveler's corpse, wondering if the ghost would do the same to everyone in the monastery.

Feng, Lau feared, would certainly try.

Bonus Scene Chapter 7: At the Home of Farmer Jiang

For seventeen years, Jiang had been alone with his dogs on his farm. His wife had passed away, and she waited for him in the next life. Not a day went by where he did not think of her. By the time the silver fox had killed four of his chickens, Jiang had only one dog left. The dog's name was Gou, and he was as wise as he was fierce.

Jiang took Brother Lau's advice and kept Gou with him at all times.

On the second evening after having gone to the monastery, Jiang went outside of his home. Gou followed close to him as Jiang checked on the chickens and the geese. He made sure the locks were secure and that the animals were all bedded down for the evening. When he had finished, Jiang went back to the house and gathered up what he needed.

With the imminent arrival of the Ghost Festival, he knew it was time to leave the regular offerings for the dead. Jiang felt it was necessary to leave more than he had in the past. On a table he had built for that purpose, he set out the offerings of food and drink by the well. He had taken some of his emergency money and bought the finest meats and liquors available. The food he prepared for the dead was better than what he had eaten throughout the entire previous year.

But if he wanted to continue to eat food, Jiang knew what he had to do in order to survive.

Like everyone else nearby, he had heard about the traveler's death. More importantly, he had learned of the gruesome nature of the man's death, and it made him think of the way the silver fox had tortured the last of the chickens.

When the meal was positioned properly on the table, Jiang stepped back to examine the setting. All looked well, and while he had no desire to be outside with the dead about, he knew the offering had to be perfect.

And from what he could see, it was.

Satisfied, Jiang hurried back into his house, Gou trotting along beside him. Once they were both inside, Jiang slammed the door shut, barred it, and retreated to his bed. He sat down and ran his hands through Gou's hair, rubbing the dog down while lost deep in thought.

A knock on the door shook him out of his daze and fear made certain he was wide awake as he called out, "Who is it?"

"Brother Bohai," the young monk answered.

Jiang frowned. It was not like Bohai to visit. Lau did quite often, but not many of the other Brothers were as willing to do so.

"What is it, Brother Bohai?" Jiang asked, not getting up. Gou had turned and faced the door.

"I wish to come in, Jiang," the monk replied, and Jiang frowned.

Gou faced the door, a low growl emanating from him. The dog's forelegs were stiff and stuck out slightly to either side. His teeth were bared, and saliva gathered in the corners of his mouth.

"I am tired, Brother Bohai," Jiang said, "I will come and speak with you tomorrow."

"No," the monk replied, "I would have you speak to me now."

Jiang stiffened. He understood why the monk's voice was strange. He was trying to hide an accent.

An accent Bohai had never spoken with before.

"Good night, Brother Bohai," Jiang said, keeping his voice steady, "I shall speak with you in the morning."

The door shook in its frame as Bohai slammed it.

"You will speak with me now!" the monk screamed. "Come outside and speak to me!"

What followed next was a torrent of screams and profanity, curses and vulgarities Jiang had never imagined could be known by one man alone.

Gou began to bark, a frenzied, insane sound that sent chills racing up Jiang's spine. The piece of wood serving as a bar on the door showed a hairline crack, then another as Bohai continued to pound upon it.

Jiang fought back the panic as it rose to a screaming crescendo in his mind, forcing himself to remain calm. He needed a weapon for protection against Brother Bohai, who seemed to be possessed by an angry ghost.

But Jiang had none. He was a farmer, and his father had been a farmer, and so on for generations. But his family had not always been farmers.

Then Jiang's frantic mind calmed, and he got to his feet.

He went to the corner where he kept the small shrine to his

ancestors. A single, and simple incense burner and a faded wooden golden flower lay on a small table. Behind the table, wrapped in ancient cloth was the item Jiang sought.

Behind him, he heard the door crack over the profanities that still spewed from Brother Bohai's mouth, and Jiang stripped the fabric off the heirloom.

It was an edged weapon set atop the end of a weighted length of wood. Its head was long, wide, and curved. The edge of the blade was dull, but still sharp enough to pierce someone's flesh.

His father had called it a 'reclining moon blade,' and altogether the weapon was as tall as Jiang. As a child, he had listened as his father told tales of an ancestor who had wielded it in battles fought long ago. But Jiang didn't need it to fight ancient bandits or invading enemies.

He needed it to kill a possessed Buddhist monk, and his hands shook as he turned to face the threat.

The wooden brace he had placed across the doorframe for extra protection shattered, as did the door itself. Gou lunged forward, jaws snapping. Bohai recoiled but remained in the house even after the dog had sunk his teeth into the man's calf.

A mad, crazed smile spread across the monk's face as he reached his hands out for Jiang. Hands bloody and shattered after his relentless assault on the door. Bohai continued forward, dragging the snarling Gou along with him, the dog refusing to let go of the man's leg.

Jiang steadied himself, brought the long weapon up and stepped forward. With a strength built from a life of disciplined work on the farm, he drove the spear deep into Bohai's chest. The weapon went in with surprising ease, a dark stain erupting on the monk's orange robes and spreading.

Bohai's chin dropped to his chest, his shoulders sagged, and Jiang found himself bearing the weight of the man at the end of the blade.

Then the monk's head snapped up, bloody teeth revealed in a gruesome smile as he said, "Alive or dead does not matter to me, I can move his flesh all the same."

The dead monk grabbed the shaft of the weapon with one broken hand and reached for Jiang with the other.

Jiang fought the urge to run blindly in fear, casting his eyes about his small home and searching for a way to escape the dead man. But the weight of the spear shifted and Jiang stumbled back.

Bohai had pulled the blade out of himself, and still dragging the dog along with him, the monk advanced on Jiang.

Bonus Scene Chapter 8: A Horrific Event

Lau hurried alongside of Brother Zhu as they made their way towards Farmer Jiang's home. One of the younger monks had reported to Lau that Bohai had left the monastery. It was an act so out of character for the anti-social Bohai that Lau had raced to Zhu's room and told him of it.

Lau had a nagging suspicion that the oddly acting man was on his way to Jiang's home, and he was fearful that his brother monk had not left of his own accord.

For several days, fear had gnawed at Lau. After the discovery of the traveler's body, and the terrifying conversation with the dead Feng, Lau had done his best to warn his fellow monks.

He had not been rewarded for his efforts.

Instead, he had been ridiculed and mocked. Granted it had been done in a gentle fashion, but the sentiment behind the statements and the looks had cut deeply. All Lau wanted to do was keep them safe. All of them.

His brethren, on the other hand, told him he was superstitious, that while ghosts most certainly existed, they could do nothing as horrible as what had been done to the traveler.

After several days of repeated rebukes, he had been spoken to by the Abbott, and Lau had been told that he needed to stop. If he did not, the Abbott would be forced to send Lau away merely to maintain the harmony within the monastery.

The other monks had increased their teasing as the Ghost Festival approached, and Lau's uneasiness became more apparent.

And since Bohai's disappearance coincided with the eve of the Ghost Festival, Lau's fear for the man was a burning knot in his stomach. He remembered Feng's statement about an increase in power with the arrival of the festival.

Although Zhu disagreed with the idea that Bohai was on his way to see Jiang because of Feng, Zhu did believe they would find the man on the road leading toward the village.

As they neared the path that led off to Jiang's farm, a terrific shout rang out in the dim light of the evening. A dog could be heard barking, the sound both ferocious and frantic. Without waiting for Zhu, Lau sprinted along the path toward Jiang's house. When he reached it, he skidded to a halt. Jiang was in front of his home, the door shattered.

The farmer's dog lunged at Brother Bohai and tore a large chunk of flesh out of the man's leg, but Bohai did nothing more than stumble. Jiang had armed himself with an ancient-looking weapon, handling it with surprising ease. Yet every blow he landed was ineffectual.

Bohai was as unfazed by the weapon as he was by the dog, and it was quite obvious the man was dead.

Zhu arrived beside Lau and made a grunt of surprise as he stared at Bohai.

"We have to drive the ghost out," Lau said, forcing his voice to remain level and without revealing his fear.

"There is no ghost possessing him!" Zhu snapped.

Bohai glanced over at them, his eyes showing nothing but whites. A bloody grin spread across his face.

"No, Little One, there is no him. This farmer here has slain the monk and sent him on," the ghost said. "I alone remain. And once I am done with this peasant, I shall deal with you."

Zhu's face paled and he shuddered as he said in disbelief, "Get out."

The ghost let out a deep, bitter laugh and replied, "No."

Jiang lunged at the dead man, but the blade was slapped away.

"Get out!" Zhu shrieked.

Lau reached out a hand, put it on Zhu's shoulder, and said in a soft voice, "I will deal with this."

A sense of calm had settled onto Lau, and the sound of the dog and Zhu faded into the background. The ghost grabbed hold of Jiang's weapon and wrenched it free. As the dead man swung the blade towards the farmer, Lau whispered, "Leave us."

Bohai stiffened. The weapon dropped to the ground with a thud, and then the dead monk did the same.

A silence filled the farm, broken after only a moment by Jiang's dog, who let out a whine, and hurried to stand beside the man. Lau glanced at Zhu and found his brother monk staring at him with surprise.

"How?" Zhu asked.

Lau shook his head. "I do not know, but I do know that we have to hurry back to the monastery."

"I fear it is too late for the monastery," Jiang said, gesturing behind the men.

Lau turned around, and a moan of despair arose from Zhu's throat as they stared at their home.

From where they stood, parts of the monastery were illuminated. Not by the light of the rising moon, but by fires that consumed some of the outlying buildings. The flames were tall and bright, the edges tinged with a light blue that reminded Lau of lightening.

The wind shifted, carrying the smell of ash and flame as well as the faint sounds of laughter mingled with screams.

Feng and his kind were butchering the monks.

Lau turned toward the path that would return him to the road.

"Where are you going?" Zhu whispered, his voice raw with fear.

"I am going home," Lau replied, pausing only for a moment. "Our brethren need us."

Jiang leaned over, picked up his weapon, and called his dog to him. Several steps carried him to Lau's side.

"Will you stay here, my friend?" Lau asked. There was no condemnation in his voice. No ridicule in the question.

Zhu hesitated, then he nodded.

"Wait for us, then," Lau said, "and we will be back for you after the sun rises."

"How do you know?" Zhu asked, his question barely audible.

"I don't," Lau replied, "but that doesn't matter."

Lau nodded to Jiang, and the two men and the dog made their way back to the monastery, where Feng and the dead awaited them.

* * *

Sherman's
Collection

Chapter 1: Charles Talks With His Mother

Charles Gottesman drank his coffee while his mother made her breakfast. She'd been eating the same thing for the past thirty years. A bowl of oatmeal, half of a kiwi, a cup of coffee, and piece of toast with a light coating of margarine. As she'd gotten older she'd added vitamins and various medications to her routine, but it was essentially the same one he remembered her adopting when he started middle-school.

When she finally brought her own coffee to the table and sat down, Charles asked if anything was new.

"Not much." His mother smiled. "Your father's off watching your siblings run in a relay race. Oh, I almost forgot. Mr. Sherman has died."

"Mr. Sherman?" Charles asked. "I didn't know he was still alive."

She nodded. "He was. Evidently he had a nurse coming to check on him each day, and she found him after he passed away yesterday."

"What's going to happen with his house and all his belongings?"

"I was speaking with Mrs. Charron, and she said he had given away most of his things. All he had left was his library and the house."

"He didn't have any family, did he?" Charles asked.

His mother shook her head. "Not that I know of."

"Are they putting his house up for sale?"

She nodded. "It should be on the market by Tuesday. Why?"

"I always loved that house," Charles said.

"That house scares the bejesus out of me," his mother said. "You would buy it?"

"Definitely," Charles answered. "I've been in an apartment for, what, two years now? Yes, two years since the divorce. I'm ready to be in a house again."

"Well," his mother said, taking a sip of coffee, "call Mrs. Charron in the morning, she's at Church right now. Her sister is the real estate agent."

"I will," Charles said. "I will."

"Anyway," his mother said, "tell me about your writing for that new magazine"

And so Charles did.

Chapter 2: The Nurse's Boyfriend

Mike sat at the computer, scrolling through the listings on Monster.com. The whole get-a-job deal was not working out for him. He still had a couple of months of unemployment left. Hell, he figured he could wait at least another month before he had to do some serious job hunting.

But Ellen wasn't letting up on it, and since she was the one carrying them both, he couldn't complain much.

At least to her.

The guys at Rocky's Tap and Grill would listen and understand.

Mike sighed and clicked on the next set of 25 jobs. Plenty of CNC machining work, but nothing nearby. Mike didn't want that much of a commute.

The tumbler on the front door's deadbolt clicked, and the door opened a moment later. Ellen stumbled in. She hung her keys up on the rack, dropped her bag on the floor, and closed the door behind her.

Mike straightened up and swung around in the chair, smiling at her.

Ellen smiled back as she took her brown hair out of its ponytail and shook it out.

"How are you doing?" Mike asked, getting up and going to her.

She gave him a hug before saying, "A little rough today."

"What's up?" he said, letting go of her, walking into the kitchen, and getting their coffee mugs down.

"You know Mr. Sherman?" she asked, slipping her sneakers off before walking into the front room. She flopped down on the couch.

"Yeah," Mike answered. He poured coffee for each of them, brought Ellen hers, and sat down in his chair. "What happened to him?"

"He died sometime last night," she answered.

"And you found him?" Mike asked.

"Yes," she sighed. "I found him. He was a nice man."

"I'm sorry, sweetheart."

"You know," Ellen said, "he used to be wealthy, but the older he got, the more he gave away. A few days ago he said that since he couldn't take it with him, he had given it away."

"Really?" Mike asked, failing completely to understand how anyone could give money away.

"Really," Ellen said. She took a sip of her coffee. "The only things he didn't get rid of were his books and some odds and ends in his library. That stuff, he told me, was supposed to stay in the house. Even after he died. I guess he had a stipulation put in that whoever buys the house, they have to leave the library in there."

"What'll happen if they don't?" Mike asked.

Ellen shrugged. "I don't know. I don't think there's any way anyone could enforce it since he's dead. You know?"

Mike nodded.

"Anyway," she said. "How was the job search?"

"I think I found a couple of places in Milford, New Hampshire that might be a good fit," he lied comfortably. "Jared's supposed to be picking me up in about an hour. I want to see how long the commute will be if I have to work a second shift."

She smiled at him. "Cool. I'll probably be in the bath when you leave. Are you going out to shoot pool afterward?"

"Probably," Mike answered.

"Okay," she said. She put her coffee down and stretched, and Mike smiled at her.

***

Mike and Jared sat on a picnic table outside of Rocky's, smoking and watching the October sunset.

"You familiar with Nashua at all?" Mike asked.

"A little," Jared answered. "Why?"

"You know where Sheridan Street is?"

Jared thought for a moment before answering, "Yeah. It's off Charlotte Avenue."

Mike nodded. "You know Ellen's been doing that visiting nurse thing, right?"

"Yeah," Jared said. "Good money, isn't it?"

"Decent," Mike said. "Decent. Anyway. One of her patients died last night."

"She find him?"

Mike tried not to get mad at Jared's interruption. "Yup, she found him. The guy used to be rich. Got rid of everything but the stuff in his library."

"Yeah?"

Mike sighed. "Yeah. Jared, would you get rid of all of your money and stuff?"

"Oh, hell, no." Jared took the last drag off of his cigarette and flipped the butt into the sand by the back door.

"Exactly my thought."

"What is?"

"That he wouldn't get rid of all the money and stuff," Mike said. "I bet he had a ton of it stashed in his library."

"Ton of what?"

"Jesus," Mike said, looking at Jared. "Are you high?"

"Little."

Mike rolled his eyes. "Anyway, he probably stashed some of his money in his books."

"So what if he did?"

"He died alone," Mike said. "Ellen told me the guy had no family. That's why he was giving everything away."

"Shit," Jared said. "So you think he might have hidden some cash in his library?"

"Exactly," Mike said with a sigh of relief. "Exactly. I bet if we went over there when it got a little darker, we could probably get in and go through the library. Guy was like ninety or something when he died. Can you imagine how much he's probably got stashed away?"

Jared shook his head. "Wow. Yeah. Do you want to do it tonight?"

"Soon as it gets dark. We should probably take a ride over and figure out where on Sheridan it is, though."

"What number is it?" Jared asked.

"Number one," Mike answered. "Number one, Sheridan Street."

Chapter 3: Mike and Jared at Mr. Sherman's

The sun had been down for a couple of hours, and Mike and Jared sat in Jared's Suburban, the lights off, but the engine running. They had the heater on low, and they were parked inside of Edgewood Cemetery near the back entrance. Sheridan Street was only thirty yards beyond the entrance.

And number one Sheridan Street was on a dead end that ran up to the wrought iron fence that surrounded the cemetery.

Not even a streetlight shone upon the old Victorian house the man had lived in.

As an added bonus, there were a good hundred yards of woods between the old man's house and his nearest neighbor.

Mike hoped there was still money inside. That was the important part of this whole deal.

"What do you think?" Jared asked. Mike's friend had sobered up, and whatever he'd taken had worn off. The man was calm and collected. Both of them were. Neither had done any house-breaking since they'd graduated high school five years earlier, but neither of them were worried about it either.

The house was guaranteed to be empty, and it was as isolated as you could get in the city. They'd picked up duffel bags at Wal-Mart. Whatever they found could be stuffed into the bags, tossed over the cemetery fence, and loaded into the Suburban.

Easy as pie.

"I think we can do this now," Mike said.

They left the vehicle running and got out into the cold night air. Their breath slipped free in slim vapor trails, and they put their gloved hands into the pockets of their extra-large hooded sweatshirts. They walked casually, talking in low voices, hoods down, but with knit caps on. It was cold enough to justify the hats, and they stepped easily from the cemetery onto Sheridan Street.

If anybody noticed them at all, Mike knew they'd look like a couple of guys out for a walk, teenagers cutting through the cemetery to get home. The two of them walked like they belonged in the neighborhood, and when a car drove by, its lights bright, neither he nor Jared looked away. They kept on walking.

Just before Sheridan Street turned into a dead end, it intersected another street, Ashland, and Mike and Jared paused to let a pick-up rattle by. When the truck's red rear lights disappeared around another corner, the two men walked across Ashland up to the Victorian.

They walked up the front steps of the wide porch, the wood creaking beneath their boots, and Mike stepped to the front door. He took hold of the doorknob and turned gently.

There was a soft click and the door opened.

"Awesome," Jared chuckled.

Mike could only nod his agreement.

A minute later they were in the house, the door closed behind them as they pulled the new duffel bags out from under their sweatshirts.

"Where do you think the library is?" Mike asked in a low voice.

"Dunno," Jared answered. "Maybe upstairs?"

Their voices echoed curiously, and then Mike realized it was because of the emptiness of the place. Hell, there weren't even any curtains or shades on the windows. The floors were all hardwood. Light from a full moon poured in through the windows and lit up the house, but it made everything colder, somehow.

There was a rumbling and a rattling from the basement, and both men froze in place.

A heartbeat later, a giant steam radiator shook and hissed into life.

Mike let out a long breath. "Damn."

"Scared me too," Jared said.

"Yeah," Mike said. "Let's find that damned library and get the hell out of here."

Jared nodded.

A large set of stairs led off from the hallway they were in, and the two of them walked up the stairs side by side. All of the doors were open on the second floor, and a moment later they found the library. It had a large window on the back wall with the moon shining directly in. The shelves were loaded with books as well curious items—a couple of old automatic pistols that looked like they came out of a World War Two movie, some swords, bayonets. Lots and lots of military stuff. Even a Nazi flag.

"Wow," Jared said.

"Right," Mike agreed. "This is crazy." Looking closer he saw a Zippo lighter. Reaching out he picked it up off of the shelf and saw that someone had etched out the word "Iwo" in old-style letters. Nodding to himself, he slipped it into his pocket.

"Do you think we can move any of this stuff?" Jared asked.

Mike nodded. "Definitely. There's a guy at that indoor flea market out in Milford that doesn't ask any questions. And he's always got a ton of military stuff."

"Okay," Jared said, opening a bag. "Let's do this."

It took the two of them less than five minutes to fill four bags with everything that looked like it might be worth something. They even checked a couple of the books to see if there was cash hidden inside, but they had no luck.

Mike and Jared each picked up a pair of bags and made for the stairs. They had nearly reached the first floor when Mike felt something cold rip through him, and he stumbled over the last step.

"Jesus Christ!" Jared snapped, almost tripping over Mike. "What the hell was that?"

"Something cold?" Mike asked.

"Yeah," Jared said, nodding and looking around. "It's like I stepped into a freezer or something."

The house shook slightly, as if an eighteen wheeler was rushing by on the street beyond. But there was nothing. Not even a car rumbling by.

"What the hell?" Mike said.

Behind them, something slammed, and together they twisted around. All Mike could see was a closed door and—

Drawers flew out of a built-in cabinet to the left of the door as the doorknob turned, the door opened and then slammed viciously closed.

Without another word, Mike turned and ran for the front door. Jared beat him to it. Jared managed to get a hold of the doorknob without letting go of either of the bags.

"Jesus!" Jared yelled. "Help me, something's trying to keep the door closed!" Jared strained against the door.

Mike threw himself forward, dropping both of his bags to the floor. Mike slipped his fingers into the barely open door and pulled back, grunting with the effort. Together they managed to push the door open wide enough for them to slip out.

They left Mike's duffel bags on the floor as they tumbled onto the porch and fell down the broad steps. Behind them, the door swung open wide and then slammed shut, the glass in the windows rattling.

They sprinted for the cemetery fence, Mike taking one of the bags from Jared and heaving it over the wrought iron as Jared did the same. Then they ran around the perimeter of the fence to the back entrance, and from there to the Suburban. When they reached the vehicle, they scrambled for the bags, tossed them into the back and piled in themselves.

Jared dropped the SUV into gear and tore out along the cemetery's road. He didn't slow down until they were on Amherst Street, aimed towards Merrimack. Jared didn't get onto the highway, driving up instead to Market Basket and parking in the well-lit lot.

Mike looked at Jared and said, "What the hell was that?"

Jared only shook his head.

"Seriously," Mike said, taking a deep breath, "was that a ghost?"

"I think so. I mean, I don't know for sure," Jared said in a low voice. "Yeah. Yeah, I think it was."

"Think it was pissed we went in there and took some stuff out?"

"No," Jared said, shaking his head. "They don't care about stuff like that. Right?"

Mike thought about it for a minute and then nodded in agreement. "Yeah. It was probably upset we were there, you know?"

Jared nodded. "Not that we took things."

"We lost the two bags I had," Mike said.

"Doesn't matter," Jared said. "That scared the hell out of me."

Mike laughed nervously. "Yeah. Me too, man."

"So, what do you want to do?" Jared said. "Do you want to try and fence the goods this weekend?"

"Yeah," Mike said. "That'll be the best deal, I think. That way we can do it together. You want to hold onto it until then?"

Jared looked into the back at the two bags. After a moment he said, "Yeah. I'll toss a tarp over'em, so nobody decides to pop a lock and go looking around the back of the car."

"Cool," Mike said. "Now we've finished with that crap, want

to grab a couple of beers?"

"Hell yeah," Jared said. "Want to go to Rocky's?"

"Damned right," Mike said, relaxing into the seat for the first time since they'd left the cemetery. "You're damned right."

Chapter 4: Mike and the Zippo

Mike had more than a few beers at Rocky's.

In fact, he had more than a few pitchers.

But he wasn't sure.

When he got home, Ellen was already asleep. She had popped an Ambien since she was still getting used to going from third shift to her own gig as a traveling nurse.

Mike didn't need an Ambien. He had at least a gallon and a half of Bud Lite in him. Easily a gallon and a half.

He'd be lucky if he didn't piss himself.

Mike attempted to hang his keys up, missed the rack twice, and shrugged, dropping them to the floor. Then he sat down on the floor to take his boots off. There was no way he was going to be able to find a chair and manage to sit in it on the first try.

No sir, not at all.

Giggling to himself and grinning, Mike managed to take first one boot, and then the other, off. Both of his socks, however, stayed in the boots.

Oh well, he thought.

He rolled from a sitting position onto his hands and knees, and then he slowly got to his feet, reaching out to the wall for support. The last thing he needed was to pass out on the floor. Ellen would wake him up with a kick in the ass and a good chewing out.

Neither of which were appealing. Plus she'd probably—

Mike tumbled to the floor, the thought cut off as he rolled onto his back, looking up at the ceiling. He laughed and stared up at the ceiling. His stomach rumbled and let out a loud belch, and he laughed again.

Shifting his weight, Mike felt something hard and uncomfortable in his front pocket. Frowning he managed to climb to his feet, leaning against the wall before reaching into the pocket and digging out the offending item.

A moment later he was holding a Zippo lighter. He looked at it for a moment, trying to remember where he had gotten it, and then he smiled.

The dead man's house on Sheridan Street.

That's where he had gotten the lighter.

Holding it in his hand he slowly made his way into the front room, using the furniture as a guide before dropping down heavily into his chair. He turned on the lamp that stood on the side-table and blinked at the light. Once his eyes had adjusted, he took out his box of cigars. From the box, he took a cigar and the snipper, trimming the cigar before closing the box up. Placing the cigar between his lips, he brought the lighter up, flipped open the lid and rolled the flint beneath his thumb.

A bright flame surged into life on the wick, and Mike lit the cigar. He drew on the cigar until it was smoking steadily. Then he closed the lighter—

But the lighter didn't close.

The lid stayed open, and the flame continued to burn brightly.

Frowning, Mike tried again.

Nothing.

He tried flipping the lid closed once more, and still it didn't move. The flame didn't even flicker.

With his free hand, Mike went to close the lid, and couldn't move it. Then he couldn't take his hand off of the lid.

He couldn't take either of his hands off of the lighter. As he looked at it, the flame grew larger, bending towards him with every breath he took. Tendrils of smokeless flame reached out towards him, carefully snaking their way through the air.

Mike tried to shake the lighter out of his hands, but nothing happened. He held it as far away as possible, and still the flames moved closer to him. He spat out the cigar onto the floor, where the small head that had been forming exploded in bright embers onto the rug which Ellen had recently bought to match the furniture.

For a moment, Mike was worried about what she would say, and then he realized the flames were drawing closer. They were two straight lines mere inches from his nose, and he could feel the heat.

A terrible heat.

Mike opened his mouth to call for Ellen, and the flames leaped forward. One of them split again and raced into his nostrils. The other surged into his throat.

The scream that rose up was devoured by the flame, and Mike fell writhing to the floor as the flames sought out his lungs.

Chapter 5: Ellen, Mike, and the Zippo

The sun was easing in around the curtains in the bedroom when Ellen's alarm went off. Groaning, she reached out, turned the alarm off, and sat up. A glance over to Mike's side of the bed showed that her boyfriend hadn't come home last night. Or at least hadn't made it into the bed.

As she stretched, she smelled the potent stench of one of his cigars, and she frowned.

Mike had made it home, obviously drunk. He knew she didn't want him smoking in the apartment. They had a deck. He could smoke out there to his heart's content even though he stank every time he was finished.

Angrily Ellen got out of bed, pulled on her bathrobe, and put her slippers on. She walked down the narrow hallway to the front room and saw Mike's bare feet before she saw him.

Great, she thought. *He didn't even manage to get on the couch.*

When she turned the corner completely, she saw a nearly whole cigar on the new rug and burn marks on it as well. Her temper flared, and she went to yell at him when she noticed he was flat on his back. His hands were frozen at his throat, his face a twisted mask of horror, his mouth open.

There were burns on his lips and nostrils, and he was dead. Obviously, painfully dead. On the floor beside him was a Zippo lighter. One that looked familiar.

Ellen's anger was gone. She was dazed, confused. She walked over to the lighter, focusing on it and not on Mike's death.

Not focusing on Mike's death.

Ellen bent down and picked up the Zippo. The word 'Iwo' was engraved on one side of the lighter. She'd seen it before. Yes. Mr. Sherman had showed it to her one day. A memento of his time in the Marine Corps he had said.

How did it get here? She thought. *Did I accidentally bring it home one day?*

I'll have to take it back, she thought. Still in a daze, she stood up and walked to the phone. She slipped the lighter into her robe's pocket, picked up the phone, and called 911.

Chapter 6: Mr. Sherman's House

Charles leaned against the side of his car as he waited for the real estate agent to show up. Around him, a pleasant autumn wind shook the brightly colored leaves of the cemetery trees, and he looked at the faded glory of Mr. Sherman's house.

When Charles had been a boy the house had still been several shades of blue, painted as only a grand Victorian Lady could be.

But that had been over thirty years earlier, and New England winters were never kind.

The sound of a car's engine turned Charles' attention to the left. A black BMW turned up the intersection with Ashland Street. The driver parked the car a little bit behind Charles's and a moment later got out.

"Charles?" the woman asked, smiling.

"That's me," Charles said, straightening up and walking to her.

"Mary Beth Holmes," she said, extending her hand.

"A pleasure," Charles said, shaking her hand warmly.

"You know," Mary Beth said, "I haven't officially listed the house yet. My sister says you grew up in the area?"

"I did," Charles nodded. "If you were to walk around the right-hand side of the house here there's a small wooded path. It runs along the edge of the cemetery and then comes out to the dead end of Adams Street. And I grew up on the corner of Adams and Hill."

"Wow," she said, smiling pleasantly. "And you always liked the house?"

"Loved it," Charles said. "I even got to go into it once when I was much younger."

"Well," Mary Beth said, reaching into a jacket pocket and pulling out a key, "you probably won't remember much about the house, but I will say it is in remarkable condition."

No, Charles thought. *I'll remember.*

But he merely smiled and fell into step beside her as Mary Beth walked up the broad, brick walkway to the front steps. As they climbed them, the wooden stairs creaked. The porch boards sighed as Charles and the real estate agent crossed.

"What's this?" Mary Beth asked, bending down and picking up something near the door. She turned to him and showed him a Zippo lighter. The word 'Iwo' was engraved in German gothic script on the brass case.

Charles frowned. "That's Mr. Sherman's."

"How do you know?" she asked.

"He showed me his library when I was here," he answered softly.

"Well, we'll have to put it back, then," Mary Beth said, turning to unlock the door. "Oh, that reminds me. Mr. Sherman put a curious stipulation in his will stating that when the house was sold, the library had to remain intact. Nothing from it was to leave the house."

"I've never heard of anything like that before."

"I know." Mary Beth chuckled as she opened the door. "It's not enforceable once the house is sold, but I am required to mention it prior to any showing. And—"

She stopped talking and looked down.

Charles saw a pair of generic duffel bags on the floor to the left of the door. The bags were packed.

"These weren't here before," Mary Beth said, stepping into the house and over to one side.

Charles followed her in and squatted down beside the bags. He opened first one, and then the other. "These are all things from his library. It looks like someone was trying to steal them."

Mary Beth's lips tightened. "I have to report this to the police."

Charles nodded, standing up. "That's fine."

"Do you want to do the showing another time?" she asked apologetically.

"No need," Charles smiled. "I already know I want the house."

Smiling in relief, Mary Beth said, "That's great. Let me call the police and then we can work out when the inspector can come."

Charles nodded and started to explore the first floor, as he had so many years before. Mary reached for her cell phone and dialed the police.

Chapter 7: December 7th, 1984

Charles walked through the snow from Joshua's house on Hooker Street, but the snow was falling faster than anything Charles had ever seen. He was bundled up in his parka and snow pants, knit cap, scarf, and mittens. His feet were in plastic bags inside of his snow boots.

But he was cold.

The temperature was almost too cold to snow. At least that's what his father had said. But the nor'easter wasn't supposed to have come until after bedtime.

That was what the radio news was reporting when Charles's father had dropped him off at Joshua's.

It was three o'clock when Charles had left Joshua's house— before Joshua's mother could wake up from her afternoon drunk and realize there was one more child to hit in the house. Besides, Charles needed to be home by three thirty. His mother and brother and sister were supposed to be home by four, and Charles had his chores to do. If he didn't, he'd get punished, and he wouldn't be allowed to go over Joshua's for a while again.

And he was the only one Joshua hung around with.

Charles had left Joshua's in plenty of time to get home. Plenty of time when it wasn't snowing so hard and so fast. Charles had only reached the edge of the cemetery when his new watch beeped that it was three thirty.

It had taken him half an hour to walk what usually took him five minutes.

Charles pushed his way through the gathering snow, a sharp wind creating huge drifts, some of them taller than Charles.

"Boy!" a voice shouted.

Charles looked around and saw the front door open on the old house across from the cemetery. Mr. Sherman's house.

Mr. Sherman stood in the doorway, waving to him.

"Boy!" the old man shouted again. "Come inside and call your parents!"

Charles was about to say 'no' when he realized he could barely move his mouth, and he was colder than he had ever been in his life. Mr. Sherman's house was frightening, almost always dark for all of Charles's life. But Charles's mother knew the old man, had gone to school with his daughter, the one who had been killed on Main Street for saying no when a guy had asked her out.

Even though fear gripped his belly when he looked at the house, Charles turned towards the old man and the open door. Charles walked through the gathering snow, stumbled, and caught himself.

A moment later, Mr. Sherman was there. He was smaller than Charles's mother, but he scooped Charles up into his arms and carried him through the snow, up the stairs, and into the house. Mr. Sherman shouldered the door closed and then carried Charles into a living room where a fire burned in a large fireplace.

Mr. Sherman set Charles down on a braided rug in front of the fire. "Warm up, boy. I'll put milk on for hot chocolate. Soon as you feel your fingers, you call your parents and tell them you're here."

Charles could only nod, and Mr. Sherman left the room. Shaking, Charles took off his hat and his scarf and his mittens, putting them out on the bricks that lined the fireplace on the floor. His hands were cold, wet and red. Charles rubbed them together and then got to his feet. He looked around and saw an old black phone by a chair. The phone was on a small table, and Charles realized everything looked perfect, like it was a picture in a book.

Charles looked at the snow dripping off his clothes and onto the rug, and then he carefully took off his jacket, snow pants, and boots. The last things were the plastic bags on his feet.

No longer in danger of ruining the room, Charles stepped over to the phone, and with tingling fingers, he dialed his house.

The phone rang twice before it was answered by his mother. "Hello?" she asked, and Charles could hear the worry in her voice.

"Hi, Mom," Charles said.

"Oh, thank God," his mother sighed. "Where are you? We called Joshua's house, but he said you'd left a while ago."

"I'm at Mr. Sherman's house," Charles said. "I got here a minute ago."

"Okay," his mother said. "Okay. Listen, you stay there. As soon as the plows go by, your father will be up there to get you. Could I speak to Mr. Sherman?"

"Um," Charles said, turning around in time to see Mr. Sherman entering the room. "Sure. Hold on. Mr. Sherman?"

"Your mother would like to speak with me, Charles?" Mr. Sherman asked.

"Yes."

"Certainly," Mr. Sherman said. He held out his hand, and Charles gave him the phone. "Hello, Tina. Yes...yes, that's fine. I'm making hot chocolate for your son now. I didn't recognize him at first. Yes...yes, of course. We'll wait for your husband."

Mr. Sherman motioned to Charles, holding the phone out.

Charles took it. "Hi, Mom."

"Hi," she said. "Everything is all set with Mr. Sherman. We'll see you soon, okay?"

"Okay."

"I love you," she said. "And make sure you're polite, okay?"

"I will, and I love you too."

Charles hung up the phone.

"The hot chocolate should be ready in a moment," Mr. Sherman smiled. "Come with me, please."

Charles dutifully followed the man out of the living room, through the hallway and into the kitchen. All of the appliances were old. Older than anything Charles had ever seen in person. A copper pot was on a burner, and a large mug was on the counter beside the stove.

"I do not have any whipped cream, I am afraid," Mr. Sherman said, turning the flame off under the pot. Using an oven mitt, the man poured warm milk into the mug. He replaced the pot onto the burner, and the oven mitt onto a hook hanging from the upper cabinet. He used a spoon to stir the milk. "Here."

Charles took the warm mug in his hands, and saw the rich chocolate color of the milk.

"Real chocolate milk." The old man smiled.

"Thank you very much," Charles said. He took a sip. The hot chocolate was fantastic. Charles drank it as quickly as politeness would allow. He could feel the warmth settle into his stomach and spread out.

"Good?" Mr. Sherman asked, smiling.

"Yes."

"Good," the old man said, gently taking the mug from Charles. Mr. Sherman rinsed it out in the sink and set it down on the counter. "Well, I'm afraid I don't get very good reception on the television when the storms are here. I don't suppose you like

496

to read, do you?"

"I love reading," Charles said.

"Excellent! What are you reading at home?"

"The Count of Monte Cristo," Charles answered.

Mr. Sherman smiled broadly. "That is fantastic, young man. I love to read as well. I even have a small library. Would you like to see it?"

"Yes," Charles said excitedly. "Do you have a lot of books?"

"A few," Mr. Sherman said, winking. "Come. I will show you the library."

Charles followed as Mr. Sherman walked out of the kitchen, back into the hallway and started up a large flight of stairs. In a minute, they were on the second floor, and Mr. Sherman was opening the door to his library, turning on the light and stepping aside so Charles could look in.

Charles blinked.

He'd never seen so many books outside of the Nashua Public Library before. Not even his school had as many books.

The walls in Mr. Sherman's library were almost completely covered with bookshelves. Books were everywhere. They were neatly arranged, and occasionally there was a sword, or a gun, or something military. In the center of the room was a large table with a writing pad and a pen. Behind the table was a tall leather chair, and there was a lamp with a green glass shade on the table beside the writing pad.

"Wow," Charles said softly. He turned and looked at Mr. Sherman. "Have you read all of these books?"

Mr. Sherman gave him a small smile and shook his head. "No, not yet."

"Where did you get all of the war stuff?" Charles asked.

"It's called militaria, young Charles," Mr. Sherman answered him, his smile fading away. "And I have gathered it over my life."

"You collect it?"

"In a manner of speaking," Mr. Sherman said. "These particular items are not what they seem to be, Charles. They're all haunted."

Charles tore his eyes away from a bugle resting on a stack of books. He looked at Mr. Sherman and tried to see if he was joking.

The old man wasn't. Mr. Sherman had a terribly serious look

on his face.

"How are they haunted?" Charles asked.

"Well," Mr. Sherman said, frowning for a moment before answering. "Do you see that lighter by the window?"

Charles looked, saw the old fashioned lighter, and nodded. "Yes."

"That lighter came from a man who was a Marine during World War Two. He was a flamethrower operator, and he often used that lighter to light his cigarettes while he was killing the enemy."

"How is it haunted?" Charles asked.

"If you use it to light a cigarette or cigar," Mr. Sherman said softly, "it will burn the air out of your lungs."

Charles felt a chill race down his spine, and he looked at the lighter nervously. Then he looked from the lighter to a sword, asking, "Are they all like that?"

"Yes," Mr. Sherman nodded. "Yes. They are all like that."

Chapter 8: Jared, November 4th, 2015

Jared felt down as he cracked open another beer.

Mike was dead.

Jared's ex-girlfriend Erica, who was friends with Mike's girl Ellen, had sent him a text that Mike had died. Died the night Jared and Mike had robbed that empty house.

That empty haunted house.

No one knew exactly what had happened. Some sort of freak natural cause, Jared thought. Hell, Mike was fine when Jared had dropped him off at the apartment. A little drunk and a little tired, but no worse than Jared had been, and Jared had managed to drive home without getting caught for driving under the influence.

But Mike was dead.

Jared shook his head and pounded back the beer. It was eight o'clock in the morning, but the building inspector had shut down the site Jared was working at, so he had the day off. And there was no one around to bitch at him for drinking first thing in the morning. One of the benefits of not being with Erica anymore.

The sex had definitely not been worth the nagging that came afterward.

Jared walked over to the fridge, got himself another beer, grabbed a half of a BLT he had left from the day before, and made his way back to the couch. He flopped down and opened the beer. He took a drink, set the can on the coffee table and opened up the BLT. As he ate, he sent text messages out to some of his and Mike's mutual friends.

Since Mike was dead, Jared had no way to contact the guy at the indoor flea market. He was pretty sure Ellen wouldn't know that guy, and he didn't want to bother her anyway since Mike was dead. Those two had liked each other, and Jared felt pretty bad about the whole thing.

For about half an hour, Jared sent out the text messages, finishing his beer and BLT and put the television on. He was watching the show "American Justice" when he finally got a text back about the guy in Milford.

"Thank God," Jared said. He dug a pen out of the mess of newspapers on the coffee table and jotted the number down on one of the papers. He muted the volume on the television before picking up his phone. He dialed the number and waited.

After a few rings, someone answered.

"Hello?"

"Hey," Jared said. "Is this Dave?"

"Yeah. Who's this?"

"Jared. I'm a friend of Mike Singer."

There was a pause. "Oh, yeah. Mike. Hey, he just died, didn't he?"

"Yeah."

"I was sorry to hear that."

"Me too."

"So," Dave said. "What's up?"

"I've got some old military stuff Mike had said you might want to buy," Jared answered.

"Sure," Dave said. "When do you want to meet up?"

"You free at all today?"

"Hold on," Dave said. Jared could hear pages being flipped. "Yeah, after four. You know where I'm at?"

"No."

"Right on the Milford Oval, you can't miss it. Says 'Milford Antiques and Collectibles' on the front."

"Okay," Jared said, writing the information down. "See you at four."

"Good."

Dave ended the call, and Jared hit end on his own phone, putting it down once more. Smiling to himself, Dave picked up the remote and turned the volume back on.

***

Mr. Sherman's house, not surprisingly, passed the house inspection with flying colors. And since the house was being sold at a rock bottom price, there was no real negotiation. Charles had a lot of money in the bank. More than enough to cover the price of the home.

In a matter of days Charles was moved in.

In all of that time, Charles hadn't gone into the library.

Mr. Sherman's lighter and the two bags he and the realtor had found in the house sat on the floor in front of the closed library door.

Charles knew that he was going to have to go to the library and put the items back. He had never doubted Mr. Sherman's statement that the items were haunted. And Charles had never possessed the urge to handle them.

But he was going to have to put them back. Of that, he felt certain. He was worried though. If the lighter had been on the porch, and the bags inside the door, had someone managed to get out of the house with something else?

The only way Charles would know would be by entering the library and putting the things back. He remembered perfectly where everything had been. He could see each item clearly, each image forever set in his memory.

And, Charles hoped, Mr. Sherman had kept some sort of list. Charles had no idea if the man had continued to collect items. If so, there might be a catalog. It was the only thing that would make sense, especially since the items were haunted. Dangerously so.

Sighing, Charles walked into the kitchen that was unchanged from the time he had stepped into it thirty years earlier at the tender age of eleven. The same oven-mitt hung from its hook. The same copper pan sat on a burner. To the left of the stove was an electric percolator Charles was sure was in perfect working order.

The old Frigidaire refrigerator hummed loudly as Charles walked to a cabinet and took down his coffee. He made a pot for himself, and once it was ready, he poured some into a mug. With the mug in hand, he made his way to the library.

For a moment, he stood in front of the door, looking down first at the bags and then back to the door. Taking a deep breath, he reached out, took hold of the curiously warm glass doorknob, and opened the door.

The library was dark, the shade pulled down on the room's solitary window.

And the library, strangely enough, was as big as he remembered it. He had always thought the size of the room was merely a product of his youth.

But it wasn't.

Charles reached into the room, found the push-button light switch, and pressed the 'on' button.

The light on the table came brightly to life, as did several new lights. These were small, recessed lights set into the tin ceiling. The lights shone down on the shelves, and Charles saw the empty spaces where items had been. He saw other items that were new to him. On the reading table, atop a fresh writing pad, was a letter and a small, leather-bound journal.

Charles stepped over the bags and into the library. He walked to the table, set his coffee mug down on a marble coaster near the lamp and sat down in the large leather chair.

He picked up the letter, found it wasn't sealed, and removed the letter from it.

Dear Friend, the letter began.

> *It is my sincere hope that you have found this home to your liking. I have maintained it to the best of my ability these past sixty years. You have, I am sure, wondered why I have made the demand that the library—and all its contents— remain intact and untouched. I do not, obviously, know what your thoughts or feelings are on the supernatural, but I must inform you that the items within this library are of the supernatural variety.*
>
> *The militaria you see on the shelves are haunted. Yes, haunted. And they are haunted in the most brutal of ways, by the men and women who carried them home. These are not the simple trophies of war you may have seen. These are infected with the hatred and murderous spirits of their previous owners. I strongly recommend you do not touch them.*
>
> *I have attempted to destroy them, but they are indestructible. I have tried burying them or casting them into deep waters, but they reappeared. How, I do not know. All I know is that people—men, women, and children—died because of my hubris. The only option, then, is to guard them.*
>
> *Thus, I must ask you to leave these items where they are. This room is special. It is a place*

of binding, a place where I can freely move and place the items without fear.

Please, leave these items here. If you cannot, I suggest you do not purchase this home for it brings with it a responsibility most cannot agree to carry.

Sincerely,
Philip Sherman

Charles set the letter down and took up his coffee. He drank the coffee for a few minutes before returning the mug to the coaster and picking up the journal.

Charles opened to the first page and saw that it was a list of items as well as an extremely accurate map of the library. Beside each item was a letter, and on the map there was a corresponding letter to mark the location of the item. The next page listed the same items, yet beside each item was the date Mr. Sherman had obtained it as well where. Occasionally, as Charles flipped through the pages, he would see a small note saying, "Obtained with the assistance of" followed by a name.

So there were others who knew of the items and what they did.

Halfway through the journal, after the last entry, there was a hastily jotted note.

Under the table.

Frowning, Charles put the journal down, and got down on his hands and knees. Tilting his head up, he looked at the underside of the table.

There, tucked into a narrow wooden shelf, was a small box, no bigger than a cigar box.

Charles reached up, took hold of the box and pulled it out.

Getting back to his feet and sitting down once more, Charles opened the box. In it was a pair of white cotton gloves and a piece of folded paper.

Charles took the paper out, opened it and read, *These gloves are to be used in the procurement of haunted items. Handle nothing without these gloves. Thomas Granger, 1954.*

Charles returned the paper to the box, closed the lid and set the box on the table in front of him. He looked at the bags lying on the floor beyond the library's threshold.

He was going to have to return those items to the shelves. Which meant he was going to have to put on the gloves. Charles remembered vividly Mr. Sherman describing the effects of the lighter, should one attempt to use it, and he wondered, with a cold twisting sensation in his stomach, what the others might do if handled improperly.

***

Jared took out the razor blade, cut a line out from the pile and proceeded to chop it up on the surface of the mirror. Alice in Chains played on the stereo, and Jared was feeling *good*.

I'll be feeling even better in a minute, he thought. Grinning, he continued to chop up the coke, making sure it was fine as it could be.

The guy Dave had given him a grand for the stuff in the bags, which meant, of course, that Dave could move it for at least ten times that amount. But hey, Jared didn't mind. He couldn't move it, so it was no use to him.

But he did keep a little something for himself.

On the coffee table, on top of the piled up newspapers, was the most badass bayonet Jared had ever seen. And he had watched a lot of war movies. Nothing had ever shown up like this bayonet. The thing was long, sharp as hell, and had a serrated edge like somebody could saw an oak tree in half with the god-damned thing.

Nope, Jared had kept that little gem for himself. Hell, he might even get out his old woodworking tools and make a stand for the blade. It was that awesome.

Reaching out, Jared gave the bayonet's handle a happy pat, and then he took a dollar bill out of his wallet. Rolling it up, he leaned over the mirror, set the improvised straw to the start of the line, closed the unoccupied nostril with a finger, and ran the straw down the length of the line as he snorted it happily.

Exhaling he leaned back against the couch, tilting his head back ever so slightly. He straightened up, dipped a finger in a glass of water and snorted a couple of drops. A heartbeat later he had the pleasant drip going down the back of his throat. With another finger, he swept up a little bit of the coke dust and rubbed it along his gums, giving himself a little freeze.

Yes, that money was well spent. Jared sighed happily.

As the buzz kicked in, Jared looked at the bayonet again.

After a moment, he reached out, grasped it by its handle and picked it up. He looked at it carefully, admiring the way the light glowed in the metal. The grip was a perfect fit. Jared grinned, imagining what it was like to stab somebody with one of—

The lights flickered, and the music cut out.

Still grinning Jared looked around, and then stopped.

In a shadow by the kitchen, he could make out a person, standing there.

Then the person stepped out. It was a man. A tall man wearing a torn and tattered uniform. There was mud caked on his boots, his eyes were sunken in his thin face, his hair bedraggled. His hands clenched and unclenched at his sides.

"Das ist nicht Ihre Bajonett," the man said his voice a deep growl.

"What?" Jared asked, thoroughly confused. Did somebody cut this coke with something?

"*Das ist nicht Ihre Bajonett!*" the man yelled, taking a step forward. "Das ist meins, du Schweinhund. Mein."

The man took another step forward, extending his right hand. "Gib es mir."

"What?" Jared said, trying to stand up and finally succeeding, still holding onto the bayonet. "Dude, I don't know what you're saying, or how in the hell you—"

"*Gib es mir! Jetzt! Schnell!*" the man howled taking another step forward, the extended hand shaking with rage.

And Jared realized he could see through the man.

He could see right through him.

"Oh, hell no," Jared said. He took a nervous step back and stumbled.

The ghost, for that was the only thing it could be, lunged forward and grabbed both of Jared's wrists. The ghost's hands were deathly cold, and Jared let out an involuntary yell. The ghost squeezed, and Jared dropped the bayonet to the floor.

The ghost pushed Jared back onto the couch and stooped down, swiftly picking up the bayonet and letting out a long, relieved sigh as he held it.

Jared could only watch, numbed by coke and beer and fear.

The ghost turned and looked at Jared with pure hate.

"Dieb," the ghost said softly. "Nicht als ein Dieb."

"Dude," Jared said, "I have no idea what you're saying. But hey, take your bayonet and go, okay? No blood, no foul."

"Blut. Ja, das Blut," the ghost said, and a terrible, foul smile played across his face.

The ghost stepped closer, and Jared tried to scramble away. He felt that cold, horrible grip wrap around his throat, and then a sharp, sudden pain in his ribs. Choking he managed to look down, only to see the bloody end of the bayonet protruding from his chest.

"Blut," the ghost whispered in Jared's ear, and he twisted the bayonet.

Chapter 9: Jared and the News

Charles sat in his recliner, a glass of beer on the table beside him and the channel 9 news on in front of him. It was six o'clock in the evening, and he had managed to get quite a bit done in regards to work. He had to double check it, but that could wait until the morning.

The 'Breaking News' banner scrolled across the screen suddenly, and Charles couldn't help but roll his eyes.

Everything was 'Breaking News', even minor fender-benders. Charles chuckled at the thought suddenly. There couldn't be fender-benders anymore. Everything was plastic. Gone were the days of big old six cylinders wrapped in steel.

Still chuckling, Charles turned his attention back to the television.

"Sam Speidel is there at the Nashua Police Station," the anchorwoman said. "Sam, what do you have for us?"

"Well, Karina," Sam said, "what we have is a fairly gruesome murder according to our inside source. The victim's identity hasn't been released yet, pending notification of his next of kin. He was found murdered in his apartment this afternoon at four thirty. His neighbors heard screaming and called the police. When the police arrived, they found the man stabbed to death.

"Our source states there were drugs and money at the scene, so this could have been drug related."

"Sam," Karina said, "is there any concern among the police that this is gang related?"

"Well, Karina," Sam said, "according to Nashua's Mayor, there is no gang problem in Nashua. The police and our source are not speaking about it."

"Is there anything we know about the victim?" Karina asked.

"The only information we have is that the victim was found in an apartment leased to a Jared Capote, age 23. We were also able to discover he had a criminal record for house breaking and fencing stolen goods."

"Sam," Karina said, "is there any information on the weapon used? I know you said he was stabbed, but are we looking at a crime of opportunity here?"

"Our source inside said the weapon used was an antique bayonet, the kind of weapon, our source said, you wouldn't want to use on your worst enemy."

Charles turned the television off and put the remote on the table. He picked up his beer and drank some of it, looking at the blank television. After a moment he put the beer down, stood up and went upstairs to the library. He turned on the light, walked to the desk and sat down.

Mr. Sherman's journal was still there.

Charles opened it and looked at the list of items and the map.

There was a place for a bayonet. A butcher's bayonet from World War One.

Charles flipped through the journal until he found the entry for the weapon.

Obtained Butcher's Bayonet from a small antique store in Wells, Maine, October 13th, 1962. Proprietor of store stated it had come from an evidence auction held by the local police department some years back. The bayonet was used to kill the previous owner, although no one was ever found to have done the killing. The only witness had reported glimpsing a tall stranger in the barn with the deceased prior to the murder.

Even with the gloves on, I could feel the energy surging through the weapon.

Purchased for the sum of $30.00 and the thanks of the proprietor who said he felt ill each time he touched it.

Charles closed the book.

There were, according to the list, twenty-three items missing from the library. Charles knew where one of them was, but that left twenty-two. Could he get them back and put them in the library?

Was it his responsibility?

And how would he track them down? The bayonet was more than likely in the Nashua Police Department's evidence room, so theoretically it was locked up, but what if someone took it out?

Shaking his head, Charles stood up. He had to think about it. He had to think about all of it.

Sighing he walked out of the library, turned out the light and headed back down to his chair and his beer. Maybe a movie to take his mind off of everything.

***

Something slammed into the wall, and Charles sat up in his bed.

The room was dark, no sunlight behind the drawn curtains.

Looking at his clock, Charles saw it was three thirteen in the morning.

Another slam shook the wall and the bed.

And the bed was against the wall his room shared with the library.

A third slam.

Charles stood up and walked barefoot out of his room and into the dimly lit hall to the closed library door. Light was coming out from the edges.

Taking a deep breath, Charles opened the door.

A man, perhaps only five and a half feet tall, stood by the shared wall, holding onto the leather chair, getting ready to ram it against the shelves, which were surprisingly undisturbed.

Charles realized he could see through parts of the man, who was smoking cheerfully.

"Why are you doing that?" Charles asked, not quite sure what to say.

The man stopped and looked over at Charles in surprise. After a moment he said, "You're not Philip."

"No," Charles agreed, "I'm not. I'm Charles. Who are you?"

"Sid," the man said, letting go of the chair and giving Charles an appraising look. "Where's Philip?"

"He's dead," Charles answered.

"Oh. Did I wake you up?"

"Yes."

"Sorry about that. It was the only way to wake Philip up most of the time."

"Why were you trying to wake him up?" Charles asked, desperately trying to figure out if he was dreaming or if he was having a conversation with a ghost.

"To talk," Sid said. He moved the chair back to the desk. "We're all curious as to how the others are going to be brought back."

"Who're you talking about?" Charles asked, confused.

"Us," Sid said, gesturing around the room. "Each item in here, every weapon or flag or whatever, someone is bound to it. And, when we're in this room, we're bound to this room. Don't ask me how or any of that crap. I don't know. Point is, none of us are happy to be in here. But, since we have to be in here, it's not fair the others aren't in here, too. We want to know how you're going to get them back."

"I didn't know I had to," Charles said.

Sid let out a deep and unpleasant laugh.

"Oh, you don't have to," Sid said, grinning maliciously around his cigarette, "but people are going to die. A lot of people. Hell, I got one and I was only out for a few hours."

"You got one?" Charles said, shaking his head, realizing he wasn't dreaming.

"Sure as shit I did. One of the little peckers that stole us out of here. Can't abide a thief," Sid said. "None of us can. That's alright, though. Burned the hell out of his lungs. Cooked him right. Wasn't too happy his girlfriend brought me back to this place. But I can't be too mad, she was good to Philip."

"Philip's nurse brought you back?" Charles asked.

"She did," Sid nodded.

She might know, Charles thought. *She might know where to start looking.*

"So," Sid said, interrupting Charles' thoughts, "got time to talk?"

Charles let out a surprised laugh. "Sure, why the hell not?"

Charles walked over to the chair and sat down as Sid sat down on the table. "Well," Charles said, "what do you want to talk about?"

"Dames and baseball," Sid grinned. "What the hell else is there to talk about?"

***

The conversation with Sid had been surreal to say the least. There'd been no explanation why Sid was visible and present and not any of the others. Charles hadn't exactly pressed the issue either.

Charles sat in his kitchen, the bowl which had contained his oatmeal was empty with his second cup of coffee now in front of him. The hour of nine had struck. Charles stifled a yawn and tried to rub the sleep out of his eyes. He'd only left the library half an hour earlier, and Charles wondered if he was going to be able to sleep at all, or if sleep would ruin him for the rest of the day.

But the question Sid had posed to him ate at his conscience.

Charles knew what the weapons were. He knew, now, what they were capable of. How could he sit back, knowing what they were, and do nothing? Mr. Sherman had left him the means to handle the weapons. Sid, Charles knew, would be more than happy to assist with whatever information he had. More than likely most of the people in the library would.

Charles shook his head at the thought.

If he hadn't seen the news about the murder, and realized the bayonet had come from Mr. Sherman's own collection, then he might not be concerned. Charles could, like Ebenezer Scrooge had with his old partner Marley, attribute his own conversation with Sid to a bad bit of potato or mustard.

Charles couldn't, though. Not that he would have anyway. Charles had always been willing to listen to arguments defending the existence of the supernatural. The early morning discussion on dames and baseball, as Sid had so succinctly put it, had made Charles a firm believer.

Now all Charles had to do was figure out how to get in touch with Mr. Sherman's nurse, and see if he could enlist her aid.

If she would believe him.

Sighing, Charles finished his coffee and put the mug down. Well, he thought, I might as well shower and face the day.

With an inward groan he pushed the chair out from the table, stood up, and cleared the dishes away.

Chapter 10: John and the Bayonet

John Henry took the murder weapon and got it ready to be filed away in the evidence locker.

John had been working as a clerk for the Nashua Police Department for over twenty years, and he could have retired, but he had a gambling habit and needed some sort of income if he was going to play the Indian casinos. And sometimes things came into the evidence room that would never be missed.

Like the bayonet.

From all the talk going around the station, the murder was a closed-room case. Literally for this one.

No sign of forced entry. No one was seen going in or out of the guy's apartment except for himself. All of his convictions were over four years old. Plus, according to the guy's employer, he was a steady worker. Never late. Didn't steal from the job sites. Didn't steal from the construction company he worked for. Worst thing the kid seemed to have done recently was get some coke and have a little party for himself.

Hell, there wasn't even any trace evidence kicking around the apartment. Everything was either the kid's or the kid's ex-girlfriend's. She had said that aside from drinking and shooting pool with a buddy of his named Mike, he hadn't done anything recently.

And Mike was dead too. John had seen that report when Detective O'Malley was proofing it in the break room. Somehow Mike's lungs had caught fire, and the guy had smothered to death. Nobody could figure it out. Technically the medical examiner said it was impossible.

But John had seen the pictures of the lungs.

They had been char-broiled.

Nope, not pretty at all.

John opened up the evidence box that had the bayonet and pulled the weapon out. He wouldn't be able to get much for it, but it was better than nothing. John needed some easy cash for the trip down to Foxwoods on the upcoming weekend.

With that in mind, he got out another evidence box, put in a ream of printer paper, and closed it up. He carefully put a fresh seal around the edges, typed up a new label, forged Detective Samuels' signature—the guy was a prick anyway—and touched everything up nicely. After that, he shredded, cut up, and dispersed the evidence of his own crime.

John took the blood-marked bayonet, still in its original evidence bag, and slipped it into his gym bag. With that done, he took one last look around the evidence locker, nodded to himself once he was sure he hadn't left anything lying around, and made his way upstairs to the time clock.

John waved to a couple of people, punched his number into the clock, and once he received the beep that said he had done it right, he left the building. In a few minutes, he was in his car and turning onto West Hollis Street. It was three thirty in the afternoon, and, if traffic was moving alright, he'd be able to catch Dave out in Milford.

The guy was always happy to buy whatever John brought to him.

And John was always happy to sell.

Chapter 11: Ellen and Charles and Mr. Sherman

It had taken some phone calls, and assurances he wasn't trying to harass the young nurse, but Charles had finally found Ellen's cell phone number. He sent her a simple text. *Hello, I knew Mr. Sherman. Would you have time to stop by his house and speak with me? I live here now. Charles.*

At five in the evening, Ellen had replied.

Yes. What time?

Charles had written back, *Anytime. I'm home all night.*

Ellen had responded with a simple, *Ok,* and that was it.

At seven o'clock on the nose, however, the doorbell had rung.

Charles had gotten out of his chair, turned off the news and hurried to the front door.

When he opened the door, he found an attractive young woman standing on the porch, her eyes bloodshot and a sense of exhaustion around her. She wore a simple gray pullover sweatshirt and a pair of jeans and sneakers. She gave him a tired smile and extended her hand.

"Hi, I'm Ellen," she said.

"Hi, Ellen, I'm Charles. Please," he said, shaking her hand and then stepping aside, "come in."

Ellen stepped in, looking around the house as he closed the door and left it unlocked.

"The place looks different with furniture in it," she said after a moment. She gave him her tired smile again. "It looks nice."

"Thank you," Charles said. "Would you care to come into the dining room?"

"Well," she said, hesitating, "can I ask what this is about? I came over because I liked Mr. Sherman a lot. He was a nice man."

"He was indeed," Charles said. "And he was a very good man. I need to talk to you about something that's going to be unpleasant, and I want to apologize in advance for it."

She looked at him warily, sliding her hands into the pocket of her hoodie, glancing over at the door quickly to make sure it was still unlocked. "What is it?"

"When I came to look at the house," Charles said, "I found an old Zippo lighter on the front porch."

Ellen relaxed slightly. "That was me. I think I accidentally brought it home one day, so I brought it back."

"Now, I do hate asking this," Charles said, swallowing nervously, "but was that the same night your boyfriend died?"

She looked at Charles coldly for a moment, and then her eyes widened slightly, and she nodded.

"Ellen," Charles said softly, "when the real estate agent and I came to the house that day when you brought the lighter back, there were two duffel bags on the floor in here. They were filled with military items from Mr. Sherman's library."

"Oh, Jesus Christ," Ellen said in a low voice. "Oh, Jesus!"

"Do you think he might have tried to steal those items?" Charles asked.

"He wouldn't have done it alone, though," she said angrily. "He would have gotten his friend Jared. They used to break into places when they were in high school. Stupid crap. Oh, God."

"Where's Jared now," Charles said. "Do you know?"

"Jared was killed..." her voice trailed off, and she looked at Charles. "This can't possibly be connected. It can't."

"Have you seen any news on how Jared was killed?" Charles asked, still keeping his tone easy.

She shook her head.

"Channel 9 was reporting he was stabbed. That an inside source with the police said he had been stabbed with a bayonet."

Again Ellen shook her head.

"I know they made it out of the house with quite a bit of stuff," Charles said. "Mr. Sherman kept an exceptionally detailed list of what was in his library. What I need to know, Ellen, is do you know of anyone they would bring the militaria to?"

"How could stealing some stuff cause them to die?" Ellen snapped. "Seriously. What, is this shit cursed or something?"

"In a way it is, Ellen," a voice said, and both Charles and Ellen screamed.

Charles, who had been standing with his back to the stairs, twisted around in time to see the thinnest outline of a shape floating slowly down towards them.

"Charles," the voice said, emanating from the center of the shape, "it has been a terribly long time."

Charles took several steps back until he almost bumped into Ellen.

The shape stopped at the bottom of the stairs, flickered into a solid form that brought a combined gasp from both Charles and

Ellen.

For the briefest of moments, Mr. Philip Sherman was standing before them. While he was clearly defined, he was not solid. Charles could see through the old man and the plain black three-piece suit he was wearing. The man looked far older than Charles remembered, and Charles was sure he was looking at Mr. Sherman the way he had been before his death.

"Come up to the library," Mr. Sherman said, fading away. "Come up to the library, and I will tell you what you need to know."

Chapter 12: In the Library with Philip Sherman

Charles Gottesman knew exactly what sort of things were in the library, and they scared him to death.

Ellen Kay, who had yet to be burdened with the information, sat in the library's sole chair. She'd been trembling ever since Mr. Sherman appeared from beyond the grave to beckon both her and Charles up to the library.

Charles stood behind the chair, gripping the top tightly and trying to stay focused on the faint mist standing in front of the door. That mist seemed to be Mr. Sherman, but around the room Charles could hear faint shuffling noises as if a great many sleepers had been awakened.

He was afraid that was exactly what had occurred.

"I'm glad you both are here," Mr. Sherman said, his voice faint. "I could never have hoped, Charles, that you would buy my home. I always believed, ever since you first came into the house, that you would be capable of guarding the items within.

"And you, Ellen, your kindness to me was more appreciated than you could ever know. I am terribly sorry for your loss. I tried desperately to chase your young man and his friend out of the house, to keep these cursed items within these walls, but I failed."

"What are you talking about?" Ellen asked softly, shaking her head. "Why is this even happening?"

"The answers to both of your questions," Mr. Sherman replied, "are one and the same. As Charles here has learned, the militaria which you see on the shelves around you is cursed, haunted. Each item here is deadly, and sometimes even wicked. Some of them are truly horrific. I am afraid the worst of them are out and abroad in society. I must ask you both to retrieve them."

"What do you mean?" Ellen asked. She looked up at Charles. "What does he mean?"

"He means," Charles answered, "we should figure out what happened to the rest of the militaria that's missing and decide how we're going to get it back."

The light went out in the room, and people laughed.

Charles knew he hadn't laughed, and he was positive Ellen hadn't either.

"Let us all out," a voice hissed close to Charles' ear. "Let us out. The world moved along well enough when we were free to roam."

"Do you know what's waiting for you, pretty girl?" a second voice asked. "Terrible things you can't even imagine. Oh, the pleasures some of us took in life, the mere mention of them would curdle milk."

The voices laughed again, and then Charles heard Sid's voice. "Get 'em back. Don't get 'em back. Whatever you decide better be the same. A few of us like things done fair and square, Charles. All of us locked up or all of us free. Doubt you'll get much peace when there's a single one of our brothers out and about. Enjoying the sights, as it were."

The light flickered and then came back on.

Ellen stifled a gasp, and Charles managed to hold back his own exclamation of surprise.

For a moment there were perhaps a dozen, maybe even more, ghosts visible in the room. All men. All different ages and races. All in military uniforms and looking hungrily at Charles and Ellen.

"Make sure it's fair," a voice said behind them, and the light flickered out again.

Chapter 13: Dave Ganz and the Militaria

Dave watched the news at eleven and listened to the replay of an early report about a murder over in Nashua. Some guy got stabbed to death with a bayonet.

Damned kids, Dave thought to himself, lighting a cigarette. *They'll kill each other with anything. For any reason.*

He wasn't surprised, though. Nashua had been getting worse for the past decade, and he was happy he'd moved out right before the end of the nineties. Of course, getting divorced and his bitch wife forcing him to sell the house had also helped with that, but he tried not to think too much about Diane. Thankfully she had died of breast cancer, and the alimony payments had finally stopped.

That's how Dave knew there was a God and that he didn't like women all that much. Or at least he didn't like bitches.

Dave chuckled to himself, popped a Hungry Man into the microwave and started it. He popped the tab on a Natty Ice, grimaced at the first swallow, but relaxed after that. It was always the first taste that was the worst. Natties were never enjoyable, but they at least became tolerable.

Dave walked over to the dining table, an old Christmas-themed tablecloth draped over it to protect the surprisingly unmarred cherry finish underneath, and looked at the militaria he'd scored. He had two good-sized duffel bags some kid named Jared had sold him, and the shit was undoubtedly hot. Even so, Dave could move it out to the stall at the flea market and hopefully sell most of it before the day was over.

Military shit always moved. Especially the Nazi stuff, and there were a couple of obviously original Nazi pieces in the bags.

Then there was the bayonet John had brought him.

Dave chuckled, shaking his head. The damned thing was still in an evidence bag and had blood dried on the steel.

John had no shame. Not that Dave did either, but seriously, the balls to lift that piece right out of the Nashua Police station.

The bayonet would not be going into the stall. That piece Dave would be selling to a private, well to do buyer who liked two things, murder weapons and to remain unknown to the rest of the world when it came to collecting.

Dave understood both, and he was well paid to find the first and even better paid to make sure the second remained a hard fact.

With that in mind, Dave took his Natty Ice with him to a heating grate in the floor. Grunting, he sat down and dragged a screwdriver and a box of latex gloves over to him. He set the drink on the floor by the grate and put on a pair of the gloves. Next he used the screwdriver to remove the screws from the grate, and then to pry the grate itself up.

Dave didn't need to look down to see the pair of snap traps baited with peanut butter he'd placed in that part of the heating system. But those were eye candy for anybody who was looking for anything in the apartment.

Keeping his hand above the traps, Dave slid his hand in and carefully took down a disposable cell phone he had velcroed up there. Easing his hand out, Dave sat back with the phone and powered it up. There was only one phone number programmed into it, the number of another disposable cell phone.

Dave hit speed dial and then speakerphone.

The phone rang perhaps a dozen times before it was answered.

"Hello, Dave."

"Hey, Elmer."

"What do you have?"

"See the news about the bayonet murder?" Dave asked.

"Yes."

"I have the bayonet."

Dave could have sworn he heard Elmer's breath pick up. "Are you serious, Dave?"

"Of course I am. You know I don't mess around."

"Of course, of course. I'm just very excited. You usually don't get your hands on such a piece so...so quickly. Could you bring it by tonight?"

"I've already got a beer in me," Dave answered. "I could do first thing tomorrow morning."

"Six?" Elmer asked.

Dave stifled a groan, thought of the money and said, "Yeah. Sure. Six is no problem."

"Very, very good, Dave," Elmer said, sounding giddy. "You will not be disappointed in your payment. I promise you that."

"I know. You never disappoint," Dave said. "See you then."

Dave hung up the phone, powered it down and returned it to its place. When he was all done putting everything back in order, he finished his beer and grunted as he got back to his feet. The microwave chirped to let him know his meal was done, and he finished his beer before tossing the can in the trash and getting the meal out of the microwave.

Carrying the black plastic tray the meal was in by its edges, Dave brought it over to the table, dropped it down on last month's copy of Maxim, and sat down in his only chair.

"Ah shit," he grumbled to himself. With a grunt he stood up, went to the already open silverware drawer and fished a relatively clean fork out. He paused long enough to get another Nattie from the fridge and returned to the table. Dave ate quickly, ignoring how hot the food was by washing each bite down with some beer.

In under eight minutes—he had eating a Hungry Man down to a science—he finished his meal and his second beer. With his dinner done, Dave pushed the tray off to one side and reached over the table to drag one of the duffel bags closer. It was time for a closer look at what he'd paid for.

Dave took each piece out of the duffel bag carefully, and soon he had a pretty impressive group in front of him. There were items Dave could identify and others he would have to go online and look up to name before he could hunt down pricing information.

One piece jumped out at him, though. It was a dull khaki canvas case with a frayed shoulder strap. The thing looked ancient, and it had a unit insignia painted on the front, an Indian head profiled in a star. The whole package was cool.

Dave pulled the case closer to him and made sure not to tear the old canvas as he undid the brass snaps. Lifting the flap, he looked inside and grinned. There was an old gas mask. Probably World War One. And it looked like all of it was there. The mask, the respirator. The whole deal.

A soft smell of onions, with a hint of garlic, seemed to drift out of the case.

A dark shape flitted by, barely visible in Dave's peripheral vision.

He snapped his head up and looked around.

Nothing.

Not a thing.

Not even a bat, like he'd had last week.

Dave coughed, his lungs hurting slightly.

Heartburn, he thought, coughing again. *Must be heartburn. Shouldn't wolf down those damned TV dinners.* He coughed again, and his eyes watered. Something cold touched his neck, and he felt the hairs stand on end.

Dave twisted around in his chair, but again he couldn't see anything.

Grumbling, he pushed the chair away from the table, coughed, and then he yawned.

He was exhausted. He needed to get some sleep, so he could deliver the bayonet to the crazy man in the morning.

Still coughing, Dave made his way towards his bedroom, a long shadow flickering along the wall behind him where no shadow should have been.

Chapter 14: Charles and the Colonist

The sound of a dog barking made Charles pause as he pulled his sweater on.

The barking wasn't coming from outside of the house, but rather from the inside.

Specifically, it sounded as though the barking was coming from the library, which wouldn't surprise Charles at all.

He finished putting his sweater on, and then he slipped his feet into his shoes, tying each lace carefully. He tried to ignore the barking, but he couldn't.

Not only was the barking continuing, but it was getting louder as well.

Charles walked out of his bedroom, closed the door and walked by the library door which shuddered as something slammed into it. On the other side, something was snarling and growling through the wood.

Charles shook his head and walked down the stairs. He was going to eat breakfast before he dealt with anything in the library.

The barking dog, however, didn't seem to like Charles ignoring him. It became frenzied, howling with rage as it seemed to attack the door.

Charles ignored the headache that was starting behind his eyes.

Instead of worrying about the dog, or about anything in the library, Charles made himself a large pot of coffee. He leaned against the counter, enjoying the smell of the coffee brewing and focusing on the sound of the percolator instead of the rabid dog in the library. After a minute of listening to both percolator and rabid dog, Charles sighed and straightened up. He pulled a loaf of bread out of the breadbox and plugged in the toaster.

A few minutes later, he was sitting at the table, eating his plain breakfast and wondering how much aspirin he was going to have to take to beat down the headache which had successfully arrived.

Four. Four should do the trick. But he had to get that dog to shut up first.

And the thought of that was terrifying to him.

Charles didn't know if anything could, or would, harm him in the library, and he wasn't keen on finding out. He supposed, however, he would have to eventually.

So why not now?

Nodding to himself, Charles stood up, finished the last of his coffee and made his way out of the kitchen, through the hallway, and up the stairs to the library. He didn't pause before opening the door, instead turning the doorknob and striding in purposefully as he clicked on the light.

Then he came to a staggering halt.

A great dane stood in the far right corner of the room, its hackles raised as a low growl rose from its long throat and slipped out between bare teeth. Around its thick neck, a broad and spiked leather collar was buckled.

Charles had no doubt about whether or not the dog could hurt him, regardless of whether it was a ghost or real.

Those teeth were real, and that dog was angry.

Charles stood straight, squared his shoulders and said in a voice far calmer than he felt, "Whose dog is this?"

The dog snarled. Charles ignored it.

"Tell me whose dog this is, or I swear to Christ, I will lock this rabid son of a bitch away," Charles snapped.

A shape stepped out of the shadows.

The man was tall. Terribly tall, perhaps six and a half feet. He was, not surprisingly, deathly pale. The man wore the clothes Charles had seen on illustrations of the early pilgrims, America's first colonists.

All his grade school memories of Puritans were shattered as he looked at the man. This was no happy Englishman at the first Thanksgiving. This Englishman, this Puritan, was strong and severe, his face hatchet-like beneath his broad-brimmed buckled hat. He wore at his side a long sword, and he carried a flintlock pistol in each hand.

This Puritan was ready for war.

"The hound is mine," the Puritan said, his English accent strong. "Thou shalt not touch him."

"I'll send him to Hell if I choose," Charles responded. "This is my house. I won't have you causing trouble while I'm here."

"I can certainly remove thee if thou wish it," the Puritan grinned.

"Funny guy," Charles said. "Muzzle the dog and leave me be for a while."

The dog vanished, and for the first time Charles saw the old leather dog collar with gleaming spikes resting on a lower shelf.

"We will speak soon," the Puritan said, and he vanished as well.

"Great," Charles sighed to himself. "I can't wait."

Turning around, he turned off the light and closed the door behind him, ignoring the snickering he heard from the dark shadows.

Chapter 15: Ellen and Her Thoughts

Ellen sat in her Volkswagen Bug, waiting for the heater to finish defrosting the windshield. She could have gotten out and scraped the windshield clean in less time, but she was having a hell of a week so far, and minutes of relative sanity were few and far between.

She had been up half the night trying to figure out if she had experienced what she thought she had at Mr. Sherman's, well, Charles's house. She could only come to the conclusion that she had.

Ellen had seen a ghost.

She had spoken with a ghost, the ghost of Mr. Sherman.

And Mike was dead.

Mike was dead because he had stolen some stupid lighter from Mr. Sherman's library, which was a little shop of horrors when you sat right down and thought about it. Not only was Mike dead, but Jared was dead too.

Mike had been killed by a lighter.

A Zippo lighter, of all things. And Jared had been killed with a bayonet he had kept.

Mr. Sherman wanted her to help Charles find out where Mike and Jared would have tried to sell the stolen stuff.

Ellen didn't want to, though. She didn't want to do anything. She didn't want to eat. She didn't want to sleep. She didn't want to work. And she didn't want to bury Mike.

She had never, ever wanted to bury Mike.

And with the car's heater blasting away at the windshield, Ellen put her face in her hands and cried again.

Chapter 16: Dave, Elmer, and the Bayonet

Dave felt like his skin was burning as he got out of his car, barely biting back a scream. Something was wrong with him, and as soon as he got his money for the bayonet he was going straight to the Southern New Hampshire Hospital in Nashua.

But he wanted his money first.

With his eyes watering and each step an agony, Dave climbed the stairs to Elmer's huge mansion in Hollis and rang the bell. In his hand, Dave held a large leather briefcase which contained the bayonet, and which in turn would be used to transport his money from Elmer's house.

Elmer paid a lot of money. He had said Dave wouldn't be disappointed.

Dave was sure he wouldn't be, but he also wanted to get looked at by a doctor.

He had woken up feeling terrible. His eyes had hurt, his armpits, his crotch. Everything it seemed. And this was supposed to be a good weekend for the flea market, too. Lots of people coming up into Milford prior to Thanksgiving.

So even though he'd felt like absolute garbage, Dave had run over to the flea market and set up the militaria. He'd also left a message for Neal asking him to price the stuff and keep an eye on it for him until he could get back from the hospital.

If he could get back from the hospital.

Sweating and panting, Dave pressed the doorbell again.

Christ, where the hell was he? That dumbass better not be asleep.

Before he could follow up with anything creative, Dave took a nervous step back as the door suddenly swung in.

Elmer was standing in front of him, grinning.

The young, wealthy man wore pajamas, slippers and a robe that probably cost more than Dave's car.

The grin dropped off of Elmer's face when he looked at Dave, though. "Dave, you don't look too hot. You okay?"

"Little sick," Dave explained. "Not contagious, though."

"I appreciate that tidbit of info," Elmer said, "but you could have called and told me you were sick."

Dave gave a weak smile. "Said I would bring it."

"And you did," Elmer said, nodding to the briefcase. "Come

on in. Fiona and the boys are at a swim meet. They won't be home for a while yet. You want anything to eat or drink?"

Dave shook his head. The mere thought of food made his stomach churn.

"You want your money," Elmer said.

Dave nodded.

"And I think you'll be wanting to get to a hospital."

Again Dave nodded.

"Fair enough. Hell," Elmer said as he walked over to a mahogany secretary and opened a drawer, "I'll call you an ambulance if you like. I'll tell Fiona you're a stranger who needed help."

"No," Dave said, shaking his head. "It's not that big of a deal. I can drive myself."

"If you say so," Elmer said. He reached into the drawer and took out a small, letter sized envelope that was fairly thick. As he closed the drawer, Dave brought the briefcase to a hall table, set it down and opened it. Dave took the bayonet out of the briefcase and exchanged it for the envelope.

Dave didn't look inside the envelope. He was never, ever discourteous with someone like Elmer. Dave could count it later. In the hospital maybe. That would help him feel better.

He put the envelope into the briefcase and closed it.

Elmer stood, utterly fascinated with the bayonet, carefully turning it over in his hands, looking at the steel through the plastic of the evidence bag.

"I have the perfect place for this," Elmer said in a soft voice a moment later. Then Elmer looked up and smiled happily at Dave. "Thank you very much, Dave. I can't tell you how thrilled I am to have gotten this piece."

Dave managed a weak smile. "You're welcome, Elmer. Now, I hate to be rude, but I need to get to a doctor or something."

"Of course, of course," Elmer said, hurrying past Dave to open the large door. "Please, enjoy your money, and feel better."

"I will," Dave said, and he stumbled down the stairs towards his car wondering if perhaps he should have taken Elmer up on the ambulance offer.

Chapter 17: Ellen at the Hospital

Ellen was in the emergency room of Southern New Hampshire Hospital, talking with Betty about the upcoming funeral and standing in the ambulance bay when the alarm came over the comm.

"We have an ambulance inbound from Amherst Street," the dispatcher said, the woman's voice echoing off of the concrete walls. "Single vehicle MVA, possible medical emergency, patient is stable. ETA five minutes."

Ellen and Betty stepped off to one side, making sure everything was cleared for the EMTs and whoever was going to be receiving the patient. The two women stood silently as the seconds ticked past. The conversation had been lost.

"All nonessential personnel clear the ER," a voice said over the speakers suddenly. "All nonessential personnel clear the ER. Inbound patient from single vehicle MVA is a code gray. I say again, inbound patient from single vehicle MVA is a code gray."

Betty's face went pale.

"What?" Ellen asked. She had never worked for Southern. She had no idea what their codes were. "Betty, what is it?"

"Code gray," Betty said, shaking her head. "Code gray is infectious disease."

"How infectious?"

Betty looked at Ellen, some of the color coming back into her face. "Ebola infectious."

"Jesus."

"Yeah."

"I'll grab a suit," Ellen said, turning away.

"Are you sure?" Betty asked, surprised.

"I'm one of the few that went through the CCD's infectious diseases course run by Saint Joseph's Hospital," Ellen said. "So yeah, I'm sure."

"Follow me," Betty said. "I'll introduce you to Priscilla. She's the nurse in charge today. I'm pretty sure she'll take all the help she can get."

Ellen followed Betty as she hurried back into the ER. The ER was organized chaos. Nonessential personnel were disappearing around corners while a trio of nurses and a doctor were being helped into awkward but necessary biohazard suits. An older woman, who looked like she could be anywhere between fifty and seventy, stood in a pair of black scrubs overseeing everything and calling out corrections as necessary.

"Priscilla," Betty said.

The woman in black turned and looked at Betty.

"Betty," Priscilla said, "you're not qualified to be in here. You could literally catch your death."

Betty grinned. "I know. This is my friend Ellen Kay. She worked at St. Joe's for a while, and she did their CDC course."

Priscilla raised an eyebrow. "Who was your teacher in the ER overall?"

"Marjorie Lozeau," Ellen answered.

Priscilla laughed. "You must have been good if you survived Marjorie. I started nursing at St. Joe's too, and Marjorie was my instructor. We've got a couple of extra suits in exam room six. Betty, help her get ready and then make sure we've got this part of the ER taped off."

Priscilla extended her hand, and Ellen shook it. "Welcome, Ellen. We all appreciate your help."

Ellen nodded and followed Betty once more.

In a few moments, Ellen found herself suited up and sweating, waiting with the other nurses and the doctor. Introductions had gone around, and Ellen had promptly put the names in the back of her mind. Ellen glanced behind her. Layers of heavy plastic sheeting had been taped up. Someone announced that the CDC was prepping a team for flight.

Then the ambulance arrived.

The doors on the back of the ambulance opened as soon as it stopped, and the two EMTs, looking remarkably calm, wheeled out the gurney. A middle-aged man lay naked on it. He was covered in second and third-degree burns and breathing through a respirator. The EMTs had already started IVs, and the patient was unconscious.

"Was the car burning?" the doctor asked as the EMTs wheeled the man into a room.

"Nope," one of the EMTs answered. "Car wasn't even that wrecked. Only reason it was called in was because a guy saw the vic's car glide into a stone wall. The witness said he could hear the vic screaming in pain. The burns weren't this bad when we got him into the bus."

The other EMT nodded his agreement before saying, "Donnie had to cut the vic's clothes off en route."

Both of the EMTs stepped back and one of the nurses, Ellen thought her name was Doreen, said, "Go into four, we've got a place for you to sit and relax until we figure this out."

"Sounds good," Donnie said, and the two EMTs got out of the way.

Ellen fell into a rhythm with the team, and soon they had the patient connected to and ready for whatever treatment was necessary. The team was beginning to relax when the patient sat up, screaming.

Which shouldn't have been possible.

The man had so much morphine in him he should have been out for hours.

"I'm blind!" the man screamed. "I'm blind!"

Ellen could see that the man's corneas looked burnt.

Chapter 18: Charles and the List

Charles had finished his writing for the morning and was sitting at his dining table. In front of him he had a legal pad, a pen in hand, and Mr. Sherman's notebook which contained the list of cursed and haunted items. The descriptions were concise and helpful, and Charles made sure he had his own list of items which were no longer within the library.

For a few, foolish moments, he had contemplated doing the necessary research in the library, but a single glance at the great dane's spiked collar had cured him of that idea.

Charles felt certain the dead within the library would be exceptionally pleased with themselves if they were able to kill him.

The thought was less than comforting.

With a sigh, Charles pushed the memory of the great dane, the pilgrim, and Sid far from his mind and focused on the items before him. He looked at the list and then drew an underline beneath the 'bayonet'. The bayonet was still out in the world, as evidenced by the murder its owner had committed. But the bayonet was in the hands of the police. Retrieving it might be difficult, although not impossible. Charles had known some bad men when he was younger, and he knew there were ways around everything.

Thus the underlining.

But there were so many things missing. Some of them were small, like the Nazi Party tie-pin. Others were large—a full Japanese "meatball" flag. There was a sailor's folding knife and a First World War gas mask. A bridle for a Civil War cavalry man's horse. The belt buckle of a British Grenadier from the Revolution. And at least a dozen more.

Charles could only hope Ellen would find out who Mike and Jared would have brought the items to—and all the items could be recovered.

What if some of the things were bought and then put away? What if they weren't handled enough to trigger the ghost? What if the damned things sat dormant for years, waiting for the right moment?

Charles sat back in the chair and looked at his cell phone.

He had given Ellen his number and asked her to text or call

as soon as she had found out anything. He knew she would. Or rather he trusted she would. He didn't know her.

Charles closed his eyes, put his pen down and rubbed at his temples, trying to ignore the ache in his neck. He needed to stay focused and concentrate on the task at hand. And that first task was finding out how to get the bayonet back.

Opening his eyes, Charles picked up his cell phone and dialed Lee Parker's from memory.

The phone rang for nearly a minute, and Charles was thinking maybe Lee was back in prison when the man answered.

"Hello?" Lee asked, sounding like he was smoking more than three packs of Camels a day now.

"Lee," Charles said, "it's Charlie."

"Charlie?"

Charles sighed. "Charles Gottesman."

"Gottesman?" Lee paused. "God's Man? Is this the damned Reverend?!"

Charles smiled in spite of himself. "Yeah, Lee, it's the Reverend."

"Hey, you old bastard!" Lee laughed and Charles could hear him light up a cigarette. "I'd heard you went straight."

"That was about ten years ago, Lee," Charles said.

"Well, hell, Rev," Lee said, "I got out a couple of months ago."

"Damn," Charles said, sitting up straight. "You did the whole thing?"

"All ten," Lee replied. "Anyway, what's up? What do you need?"

"I need to find out if something can be gotten out of evidence?"

Lee laughed. "Shit, Rev, you haven't changed at all."

"That's not true," Charles answered.

"Oh no?"

"Nope," Charles said, grinning, "I don't have cops parked outside my apartment anymore."

Lee let out a laugh that caused Charles to hold the phone away from his ear for a moment. When he brought it back, Lee was saying, "So you need to get something out of evidence?"

"Yeah."

"What station?"

"Nashua."

Lee exhaled loudly. "You might be in luck."

"How's that?"

"Depending on what it is, and what you're willing to pay, the clerk in the evidence room, this guy named John, he's got a serious gambling habit."

"Shit."

"Yup," Lee said. "Guy can't even show his face in Boston anymore. Portuguese have run him out, and the Irish won't let him step into Southie. Italians have already said they'll take his kneecaps if he so much as switches cabs in the North End."

"What'd he do?"

"Ran out on the vig with the numbers," Lee answered. "Paid it back later, you know, but his Boston visitor's pass has been permanently revoked."

"So," Charles said, "guy's always looking for cash?"

"Exactly."

"You want to reach out to him for me?"

"Sure," Lee answered. "Not a problem at all. You want me to broker or just make the connection?"

"Just the connection," Charles said. "Where are you drinking now?"

"Polish American Club on School Street," Lee said.

"Okay," Charles said. "I'll call and put something on the books for you."

"You don't have to."

"I know," Charles replied. "Listen, you've got my number on your cell now. Give me a holler when we can make the connection. And don't be a stranger. We can sit down in the Club and have a couple of drinks soon."

"I like that idea," Lee said. "Give me a day or two, Rev, and you'll have a new friend."

"Thanks, Lee," Charles said, and ended the call.

He put the cell on the table and wondered when Ellen was going to call.

Chapter 19: Elmer Hoyt and the Bayonet

Fiona and the boys were still at the swim meet. In fact, they'd be at the swim meet until Sunday night, since the meet was in Burlington, Vermont.

Which was fine with Elmer. He loved his family dearly, but he hated having to lock the room to his museum all of the time. Or, as Fiona called it, his museum of Hate.

Elmer grinned at the thought.

Per usual, Fiona was on the mark.

Holding the bayonet in his hand, Elmer walked down the long hallway to the basement stairs, and then he traveled down them and into the finished basement. At the far end of the basement was the door which served as the barrier and entrance to his museum. There was a palm scanner to the right of the door, and he put his palm on it. The lock clicked softly, and the entire door moved back an inch before sliding to the right, into the wall.

A large room was revealed, all of the lights coming softly to light, glowing brighter until they reached the appropriate level. All of Elmer's many prizes were protected in museum cases, each one sealed and in a controlled atmosphere. Each item bore a specific label as well, detailing exactly what it was used for, when it was used, how it was used, upon whom it was used, and—perhaps most importantly—who had used it.

In a decade, Elmer had managed to gather nearly a thousand murder weapons and he had plenty of room to grow as well.

These weren't reproductions. Oh no. That wouldn't work at all. These were the real deal, carefully cultivated. He had half a dozen disposable cell phones with people who were willing to find and sell anything.

Elmer made his way to the back and turned left into another aisle. At the center of a shelving system, there was an unoccupied space. He opened the glass door, put the bayonet in its evidence bag down upon the black velvet and closed the door. Elmer pressed the small button sealing the door and turned away.

A chill ran along his spine as he wandered through his museum, a pleasant thrill of fear at the gathered items. A brown extension cord used to garrote a young man, an empty bottle of bleach that had been used to make a chemical weapon to kill a homeless woman squatting in a shed.

Elmer smiled.

Yes, he enjoyed the museum and the way it made him feel.

He would have plaques made up for the bayonet, once he had all of the correct information on the murder. He would be back later, though, to get a better look at the bayonet and to get it out of its evidence bag.

Whistling happily, Elmer walked out of the museum and closed the door behind him.

Chapter 20: Ellen and the CDC Report

Ellen and the rest of the team sat outside the sealed off area in a room of their own. The rest of the ER continued on with its normal, busy weekend schedule of repairing the damage of fights and car accidents. Ellen and the team had worked for hours stabilizing the man and trying to keep him comfortable. He couldn't be moved to the burn unit until he was cleared, and the CDC was in the room with him, running tests and trying to find out what was wrong.

Her thoughts were interrupted by a knock on the door.

"Come in," the doctor said.

The door opened, and one of the CDC doctors came into the room, smiling at everyone. Ellen instantly relaxed.

"Good news for you guys," the CDC doctor said. "This is not an infectious disease."

"Thank God," one of the nurses murmured.

"Indeed," the CDC doctor said.

"What is it then?" Ellen asked.

The doctor looked at her, and the smile faded away. "Those are chemical burns. In fact, I'd go so far as to say he was in a chemical attack."

"How's that possible?" Doreen asked.

"That I don't know," the CDC doctor said, "but if he makes it through, I plan on asking him. Right now he has a very, very slim chance of surviving. If he does, he will need extensive burn treatments and he'll be permanently blind."

"Are you sure it's from a chemical attack?" the ER doctor asked.

The CDC doctor nodded. "I did a lot of work with Doctors Without Borders when I was younger. Some African warlords had managed to get their hands on mustard gas and the patient in there has the same exact wounds as someone who was exposed to a heavy dose of it. The weapons were from right around World War One. But even though they were old, they weren't any less effective."

"But how did this man get exposed to it?" someone asked. "I mean, he was driving, right?"

"Yes," the CDC doctor said. "We've got the car quarantined, and the police are getting a search warrant for the victim's house.

We need to see if anything is in there and if anyone else might have been exposed to it as well."

"Was he a chemist or something?" Doreen asked. "Could he have accidentally set something off?"

"No," the CDC doctor responded. "He was a pawnbroker. Evidently the police know of him. He's been reported as knowingly buying stolen goods, but the police haven't been able to make anything stick. We're concerned he may have gotten more than he bargained for with something and that it might affect others."

Ellen's heart had skipped a beat when the doctor had said 'pawnbroker,' and she asked, "Was he here in Nashua?"

"His shop?" the CDC doctor asked, and Ellen nodded. "No. He lived in and operated a shop out of Milford."

Milford.

Mike used to talk about a man he knew out in Milford, a pawnbroker he used to bring electronics to when he would steal merchandise back in high school.

The patient must have been contacted by Jared, and Jared must have sold the guy everything. Everything except the bayonet. The bayonet had finished Jared off. But the rest of it, the rest of it might be at the patient's house.

At least one thing was. Whatever had been used to hold the mustard gas, she knew. And whatever it was might well end up killing the man.

"So," the CDC doctor was saying, "basically, you're all clear to go. Make sure you stop by and see my team members. They're going to do a basic wipe. I want to be absolutely positive there was no residue on the victim while you were handling him."

Ellen stood up with the others and followed them out of the room to where a member of the CDC team stood with reactive wipes. Ellen stood in line patiently, had her hands and her neck swiped, was pleased to see there was no reaction, and then made her way out into the rest of the ER.

Priscilla was at the center command corral with Betty, and the two women smiled at her.

"How are you holding up?" Betty asked.

"Tired," Ellen answered. "Really, really tired."

"I'm not surprised," Priscilla said. "Any big event wears you down. You're welcome to crash in a room for a while if you want.

I'm hoping it won't be too busy."

"Thanks," Ellen smiled wearily. "If I can grab a quick shower that would be perfect."

"Come on," Betty said, "I'll bring you to a room. Let me grab your stuff for you."

Betty left, and Priscilla was called away, leaving Ellen alone for a minute at the corral. The ER went on about its business, and she listened to the comforting, if hectic, sounds around her. Part of her missed the fast pace of the ER environment, and she wondered if it might be good to get hired as an ER nurse somewhere to take her mind off of Mike for a while.

Betty came back with a plastic drawstring bag that contained everything Ellen had worn into the ER. Ellen took the bag from her friend and then followed her out into a back room, one with only a gurney and a small bathroom with a shower. There were linens on the gurney, as well as a pillow.

"Go ahead and crash here for a while, Ellen," Betty said, flipping the light on for her. "I've got about three more hours left in my shift. Do you want me to wake you up when I'm done?"

"Please," Ellen said.

"Okay."

Betty gave Ellen a small wave, and Ellen returned it as Betty closed the door behind her.

Sighing Ellen dropped her bag on the gurney and opened it. She took out her cell, fought the urge to see if there were any texts from Mike, and sent a quick text to Charles.

I think I know who the pawnbroker is. Ran a shop out of Milford.

Within a minute, she had a response.

Great. Will check on it now. You okay?

She wrote back and added, *Tired. Will talk later.*

Ellen put her phone on 'silent' and got ready for her shower.

Chapter 21: Charles on the Milford Oval

Charles sat in a hard, uncomfortable chair inside a small coffee shop on the Milford Oval. He was able to look out the front window at the pawnshop as he drank a cup of strong black coffee.

Several police officers stood outside the pawnshop while a few plain-clothes officers walked back and forth from the shop to a mobile crime scene truck. Around the oval, people had stopped and were watching the events with the same morbid curiosity as witnesses to accidents.

The longer the police stayed, the busier the coffee shop became.

And the louder the customers talked.

"Any idea what's going on?" someone asked.

"Nope," answered a second.

"I do," said a third. "Mulvey said that the old pawnbroker crashed his car out in Hollis. Depot Road maybe?"

"So what are they looking for?" a fourth voice asked. "A still? They think that old bastard was making his own shine or something?"

Laughter answered the question.

"No," said another voice. "He's got burns on him. Heard the EMTs talking when they were gassing up over at the Mobil station. They're trying to figure out what burned him."

"Wasn't his car?" the second voice asked.

"Naw," answered the gas station voice. "They think he was exposed to something."

"Coulda been anything," the first voice said. "Guy buys anything you bring in there, or just about."

"They checked his stall out at the flea market yet?" someone asked.

"Why would they?" replied another. "Last time he put anything new in was about a week ago, and that was a bunch of toys from Star Wars."

The conversation continued on, but Charles was focused.

He'd seen a sign for an indoor flea market on the way up Amherst Street, right when he came over the town line between Hollis and Milford. It had to be the one the people were talking about. He needed to see. Charles twisted in his seat, caught the eye of his less than enthusiastic waitress and motioned for the check.

As she was bringing it over to him, Charles caught another bit of information.

"Well," someone said, "they wouldn't be able to check the flea market today anyway. Old Grayson's sister passed up in Concord, and he's shut the place down for the rest of the week. Doubt they'd be able to get a warrant for Grayson's easy anyway. Not with the judges all being allowed to hunt on his land, even when it ain't the season."

There were grumbles of agreement, and Charles felt his hopes sink as he took the check. He fished a ten-dollar bill out of his wallet, as well as a five, and left the smaller bill for the tip. With the check in hand, he walked up to the register and waited to pay, wondering what he might be able to do about the pawnbroker's shop, his stall in the flea market, and hell, there had to be a house somewhere.

Soon Charles had his change in hand and was walking along the sidewalk to his car, trying to think of how to see what the pawnbroker had.

The twenty-minute ride from the Milford Oval to his house on Sheridan Street didn't give Charles any other ideas, but when he unlocked his door and stepped inside he realized instantly something was wrong.

The house wasn't right.

He closed the door behind him and then stood perfectly still in the hallway. Charles tilted his head to one side and listened. After a moment, he could hear the hum of the refrigerator in the kitchen, the hiss of the heaters. But that wasn't it. There was still something else.

He looked into the den and saw books which had been stacked on the coffee table standing on end instead. A glance into the dining room showed all of the curtains to have been drawn. From the kitchen, the overhead light cast its glow onto the hardwood floor of the hallway.

Slowly, ever so slowly, Charles looked up the stairs, and he saw the library door standing wide open.

And he knew that to be wrong.

Charles had closed the library before leaving the house. Hell. He made sure the library door was closed all of the time.

Which means something in the house had opened it. And if

something had opened it, then somehow something had managed to get out and wander around the house.

And there was no way in hell Charles was going to be able to live with that. It was bad enough having the damned things in the library, but he couldn't have them rambling about the house.

The place wasn't theirs, and they sure as hell weren't striking him as a particularly pleasant group of individuals to have around.

Charles was going to have to go upstairs and close the door, and he was going to have to get some sort of a lock to—

"Are you coming up, Charles?" a voice asked.

Charles looked up and saw a woman standing in the doorway of the library. She was a middle-aged woman, on the plump side, and she wore a nurse's uniform. Her face was pretty, and the nurse's hat was cocked jauntily to one side. She looked like she had stepped out of a World War Two movie.

"Come on up, Charles," she said, and he realized her voice was husky. Sultry and seductive all in one desperate breath.

Charles took an involuntary step forward, and the smile she gave him sent a shiver of pleasure down his spine. He took a second step, and then a third. The sheer sensuality in the woman's smile seemed to increase a thousandfold with every step. Soon Charles found himself at the top of the stairs, holding onto the banister and breathing heavily, looking at the woman.

She was stunningly beautiful up close.

Charles was having a difficult time breathing as he took a step closer.

"Rose!" a voice snapped.

Charles couldn't look away from her, even as the sensual smile on her face twisted into a snarl. She stepped back into the room.

"Get back, Rose," the voice said again, and Charles realized it was Mr. Sherman talking.

"Mind your business, Philip," Rose spat.

"This is my business, Rose," Mr. Sherman replied. "Now go back into the library and behave yourself."

"Bastard," she hissed and disappeared.

Instantly Charles was gasping, suddenly realizing he hadn't been breathing well at all. He staggered forward and pulled the library door closed. He looked around the hallway and saw a faint mist fading away. Charles turned his attention back to the library door and looked at it. There was an old keyhole in the brass door plate, but no key as far as he—

Something clinked in the bathroom.

"Jesus," Charles said softly. Worried something else was out, he made his way quietly to the bathroom.

There, on the tiled floor, was a small skeleton key.

Charles looked around the bathroom and realized the key had probably been on the ledge of the molding above the door. On the inside ledge.

Mr. Sherman had probably put it up there years before. A precaution. And now, Charles was certain, Mr. Sherman had pushed the key off of the ledge. A way to keep Charles safe.

Let's see if it works, Charles thought. He bent down and picked up the key. He brought it to the closed library door, and with a slight tremble in his hand, Charles slid the key in and turned it.

The sound of a tumbler locking into place was a beautiful, powerful sound, and Charles sighed with relief. He took the key out and put it on the ledge above the library door.

I need coffee, he thought and turned away from the library to walk back down the stairs.

Chapter 22: Charles and Mr. Sherman, May 1984

Charles was running as fast as he could, but he knew he wouldn't be able to outrun Dylan and Kevin on their bikes. Plus, Charles had his book bag, and they had dumped theirs in Dylan's front yard before racing after him.

Charles hadn't backed down at lunch when they wanted his chocolate milk, and now they were going to beat the hell out of him.

He knew it.

But he was so close to home.

He needed to get onto Adams Street, to get to the end of Sheridan and through the path.

Behind him, Charles heard Dylan and Kevin letting out war whoops as they gained on him.

Ahead of Charles was Mr. Sherman's house and Mr. Sherman was out in the yard, watering his flowerbeds. When Mr. Sherman caught sight of Charles running, he stopped watering the plants and asked, "Why are you running, Charles? Is something wrong?"

Charles couldn't answer. He was out of breath, and he knew the boys were getting too close.

Evidently Mr. Sherman realized what was going on as well as he said, "Come into my yard, Charles. Catch your breath."

Charles nearly cried with relief as he turned into Mr. Sherman's yard, stumbling and falling into a patch of perfect grass. Mr. Sherman let him lay there as he watered the plants, and as the two boys rode up to the edge of Mr. Sherman's property to grin maliciously at Charles.

"Come on, Charlie," Dylan sneered. "You need to come off that old guy's property. That isn't nice."

"Leave," Mr. Sherman said, not even looking at the boys. He merely continued to water his plants.

"What?" Kevin asked. He was older, and his father was a detective on the Nashua Police force. Kevin got away with anything he wanted.

"Leave," Mr. Sherman said again.

Kevin and Dylan laughed.

"You can't make us," Dylan laughed.

"Yeah," Kevin said, "we're on the street."

"True. Very true," Mr. Sherman said.

Charles sat up and looked nervously at Dylan and Kevin.

"The longer we wait," Kevin said, "the worse it's going to be, Charlie."

"Is that so?" Mr. Sherman asked. "Well then, we mustn't have you waiting."

And Mr. Sherman sprayed them both with the garden hose.

The day was cold, and Charles could only imagine how much colder the water was. If he judged its temperature by the way Dylan and Kevin screamed in outrage, it was a lot colder.

Mr. Sherman continued to spray the two boys and their bikes until they had taken off back towards Dylan's house.

Charles looked at Mr. Sherman, and the man smiled at him.

"I dislike bullies," Mr. Sherman said. "Would you like some lemonade before you go home?"

"Yes, please," Charles said, standing up and looking back the way the two boys had gone.

"Don't worry about them for now," Mr. Sherman said. "They won't come back. Not to here, and they won't be looking for you for a while at least."

Charles followed Mr. Sherman into the man's house, taking a seat on the couch in the man's den. Mr. Sherman went into the kitchen and returned a moment later with a tall glass of lemonade for each of them.

"Why were they chasing you?" Mr. Sherman asked.

"I wouldn't give Kevin my chocolate milk at school."

"Of course," Mr. Sherman said, shaking his head. "They may try tomorrow you know."

"I know," Charles said. "They'll probably try at lunch."

"What will you do?"

"Fight," Charles said, looking at Mr. Sherman. "It's what I have to do sometimes."

"I understand," Mr. Sherman said. "I've had to fight before as well. It is never a pleasurable experience for me. And, from what I can hear in your voice, it's not a pleasant one for you either."

Charles shook his head. "No. It's not."

"Good. I—"

Something crashed upstairs and Charles looked to the stairwell as Mr. Sherman straightened up. Mr. Sherman put his drink down and stood up.

"I fear my cat may have gotten into my library," Mr. Sherman said. "I'll have to go up and check. Will you wait here, Charles?"

"Yes," Charles answered.

"Thank you."

With stiff steps, Mr. Sherman walked out of the den and turned up the stairs. Charles drank his lemonade happily, nearly finishing it before he heard a door close and then Mr. Sherman's footsteps on the stairs. A moment later the man stepped back into the den, breathing hard, his hair slightly disarrayed.

"Are you okay?" Charles asked.

Mr. Sherman nodded, smiling. "My cat was more troublesome than usual. She didn't want to get out of the room."

"Oh," Charles said.

"So, Charles," Mr. Sherman said, sitting down once again, "tell me what you're reading now."

Charles finished his lemonade and told Mr. Sherman about John Steinbeck and a book called *Tortilla Flat*.

Chapter 23: Elmer and the German

Elmer was sitting at his desk, leaning back into the exceptional comfort of his leather chair and looking at world news on his primary screen. His secondary screen, which showed all of the various feeds from his security systems, was on his right, in his line of sight. If there was a flicker of movement, the barest hint of motion, his cameras picked it up, and a small alarm light flashed.

Even the museum had several cameras installed, to make sure no one got in there and took anything. That might have been paranoid for most people, but not for Elmer. He'd put a lot of time and money into that collection.

So when camera 4's alarm went off and said there was motion in the museum, specifically in the back section where he had put the bayonet, Elmer became distressed.

In a moment he was up, out of his chair and moving towards the museum. Thirty seconds after reaching the door he was through the security protocol and into the museum itself.

Elmer walked rapidly to the display where he'd—

Elmer stopped and tried not to gape at the giant of a man standing in front him.

Although Elmer could see through parts of the man, there was no denying the stranger was huge and wore an antique military uniform.

And the man was angry.

He glared at Elmer and pointed at the bayonet behind the sealed glass door.

"*Why is my bayonet there?*" the man demanded.

Elmer shook his head. The man was speaking German. German.

"*Um, your...your bayonet?*" Elmer asked, trying to remember his German. It had been years since he had spoken the language on a regular basis.

"*Yes! My bayonet!*"

"*I bought your bayonet today. Someone was killed with it.*"

The stranger laughed, a cold laugh that caused Elmer's balls to shrink up against him.

"*Someone?*" the stranger grinned. "*How about thousands of someones? I have killed many men with that blade. Cut through many lives, sorting out the chaff. Winnowing, as it were."*

Elmer straightened up. "You killed him?"

"I killed them all."

"That's wonderful," Elmer said softly, and the stranger's grin was replaced with a smile.

"I think so. What is your name, boy?" the man asked.

"Elmer Hoyt."

"Elmer Hoyt, I am Captain Ernst von Epp. I do not wish to be here, Elmer," Captain Epp said. *"I cannot kill when stuck in one place."*

"If I let you out, you might be locked away somewhere I can't help you."

"I have been before," Captain Epp grumbled. *"It was an unpleasant experience. And how, Herr Hoyt, can you help me?"*

Elmer licked his lips excitedly, asking, "What if I was to bring someone to you. Would that be as good?"

The German ghost smiled. *"Yes. But why? Why would you?"*

"So I could watch," Elmer answered honestly.

Captain Epp laughed, the sound deep but disturbingly hollow at the same time. *"You like to watch death, do you?"*

Elmer nodded, thinking of all of the YouTube videos he watched when the boys and Fiona weren't around.

"There are more, you know," Captain Epp said after a moment.

"More what?"

"More like me. Dozens of us. Trapped and bound to our past, murdering in our undead future."

"Where?" Elmer said excitedly. "Where?"

"I do not know. But there were many of us, Herr Hoyt, and you could watch dozens die in different ways."

Elmer nodded. He would have to find out where Dave had gotten the bayonet. He would know where the others came from. He would. He looked to Captain Epp, "I will find them. Now, do you need someone for tonight?"

The ghost laughed, and Elmer laughed too.

He hadn't been this happy since his youngest was born.

This was turning out to be better than anything Elmer could ever have dreamed of.

Chapter 24: Ellen and the Apartment

At three o'clock in the morning, the smoke detector in the kitchen went off, snapping Ellen up and out of a fitful sleep.

She threw the blankets off and hurried out of the room, turning on lights as she went. She dragged a chair from the table and into the kitchen so she could climb up and hit the silence button.

Ellen couldn't smell smoke anywhere. The place was—

And then she smelled it. The heavy, sweet smell of the cigars Mike had loved to smoke when he still had a job and could afford them.

Carefully Ellen climbed down off of the chair and stepped out of the kitchen. She walked into the den and in the dim light of the moon spilling into the room, she saw a shape sitting in Mike's easy chair. Cigar smoke curled up towards the ceiling, fluorescent in the moonlight. The large, glowing tip of the cigar caught her eye.

Ellen stood completely still, watching as an arm reached up and the transparent hand removed the cigar from the mouth. The arm went to the armrest, the hand pale in the moonlight, the cigar smoking lazily.

"Hello, Doll." It was Mike's voice, although it sounded rough. Hoarse.

"Mike," she said softly.

"Mike," he answered, and even through the painful distortion of his voice, she could hear the humor in his answer. "You know, Doll, you need to leave this alone."

Ellen blinked, confused. "Leave what alone?"

"The lighter. The stuff Jared and I boosted from the old man's house. That shit's poison, Ellen," he said, all of the levity gone from his voice. He took a drag off of the cigar. "I'm dead because of that shit. You know it as well as I do. Hell. Jared's dead too. Lots of folks are dead from those damned things. I don't want you to be one of them."

"But they have to be found," Ellen said softly. "They have to be brought back."

"They do," Mike agreed. "But that doesn't mean you have to do it."

"If not me, then who?" Ellen asked. And she realized she was having the same argument she always had with Mike whenever she wanted to do volunteer work or take care of a patient in a dangerous section of town. He had always been protective, and he was still being protective, even in death.

"There's already the guy that bought the old man's house," Mike answered. "Let him do it."

"I can't."

"You need to," Mike whispered.

There was a hissing sound, and Ellen stumbled back, closing her eyes as she started to fall.

She woke up in bed, her alarm going off.

What a bizarre dream, Ellen thought as she sat up and turned the alarm off. She got out of bed and headed out into the kitchen to start the coffee before her shower.

She nearly walked into a chair standing beneath the smoke detector.

In the air she could smell cigar smoke, and a quick look at the den showed the stub of a fresh cigar stubbed out in Mike's eagle ashtray.

Ellen swallowed dryly and grabbed hold of her racing thoughts.

She couldn't stay in the apartment. Not if Mike was going to show up. She couldn't be afraid to leave her bedroom and—

"Shit."

What if he showed up in the bedroom?

Ellen left the den, walked back to the bedroom and picked up her phone. She scrolled through her contacts. She needed to find someone who wasn't married or living with a partner.

There wasn't anyone.

Not a single person.

All of her friends, both female and male, were in relationships, and she wasn't going to ask to sleep over because she was afraid of ghosts.

Ghosts.

There was one person she could call. She didn't know him very well, but she didn't get a creepy vibe off of him, and she could always lock the bedroom door somehow.

If Charles would even think about having her over.

For a moment she thought about his house, about the things in the library. Even with the things locked away Charles's library

Ellen would rather be in his house than with Mike in the apartment.

Anything would be better than waking up to Mike's ghost.

She couldn't deal with that. Not again.

Ellen scrolled through her contacts, found his number, and called Charles Gottesman.

Chapter 25: Where to Sleep

Charles was exhausted.

Someone had been a complete and utter pain in the ass in the library, pretty much through the whole night. He'd finally been forced to come down and catch a couple of interrupted hours of sleep on the couch.

He sat in his recliner and looked through the journal Mr. Sherman had kept regarding the objects, and he found the entry he was looking for.

Nurse's cap. Found in the debris of the USS Pirate following sinking of the ship by a mine. Wonsan Harbor, Korea, 1950. Twelve missing sailors, one missing nurse (Rose McCourtland), and one dead. Since the nurse's cap was recovered, there have been eleven deaths related to 'dry' drowning in the cap's presence. Purchased at an estate sale, 1990, Bar Harbor, Maine.

Drowning, Charles thought. *The bitch was trying to drown me.*

I need to figure out how to control them.

Charles flipped through the pages, looking for some way to gain control when his cell phone rang.

With a grunt, he leaned forward, took the phone off the coffee table and looked at the caller ID.

Ellen.

"Hello?" he asked as he answered it.

"Charles," she said. "It's Ellen."

"Is everything okay?" he asked, straightening up. He could hear fear in her voice.

"No. I had a bad night."

"Me too," Charles said. "I'm very sorry to hear it. Can I do anything?"

"Well," she said nervously, "this is kind of strange, but do you happen to have an extra room?"

"I have several," Charles answered. "Do you need to stay here for a while?"

"You don't mind?" she asked, relief flooding into her voice. "I mean, it's not too strange, is it?"

"Ellen," Charles said, "I think you and I both know what's too strange. When do you want to come over?"

"Now," she answered. "I want to throw some stuff into a bag and come over now."

"Then come over," Charles told her. "I'll go unlock the front door and get some coffee going."

"Thank you," Ellen said. "Thank you."

"You're welcome," Charles said. "And don't worry about it. This is going to be good for me, too."

Chapter 26: Elmer visits Dave in the Hospital

Elmer was excited.

No, scratch that. He was beyond excited. There wasn't even a word for what he was right now.

He parked his car in the back lot of the hospital parking lot. He got out and stretched, trying to calm himself down. It wouldn't look good to go bopping into the hospital to visit his "father" in ICU. Which is where they were currently keeping Dave.

Finding out where the pawnbroker was and what had happened to him had been a chore and a half.

Oh, well. Elmer locked the car, stuffed his keys into his coat pocket and his hands in after his keys. *Time to go.*

He walked at a slow and steady pace, like someone visiting a terribly sick relative ought to be doing. He could run. God no. If somebody saw him, and then heard the questions he was going to ask Dave, Elmer might find himself being evaluated in the ER in regards to his own sanity.

But he was more than sane. Much more than sane.

Life had dealt Elmer a royal flush in the form of Captain Epp, and Elmer only had to play the hand right to get the whole pot.

Oh, yes. Everything was his for the taking.

Murder weapons he could feed.

A shiver of excitement raced along his spine, and Elmer realized how quickly he was walking. He had to slow down.

Elmer forced himself to slow down, to breathe deeply and think only of making it into the building. A minute later, he was passing through the revolving doors and walking purposefully down the hallway towards the elevators. When he reached them, he glanced at the signs and saw he was standing in front of the proper elevators to take him to the fourth floor and the ICU wing.

Elmer pressed the button and waited for the elevator. In a moment it was there and he was stepping in and pressing the "4" button. The door closed and Elmer stood straight, waiting.

At each floor the elevator slowed down, as if to make a stop, and then it continued on.

Elmer was nervous even though he knew no one could challenge what he would say. No one at all.

The doors opened and Elmer stepped out onto the fourth

floor. A sign pointed to the left, showing the way to ICU. Elmer followed the sign and reached a pair of locked doors. Outside of them was a hard lined phone. Elmer picked up the phone and put it to his ear. A moment later there was a chime and a woman. "ICU, who are you here to see?"

"Hi, I'm here to see my father, Dave Ganz."

"Hold, please," the woman said.

A moment later the door opened up and a doctor stepped out. She smiled at Elmer, extending her hand.

"Hello, I'm Doctor Coryell," she said. "I'm sorry we've had to meet under these circumstances."

"Me too, doctor," Elmer replied. "Can you tell me what's happened exactly? I've gotten all sorts of confusing stories, from my father being drunk and crashing his car to him being attacked by Afghanis with acid. All I know for certain is he was in some sort of accident, and he's been brought here and placed in ICU."

"Well," Doctor Coryell said, "your father was in a single vehicle car accident. But he wasn't drunk. In fact, we're not exactly sure what happened. We've done some tests and sent some blood work out to try and identify any issues we might not be able to see, but other than that, we don't know what's going on. All we do know is he has severe second and third degree chemical burns on over eighty percent of his body, and his corneas were exposed to whatever it was as well, leaving him permanently blind."

"God damnit," Elmer said, honestly shocked.

"Yes," the doctor said, nodding her agreement. "So I wanted to warn you we have your father pretty well wrapped up at this moment. We're treating his chemical burns the best way we can right now, and we're hoping we can save him. His body has experienced a severe shock, though, and if he does pull through the shock, he may well succumb to an infection due to the burns."

"I understand," Elmer said softly.

"Okay," Doctor Coryell said, nodding. "Follow me."

She led the way, swiping her safety badge over a keypad. A red light flipped to green, the door lock clicking loudly. She opened the door and held it for him. He followed her into the ICU where there were other patients, four altogether, with one or two relatives sitting with them.

Except for Dave.

No one was sitting with Dave.

The man looked like a mummy, wrapped protectively in some sort of material, his eyes bandaged and tubes running into his mouth and his hands. Machines beeped steadily, and Elmer wondered how in the hell he was going to get Dave to talk.

Even if he did manage to get something good and coherent out of him, Elmer would have to worry about the ICU staff overhearing things. Not that they would be able to make sense out of much of anything when it came to the death items, but Elmer did enjoy keeping a low profile as often as possible.

"Please come get us if you need anything or if you have any questions," Doctor Coryell said at the door to Dave's room.

"I will," Elmer replied, and he went into the room.

He smelled disinfectants and medicines and death. Half a dozen machines were clicking and making soft sounds, all of them performing vital functions. If it weren't for the machines, Dave would not only look dead, but be dead.

Only by the grace of God, it seemed, was Dave still alive.

But that was good.

Elmer needed Dave alive. He needed Dave to come to consciousness long enough for the man to tell him if he knew of the other items. And if he did, where the hell they were.

Elmer walked close to Dave and leaned over the man, his back to the staff in the center of the ICU hub. He needed them to think he was worried about his 'father'. A moment later, Elmer straightened up and walked around the bed to the room's single chair.

He sat down, pulled a battered copy of *Salem's Lot* out of his jacket pocket, and read, waiting for Dave to wake up.

Chapter 27: John and Lee have a Chat

A knock sounded on John's apartment door.

A hard, heavy knock that sent a ripple of fear through John.

He picked up his .38 from the coffee table, held the weapon at his side, and went and stood by the side of the door.

"Who is it?" he asked.

"John, it's Lee."

"Lee?" John asked. "Lee who?"

"Lee Parker."

John stiffened, put the pistol on the TV cabinet, and opened the door. "Hey, Lee, come on in."

"Thanks," Lee said, walking in and going to the couch. He sat down, looked at John's coffee, and picked it up, taking a long drink. "Sit down, John."

John went and sat down in his chair. "What's going on, Lee?"

"Nothing much," Lee answered.

"I'm paid up with everybody."

"I'm not here about any of that."

John relaxed a little. "Oh. So, what can I do for you?"

Lee finished John's coffee and set the empty mug back on the table. "You still moving stuff out of evidence?"

"Once in a while," John said.

"Good," Lee said, looking steadily at him. "I got a friend who needs you to move something for him. He'll pay."

John sighed with relief. "Sure thing, Lee. That's not a problem at all."

"I'll give him your number. Make sure you give him what he wants."

John nodded.

"I will not be a happy man if I have to come back and talk to you about this," Lee said in a cold voice.

John swallowed nervously, looking at the thin, harsh man sitting across from him. Lee wore an old leather jacket over a sweater and a pair of faded jeans with Wellington boots. Somewhere, Lee would have a knife. Not a very big one, John knew. Nothing big enough to violate Lee's parole. That hadn't ever been Lee's style.

"I didn't know you were out yet," John said, smiling anxiously. "I don't think anybody does."

"Most don't," Lee said. He picked up John's cigarettes and lighter off of the coffee table. He shook out a cigarette, lit it, and then pocketed both the lighter and the cigarettes.

John didn't say anything.

Lee stood up, looked around and said, "I'm leaving. I'll give him the number. Make sure you give him whatever he wants."

"Sure, Lee," John said. "Sure."

Lee nodded, walked to the front door, and left.

When the door clicked shut, John shuddered and relaxed into the chair. He hoped Lee's friend would call soon and there wouldn't be any more conversations with Lee.

Ever.

With trembling hands, John got up, locked the front door, and made himself more instant coffee.

Chapter 28: Charles and Ellen and the Library

Charles greeted Ellen at the door as she crossed the porch carrying a couple of bags.

"How are you holding up?" he asked her, closing the door behind her.

She shook her head. "Not good."

"What's going on?" he asked, taking a bag from her and leading the way up the stairs.

"My dead boyfriend showed up last night and told me to stay away from this whole fiasco," Ellen replied tiredly.

"Oh."

"Yeah."

Charles brought her to one of the front bedrooms. Inside he had set up his old camping cot and thrown a spare area rug down on the floor. He had managed to get shades up when he first moved in, and he had taken a floor lamp and put it in there as well.

"Sorry I don't have any more furniture," Charles said, "but I've been living in a small apartment for the past couple of years."

"Don't worry about it." Ellen smiled. "I'm thankful you're doing this for me. We don't know each other, and this is a big thing you're doing."

"Well, if you're being visited by the dead," Charles said, "I guess we're in this together."

Charles stepped aside to let her into the room and waited as she put her bags down on the cot.

"So," she said. "How come you didn't sleep well?"

"My tenants in the library," Charles said bitterly. "One of them tried to kill me."

"Oh. Wow."

"It was a disturbing experience," Charles said. "I was going through Mr. Sherman's journal, trying to find a reference to anything that might tell me how to control the difficult ones."

"Did you find anything?" Ellen asked.

"No," Charles said, shaking his head. "Not yet. Do you want some coffee?"

"Yes, please," Ellen answered. "That'd be great."

"Okay, follow me," he said. Charles led her back downstairs and into the kitchen, gesturing towards the table as he said,

"Take a seat."

"Thanks," Ellen said and sat down.

"I don't have any cream," Charles said as he made the coffee, "but I do have sugar."

"That's okay, I like it black."

"Excellent," Charles smiled. "I'm hoping to get out to Milford again in the next couple of days, see if I can't find the pawnbroker's booth. If we're lucky, everything should be there."

"If we're lucky."

Charles nodded, sitting down at the table. "I haven't had a roommate in about ten years, so I'm a little rusty on the whole thing. I've got a washer and dryer in the basement, and plenty of room in the fridge, and cabinets for whatever you want to buy. I read a whole lot and write too, so I'm a pretty quiet guy. The only disturbance, of course, is going to be from the library."

"We'll figure that out," Ellen said. "Don't worry about it. I like my sleep. I don't get enough of it. I sure as hell don't want to have to suffer because I'm rooming with irritable ghosts."

Charles grinned at her. "Sounds good to me."

In a few moments, the coffee was ready, and Charles poured them each a mugful.

"Do you want to come up to the library with me?" Charles asked her before taking a sip of his coffee. "I'm going to poke around and see if there's anything up there that might help."

"Sure," Ellen said. "I called a friend to cover my visits today, so there's nothing for me to do. Mike's family decided yesterday to not let me help with the burial planning. In fact, they sent a happy little email saying it might be better if I didn't show up to the wake since we weren't married or anything."

"I'm sorry to hear that," Charles said.

Ellen shrugged her shoulders as she stood, her eyes red with lack of sleep and unspilled tears. "I know he loved me. That's all I need. I may want to see the burial, but I don't need to."

Charles could only nod before leading the way to the library.

The library was quiet, thankfully, when they entered.

"Let me grab another chair," Charles said. "You can sit on that one if you like."

"Thanks." Ellen smiled, and she sat down, brushing a loose lock of hair out of her eyes.

Charles went into his own room, grabbed the ladder-back

Shaker chair by his dresser, and carried it into the library, setting it down on the desk across from Ellen.

"So," she said, looking around. "We need to figure out if there's a way to lock down some of the nastier things in here?"

"Yes, exactly," Charles said.

"Well," Ellen said, "is there anything in here that looks like it might work?"

The library, while being a good size, wasn't so large that they couldn't look at all of the shelves from where they sat at the desk. Charles was carefully moving his eyes over each shelf when Ellen spoke.

"There," she said, getting up and pointing. "That box on the bottom shelf."

Charles looked where she was pointing and stood up, catching sight of a box that took up an entire bottom shelf. He hadn't noticed it before, and he probably would have looked right past it again. Mr. Sherman had stacked books upon the box, and the box's wood was the same color as the shelves.

Charles and Ellen walked over to the shelf together, and they both sat down on the floor. In silence, they pulled the books off of the box, stacking them neatly on the floor beside them. As soon as the box was clear, and they pulled it out off of the shelf.

"Go ahead," Ellen said, looking at him. "You can do the honors."

"Thanks," Charles said wryly.

"No problem." Ellen grinned.

Charles took hold of the lid and lifted it up, the top heavy. When he got it opened completely, Charles saw why.

The entire box was lined with what looked like lead.

Within the box's narrow confines were a few items. A folded letter, a small knife, a couple coins, and a bronze ring.

Charles felt the hair on the back of his neck rise up, and it seemed as though he heard a low growl. He closed the box and looked at Ellen.

"Want to finish this downstairs in the dining room?" he asked.

Her eyes had widened slightly, and she nodded.

Together they stood up, grabbed their coffees and left the room. He locked the door, put the key away and followed Ellen down into the dining room. His notebook and Mr. Sherman's journal were still on the table where he had left them. Charles took a seat, and Ellen sat down on his right.

"Did you hear a dog growl?" she asked after a minute.

"Yeah," Charles said. "That's the puritan's great dane."

"Okay. I don't want to meet either of them."

"Understood. I didn't want to meet them to begin with."

"No doubt," she sighed. "So, that's Mr. Sherman's journal?"

"Yes," Charles nodded. "I want to see if there's anything in here about the items that were up in the box."

"Did he keep notes on the other stuff?"

Charles nodded again.

"Well," Ellen said, "he probably kept notes on those too."

"I hope so," Charles said. "I hope like hell the box works."

"Me too," Ellen said, taking a sip of her coffee. "Me too."

Chapter 29: Elmer and Dave in the ICU

Elmer had very little time left.

Fiona and the boys would be home by six o'clock in the evening, which meant Elmer would have to be there to greet them, or else Fiona would be worried about him. When Fiona was worried, life was unpleasant.

Elmer sat close to Dave and wondered if the man was ever going to come out of the coma the doctors had induced.

Elmer doubted it.

The doctors hadn't passed on any uplifting information. In fact, a Doctor Cho had informed Elmer he might want to start considering funeral arrangements and had even sent a social worker to talk to him.

No, Elmer sighed. It didn't seem like old Dave was going to be able to pull out of it. Which meant Elmer was going to have to do some legwork. Or rather, he was going to have to hire a private detective to do some legwork. Fiona would be worried if Elmer went out and about—which was completely out of character. There was a reason Elmer worked from home.

He didn't like people much.

His two days in the ICU had tested his patience.

He had seen one woman die, and another one was on her way out. Good God, the amount of bitching and complaining that went on was enough to want him to put them all out of their misery.

Elmer let out a long, slow breath and focused on the goal. He needed to obtain all of those items Captain Epp had spoken of.

Elmer needed them.

This was far beyond want. That's what Fiona couldn't understand about his museum of hate. Elmer didn't want the items, he needed them. When he found out one was available for purchase, he had to have it.

It was as simple as that.

Dave moved on the bed.

Ever so slightly, but he had moved.

Elmer straightened up, risked a glance out to the nurses' station to make sure no one was watching, and got far closer to Dave than they had said was okay.

"Dave," Elmer said in a low voice, barely audible over the

various noises of the machines connected to the old pawnbroker.

Dave moved again, his head turning gingerly towards the sound of Elmer's voice.

Elmer's heart beat rapidly. "Dave, can you hear me?"

The heart monitor beeped rapidly.

Dave nodded.

"Dave, it's Elmer. Where did you get the bayonet from?"

Dave mumbled something around the breathing tube in his mouth, and Elmer leaned even closer. Elmer clenched the arms of the chair, fighting the desire to rip the breathing tube right out of Dave's mouth.

"Dave!" Elmer hissed. "Where did you get it from?!"

An alarm sounded on one of the machines, and movement at the nurses' station caught Elmer's eye. The nurses rushed towards the room, and the doctor on duty came out of another patient's room.

Swearing vehemently under his breath, Elmer pushed himself back and away from Dave's side, making room for the medical staff.

Someone asked him to leave, and Elmer nodded, getting up and stalking out of the room, and out of ICU altogether. Dave was flat-lining. There wasn't any more to learn here. Elmer was going to have to hire someone.

Stuffing his hands deep into his pockets, Elmer made his way to the parking garage, wondering who he should call.

Chapter 30: Charles and John Talk about the Bayonet

Charles had received a text from Lee that read, *John,* and the man's cell phone number.

Charles parked his car in the lot of St. Philip's Greek Orthodox Church, directly across from the Nashua Police Station. He looked at the time and saw it was four o'clock in the afternoon on the nose. Charles called John's cell.

After two rings, the phone was answered, and a cautious voice asked, "Hello?"

"John?" Charles asked.

"Yes."

"This is Charles. I'm Lee Parker's friend."

There was a pause, and Charles could hear the man's breath quicken.

"Oh," John said. "Yes. Yes. Lee said you would be calling."

"I'm calling," Charles said. He kept his tone neutral, his voice low. "I need something out of the evidence room."

"Sure," John said. "If I can."

"No," Charles said evenly. "There is no 'if' here, John."

"Um, okay," John said. "What do you need?"

"A bayonet came in from a murder. I need the bayonet."

There was a long pause before John answered. "I can't get that out of evidence for you."

"John," Charles said, "that's not what I want to hear from you. Try another answer."

The next pause was even longer, and for a moment Charles thought the man had hung up on him.

"It's not here," John said. "I, I already sold it."

"To whom, John?" Charles said.

"I—"

"Don't tell me you can't, John," Charles said, his old temper flaring, "because I swear to Christ that I will make sure you drink your food for the rest of your life."

"A pawnbroker," John said. "A pawnbroker in Milford. Guy's name is Dave Ganz. Runs a little shop on the oval. I sold it to him a couple of days ago. I don't know if he'll still have it or not. He tends to move stuff pretty quickly."

A cold rage swept over Charles. This ass had put someone else's life at risk because he needed cash.

"Um, are you going to clear me with Lee?" John asked.

"We'll see," Charles said, and he ended the call.

Dropping the phone into the console, he closed his eyes and got his temper under control. The man couldn't know what the bayonet did. A few days earlier Charles wouldn't have known.

Opening his eyes, Charles picked up his phone and sent a quick text to Lee. *All good. Thanks.*

Charles put the phone down, started the engine, and drove out of the parking lot. He needed to see what Dave Ganz had at the flea market. He needed to do it soon.

Chapter 31: Ellen and the Music Box

Ellen used the spare key Charles had given her to get into the house, putting her bag down on the floor by the front door and automatically looking for the peg to hang her keys on.

But she wasn't in her apartment, so there was no peg to hang them on.

With a sigh, she dropped the keys on her bag, locked the door, and made her way upstairs to her bedroom. She'd managed to bring a few more belongings over from the apartment, but only when Charles or Betty had been able to help her. Ellen grabbed a change of clothes and went to the bathroom, took a quick shower, and got dressed. She didn't bother with make-up or doing anything with her hair other than blow-drying it.

She had no reason for anything.

Ellen pushed those thoughts out of her mind, picked up her dirty laundry and dropped it into the hamper. She opened the door to leave the bathroom and stopped.

She could hear music.

A soft, beautiful, classical piece sounded like it was coming from a music box.

Ellen looked to the right and saw the library door.

The music was coming through the door, and Ellen wanted to hear it better. She knew she could hear it better in the library.

Of course, she could listen to it better in the library. She could leave the light off and sit in the leather chair, and listen to the music.

She could open the door. Charles had put the key up on the top of the door jamb. She had seen him. She would have to grab the chair out of his room so she could reach it. A small part of her told her she shouldn't get the key, she shouldn't go into the room. She should go downstairs and ignore the music.

Ellen ignored that part of her.

She went into Charles' room, found the chair, and brought it out into the hallway. The music continued to play as she fetched the key, got it down, and unlocked the door.

The music got louder the instant she opened the door, and she sighed happily. Ellen left the key in the lock and the light off, walking into the library guided by the small bit of light spilling in from the hallway.

She went to the leather chair and dropped down into it, closing her eyes and listening happily. Somewhere she'd heard the music before. Probably in a hospital or an elevator. *Or both*, she thought with a happy smile.

It was such happy music. She didn't need to think about anything. She didn't need to worry about anything. Ellen knew she had things to worry about, of course. Everyone did. But she didn't have to when the music was playing.

The library was a little colder than she remembered, and for a moment she thought about getting up and getting a blanket from her room, but then she decided not to. She'd be okay with a little bit of cold, and besides, she didn't want to miss any of the music.

No, she couldn't miss a single note.

Ellen kept her eyes closed and ignored the increasing chill in the room. Even when she started to first tremble, and then to shake, she pushed the cold out of her mind and focused on the music.

Ellen smiled to herself and listened.

Faintly she heard a voice as if someone was calling to her. Then the door slammed shut, leaving her to the music.

***

Charles pulled in beside Ellen's Volkswagen Bug and shut his car down. He pocketed his keys as he climbed out, and when he closed the door, he realized something was wrong. The glass in the house windows seemed to be vibrating in their frames.

He sprinted for the door, which opened for him. Faintly he heard Mr. Sherman say, "The library."

Charles heard music as he raced into the house. He took the stairs two at a time, pushing the music out of his thoughts. He knew instinctively the music was the problem.

Suddenly a memory leaped forward, a flashing picture of one of Mr. Sherman's journal pages. A music box found amongst the belongings of a revolutionary war soldier who had died of exposure at Valley Forge.

The music grew louder, trying to push deep into Charles' mind as he reached the second floor. He pushed aside his chair and threw open the door, the key clattering to the floor. He saw

Ellen in the chair, curled up in a fetal position. Her lips were blue, as were her eyes, the whites of which were showing in a slim gap between the eyelids. She was pale, far too pale.

Hypothermia. Charles looked around the room and spotted the music box playing on a shelf on the back wall. The faint image of a soldier sat in front of it, wrapped in rags and the remnants of a blanket, his kerchiefed head topped with a three corner hat. He had rotten teeth and glared as Charles hurried forward.

The ghost said nothing as Charles seized the music-box, a small, heavily carved wooden box with the lid open and the delicate instrument playing within. The lid wouldn't close, and Charles could feel the cold seeping into him. A desire built, calling him to sit on the floor and listen. To do nothing more than to listen.

The floor, Charles thought. Looking down, he saw the lead lined box, dropped to his knees so heavily the pain shattered the desire to listen, and he opened the box.

Behind him the ghost screamed, a sound that ripped through Charles' thoughts even as he dropped the music-box into small ghost prison and slammed the top down.

The music stopped instantly.

Charles snatched up the key to the door and got to his feet, hobbling with pain over to where Ellen sat. He didn't bother trying to lift her up, he merely pushed the chair out of the library, its old brass wheels squealing. A moment later, he had her and the chair in the hallway, and he was locking the door. He put the key in his pocket and managed to pick up Ellen.

Leaning heavily against the wall, Charles managed to make it down the stairs and into the den. He put Ellen on the couch, started a fire in the fireplace, and turned his attention back to her. Her skin was cold and unnatural to the touch, but she was still breathing.

As the fire grew, Charles sat down on the couch, pulled Ellen against him, and then covered them both with an old comforter off of the back of the couch. His body heat would be the best thing for her. He rubbed her arms and hands, keeping as much contact as possible with her body.

Long minutes passed before a murmur escaped her lips.

A few more minutes after that, she asked in a small voice, "Why am I so cold?"

"You went into the library," Charles answered softly.

"Oh, Jesus, I did, didn't I?" she groaned, shivering against him.

Charles was sweating from the heat of the fire as well as the comforter and Ellen.

"I hate to ask," she said after a few more minutes, "but are we going to be safe here? I don't want to see Mike, but if the alternative's dying, then I'll have to go back."

"Understood," Charles said. "There has to be a way, and it might be as simple letting them know who's in charge. I haven't finished reading all of Mr. Sherman's journal yet. Maybe there's something in there."

Ellen's shivering subsided, and she sat up, pulling the comforter around her as she twisted on the couch to face Charles.

"Thanks," she said. "How did you know that body heat worked best?"

"I do a lot of research," Charles smiled, "on a lot of different things. I had to write about hypothermia once."

"You remembered that?" she asked.

He nodded. "I remember lots of things. Too many things, when it comes right down to it."

Ellen shook her head. "No, Charles, you keep on remembering stuff. It definitely came in handy today."

"You hungry?" Charles asked, standing up.

"A little. I bought some chicken noodle soup the other day. I'll make that in a bit."

"I'll get it," he smiled. "Stay on the couch and get warm."

Charles left the room and went to the kitchen. As he went about getting the soup ready for her, there was a whisper from behind him. Charles turned slowly around and saw nothing.

"Charles," Mr. Sherman whispered. The word came from directly in front of Charles.

Charles took an involuntary step back, bumping into the countertop.

"Ah, good," Mr. Sherman said, his voice still low. "There are times when I try to speak to you or Ellen, and neither of you responds. I can only assume I am not strong enough at those moments."

Charles waited in silence.

"Charles, I left the library open because I would visit with the dead. I was fascinated by history. They are egotistical, which is part of the reason why they are bound to those objects. They lack the imagination to see the world without them. You must either bind them all to the room permanently, or stroke their egos. Do you understand?"

"Yes," Charles answered softly.

"So long as you ignore them, they will, like petulant children, demand your attention. When they demand it, however, they might kill you or Ellen. They are violent, as you know. Take steps to ensure they will not be violent with you and Ellen."

Charles waited again, but after a few minutes there was nothing else. Either Mr. Sherman had passed along the information he had wanted to, or else he had lost the energy to do so.

Turning back around to the pot he had taken out, Charles prepared the soup with shaking hands.

Chapter 32: Elmer and the Investigator

Fiona and the boys were home.

Elmer was pleased they were back, that Owen had taken first in his age group, and that Ryan had taken third in his own, but their return prevented Elmer from conducting certain business transactions from the safety of his house.

Which meant Elmer was going to have to go out.

Occasionally he did go out, and when he did, it was to take a drive to clear his thoughts. More often than not, he picked up some small item for the museum of hate, but his leaving was so rare an event, Fiona usually questioned him about it.

Thankfully she was too tired from the swim meet and the travel to say anything more than goodbye when Elmer told her he was going for a drive. The boys were at school, and Fiona had a bloody mary, and was trying to take the edge off of a hectic return to school.

Elmer took the black BMW when he went out, the car as common as a Ford when he drove through Hollis. Elmer wasn't leaving Hollis. In fact, he was meeting the investigator at the Country Kitchen for coffee and to iron out the details.

Elmer pulled into the lot for the restaurant, parked, and went in. He smiled pleasantly at the waitress who greeted him and made his way to the table nearest the door where an older man waited. The man, perhaps in his fifties, drank coffee from a ceramic mug and read a carefully folded newspaper. The man had steel gray hair cut short, and he wore a simple dark blue sweater, khaki pants, and a pair of black shoes.

The man glanced up over the top of his newspaper and smiled pleasantly. He put the paper down and extended his hand. "Elmer?"

"Yes," Elmer said, shaking the offered hand and sitting down across from the man.

"Roger," the man said before taking another sip of his coffee.

Before Elmer could say anything, the waitress came over and topped off Roger's mug without asking Elmer for anything.

Elmer, who was going to say no to any question about food, was still surprised.

Roger smiled. "I assumed you weren't the type of person to eat in a little diner like this. I told the waitress I was expecting company, but you wouldn't want to be bothered about food."

Elmer straightened up in his chair and found himself smiling. "That's exactly right, Roger."

"So," Roger said, sipping his coffee, "what exactly do you want to be bothered about, Elmer?"

For a moment, Elmer wondered how much he should tell Roger, and then he decided to tell him about everything except the ghost.

"I collect items which were used to commit murders," Elmer said. "Recently I acquired a bayonet that was used in a locked-door murder. I have reason to believe the bayonet came from a collection similar to my own, and, quite frankly, Roger, I want that collection. I attempted to find out how the bayonet was obtained by the man who sold it to me, but he died yesterday before I could do so."

"You would like me to find the individual who sold the bayonet to your own contact?" Roger asked.

"Exactly."

"You do understand you purchased an item that was more than likely stolen?"

"Of course."

Roger nodded and took a longer drink from his mug. "Well, since we both know you have participated in a crime by receiving stolen goods, I am going to have to ask for more than my usual fee for the job. This will be to help defray any costs I might incur should I be arrested as well."

Elmer hadn't considered the being arrested angle, but he nodded in agreement.

"Good," Roger said. "I'm requesting seventy-five dollars an hour, plus expenses. I will present receipts for anything I purchase while on the clock for you. This can range from a sandwich at a pizza place to filling the tank on my car. It will not be for new pants or shoes or anything like that unless, of course, something happens to those items while I'm actively working on the job. I will give you a phone number of a disposable phone so you can contact me at any time of the day or night if you learn something new. I will contact you as soon as I have solid information. Do not harass me with calls inquiring as to the status of the investigation. I will stop working for you."

"Understood."

"Excellent." Roger smiled. He reached into his back pocket, took out a small business card, and flipped it over. On the back, a cell number was written. "This is the number."

"Thank you," Elmer said, putting the number away in his wallet.

"Who did you buy the bayonet from?" Roger asked.

"David Ganz."

Roger took a small notebook from under his newspaper, and jotted the name down. "Did he own a business?"

"Pawn shop in Milford."

"Okay. Where did he die?"

"Southern New Hampshire Hospital in Nashua."

Roger nodded, looked up, and smiled pleasantly. "Okay, Elmer. I'll call you soon."

Elmer returned the smile, stood up, and left the restaurant. He was excited. In fact, he wanted to get home as soon as possible, so he could share the news with Captain Epp. Perhaps, when Fiona and the boys went out to practice, he could bring someone home for Captain Epp.

Yes, that seemed like a fantastic idea.

Humming to himself, Elmer tossed the BMW's key from hand to hand, looking forward to the evening.

Chapter 33: Mr. Sherman's House, 1989

Charles walked up the dead end of Sheridan Street, heading towards the path that would lead to Adams Street when he heard a yell followed by a crash.

Both sounds came from Mr. Sherman's house.

Mr. Sherman lived alone.

Charles ran straight across Mr. Sherman's well-kept lawn to the porch stairs. He hurried up the stairs and knocked on the door.

A groan answered his knock, and Charles cautiously tried the doorknob.

It turned, and the latch clicked loudly.

Charles pushed the door open, calling out, "Mr. Sherman? It's Charles Gottesman!"

As the door opened all of the way, Charles saw Mr. Sherman lying in a heap at the bottom of the stairs. At the top of the stairs, he caught sight of the library door open, the light on.

Charles hurried to Mr. Sherman's side and knelt down beside the man. There was a trickle of blood coming from a small cut on top of a welt that was rising on Mr. Sherman's forehead. Mr. Sherman's bottom lip was swelling too, and the man groaned once more before opening his eyes. For a moment, the eyes seemed to roll in different directions before they focused on Charles.

"Charles," Mr. Sherman said in a low voice. "I left the front door unlocked."

"Yes."

"Well," Mr. Sherman smiled, managing to sit up. "It seems that becoming forgetful in my old age has its benefits."

Charles stood up and held out his hands to Mr. Sherman. The man nodded, took hold of Charles' hands, and together they managed to get Mr. Sherman to his feet. The man swayed, reaching a hand out to touch the wall and steady himself.

A soft click drifted down the stairs, and Charles looked up.

The door to the library was closed.

Charles blinked, looked again, and saw the door was closed.

"Mr. Sherman," Charles said, still looking at the library door.

"Yes?"

"The library door. It was open when I came in."

Mr. Sherman looked up at the library and sighed. "Yes, Charles. Yes. It closes itself occasionally, although I wish it wouldn't. Now, Charles, let us get a cup of tea, shall we? I don't believe that I have a concussion, but if you would be kind enough to sit with me long enough for a cup of tea, I would appreciate it."

Charles looked at the door, shook his head, and then followed Mr. Sherman into the kitchen.

Chapter 34: Charles in the Library

Ellen was asleep in her room when Charles opened up the library and walked in.

The room felt uncomfortably silent as he sat down in the chair and put his hands on the desk. He took a deep breath, let it out slowly, and then asked out loud, "Does anyone wish to speak?"

The silence grew heavier.

Charles waited.

Minutes passed, and then he heard a sigh.

A shape appeared in the doorway, faint at first, but slowly it gained definition until a young boy of perhaps ten or twelve stood there. He wore homespun clothes and looked as though he could have been from the late eighteen hundreds.

"Hello," Charles said.

The boy looked at him, his face pale, his hair blonde. After a moment the boy said, "Hello."

"Will you talk to me?"

The boy crossed his arms over his chest and asked, "Will you listen?"

Charles felt his eyebrows rise, but he managed to keep his tone neutral. "Yes. What will you tell me?"

The boy grinned, a bit of malice in his eyes. "I will tell you what it's like when you scalp a man."

Charles merely breathed and nodded.

"I'll tell you how to make one of the red men scream, even though he won't want to."

Charles nodded again.

"I will tell you," the boy said, looking at Charles and lowering his voice, "what the flesh of man tastes like, both raw and roasted."

"I'm listening," Charles said softly.

"I'm Thomas," the boy said happily, sitting down on the floor, "and I died in 1876."

Charles listened.

Chapter 35: Elmer hears from Roger

Two days after Elmer had met Roger at the restaurant, Elmer's business line rang.

The caller ID showed a cell number Elmer didn't recognize until he realized it was the number on the back of the card Roger had given him.

Elmer hurriedly answered the phone.

"Hello?"

"Hello, Elmer," Roger said. "I have some news for you."

"Wow," Elmer said, leaning back in his chair, "that was fast."

"Thank you. The information is pretty straightforward, Elmer. There's an evidence clerk at the Nashua Police Department who has a gambling problem. He scratches that itch with things he sells from evidence. He sold the bayonet to David Ganz. He doesn't know anything about the bayonet after that."

"Damn," Elmer said, shaking his head.

"That's not the end of it," Roger said easily. "Looks like the bayonet was used to kill a man named Jared Capote. Like you said, Jared Capote's murder is a locked room case. That's why the clerk thought it was okay to sell the weapon. When I looked a little more at Jared, I saw his friend Mike Singer died the day before. No exact details were available. However, Mike was living with his girlfriend at the time, a woman named Ellen Kay. Are you following all of this?"

"Yes."

"Good. Now, Ellen Kay works as a visiting nurse, and the day Mike Singer died, she found one of her patients dead. That man was Philip Sherman. A few days later, when Mr. Sherman's house was being shown for a quick sale, the real estate agent called the police to say there had been a break-in. Mr. Sherman's library had been left intact, and part of the sale of the house included the stipulation that nothing in the library could be removed. While the police didn't have a list of items which had been stolen from the library, they could see things were indeed missing. Those things, Elmer, were military items. Collectibles and such.

"Now I did a little digging on both Jared Capote and Mike Singer, and it turns out they had a couple of breaking and entering charges back from their high school days. Put two and two together, and you've got a couple of guys looking to make a quick buck. The best I can figure is Mike learned of Mr. Sherman's death from his girlfriend, Ellen. Mike probably heard the library was the only thing still there, and since Mr. Sherman was ninety-five when he passed away, Mike probably thought there was some money or something worthwhile in the library.

"Mike then must have gotten in touch with Jared; they got into the house, and then got away with a couple of bags of material. Evidently Jared decided to keep the bayonet for himself, but nothing else. That means he moved the material or whoever killed him took the material. Either way, some of that material is missing."

"There must also be some at Mr. Sherman's house," Elmer said excitedly. "Is the house still for sale?"

"No, it's been purchased. The new owner is a man named Charles Gottesman. He's a writer. General non-fiction, essentially."

"Do you have the address?" Elmer asked.

"I do," Roger said. "It's number one Sheridan Street in Nashua."

"Excellent!" Elmer said, writing the information down. "This is superb work, Roger. Could you please send me an invoice by email? Payment via cash?"

"Yes, please, Elmer," Roger chuckled. "The invoice is already in your inbox."

"Good. Thanks, Roger."

"You're welcome."

Elmer ended the call and put his phone down on the desk. He turned the chair and looked at the video feeds from the museum. He frowned. He still had to clean up after Captain Epp. The ghost had made a mess with the stranger Elmer had managed to get into the house.

Oh, well. Elmer smiled. *It was worth it, and there are plenty of ways to dismember a body and get rid of it.*

Plenty of ways.

Chapter 36: Charles and Ellen at the Flea Market

Charles and Ellen sat in her Volkswagen in the parking lot of the old mill that served as the Milford Flea Market. Charles occasionally went to the flea market, looking for older books to use for research. Today he and Ellen had a list of the missing items, as well as a sincere hope the items hadn't been sold.

Charles had taken out quite a bit of cash from his rainy day fund, and he was carrying the white gloves that had been hidden beneath Mr. Sherman's desk.

"Are you ready?" Charles asked.

"To go hunting for haunted items in a flea market?" Ellen asked with a shaky laugh. "Sure, I'm ready."

"Right," Charles said, shaking his head. "Yeah, I'm not ready either."

"No use in sitting here," Ellen said.

"No. Definitely not." Charles reached into his jacket's inner pocket and pulled out the gloves and the cash. He split the pile of cash in two, and handed one-half to Ellen.

"Gee, thanks, Dad," she said, grinning.

"You're welcome," Charles smiled back. He then handed her the right glove. "I probably should have been using this the whole time, but I was pretty stupid."

"What, the gloves?"

Charles nodded. "They're supposed to act as a buffer of some sort between the item and your skin. The gloves are supposed to protect you from the worst of the item's influence."

"We're going to look like Michael Jackson, you know," she said.

"I'm surprised you even know who he is," Charles laughed.

"He made *Thriller*," Ellen smiled. "*Thriller*. That's all I have to say about that."

"Well, now we're suitably prepared," Charles said, "shall we go in?"

"Sure," Ellen said, swallowing nervously. "Let's get this done."

They got out of the car, closed the doors, and made their way into the flea market with a few other people.

"Shoot me a text if you find anything," Charles said as they entered the building, pausing in the stairwell. "I'll do the same."

Ellen nodded, put her purse straps over her shoulder, and walked forward to prowl through the booths on the first floor. Charles walked up the stairs to the second floor and started his own search.

Chapter 37: Wayne Broderick and Dave's Stuff

Wayne didn't bother looking around when he "Irished up" his coffee. None of the other sellers at the flea market would care, and if a buyer had a problem with him drinking, then Wayne wouldn't sell to them. But that was pretty rare. Most of the folks who bought from him were either old school New Englanders who didn't much care about anything, or trendy kids who thought he was, what was it, ah, yes, "Edgy."

Idiots.

Wayne looked at the flask that held his whiskey. It was a beautiful silver piece that had been engraved with two words, My Lai. The words pulled at his memory, but he couldn't figure out what they meant. He had no idea who Lai had been, or why they were important, but hey, to each his own.

Wayne would be damned if his whiskey didn't taste *better* from the flask. Which was funny because he found the damned thing with all of the other military crap Dave had asked him to watch over.

Dave, Wayne thought. *Poor Dave.*

Wayne uncapped the flask, took a long pull from it to honor Dave, and then he capped the flask and put it away. He leaned back in the battered old recliner that served as his throne, surrounded by the various bits and pieces of old junk he sold. Some of it was good, some of it was bad. Wayne didn't know. He didn't follow the Antiques Roadshow or read any of the magazines about antiques.

Wayne read people.

Most people told you exactly what they were willing to pay as soon as they saw an item. Some could be hooked for a little more, others would haggle down. Some were unreadable, but those were few and far between, and they usually laughed at the price he threw at them. When that happened, Wayne would grin and ask what they'd be willing to pay for it.

Wayne had a good time, bought most of his stuff at the end of estate sales and cleaned out barns and cellars and attics. He had his pension from the Navy, his pension from his twenty years with the State. The money he made selling junk was drinking money and funds for the occasional trip down to Foxboro to watch the Patriots play.

No, Wayne didn't have any pressure from anybody for anything.

He took a drink of his coffee and grinned.

Damned if that coffee didn't taste just right with the whiskey.

A Chinese couple walked by, and a surge of hate flared within him, taking him aback.

What the hell? Wayne thought. He'd worked with a lot of Chinese over the years, hated haggling with them, but he didn't hate them.

He turned his head to watch the couple as they stopped to look at some lamps in Joan's stall across the aisle. They were young, fashionable. Wayne felt the surge of hate once more. It rose from deep within his stomach, and he literally had to fight the urge to grab hold of a knife from Dave's collection.

Wayne wanted to stab them.

He wanted to stab them to death.

Wayne forced himself to look away, and he felt the desire subside. With a shaking hand he lifted up his coffee and took a drink, the whiskey settling his nerves.

Jesus Christ, he thought. *What the hell is going on?*

He looked over at the table he'd put all of Dave's stuff on, the military crap the man had wanted to move. Something about it was wrong. Something about the damned things twisted his stomach.

Wayne shook his head and took another drink of his coffee.

If he didn't sell most of Dave's stuff today, he'd sell the lot wholesale to Tim over at the Army Surplus store.

Well, everything but the flask, Wayne thought with a grin.

He took the flask out of his pocket, added another splash of whiskey, and hoped the first customer wouldn't be any sort of Asian.

Chapter 38: Charles and Wayne

Charles saw the militaria after wandering about the second floor for nearly fifteen minutes. He paused long enough to send Ellen a quick text and then made his way directly to the tables.

Three tables stood in a straight line, battered old folding tables that looked like they'd been cast out of a Church bingo hall. All sorts of items stood neatly on the tables, everything from old oil cans to ancient copies of Harper's Weekly and the Saturday Evening Post. The last table on the left, however, had nearly everything that was missing from the library.

Behind the chairs, seated in a recliner that looked as old as the man who sat in it, was a man who was probably somewhere between sixty and ninety. He had a full, gray beard that reached down to his chest, a bald head, steel-rimmed glasses and a flannel shirt of indeterminate color beneath a pair of faded overalls. In one hand, he held a mug of coffee that proudly proclaimed, "Navy Veteran," and in the other he held an uncapped silver flask he was tipping over the mug.

From the faint smell, it was whiskey. Then Charles got a better look at the flask as the man shifted it around to cap it.

The flask was engraved with the words "My Lai."

The flask was part of the militaria, too, but the man seemed to be happy using it for its original purpose. Charles wondered when the ghost would start to work on the man.

Charles went up and stood in front of the militaria and looked down at the items. His stomach dropped, churning because he stood so close to them. He had read about them all, knew about each one and what it was capable of doing.

He took the list he had made out of his pocket and started checking them off mentally. A short, modern knife was taken from the first Gulf War. The flask, the old man had. A Nazi battle flag. A Japanese pack of cigarettes. A pair of Soviet sunglasses. A single gauntlet. The iron killing point of a Zulu spear.

"Do you see anything you like?" the old man asked.

Charles looked up, smiling and tucking the list away. Ellen came hurrying to stand beside him, smiling as she said, "There you are."

"Here I am," Charles said. He turned and looked at the old man. "Yes. I'm interested in all of them."

"Are you now?" the old man grinned, his teeth all present, but yellow and crooked. "I would be pleased to sell you each and every piece."

"I'm glad to hear that," Charles said. "But I want to buy your flask, too."

"What?" the old man laughed. "Hell, son, the flask ain't for sale. Just what you see on the tables."

Charles smiled and stepped over to the right to stand directly in front of the man, only the center table and its assorted junk separating them. "I know you'll sell that to me."

"Really, son?" the old man asked.

"Really," Charles said, lowering his voice slightly, forcing the older man to lean forward in his chair.

"Why is that?"

"Because I know what that damned thing is doing to you," Charles answered.

The old man blinked, started to say something, and then he stopped. Charles continued.

"That flask you're using," Charles said, speaking even softer. "It has two words on it, My Lai. That's the name of a village in Vietnam."

The man's face paled above his beard, eyes flicking down to the flask in his lap.

"Ah," Charles said, "you know the name. Didn't realize it before?"

The man shook his head ever so slightly.

"It makes you hate," Charles said, looking steadily at the man. "It makes you hate. First it makes you hate Asians. Chinese, Japanese, Vietnamese. Honestly, the flask can't tell the difference between any of them. It hates them all. Because it hates them, and you hold it, you hate them. Soon you'll want to do something more than hate them. Then you will do something more."

"Jesus Christ," the man said, putting the flask on the table in front of him and wiping his hand off on his pants leg.

"All of those things are like that," Charles said, nodding at the other militaria. "Every last one."

Thin beads of sweat appeared on the older man's brow.

"You've felt it, haven't you?" Ellen said, stepping close to Charles, looking at the old man.

The old man nodded. "I can feel there's something wrong with all of it. Every last one that Dave asked me to sell for him. Before he got sick and died."

"Have you sold any of the pieces at all?" Ellen asked him. "I think there's one missing."

Charles looked at the militaria, did a mental scan, and then nodded his agreement, turning back to the old man. "There's a gas mask that's not there."

"Nothing. I didn't sell anything from that pile. But if Dave had it, and it wasn't here, it'd be at his house," the old man said.

Charles felt his shoulders drop. How the hell were they going to get into the dead man's house? He didn't want to break in, but he might have to.

"I've got a key," the old man said, straightening up in his chair and giving the flask a wary look. "I don't know if that'll help at all, but I've got a key."

"That," Ellen said, smiling at the man, "would be a great help."

"How much do you want for all of it, before we get carried away here?" Charles asked.

The old man gave a wry grin. "If I didn't have to keep up appearances here, I'd give you the lot. As is, pass me a hundred if you can swing it, and everyone'll think I took you."

"Sounds good to me," Charles said, nodding with relief. "I'm Charles."

"Wayne," the old man said. "Got a bag or something for all of that?"

"I do," Ellen said, taking off her purse and opening it, pulling out a pair of large duffel bags.

"Good," Wayne said. "Let's get this stuff in there, and then I'll see if Joan can spot my stuff for a bit. I'll run you over to Dave's."

"Thank you," Charles said. He took a hundred off of the roll in his pocket and handed it over to Wayne.

"Don't thank me yet," Wayne said, folding the bill and stuffing it into his own pocket. "Dave wasn't the cleanest man I'd ever met, and we may have one hell of a time finding anything in that sty of his."

Chapter 39: Charles and Ellen at Home

"He wasn't lying," Ellen said from her seat on the couch.

"What was that?" Charles asked.

"Wayne," she said. "He wasn't lying about that place being dirty."

Charles chuckled, shaking his head. "No. He definitely wasn't."

"What amazed me, though," she continued, "was he said it looked like the place had been gone through."

"Yeah," Charles said, "I don't know how anyone could tell the difference. I'm curious what they were looking for. Nothing seemed to be taken."

"Do you think that maybe they were after the ghost stuff?" Ellen asked.

Charles shook his head. "I sure as hell hope not. I don't want to think about someone else out there hunting for those things. I know Mr. Sherman collected them to keep them out of the world, but I don't know about other people."

"Definitely a disturbing thought," Ellen said, closing her eyes and settling back against the couch.

"Definitely," Charles said. "But at least we got the gas mask back. And the other stuff."

Ellen nodded. "The only thing missing is the bayonet."

"Yeah," Charles sighed. "I was hoping the damned thing was going to be in that house."

"Me too."

Charles massaged his temples and closed his eyes. After a moment, he opened them again and sighed. "I have to put those things back."

"I know."

"I don't want to go in there," Charles said softly. "That library scares the absolute hell out of me."

"I know." She paused and then added, "Do you want me to come up with you?"

"No, thank you," Charles said, smiling at her. "I'm going to try and engage one of them in conversation again."

"That's strange, you know," Ellen said.

"What's that?"

"Coddling a ghost," she said, shaking her head. "I mean,

they're dead. I don't get any of it."

"Neither do I," Charles said, "but if talking with them keeps them from trying to kill us, then I'll talk to them."

"True," Ellen sighed. "Anyway, I was going to run over to my apartment, get a couple of little things out of there."

"Do you want me to come with you?" Charles asked.

"No," Ellen answered. "I should be okay. I'm going to need to do it alone at some point anyway. It might as well be at a time when I choose it."

"Okay," Charles said. "You can call or text me if you need anything."

"I will, thanks," Ellen smiled. She got up off of the couch and stretched. "I'll talk to you soon, Charles."

"Sounds good," Charles said, returning the smile. He watched her leave the room and heard the door open and close behind her. He turned his attention to the duffel bags by the fireplace and stifled a small wave of fear.

Standing up, he walked over to the bags, picked them up, and went to the library. In a moment, he had the door open, and the light on, and he was setting the bags on the desk. From his jacket pocket he took out the gloves, put them on, and returned the various items to the shelves.

It didn't take him long, and soon he was taking the gloves off and sitting down in the chair and looking about the library.

"Hello," he said shortly. "I'm here. Does anyone wish to speak?"

"Why did you stop me?" a voice asked from a corner.

Charles felt a shiver of fear at the sound of the voice. There was a deep rage under the words, and Charles wondered if he was going to have to lock the item up.

He kept a firm expression on his face as he turned to face the voice.

A young man had materialized, nearly fully formed, and wearing the old olive drab green uniform of a United States soldier from Vietnam.

"I stopped you," Charles said, "because you can't be killing people now."

"I can kill whenever I want," the ghost snapped.

Charles took a deep breath and said, "Can you tell me why?"

The ghost grinned. "There's a saying I learned when all those assholes were protesting in the States. They had Mao's little red book, you know?"

Charles did, so he nodded.

"Anyway," the ghost said, "the saying is, power stems from the barrel of a gun."

"My father," Charles said, "always said the strongest man in the world is the man standing in front of you with a gun."

"Damned right," the ghost laughed. "Your dad a soldier?"

"He was," Charles said, "crew chief on a Huey. 1967 to 1969."

The ghost nodded, seeming to relax slightly. "Your dad saw some shit then."

"He did. Talks about it every once in a while when he's got a good drunk on."

Again the ghost nodded. "We saw some shit. Some serious shit. That's why we cut all those bastards down in My Lai. We were tired of it."

"Yeah?"

"Yeah," the ghost said.

Charles watched the ghost pull a pack of cigarettes out, fish one out and light it. The entire thing was odd. Disturbingly familiar, and at the same time painfully surreal. Charles could even smell, ever so faintly, the cigarette smoke.

"Yeah, yeah it was," the ghost said. "You heard stories about what happened to prisoners. You heard stories of what the guys did when they got a couple of VC or NVA. You tried not to take prisoners. Too much bullshit. But at My Lai, well, we were sick of all the bullshit by then."

The ghost exhaled and looked at Charles.

"Did you ever see what a shotgun does to a kid?"

Charles shook his head.

The ghost grinned. "Well, let me tell you about it."

And the ghost did.

Chapter 40: Ellen at the Apartment

As soon as Ellen stepped into the apartment, she could smell smoke. With it was the sickeningly sweet smell of roast pork. The smell of someone who has literally been cooked.

She ran into the kitchen and threw up into the sink.

The smell was terrible, and she felt an urge to open the windows as she ran the faucet and the disposal to clean up the vomit in the sink.

But opening the windows would take time, and she wanted to spend as little as possible in the apartment. She needed a couple of sets of scrubs and a few photographs. Plus, her winter coat. It was getting cold—

"Hello Ellen," Mike said from the den.

Ellen straightened up, stiffening. She swallowed nervously and fought the urge to run.

"Aren't you going to say hello to me?" he asked.

Ellen walked out of the kitchen and looked into the den. The room was unnaturally dim, and once more, she could see her dead boyfriend sitting in his chair.

"Hello," Ellen said softly. There was a chill in the room suddenly, and she folded her arms over her chest.

"Why aren't you here anymore?" he asked. She could see a cigar in his hand, the tip glowing strangely.

"Because you're here," Ellen answered. "You're dead, Mike. You need to go and be dead."

"I am being dead," Mike replied, a hint of anger creeping into his voice. "I can't get much deader than I am, Ellen."

"I can't be here," she said. "I can't. I want to get a couple of things and get out of here."

"Where are you staying?" Mike asked, jealousy and suspicion joining the anger in his words.

"With a friend," she answered.

"A friend with benefits?" he sneered.

"Seriously, Mike?" Ellen shook her head. "I can't believe I'm having an argument with my dead boyfriend."

Mike's ashtray hurtled by her, shattering against the wall, ashes spraying out.

"Yes, seriously," he hissed. The lights flickered in the kitchen and the temperature plummeted. "Where the hell are you staying?"

Ellen didn't answer. She turned and started towards the hallway when the bulbs in the kitchen exploded.

"Where are you staying?!" Mike screamed.

She'd buy new scrubs, Ellen thought. Ellen turned away from the hallway and walked to the front door. Something cold rushed through her, and a moment later Mike's disembodied voice came from in front of her as she grabbed the doorknob.

"Who says you can leave?" he hissed.

Ellen tried to turn the knob, but it wouldn't budge. A spike of panic ripped through her, but she shoved it aside.

"Let me out, Mike," Ellen said firmly.

"Why?" he demanded. "Who are you going to go see?"

"Let me out, Mike," she said again, trying the knob and finding it still immovable.

"Why?"

"Because I want to go," she said, and suddenly a wave of sadness swept over her. "Because you're dead, Mike. Because you're dead."

There was a long moment of silence before Mike spoke again.

"I am dead," he said softly. "I am."

Ellen tried the doorknob again, and it turned easily in her hand.

She opened the door and left the apartment, closing it behind her, but not bothering to lock it.

There was nothing in the apartment she wanted anymore.

Chapter 41: Elmer and Charles have a Conversation

Elmer parked his car across from One Sheridan Street, put on his best smile, and got out of his car. He straightened up, made sure his suit coat and tie were perfect, and walked across the street and up the path and stairs to the front door. An old fashioned doorbell was on the right, and he turned the key-shaped handle. The bell rang loudly beyond the door.

A few moments passed, and then through the door, Elmer heard, "I'm coming!"

A brief moment after that, the door opened, and a man in his forties stood in the doorway. He had short black hair with random strands of white, and he wore a sweater and a pair of black pants as well as house slippers.

"May I help you?" the man asked.

"Yes," Elmer said, extending his head. "I'm Elmer Hoyt."

"Hello, Elmer," the man said, shaking his hand.

"Are you Charles Gottesman?"

"I am," Charles said.

"May I come in? I'd like to discuss the library you purchased," Elmer smiled.

"I'm afraid you can't come in," Charles said, standing firmly in front of Elmer and barring any entrance.

Elmer blinked, but managed to keep the smile on his face. "I'm interested in purchasing some of the items within."

"They're not for sale," Charles replied.

"I'm willing to pay a considerable amount for them," Elmer said, still smiling.

"That's excellent, but unfortunate," Charles said, a cold look on his face. "Nothing in this house is for sale. I'm sorry you wasted your time, Mr. Hoyt, but you need to leave."

Elmer's smile disappeared, and he felt anger boiling up. "You don't understand, Mr. Gottesman. I want to purchase your militaria."

"I understand you perfectly well," Charles said. "What you're not understanding is that it is not, and will not be, for sale. If you don't leave, Mr. Hoyt, I will call the police, and they will help you leave."

"Mr. Gottesman," Elmer said, unable to keep the anger out of his voice. "I want those items for my collection. Name your price."

"Mr. Hoyt," Charles said, "I'm going to give you some advice about items like the ones in my house. They're dangerous. Exceptionally so. They're not to be handled lightly."

"I know exactly what they are like," Elmer snapped. "I need to add yours to my collection."

"They're not toys," Charles said. "Each and every one of those items can kill. Misjudging the things that inhabit them, that are attached to them, can make you a victim before the dust settles on your shelves."

"I think I can handle such things, Mr. Gottesman," Elmer snarled.

"Well then, I wish you the best of luck with your collection. Good day, Mr. Hoyt," Charles said. "I'm going to call the police now."

"Goddamn you!" Elmer snarled as the door closed.

Clenching his fists, Elmer turned around and stormed down the stairs and back to his car. He needed those items. He needed them. He needed to find someone who would break-in and steal them for him. But he hadn't had to do that for years. He didn't even know anyone in that business anymore.

Perhaps Roger would know, Elmer thought. Angrily he got into his car, slamming the door shut and starting the engine. Soon he was turning around in Gottesman's driveway and headed home.

Elmer had to call Roger.

Roger would be able to help.

Chapter 42: Charles and Ellen at Home

Charles and Ellen sat at the dining table. She had been quiet when she'd gotten back from the apartment. Charles had cooked a simple dinner of fried potatoes and bacon, an old German recipe he had learned from his grandmother. Ellen had eaten quietly, and now she sat with her hands wrapped around her mug of coffee.

"Did you see Mike?" Charles asked gently.

Ellen nodded.

"Are you okay?"

She shook her head.

"Is there anything I can do?"

Again she shook her head, giving him a small smile and blinking back a few tears. "No thank you, Charles. I don't even know how to explain the situation, it's so, so bizarre."

Charles could only nod.

She took a sip of her coffee and asked, "Did you speak with any of them?"

"I did," Charles said. "I spoke with the ghost attached to the flask Wayne was drinking from."

"How was that?"

"Brutal," Charles said uncomfortably. "Brutal. I don't doubt I'll have nightmares from the things I've heard."

"I'm sorry," Ellen said.

"So am I," he sighed. "Oh, I also had someone show up and ask if he could buy the items in the library."

"What?" Ellen asked. "How the hell did he find out about it?"

"I didn't ask," Charles said. "I told him no."

"How did he take that?"

"Not well. He was extremely upset when he left."

"Well," Ellen said, "here's hoping he doesn't try to break in."

"True," Charles said. "I'd hate to try and explain that to the police. Anyway, do you want some more coffee?"

"Yes, please," Ellen said. She held her mug out to Charles.

"You know," Charles said, taking the mug from her, "we're only missing the bayonet now."

"I know," Ellen said. "Here's hoping it never pops back up."

"Very, very true," Charles agreed, and he walked back to the kitchen for the coffee.

Once he reached the kitchen and started to pour the coffee Charles stopped, straightening up. "Holy shit."

Leaving the mugs in the kitchen Charles hurried back into the den. "Ellen."

"You okay?" she asked, sitting up.

"Yes," he said hurriedly. "I just realized something. I think Elmer may have the bayonet."

"What? Why?"

"How else would he know about the collection?" Charles said. "He must have spoken with the pawnbroker or possibly even the ghost attached to the bayonet."

"Jesus," Ellen said, getting to her feet. "Do you know where he lives?"

"No," Charles said, taking out his cell phone and bringing up Lee's number, "but I'm sure I can find out."

Chapter 43: Elmer and Captain Epp

Elmer was furious.

Roger had been less than helpful.

The man had flat out refused to assist Elmer in finding someone to break into Charles Gottesman's house and steal the items.

The few men he had known were either no longer in the state or were tenants in one of the state's correctional facilities. The one man he had been able to reach, Lee Parker, who had never flinched at anything before he had gone to prison, had laughed at him when Elmer had told him that it was a house belonging to Charles Gottesman.

Then Lee had hung up the phone.

Elmer knew better than to call Lee back. He'd heard of someone who had done that before. The gentleman had ended up in the hospital with severe facial fractures. No, Elmer was going to have to figure out how to do the dirty work himself.

First, he needed to calm down. He needed to relax and figure out how exactly he was going to get the items out of Gottesman's house.

Elmer walked over to his bar, poured himself a healthy dose of bourbon, and drank it. The liquor was hot in his throat and belly, and he breathed in the deep scent of it. He closed his eyes, took in a long, deep breath, and exhaled slowly.

I need my museum, he thought.

Elmer put the glass down on the bar and left the room, making his way to the door of the museum. For a moment, he wondered where his family was, and then he remembered Fiona saying something about going to Target to look at Christmas decorations.

Elmer rolled his eyes at the thought of shopping in public and finally reached the museum's door. He let himself in and strolled along the shelves as the door closed and locked behind him. Occasionally he paused, looking at a piece and smiling happily. Between the murder weapons and the bourbon, he was starting to feel good.

Soon he found himself approaching the display case that held the bayonet to which Captain Epp was attached. Elmer grinned at the tiled floor. There wasn't a single drop of blood that could be seen. Not a single strand of DNA would show up. He had studied murder scenes and murder scene cleanups over the years, and he knew he had done a professional job.

Butchering the victim's body had been difficult. Elmer had never enjoyed handling raw meat, but after about twenty minutes he had gotten into the swing of it. He had managed to cut the man down into extremely small, manageable pieces. He had then dissolved them a little bit at a time in the private bathroom off of his office. The bones had been easily ground up and disposed of during his occasional drives.

Yes, everything had gone extremely well. He had made sure to save the recording of the murder, burying it deep in an external hard-drive that could be wiped with an industrial magnet the instant something went wrong.

Elmer couldn't wait to find another victim for Captain Epp.

In fact, Elmer thought, *that's what I should do this evening.*

Humming to himself Elmer opened the case for the bayonet and took it out. He held it in his hands, enjoying the weight of it. Enjoying the fact it had been used to kill, and so recently at that.

Elmer turned the weapon over in his hands, wondering what it had been like for Captain Epp to use it on the battlefield. The carnage must have been amazing, the slaughtering of thousands by machine guns and artillery, and then the up close and personal killing. A type of killing Captain Epp was so skilled in.

Grinning to himself Elmer held onto the bayonet and walked out of the museum. He made his way to the back door, pausing to pour himself a fresh drink. He took both the bayonet and the drink onto the porch and stood by one of the chairs, enjoying the cold air. Elmer took a sip and looked at the bayonet.

"Why are you holding it?"

Elmer looked up and saw Captain Epp standing in front of him. "Ah, Captain. I was wondering what it was like to use this weapon in battle."

"Were you? What in particular, Herr Hoyt, were you wondering about?"

"Well," Elmer said cheerfully, "I was wondering what it looked like when you used a bayonet like this on someone's stomach."

"Ah," Captain Epp smiled, reaching out and gently taking the bayonet from Elmer. *"That was always an interesting*

experience. *You see, most of my comrades ground the backs down. They believed war was terrible enough without a blade such as this affixed on the end of our rifles."*

"Is that so?"

"It is. I disagreed with them."

"I'm not surprised. I disagree with them as well."

Captain Epp smiled. *"Do you?"*

"Of course," Elmer said. "War can never be terrible enough."

"I agree," Captain Epp chuckled.

"I contacted a Mr. Gottesman today," Elmer said.

Captain Epp frowned. *"Who is he?"*

"He has the collection of items similar to your bayonet," Elmer said, frowning. "He has no intention of selling any of them to me."

"And what shall you do about that?"

"There is nothing I can do," Elmer said bitterly. "I have no way to get them."

"You are giving up that easily?"

"No," Elmer said. "I must simply find another way. It may take some time, as well as finding another victim for you. I confess myself disappointed with my own failure, but I will succeed eventually."

"Ah. I am not a patient man, Herr Hoyt," Captain Epp said with a grim smile. *"However, what were we discussing?"*

"War," Elmer said, a smile returning to his face. "We were discussing how war can never be terrible enough."

"Yes," Captain Epp said, nodding, *"yes. And I must say, Herr Hoyt, I agree completely."*

Elmer smiled, and then his smile slipped away as Captain Epp stepped forward and thrust the bayonet deep into his stomach.

The pain was more than anything Elmer had ever experienced before. He would have fallen to the floor if the ghost had not taken hold of him by a shoulder. Then Elmer screamed as Captain Epp slowly, ever so slowly, twisted the bayonet in the wound.

Elmer could feel his intestines being wrapped around the blade and its ridges.

"I agree, Herr Hoyt, that war can never be terrible enough," Captain Epp said softly, smiling pleasantly at him. *"And I have*

never stopped being at war."

***

Charles and Ellen got out of her car as a scream ripped through the cold air.

Without a word, they raced towards the sound, running around the side of the large house which Lee Parker had told Charles belonged to Elmer Hoyt. The house was huge and modern, an eyesore when compared to the colonial homes Charles and Ellen had passed on their way.

When they turned the corner, Charles saw Elmer Hoyt lying on his side on a large porch. Standing above him was a large German soldier wearing what Charles knew was a World War One uniform. The soldier held the bayonet, blood dripping from it.

The German stepped towards Charles, and Ellen slipped around the man to check on Elmer Hoyt. Charles focused on the German, catching sight of Ellen out of the corner of his eye as she took off her jacket and pressed down on Hoyt's stomach. Then all of Charles' attention was on the German, the ghost grinning, raising the bayonet and laughing.

Charles pulled on the white gloves.

When the German saw them, he snarled and turned towards Ellen.

Charles lunged forward, wrapping both hands around the hilt of the weapon as the German let out a horrific scream of rage. The two of them wrestled for a moment before the German twisted the bayonet towards Charles, pushing it ever closer to him.

The bayonet plunged downwards, cutting through the thick muscle of Charles's left shoulder.

Charles screamed, yet didn't let go of the weapon.

The German let out one more howl of rage, trying to jerk the weapon free.

"The box," Charles gasped, "get the box!"

Ellen turned, sprinting back around the house.

"Welche Box, guter Herr?" the German hissed at Charles.

Charles couldn't understand the German, and he didn't want to. The ghost was incredibly strong, trying to twist the weapon in

599

the wound. It took all of Charles' effort to stop him.

"Ich bin dein Tod, umarme mich," the ghost said, leaning in close, grinning at him with crooked teeth. *"Umarme mich!"*

"Charles!" Ellen called out to him.

Charles didn't look at her, he was gasping with the effort, the German pushing him back a step.

And then Ellen was beside him.

She dropped the box to the ground, and said, "Don't look."

Charles closed his eyes.

A sharp, incredible pain blazed across his wounded shoulder and suddenly the bayonet was free.

"Du dumme Schlampe!" the German screamed.

Ellen wrapped her hands around Charles' own and together they forced the weapon towards the box. She freed one hand, flipped up the box, and managed to thrust the bayonet into the box. Ellen slapped the lid closed, the German's screams of rage ending abruptly.

Charles collapsed to his knees, Ellen hurrying to his side. Blood was seeping into his clothing.

"Charles," she said. "Charles, look at me."

Charles did so.

She smiled at him. "Listen to me. This is not severe, but it is going to need stitches. I can do that at home, but it's not going to be terribly pleasant. Do you understand?"

"Yes," Charles said, clenching his teeth against the pain. "Hoyt?"

"Alive, but he needs medical attention. I did what I could," Ellen replied, helping Charles get to his feet. She bent down and picked up the box. "I'll call the hospital and then they'll send an ambulance. If I call an emergency line they'll trace my phone."

Charles nodded, and Ellen led him down off of the porch, back around the house and to the Volkswagen. She helped him get into the car, put the box at his feet and buckled Charles in.

A moment later, she was in the car, closing the door and starting the engine with one easy, fluid motion. The engine rumbled, and she turned the headlights on before looking at Charles and smiling.

Charles found he was shivering, and he swallowed nervously. "What are you smiling about?"

"I realized something," she said, checking the mirrors before pulling out onto the road.

"What's that?"

"At least we got the bayonet back," Ellen said, laughing.

Unable to stop himself, Charles laughed too. "Yes, yes we did."

* * *

Bonus Scene Chapter 1: The Antique Store, Norwich, Connecticut, 1958

Philip sat in his car, the engine off and the Ford parked in front of the Norwich, Connecticut Library. The clock on city hall struck nine in the morning, and soon Blackwell's Antiques on Washington Street would open.

In the shop was another item to collect.

An old Sharps rifle, from what Philip had been able to gather.

One with typical, murderous intent.

Philip considered starting the engine again, just to get a little heat in, but he might get too comfortable. He might decide that it could wait another day or two.

He'd done it before, and with disastrous consequences.

No, he thought, sighing. *No, I have to do it today.*

Philip flexed his hands in his gloves, stretching the leather, and then he took the key out of the ignition, put it into the inner pocket of his overcoat and opened the door.

A harsh, bitter wind coursed down Main Street, biting at his exposed face and ears.

But it wasn't colder than Korea. Not even close. And Philip had made the long, treacherous march down from the Chosin Reservoir.

He could walk half a block up to the antique store.

Glancing both ways and seeing that the road was free of traffic, Philip crossed Main Street, walked to the intersection with Washington Street and turned left. He moved at a steady pace and moments later, he found himself standing at the storefront for Blackwell Antiques.

Some old colonial pewter and a pair of matching Federal side chairs occupied one window, with the pewter on top of a piecrust tea table. In the other window hung an American primitive painting along with an old sailor's chest well decorated with primitive nautical themes.

The plain white and black sign in the store's glass front door read 'Open.'

Philip stepped into the small alcove, opened the door and heard a small bell chime brightly as he walked into the shop.

The antique store was packed with goods, as was usual with New England antique stores. A wide range of items of dubious value set close to one another on shelves and tables. At the far end of the store was a counter, and behind that counter was a young man, perhaps twenty years old.

The young man looked up from the paper he was reading as Philip walked in.

"Good morning," Philip said, taking his gloves off and sliding them into his pockets.

"Morning," the young man replied, and he went back to his paper.

Philip ignored the items around him and walked to the counter, behind which were shelves that held antiques the owner obviously knew were of some worth. On the top most shelf, nearly at the ceiling, was what Philip had come. The Sharps rifle.

When Philip reached the desk, the young man looked at Philip and gave him a tight smile. "Yes?"

"Hello," Philip said, "my name is Philip Sherman. I called yesterday and spoke with a Henry Blackwell about purchasing the Sharps rifle."

The young man frowned and then after a moment he looked around the counter and found a small note. He picked it up, read it and his eyebrows raised up. "Well," the young man said after a moment, "I didn't think that Mr. Blackwell would ever sell that rifle. He is particularly attached to it."

"I can understand," Philip smiled. "It is a rare and an exceptional piece."

Again the young man gave him a tight smile. Then, after having set the paper back down on the counter, the young man turned around and reached up, taking the rifle down off of the shelf. As he turned back around with the weapon, Philip opened up his coat, slipped a hand into his other inner pocket and withdrew a pair of white cotton gloves.

Philip put the gloves on carefully, relaxing slightly as he did so.

The young man stepped up to the counter and then the bell over the front door chimed, and he looked up. The young man started to smile, but then it faltered as he said, "Ah, Mr. Blackwell."

Philip turned and looked as an older man hurried into the store. The man's short gray hair was disheveled, and he was remarkably unkempt. The man had neither shaved nor dressed himself properly. The man's shirttails were out, his shoes untied, and he was wearing neither jacket nor waistcoat.

"Mr. Blackwell, are you alright?" the young man asked, still holding onto the rifle.

"I'm not selling that!" Mr. Blackwell said shrilly.

Philip looked back to the young man and saw his hands clench tightly on the weapon. Gently Philip said, "Put that on the counter, son."

The young man didn't seem to hear him, his eyes starting to glaze over as they flickered from left to right rapidly.

Mr. Blackwell came to a stop a few feet from Philip, panting. "Thurber," Mr. Blackwell said, "put the rifle on the counter. Please."

But young Thurber wasn't listening to either one of them, which was evident as he tilted his head slightly to the right, nodding.

"Thurber," Philip said in a commanding voice, "put the damned rifle down!"

Thurber's eyes snapped over to Philip, his lip curled into a sneer, and he cocked the weapon.

"It's not loaded," Mr. Blackwell started to say, but Philip wasn't paying attention to the man.

Thurber brought the rifle up quickly to his shoulder, taking aim at Mr. Blackwell even as Philip launched himself forward. He grabbed hold of the barrel with both hands and pushed it up even as Thurber squeezed the trigger. The rifle roared in the close confines of the store, shattering a brass and crystal chandelier. Shards of the crystal scattered through the room, one piece cutting a path across Philip's forehead.

As the blood trickled down in front of his eyes, Philip wrested the weapon out of Thurber's hands.

Thurber stumbled back while Mr. Blackwell was howling in pain, obviously struck by some sort of shrapnel. And as Philip got a firm grasp of the Sharps rifle he was able to see who the young man had been listening to.

A great, giant ghost of a man stood on the other side of the counter, glaring at Philip. The man wore an old Confederate uniform, crossed sabers on his forage cap.

"Who the hell are you, you son of a bitch?" the man snarled, his voice carrying with it the faintest hint of a Southern accent.

Philip didn't answer. It wasn't time to. He had to concentrate. He looked to Mr. Blackwell, who was hurrying to the counter to check on Thurber, who had sat down heavily on an old chair.

"Is he alright?" Philip asked.

"Answer me!" the ghost screamed at Philip.

"Dazed," Mr. Blackwell said. He looked at Philip and saw that he was still holding the rifle. His face blanched, and he said, "How can you hold it?"

"The gloves," Philip answered.

"Take the god-damned things off," the ghost spat. "Take them off and hold my rifle."

Philip ignored him.

Mr. Blackwell looked from the rifle to Thurber, and then to Philip. "Will you be able to handle it?"

"Handle it?" Philip asked with a surprised chuckle. "No. But I'll be able to get it somewhere safe."

"I'll gut you, you son bastard," the ghost said, sliding through the counter and standing in front of Philip. "I will find a way to gut you."

"He's talking to you," Mr. Blackwell said simply.

Philip nodded.

"He's a right old bastard is what he is," Mr. Blackwell said tiredly, "but he's been a friend at times. Ever since I was a boy and I found the rifle in my grandfather's house. My grandfather killed a few men with it, and then himself. But they never found the rifle. Sergeant Hill told me what he'd done with my grandfather. I don't know why he never had me do it."

"He was a good boy," the ghost said. "You can tell him that. But you're a bad man, and bad men end badly."

"The sergeant," Philip said, "tells me that you were a good boy. I, however, should not expect any consideration."

Mr. Blackwell laughed, took a pocket square out of a pants pocket and dabbed at a cut on his cheek. "No, I imagine he won't give you any."

Thurber looked at the men dazedly. "Why was the rifle loaded?"

"It's always loaded," Mr. Blackwell answered. He looked at Philip and asked, "How did you know about the rifle?"

"Yes," Sergeant Hill hissed, "how did you know?"

Philip ignored the ghost but answered Mr. Blackwell. "I've been going through the papers for years now, looking for curious deaths. When I read of your grandfather's I dug a little more. Now, I hate to be rude, Mr. Blackwell, but I should like to put this away in my car and get it somewhere safe. I dislike holding onto it anymore than I have to."

"Understood, sir," Mr. Blackwell said, straightening up. "Good luck."

"Thank you," Philip said, and he turned his back on Mr. Blackwell and Thurber. As he walked out of the antique shop, the ghost of Sergeant Hill was fairly dragged along with him, screaming as he went. When they got to Philip's car, and he opened the trunk, the ghost was quite literally frothing at the mouth.

Philip continued to ignore him as he took out his key ring, selected a small lock key, and unlocked a long, lead lined box. Into the box, he put the rifle, and he closed the lid, locking it securely once more.

And it was silent.

The lead kept the ghost within.

Philip sighed as he closed the trunk. He had read in some occult books that lead worked to bind restless spirits, but the Sharps rifle was the first real test of that theory. And Philip was exceptionally glad it had worked.

A two-hour drive back to Nashua with Sergeant Hill screaming profanities at him would have been a decidedly unpleasant experience.

Bonus Scene Chapter 2: Old South Cemetery, Hollis, New Hampshire, 1964

Philip crept from headstone to headstone, staying as low as he could. For the entire day, he had been tracking the man, and now the man was in the cemetery. The man either had a victim in the cemetery already, or he was waiting for one.

Philip had to stop him either way. In his right hand, Philip carried a shortened police baton, cut to size by a friend of his on the Nashua Police Department.

Ahead, the unknown man was speaking softly in Latin, which is what had first grabbed Philip's attention earlier in the morning. What had kept Philip's attention, however, was the ancient brass ring on the man's left index finger. It was engraved with a rough eagle with a cross above it. An early Roman Legionary ring.

And it was there that the pieces had fallen together.

In the Gilson Road Cemetery, the Nashua Police had found a young woman beaten to death with an iron pole. She had been stripped naked and her head tied into the fork of a tree.

In Woodlawn Cemetery, a second young woman had been found, killed the same way and her head tied into the fork of a tree as well.

The deaths were consistent with a style of punishment doled out by Caesar's Legions in ancient Rome. Thus the Latin had caught Philip's ear, and the ring had assured him the man was indeed the killer, albeit unwillingly.

Whoever was still attached to the ring had a taste for murder, as so many of them had. And whoever it was happened to be living vicariously through this young man.

Philip only hoped that he wouldn't have to kill the man to get the ring away from him. But the murders had to stop, and if killing the man would ensure no more people were needlessly killed by someone being possessed by the ring, then so be it.

Philip had killed before, and he knew he would have to kill again.

He moved forward again until he found himself across from the outer stone wall and looking down into the small cemetery. In the center of the headstones, as the halfmoon's light spilled out on the new grass, Philip could see a man dragging a naked young woman towards the far edge. A glance there showed a tree with the necessary fork in it, and a large iron bar leaned against an ancient headstone.

Yes. This is who I've been looking for, Philip thought. *I need to wait.*

And so Philip waited, as terrible as it was. He waited for the man to bring the woman to the tree and slap her back into consciousness. She screamed and fought the man as he started to bind her head into the fork of the tree and its limb, but there was no one to hear her. The cemetery was too far removed from town. The road too abandoned at night.

But she wasn't alone, although she didn't know it.

As soon as the man started his binding, Philip took a grip on the baton and sprinted forward. He brought the baton crashing down at the base of the man's skull and spine, yet the man turned at the last moment, and what would have been a debilitating, if not an outright crippling blow, merely shattered the man's jaw.

The man stumbled back, screaming in rage and fury, spitting out blood and broken teeth as he lunged at Philip.

Philip sidestepped the man's attack and brought the baton down again, breaking the man's left arm at the bicep. Quickly Philip struck twice more, in the chest region, the second blow cracking his sternum and causing the man to slip slightly, crashing into a headstone and tumbling down.

Philip didn't waste time checking on the young woman. He would do that after. He needed to keep the pressure on the possessed. At any moment, the man might gain the upper hand, and that would prove to be fatal for both Philip and the young woman.

Leaping forward, Philip struck again with the baton as the man raised a hand to grasp a headstone. Philip smashed the man's fingers, eliciting another howl of pain and rage. A torrent of Latin, which Philip couldn't understand, flowed from the man's mouth as he lashed out with a foot, the heel of which caught Philip in the thigh and deadened his muscle momentarily.

Dropping to a knee and gasping in pain, Philip still managed to dodge another kick before slamming the baton into the man's groin. The man let out a cough, followed by vomit, as he grasped his balls while collapsing to the grass.

As quickly as he could, Philip pulled his cotton gloves out of his pocket, slipped them on and grabbed hold of the man's left hand. He pulled on the ring.

It stayed there.

In his ears, Philip heard someone laughing, saying something in Latin. It wasn't the man on the ground. He was insensible with pain, unable to talk.

The voice continued to laugh.

But this wasn't Philip's first time to the carnival, as the saying went.

From his pocket Philip dug out a sailor's folding knife, opened it with a flick of his wrist, and before the unseen Latin speaker could finish expressing outrage at the sight of the weapon, cut the man's finger off.

Philip ripped the ring off of the finger and dropped the finger onto the grass beside the man. The man's blood did not stain the white cotton gloves.

Standing up, Philip held onto the ring tightly, folded the knife and put it away before hurrying over to the young woman, who stood clawing at the bindings that were half finished.

"Calm down," Philip said gently, freeing her, "calm down. Where are your clothes?"

"His car," she managed to say after a moment, forcing herself into calm.

"Where's that?"

"Dow Road."

"Alright," Philip said, "I'll bring you there. You can get your clothes and then I'll take you home."

"What about him?" she asked, pointing at the man.

"What about him?" Philip asked.

"Shouldn't we call the police?"

Philip shook his head. "He'll be dead soon."

"How do you know?" she asked fearfully, looking at the man.

"One way or another," Philip said softly, "he'll be dead soon."

Bonus Scene Chapter 3: Sullivan Farm, Brookline, New Hampshire, 1969

The wind shook the car as Philip pulled into the long driveway that led up to the white farmhouse. The main house and its country red barn stood atop a small hill. A chicken coop sprawled out to the right, and a paddock could be glimpsed behind the barn and stretching over to the back of the house.

And while the sun was rapidly setting behind the apple orchard on the west of the property, there were no lights on in the house. Nor in the barn. A battered green pickup truck was parked by the side door to the house, but there was no one that Philip could see or hear.

That was a decidedly bad sign.

Philip pulled into the driveway behind the pickup, turned off the ignition and got out of the car. The wind ripped the door out of his hand and slammed it shut.

He looked at the stairs leading to the house's side door and took a deep breath, getting ready to go up and knock on the door when he heard music.

Soft music, someone picking out a pleasant tune on a guitar.

The sound came from the barn and as Philip turned to face the barn, he knew the sound wasn't right. He'd heard enough of the dead to know when they were doing something. And this music was being made by the dead.

But Philip had never heard the dead without actually touching an object he was collecting. *I can't tell*, he thought, *if this is a good or a bad thing.*

I'll need to worry about that later, Philip thought. He started walking towards the barn, where the giant sliding door was open a few feet. When he reached the door, he didn't bother peeking in, he had a fair idea of what to expect.

Philip walked into the barn and saw a middle-aged man hanging from one of the rafters. Beneath the man's gently swaying work boots was a turned over milking stool. In the stalls around the barn, cows stood, lazily looking at Philip as they chewed their cuds.

The music came from the ghost of a young man standing beside the door to a small shop, playing his guitar happily, smiling at the body hanging from the ceiling.

Philip went to the body and looked around for the letter. He knew that it was somewhere on the man, either a pocket or in his hands.

And there it was held loosely in the man's left hand.

"What are you doing here?" a voice asked suddenly, and when Philip looked up, he realized the ghost of the young man was standing right next to him, fuming. "Who are you? Why can you hear me?"

Philip didn't answer, reaching into his pockets instead and taking out his gloves.

"Who are you?!" the young man demanded, and Philip felt waves of sadness roll over him. The sadness battered at his thoughts and images of Korea flooded into his mind. Not his own battles, but those of the young man. Units falling back against the initial attack of the North Koreans. Being captured and sent north. Surviving years of torment.

Coming home and not being able to change.

Nothing helped.

Nothing.

Writing the letter, explaining why. Writing the letter and holding onto it as he climbed onto the top of the desk chair he'd sat in as a boy, and hanging himself from one of the exposed beams in his bedroom.

Philip gasped and stumbled backward, nearly dropping his gloves.

"You need to get out," the ghost snarled. "You need to leave. They're all mine, and you want to take them away from me. There's a whole family left. A whole family. They'll all understand soon enough."

Philip didn't respond, pulling on his gloves instead and straightening up. The ghost sent fresh waves of despair rolling over Philip, but Philip was reinforced. The gloves helped, somehow, to blunt the worst of the despair.

Delicately, Philip opened the dead man's hand and freed the letter. Philip didn't read the letter, didn't even allow himself a glimpse of the words within as he folded the paper.

"What are you doing with that?" the ghost said. "What are you doing with me?"

Philip continued to ignore the ghost, whose questioning increased in volume the more Philip remained silent. When

Philip and his ill-tempered guest reached the car's trunk, Philip opened it, and unlocked the lead-lined carrying case within.

The ghost howled in rage as Philip put the letter into the case, then closed and locked the lid. Philip closed the trunk and sat down on the bumper, his hands shaking as he removed his gloves and put them back into his coat's inner pocket.

Why did I hear this one? Philip asked. *I wasn't even touching the letter. I wasn't even close enough to it.*

Shaking his head, Philip stood up. *I'll have to call Thomas when I get home.*

With that thought in mind, Philip stood up and walked to the driver's side door of the car.

***

When Philip got home, neither Eleanor nor their daughter Samantha was home, which was a good thing. He hated having to tell the girl that she couldn't go into the library. He'd always locked the door, but she was a teenager. And that, more than anything, would lead her to attempt to get into the library.

Which would be disastrous, if not outright deadly.

Eleanor understood what the items were and what they had done, even though she had no desire to have them in the house. It was only after Philip had lined the library with lead behind the bookshelves and put them in the door, as well as having a theoretically 'unpickable' lock in the doorknob that she relaxed slightly.

At some point, Philip hoped to find someone who could take the items off his hands so he didn't have to constantly fear his daughter entering the library.

Until then, however, he had a responsibility. The things had to be kept away from society. Locked up and carefully guarded.

When Philip had finished backing his car into the driveway, he got the letter out of the box and went inside the house. He hurried up the stairs, unlocked the library, turned the light on and went in. After placing the letter in a small glass case, Philip stripped off his gloves, put them on the desk and sat down heavily in his chair.

He let out a long sigh and then straightened up, uncapping his brandy and pouring himself a healthy dose. Sitting back again, he held the brandy snifter in his left hand, rolling the liquid around in the glass, warming it with his own body heat. After a few minutes of silence, he took a small sip, then picked up the receiver and dialed the operator. When a young woman answered he asked for a long distance operator. Once transferred to the long distance operator, he gave the woman Thomas' phone number and waited while she connected them.

After half a dozen rings, Thomas picked up.

"Hello?"

"Hello Thomas," Philip said, "it's Philip Sherman."

"Ah, Philip!" Thomas said happily. "How are you, young man?"

"I'm well overall, but I'm confused," Philip said. "I heard one of the ghosts today."

There was a pause before Thomas said, "And this was, I suppose before you were actually handling the item?"

"Yes, exactly."

"Ah. And you would like to know why?"

"Yes."

"You see," Thomas began, "you have come into contact with so many of the items that the world is growing thin around you. When you are near a strong ghost, you will know it. The more you work with these items, the thinner the membrane, as it is, will become around you. You need to start disciplining yourself, Philip, you need to be prepared to ignore things that others will neither see nor hear."

"So this is going to get worse?" Philip asked with a sigh.

"Exactly," Thomas said sympathetically. "In several years you will be able to see even the slightest of shades lurking around a building or person. It drives some of the collectors mad, but I believe that you are made of sterner stuff than most. You will do fine, Philip."

Philip chuckled. "Thank you for the vote of confidence, Thomas."

"You're welcome," Thomas said. "Now, tell me, what is it you gathered today?"

"Do you remember the story of the suicide letter?" Philip asked.

"Yes, of course," Thomas said. "They say that it somehow worked its way all the way back into the United States. Is that what you found?"

"I did."

"With another victim?"

"I'm afraid so," Philip answered, taking a sip of his brandy.

"Tell me, what is next?"

"Well," Philip said, "I've heard rumor of a French Foreign Legion hat that slowly drives the owner mad with thirst."

"And you've started your research?"

"Of course," Philip chuckled, the brandy warming his stomach and his limbs. "Of course I have."

Bonus Scene Chapter 4: Philip Sherman's Library, Nashua, NH, 1980

Philip sat alone in his library.

All of the whiskey was gone, most of the brandy too.

Eleanor was at her sister's house in Milford.

Samantha was buried in Edgewood Cemetery, directly across from the front door of the house, separated only by the wrought iron fence that wrapped around the cemetery.

He and Eleanor had buried their daughter last week. The girl murdered in front of the grocery store after turning down a man's advances.

Philip took another drink and looked around the room at the things he had collected over the years. The dangerous, terrible things he had sought to remove from the world to keep his daughter safe. To keep everyone's sons and daughters safe.

Yet it hadn't mattered in the end.

The murderer wasn't possessed by some ghost bound to the knife that he had used. No, the man had simply gone into the grocery store, stolen a carving knife and killed Samantha as she waited for the bus.

That was all.

Nothing more.

He looked around the library and realized that a great many of the dead were out of their hiding places and looking at him. Several with sympathy, others sneering as they reveled in his pain. Philip wanted to destroy them all, but the items to which the dead were bound could not be destroyed.

The ghosts could be locked away and silenced in tombs of lead, but they couldn't be destroyed.

Philip could be, though, and he was sure that his daughter's death would break him. It had already broken his wife.

He honestly didn't know if she would ever come back from her sister's house.

"Will you go and visit your daughter?" a voice whispered the tone cold and belittling. "Shall you go and weep over her grave?"

Philip looked up and found the owner of the voice standing in front of the desk.

A First World War pilot who was eternally bound to the pale white silk scarf that he had worn in combat.

Ward.

The ghost's name was Ward.

"Shall you go weeping through the cemetery?" Ward grinned. "I would like to see that. Could you perhaps wear my scarf out, I would love to help you mourn your daughter. If you wore my scarf long enough, well, you could even join her."

A few other ghosts laughed and chimed in their agreement.

Philip stood up and grasped onto the desk to keep his balance. He was drunk. Far more drunk than he had been in a long time. But drunk or not, he knew what he wanted to do.

From a plain wooden box, Philip removed his gloves and put them on.

The laughter in the room stopped as the ghosts watched him.

Philip walked slowly over to one of the bookshelves, and he took down a large encyclopedia and brought it back to the desk. This he opened to reveal that the interior of the encyclopedia had been cut out, leaving enough room for a rough box made of lead.

"What are you doing?" Ward asked angrily.

"I'm shutting your mouth," Philip said, his words slurring only slightly. When he opened the box, a slew of voices screamed at him, the sound causing him to wince, but that was all.

Ignoring the angry screams and howls, Philip walked to where Ward's scarf was on a shelf, took it down and carried it back to the desk.

"You wouldn't dare to put me in there," Ward snapped.

Philip ignored him, folding the scarf tightly before placing it into the lead box. As he closed the lid, Ward's screams joined those of the others whom Philip had essentially imprisoned.

But with the closing of the lid came blessed silence.

Philip shut the encyclopedia, brought it back to the shelf and returned it to its place. With that done, he walked out of the library and closed the door behind him. He didn't bother locking the door.

There wasn't a reason to anymore.

Holding onto the railing, Philip managed to make his way down to the hallway, and then out the front door. In a few minutes, he had entered Edgewood Cemetery through the back gate and found himself standing at Samantha's grave. Sinking down to his knees, Philip put his face in his hands and wept, wondering once more if what he did for the world really mattered anymore.

And perhaps, just perhaps, he thought, *I should set the ghosts free.*

But the thought left as quickly as it had come, and Philip remained at the grave of his daughter, weeping as the sun set.

* * *

If you enjoyed the book, please leave a review. Your reviews inspire us to continue writing about the world of spooky and untold horrors!

Check out these best-selling books from our talented authors

Ron Ripley (Ghost Stories)
- Berkley Street Series Books 1 – 9
  www.scarestreet.com/berkleyfullseries
- Moving in Series Box Set Books 1 – 6
  www.scarestreet.com/movinginboxfull

A. I. Nasser (Supernatural Suspense)
- Slaughter Series Books 1 – 3 Bonus Edition
  www.scarestreet.com/slaughterseries

David Longhorn (Sci-Fi Horror)
- Nightmare Series: Books 1 – 3
  www.scarestreet.com/nightmarebox
- Nightmare Series: Books 4 – 6
  www.scarestreet.com/nightmare4-6

Sara Clancy (Supernatural Suspense)
- Banshee Series Books 1 – 6
  www.scarestreet.com/banshee1-6

For a complete list of our new releases and best-selling horror books, visit www.scarestreet.com/books

See you in the shadows,
Team Scare Street